I0688100

James Cook, James King, David L. Purves

Voyages Round the World

James Cook, James King, David L. Purves

Voyages Round the World

ISBN/EAN: 9783337189464

Printed in Europe, USA, Canada, Australia, Japan

Cover: Foto ©Andreas Hilbeck / pixelio.de

More available books at **www.hansebooks.com**

VOYAGES ROUND THE WORLD

BY

CAPTAIN JAMES COOK

EDITED, WITH NOTES, ETC., BY

D. LAING PURVES,

NEW YORK:
R. WORTHINGTON, 770 BROADWAY.
1883.

G420
.C65P9

COOK'S VOYAGES ROUND THE WORLD.

[It may here be mentioned that, save for the episode of the first sojourn at Otaheite, taken below from Dr Hawkesworth's account almost at full length, the synopsis of the famous discoverer's first two voyages is taken from the third volume of "Maritime and Inland Discovery," pp. 28–69, in Dr Lardner's well-known but now not very easily attainable "Cabinet Cyclopædia." Chapters III. and IV. of Book V. runs as follows; and they are none the less valuable, as introducing some brief preliminary record of a man whom England, without any injustice to earlier or later names, may honestly regard as her greatest navigator and her most indefatigable and successful discoverer. We give the text of the "Cyclopædia," except for a few changes necessitated by severance from the context, precisely as we find it after two-and-forty years.]

COOK'S FIRST VOYAGE.

"THE interests of science and the acquisition of geographical knowledge entered largely into the motives of the circumnavigations [we have] related. But the first expedition of importance, fitted out wholly for scientific objects, was that entrusted to the command of the celebrated Captain James Cook. This great navigator was born of humble parents : his father was an agricultural labourer, whose steady conduct was at length rewarded by his employer with the situation of hind or under-steward. As he had nine children, and his means were slender, he was unable to assist materially their individual exertions to procure a livelihood. James, when thirteen years of age, was apprenticed to a shopkeeper at Straiths, a fishing town not far from Whitby; but the predilection of young Cook for the sea was soon manifested with that strength of inclination which is sure to accompany peculiar talents.

He engaged himself for seven years with the owners of some ships employed in the coal trade; and, when the period of his engagement was expired, he was promoted by his employers to the rank of mate of one of their vessels. The coal trade of England, being chiefly carried on near a singularly dangerous coast, where unceasing vigilance is required on the part of the seamen, constitutes the best school of practical mariners in the world. Cook, who obeyed his own inclinations when he turned sailor, profited, no doubt, in the highest degree, from the opportunities which his coasting voyages afforded him of becoming acquainted with the practical part of navigation. At length, being in the Thames in 1755, when impressments were carried on to a great extent, he resolved to anticipate the impending necessity, and offered himself to serve on board the Eagle, a man-of-war of 60 guns.

Shortly after, the friends and patrons of his family in Yorkshire having warmly recommended his interests to the care of Mr Osbaldiston, the member for Scarborough, and Captain (afterwards Sir Hugh) Palliser, who commanded the Eagle, reporting well of his conduct and capacity, he was appointed master of the Mercury, a small vessel which soon afterwards joined the fleet of Sir Charles Saunders in the Gulf of St Lawrence. Here the talents and resolution of Cook soon became conspicuous.

"It was found necessary, in order that the fleet might co-operate with the army under General Wolfe, that it should take up a position along the shore in front of the French encampments; but before this manœuvre could be put in execution, the channel of the river was to be sounded. This difficult task required the union of more than ordinary intelligence and intrepidity, and Cook was the person selected for the purpose. For several nights he carried on his operations unperceived; but at length the enemy discovered his movements, and, sending out a great number of boats after it grew dark, attempted to surround and cut him off. Cook pushed for the Isle of Orleans; and so narrowly did he escape being captured, that as he stepped on shore from the bow of his boat, the Indians in pursuit of him entered at the stern; and the boat itself, which was a pinnace belonging to a man-of-war, was carried off by the enemy. Cook, however, had accomplished his task, and laid before the Admiral of the fleet a survey of the channel, which was found to be both full and accurate. After the conquest of Quebec he was appointed to examine the more difficult portions of the River St Lawrence, with the navigation of which the English had but little acquaintance. His zeal and abilities soon after procured him an appointment as master to the Northumberland, which bore the Commodore's flag at Halifax. Here he found leisure to apply himself to the study of elementary mathematics, and to improve

those talents as a practical hydrographer of which he had given such ample proofs in his first rude essays. An opportunity also soon occurred of displaying his improvement by surveying a part of the coast of Newfoundland. This island had lately fallen into the power of the English; and its importance as a fishing station being fully appreciated by Sir Hugh Palliser, who was appointed governor in the year 1764, he strongly represented to Government the necessity of making an accurate survey of its coasts; and, accordingly, by his recommendation, Cook was appointed marine surveyor of Newfoundland and Labrador, and the Grenville schooner was placed under his command for this purpose. The manner in which Cook executed this task confirmed the high opinion already entertained of his zeal and ability. A short paper which he communicated to the Royal Society on an eclipse of the sun observed in Newfoundland, and the longitude of the place as calculated from it, procured him the character of a respectable mathematician.

"But still higher honours awaited him. The transit of the planet Venus over the sun's disc, calculated to take place in 1769, was looked forward to by the scientific world with much anxious interest; and it was earnestly desired that all the advantage which could be derived to science from so rare a phenomenon might be secured by observing it in distant quarters of the globe. In accordance with this view, the Royal Society presented an address to the King, setting forth the advantage of observing the transit in the opposite hemisphere, their inability to fit out an expedition for the purpose, and praying his Majesty to equip a vessel to be despatched to the South Sea under their direction. This petition was at once complied with. The person at first designed to command the expedition was Mr Dalrymple, chief hydrographer to the Admiralty, and no less celebrated for his geographical knowledge than for his zeal in maintaining the existence of an Australian continent. Dalrymple had never held a commission in his Majesty's navy; and the experience of Dr Halley had proved that one so circumstanced cannot expect obedience from a crew subjected to the discipline of the navy. The pride of the profession scorns to submit to those who have not acquired their authority by passing through the ordinary routine of promotion. Dalrymple, however, refused to engage in the expedition unless with the amplest powers of a commander. The Admiralty, on the other hand, were unwilling to entrust him with powers which might embroil him with his officers. Neither party would yield; and, while the affair thus remained in suspense, Cook was proposed. Inquiries were then made as to his abilities; and, as all who knew him spoke favourably of him; and great confidence is usually felt in the steady and concentrated talents of the self-taught, he was chosen to command the expedition, being first promoted to the rank of lieutenant.

"It is a proof of Cook's natural strength of understanding, that his mind was not enslaved by habits, but that he was always ready to introduce innovations into his practice whenever they were recommended by common sense and experience. Instead of selecting a frigate, or vessel of that description, for his voyage, he chose a vessel built for the coal trade, with the sailing qualities of which he was well acquainted. He justly represented, that a ship of this kind was more capable of carrying the stores requisite for a long voyage; was exposed to less hazard in running near coasts—an object of great importance in a voyage of discovery; was less affected by currents; and, in case of any accident, might without much difficulty or danger, be laid on shore to undergo repairs. The ship which he chose was of 360 tons' burden, and named the Endeavour. No pains were spared by the Admiralty in fitting her out for the voyage; and, as the improvement of science was its main object, persons qualified to attain the desired end were appointed to accompany the expedition. Mr Green

was named by the Royal Society as the astronomer; Dr Solander, a learned Swede and pupil of Linnæus, went as naturalist; Mr (afterwards Sir Joseph) Banks, a gentleman of large fortune, and at that time very young, who afterwards reflected so much lustre on his country by devoting a long life and ample means to the interests of learning, renounced the ease to which his affluence entitled him, and commenced his active and honourable career by a voyage round the world. Being accompanied by able draughtsmen, and being himself zealously attached to the study of natural history, and amply provided with everything conducive to the gratification of his favourite pursuit; being at the same time of a lively, open, liberal, and courageous temper, his company was no less agreeable than it was advantageous. Before the preparations were completed, Captain Wallis returned from his voyage round the world; and having been advised to fix on some spot in the South Sea conveniently situated for the erection of an observatory, he named Port Royal in King George the Third's Island as a place well adapted for that purpose.

"Everything being now prepared, Lieutenant Cook sailed from Plymouth on the 26th of August 1768. He touched at Rio Janeiro, where the Portuguese Governor, no less ignorant than suspicious, was much at a loss to comprehend the object of the expedition; nor, after much trouble, was he able to form a juster idea of it, than that it was intended to observe the north star passing through the south pole. It was only by stealth that Mr Banks could go ashore, though nature seemed here to teem with the objects of his research, and brilliant butterflies flew round the ship to the height of the mast. In leaving this port, Cook, after the example of Byron, sailed over the position which had been assigned by Cowley to Pepys' Island, and finally dispelled all belief in its existence. He then directed his course through the Straits of Le Maire, to pass round Cape Horn.

"The naturalists of the expedition

landed on Tierra del Fuego, and, crossing a morass and some low woods, ascended the highest eminence they could descry. It was now midsummer in this region, and the temperature during the day was moderately warm, but as night approached snow fell in great quantities, and the cold became excessive. The exploring party, who had incautiously advanced too far, were unable to effect their return to the shore before sunset, and were obliged to spend the night exposed to all the inclemency of the weather, in a singularly desolate and unsheltered region. Dr Solander, who, having travelled in the north of Europe, was well acquainted with the fatal effects of cold on the constitution, repeatedly admonished his companions to resist the first approach of drowsiness, as the sleep superinduced by cold is sure to prove fatal; but he was the first to feel the dangerous torpor he predicted, and entreated his companions to allow him to lie down and take his rest; but they, fortunately instructed by his lessons, persisted in dragging him along, and thus saved his life. On reaching the woods in their descent, they kindled a fire, round which they spent the night; and when the sun rose, they made their way to the ships; but two of the party, servants of Mr Banks, who lay down to rest in the snow, were found dead the next morning.

"The voyage round Cape Horn into the Pacific occupied thirty-four days; and Cook, who was rather fortunate in his weather, seems to think it preferable to the passage through the Straits of Magellan. In his voyage through the ocean, he descried some small islands, of the group which had been previously visited by Wallis and Bougainville. He proceeded, however, direct to the place of his destination, not allowing himself to be detained by unimportant discoveries."

[The account of Cook's first stay at Otaheite, and his transactions with the natives there, is altogether too curious and interesting to be dismissed with the curt notice Dr Lardner ac-

cords to it; and we take the following particular narration from Dr Hawkesworth's Collection of Voyages, as reproduced by Kerr in his well-known History of Voyages and Travels (Edinburgh, 1814; vol. xii., p. 423, *ad finem*). The section headings have not been regarded, the entire narrative being treated as what it really is —one consecutive story.]

About 1 o'clock on Monday the 10th April, some of the people who were looking out for the island to which we were bound, said they saw land ahead, in that part of the horizon where it was expected to appear; but it was so faint, that whether there was land in sight or not remained a matter of dispute till sunset. The next morning, however, at 6 o'clock, we were convinced that those who said they had discovered land were not mistaken; it appeared to be very high and mountainous, extending from W. by S. half S. to W. by N. half N., and we knew it to be the same that Captain Wallis[1] had called King George the Third's Island. We were delayed in our approach to it by light airs and calms, so that in the morning of the 12th we were but little nearer than we had been the night before; but about seven a breeze sprung up, and before eleven several canoes were seen making towards the ship. There were but few of them, however, that would come near; and the people in those that did, could not be persuaded to come on board. In every canoe there were young plantains, and branches of a tree which the Indians call "E' Midho;" these, as we afterwards learned, were brought as tokens of peace and amity; and the people in one of the canoes handed them up the ship's side, making signals at the same time with great earnestness, which we did not immediately understand. At length we guessed that they wished these symbols should be placed in some conspi-

---

[1] Who had circumnavigated the globe in 1766-1768 in the Dolphin, and come into hostile contact with the natives of Otaheite.

cuous part of the ship; we therefore immediately stuck them among the rigging, at which they expressed the greatest satisfaction. We then purchased their cargoes, consisting of cocoa-nuts, and various kinds of fruit, which, after our long voyage, were very acceptable.

We stood on with an easy sail all night, with soundings from twenty-two fathoms to twelve; and about 7 o'clock in the morning we came to an anchor in thirteen fathoms in Port Royal Bay, called by the natives Matavai. We were immediately surrounded by the natives in their canoes, who gave us cocoa-nuts, fruit resembling apples, bread-fruit, and some small fishes, in exchange for beads and other trifles. They had with them a pig, which they would not part with for anything but a hatchet, and therefore we refused to purchase it; because, if we gave them a hatchet for a pig now, we knew they would never afterwards sell one for less, and we could not afford to buy as many as it was probable we should want at that price. The bread-fruit grows on a tree that 's about the size of a middling oak. Its leaves are frequently a foot and a half long, of an oblong shape, deeply sinuated like those of the fig-tree, which they resemble in consistence and colour, and in the exuding of a white milky juice upon being broken. The fruit is about the size and shape of a child's head, and the surface is reticulated not much unlike a truffle. It is covered with a thin skin, and has a core about as big as the handle of a small knife. The eatable part lies between the skin and the core; it is as white as snow, and somewhat of the consistence of new bread. It must be roasted before it is eaten, being first divided into three or four parts. Its taste is insipid, with a slight sweetness somewhat resembling that of the crumb of wheaten bread mixed with a Jerusalem artichoke. Among others who came off to the ship was an elderly man, whose name, as we learned afterwards, was Owhaw, and who was immediately known to Mr Gore, and several others who had been

here with Captain Wallis; as I was informed that he had been very useful to them, I took him on board the ship with some others, and was particularly attentive to gratify him, as I hoped he might also be useful to us.

As our stay here was not likely to be very short, and as it was necessary that the merchandise which we had brought for traffic with the natives should not diminish in its value, which it would certainly have done if every person had been left at liberty to give what he pleased for such things as he should purchase; at the same time that confusion and quarrels must necessarily have arisen from there being no standard at market; I drew up the following rules, and ordered that they should be punctually observed:

Rules to be observed by every person in or belonging to his Majesty's bark the Endeavour, for the better establishing a regular and uniform trade for provision, &c. with the inhabitants of King George's Island.

I. To endeavour, by every fair means, to cultivate a friendship with the natives; and to treat them with all imaginable humanity.

II. A proper person or persons will be appointed to trade with the natives for all manner of provisions, fruit, and other productions of the earth; and no officer or seaman, or other person belonging to the ship, excepting such as are so appointed, shall trade or offer to trade for any sort of provision, fruit, or other production of the earth, unless they have leave so to do.

III. Every person employed on shore, on any duty whatsoever, is strictly to attend to the same; and if by any neglect he loseth any of his arms or working tools, or suffers them to be stolen, the full value thereof will be charged against his pay, according to the custom of the navy in such cases, and he shall receive such further punishment as the nature of the offence may deserve.

IV. The same penalty will be inflicted on every person who is found to embezzle, trade, or offer to trade, with any part of the ship's stores of what nature soever.

V. No sort of iron, or anything that is made of iron, or any sort of cloth, or other useful or necessary articles, are to be given in exchange for anything but provision.

J. Cook.

As soon as the ship was properly secured, I went on shore with Mr Banks and Dr Solander, a party of men under arms, and our friend Owhaw. We were received from the boat by some hundreds of the inhabitants, whose looks at least gave us welcome, though they were struck with such awe, that the first who approached us crouched so low that he almost crept upon his hands and knees. It is remarkable, that he, like the people in the canoes. presented to us the same symbol of peace that is known to have been in use among the ancient and mighty nations of the northern hemisphere—the green branch of a tree. We received it with looks and gestures of kindness and satisfaction; and observing that each of them held one in his hand, we immediately gathered every one a bough, and carried it in our hands in the same manner.

They marched with us about half a mile towards the place where the Dolphin had watered, conducted by Owhaw; they then made a full stop, and having laid the ground bare, by clearing away all the plants that grew upon it, the principal persons among them threw their green branches upon the naked spot, and made signs that we should do the same. We immediately showed our readiness to comply, and to give a greater solemnity to the rite, the marines were drawn up, and marching in order, each dropped his bough upon those of the Indians, and we followed their example. We then proceeded, and when we came to the watering-place it was intimated to us by signs that we might occupy that ground; but it happened not to be fit for our purpose. During our walk they had shaken off their first timid sense of our superiority, and were become familiar: they went with us from the watering-place and took a circuit through the woods; as we went along, we distributed beads and other small presents among them, and had the satisfaction to see that they were much gratified. Our circuit was not less than four or five miles, through groves of trees, which were loaded with cocoa-nuts and bread-fruit, and afforded the most grateful shade. Under these trees were the habitations of the people, most of them being only a roof without walls; and the whole scene realised the poetical fables of Arcadia. We remarked, however, not without some regret, that in all our walk we had seen only two hogs, and not a single fowl. Those of our company who had been here with the Dolphin told us, that none of the people whom we had yet seen were of the first class; they suspected that the chiefs had removed, and upon carrying us to the place where what they called the Queen's Palace had stood, we found that no traces of it were left. We determined therefore to return in the morning, and endeavour to find out the *noblesse* in their retreats.

In the morning, however, before we could leave the ship, several canoes came about us, most of them from the westward, and two of them were filled with people who by their dress and deportment appeared to be of a superior rank. Two of these came on board, and each singled out his friend; one of them, whose name we found to be Matahah, fixed upon Mr Banks, and the other upon me: this ceremony consisted in taking off great part of their clothes and putting them upon us. In return for this, we presented each of them with a hatchet and some beads. Soon after they made signs for us to go with them to the places where they lived, pointing to the SW.; and as I was desirous of finding a more commodious harbour, and making further trial of the disposition of the people, I consented.

I ordered out two boats, and with Mr Banks and Dr Solander, the other gentlemen, and our two Indian friends, we embarked for our expedition. After rowing about a league, they made signs that we should go on shore, and gave us to understand that this was the place of their residence. We accordingly landed, among several hundreds of the natives, who conducted us into a house of much greater length than any we had seen. When we entered, we saw a middle-aged man, whose name was afterwards discovered to be Tootahah; mats were immediately spread, and we were desired to sit down over against him. Soon after we were seated, he ordered a cock and hen to be brought out, which he presented to Mr Banks and me; we accepted the present, and in a short time each of us received a piece of cloth, perfumed after their manner, by no means disagreeably, which they took great pains to make us remark. The piece presented to Mr Banks was eleven yards long and two wide; in return for which, he gave a laced silk neckcloth, which he happened to have on, and a linen pocket handkerchief. Tootahah immediately dressed himself in his new finery, with an air of perfect complacency and satisfaction. But it is now time that I should take some notice of the ladies.

Soon after the interchanging of our presents with Tootahah, they attended us to several large houses, in which we walked about with great freedom: they snowed us all the civility of which, in our situation, we could accept; and, on their part, seemed to have no scruple that would have prevented its being carried further. The houses, which as I have observed before, are all open, except a roof, afforded no place of retirement; but the ladies, by frequently pointing to the mats upon the ground, and sometimes seating themselves and drawing us down upon them, left us no room to doubt of their being much less jealous of observation than we were.

We now took leave of our friendly chief, and directed our course along the shore. When we had walked about a mile, we met, at the head of a great number of people, another chief, whose name was Tubourai Tamaide,

with whom we were also to ratify a treaty of peace, with the ceremony of which we were now become better acquainted. Having received the branch which he presented to us, and given another in return, we laid our hands upon our left breasts and pronounced the word "Taio," which we supposed to signify friend. The chief then gave us to understand that if we chose to eat he had victuals ready for us. We accepted his offer, and dined very heartily upon fish, bread-fruit, cocoa-nuts, and plantains, dressed after their manner; they ate some of their fish raw, and raw fish was offered to us, but we declined that part of the entertainment.

During this visit a wife of our noble host, whose name was Tomio, did Mr Banks the honour to place herself upon the same mat close by him. Tomio was not in the first bloom of her youth, nor did she appear to have been ever remarkable for her beauty; he did not, therefore, I believe, pay her the most flattering attention. It happened, too, as a further mortification to this lady, that seeing a very pretty girl among the crowd, he, not adverting to the dignity of his companion, beckoned her to come to him. The girl, after some entreaty complied, and sat down on the other side of him; he loaded her with beads and every showy trifle that would please her. His princess, though she was somewhat mortified at the preference that was given to her rival, did not discontinue her civilities, but still assiduously supplied him with the milk of the cocoa-nut, and such other dainties as were in her reach. This scene might possibly have become more curious and interesting if it had not been suddenly interrupted by an interlude of a more serious kind. Just at this time, Dr Solander and Mr Monkhouse complained that their pockets had been picked. Dr Solander had lost an opera-glass in a shagreen case, and Mr Monkhouse his snuff-box. This incident unfortunately put an end to the good-humour of the company. Complaint of the injury was made to the chief; and, to give it weight, Mr Banks started up and hastily struck the butt end of his firelock upon the ground. This action, and the noise that accompanied it, struck the whole assembly with a panic; and every one of the natives ran out of the house with the utmost precipitation, except the chief, three women, and two or three others who appeared by their dress to be of a superior rank.

The chief, with a mixture of confusion and concern, took Mr Banks by the hand, and led him to a large quantity of cloth which lay at the other end of the house; this he offered to him piece by piece, intimating by signs, that if that would atone for the wrong which had been done, he might take any part of it, or, if he pleased, the whole. Mr Banks put it by, and gave him to understand that he wanted nothing but what had been dishonestly taken away. Toubourai Tamaide then went hastily out, leaving Mr Banks with his wife Tomio, who, during the whole scene of terror and confusion, had kept constantly at his side, and intimating his desire that he should wait there till his return. Mr Banks accordingly sat down and conversed with her, as well as he could by signs, about half an hour. The chief then came back with the snuff-box and the case of the opera-glass in his hand, and, with a joy in his countenance that was painted with a strength of expression which distinguishes these people from all others, delivered them to the owners. The case of the opera-glass, however, upon being opened, was found to be empty; upon this discovery, his countenance changed in a moment; and catching Mr Banks again by the hand, he rushed out of the house without uttering any sound, and led him along the shore, walking with great rapidity. When they had got about a mile from the house, a woman met him and gave him a piece of cloth, which he hastily took from her, and continued to press forward with it in his hand. Dr Solander and Mr Monkhouse had followed them, and they came at length to a house where they were received by a woman,

to whom he gave the cloth, and intimated to the gentlemen that they should give her some beads. They immediately complied; and the beads and cloth being deposited upon the floor, the woman went out, and in about half-an-hour returned with the opera-glass, expressing the same joy upon the occasion that had before been expressed by the chief. The beads were now returned, with an inflexible resolution not to accept them; and the cloth was with the same pertinacity forced upon Dr Solander as a recompense for the injury that had been done him. He could not avoid accepting the cloth, but insisted in his turn upon giving a new present of beads to the woman. It will not perhaps be easy to account for all the steps that were taken in the recovery of this glass and snuff-box; but this cannot be thought strange, considering that the scene of action was among a people whose language, policy, and connections are even now but imperfectly known. Upon the whole, however, they show an intelligence and influence which would do honour to any system of government, however regular and improved. In the evening, about 6 o'clock, we returned to the ship.

On the next morning, Saturday the 15th, several of the chiefs whom we had seen the day before came on board, and brought with them hogs, breadfruit, and other refreshments, for which we gave them hatchets and linen, and such things as seemed to be most acceptable.

As in my excursion to the westward I had not found any more convenient harbour than that in which we lay, I determined to go on shore and fix upon some spot, commanded by the ship's guns, where I might throw up a small fort for our defence, and prepare for making our astronomical observation. I therefore took a party of men and landed without delay, accompanied by Mr Banks, Dr Solander, and the astronomer, Mr Green. We soon fixed upon a part of the sandy beach on the NE. point of the bay, which was in every respect convenient for our purpose, and not near any habitation of the natives.   Having marked out the ground that we intended to occupy, a small tent belonging to Mr Banks was set up, which had been brought on shore for that purpose; by this time a great number of the people had gathered about us, but, as it appeared, only to look on, there not being a single weapon of any kind among them.   I intimated, however, that none of them were to come within the line I had drawn, except one, who appeared to be a chief, and Owhaw.   To these two persons I addressed myself by signs, and endeavoured to make them understand that we wanted the ground which we had marked out to sleep upon for a certain number of nights, and that then we should go away.   Whether I was understood, I cannot certainly determine; but the people behaved with a deference and respect that at once pleased and surprised us; they sat down peaceably without the circle, and looked on, without giving us any interruption, till we had done, which was upwards of two hours.   As we had seen no poultry, and but two hogs, in our walk when we were last on shore at this place, we suspected that upon our arrival they had been driven farther up the country; and the rather, as Owhaw was very importunate with us, by signs, not to go into the woods, which, however, and partly for these reasons, we were determined to do. Having therefore appointed the thirteen marines and a petty officer to guard the tent, we set out, and a great number of the natives joined our party.   As we were crossing a little river that lay in our way, we saw some ducks, and Mr Banks, as soon as he had got over, fired at them, and happened to kill three at one shot.   This struck [the natives] with the utmost terror, so that most of them fell suddenly to the ground as if they also had been shot at the same discharge.   It was not long, however, before they recovered from their fright, and we continued our route; but we had not gone far before we were alarmed by the report of two pieces, which were fired by the guard at the tent.

We had then straggled a little distance from each other, but Owhaw immediately called us together, and by waving his hand, sent away every Indian who followed us except three, each of whom, as a pledge of peace on their part, and an entreaty that there might be peace on ours, hastily broke a branch from the trees, and came to us with it in their hands.   As we had too much reason to fear that some mischief had happened, we hastened back to the tent, which was not distant above half-a-mile; and when we came up, we found it entirely deserted, except by our own people.

It appeared that one of the Indians who remained about the tent after we left it, had watched his opportunity, and, taking the sentry unawares, had snatched away his musket.   Upon this the petty officer, a midshipman, who commanded the party—perhaps from a sudden fear of further violence, perhaps from the natural petulance of power newly acquired, and perhaps from a brutality in his nature—ordered the marines to fire.   The men, with as little consideration or humanity as the officer, immediately discharged their pieces among the thickest of the flying crowd, consisting of more than a hundred; and, observing that the thief did not fall, pursued him and shot him dead.   We afterwards learned that none of the others were either killed or wounded.   Owhaw, who had never left us, observing that we were now totally deserted, got together a few of those who had fled, though not without some difficulty, and ranged them about us.   We endeavoured to justify our people as well as we could, and to convince the Indians that if they did no wrong to us, we should do no wrong to them.   They went away without any appearance of distrust or resentment; and having struck our tent, we returned to the ship, but by no means satisfied with the transactions of the day.

Upon questioning our people more particularly, whose conduct they soon perceived we could not approve, they alleged that the sentinel whose musket was taken away, was violently assaulted and thrown down, and that a push was afterwards made at him by the man who took the musket, before any command was given to fire. It was also suggested, that Owhaw had suspicions, at least, if not certain knowledge, that something would be attempted against our people at the tent, which made him so very earnest in his endeavours to prevent our leaving it. Others imputed his importunity to his desire that we should confine ourselves to the beach : and it was remarked that neither Owhaw, nor the chiefs who remained with us after he had sent the rest of the people away, would have inferred the breach of peace from the firing at the tent, if they had had no reason to suspect that some injury had been offered by their countrymen ; especially as Mr Banks had just fired at the ducks. And yet that they did infer a breach of peace from that incident, was manifest from their waving their hands for the people to disperse, and instantly pulling green branches from the trees. But what were the real circumstances of this unhappy affair, and whether either, and which of these conjectures were true, could never certainly be known.

The next morning but few of the natives were seen upon the beach, and not one of them came off to the ship. This convinced us that our endeavours to quiet their apprehensions had not been effectual ; and we remarked with particular regret, that we were deserted even by Owhaw, who had hitherto been so constant in his attachment, and so active in renewing the peace that had been broken. Appearances being thus unfavourable, I warped the ship nearer to the shore, and moored her in such a manner as to command all the N E. part of the bay, particularly the place which I had marked out for building a fort. In the evening, however, I went on shore with only a boat's crew, and some of the gentlemen. The natives gathered about us, but not in the same number as before. There were, I believe, between thirty and forty, and they trafficked with us for cocoa-nuts and

other fruit, to all appearance as friendly as ever.

On the 17th, early in the morning, we had the misfortune to lose Mr Buchan, the person whom Mr Banks had brought out as a painter of landscapes and figures. He was a sober, diligent, and ingenious young man, and greatly regretted by Mr Banks ; who hoped, by his means, to have gratified his friends in England with representations of this country and its inhabitants, which no other person on board could delineate with the same accuracy and elegance. He had always been subject to epileptic fits, one of which seized him on the mountains of Tierra del Fuego ; and this disorder being aggravated by a bilious complaint which he contracted on board the ship, at length put an end to his life. It was at first proposed to bury him on shore, but Mr Banks thinking that it might perhaps give offence to the natives, with whose customs we were then wholly unacquainted, we committed his body to the sea, with as much decency and solemnity as our circumstances and situation would admit.

In the forenoon of this day we received a visit from Tubourai Tamaide, and Tootahah, our chiefs, from the west : they brought with them, as emblems of peace, not branches of plantain, but two young trees, and would not venture on board till these had been received ; having probably been alarmed by the mischief which had been done at the tent. Each of them also brought, as propitiatory gifts, some bread-fruit, and a hog ready dressed. This was a most acceptable present, as we perceived that hogs were not always to be got ; and in return we gave to each of our noble benefactors a hatchet and a nail. In the evening we went on shore and set up a tent, in which Mr Green and myself spent the night, in order to observe an eclipse of the first satellite of Jupiter ; but the weather becoming cloudy, we were disappointed.

On the 18th, at daybreak, I went on shore, with as many people as could possibly be spared from the ship, and began to erect our fort. While some were employed in throwing up entrenchments, others were busy in cutting pickets and fascines, which the natives, who soon gathered round us as they had been used to do, were so far from hindering, that many of them voluntarily assisted us, bringing the pickets and fascines from the wood where they had been cut, with great alacrity. We had, indeed, been so scrupulous of invading their property, that we purchased every stake which was used upon this occasion, and cut down no tree till we had first obtained their consent. The soil where we constructed our fort was sandy, and this made it necessary to strengthen the entrenchments with wood; three sides were to be fortified in this manner; the fourth was bounded by a river, upon the banks of which I proposed to place a proper number of water-casks. This day we served pork to the ship's company for the first time, and the Indians brought down so much bread-fruit and cocoa-nuts, that we found it necessary to send away part of them unbought, and to acquaint them by signs, that we should want no more for two days to come. Everything was purchased this day with beads; a single bead, as big as a pea, being the purchase of five or six cocoa-nuts, and as many of the bread-fruit. Mr Banks's tent was got up before night within the works, and he slept on shore for the first time. Proper sentries were placed round it, but no Indian attempted to approach it the whole night.

The next morning, our friend Tubourai Tamaide made Mr Banks a visit at the tent, and brought with him not only his wife and family, but the roof of a house, and several materials for setting it up, with furniture and implements of various kinds, intending, as we understood him, to take up his residence in our neighbourhood. This instance of his confidence and good-will gave us great pleasure, and we determined to strengthen his attachment to us by every means in our power. Soon after his arrival he took Mr Banks by the hand, and leading him out of the line, signified that he should accompany him into the woods. Mr Banks readily consented, and having walked with him about a quarter of a mile, they arrived at a kind of awning which he had already set up, and which seemed to be his occasional habitation. Here he unfolded a bundle of his country cloth, and taking out two garments, one of red cloth, and the other of very neat matting, he clothed Mr Banks in them, and without any other ceremony immediately conducted him back to the tent. His attendants soon after brought him some pork and bread-fruit, which he ate, dipping his meat into salt water instead of sauce; after his meal he retired to Mr Banks's bed, and slept about an hour. In the afternoon, his wife Tomio brought to the tent a young man about two-and-twenty years of age, of a very comely appearance, whom they both seemed to acknowledge as their son, though we afterwards discovered that he was not so. In the evening, this young man and another chief, who had also paid us a visit, went away to the westward, but Tubourai Tamaide and his wife returned to the awning in the skirts of the wood.

Our surgeon, Mr Monkhouse, having walked out this evening, reported that he had seen the body of the man who had been shot at the tents, which he said was wrapped in cloth, and placed on a kind of bier, supported by stakes, under a roof that seemed to have been set up for the purpose; that near it were deposited some instruments of war, and other things, which he would particularly have examined but for the stench of the body, which was intolerable. He said, that he saw also two more sheds of the same kind, in one of which were the bones of a human body that had lain till they were quite dry. We discovered, afterwards, that this was the way in which they usually disposed of their dead.

A kind of market now began to be kept just without the lines, and was plentifully supplied with everything but pork. Tubourai Tamaide was our constant guest, imitating our manners, even to the using of a knife and fork, which he did very handily.

As my curiosity was excited by Mr Monkhouse's account of the situation of the man who had been shot, I took an opportunity to go with some others to see it. I found the shed under which his body lay, close by the house in which he resided when he was alive, some others being not more than ten yards distant; it was about fifteen feet long, and eleven broad, and of a proportionable height; one end was wholly open, and the other end, and the two sides, were partly enclosed with a kind of wicker work. The bier on which the corpse was deposited was a frame of wood like that in which the sea-beds, called cots, are placed, with a matted bottom, and supported by four posts, at the height of about five feet from the ground. The body was covered first with a mat, and then with white cloth; by the side of it lay a wooden mace, one of their weapons of war, and near the head of it, which lay next to the close end of the shed, lay two cocoa-nut shells, such as are sometimes used to carry water in; at the other end a bunch of green leaves, with some dried twigs, all tied together, were stuck in the ground, by which lay a stone about as big as a cocoa-nut. Near these lay one of the young plantain trees, which are used for emblems of peace, and close by it a stone axe. At the open end of the shed also hung, in several strings, a great number of palm-nuts, and without the shed was stuck upright in the ground the stem of a plantain tree about five feet high, upon the top of which was placed a cocoa-nut shell full of fresh water. Against the side of one of the posts hung a small bag, containing a few pieces of bread-fruit ready roasted, which were not all put in at the same time, for some of them were fresh; and others stale. I took notice that several of the natives observed us with a mixture of solicitude and jealousy in their countenances, and by their gestures expressed uneasi-

ness when we went near the body, standing themselves at a little distance while we were making our examination, and appearing to be pleased when we came away.

Our residence on shore would by no means have been disagreeable if we had not been incessantly tormented by the flies, which, among other mischief, made it almost impossible for Mr Parkinson, Mr Bank's natural history painter, to work; for they not only covered his subject so as that no part of its surface could be seen, but even ate the colour off the paper as fast as he could lay it on. We had recourse to mosquito-nets and fly-traps, which, though they made the inconvenience tolerable, were very far from removing it.

On the 22d, Tootahah gave us a specimen of the music of this country: four persons performed upon flutes, which had only two stops, and therefore could not sound more than four notes by half tones. They were sounded like our German flutes, except that the performer, instead of applying it to his mouth, blew into it with one nostril, while he stopped the other with his thumb. To these instruments four other persons sung, and kept very good time; but only one tune was played during the whole concert.

Several of the natives brought us axes, which they had received from on board the Dolphin, to grind and repair; but among others there was one which became the subject of much speculation, as it appeared to be French. After much inquiry, we learned that a ship had been here between our arrival and the departure of the Dolphin, which we then conjectured to have been a Spaniard, but afterwards knew to have been the Boudeuse, commanded by M. de Bougainville.

On the 24th, Mr Banks and Dr Solander examined the country for several miles along the shore to the eastward. For about two miles it was flat and fertile; after that the hills stretched quite to the water's edge, and a little farther ran out into the sea, so that they were obliged to climb over them. These hills, which were barren, continued for about three miles more, and then terminated in a large plain, which was full of good houses, and people who appeared to live in great affluence. In this place there was a river, much more considerable than that at our fort, which issued from a deep and beautiful valley, and where our travellers crossed it, though at some distance from the sea, was near 100 yards wide. About a mile beyond this river the country became again barren, the rocks everywhere projecting into the sea, for which reason they resolved to return. Just as they had formed this resolution, one of the natives offered them refreshment, which they accepted. They found this man to be of a kind that has been described by various authors as mixed with many nations, but distinct from them all. His skin was of a dead white, without the least appearance of what is called complexion, though some parts of his body were in a small degree less white than others; his hair, eyebrows, and beard were as white as his skin; his eyes appeared as if they were blood-shot, and he seemed to be very short-sighted. At their return they were met by Tubourai Tamaide and his women, who, at seeing them, felt a joy which not being able to express, they burst into tears, and wept some time before their passion could be restrained.

This evening Dr Solander lent his knife to one of these women, who neglected to return it, and the next morning Mr Banks's also was missing. Upon this occasion I must bear my testimony that the people of this country, of all ranks, men and women, are the arrantest thieves upon the face of the earth. The very day after we arrived here, when they came on board us, the chiefs were employed in stealing what they could in the cabin, and their dependants were no less industrious in other parts of the ship: they snatched up everything that it was possible for them to secrete, till they got on shore, even to

the glass ports, two of which they carried off undetected. Tubourai Tamaide was the only one except Tootahah who had not been found guilty, and the presumption, arising from this circumstance, that he was exempt from a vice of which the whole nation besides were guilty, could not be supposed to outweigh strong appearances to the contrary. Mr Banks, therefore, though not without some reluctance, accused him of having stolen his knife. He solemnly and steadily denied that he knew anything of it; upon which Mr Banks made him understand that whoever had taken it, he was determined to have it returned. Upon this resolute declaration, one of the natives who was present produced a rag in which three knives were very carefully tied up. One was that which Dr Solander had lent to the woman, another was a table knife belonging to me, and the owner of the third was not known. With these the chief immediately set out in order to make restitution of them to their owners at the tents. Mr Banks remained with the women, who expressed great apprehensions that some mischief was designed against their lord. When he came to the tents, he restored one of the knives to Dr Solander and another to me, the third not being owned, and then began to search for Mr Banks's in all the places where he had ever seen it. After some time, one of Mr Banks's servants, understanding what he was about, immediately fetched his master's knife, which it seems he had laid by the day before, and till now knew nothing of its having been missed. Tubourai Tamaide, upon this demonstration of his innocence, expressed the strongest emotions of mind, both in his looks and gestures; the tears started from his eyes, and he made signs with the knife, that, if he was ever guilty of such an action as had been imputed to him, he would submit to have his throat cut. He then rushed out of the lines, and returned hastily to Mr Banks, with a countenance that severely reproached him with his suspicions. Mr Banks soon understood that the knife had been received from his servant, and was scarcely less affected at what had happened than the chief; he felt himself to be the guilty person, and was very desirous to atone for his fault. The poor Indian, however violent his passions, was a stranger to sullen resentment; and upon Mr Banks's spending a little time familiarly with him, and making him a few trifling presents, he forgot the wrong that had been done him, and was perfectly reconciled.

Upon this occasion it may be observed that these people have a knowledge of right and wrong from the mere dictates of natural conscience; and involuntarily condemn themselves when they do that to others which they would condemn others for doing to them. That Tubourai Tamaide felt the force of moral obligation, is certain; for the imputation of an action which he considered as indifferent, would not, when it appeared to be groundless, have moved him with such excess of passion. We must indeed estimate the virtue of these people by the conformity of their conduct to what in their opinion is right; but we must not hastily conclude that theft is a testimony of the same depravity in them that it is in us, in the instances in which our people were sufferers by their dishonesty; for their temptation was such as to surmount, would be considered as a proof of uncommon integrity among those who have more knowledge, better principles, and stronger motives to resist the temptations of illicit advantage. An Indian among penny knives and beads, or even nails and broken glass, is in the same state of trial with the meanest servant in Europe among unlocked coffers of jewels and gold.

On the 26th I mounted six swivel guns upon the fort, which I was sorry to see struck the natives with dread. Some fishermen who lived upon the point removed farther off, and Owhaw told us, by signs, that in four days we should fire great guns.

On the 27th, Tubourai Tamaide, with a friend, who ate with a voracity that I never saw before, and the three women that usually attended him, whose names were Terapo, Tirao, and Omie, dined at the fort. In the evening they took their leave, and set out for the house which Tubourai Tamaide had set up in the skirts of the wood; but in less than a quarter of an hour he returned in great emotion, and hastily seizing Mr Banks's arm, made signs that he should follow him. Mr Banks immediately complied, and they soon came to a place where they found the ship's butcher, with a reaping-hook in his hand. Here the chief stopped, and, in a transport of rage which rendered his signs scarcely intelligible, intimated that the butcher had threatened, or attempted, to cut his wife's throat with the reaping-hook. Mr Banks then signified to him, that if he could fully explain the offence, the man should be punished. Upon this he became more calm, and made Mr Banks understand that the offender, having taken a fancy to a stone hatchet which lay in his house, had offered to purchase it of his wife for a nail; that she having refused to part with it upon any terms, he had catched it up, and throwing down the nail, threatened to cut her throat if she made any resistance. To prove this charge, the hatchet and the nail were produced; and the butcher had so little to say in his defence, that there was not the least reason to doubt of its truth.

Mr Banks having reported this matter to me, I took an opportunity, when the chief and his women, with other Indians, were on board the ship, to call up the butcher, and after a recapitulation of the charge and the proof, I gave orders that he should be punished, as well to prevent other offences of the same kind, as to acquit Mr Banks of his promise. The Indians saw him stripped and tied up to the rigging with a fixed attention, waiting in silent suspense for the event; but as soon as the first stroke was given, they interfered with great agitation, earnestly entreating that the rest of the punishment might be remitted. To this, however, for many reasons, I could not consent; and when they found that they could not prevail by their intercession, they gave vent to their pity by tears.

Their tears, indeed, like those of children, were always ready to express any passion that was strongly excited, and, like those of children, they also appeared to be forgotten as soon as shed; of which the following, among many others, is a remarkable instance. Very early in the morning of the 28th, even before it was day, a great number of them came down to the fort, and Terapo being observed among the women on the outside of the gate, Mr Banks went out and brought her in; he saw that the tears then stood in her eyes, and as soon as she entered they began to flow in great abundance. He inquired earnestly the cause, but instead of answering, she took from under her garment a shark's tooth, and struck it six or seven times into her head with great force; a profusion of blood followed, and she talked loud, but in a most melancholy tone, for some minutes, without at all regarding his inquiries, which he repeated with still more impatience and concern, while the other Indians, to his great surprise, talked and laughed, without taking the least notice of her distress. But her own behaviour was still more extraordinary. As soon as the bleeding was over, she looked up with a smile, and began to collect some small pieces of cloth, which during her bleeding she had thrown down to catch the blood; as soon as she had picked them all up, she carried them out of the tent, and threw them into the sea, carefully dispersing them abroad, as if she wished to prevent the sight of them from reviving the remembrance of what she had done. She then plunged into the river, and after having washed her whole body, returned to the tents with the same gaiety and cheerfulness as if nothing had happened.

It is not indeed strange that the sorrows of these artless people should be transient, any more than that their passions should be suddenly and strongly expressed. What they feel they have never been taught either to disguise or suppress, and having no habits of thinking which perpetually recall the past, and anticipate the future, they are affected by all the changes of the passing hour, and reflect the colour of the time, however frequently it may vary. They have no project which is to be pursued from day to day, the subject of unremitted anxiety and solicitude, that first rushes into the mind when they awake in the morning, and is last dismissed when they sleep at night. Yet, if we admit that they are upon the whole happier than we, we must admit that the child is happier than the man, and that we are losers by the perfection of our nature, the increase of our knowledge, and the enlargement of our views.

Canoes were continually coming in during all this forenoon, and the tents at the fort were crowded with people of both sexes from different parts of the island. I was myself busy on board the ship, but Mr Mollineux, our master, who was one of those that made the last voyage in the Dolphin, went on shore. As soon as he entered Mr Banks's tent, he fixed his eyes upon one of the women, who was sitting there with great composure among the rest, and immediately declared her to be the person who at that time was supposed to be the queen of the island; she also, at the same time, acknowledging him to be one of the strangers whom she had seen before. The attention of all present was now diverted from every other object, and wholly engaged in considering a person who had made so distinguished a figure in the accounts that had been given of this island by its first discoverers; and we soon learned that her name was Oberea. She seemed to be about forty years of age, and was not only tall, but of a large make; her skin was white, and there was an uncommon intelligence and sensibility in her eyes. She appeared to have been handsome when she was young, but at this time little more than memorials of her beauty were left.

As soon as her quality was known, an offer was made to conduct her to the ship. Of this she readily accepted, and came on board with two men and several women, who seemed to be all of her family. I received her with such marks of distinction as I thought would gratify her most, and was not sparing of my presents, among which this august personage seemed particularly delighted with a child's doll. After some time spent on board, I attended her back to the shore; and as soon as we landed, she presented me with a hog, and several bunches of plantains, which she caused to be carried from her canoes up to the fort in a kind of procession, of which she and myself brought up the rear. In our way to the fort we met Tootahah, who, though not king, appeared to be at this time invested with the sovereign authority. He seemed not to be well pleased with the distinction that was shown to the lady, and became so jealous when she produced her doll, that to propitiate him it was thought proper to compliment him with another. At this time he thought fit to prefer a doll to a hatchet; but this preference arose only from a childish jealousy, which could not be soothed but by a gift of exactly the same kind with that which had been presented to Oberea; for dolls in a very short time were universally considered as trifles of no value.

The men who had visited us from time to time had, without scruple, eaten of our provisions; but the women had never yet been prevailed upon to taste a morsel. To day, however, though they refused the most pressing solicitations to dine with the gentlemen, they afterwards retired to the servants' apartment, and ate of plantains very heartily; a mystery of female economy here, which none of us could explain.

On the 29th, not very early in the forenoon, Mr Banks went to pay his court to Oberea, and was told that she was still asleep under the awning of her canoe. Thither, therefore, he went, intending to call her up, a liberty which he thought he might take without any danger of giving offence. But, upon looking into her chamber, to his great astonishment he found her in bed with a handsome young fellow about five-and-twenty, whose name was Obadée. He retreated with some haste and confusion, but was soon made to understand that such amours gave no occasion to scandal, and that Obadée was universally known to have been selected by her as the object of her private favours. The lady being too polite to suffer Mr Banks to wait long in her antechamber, dressed herself with more than usual expedition, and, as a token of special grace, clothed him in a suit of fine cloth, and proceeded with him to the tents. In the evening Mr Banks paid a visit to Tubourai Tamaide, as he had often done before, by candle light, and was equally grieved and surprised to find him and his family in a melancholy mood, and most of them in tears. He endeavoured in vain to discover the cause, and therefore his stay among them was but short. When he reported this circumstance to the officers at the fort, they recollected that Owhaw had foretold that in four days we should fire our great guns; and as this was the eve of the third day, the situation in which Tubourai Tamaide and his family had been found, alarmed them. The sentries, therefore, were doubled at the fort, and the gentlemen slept under arms; at two in the morning, Mr Banks himself went round the point, but found everything so quiet that he gave up all suspicions of mischief intended by the natives as groundless. We had, however, another source of security; our little fortification was now complete. The north and south sides consisted of a bank of earth four feet and a half high on the inside, and a ditch without, ten feet broad and six deep; on the west side, facing the bay, there was a bank of earth four feet high, and palisadoes upon that, but no ditch, the works here being at high-water mark; on the east side, upon the bank of the river, was placed a double row of water-casks filled with water ; and, as this was the weakest side, the two 4-pounders were planted there, and six swivel guns were mounted so as to command the only two avenues from the woods. Our garrison consisted of about five-and-forty men with small arms, including the officers, and the gentlemen who resided on shore ; and our sentries were as well relieved as on the best regulated frontier in Europe.

We continued our vigilance the next day, though we had no particular reason to think it necessary ; but about 10 o'clock in the morning, Tomio came running to the tents, with a mixture of grief and fear in her countenance, and taking Mr Banks, to whom they applied in every emergency and distress, by the arm, intimated that Tubourai Tamaide was dying, in consequence of something which our people had given him to eat, and that he must instantly go with her to his house. Mr Banks set out without delay, and found his Indian friend leaning his head against a post in an attitude of the utmost languor and despondency ; the people about him intimated that he had been vomiting, and brought out a leaf folded up with great care, which, they said, contained some of the poison, by the deleterious effects of which he was now dying. Mr Banks hastily opened the leaf, and upon examining its contents, found them to be no other than a chew of tobacco, which the chief had begged of some of our people, and which they had indiscreetly given him. He had observed that they kept it long in the mouth, and being desirous of doing the same, he had chewed it to powder and swallowed the spittle. During the examination of the leaf and its contents, he looked up at Mr Banks with the most piteous aspect, and intimated that he had but a very short time to live. Mr Banks, however, being now master of his disease, directed him to drink plentifully of cocoa-nut milk, which in a short time put an end to his sickness and apprehensions ; and he spent the day at the fort with that uncommon flow of cheerfulness and good-humour which is always produced by a sudden and unexpected relief from pain either of body or mind.

Captain Wallis having brought home one of the adzes which these people—having no metal of any kind—make of stone, Mr Stevens, the Secretary to the Admiralty, procured one to be made of iron in imitation of it, which I brought out with me, to show how much we excelled in making tools after their own fashion. This I had not yet produced, as it never happened to come into my mind. But on the 1st of May, Tootahah, coming on board about 10 o'clock in the forenoon, expressed a great curiosity to see the contents of every chest and drawer that was in my cabin. As I always made a point of gratifying him, I opened them immediately ; and having taken a fancy to many things that he saw, and collected them together, he at last happened to cast his eye upon this adze. He instantly snatched it up with the greatest eagerness, and, putting away everything which he had before selected, he asked me whether I would let him have that. I readily consented ; and, as if he was afraid I should repent, he carried it off immediately in a transport of joy, without making any other request, which, whatever had been our liberality, was seldom the case.

About noon, a chief who had dined with me a few days before, accompanied by some of his women, came on board alone. I had observed that he was fed by his women, but I made no doubt that upon occasion he would condescend to feed himself. In this, however, I found myself mistaken. When my noble guest was seated, and the dinner upon the table, I helped him to some victuals. As I observed that he did not immediately begin his meal, I pressed him to eat ; but he still continued to sit motionless like a statue, without attempting to put a single morsel into his mouth, and would certainly have gone without his dinner if one of the servants had not fed him.

In the afternoon of Monday the 1st of May we set up the observatory, and took the astronomical quadrant, with some other instruments, on shore, for the first time. The next morning, about 9 o'clock, I went on shore with Mr Green to fix the quadrant in a situation for use, when, to our inexpressible surprise and concern, it was not to be found. It had been deposited in the tent which was reserved for my use, where, as I passed the night on board, nobody slept. It had never been taken out of the packing-case, which was eighteen inches square, and the whole was of considerable weight; a sentinel had been posted the whole night within five yards of the tent door, and none of the other instruments were missing. We at first suspected that it might have been stolen by some of our own people, who, seeing a deal box, and not knowing the contents, might think it contained nails, or some other subjects of traffic with the natives. A large reward was therefore offered to any one who could find it, as without this we could not perform the service for which our voyage was principally undertaken. Our search in the meantime was not confined to the fort and places adjacent, but as the case might possibly have been carried back to the ship, if any of our own people had been the thieves, the most diligent search was made for it on board. All the parties, however, returned without any news of the quadrant. Mr Banks, therefore, who upon such occasions declined neither labour nor risk, and who had more influence over the Indians than any of us, determined to go in search of it into the woods; he hoped that if it had been stolen by the natives he should find it wherever they had opened the box, as they would immediately discover that to them it would be wholly useless; or, if in this expectation he should be disappointed, that he might recover it by the ascendancy he had acquired over the chiefs. He set out, accompanied by a midshipman and Mr Green, and as he was crossing the river he was met by Tubourai Tamaide, who immediately made the figure of a triangle with three bits of straw upon his hand. By this Mr Banks knew that the Indians were the thieves; and that, although they had opened the case, they were not disposed to part with the contents. No time was therefore to be lost, and Mr Banks made Tubourai Tamaide understand that he must instantly go with him to the place whither the quadrant had been carried. He consented, and they set out together to the eastward, the chief inquiring at every house which they passed after the thief by name. The people readily told him which way he was gone, and how long it was since he had been there. The hope which this gave them, that they should overtake him, supported them under their fatigue; and they pressed forward, sometimes walking, sometimes running, though the weather was intolerably hot. When they had climbed a hill at the distance of about four miles, their conductor showed them a point full three miles farther, and gave them to understand that they were not to expect the instrument till they had got thither. Here they paused; they had no arms, except a pair of pistols which Mr Banks always carried in his pocket. They were going to a place that was at least seven miles distant from the fort, where the Indians might be less submissive than at home, and to take from them what they had ventured their lives to get, and what, notwithstanding our conjectures, they appeared desirous to keep. These were discouraging circumstances, and their situation would become more critical at every step. They determined, however, not to relinquish their enterprise, nor to pursue it without taking the best measures for their security that were in their power. It was therefore determined that Mr Banks and Mr Green should go on, and that the midshipman should return to me, and desire that I would send a party of men after them, acquainting me, at the same time, that it was impossible they should return till it was dark. Upon receiving this message, I set out with such a party as I thought sufficient for the occasion, leaving orders, both at the ship and at the fort, that no canoe should be suffered to go out of the bay, but that none of the natives should be seized or detained.

In the meantime, Mr Banks and Mr Green pursued their journey, under the auspices of Tubourai Tamaide, and in the very spot which he had specified, they met one of his own people, with part of a quadrant in his hand. At this most welcome sight they stopped ; and a great number of Indians immediately came up, some of whom pressing rather rudely upon them, Mr Banks thought it necessary to show one of his pistols, the sight of which reduced them instantly to order. As the crowd that gathered round them was every moment increasing, he marked out a circle in the grass, and they ranged themselves on the outside of it, to the number of several hundreds, with great quietness and decorum. Into the middle of this circle, the box, which was now arrived, was ordered to be brought, with several reading glasses, and other small matters, which in their hurry they had put into a pistol-case that Mr Banks knew to be his property— it having been some time before stolen from the tents, with a horse pistol in it, which he immediately demanded, and which was all restored.

Mr Green was impatient to see whether all that had been taken away was returned, and upon examining the box found the stand, and a few small things of less consequence wanting. Several persons were sent in search of these, and most of the small things were returned. But it was signified that the thief had not brought the stand so far, and that it would be delivered to our friends as they went back ; this being confirmed by Tubourai Tamaide, they prepared to return, as nothing would then be wanting but what might easily be supplied ; and after they had advanced about two miles, I met them with my party, to our mutual satisfaction, congratulating each other upon the recovery of the quadrant, with a pleasure proportioned to the importance of the event.

About 8 o'clock, Mr Banks, with Tubourai Tamaide, got back to the fort ; when, to his great surprise, he found Tootahah in custody, and many of the natives in the utmost terror and distress, crowding about the gate. He went hastily in, some of the Indians were suffered to follow him, and the scene was extremely affecting. Tubourai Tamaide pressing forward, ran up to Tootahah, and catching him in his arms, they both burst into tears, and wept over each other, without being able to speak ; the other Indians were also in tears for their chief, both he and they being strongly possessed with the notion that he was to be put to death. In this situation they continued till I entered the fort, which was about a quarter of an hour afterwards. I was equally surprised and concerned at what had happened, the confining Tootahah being contrary to my orders, and therefore instantly set him at liberty. Upon inquiring into the affair, I was told, that my going into the woods with a party of men under arms, at a time when a robbery had been committed, which it was supposed I should resent in proportion to our apparent injury by the loss, had so alarmed the natives, that in the evening they began to leave the neighbourhood of the fort, with their effects ; that a double canoe having been seen to put off from the bottom of the bay by Mr Gore, the second lieutenant, who was left in command on board the ship, and who had received orders not to suffer any canoe to go out, he sent the boatswain with a boat after her to bring her back ; that as soon as the boat came up, the Indians, being alarmed, leaped into the sea and that, Tootahah being unfortunately one of the number, the boatswain took him up and brought him to the ship, suffering the rest of the people to swim on shore ; that Mr Gore, not sufficiently attending to the order that none of the people should be confined, had sent him to the fort, and Mr Hicks, the first lieutenant, who commanded there, receiving him in charge from Mr Gore, did not think himself at liberty to dismiss him. The notion that we intended to put him to death had possessed him so strongly, that he could not be persuaded to the contrary till by my orders he was led out of the fort. The people received him as they would have done a father in the same circumstances, and every one pressed forward to embrace him. Sudden joy is commonly liberal, without a scrupulous regard to merit ; and Tootahah, in the first expansion of his heart, upon being unexpectedly restored to liberty and life, insisted upon our receiving a present of two hogs ; though, being conscious that upon this occasion we had no claim to favours, we refused them many times.

Mr Banks and Dr Solander attended the next morning in their usual capacity of market-men ; but very few Indians appeared, and those who came brought no provisions. Tootahah, however, sent some of his people for the canoe that had been detained, which they took away. A canoe having also been detained that belonged to Oberea, Tupia, the person who managed her affairs when the Dolphin was here, was sent to examine whether anything on board had been taken away ; and he was so well satisfied of the contrary, that he left the canoe where he found it, and joined us at the fort, where he spent the day, and slept on board the canoe at night. About noon, some fishing-boats came abreast of the tents, but would part with very little of what they had on board ; and we felt the want of cocoanuts and bread-fruit very severely. In the course of the day, Mr Banks walked out into the woods, that by conversing with the people he might recover their confidence and goodwill. He found them civil, but they all complained of the ill-treatment of their chief, who, they said, had been beaten and pulled by the hair. Mr Banks endeavoured to convince them that he had suffered no personal violence, which, to the best of our knowledge, was true ; yet, perhaps, the boatswain had behaved with a brutality

which he was afraid or ashamed to acknowledge. The chief himself being probably, upon recollection, of opinion that we had ill-deserved the hogs which he had left with us as a present, sent a messenger in the afternoon to demand an axe and a shirt in return ; but as I was told that he did not intend to come down to the fort for ten days, I excused myself from giving them till I should see him, hoping that his impatience might induce him to fetch them, and knowing that absence would probably continue the coolness between us, to which the first interview might put an end.

The next day we were still more sensible of the inconvenience we had incurred by giving offence to the people in the person of their chief ; for the market was so ill supplied that we were in want of necessaries. Mr Banks therefore went into the woods to Tubourai Tamaide, and with some difficulty persuaded him to let us have five baskets of bread-fruit ; a very seasonable supply, as they contained above 120. In the afternoon another messenger arrived from Tootahah for the axe and shirt. As it was now become absolutely necessary to recover the friendship of this man, without which it would be scarcely possible to procure provisions, I sent word that Mr Banks and myself would visit him on the morrow, and bring what he wanted with us.

Early the next morning he sent again to remind me of my promise, and his people seemed to wait, till we should set out, with great impatience. I therefore ordered the pinnace, in which I embarked with Mr Banks and Dr Solander about 10 o'clock. We took one of Tootahah's people in the boat with us, and in about an hour we arrived at his place of residence, which is called Eparre, and is about four miles to the westward of the tents.

We found the people waiting for us in great numbers upon the shore, so that it would have been impossible for us to have proceeded, if way had not been made for us by a tall well-looking man, who had something like a turban about his head, and a long white stick in his hand, with which he laid about him at an unmerciful rate. This man conducted us to the chief, while the people shouted round us, "Taio Tootahah,"—"Tootahah is your friend." We found him, like an ancient patriarch, sitting under a tree, with a number of venerable old men standing round him. He made a sign to us to sit down, and immediately asked for his axe; this I presented to him, with an upper garment of broad cloth, made after the country fashion, and trimmed with tape, to which I also added a shirt. He received them with great satisfaction, and immediately put on the garment; but the shirt he gave to the person who had cleared the way for us upon our landing, who was now seated by us, and of whom he seemed desirous that we should take particular notice. In a short time, Oberea, and several other women whom we knew, came and sat down among us. Tootahah left us several times, but after a short absence returned; we thought it had been to show himself in his new finery to the people, but we wronged him, for it was to give directions for our refreshment and entertainment. While we were waiting for his return the last time he left us, very impatient to be dismissed, as we were almost suffocated in the crowd, word was brought us that he expected us elsewhere. We found him sitting under the awning of our own boat, and making signs that we should come to him. As many of us, therefore, went on board as the boat would hold, and he then ordered bread-fruit and cocoa-nuts to be brought, of both which we tasted, rather to gratify him than because we had a desire to eat. A message was soon after brought him, upon which he went out of the boat, and we were in a short time desired to follow. We were conducted to a large area or court-yard, which was railed round with bamboos about three feet high, on one side of his house, where an entertainment was provided for us, entirely new. This was a wrestling-match.

At the upper end of the area sat the chief, and several of his principal men were ranged on each side of him, so as to form a semicircle; these were the judges, by whom the victor was to be applauded. Seats were also left for us, at each end of the line; but we chose rather to be at liberty among the rest of the spectators.

When all was ready, ten or twelve persons, whom we understood to be the combatants, and who were naked, except a cloth that was fastened about the waist, entered the area, and walked slowly round it, in a stooping posture, with their left hands on their right breasts, and their right hands open, with which they frequently struck the left fore-arm so as to produce a quick smart sound. This was a general challenge to the combatants whom they were to engage, or any other person present. After these followed others, in the same manner; and then a particular challenge was given, by which each man singled out his antagonist. This was done by joining the finger ends of both hands, and bringing them to the breast, at the same time moving the elbows up and down with a quick motion. If the person to whom this was addressed accepted the challenge, he repeated the signs, and immediately each put himself into an attitude to engage. The next minute they closed, but, except in first seizing each other, it was a mere contest of strength; each endeavoured to lay hold of the other, first by the thigh, and if that failed by the hand, the hair, the cloth, or elsewhere as he could. When this was done they grappled, without the least dexterity or skill, till one of them, by having a more advantageous hold, or greater muscular force, threw the other on his back. When the contest was over, the old men gave their plaudit to the victor in a few words, which they repeated together in a kind of tune; his conquest was also generally celebrated by three huzzas. The entertainment was then suspended for a few minutes, after which another couple of wrestlers came forward and engaged in the same manner. If it happened that neither was thrown, after the contest had continued about a minute, they parted, either by consent or the intervention of their friends; and in this case each slapped his arm, as a challenge to a new engagement, either with the same antagonist or some other. While the wrestlers were engaged, another party of men performed a dance, which lasted also about a minute; but neither of these parties took the least notice of each other, their attention being wholly fixed on what they were doing. We observed with pleasure, that the conqueror never exulted over the vanquished, and that the vanquished never repined at the success of the conqueror; the whole contest was carried on with perfect good-will and good-humour, though in the presence of at least 500 spectators, of whom some were women. The number of women, indeed, was comparatively small; none but those of rank were present; and we had reason to believe that they would not have been spectators of this exercise but in compliment to us.

This lasted about two hours; during all which time, the man who had made a way for us when we landed, kept the people at a proper distance, by striking those who pressed forward very severely with his stick. Upon inquiry we learned that he was an officer belonging to Tootahah, acting as master of the ceremonies. It is scarcely possible, for those who are acquainted with the athletic sports of very remote antiquity, not to remark a rude resemblance of them in this wrestling-match among the natives of a little island in the midst of the Pacific Ocean. And female readers may recollect the account given of them by Fenelon in his Telemachus, where, though the events are fictitious, the manners of the age are faithfully transcribed from authors by whom they are supposed to have been truly related.

When the wrestling was over, we were given to understand that two hogs, and a large quantity of breadfruit, were preparing for our dinner; which, as our appetites were now keen, was very agreeable intelligence. Our host, however, seemed to repent of his liberality; for, instead of setting his two hogs before us, he ordered one of them to be carried into our boat: at first we were not sorry for this new disposition of matters, thinking that we should dine more comfortably in the boat than on shore, as the crowd would more easily be kept at a distance; but when we came on board, he ordered us to proceed with his hog to the ship. This was mortifying, as we were now to row four miles while our dinner was growing cold; however, we thought fit to comply, and were at last gratified with the cheer that he had provided, of which he and Tubourai Tamaide had a liberal share.

Our reconciliation with this man operated upon the people like a charm; for he was no sooner known to be on board, than bread-fruit, cocoa-nuts, and other provisions were brought to the fort in great plenty. Affairs now went on in the usual channel; but pork being still a scarce commodity, our master, Mr Mollineux, and Mr Green, went in the pinnace to the eastward, on the 8th, early in the morning, to see whether they could procure any hogs or poultry in that part of the country. They proceeded in that direction twenty miles; but though they saw many hogs, and one turtle, they could not purchase either at any price. The people everywhere told them, that they all belonged to Tootahah, and that they could sell none of them without his permission. We now began to think that this man was indeed a great prince; for an influence so extensive and absolute could be acquired by no other. And we afterwards found that he administered the government of this part of the island, as sovereign, for a minor whom we never saw all the time that we were upon it. When Mr Green returned from this expedition he said he had seen a tree of a size which he was afraid to relate, it being no less than sixty yards in circumference; but Mr Banks and Dr Solander soon explained to him that it was a species of the fig, the branches of which, bending down, take fresh root in the earth, and thus form a congeries of trunks, which being very close to each other, and all joined by a common vegetation, might easily be mistaken for one.

Though the market at the fort was now tolerably supplied, provisions were brought more slowly; a sufficient quantity used to be purchased between sun-rise and eight o'clock, but it was now become necessary to attend the greatest part of the day. Mr Banks, therefore, fixed his little boat up before the door of the fort, which was of great use as a place to trade in. Hitherto we had purchased cocoa-nuts and bread-fruit for beads; but the market becoming rather slack in these articles, we were now, for the first time, forced to bring out our nails. One of our smallest size, which was about four inches long, procured us twenty cocoa-nuts, and bread-fruit in proportion, so that in a short time our first plenty was restored.

On the 9th, soon after breakfast, we received a visit from Oberea, being the first that she had made us after the loss of our quadrant and the unfortunate confinement of Tootahah; with her came her present favourite, Oba-dée, and Tupia. They brought us a hog and some bread-fruit, in return for which we gave her a hatchet. We had now afforded our Indian friends a new and interesting object of curiosity— our forge, which, having been set up some time, was almost constantly at work. It was now common for them to bring pieces of iron, which we suppose they must have got from the Dolphin, to be made into tools of various kinds; and as I was very desirous to gratify them, they were indulged, except when the smith's time was too precious to be spared. Oberea, having received her hatchet, produced as much old iron as would have made another, with a request that another might be made of it; in this, however, I could not gratify her, upon which she brought out a broken axe, and desired it might be mended. I was glad of an opportunity to compromise the difference between us; her axe was mended, and she appeared to be con-

tent. They went away at night, and took with them the canoe, which had been a considerable time at the point, but promised to return in three days.

On the 10th, I put some seeds of melons and other plants into a spot of ground which had been turned up for the purpose; they had all been sealed up by the person of whom they were bought, in small bottles, with rosin; but none of them came up except mustard; even the cucumbers and melons failed, and Mr Banks is of opinion that they were spoiled by the total exclusion of fresh air.

This day we learned the Indian name of the island, which is Otaheite, and by that name I shall hereafter distinguish it. But after great pains taken we found it utterly impossible to teach the Indians to pronounce our names; we had, therefore, new names, consisting of such sounds as they produced in the attempt. They called me "Toote;" Mr Hicks, "Hete;" Mollineux they renounced in absolute despair, and called the master "Boba," from his christian name Robert; Mr Gore was "Toarro;" Dr Solander, "Torano;" and Mr Banks, "Tapane;" Mr Green, "Eteree;" Mr Parkinson, "Patini;" Mr Sporing, "Polini;" Petersgill, "Pedrodero;" and in this manner they had now formed names for almost every man in the ship. In some, however, it was not easy to find any traces of the original, and they were perhaps not mere arbitrary sounds, formed upon the occasion, but significant words in their own language. Monkhouse, the midshipman who commanded the party that killed the man for stealing the musket, they called "Matte;" not merely by an attempt to imitate in sound the first syllable of Monkhouse, but because "Matte" signifies dead; and this might probably be the case with others.

Friday, the 12th of May, was distinguished by a visit from some ladies whom we had never seen before, and who introduced themselves with very singular ceremonies. Mr Banks was trading in his boat at the gate of the fort as usual, in company with Tootahah, who had that morning paid him a visit, and some other of the natives. Between 9 and 10 o'clock, a double canoe came to the landing-place, under the awning of which sat a man and two women. The Indians that were about Mr Banks made signs that he should go out to meet them, which he hasted to do; but by the time he could get out of the boat, they had advanced within ten yards of him; they then stopped, and made signs that he should do so too, laying down about a dozen young plantain-trees, and some other small plants. He complied, and, the people having made a lane between them, the man, who appeared to be a servant, brought six of them to Mr Banks by one of each at a time, passing and repassing six times, and always pronouncing a short sentence when he delivered them. Tupia, who stood by Mr Banks, acted as his master of the ceremonies, and, receiving the branches as they were brought, laid them down in the boat. When this was done, another man brought a large bundle of cloth, which having opened, he spread piece by piece upon the ground, in the space between Mr Banks and his visitors. There were nine pieces, and having laid three pieces one upon another, the foremost of the women, who seemed to be the principal, and who was called Oorattooa, stepped upon them, and taking up her garments all around her to the waist, turned about, with great composure and deliberation, and with an air of perfect innocence and simplicity, three times. When this was done, she dropped the veil, and stepping off the cloth, three more pieces were laid on, and she repeated the ceremony, then stepping off as before; the last three were laid on, and the ceremony was repeated in the same manner the third time. Immediately after this the cloth was rolled up, and given to Mr Banks as a present from the lady, who, with her friend, came up and saluted him. He made such presents to them both as he thought would be most acceptable, and after having stayed about an hour they went away. In the evening the gentlemen at the fort had a visit from Oberea, and her favourite female attendant, whose name was Otheothea, an agreeable girl, whom they were the more pleased to see, because, having been some days absent, it had been reported she was either sick or dead.

On the 13th, the market being over about 10 o'clock, Mr Banks walked into the woods with his gun, as he generally did, for the benefit of the shade in the heat of the day. As he was returning, he met Tubourai Tamaide, near his occasional dwelling, and stopping to spend a little time with him, he suddenly took the gun out of Mr Banks's hand, cocked it, and holding it up in the air, drew the trigger; fortunately for him it flashed in the pan. Mr Banks immediately took it from him, not a little surprised how he had acquired sufficient knowledge of a gun to discharge it, and reproved him with great severity for what he had done. As it was of infinite importance to keep the Indians totally ignorant of the management of fire-arms, he had taken every opportunity of intimating that they could never offend him so highly as by even touching his piece; it was now proper to enforce this prohibition, and he therefore added threats to his reproof. The Indian bore all patiently; but the moment Mr Banks crossed the river, he set off with all his family and furniture for his house at Eparre. This being quickly known from the Indians at the fort, and great inconvenience being apprehended from the displeasure of this man, who upon all occasions had been particularly useful, Mr Banks determined to follow him without delay, and solicit his return. He set out the same evening accompanied by Mr Mollineux, and found him sitting in the middle of a large circle of people, to whom he had probably related what had happened, and his fears of the consequences. He was himself the very picture of grief and dejection, and the same passions were strongly marked in the countenances of all the people that surrounded him.

When Mr Banks and Mr Mollineux went into the circle, one of the women expressed her trouble as Terapo had done upon another occasion, and struck a shark's tooth into her head several times till it was covered with blood. Mr Banks lost no time in putting an end to this universal distress; he assured the chief that everything which had passed should be forgotten, that there was not the least animosity remaining on one side, nor anything to be feared on the other. The chief was soon soothed into confidence and complacency, a double canoe was ordered to be got ready, they all returned together to the fort before supper, and, as a pledge of perfect reconciliation, both he and his wife slept all night in Mr Banks's tent. Their presence, however, was no palladium; for, between 11 and 12 o'clock, one of the natives attempted to get into the fort by scaling the walls, with a design, no doubt, to steal whatever he should happen to find. He was discovered by the sentinel, who happily did not fire, and he ran away much faster than any of our people could follow him. The iron and iron-tools which were in continual use at the armourer's forge that was set up within the works, were temptations to theft which none of these people could withstand.

On the 14th, which was Sunday, I directed that divine service should be performed at the fort. We were desirous that some of the principal Indians should be present; but when the hour came, most of them were returned home. Mr Banks, however, crossed the river, and brought back Tubourai Tamaide and his wife Tomio, hoping that it would give occasion to some inquiries on their part, and some instruction on ours. Having seated them, he placed himself between them, and during the whole service they very attentively observed his behaviour, and very exactly imitated it; standing, sitting, or kneeling, as they saw him do. They were conscious that we were employed about somewhat serious and impor-

tant, as appeared by their calling to the Indians without the fort to be silent; yet when the service was over, neither of them asked any questions, nor would they attend to any attempt that was made to explain what had been done.

On the 14th and 15th, we had another opportunity of observing the general knowledge which these people had of any design that was formed among them. In the night between the 13th and 14th, one of the water-casks was stolen from the outside of the fort. In the morning there was not an Indian to be seen who did not know that it was gone; yet they appeared not to have been trusted, or not to have been worthy of trust; for they seemed all of them disposed to give intelligence where it might be found. Mr Banks traced it to a part of the bay where he was told it had been put into a canoe; but, as it was not of great consequence, he did not complete the discovery. When he returned, he was told by Tubourai Tamaide that another cask would be stolen before the morning. How he came by this knowledge it is not easy to imagine; that he was not a party in the design is certain, for he came with his wife and family to the place where the water-casks stood, and placing their beds near them, he said he would himself be a pledge for their safety, in despite of the thief. Of this, however, we would not admit, and making them understand that a sentry would be placed to watch the casks till the morning, he removed the beds into Mr Banks's tent, where he and his family spent the night, making signs to the sentry when he retired, that he should keep his eyes open. In the night this intelligence appeared to be true; about 12 o'clock the thief came, but discovering that a watch had been set, he went away without his booty.

Mr Banks's confidence in Tubourai Tamaide had greatly increased since the affair of the knife, in consequence of which he was at length exposed to temptations which neither his integrity nor his honour was able to resist.

They had withstood many allurements, but were at length ensnared by the fascinating charms of a basket of nails. These nails were much larger than any that had yet been brought into trade, and had, with perhaps some degree of criminal negligence, been left in a corner of Mr Banks's tent, to which the chief had always free access. One of these nails Mr Banks's servant happened to see in his possession, upon his having inadvertently thrown back that part of his garment under which it was concealed. Mr Banks being told of this, and knowing that no such thing had been given him either as a present or in barter, immediately examined the basket, and discovered that out of seven nails five were missing. He then, though not without great reluctance, charged him with the fact, which he immediately confessed, and, however he might suffer, was probably not more hurt than his accuser. A demand was immediately made for restitution; but this he declined, saying that the nails were at Eparre. However, Mr Banks appearing to be much in earnest, and using some threatening signs, he thought fit to produce one of them. He was then taken to the fort, to receive such judgment as should be given against him by the general voice. After some deliberation, that we might not appear to think too lightly of his offence, he was told, that if he would bring the other four nails to the fort, it should be forgotten. To this condition he agreed; but I am sorry to say he did not fulfil it. Instead of fetching the nails, he removed with his family before night, and took all his furniture with him.

As our long-boat had appeared to be leaky, I thought it necessary to examine her bottom, and to my great surprise, found it so much eaten by the worms, that it was necessary to give her a new one. No such accident had happened to the Dolphin's boats, as I was informed by the officers on board, and therefore it was a misfortune that I did not expect. I feared that the pinnace also might be nearly in the same condition, but, upon examining her, I had the satisfaction to find that not a worm had touched her, though she was built of the same wood, and had been as much in the water. The reason of this difference I imagine to be that the long-boat was payed with varnish of pine, and the pinnace painted with white lead and oil; the bottoms of all boats, therefore, which are sent into this country should be painted like that of the pinnace, and the ships should be supplied with a good stock, in order to give them a new coating when it should be found necessary.

Having received repeated messages from Tootahah, that if we would pay him a visit he would acknowledge the favour by a present of four hogs, I sent Mr Hicks, my first lieutenant, to try if he could not procure the hogs upon easier terms, with orders to show him every civility in his power. Mr Hicks found that he was removed from Eparre to a place called Tettahah, five miles farther to the westward. He was received with great cordiality; one hog was immediately produced, and he was told that the other three, which were at some distance, should be brought in the morning. Mr Hicks readily consented to stay; but the morning came without the hogs; and it not being convenient to stay longer, he returned in the evening with the one he had got.

On the 25th, Tubourai Tamaide and his wife Tomio made their appearance at the tent, for the first time since he had been detected in stealing the nails. He seemed to be under some discontent and apprehension, yet he did not think fit to purchase our countenance and good-will by restoring the four which he had sent away. As Mr Banks and the other gentlemen treated him with a coolness and reserve which did not at all tend to restore his peace or good-humour, his stay was short, and his departure abrupt. Mr Monkhouse, the surgeon, went the next morning in order to effect a reconciliation, by persuading him to bring down the nails ; but he could not succeed.

On the 27th, it was determined that we should pay our visit to Tootahah, though we were not very confident that we should receive the hogs for our pains. I therefore set out early in the morning, with Mr Banks and Dr Solander, and three others, in the pinnace. He was now removed from Tettahah, where Mr Hicks had seen him, to a place called Atahourou, about six miles farther ; and as we could not go above half-way thither in the boat, it was almost evening before we arrived. We found him in his usual state, sitting under a tree, with a great crowd about him. We made our presents in due form, consisting of a yellow stuff petticoat and some other trifling articles, which were graciously received ; a hog was immediately ordered to be killed and dressed for supper, with a promise of more in the morning. However, as we were less desirous of feasting upon our journey than of carrying back with us provisions, which would be more welcome at the fort, we procured a reprieve for the hog, and supped upon the fruits of the country. As night now came on, and the place was crowded with many more than the houses and canoes would contain, there being Oberea, with her attendants, and many other travellers whom we knew, we began to look out for lodgings. Our party consisted of six. Mr Banks thought himself fortunate in being offered a place by Oberea in her canoe, and wishing his friends a good-night, took his leave. He went to rest early, according to the custom of the country, and taking off his clothes, as was his constant practice, the nights being hot, Oberea kindly insisted upon taking them into her own custody, for otherwise, she said, they would certainly be stolen. Mr Banks, having such a safe guard, resigned himself to sleep with all imaginable tranquillity ; but waking about 11 o'clock, and wanting to get up, he searched for his clothes where he had seen them deposited by Oberea

when he lay down to sleep, and soon perceived that they were amissing. He immediately awakened Oberea, who, starting up and hearing his complaint, ordered lights, and prepared in great haste to recover what he had lost. Tootahah himself slept in the next canoe, and being soon alarmed, he came to them, and set out with Oberea in search of the thief. Mr Banks was not in a condition to go with them, for of his apparel scarce anything was left him but his breeches. His coat and his waistcoat, with his pistols, powder-horn, and many other things that were in the pockets, were gone. In about half-an-hour his two noble friends returned, but without having obtained any intelligence of his clothes or of the thief. At first he began to be alarmed ; his musket had not indeed been taken away, but he had neglected to load it. Where I and Dr Solander had disposed of ourselves he did not know ; and therefore, whatever might happen, he could not have recourse to us for assistance. He thought it best, however, to express neither fear nor suspicion of those about him ; and giving his musket to Tupia, who had been waked in the confusion and stood by him, with a charge not to suffer it to be stolen, he betook himself again to rest, declaring himself perfectly satisfied with the pains that Tootahah and Oberea had taken to recover his things, though they had not been successful. As it cannot be supposed that in such a situation his sleep was very sound, he soon after heard music, and saw lights at a little distance on shore. This was a concert or assembly, which they call a Heiva, a common name for every public exhibition ; and as it would necessarily bring many people together, and there was a chance of my being among them with his other friends, he rose and made the best of his way towards it. He was soon led by the lights and the sound to the hut where I lay, with three other gentlemen of our party ; and easily distinguishing us from the rest, he made up to us more than half naked, and told us his melancholy story. We gave him such comfort as the unfortunate generally give to each other, by telling him that we were fellow-sufferers. I showed him that I was myself without stockings, they having been stolen from under my head, though I was sure I had never been asleep; and each of my associates convinced him by his appearance that he had lost a jacket. We determined nevertheless to hear out the concert, however deficient we might appear in our dress. It consisted of three drums, four flutes, and several voices. When this entertainment, which lasted about an hour, was over, we retired again to our sleeping places, having agreed that nothing could be done toward the recovery of our things till the morning.

We rose at daybreak, according to the custom of the country. The first man that Mr Banks saw was Tupia, faithfully attending with his musket; and soon after, Oberea brought him some of her country clothes as a succedaneum for his own; so that when he came to us he made a most motley appearance, half Indian and half English. Our party soon got together, except Dr Solander, whose quarters we did not know, and who had not assisted at the concert. In a short time Tootahah made his appearance, and we pressed him to recover our clothes; but neither he nor Oberea could be persuaded to take any measure for that purpose, so that we began to suspect that they had been parties in the theft. About 8 o'clock we were joined by Dr Solander, who had fallen into honester hands, at a house about a mile distant, and had lost nothing. Having given up all hope of recovering our clothes, which indeed were never afterwards heard of, we spent all the morning in soliciting the hogs which we had been promised; but in this we had no better success. We therefore, in no very good humour, set out for the boat about 12 o'clock, with only that which we had redeemed from the butcher and the cook the night before.

As we were returning to the boat, however, we were entertained with a sight that in some measure compensated for our fatigue and disappointment. In our way we came to one of the few places where access to the island is not guarded by a reef, and consequently a high surf breaks upon the shore. A more dreadful one indeed I had seldom seen. It was impossible for any European boat to have lived in it; and if the best swimmer in Europe had by any accident been exposed to its fury, I am confident that he would not have been able to preserve himself from drowning, especially as the shore was covered with pebbles and large stones. Yet in the midst of these breakers were ten or twelve Indians swimming for their amusement. Whenever a surf broke near them they dived under it, and, to all appearance with infinite facility, rose again on the other side. This diversion was greatly improved by the stern of an old canoe, which they happened to find upon the spot. They took this before them, and swam out with it as far as the outermost breach; then two or three of them, getting into it, and turning the square end to the breaking wave, were driven in towards the shore with incredible rapidity, sometimes almost to the beach; but generally the wave broke over them before they got half way, in which case they dived, and rose on the other side with the canoe in their hands. They then swam out with it again, and were again driven back, just as our holiday youth climb the hill in Greenwich Park for the pleasure of rolling down it. At this wonderful scene we stood gazing for more than half-an-hour, during which time none of the swimmers attempted to come on shore, but seemed to enjoy their sport in the highest degree. We then proceeded on our journey, and late in the evening got back to the fort.

Among other Indians that had visited us, there were some from a neighbouring island which they called Eimeo or Imao, the same to which Captain Wallis had given the name of the Duke of York's Island; and they gave us an account of no less than two-and-twenty islands that lay in the neighbourhood of Otaheite.

As the day of observation now approached, I determined, in consequence of some hints which had been given me by Lord Morton, to send out two parties to observe the transit from other situations, hoping that if we should fail at Otaheite, they might have better success. We were, therefore, now busily employed in preparing our instruments, and instructing such gentlemen in the use of them as I intended to send out. On Thursday the 1st of June, the Saturday following being the day of the transit, I despatched Mr Gore in the long-boat to Imao, with Mr Monkhouse and Mr Sporing, a gentleman belonging to Mr Banks, Mr Green having furnished them with proper instruments. Mr Banks himself thought fit to go upon this expedition; and several natives, particularly Tubourai Tamaide and Tomio, were also of the party. Very early on the Friday morning, I sent Mr Hicks, with Mr Clerk and Mr Petersgill, the master's mates, and Mr Saunders, one of the midshipmen, in the pinnace to the eastward, with orders to fix on some convenient spot at a distance from our principal observatory, where they also might employ the instruments with which they had been furnished for the same purpose.

The long-boat not having been got ready till Thursday in the afternoon, though all possible expedition was used to fit her out, the people on board, after having rowed most part of the night, brought her to a grappling just under the land of Imao. Soon after daybreak they saw an Indian canoe, which they hailed, and the people on board showed them an inlet through the reef, into which they pulled, and soon fixed upon a coral rock, which rose out of the water about 150 yards from the shore, as a proper situation for their observatory. It was about eighty yards long and twenty broad, and in the middle of it was a bed of white sand, large enough for the tents to stand upon. Mr Gore and his assistants immediately began to set them up, and make other necessary preparations for the important business of the next day. While this was doing, Mr Banks, with the Indians of Otaheite, and the people whom they had met in the canoe, went ashore upon the main island to buy provisions; of which he procured a sufficient supply before night. When he returned to the rock he found the observatory in order, and the telescopes all fixed and tried. The evening was very fine, yet their solicitude did not permit them to take much rest in the night; one or other of them was up every half-hour, who satisfied the impatience of the rest by reporting the changes of the sky—now encouraging their hope by telling them that it was clear, and now alarming their fears by an account that it was hazy.

At daybreak they got up, and had the satisfaction to see the sun rise without a cloud. Mr Banks then wishing the observers, Mr Gore and Mr Monkhouse, success, repaired again to the island, that he might examine its produce and get a fresh supply of provisions. He began by trading with the natives, for which purpose he took his station under a tree; and to keep them from pressing upon him in a crowd, he drew a circle round him, which he suffered none of them to enter. About 8 o'clock he saw two canoes coming towards the place, and was given to understand by the people about him that they belonged to Tarrao, the king of the island, who was coming to make him a visit. As soon as the canoes came near the shore, the people made a lane from the beach to the trading-place, and his majesty landed with his sister, whose name was Nuna. As they advanced towards the tree where Mr Banks stood, he went out to meet them, and, with great formality, introduced them into the circle from which the other natives had been excluded. As it is the custom of these people to sit during all their conferences, Mr Banks unwrapped a kind of turban of Indian cloth, which he wore upon his head instead of a hat, and spreading it upon the ground, they all sat down upon it together. The royal present was then brought, which consisted of a hog and a dog, some bread-fruit, cocoa-nuts, and other articles of the like kind. Mr Banks then despatched a canoe to the observatory for his present, and the messengers soon returned with an adze, a shirt, and some beads, which were presented to his majesty, and received with great satisfaction. By this time Tubourai Tamaide and Tomio joined them from the observatory. Tomio said that she was related to Tarrao, and brought him a present of a long nail, at the same time complimenting Nuna with a shirt.

The first internal contact of the planet with the sun being over, Mr Banks returned to the observatory, taking Tarrao, Nuna, and some of their principal attendants, among whom were three very handsome young women, with him. He showed them the planet upon the sun, and endeavoured to make them understand that he and his companions had come from their own country on purpose to see it. Soon after Mr Banks returned with them to the island, where he spent the rest of the day in examining its produce, which he found to be much the same with that of Otaheite. The people whom he saw there also exactly resembled the inhabitants of that island, and many of them were persons whom he had seen upon it; so that all those whom he had dealt with knew of what his trading articles consisted, and the value they bore. The next morning, having struck the tents, they set out on their return, and arrived at the fort before night.

The observation was made with equal success by the persons whom I had sent to the eastward, and at the fort. There not being a cloud in the sky from the rising to the setting of the sun, the whole passage of the planet Venus over the sun's disc was observed with great advantage by Mr Green, Dr Solander, and myself. Mr Green's telescope and mine were of the same magnifying power, but that of Dr Solander's was greater. We all saw an atmosphere or dusky cloud round the body of the planet, which very much disturbed the times of contact, especially of the internal ones; and we differed from each other in our accounts of the times of the contacts much more than might have been expected. According to Mr Green,

	Ho.	Min.	Sec.	
The first external contact, or first appearance of Venus on the Sun, was . .	9	25	42	Morning.
The first internal contact, or total emersion, was . .	9	44	4	
The second internal contact, or beginning of the emersion, . .	3	14	8	Afternoon.
The second external contact, or total emersion, . . .	3	32	10	

The latitude of the observatory was found to be 17° 29′ 15″, and the longitude 149° 32′ 30″ W. of Greenwich.

But if we had reason to congratulate ourselves upon the success of our observation, we had scarce less cause to regret the diligence with which that time had been improved by some of our people to another purpose. While the attention of the officers was engrossed by the transit of Venus, some of the ship's company broke into one of the store-rooms and stole a quantity of spike nails, amounting to no less than one hundredweight. This was a matter of public and serious concern; for these nails, if circulated by the people among the Indians, would do us irreparable injury, by reducing the value of iron, our staple commodity. One of the thieves was detected, but only seven nails were found in his custody. He was punished with two dozen lashes, but would impeach none of his accomplices.

On the 5th we kept his Majesty's birthday; for, though it is the 4th, we were unwilling to celebrate it during the absence of the two parties who had been sent out to observe the transit. We had several of the Indian chiefs at our entertainment, who drank his Majesty's health by the name of "Kihiargo," which was the nearest imitation they could produce of King George.

About this time died an old woman of some rank, who was related to Tomio, which gave us an opportunity to see how they disposed of the body, and confirmed us in our opinion that these people, contrary to the present custom of all other nations now known, never bury their dead. In the middle of a small square, neatly railed in with bamboo, the awning of a canoe was raised upon two posts, and under this the body was deposited upon such a frame as has before been described. It was covered with fine cloth, and near it was placed bread-fruit, fish, and other provisions. We supposed that the food was placed there for the spirit of the deceased, and consequently that these Indians had some confused notion of a separate state; but upon our applying for further information to Tubourai Tamaide, he told us that the food was placed there as an offering to their gods. They do not, however, suppose that the gods eat, any more than the Jews supposed that Jehovah could dwell in a house. The offering is made here upon the same principle as the temple was built at Jerusalem—as an expression of reverence and gratitude, and a solicitation of the more immediate presence of the Deity. In the front of the area was a kind of stile, where the relations of the deceased stood to pay the tribute of their sorrow; and under the awning were innumerable small pieces of cloth, on which the tears and blood of the mourners had been shed; for in their paroxysms of grief it is a universal custom to wound themselves with the shark's tooth. Within a few yards two occasional houses were set up, in one of which some relations of the deceased constantly resided, and in the other the chief mourner—who is always a man, and who keeps there a very singular dress, in which a ceremony is performed that will be described in its

turn. Near the place where the dead are thus set up to rot, the bones are afterwards buried.

Having observed that bread-fruit had for some days been brought in less quantities than usual, we inquired the reason, and were told, that there being a great show of fruit upon the trees, they had been thinned all at once, in order to make a kind of sour paste, which the natives call "mahie," and which, in consequence of having undergone a fermentation, will keep a considerable time, and supply them with food when no ripe fruit is to be had.

On the 10th, the ceremony was to be performed in honour of the old woman whose sepulchral tabernacle has been described, by the chief mourner; and Mr Banks had so great a curiosity to see all the mysteries of the solemnity, that he determined to take a part in it, being told that he could be present upon no other condition. In the evening, therefore, he repaired to the place where the body lay, and was received by the daughter of the deceased, and several other persons, among whom was a boy about fourteen years old, who were to assist in the ceremony. Tubourai Tamaide was to be the principal mourner; and his dress was extremely fantastical, though not unbecoming. Mr Banks was stripped of his European clothes, and, a small piece of cloth being tied round his middle, his body was smeared with charcoal and water, as low as the shoulders, till it was as black as that of a Negro. The same operation was performed upon several others, among whom were some women, who were reduced to a state as near to nakedness as himself; the boy was blacked all over, and then the procession set forward. Tubourai Tamaide uttered something, which was supposed to be a prayer, near the body, and did the same when he came up to his own house. When this was done, the procession was continued towards the fort, permission having been obtained to approach it upon this occasion. It is the custom of the Indians to fly from these processions with the utmost precipitation, so that as soon as those who were about the fort saw it at a distance, they hid themselves in the woods. It proceeded from the fort along the shore, and put to flight another body of Indians, consisting of more than 100, every one hiding himself under the first shelter that he could find. It then crossed the river, and entered the woods, passing several houses, all which were deserted, and not a single Indian could be seen during the rest of the procession, which continued more than half-an-hour. The office that Mr Banks performed was called that of the Nineveh, of which there were two besides himself; and the natives having all disappeared, they came to the chief mourner, and said, "Imitata"—"There are no people," after which the company was dismissed to wash themselves in the river, and put on their customary apparel.

On the 12th, complaint being made to me by some of the natives that two of the seamen had taken from them several bows and arrows, and some strings of plaited hair, I examined the matter, and finding the charge well supported, I punished each of the criminals with two dozen lashes. Their bows and arrows have not been mentioned before, nor were they often brought down to the fort. This day, however, Tubourai Tamaide brought down his, in consequence of a challenge which he had received from Mr Gore. The chief supposed it was to try who could send the arrow farthest; Mr Gore, who best could hit a mark; and as Mr Gore did not value himself upon shooting to a great distance, nor the chief upon hitting a mark, there was no trial of skill between them. Tubourai Tamaide, however, to show us what he could do, drew his bow, and sent an arrow, none of which are feathered, 274 yards, which is something more than a seventh, and something less than a sixth part of a mile. Their manner of shooting is somewhat singular; they kneel down, and, the moment the arrow is discharged, drop the bow.

Mr Banks, in his morning walk this day, met a number of the natives, whom, upon inquiry, he found to be travelling musicians; and having learned where they were to be at night, we all repaired to the place. The band consisted of two flutes and three drums, and we found a great number of people assembled upon the occasion. The drummers accompanied the music with their voices, and, to our great surprise, we discovered that we were generally the subject of the song. We did not expect to have found among the uncivilised inhabitants of this sequestered spot, a character which has been the subject of such praise and veneration where genius and knowledge have been most conspicuous; yet these were the bards or minstrels of Otaheite. Their song was unpremeditated, and accompanied with music; they were continually going about from place to place, and they were rewarded by the master of the house, and the audience, with such things as one wanted and the other could spare.

On the 14th, we were brought into new difficulties and inconvenience by another robbery at the fort. In the middle of the night, one of the natives contrived to steal an iron coalrake that was made use of for the oven. It happened to be set up against the inside of the wall, so that the top of the handle was visible from without; and we were informed that the thief, who had been seen lurking there in the evening, came secretly about three o'clock in the morning, and, watching his opportunity when the sentinel's back was turned, very dexterously laid hold of it with a long crooked stick, and drew it over the wall. I thought it of some consequence, if possible, to put an end to these practices at once, by doing something that should make it the common interest of the natives themselves to prevent them. I had given strict orders that they should not be fired upon, even when detected in these attempts, for which I had many reasons. The common sentinels were by no means fit to be entrusted with a power of life and death, to be exerted whenever they should think fit, and I had already experienced that they were ready to take away the lives that were in their power upon the slightest occasion; neither, indeed, did I think that the thefts which these people committed against us, were, in them, crimes worthy of death. That thieves are hanged in England, I thought no reason why they should be shot in Otaheite, because, with respect to the natives, it would have been an execution by a law *ex post facto*. They had no such law among themselves, and it did not appear to me that we had any right to make such a law for them. That they should abstain from theft, or be punished with death, was not one of the conditions under which they claimed advantages of civil society, as it is among us; and I was not willing to expose them to fire-arms loaded with shot, neither could I perfectly approve of firing only with powder. At first, indeed, the noise and the smoke would alarm them, but when they found that no mischief followed, they would be led to despise the weapons themselves, and proceed to insults which would make it necessary to put them to the test, and from which they would be deterred by the very sight of a gun, if it was never used but with effect.

At this time, an accident furnished me with what I thought a happy expedient. It happened that above twenty of their sailing canoes were just come in with a supply of fish. Upon these I immediately seized, and, bringing them into the river behind the fort, gave public notice that except the rake, and all the rest of the things which from time to time had been stolen, were returned, the canoes should be burned. This menace I ventured to publish, though I had no design to put it into execution, making no doubt but that it was well known in whose possession the stolen goods were, and that, as restitution was thus made a common cause, they would all of them in a short time be brought back. A list of the things was made out, consisting principally of the rake, the musket which had been taken from the marine when the Indian was shot, the pistols which Mr Banks lost with his clothes at Atahourou, a sword belonging to one of the petty officers, and the water cask. About noon the rake was restored, and great solicitation was made for the release of the canoes; but I still insisted upon my original condition. The next day came, and nothing further was restored, at which I was much surprised, for the people were in the utmost distress for the fish, which in a short time would be spoilt; I was, therefore, reduced to a disagreeable situation, either of releasing the canoes, contrary to what I had solemnly and publicly declared, or detaining them, to the great injury of those who /were innocent, without answering any good purpose to ourselves. As a temporary expedient I permitted them to take the fish, but still detained the canoes. This very license, however, was productive of new confusion and injury; for, it not being easy at once to distinguish to what particular person the several lots of fish belonged, the canoes were plundered, under favour of this circumstance, by those who had no right to any part of their cargo. Most pressing instances were still made that the canoes might be restored; and I, having now the greatest reason to believe either that the things for which I detained them were not in the island, or that those who suffered by their detention had not sufficient influence over the thieves to prevail upon them to relinquish their booty, determined at length to give them up, not a little mortified at the bad success of my project.

Another accident also about this time was, notwithstanding all our caution, very near embroiling us with the Indians. I sent the boat on shore, with an officer, to get ballast for the ship; and, not immediately finding stones convenient for the purpose, he began to pull down some part of an enclosure where they deposited the bones of their dead. This the Indians violently opposed, and a messenger came down to the tents to acquaint the officers that they would not suffer it. Mr Banks immediately repaired to the place, and an amicable end was soon put to the dispute, by sending the boat's crew to the river, where stones enough were to be gathered without a possibility of giving offence. It is very remarkable, that these Indians appeared to be much more jealous of what was done to the dead than the living. This was the only measure in which they ventured to oppose us, and the only insult that was offered to any individual among us was upon a similar occasion. Mr Monkhouse happening one day to pull a flower from a tree which grew in one of their sepulchral enclosures, an Indian, whose jealousy had probably been upon the watch, came suddenly behind him, and struck him. Mr Monkhouse laid hold of him, but he was instantly rescued by two more, who took hold of Mr Monkhouse's hair and forced him to quit his hold of their companion, and then ran away without offering him any further violence.

In the evening of the 19th, while the canoes were still detained, we received a visit from Oberea, which surprised us not a little, as she brought with her none of the things that had been stolen, and knew that she was suspected of having some of them in her custody. She said, indeed, that her favourite Obadée, whom she had beaten and dismissed, had taken them away; but she seemed conscious that she had no right to be believed. She discovered the strongest signs of fear, yet she surmounted it with astonishing resolution; and was very pressing to sleep with her attendants in Mr Banks's tent. In this, however, she was not gratified; the affair of the jacket was too recent, and the tent was, besides, filled with other people. Nobody else seemed willing to entertain her; and she therefore, with great appearance of mortification and disappointment, spent the night in her canoe. The next morning early, she returned to the fort, with her canoe and everything that it contained, putting herself wholly into our power, with something like greatness of mind, which excited our wonder and admiration. As the most effectual means to bring about a reconciliation, she presented us with a hog, and several other things, among which was a dog. We had learned that these animals were esteemed by the Indians as more delicate food than their pork; and upon this occasion we determined to try the experiment. The dog, which was very fat, we consigned over to Tupia, who undertook to perform the double office of butcher and cook. He killed him by holding his hands close over his mouth and nose, an operation which continued above a quarter of an hour. While this was doing, a hole was made in the ground about a foot deep, in which a fire was kindled, and some small stones placed in layers alternately with the wood to heat; the dog was then singed by holding him over the fire, and, by scraping him with a shell, the hair taken off as clean as if he had been scalded in hot water. He was then cut up with the same instrument, and his entrails, being taken out, were sent to the sea, where, being carefully washed, they were put into cocoa-nut shells, with what blood had come from the body. When the hole was sufficiently heated, the fire was taken out, and some of the stones, which were not so hot as to discolour anything that they touched, being placed at the bottom, were covered with green leaves. The dog, with the entrails, was then placed upon the leaves, and other leaves being laid upon them, the whole was covered with the rest of the hot stones, and the mouth of the hole close stopped with mould. In somewhat less than four hours it was again opened, and the dog taken out excellently baked; and we all agreed that he had made a very good dish. The dogs which are here bred to be eaten, taste no animal food, but are kept wholly upon bread-fruit, cocoa-nuts, yams, and other vegetables of the like kind. All the flesh and fish eaten by the inhabitants is dressed in the same way.

On the 21st, we were visited at the fort by a chief, called Oamo, whom we had never seen before, and who was treated by the natives with uncommon respect. He brought with him a boy about seven years old, and a young woman about sixteen; the boy was carried upon a man's back, which we considered as a piece of state, for he was as well able to walk as any present. As soon as they were in sight, Oberea and several other natives who were in the fort went out to meet them, having first uncovered their heads and bodies as low as the waist. As they came on, the same ceremony was performed by all the natives who were without the fort. Uncovering the body, therefore, is in this country probably a mark of respect; and as all parts are here exposed with equal indifference, the ceremony of uncovering it from the waist downwards, which was performed by Oorattooa, might be nothing more than a different mode of compliment adapted to persons of a different rank. The chief came into the tent, but no entreaty could prevail upon the young woman to follow him, though she seemed to refuse contrary to her inclination. The natives without were indeed all very solicitous to prevent her; sometimes, when her resolution seemed to fail, almost using force. The boy also they restrained in the same manner; but Dr Solander, happening to meet him at the gate, took him by the hand, and led him in before the people were aware of it. As soon, however, as those that were within saw him, they took care to have him sent out.

These circumstances having strongly excited our curiosity, we inquired who they were, and were informed that Oamo was the husband of Oberea, though they had been a long time separated by mutual consent; and that the young woman and the boy were their children. We learned also, that the boy, whose name was Terridiri, was heir-apparent to the sovereignty of the island, and that his sister was intended for his wife, the marriage being deferred only till he should arrive at a proper age. The sovereign at this time was a son of Whappai, whose name was Outou, and who, as before has been observed, was a minor. Whappai, Oamo, and Tootahah, were brothers; Whappai was the eldest, and Oamo the second; so that, Whappai having no child but Outou, Terridiri, the son of his next brother Oamo, was heir to the sovereignty. It will, perhaps, seem strange that a boy should be sovereign during the life of his father; but, according to the custom of the country, a child succeeds to a father's title and authority as soon as it is born. A regent is then elected, and the father of the new sovereign is generally continued in his authority, under that title, till his child is of age; but, at this time, the choice had fallen upon Tootahah, the uncle, in consequence of his having distinguished himself in a war. Oamo asked many questions concerning England and its inhabitants, by which he appeared to have great shrewdness and understanding.

On Monday the 26th, about 3 o'clock in the morning, I set out in the pinnace, accompanied by Mr Banks, to make the circuit of the island, with a view to sketch out the coast and harbours. We took our route to the eastward, and about eight in the forenoon we went on shore, in a district called Oahounue, which is governed by Ahio, a young chief, whom we had often seen at the tents, and who favoured us with his company to breakfast. Here also we found two other natives of our old acquaintance, Tituboalo and Hoona, who carried us to their houses, near which we saw the body of the old woman at whose funeral rites Mr Banks had assisted, which had been removed hither from the spot where it was first deposited—this place having descended from her by inheritance to Hoona, and it being necessary on that account that it should lie here. We then proceeded on foot, the boat attending within call, to the harbour in which Mr Bougainville lay, called Ohidea, where the natives showed us the ground upon which his people pitched their tent, and the brook at which they watered, though no trace of them remained, except the holes where the poles of the tent had been fixed, and a small piece of potsherd which Mr Banks found in looking narrowly about the spot. We met, however, with Orette, a chief who was their principal friend, and whose brother Outorrou went away with them. This harbour lies on the west side of a great bay, under shelter of a small island called Boourou, near which is another called Taawir-rii. The breach in the reefs is here very large, but the shelter for the ships is not the best.

Soon after we had examined this place we took boat, and asked Titu-boalo to go with us to the other side of the bay; but he refused, and ad-vised us not to go, for he said the country there was inhabited by people who were not subject to Tootahah, and who would kill both him and us. Upon receiving this intelligence, we did not, as may be imagined, relin-quish our enterprise; but we imme-diately loaded our pieces with ball. This was so well understood by Titu-boalo as a precaution, which rendered us formidable, that he now consented to be of our party. Having rowed till it was dark, we reached a low neck of land, or isthmus, at the bottom of the bay, that divides the island into two peninsulas, each of which is a dis-trict or government wholly indepen-dent of the other. From Port Royal, where the ship was at anchor, the coast trends E. by S. and ESE. ten miles, then S. by E. and S. eleven miles to the isthmus. In the first direction the shore is in general open to the sea; but in the last it is covered by reefs of rocks, which form several good harbours, with safe anchorage, in six-teen, eighteen, twenty, and twenty-four fathoms of water, with other con-veniences. As we had not yet got into our enemy's country, we deter-mined to sleep on shore. We landed, and, though we found but few houses, we saw several double canoes, whose owners were well known to us, and who provided us with supper and lodging, of which Mr Banks was in-debted for his share to Oorattooa, the lady who had paid him her compli-ments in so singular a manner at the fort.

In the morning we looked about the country, and found it to be a marshy flat, about two miles over, across which the natives haul their canoes to the corresponding bay on the other side. We then prepared to continue our route for what Tituboalo called the other kingdom. He said that the name of it was Tiarrabou, or Otaheite Ete; and that of the chief who go-verned it, Waheatua. Upon this oc-casion, also, we learned that the name of the peninsula where we had taken our station was Opoureonu, or Ota-heite Nue. Our new associate seemed to be now in better spirits than he had been the day before. The people in Tiarrabou would not kill us, he said; but he assured us that we should be able to procure no victuals among them; and indeed we had seen no bread-fruit since we set out.

After rowing a few miles, we landed in a district which was the dominion of a chief called Marnitata, "the bury-ing-place of men," whose father's name was Pahairedo, "the stealer of boats." Though these names seemed to favour the account that had been given by Tituboalo, we soon found that it was not true. Both the father and the son received us with the greatest civility, gave us provisions, and, after some delay, sold us a very large hog for a hatchet. A crowd soon gathered round us, but we saw only two people that we knew; neither did we observe a single bead or or-nament among them that had come from our ship, though we saw several things which had been brought from Europe. In one of the houses lay two 12-pound shot, one of which was marked with the broad arrow of Eng-land, though the people said they had them from the ships that lay in Bou-gainville's harbour.

We proceeded on foot till we came to the district which was immediately under the government of the principal chief, or king, of the peninsula, Waheatua. Waheatua had a son, but whether, according to the custom of Opoureonu, he administered the government as regent or in his own right, is uncertain. This district consists of a large and fertile plain watered by a river so wide that we were obliged to ferry over it in a canoe; our Indian train, however, chose to swim, and took to the water with the same facility as a pack of hounds. In this place we saw no house that appeared to be inhabited, but the ruins of many that had been very large. We proceeded along the shore, which forms a bay called Oaitipeha, and at last found the chief sitting near some pretty canoe awnings, under which, we supposed, he and his attendants slept. He was a thin old man, with a very white head and beard, and had with him a comely woman, about five-and-twenty years old, whose name was Toudidde. We had often heard the name of this woman, and, from report and observation, we had reason to think that she was the Oberea of this peninsula. From this place—between which and the isthmus there are other harbours, formed by the reefs that lie along the shore, where shipping may lie in perfect security, and from whence the land trends SSE. and S. to the SE. part of the island—we were accompanied by Tearee, the son of Waheatua, of whom we had purchased a hog. The country we passed through appeared to be more cultivated than any we had seen in other parts of the island; the brooks were everywhere banked into narrow channels with stone, and the shore had also a facing of stone, where it was washed by the sea. The houses were neither large nor numerous, but the canoes that were hauled up along the shore were almost innumerable, and superior to any that we had seen before, both in size and make. They were longer, the sterns were higher, and the awnings were supported by pillars. At almost every point there was a sepulchral building, and there were many of them also in-

land. They were of the same figure as those in Opoureonu, but cleaner and better kept, and decorated with many carved boards, which were set upright, and on the top of which were various figures of birds and men. On one, in particular, there was the representation of a cock, which was painted red and yellow, to imitate the feathers of that animal; and rude images of men were, in some of them, placed one upon the head of another. But in this part of the country, however fertile and cultivated, we did not see a single bread-fruit; the trees were entirely bare, and the inhabitants seemed to subsist principally upon nuts which are not unlike a chestnut, and which they call Ahee.

When we had walked till we were weary, we called up the boat, but both our Indians, Tituboalo and Tuahow, were missing. They had, it seems, stayed behind at Waheatua's, expecting us to return thither, in consequence of a promise which had been extorted from us, and which we had it not in our power to fulfil. Tearee, however, and another, embarked with us, and we proceeded till we came abreast of a small island called Otooareite. It being then dark, we determined to land, and our Indians conducted us to a place where they said we might sleep. It was a deserted house, and near it was a little cave in which the boat might lie with great safety and convenience. We were, however, in want of provisions, having been very sparingly supplied since we set out; and Mr Banks immediately went into the woods to see whether any could be procured. As it was dark he met with no people, and could find but one house that was inhabited. A bread-fruit and a half, a few ahees, and some fire, were all that it afforded; upon which, with a duck or two and a few curlews, we made our supper, which, if not scanty, was disagreeable by the want of bread, with which we had neglected to furnish ourselves, as we depended upon meeting with bread-fruit. We took up our lodging under the awning of a canoe belonging to Tearee, which followed us.

The next morning, after having spent some time in another fruitless attempt to procure a supply of provisions, we proceeded round the south-east point, part of which is not covered by any reef, but lies open to the sea; and here the hill rises directly from the shore. At the southernmost part of the island the shore is again covered by a reef, which forms a good harbour, and the land about it is very fertile. We made this route partly on foot and partly in the boat. When we had walked about three miles, we arrived at a place where we saw several large canoes and a number of people with them, whom we were agreeably surprised to find were of our intimate acquaintance. Here, with much difficulty, we procured some cocoa-nuts, and then embarked, taking with us Tuahow, one of the Indians who had waited for us at Waheatua's, and had returned the night before, long after it was dark.

When we came abreast of the south-east end of the island we went ashore, by the advice of our Indian guide, who told us that the country was rich and good. The chief, whose name was Mathiabo, soon came down to us, but seemed to be a total stranger both to us and to our trade. His subjects, however, brought us plenty of cocoa-nuts and about twenty bread-fruit. The bread-fruit we bought at a very dear rate, but his excellency sold us a pig for a glass bottle, which he preferred to everything else that we could give him. We found in his possession a goose and a turkey-cock, which, we were informed, had been left upon the island by the Dolphin; they were both enormously fat, and so tame that they followed the Indians, who were fond of them to excess, wherever they went.

In a long house in this neighbourhood we saw what was altogether new to us. At one end of it, fastened to a semicircular board, hung fifteen human jaw-bones; they appeared to be fresh, and there was not one of them that wanted a single tooth. A sight so extraordinary strongly excited our curiosity, and we made many in-quiries about it; but at this time could get no information, for the people either could not or would not understand us.

When we left this place, the chief, Mathiabo, desired leave to accompany us, which was readily granted. He continued with us the remainder of the day, and proved very useful by piloting us over the shoals. In the evening we opened the bay on the north-west side of the island, which answered to that on the south-east, so as at the isthmus, or carrying-place, almost to intersect the island, as I have observed before; and when we had coasted about two-thirds of it we determined to go on shore for the night. We saw a large house at some distance, which, Mathiabo informed us, belonged to one of his friends; and soon after several canoes came off to meet us, having on board some very handsome women, who, by their behaviour, seemed to have been sent to entice us on shore. As we had before resolved to take up our residence here for the night, little invitation was necessary. We found that the house belonged to the chief of the district, whose name was Wiverou; he received us in a very friendly manner, and ordered his people to assist us in dressing our provision, of which we had now got a tolerable stock. When our supper was ready, we were conducted into that part of the house where Wiverou was sitting in order to eat it. Mathiabo supped with us, and Wiverou calling for his supper at the same time, we ate our meal very sociably, and with great good humour. When it was over we began to inquire where we were to sleep, and a part of the house was shown us, of which we were told we might take possession for that purpose. We then sent for our cloaks, and Mr Banks began to undress, as his custom was; and, with a precaution which he had been taught by the loss of the jackets at Atahourou, sent his clothes aboard the boat, proposing to cover himself with a piece of Indian cloth. When Mathiabo perceived what was doing, he also pretended to want a cloak; and, as he had behaved very well, and done us some service, a cloak was ordered for him. We lay down, and observed that Mathiabo was not with us; but we supposed that he was gone to bathe, as the Indians always do before they sleep. We had not waited long, however, when an Indian, who was a stranger to us, came and told Mr Banks that the cloak and Mathiabo had disappeared together. This man had so far gained our confidence that we did not at first believe the report; but it being soon after confirmed by Tuahow, our own Indian, we knew no time was to be lost.

As it was impossible for us to pursue the thief with any hope of success, without the assistance of the people about us, Mr Banks started up, and telling our case, required them to recover the cloak; and to enforce this requisition, showed one of his pocket-pistols, which he always kept about him. Upon the sight of the pistol, the whole company took the alarm, and, instead of assisting to catch the thief, or recover what had been stolen, began with great precipitation to leave the place; one of them, however, was seized, upon which he immediately offered to direct the chase. I set out therefore with Mr Banks, and though we ran all the way, the alarm had got before us, for in about ten minutes we met a man bringing back the cloak, which the thief had relinquished in great terror; and as we did not then think fit to continue the pursuit, he made his escape. When we returned, we found the house, in which there had been between 200 and 300 people, entirely deserted. It being, however, soon known that we had no resentment against anybody but Mathiabo, the chief, Wiverou, our host, with his wife and many others, returned and took up their lodgings with us for the night. In this place, however, we were destined to more confusion and trouble; for about 5 o'clock in the morning our sentry alarmed us with an account that the boat was missing. He had seen her, he said, about half-an-hour before, at her

grappling, which was not above fifty yards from the shore; but, upon hearing the sound of oars, he had looked out again, and could see nothing of her. At this account we started up greatly alarmed, and ran to the water-side. The morning was clear and star-light, so that we could see to a considerable distance, but there was no appearance of the boat. Our situation was now such as might justify the most terrifying apprehensions; as it was a dead calm, and we could not therefore suppose her to have broken from her grappling, we had great reason to fear that the Indians had attacked her, and, finding the people asleep, had succeeded in their enterprise. We were but four, with only one musket and two pocket-pistols, without a spare ball or charge of powder for either. In this state of anxiety and distress we remained a considerable time, expecting the Indians every moment to improve their advantage—when to our unspeakable satisfaction, we saw the boat return, which had been driven from her grappling by the tide; a circumstance to which, in our confusion and surprise, we did not advert. As soon as the boat returned, we got our breakfast, and were impatient to leave the place, lest some other vexatious accident should befall us. It is situated on the north side of Tiarrabou, the south-east peninsula, or division, of the island, and at the distance of about five miles south-east from the isthmus, having a large and commodious harbour, inferior to none in the island, about which the land is very rich in produce. Notwithstanding we had little communication with this division, the inhabitants everywhere received us in a friendly manner; we found the whole of it fertile and populous, and, to all appearance, in a more flourishing state than Opoureonu, though it is not above one-fourth part as large.

The next district in which we landed, was the last in Tiarrabou, and governed by a chief, whose name we understood to be Omoe. Omoe was building a house, and being therefore very desirous of procuring a hatchet, he would have been glad to have purchased one with anything that he had in his possession; it happened, however, rather unfortunately for him and us, that we had not one hatchet left in the boat. We offered to trade with nails, but he would not part with anything in exchange for them. We therefore re-embarked, and put off our boat; but the chief being unwilling to relinquish all hope of obtaining something from us that would be of use to him, embarked in a canoe, with his wife Whanno-ouda, and followed us. After some time, we took them into the boat, and when we had rowed about a league, they desired we would put ashore. We immediately complied with his request, and found some of his people, who had brought down a very large hog. We were as unwilling to lose the hog, as the chief was to part with us, and it was indeed worth the best axe we had in the ship; we therefore hit upon an expedient, and told him that if he would bring his hog to the fort at Matavai—the Indian name for Port Royal Bay—he should have a large axe and a nail into the bargain for his trouble. To this proposal, after having consulted with his wife, he agreed, and gave us a large piece of his country-cloth as a pledge that he would perform his agreement, which, however, he never did.

At this place we saw a very singular curiosity. It was the figure of a man, constructed of basket-work, rudely made, but not ill designed; it was something more than seven feet high, and rather too bulky in proportion to its height. The wicker skeleton was completely covered with feathers, which were white where the skin was to appear, and black in the parts which it is their custom to paint or stain, and upon the head where there was to be a representation of hair. Upon the head also were four protuberances, three in front and one behind, which we should have called horns, but which the

Indians dignified with the name of "Tate Ete"—little men. The image was called Manioe, and was said to be the only one of the kind in Otaheite. They attempted to give us an explanation of its use and design, but we had not then acquired enough of their language to understand them. We learned, however, afterwards, that it was a representation of Mauwe, one of their Eatuas, or gods of the second class.

After having settled our affairs with Omoe, we proceeded on our return, and soon reached Opoureonu, the north-west peninsula. After rowing a few miles, we went on shore again, but the only thing we saw worth notice, was a repository for the dead, uncommonly decorated. The pavement was extremely neat, and upon it was raised a pyramid, about five feet high, which was entirely covered with the fruits of two plants peculiar to the country. Near the pyramid was a small image of stone, of very rude workmanship, and the first instance of carving in stone that we had seen among these people. They appeared to set a high value upon it, for it was covered from the weather by a shed that had been erected on purpose.

We proceeded in the boat, and passed through the only harbour, on the south side of Opoureonu, that is fit for shipping. It is situated about five miles to the westward of the isthmus, between two small islands that lie near the shore, about a mile distant from each other; and affords good anchorage in eleven and twelve fathoms water. We were now not far from the district called Paparra, which belonged to our friends Oamo and Oberea, where we proposed to sleep. We went on shore about an hour before night, and found that they were both absent, having left their habitations to pay us a visit at Matavai. This, however did not alter our purpose; we took up our quarters at the house of Oberea, which, though small, was very neat, and at this time had no inhabitant but her father, who received us with looks that bid us welcome. Having taken possession, we were willing to improve the little day-light that was left us, and therefore walked out to a point upon which we had seen, at a distance, trees that are here called "etoa," which generally distinguish the places where these people bury the bones of their dead. Their name for such burying-grounds, which are also places of worship, is "morai." We were soon struck with the sight of an enormous pile, which, we were told, was the Morai of Oamo and Oberea, and the principal piece of Indian architecture in the island. It was a pile of stone-work, raised pyramidically, upon an oblong base, or square, two hundred and sixty-seven feet long, and eighty-seven wide. It was built like the small pyramidal mounts upon which we sometimes fix the pillar of a sun-dial, where each side is a flight of steps; the steps, however, at the sides, were broader than those at the ends, so that it terminated not in a square of the same figure with the base, but in a ridge, like the roof of a house. There were eleven of these steps, each of which was four feet high, so that the height of the pile was forty-four feet; each step was formed of one course of white coral-stone, which was neatly squared and polished; the rest of the mass, for there was no hollow within, consisted of round pebbles, which, from the regularity of their figure, seemed to have been wrought. Some of the coral-stones were very large; we measured one of them, and found it three feet and a half by two feet and a half. The foundation was of rock stones, which were also squared; and one of them measured four feet seven inches by two feet four. Such a structure, raised without the assistance of iron-tools to shape the stones, or mortar to join them, struck us with astonishment. It seemed to be as compact and firm as it could have been made by any workman in Europe, except that the steps, which range along its greatest length, are not perfectly straight, but sink in a kind of hollow in the middle, so that the whole surface, from end to end, is not a right line, but a curve. The quarry stones, as we saw no quarry in the neighbourhood, must have been brought from a considerable distance; and there is no method of conveyance here but by hand. The coral must also have been fished from under the water, where, though it may be found in plenty, it lies at a considerable depth, never less than three feet. Both the rock-stone and the coral could be squared only by tools made of the same substance, which must have been a work of incredible labour; but the polishing was more easily effected by means of the sharp coral sand, which is found everywhere upon the sea-shore in great abundance. In the middle of the top stood the image of a bird, carved in wood; and near it lay the broken one of a fish, carved in stone. The whole of this pyramid made part of one side of a spacious area or square, nearly of equal sides, being 360 feet by 354, which was walled in with stone, and paved with flat stones in its whole extent; though there were growing in it, notwithstanding the pavement, several of the trees which they call "etoa," and plantains. About a hundred yards to the west of this building, was another paved area or court, in which were several small stages raised on wooden pillars, about seven feet high, which are called by the Indians "ewattas,"[1] and seem to be a kind of altars, as upon these are placed provisions of all kinds as offerings to their gods. We have since seen whole hogs placed upon them, and we found here the skulls of above fifty, besides the skulls of a great number of dogs.

The principal object of ambition among these people is to have a magnificent Morai, and this was a striking memorial of the rank and power of Oberea. It has been remarked that we did not find her invested with the same authority she exercised

---

[1] Subsequently described in the account of the stay at Tongataboo (Voyage III.) under the designation of "whattas."

when the Dolphin was at this place, and we now learned the reason of it. Our way from her house to the Morai lay along the seaside, and we observed everywhere under our feet a great number of human bones, chiefly ribs and vertebræ. Upon inquiring into the cause of so singular an appearance, we were told that in the then last month of Owarahew, which answered to our December, 1768, about four or five months before our arrival, the people of Tiarrabou, the SE. peninsula which we had just visited, made a descent at this place, and killed a great number of people, whose bones were those that we saw upon the shore; that upon this occasion Oberea and Oamo, who then administered the government for his son, had fled to the mountains; and that the conquerors burned all the houses, which were very large, and carried away the hogs and what other animals they found. We learned also that the turkey and goose which we had seen when we were with Mathiabo, the stealer of cloaks, were among the spoils. This accounted for their being found among people with whom the Dolphin had little or no communication; and upon mentioning the jawbones which we had seen hanging from a board in a long house, we were told that they also had been carried away as trophies, the people here carrying away the jaw-bones of their enemies, as the Indians of North America do the scalps.

After having thus gratified our curiosity, we returned to our quarters, where we passed the night in perfect security and quiet. By the next evening we arrived at Atahourou, the residence of our friend Tootahah, where, last time we passed the night under his protection, we had been obliged to leave the best part of our clothes behind us. This adventure, however, seemed now to be forgotten on both sides. Our friends received us with great pleasure, and gave us a good supper and a good lodging, where we suffered neither loss nor disturbance.

The next day, Saturday, July the 1st, we got back to our fort at Matavai, having found the circuit of the island, including both peninsulas, to be about thirty leagues. Upon our complaining of the want of bread-fruit, we were told that the produce of the last season was nearly exhausted, and that what was seen sprouting upon the trees would not be fit to use in less than three months. This accounted for our having been able to procure so little of it in our route. While the bread-fruit is ripening upon the flats, the inhabitants are supplied in some measure from the trees which they have planted upon the hills to preserve a succession; but the quantity is not sufficient to prevent scarcity. They live therefore upon the sour paste which they call "mahie," upon wild plantains, and ahee-nuts, which at this time are in perfection. How it happened that the Dolphin, which was here at this season, found such plenty of bread-fruit upon the trees I cannot tell, except the season in which they ripen varies.

At our return, our Indian friends crowded about us, and none of them came empty-handed. Though I had determined to restore to their owners the canoes which had been detained, it had not yet been done; but I now released them as they were applied for. Upon this occasion I could not but remark with concern that these people were capable of practising petty frauds against each other, with a deliberate dishonesty which gave me a much worse opinion of them, than I had ever entertained from the robberies they committed under the strong temptation, to which a sudden opportunity of enriching themselves with the inestimable metal and manufactures of Europe exposed them. Among others who applied to me for the release of a canoe was one Potattow, a man of some consequence, well known to us all. I consented, supposing the vessel to be his own, or that he applied on behalf of a friend. He went immediately to the beach, and took possession of one of the boats, which, with the assistance of his people, he began to carry off; upon this, however, it was eagerly claimed by the right owners, who, supported by the other Indians, clamorously reproached him for invading their property, and prepared to take the canoe from him by force. Upon this he desired to be heard, and told them that the canoe did indeed once belong to those who claimed it; but that I, having seized it as a forfeit, had sold it to him for a pig. This silenced the clamour; the owners, knowing that from my power there was no appeal, acquiesced; and Potattow would have carried off his prize if the dispute had not fortunately been overheard by some of our people, who reported it to me. I gave orders immediately that the Indians should be undeceived; upon which the right owners took possession of their canoe, and Potattow was so conscious of his guilt that neither he nor his wife, who was privy to his knavery, could look us in the face for some time afterwards.

On the 3d, Mr Banks set out early in the morning, with some Indian guides, to trace our river up the valley from which it issues, and examine how far its banks were inhabited. For about six miles they met with houses, not far distant from each other, on each side of the river, and the valley was everywhere about 400 yards wide from the foot of the hill on one side to the foot of that on the other. But they were now shown a house which they were told was the last that they would see. When they came up to it, the master of it offered them refreshments of cocoa-nuts and other fruits, of which they accepted. After a short stay, they walked forward for a considerable time. In bad way it is not easy to compute distances, but they imagined that they had walked about six miles farther, following the course of the river, when they frequently passed under vaults formed by fragments of the rock, in which they were told people who were benighted frequently passed the night. Soon after they found the river banked by steep rocks, from which a cascade falling with great violence, formed a pool so steep that the Indians said they could not pass it. They seemed, indeed, not much to be acquainted with the valley beyond this place, their business lying chiefly upon the declivity of the rocks on each side, and the plains which extended on their summits, where they found plenty of wild plantain, which they called Vae. The way up these rocks from the banks of the river was in every respect dreadful; the sides were nearly perpendicular, and in some places 100 feet high; they were also rendered exceeding slippery by the water of innumerable springs which issued from the fissures on the surface. Yet up these precipices a way was to be traced by a succession of long pieces of the bark of the *Hibiscus tiliaceus*, which served as a rope for the climber to take hold of, and assisted him in scrambling from one ledge to another, though upon these ledges there was footing only for an Indian or a goat. One of these ropes was nearly thirty feet in length, and their guides offered to assist them in mounting this pass, but recommended another, at a little distance lower down, as less difficult and dangerous. They took a view of this "better way," but found it so bad that they did not choose to attempt it, as there was nothing at the top to reward their toil and hazard but a grove of the wild plantain or Vae tree, which they had often seen before.

During this excursion Mr Banks had an excellent opportunity to examine the rocks, which were almost everywhere naked, for minerals; but he found not the least appearance of any. The stones everywhere, like those of Madeira, showed manifest tokens of having been burned; nor is there a single specimen of any stone among all those that were collected in the island upon which there are not manifest and indubitable marks of fire, except, perhaps, some small pieces of the hatchet-stone, and even of that other fragments were collected which were burned almost to a pumice. Traces of fire are also manifest

In the very clay upon the hills; and it may therefore not unreasonably be supposed that this and the neighbouring islands are either shattered remains of a continent, which some have supposed to be necessary in this part of the globe to preserve an equilibrium of its parts, which were left behind when the rest sank by the mining of a subterraneous fire, so as to give a passage to the sea over it; or were torn from rocks which, from the creation of the world, had been the bed of the sea, and thrown up in heaps to a height which the waters never reach. One or other of these suppositions will perhaps be thought the more probable, as the water does not gradually grow shallow as the shore is approached, and the islands are almost everywhere surrounded by reefs which appear to be rude and broken, as some violent concussion would naturally leave the solid substance of the earth.

On the 4th, Mr Banks employed himself in planting a great quantity of the seeds of water-melons, oranges, lemons, limes, and other plants and trees which he had collected at Rio de Janeiro. For these he prepared ground on each side of the fort, with as many varieties of soil as he could choose; and there is little doubt that they will succeed. He also gave liberally of these seeds to the Indians, and planted many of them in the woods. Some of the melon seeds having been planted soon after our arrival, the natives showed him several of the plants, which appeared to be in the most flourishing condition, and were continually asking him for more.

We now begin to prepare for our departure, by bending the sails and performing other necessary operations on board the ship—our water being already on board, and the provisions examined. In the meantime we had another visit from Oamo, Oberea, and their son and daughter; the Indians expressing their respect by uncovering the upper parts of their body as they had done before. The daughter, whose name we understand to be Toimata, was very desirous to see the fort, but her father would by no means suffer her to come in. Tearee, the son of Waheatua, the sovereign of Tiarrabou, the south-east peninsula, was also with us at this time; and we received intelligence of the landing of another guest, whose company was neither expected nor desired. This was no other than the ingenious gentleman who contrived to steal our quadrant. We were told that he intended to try his fortune again in the night; but the Indians all offered zealously to assist us against him, desiring that, for this purpose, they might be permitted to lie in the fort. This had so good an effect, that the thief relinquished his enterprise in despair.

On the 7th, the carpenters were employed in taking down the gates and palisadoes of our little fortification, for fire-wood on board the ship; and one of the Indians had dexterity enough to steal the staple and hook upon which the gate turned. He was immediately pursued, and after a chase of six miles, he appeared to have been passed, having concealed himself among some rushes in the brook. The rushes were searched, and though the thief had escaped, a scraper was found which had been stolen from the ship some time before; and soon after our old friend Tubourai Tamaide brought us the staple. On the 8th and 9th we continued to dismantle our fort, and our friends still flocked about us; some, I believe, sorry at the approach of our departure, and others desirous to make as much as they could of us while we stayed. We were in hopes that we should now leave the island without giving or receiving any other offence, but it unfortunately happened otherwise. Two foreign seamen having been out with my permission, one of them was robbed of his knife, and endeavouring to recover it, probably with circumstances of great provocation, the Indians attacked him and dangerously wounded him with a stone; they wounded his companion also slightly on the head, and then fled into the mountains. As I should have been sorry to take any further notice of the affair, I was not displeased that the offenders had escaped; but I was immediately involved in a quarrel which I very much regretted, and which yet it was not possible to avoid.

In the middle of the night between the 8th and 9th, Clement Webb and Samuel Gibson, two of the marines, both young men, went privately from the fort, and in the morning were not to be found. As public notice had been given that all hands were to go on board on the next day, and that the ship would sail on the morrow of that day or the day following, I began to fear that the absentees intended to stay behind. I knew that I could take no effectual steps to recover them without endangering the harmony and goodwill which at present subsisted among us, and therefore determined to wait a day for the chance of their return. On Monday morning the 10th, the marines, to my great concern, not being returned, an inquiry was made after them of the Indians, who frankly told us that they did not intend to return, and had taken refuge in the mountains, where it was impossible for our people to find them. They were then requested to assist in the search, and after some deliberation, two of them undertook to conduct such persons as I should think proper to send after them to the place of their retreat. As they were known to be without arms, I thought two would be sufficient, and accordingly despatched a petty officer and a corporal of marines, with the Indian guides, to fetch them back. As the recovery of these men was a matter of great importance, as I had no time to lose, and as the Indians spoke doubtfully of their return—telling us that they had each of them taken a wife, and were become inhabitants of the country,—it was intimated to several of the chiefs who were in the fort with their women, among whom were Tubourai Tamaide, Tomio, and Oberea, that they would not be permitted to leave it till our deserters were brought back. This precaution I thought the more necessary, as, by concealing them a few days, they might compel me to go without them; and I had the pleasure to observe that they received the intimation with very little signs either of fear or discontent, assuring me that my people should be secured and sent back as soon as possible. While this was doing at the fort, I sent Mr Hicks in the pinnace to fetch Tootahah on board the ship; which he did, without alarming either him or his people. If the Indian guides proved faithful and in earnest, I had reason to expect the return of my people with the deserters before evening. Being disappointed, my suspicions increased; and night coming on, I thought I was not safe to let the people whom I had detained as hostages continue at the fort, and I therefore ordered Tubourai Tamaide, Oberea, and some others, to be taken on board the ship. This spread a general alarm, and several of them, especially the women, expressed their apprehensions with great emotion and many tears when they were put into the boat. I went on board with them, and Mr Banks remained on shore, with some others whom I thought it of less consequence to secure.

About 9 o'clock Webb was brought back by some of the natives, who declared that Gibson and the petty officer and corporal would be detained till Tootahah should be set at liberty. The tables were now turned upon me, but I had proceeded too far to retreat. I immediately despatched Mr Hicks in the long-boat with a strong party of men, to rescue the prisoners, and told Tootahah that it behoved him to send some of his people with them, with orders to afford them effectual assistance, and to demand the release of my men in his name, for that I should expect him to answer for the contrary. He readily complied; this party recovered my men without the least opposition, and, about 7 o'clock in the morning, returned with them to the ship, though they had not been able to recover the arms which had been taken from them when they were seized. These, however, were brought on board in less than half-an-hour, and the chiefs were immediately set at liberty.

When I questioned the petty officer concerning what had happened on shore, he told me that neither the natives who went with them, nor those whom they met in their way, would give them any intelligence of the deserters, but, on the contrary, became very troublesome; that, as he was returning for further orders to the ship, he and his comrade were suddenly seized by a number of armed men, who, having learned that Tootabah was confined, had concealed themselves in a wood for that purpose, and who having taken them at a disadvantage, forced their weapons out of their hands, and declared that they would detain them till their chief should be set at liberty. He said, however, that the Indians were not unanimous in this measure; that some were for setting them at liberty, and others for detaining them; that an eager dispute ensued, and from words they came to blows, but the party for detaining them at length prevailed; that soon after Webb and Gibson were brought in by a party of the natives as prisoners, that they also might be secured as hostages for the chief; but that it was after some debate resolved to send Webb to inform me of their resolution, to assure me that his companions were safe, and direct me where I might send my answer. Thus it appears that, whatever were the disadvantages of seizing the chiefs, I should never have recovered my men by any other method. When the chiefs were set on shore from the ship, those at the fort were also set at liberty, and, after staying with Mr Banks about an hour, they all went away. Upon this occasion, as they had done upon another of the same kind, they expressed their joy by an undeserved liberality, strongly urging us to accept of four hogs. These we absolutely refused as a present, and they as absolutely refusing to be paid for them, the hogs did not change masters. Upon examining the deserters, we found that the account which the Indians had given

of them was true,—they had strongly attached themselves to two girls, and it was their intention to conceal themselves till the ship had sailed, and take up their residence upon the island. This night everything was got off from the shore, and everybody slept on board.

Among the natives who were almost constantly with us, was Tupia, whose name has been often mentioned in this narrative. He had been, as I have before observed, the first minister of Oberea, when she was in the height of her power. He was also the chief tahowa or priest of the island, consequently well acquainted with the religion of the country, as well with respect to its ceremonies as principles. He had also great experience and knowledge in navigation, and was particularly acquainted with the number and situation of the neighbouring islands. This man had often expressed a desire to go with us, and on the 12th, in the morning, having, with the other natives, left us the day before, he came on board with a boy about thirteen years of age, his servant, and urged us to let him proceed with us on our voyage. To have such a person on board was certainly desirable for many reasons; by learning his language, and teaching him ours, we should be able to acquire a much better knowledge of the customs, policy, and religion of the people, than our short stay among them could give us: I therefore gladly agreed to receive them on board. As we were prevented from sailing to-day, by having found it necessary to make new stocks to our small and best bower anchors, the old ones having been totally destroyed by the worms, Tupia said he would go once more on shore, and make a signal for the boat to fetch him off in the evening. He went accordingly, and took with him a miniature picture of Mr Banks's to show his friends, and several little things to give them as parting presents.

After dinner, Mr Banks, being desirous to procure a drawing of the Morai belonging to Tootahah at

Eparre, I attended him thither, accompanied by Dr Solander, in the pinnace. As soon as we landed, many of our friends came to meet us, though some absented themselves in resentment of what had happened the day before. We immediately proceeded to Tootahah's house, where we were joined by Oberea, with several others who had not come out to meet us, and a perfect reconciliation was soon brought about; in consequence of which they promised to visit us early the next day, to take a last farewell of us, as we told them we should certainly set sail in the afternoon. At this place, also, we found Tupia, who returned with us, and slept this night on board the ship for the first time.

On the next morning, Thursday the 13th of July, the ship was very early crowded with our friends, and surrounded by a multitude of canoes, which were filled with the natives of an inferior class. Between eleven and twelve we weighed anchor, and as soon as the ship was under sail, the Indians on board took their leaves, and wept, with a decent and silent sorrow, in which there was something very striking and tender. The people in the canoes, on the contrary, seemed to vie with each other in the loudness of their lamentations, which we considered rather as affectation than grief. Tupia sustained himself in this scene with a firmness and resolution truly admirable. He wept, indeed, but the effort that he made to conceal his tears concurred with them to do him honour. He sent his last present, a shirt, by Otheothea, to Potomia, Tootahah's favourite mistress, and then went with Mr Banks to the masthead, waving to the canoes as long as they continued in sight.

Thus we took leave of Otaheite and its inhabitants, after a stay of just three months. For much the greater part of the time we lived together in the most cordial friendship, and a perpetual reciprocation of good offices. The accidental differences which now and then happened could not be more sincerely regretted on their part, than they were on ours. The principal causes were such as necessarily resulted from our situation and circumstances, in conjunction with the infirmities of human nature; from our not being able perfectly to understand each other; and from the disposition of the inhabitants to theft, which we could not all times bear with or prevent. They had not, however, except in one instance, been attended with any fatal consequence; and to that accident were owing the measures I took to prevent others of the same kind. I hoped indeed to have availed myself of the impression which had been made upon them by the lives sacrificed in their contest with the Dolphin, so as that the intercourse between us should have been carried on wholly without bloodshed; by this hope all my measures were directed during the whole of my continuance at the island; and I sincerely wish that whoever shall next visit it may be still *more* fortunate. Our traffic here was carried on with as much order as in the best regulated market in Europe. It was managed principally by Mr Banks, who was indefatigable in procuring provision and refreshments while they were to be had; but during the latter part of our time they became scarce, partly by the increased consumption at the fort and ship, and partly by the coming on of the season in which cocoa-nuts and bread-fruit fail. All kinds of fruit we purchased for beads and nails, but no nails less than forty-penny were current. After a very short time we could never get a pig of more than ten or twelve pounds for less than a hatchet; because, though these people set a high value upon spike-nails, yet, these being an article with which many people in the ship were provided, the women found a much more easy way of procuring them than by bringing down provisions. The best articles for traffic here are axes, hatchets, spikes, large nails, looking-glasses, knives, and beads, for some of which, everything that the natives have may be procured. They are, indeed, fond of fine linen cloth, both white and printed ; but an axe worth half-a-crown will fetch more than a piece of cloth worth twenty shillings.

[Although the account in the Cabinet Cyclopædia of Cook's stay at Otaheite has been in great measure anticipated, some particulars there go beyond what Dr Hawkesworth himself relates, founding his narrative on the observations and memoranda of the distinguished navigator.]

"The mild and judicious conduct of Cook completely won the confidence of the Otaheitans, and enabled him to form a more accurate opinion of their character than the voyagers who had previously visited their island. They were remarkably friendly and affectionate, and indeed their attachments alone seemed exempted from the characteristic levity which prevented them from fixing their attention on the same object for any length of time. They are a handsome people, finely made, and with open vivacious countenances ; their ingenuity was in nothing more conspicuous than in the fine cloth, or rather paper, which they made of the inner bark of a tree. The garments of this material, which they wore, were becoming and even elegant, and were arranged by the women so as to produce an effect little short of the classic draperies of antiquity. Their houses were little more than sheds, erected in the neighbourhood of the trees under which they reclined and took their meals during the day. These habitations stood very thick in the groves which cover the low margin of the island. High mountains rose behind, and a number of small streams stole down the declivities to the sea-shore; the whole presenting, from a distance, a most enchanting picture.

" It was conjectured by M. de Bougainville that the inhabitants of Otaheite were composed of two different races, and that one of these was in a servile condition. Cook also notices the superiority of the chiefs in figure and appearance, but does not venture to ascribe this difference to any circumstances of origin or descent. He does not seem to have observed the power which the chiefs usually exercised over their retainers, and which the French navigator, with perhaps too little reason, seems to have considered as absolutely despotic. But the king, it was evident, though treated with respect by all, possessed no power but what was derived from the voluntary attachment of the chiefs, whose obedience or support in every enterprise could be secured only by consulting them. The rule of succession among these islanders is singular in the extreme. The son, as soon as he is born, succeeds to the authority of his father, who at once becomes only a regent instead of a king, if he be fitted for that office. Associations of a licentious character existed among the chief persons in these islands, and among other bad effects, tended to encourage the crime of infanticide ; a crime to which the law of inheritance just mentioned may have held out some inducement, as the ambition of the parent was at once blighted by the birth of a son.

" At the time of Cook's visit, the sovereignty had devolved on a boy only seven years old, the son of Oamo and Oberea, the latter of whom had figured so conspicuously in Captain Wallis's narrative as queen of the island. She lived separate from her husband, and though still treated as a noble, no longer enjoyed the same degree of power and consideration which had rendered her friendship so valuable to the commander of the Dolphin. As a further proof of the progress made by these islanders towards civilisation, it deserves to be remarked, that their women were not condemned to labour, as is usually the case amongst rude nations. They had, indeed, abundance of domestic occupation, in making and dyeing their cloth, preparing the meals, and similar offices ; but though they were not permitted to eat with the men, they were in general treated with respect and attention.

" When M. de Bougainville arrived here, he found the islanders already acquainted with the use of iron, which they called 'aouri,' a name which he supposed them to have learned from the English who had preceded him; but Captain Wallis observed that they were not wholly ignorant of that metal in his time, though he does not mention by what name they called it; for as soon as they were presented with iron nails, they began to sharpen them, while they took no such pains with pieces of brass and copper. Cook circumnavigated and surveyed the coasts of Otaheite, which he found to have a circumference of about thirty leagues; and after a stay of about three months he prepared to depart. In leaving the affectionate islanders, he remarks, 'that, allowing for their theft, they need not fear a comparison with any people on earth.' A native named Tupia, one of Oberea's ministers, and well instructed in all the learning of his countrymen, offered to accompany the English, and the proposal was readily accepted. The Otaheitans, it appeared, sometimes ventured 200 or 300 miles through the ocean in their open canoes; and Tupia had a vague knowledge of above eighty islands, the position of many of which he attempted to describe. He was well acquainted with the heavens; and, in every part of the subsequent voyage in the Endeavour, he was enabled to point out the direction of his native island.

"On leaving Otaheite, Cook visited the neighbouring islands of Ulietea, Borabora, Otahah, Huaheine, and Raiataia. Tupia related, that in the time of his grandfather a friendly ship had called at the last named island, and he also stated that a ship had been wrecked on a low island called Oanna. These ships were probably those of Admiral Roggewein's squadron, and Oanna may have been the Schadelyk or Pernicious Island of that navigator. At Huaheine, Cook contracted a friendship with Oree, the old chief of the island, from whom he experienced unremitting kindness, and to whom, at his departure, he gave, along with some valuable presents, a small bag containing coins and medals, and a pewter plate with an inscription, as a memorial of his visit to this part of the world. These gifts the old chief promised to keep in safety. The people of Borabora had invaded some of the islands in the neighbourhood, and with such success that they were looked upon as invincible, and were become objects of dread to the simple islanders. Tupia was anxious that the English should terrify those haughty conquerors, and exhibit their superiority by firing great guns at Borabora; and at length, to calm his importunity, a ball was fired towards the island when the ship was at least seven leagues distant from the shore. To the group of islands which Cook now quitted, he gave the collective name of the Society Islands.

"After sailing four days to the west and south-west, an island was discovered to which Tupia gave the name of Oheteroa. The natives crowded on the shore to resist the landing of the strangers. They were a handsome, vigorous people, and seemed far to excel the natives of the Society Islands in the beauty of their dress. The cloth was dyed in various patterns, and of several colours, though bright yellow seemed to predominate. Their robes being collected round their waist by a belt of red cloth, gave them a gay and warlike appearance. Some had caps made of the feathers of the tropic bird, while others wore small turbans of a very elegant appearance. Their canoes were well constructed, and, as well as the javelins, were carved in a manner highly creditable to their taste and ingenuity. But no anchorage could be found near the island; and as the natives seemed bent on hostility, our navigators gave up all thoughts of cultivating an acquaintance with them, and pursued their voyage.

"On the 15th of August they sailed from Oheteroa, and in the beginning of October perceived, in the colour of the sea, in the weeds with which it was covered, and the birds which flew around them, unequivocal signs of the proximity of land. At length, on the 6th of that month, land was distinctly seen stretching to a great extent in the horizon ; several ranges of hills were distinguished rising one above another, and a chain of mountains of an enormous height terminated the picture in the rear. The general opinion was, that they had discovered the 'Terra Australia Incognita,' but it was soon perceived that this must be a part of New Zealand or Staaten Land, discovered by Abel Tasman in 1642. A party who went on shore in order to open an intercourse with the natives met with no success. They were fierce, and obstinately hostile ; but it was discovered, to the surprise and pleasure of our navigators, that when Tupia spoke to them in his native language, he was perfectly understood. In a quarrel which ensued, one of them was killed, and his dress appeared, on examination, to correspond exactly with the drawing appended to Tasman's voyage. As it was found impossible to commence an amicable correspondence with them by gentle means, it was determined to resort to force, and, according to the method followed by the first Spanish navigators, to capture the Indians first, in order to have an opportunity of treating them with kindness. This plan of proceeding can hardly be justified upon principles of reason or morality, and it has never been attended with such unequivocal success as to palliate its demerits. Two canoes were seen entering the bay, and the ship's boats proceeded immediately to intercept them ; in one, the natives escaped by paddling ; but those in the other, which was a sailing canoe, finding it impossible to get off, boldly prepared for battle. Of seven Indians who were in the canoe, four were killed on the first discharge of musketry, and the other three, who were all young, immediately jumped overboard, and attempted to save themselves by swimming ; they were, however, overtaken and picked up by the boat, though not without some difficulty. They expected to be put to death at once ; but as the studious

kindness with which they were treated soon convinced them of their error, their consternation gave way to transports of joy. They conversed freely with Tupia ; and after having been kept a day on board the ship, were again sent ashore.

"The account which the boys gave to their countrymen of their treatment on board the ship led to a correspondence, which did not, however, bear the appearance of confirmed friendship. The New Zealanders still maintained a fierce and independent carriage, and acted so little in concert, that the behaviour of different individuals was often of a totally opposite character ; but their distrust could not be generally overcome, nor an intercourse established which was likely to prove safe and advantageous. An attempt was made by them to carry off Tayeto, Tupia's boy, and they nearly succeeded ; but guns being fired at the canoe as it paddled off, the natives, in a moment of fear, let go their hold, and the boy leaped into the water. The New Zealanders made great exertions to secure their prize, but the ship's boats finally succeeded in picking up the youth, whose terror at the violent conduct of these savages was increased by the conviction which our navigators had obtained, that they were cannibals, and even that they regarded human flesh as a dainty.

"This bay, in which no provisions could be procured, was named Poverty Bay ; and our voyagers, on leaving it, proceeded along the coast towards the north. They gave the name of Mercury Bay to the inlet in which they anchored while observing a transit of that planet over the sun. They were surprised to find that the natives, notwithstanding their ferocity, were not unacquainted with the art of cultivating the ground. They had gardens, in which they reared gourds and several kinds of fruits. A decked canoe also was found on this shore, which indicated their proficiency in maritime affairs. Their 'heppahs' or hamlets were forts neatly constructed on elevated situations, defended by lines and trenches, and accessible only by a steep and narrow entrance. They had no knowledge of iron when our voyagers first touched here, although iron sand was found in the beds of several streams. The women were thickly painted with oil and red ochre, and the men were tattooed after the usual fashion of the South Seas. They were strong and active, not deficient in intelligence, or in sentiments of generosity, notwithstanding the cruelty of disposition engendered by their habits of continual warfare. Tupia conversed much with their priests; and from the superiority of his knowledge and the variety of his superstitious lore, he was regarded by them with peculiar respect and veneration.

"In prosecuting his examination of the coast towards the north, Cook entered a deep inlet terminating in a large river, which he explored to the distance of fourteen miles; from the magnitude of this river, and the general appearance of the country round it, he named it the Thames. The timber which grew here was of enormous size, trees being seen nearly twenty feet in girth six feet from the ground, and above eighty feet in height to the branches.

"Having finished the examination of the north-western shore of New Zealand, Cook experienced such severe gales, though it was now midsummer in these latitudes, that in five weeks he did not advance above fifty leagues in his course along the western shore. He at length reached a secure and capacious harbour, which he named Queen Charlotte's Sound. The country was here taken possession of, and the sound carefully surveyed. Wood, water, and fish were in the greatest abundance, the natives friendly, and plants of an anti-scorbutic quality were gathered on the shore, which soon restored the crew to perfect health. Here our voyagers were particularly struck with the exquisite warbling of the birds, which, like our nightingales, sing only during the night.

"On ascending a height in the neighbourhood of the sound, Cook was surprised on descrying the sea to the south-east, and thus found that the land, the continuity of which he had not before suspected, was divided by a strait. Passing through this strait, to which geographers have unanimously given the name of its discoverer, he directed his course towards the north till he arrived near the point where his examination of this country had commenced. He then resumed his course to the south-east, and followed the coast of the southernmost of the two islands comprised under the name of New Zealand, returning again from the south to Queen Charlotte's Sound. The southern island, or, as the natives call it, Tavai Poenammoo, is a rugged country, with mountains of prodigious height, and covered with snow the greater part of the year. The inhabitants also, though not more fierce, are ruder than their northern neighbours. They differ likewise in dialect from the inhabitants of Eaheinomauwe, as the northern island is called, where, as the climate is more genial and the soil more luxuriant, the population is considerably greater, and the arts as well as the institutions of rude society much more advanced.

"Of the natives of New Zealand Cook entertained a highly favourable opinion, notwithstanding their cannibalism, of which he saw numerous incontestable proofs. He could not collect from them any tradition respecting the arrival of Tasman on their shores, but they heard of a country called Ulimaroa, situated NW. by W., where the people ate hogs, and whence some canoes seemed to have accidently arrived in their country. The circumnavigation of New Zealand was the first grand discovery of Cook. When Tasman touched on that country, he imagined it to be a part of the great Terra Australis, or continent supposed to extend to the South Pole. Our navigator was satisfied with having disproved this supposition; and as the lateness of the season would not permit him to continue his researches in higher latitudes, he determined to direct his course to the eastern coast of New Holland, respecting which the learned world was still in total ignorance.

"He took leave of New Zealand on the 31st of March 1770, and in twenty days discovered the coast of New Holland, at no great distance from the point where the survey of Tasman had terminated. In proceeding to the north, an inlet was entered, in which the ship rode securely for some days. Inhabitants were seen, but, from their shyness and timidity, they could not be induced to approach the strangers; they seemed to be sunk in that brutal condition which is insensible even to the promptings of curiosity. From the variety of new plants collected here by the naturalists of the expedition, this inlet received the name of Botany Bay. No rivers were discovered by Cook in his voyage along this coast, which has since been found abundantly supplied with fine streams. The natives, wherever they were seen, manifested the same repugnance to the strangers, and the same indifference to the trinkets presented to them. Towards the north the country grew more hilly, and the navigation of the coast became more dangerous and intricate.

"No accident had yet occurred in a voyage of 2000 miles along a coast hitherto unexplored; but in Lat. 16° S., a high headland being in sight, which from the circumstance was afterwards named Cape Tribulation, the ship during the night struck on some coral rocks with so much force that there seemed imminent danger of her going to pieces. The planks which formed her sheathing were seen floating off, and the water rushed in with such impetuosity that, though all the pumps were manned, the leak could hardly be kept under. As day broke, land was descried eight leagues distant, without an island between to which the boats might convey the crew in case of the ship's foundering. The guns and all the stores that could be spared were thrown overboard, and preparations were made to heave the ship off the rocks, although it was thought probable that she would sink soon after. On the following night,

however, she was got afloat, and, to the surprise of all, it was found that the leakage did not increase. By constant exertion and cool perseverance the ship was navigated to a small harbour opportunely discovered on the coast—the only harbour, indeed, seen by our people during the whole voyage, which could have afforded them the same relief. On examining the injury done to the vessel, it was found that a large piece of the coral rock, having forced its way through the timbers, had remained fixed in the aperture; but for this providential circumstance the ship must have sunk the moment she was got off the reef.

"The cove in which our navigators found shelter is situated at the mouth of a small stream, to which was given the name of Endeavour River. Here the natives appeared rather more familiar, but they set little value on anything offered to them, except food. When some turtle, which they coveted, was refused them, they avenged the affront by setting fire to the long grass near the tents, an action which had nearly been attended with disagreeable consequences. Mr Banks and Dr Solander found here abundance of employment; almost everything connected with the animal and vegetable kingdoms being absolutely new. Our naturalists were particularly pleased with the animal called by the natives kangaroo. They saw several at a distance, but a long time elapsed before they could succeed in shooting one.

"The ship being repaired, our voyagers left the harbour; and, after much patient labour and anxiety, at length gained the deep sea, having been three months entangled within the reefs. They now prosecuted their voyage to the north, flattering themselves that the danger was gone by, when the wind abated, and the ship was found to be drifting fast towards the reefs which lined this coast nearly in its whole extent, and on which the great waves of the Southern Ocean break with a tremendous surf. Her destruction seemed inevitable, when a narrow channel through the reefs was descried at no great distance; and although the attempt was attended with great risk, yet the ship was steered to run through it. Having thus entered from necessity a second time within the reef, Cook resolved to persevere through all difficulties in following the coast lest he might lose the strait that separates New Holland from New Guinea, 'if,' as he doubtfully expresses it, 'such a strait there be.' He at length reached a point of land from which he could discern an open sea to the south-west, and was thus convinced that he had found the strait in question. He then landed, and in the name of his Sovereign took possession of the immense line of coast that he had discovered, to which he gave the name of New South Wales. The little island on which the ceremony was performed received the name of Possession Island.

"The crew of the Endeavour had suffered so much from sickness and fatigue that it was not deemed advisable to prolong the voyage by an examination of the coasts of New Guinea. Our navigator, therefore, held his course for Batavia, where he wished to refit his vessel; but the noxious climate of this place proved more fatal to the men than all their preceding hardships—scarcely ten remained in a condition to do duty. Tupia and his poor boy Tayeto, who had been afflicted with the scurvy during the whole voyage, were among the first victims to the pestilential air of Batavia. The seeds of illness lingered in the ship long after she had left the place; and before her arrival at the Cape she had lost no less than thirty persons, among whom were Mr Green the astronomer, Dr Solander, and the surgeon; the life of Mr Banks also was for some time despaired of. On the 10th of June, land, which proved to be the Lizard, was discovered by the same boy who had first seen New Zealand; and on the 12th, Cook came to an anchor in the Downs, having been employed two years and eleven months in his voyage round the earth."

COOK'S SECOND VOYAGE.

"The first important discovery made by Cook was effected by the circumnavigation of New Zealand. When Tasman described that country, he supposed it to be a part of the great Terra Australis Incognita, extending probably across the southern Pacific Ocean; but Cook's voyage at once overturned this theory. An opinion, however, which has long existed, cannot be at once dispelled, although utterly groundless; and many still continued to believe in the existence of a southern continent, although Cook's discoveries had cut off the connection between their theory and the facts which hitherto had been adduced in its support. But to set the question of a southern continent completely at rest, another expedition was necessary; and the English Government, having now made the advancement of science the object of national exertions, resolved to continue their laudable researches. The King was partial to the scheme; and the Earl of Sandwich, who was at the head of the Admiralty, possessed a mind sufficiently liberal and comprehensive to second effectively the wishes of his Sovereign.

"Captain Cook was named at once as the fittest person to command the new expedition. Two ships, the Resolution and the Adventure, the former of 462, the latter of 336 tons burthen, were fitted out for the voyage; and, that no opportunity might be lost to science from the want of persons capable of observing nature under every aspect, astronomers and naturalists of eminent ability were engaged to accompany the expedition; Messrs Wales and Bayley proceeding in the former, Reinhold Forster and his son in the latter, capacity. The ships were amply stored and provided for a long and difficult voyage, particularly with anti-scorbutics, and whatever was thought likely to preserve the health of the crews. Cook sailed from Plymouth on the 13th of July 1772, on his second voyage of discovery. On his arrival at the Cape of Good Hope, he was induced, by the entreaties of Mr Forster, to allow the celebrated naturalist Sparmann to join the expedition. He now directed his course to the south, in search of the land said to have been discovered by the French navigator Bouvet, but violent gales drove him far to the east of the meridian in which it was supposed to lie. After long struggling with adverse winds, he at length reached the same meridian, some leagues to the south of the latitude assigned to Cape Circumcision. Having thus proved that the land said to have been seen by Bouvet, if it existed at all, was certainly no part of a southern continent, he continued his course to the south and east.

"On the 10th of December our navigators first met with islands of ice, and on the following days these occurred in greater numbers and of larger size; some of them were nearly two miles in circuit, and sixty feet high; yet such was the force of the waves, that the sea broke quite over them. This was at first view a gratifying spectacle, but the sentiment of pleasure was soon swallowed up in the horror which seized on the mind from the contemplation of danger; for a ship approaching these islands on the weather side would be dashed to pieces in a moment. Amidst the obstructions to which our navigators were exposed from the ice islands continually succeeding one another, they derived the advantage of having an abundant supply of fresh water; large masses of ice were carried off, and stowed on deck, and the water pro-

duced from its melting was found perfectly sweet and well tasted.

"On the 17th of January 1773, our navigators had reached the Latitude of 67° 15′ S., and they saw the ice extending from east to west-south-west, without the least appearance of an opening. It was vain, therefore, to persist any longer in a southerly course; and as there was some danger of being surrounded by the ice, prudence dictated a retreat to the north. On the 8th of February, the weather being extremely thick and hazy, it was found that the Adventure had parted company; the rendezvous appointed in case of this accident, was Queen Charlotte's Sound in New Zealand, and thither Cook directed his course. In the Latitude of 62° S., on the 17th of the same month, between midnight and 3 o'clock in the morning, lights were seen in the heavens, similar to those that are known in the northern hemisphere by the name of the Aurora Borealis. Captain Cook had never heard that the Aurora Australis had been seen before, but the same phenomenon was witnessed repeatedly in the sequel of this voyage. During his run to the eastward in this high latitude, he had ample reason to conclude that no land lay to the south, unless at a very great distance. At length, after having been 117 days at sea, during which time he had sailed 3660 leagues without having come once within sight of land, he saw the shores of New Zealand on the 25th of March, and on the following day came to an anchor in Dusky Bay. Notwithstanding the length and hardships of his voyage, there was no sickness in the ship; the attention which he paid to the health of the men, by enforcing cleanliness, by keeping the vessel dry and well ventilated, and by the judicious use of anti-scorbutic diet, being attended with complete success. Having surveyed Dusky Bay, he proceeded to Queen Charlotte's Sound, where Captain Furneaux had arrived before him.

"The Adventure, after parting company with the Resolution, had followed a more northerly course, and traced the coasts of Van Dieman's Land along the southern and eastern shores. Captain Furneaux reported, "that in his opinion there are no straits between this land and New Holland, but a very deep bay." Cook had intended to investigate this point, but, considering it to be now settled by the judgment of his colleague, he resolved to prosecute his researches to the east, between the Latitudes of 41° and 46°. But before he left Queen Charlotte's Sound, he succeeded in establishing a friendly and mutually advantageous intercourse with the natives. He endeavoured to give them substantial proofs of his kind intentions, by making an addition to their stock of useful animals. He put on shore a ewe and ram, and also two goats, a male and female. A garden also was dug, and a variety of seeds of culinary vegetables, adapted to the climate, were sown in it.

"Although it was the winter season, Cook determined not to lose his time in utter inactivity. His ships being sound, and his crews healthy, he thought that he might safely proceed to examine the Southern Ocean within the Latitude of 46°; and then, refreshing at some of the islands between the tropics, return in the summer season to carry his researches to a higher latitude. His voyage from New Zealand towards the east was not productive of any interesting discoveries, nor diversified by any but the ordinary details of navigation. He felt convinced, from the great sea that rolled from the south, that no land of any extent could lie near him in that direction. When he had advanced so far as to find himself to the north of Carteret's track, he could no longer entertain any hope of finding a continent; and this circumstance, with the sickly state of the Adventure's crew, induced him to direct his course to the Society Islands. During this part of his voyage, he saw a number of those small low islands which compose the Dangerous Archipelago of Bougainville.

"The ships narrowly escaped destruction by drifting on the coral reefs at Otaheite; they were saved only by the promptness of their commander, and the unremitting exertions of the crew. On the 24th of August they anchored in their old station in Matavai Bay. The men on board the Resolution were at this time in perfect health; but the crew of the Adventure, on the other hand, suffered dreadfully from the scurvy, though the two ships were equipped alike, and the same precautionary system to preserve the health of the men was prescribed to both; but zeal on the part of the officers was requisite to give efficacy to the orders, and their example was necessary to encourage the men to sacrifice old habits in order to preserve their constitutions.

"During this visit to Otaheite, our navigators obtained a more intimate acquaintance with the manners and character of the natives. Of their religious doctrines they were unable to acquire a distinct knowledge; but they ascertained that human victims were often sacrificed to their gods. They also witnessed the "Heavas" or dramatic representations of the people, and found them not devoid of archness and ingenuity. The performance was generally extemporaneous, founded upon some incidents presented at the moment, and in which our navigators usually made a prominent figure. Otoo, the present king of Otaheite, a man of fine figure but of remarkably timid disposition, contracted an intimate friendship with Captain Cook. Oberea, who, when the island was first visited by Captain Wallis, was so conspicuous a character, was now reduced to an humble station, and had declined as much in personal appearance as in rank. It is remarkable that few inquiries were made after Tupia, who had accompanied Cook in his former voyage, or after Aootooroo, the native of Otaheite, who had accompanied Bougainville to Europe; but, though the islanders were neglectful of their own countrymen, they were uniformly solicitous in inquiring after Mr Banks.

"On leaving Otaheite, Cook visited the other islands of the group, where he found provisions in greater abundance. Oree, the chief of Huaheine, evinced towards him the most affectionate regard. Omai, a native of Ulietea, being desirous to accompany the English, was admitted by Captain Furneaux on board the Adventure; he was not of the higher class, and, consequently, not a favourable specimen of these islanders as far as regarded person and deportment; but his docility and general propriety of conduct eventually justified the choice of Captain Furneaux. A young native of Borabora, named Hete-Hete, or Oedidee (as our great navigator named him), was at the same time allowed by Captain Cook to embark in the Resolution.

"On quitting the Society Islands, Cook directed his course to the west, where he had reason to believe, from the accounts of the natives, that much yet remained to be explored. At the island named Middleburg by Roggewein, he was well treated by a chief called Tioony; at Amsterdam Island his reception was equally favourable. The language of these islanders differed but little from that of Otaheite, and they were evidently of the same race. Some of our navigators thought them much handsomer; but others, and among these Cook himself, were of a different opinion. The men were grave and stately; but the women, on the contrary, were remarkably vivacious, and prattled unceasingly to the strangers, regardless of the mortifying fact that the latter could not understand them. But these people were chiefly distinguished from the natives of the Society Islands by their superior industry. On the Island of Amsterdam, Captain Cook was struck with admiration, when he surveyed the cultivation and the beauty of the scene; he thought himself transported into the most fertile plains of Europe; there was not an inch of waste ground. The roads or paths occupied no more space than was absolutely necessary, and the fences did not take up above four inches each; nor was this small portion of ground wholly lost, for the fences themselves contained in general useful trees or plants. The scene was everywhere the same; and nature, assisted by a little art, nowhere assumed a more splendid appearance than in these islands.

"Cook now directed his course again to New Zealand; but, on approaching that country, the ships had to encounter a succession of severe gales and continued bad weather, during which the Adventure was again lost sight of and never afterwards rejoined. On the 3d of November the Resolution anchored in Queen Charlotte's Sound. The winter had been spent not unprofitably in revictualling the ships, restoring the health of the crews, and obtaining a more accurate knowledge of the islands between the tropics. And now, as summer approached, it was Cook's intention to run from New Zealand, where wood and water were to be procured in abundance, and to explore the high southern latitudes from west to east, in which course he might reckon upon having the winds and currents in his favour. While the Resolution lay in Queen Charlotte's Sound, indubitable proofs presented themselves that cannibalism was common among the natives. One of them who carried some human flesh in his canoe, was allowed to broil and eat it on board the Resolution, in order to satisfy the doubts of some of the officers. Oedidee, who witnessed all this, was shocked beyond measure at the spectacle. At first he stood motionless as a statue, but his horror at length gave way to rage, which vented itself not only on the New Zealander, but on the officers who had encouraged him; and he could not be induced even to touch the knife which had been employed to cut the human flesh.

"On the 26th of November, Cook sailed to prosecute his examination of the Antarctic seas. His crew were in good health and high spirits, not at all dejected by the arduous task which was before them. In a few days they crossed the antipodes of London, and were thus on the point of the globe which was most distant from their home. The first ice island was seen on the 12th of December; and, on the 30th of that month, our navigators had reached the 71st degree of southern latitude; but here the ice was so compact that it was impossible to proceed any further towards the south; and it was also obvious that no continent existed in that direction but what must be inaccessible from the ice. It was Cook's intention to winter again within the tropic; but in proceeding thither, he wished to satisfy himself as to the southern land said to have been discovered by Juan Fernandez. He sailed sufficiently near the position assigned to that supposed continent to assure himself that it could not have been anything more than an island of moderate size. He now directed his course in search of Davis's Land or Easter Island, which had been sought in vain by Byron, Carteret, and Bougainville. Cook, however, succeeded better, and made the island on the 11th of March 1774. The natives were found to speak a language radically the same with that of Otaheite, and which thus reaches across the Pacific Ocean from New Zealand to the sequestered islands in the East. Easter Island was found to be remarkably barren, ill supplied with water, and wholly without wood. But the attention of the English was forcibly attracted by the great statues seen on the island by Roggewein. About fifteen yards from the landing-place was found a perpendicular wall of square hewn stones, about eight feet in height, and nearly sixty in length; another wall parallel to the first, and about forty feet distant from it, was raised to the same height; the whole area between the walls was filled up and paved with square stones of blackish lava. The stones of the walls were so carefully fitted as to make a durable piece of architecture. In the midst of the area was a pillar consisting of a single stone, about twenty feet high and about five feet wide, representing the human figure down to the waist. The workmanship was rude but not bad; nor were the features of the face ill formed, but the ears were long beyond proportion. On the top of the head was placed upright a huge round cylinder of stone, above five feet in height and in diameter; this cap, which resembled the head-dress of an Egyptian divinity, was formed of a kind of stone different from that which composed the rest of the pillar, and had a hole on each side, as if it had been made round by turning. It appeared as difficult to explain how the natives of this island, who were but few in number, could carve such huge statues with no better tools than those made of bones or shells, or how they raised them on their pedestals when finished, as to divine for what purpose they undertook such gigantic labours; for it did not appear that the statues were objects of worship; yet on the eastern side of the island they were numerous enough to employ the male population of the island for many centuries in their construction. The skill of this people in carving was still more manifest in the ornaments of their canoes, and in small wooden figures, of which the English brought home many curious specimens.

"From Easter Island Cook directed his course to the Marquesas, discovered by Mendana in 1595; and on the 6th of April he got sight of one island of the group, which was, however, a new discovery, and received, from the gentleman who first descried it, the name of Hood's Island. The other islands seen by Mendana, St Pedro, Dominica, and St Christiana, were afterwards discovered in succession. The ship with much difficulty anchored in Mendana's Port in the last-mentioned island. Magdalena, the fifth island of the group, was seen only at a distance. Of the inhabitants of these islands Captain Cook tells us, that collectively they are without exception the finest race of people in this sea; for fine shape and regular features they perhaps surpass all other nations. Nevertheless the affinity of their language to that spoken in Otaheite and the Society Islands shows that they are originally of the same nation. Oedidee could converse with them tolerably well, though the English could not, and it was obvious that their languages were nearly the same. In their manners and arts the people resembled the natives of Otaheite, but appeared to be rather less ingenious and refined. Forts, or strongholds, were seen on the summits of the highest hills; but they were not visited by the English, who had not become sufficiently acquainted with the natives to venture into the interior.

"Cook, having rediscovered the Marquesas of Mendana, proceeded to Otaheite, and passing by a group, to which he gave the name of Palliser's Islands, and some others which had been seen by Byron, he anchored in Matavai Bay on the 22d of April. At this time there were no sick on board; but as the island seemed to abound with provisions, our navigator was willing to prolong his stay here. His original stock in trade was, indeed, now exhausted; but he found that the people of Otaheite set a great value on the red parrot feathers, of which he had brought a considerable supply from Amsterdam and Middleburg Islands. He thus accidentally learned an advantageous and easy course of traffic in the South Sea.

"Among other entertainments with which our navigators were treated during this visit to Otaheite was a grand naval review. The vessels of war consisted of 160 great canoes, from fifty to ninety feet in length; they were decorated with flags and streamers; and the chiefs, together with all those who were on the fighting stages, were dressed in their war habits. The whole fleet made a noble appearance, such as our voyagers had never before seen, and could not have expected in this part of the world. Besides the vessels of war, there were 170 sail of smaller double canoes, which seemed to be designed for transports and victuallers. Upon each of them was a small house or shed; and they were rigged with a mast and sail, which was not the case with the war canoes. Captain Cook estimated, at a moderate computation, that there could not be less than 7760 men in the fleet; but the immense number of natives assembled as spectators astonished the English more than the splendour of the armament, and they were still further surprised to learn that this fleet was the naval force of only one of the twenty districts into which the island is divided. On these equivocal grounds they were led to form an extremely exaggerated calculation of the population of Otaheite, which they estimated to be at least 200,000 souls; a number exceeding the truth, perhaps, in the proportion of ten to one.

"From Otaheite our navigators proceeded to visit the Society Islands, at Huaheine. Cook was affectionately received by the old chief Oree, who still carefully preserved the medals, coins, and pewter plate with an inscription commemorating the voyage, which our commander had given him on his former visit. Oedidee, who for seven months had been the faithful companion of our voyagers, and had made with them the tour of the Pacific, was put on shore at Ulietea. He left the English with regret demonstrative of a strong attachment to them; and nothing could have torn him from them but the fear of never returning to his native country. He was a fine young man, of a docile and humane disposition, and of the better class of natives, being nearly related to Opoony, the formidable chief of Borabora. But from his inexperience and imperfect acquaintance with the traditionary knowledge of his countrymen, but little could be learned from him respecting their history.

"Cook again directed his course to the west, and repeated his visit to the Friendly Islands. This name he gave to a group extending through about three degrees of latitude and two degrees of longitude, and comprising Anamooka, which Tasman, who first discovered it, named Rotterdam, Tongataboo or Amsterdam, Eaoowee or Middleburg, and Pylstart Islands. But this appellation, to which these islands were entitled by the firm alliance and friendship which seemed to exist among their inhabitants, and their courteous behaviour to strangers, might perhaps be extended much farther, so as to include the Boscawen and Keppel Isles discovered by Captain Wallis, and inhabited by people of the same friendly manners.

" Pursuing their course to the west, our navigators discovered on the 16th of July, land, which was justly conjectured to be the 'Terra Australis del Espirito Santo' of Quiros. After exploring the coast for a few days, Cook came to an anchor in a harbour in the Island of Mallicolo. The inhabitants of this island were the most ugly and deformed race which our navigators had yet seen, and differed in every respect from the other inhabitants of the Southern Ocean. They were dark coloured, of small stature, with long heads, flat faces, and countenances resembling that of a monkey. Their language, also, was found not to have any discoverable affinity with that prevailing through the islands with which the English had any acquaintance. This people differed likewise from the great Polynesian race not more by their language and figure than by their scrupulous honesty. As our navigators proceeded towards the south from Mallicolo, they passed by a group which Cook named Shepherd's Isles. Farther to the south was discovered a large island agreeably diversified with woods and lawns over the whole surface, and exhibiting a most beautiful and delightful prospect. This our navigator named Sandwich Island in compliment to his friend and patron the Earl of Sandwich. Still farther to the south was seen another large island, called by the natives Erromango, which he coasted for three days, and then came to an anchor in the intention of procuring a supply of wood and water. This, however, could not be effected without a violent conflict with the natives, who were both fierce and treacherous. It was observed that they differed from the inhabitants of Mallicolo both in language and physical conformation; they were well shaped and had tolerable features, but dark coloured, and with hair crisp and somewhat woolly. From this place Cook sailed for an island which had been descried some time before at a distance. He found that it was called Tanna by the inhabitants, from whom also he learned the names of three other islands in its neighbourhood, Inmer, Erronan, and Anaton. Two languages were found to be spoken in Tanna; one of them, which was said to have been introduced from Erronan, was nearly the same with that of the Friendly Islands; the other, which our navigators considered peculiar to Tanna, Erromango, and Anaton, was different from any they had hitherto met with in the course of their researches. The people at Tanna were well proportioned, but not robust. They had good features and agreeable countenances. Though active, and fond of martial exercises, they seemed incapable of patient labour. It appeared that they practised circumcision, and that they were eaters of human flesh; though, as their island abounded with hogs and fowls, and a variety of fruits, they could not be driven by necessity to adopt this horrid practice.

"Captain Cook devoted above a month to the survey of this archipelago, with which previous navigators had made but a superficial acquaintance. The northern islands were discovered in 1606 by Quiros, who supposed them to be portions of the great southern continent. Bougainville, in 1768, dispelled this idea, though he did not proceed to examine the islands near which he sailed; but Captain Cook, besides ascertaining the extent and situation of the islands already known, explored the whole group; and, conceiving that in consequence he had a right to name them, bestowed on them the appellation of the New Hebrides.

"The season was now approaching when it would be necessary to resume his researches in a high southern latitude, and he hastened therefore to New Zealand, where he intended to refresh his people and prepare for a navigation of considerable length. He sailed from the New Hebrides on the 1st of September, and on the 4th discovered land, near which the Resolution came to anchor the next day. The inhabitants were a strong, active, and handsome race, bearing some resemblance to the people of Tanna, and those of the Friendly Isles. The same mixed character was observed in their language. They had never seen Europeans before, but were friendly and obliging in their behaviour; and what is still more remarkable in the South Seas, strictly honest in all their dealings. To this island Captain Cook gave the name of New Caledonia; and though compelled by necessity to leave it before it was fully surveyed, he had, nevertheless, examined it sufficiently to prove, that, excepting New Zealand, it is perhaps the largest island in the South Pacific Ocean. As the Resolution pursued her course from New Caledonia, land was discovered, which, on a nearer approach, was found to be an island of good height, and about five leagues in circuit. It was uninhabited, and probably our English navigators were the first persons who had ever set foot on it. In its vegetable productions it bore a close resemblance to New Zealand. The flax plant of that country was here particularly luxuriant; but the chief produce of the island was a majestic species of pine, of such a size that, breast high, two men could scarcely clasp the trunk. This little spot was named Norfolk Island. Its fine woods and fertile soil allured, some years later, a party of British settlers; who finally abandoned it, however, from the inaccessible nature of its coast.

"On the 18th of October the Resolution came to anchor in Queen Charlotte's Sound. This was the third time of touching at New Zealand during this voyage. On searching for the bottle which Cook had left behind on his last visit, containing the particulars of his arrival, it was found to have been taken away; and from other circumstances it was evident that the Adventure had visited the harbour after the Resolution had left it. While the Resolution remained here, the intercourse maintained with the natives was of the most friendly description. Captain Cook continued his efforts to stock the island with useful animals, and for that purpose ordered a boar and sow to be put on shore.

"On the 10th of November he left New Zealand to pursue his voyage to the east. Towards the close of that month, he had reached the Latitude of 55° 48' S., when, deeming it useless to search any longer for a continent in that direction, he bore away for Cape Horn; and on the 17th of December had sight of Tierra del Fuego. This is the first instance of a run quite across the Southern Pacific. It now only remained for our navigator to cross also the Southern Atlantic to the point whence he had commenced his explorations. Having completed his examination of Tierra del Fuego and Staaten Land, he proceeded towards the east; and, after a voyage of ten days, land was seen at a distance, nearly covered with snow. On approaching the shore, it was found to be terminated in many places by perpendicular ice cliffs of considerable height. Pieces continually broke off with a noise like the report of cannon, and floated out to sea. The general aspect of the country was savage and horrid in the extreme. The wild rocks raised their lofty summits till they were lost in the clouds, and the valleys lay covered with everlasting snow. Our navigator, who at first view of this land supposed that it might be a continent, confesses that he was not much disappointed on discovering his error; 'for to judge of the bulk by the sample, it would not be worth discovering.' In Latitude 59°, and about eight degrees to the east of New Georgia, as this inhospitable shore was named, land was again seen, presenting an elevated coast, whose lofty snow-clad summits reached above the clouds. To this bleak region Cook gave the name of the Southern Thule, as it was the most southern land which had yet been discovered; but on leaving the coast he gave to the whole country the general appellation of Sandwich Land, which he concluded to be either a group of islands or a point of the southern continent. But the great quantities of ice which he met with led him to infer the existence of a large tract of land near the South Pole. He now sailed as far as the latitude assigned to Bouvet's supposed discovery; but no indications of land occurred, nor was it possible to believe any longer in the existence of Cape Circumcision.

"Cook had now made a circuit of the Southern Ocean in a high latitude, and traversed it in such a manner as to demonstrate that no southern continent existed unless near the Pole, and beyond the reach of navigation. During this circumnavigation of the globe, from the time of his leaving the Cape of Good Hope to his return to it again, he had sailed no less than 20,000 leagues. On the 13th of July 1775, he landed at Portsmouth, having been absent from Great Britain three years and eighteen days, during which time, and under all changes of climate, he had lost but four men, and only one of them by sickness.

"It has been related above that Captain Cook, on approaching New Zealand for the second time in the course of this voyage, lost sight of the Adventure, and never joined company with that ship again. Captain Furneaux was long baffled by adverse winds in his attempt to reach Queen Charlotte's Sound, which was appointed the rendezvous for the ships in case of separation. At length, on the 30th of November, the Adventure got safe into the desired port. The Resolution not being there, Captain Furneaux and his company began to entertain doubts of her safety; but on going on shore they observed on an old stump of a tree these words cut out—'Look underneath.' They dug accordingly, and soon found a bottle corked and waxed down, with a letter in it from Captain Cook, signifying his arrival on the 3d and departure on the 24th. Great exertions were now made to get the Adventure ready for sea, and on the 17th of December, the preparations being completed, Mr Rowe, a midshipman, with nine men, were sent in the large cutter to gather a stock of wild greens for the ship's company. As the boat did not return the same evening nor the next morning, and the ship was now ready for sea, Mr Burney, the second lieutenant, proceeded in search of her in the launch, manned with the boat's crew and ten marines. The launch proceeded, firing guns into all the coves by way of signals, but no traces of the cutter were found till they reached Grass Cove. Here a great many baskets were seen lying on the beach tied up; when cut open, some of them were found to be full of roasted flesh, and some of fern root, which served the natives for bread. On further search, some shoes were picked up and a hand, which was immediately known to have belonged to Thomas Hill, one of the forecastle men, the initials of his name being marked on it with an Otaheitan tatooing instrument. The natives were collected in considerable numbers round Grass Cove, shouting and inviting the English to land, but evidently with no friendly intentions. From their numbers, and the suspicion which their conduct excited in our people, Lieutenant Burney did not deem it prudent to trust himself among them; but he pursued his examination far enough to obtain a melancholy certainty as to the fate of his unfortunate companions. 'On the beach,' he says, 'were two bundles of celery, which had been gathered for loading the cutter; a broken oar was stuck upright in the ground, to which the natives had tied their canoes, a proof that the attack had been made here. I then searched all along at the back of the beach to see if the cutter was there. We found no boat, but instead of her such a shocking scene of carnage and barbarity as can never be mentioned nor thought of but with horror; for the heads, hearts, and lungs of several of our people were seen lying on the beach; and, at a little distance, the dogs gnawing their entrails.' The men who had thus fallen victims to the barbarity of the natives were among the healthiest and best of the ship's crew.

"The Adventure was detained in the sound four days after this lamentable occurrence, during which time no natives were seen. On the 23d of December, however, she got to sea; and in little more than a month reached Cape Horn, being favoured by a strong current running to the east, and by westerly winds which blow continually in the summer season in the great ocean. Captain Furneaux continued his course eastward to the Cape of Good Hope, where he refitted his ship and refreshed his people. He then sailed for England, and anchored at Spithead on the 14th of July 1774.

"In 1769 some discoveries of importance were made in the South Seas by a French mercantile adventurer. Two ships were fitted out in Bengal by MM. Law and Chevalier for a trading voyage to Peru, and were placed under the command of M. de Surville. While he was preparing to embark, news arrived in India that the English had discovered in the South Sea, 700 leagues from Peru, and in Lat. 27° S., an island exceedingly rich, and inhabited by Jews. This story gained credit, being congenial to the avaricious cravings of mankind; and even those who suspected fiction in the mention of Jews were still willing to believe that the newly-discovered country was eminently rich. Surville, touching at the Bashee Islands, carried off three of the natives to supply the deficiencies of his crew, thus furnishing a conspicuous example of that overbearing violence which has almost universally forced weak and uncivilised nations to regard Europeans as their natural enemies. In running to the south-east from New Guinea he discovered land, to which he gave the name of the Land of the Arsacides, and which was, in fact, a part of that long chain of islands that had already been seen by Bougainville, who gave the name of Louisiade to the portion which he had examined. Surville, in his intercourse with the natives, found them to be of a fierce, intractable, and treacherous disposition, and chose to designate them Arsacides, a name which he supposed to be equivalent to the word assassins. Surville afterwards visited New Zealand, and anchored in a bay, to which he gave the name of Lauriston. Captain Cook, who named it Double Bay, was at the same time employed in surveying its shores, yet these two navigators did not meet nor descry each other. The French commander, having lost his boat while anchoring here, went on shore with an armed party to punish the natives, whom he supposed to have stolen it. In a short time he burned several villages, and carried off a native chief. This outrage, perpetrated by some of the first Europeans who visited them, was soon afterwards repaid with cruel reprisals by the New Zealanders. The chief died at Juan Fernandez, and Surville was drowned while going on shore at Valparaiso.

"The Land of the Arsacides, which Surville had coasted on the north-eastern side, was again discovered in 1789 by Lieutenant Shortland of the British navy on his voyage from Port Jackson to the East Indies. He followed its southern shores, to which he gave the name of New Georgia, and passed through the Straits of Bougainville, which he named from himself, being apparently ignorant of the discoveries of the French navigators. The chain of large islands thus seen successively and partially by Bougainville, Surville, and Shortland, and which stretch from north-west to south-east, between New Guinea and the New Hebrides, are unquestionably the Salomon Islands of the early Spanish navigators. The Egmont Island of Carteret, who sought the Salomon Islands, and who approached them very closely without being aware of it, may be considered as belonging to the archipelago.

"It has been already mentioned that Bougainville brought home with him to France a native of Otaheite named Aootooroo. When the fame of Cook's discoveries began to excite a general interest in Europe, Captain Marion du Fresne, animated with a desire to emulate the glory of the English navigator, offered to take back the Otaheitean to his native land from the Isle of France at his own expense. The offer was accepted, and Kerguelen, a navigator of some note, was commissioned to carry Aootooroo to the Isle of France, and then to proceed to examine more carefully the southern part of the Atlantic Ocean. The Otaheitean died at Madagascar, but Marion did not on that account relinquish his plans, but proceeded in the ardent hope of making some important discoveries. He arrived at New Zealand without any accident, and anchored in the Bay of Islands, where his people lived on terms of familiarity, and apparently of cordial friendship with the natives; but some offence was given unawares to the passionate and capricious savages. Marion was murdered, with sixteen officers and men who had accompanied him on shore. Another party of eleven men, who were employed cutting wood in a different quarter, were at the same time set upon suddenly, and only one escaped to the ships to relate the dismal fate of his companions. When the French landed to seek the remains of their unfortunate commander, the natives insultingly cried to them from their fastnesses, 'Tacowry (the chief of the district) has killed and eaten Marion.' After this melancholy accident the ships returned to the Isle of France under the command of M. Duclesmeur, all plans of discovery being abandoned.

"Kerguelen, in the meantime, sailed from the Isle of France in January 1772; and, on the 12th of February, discovered in Lat. 50° 5' S., high land, near the coast of which he remained six days. During this time he was separated from the corvette which accompanied him. To the bleak and sterile shores which he had discovered he gave his own name; took formal possession of them for his sovereign; and, on his return to France, described their appearance in such glowing terms, that Louis XV., deceived by his representations, hung to his button-hole, with his own hand, the cross of St Louis. Kerguelen's enemies, however, insisted that he had seen ice at a distance, and mistaken it for land; they called on him to show some of the productions of the country as a proof of his discovery, and insinuated that he had purposely got rid of his comrade that he might be at liberty to indulge in gross fictions. The King, however, afforded him the means of refuting these aspersions. Kerguelen sailed again to the Southern Atlantic, and, in December 1773, again discovered land: by the 6th of January following he had traced its coasts above eighty leagues. It was, however, a barren, inhospitable, and, in general, an unapproachable shore, affording nothing that could satisfy the French nation of the importance of his discoveries. On his return he was accused of culpable indifference to the safety of his men and officers, or rather of purposely exposing those whom he disliked to dangers which eventually proved fatal. Being unable to exculpate himself, he was deprived of his rank and thrown into prison.

"No expedition, fitted out for the purpose of maritime discovery, had ever equalled that from which Captain Cook had now returned, in the magnitude and arduous nature of its peculiar object; and none had ever so completely answered its intentions and performed its task with so little loss of life or injury to the ships. The success of Cook's voyage was gratifying in the highest degree to those who had patronised the undertaking. The Earl of Sandwich was still at the head of the Admiralty, and felt naturally disposed to reward liberally one whose courage and skill had so well justified his expectations. Cook was immediately raised to the rank of post captain, and obtained a more substantial mark of favour, being appointed one of the captains of Greenwich Hospital, which afforded him a liberal maintenance and repose from his professional labours. In February 1776, only a few months after his return, he was elected a Fellow of the Royal Society; and on the evening of his first appearance there, a paper was read containing an account of the method he had taken to preserve the health of the crew of his Majesty's ship, the Resolution, during her voyage round the world. The humane and successful attention which Cook bestowed on his ship's company was soon after rewarded by the Copley medal, a prize annually bestowed by the Royal Society on the author of the best experimental paper of the year. In the discourse which the president, Sir John Pringle, delivered on the occasion of bestowing the medal, he uses the following emphatic expressions:

" 'What inquiry can be so useful as that which has for its object the saving the lives of men? and where shall we find one more successful than that before us? Here are no vain boastings of the empiric, nor ingenious and delusive theories of the dogmatist; but a concise and artless, and an uncontested, relation of the means by which, under divine favour, Captain Cook, with a company of 118 men, performed a voyage of three years and eighteen days, throughout all the climates from Lat. 52° N., to 71° S., with the loss of only one man by sickness. I would now inquire of the most conversant with the bills of mortality, whether, in the most healthy climate and the best condition of life, they have ever found so small a number of deaths within that space of time? How great and agreeable, then, must our surprise be, after perusing the histories of long navigations in former days, when so many perished by marine diseases, to find the air of the sea acquitted of all malignity; and, in fine, that a voyage round the world may be undertaken with less danger perhaps to health than a common tour in Europe.'

"The great question as to the existence of a southern continent was finally set at rest by the result of this voyage; not but that immense tracks of land might exist in the neighbourhood of the South Pole. But Cook's researches reduced the limits of the southern continent, if it exist at all within such high latitudes, as completely to dispel all those hopes of unbounded wealth and fertility with which imagination had hitherto graced that undiscovered country. One grand problem still divided the opinions of speculative geographers, and eluded every attempt made at a practical solution. The English nation had always felt a peculiar interest in the question of a north-west passage. Their earliest and most constant efforts in the career of discovery were directed towards Hudson's and Baffin's Bays, in search of a communication with the Pacific Ocean, so that they might sail by a shorter navigation to China and Japan. In consequence of the disputes between Mr Dobbs and Captain Middleton, respecting the feasibility of the scheme, the agitation of the question was tolerably recent in the public mind, and, Government adopting the views of the former gentleman, a reward of £20,000 was offered by Act of Parliament to those who should discover the desired passage.

"The British Government, captivated with the glory that might result from expeditions destined for the improvement of science, resolved now to direct its exertions towards the north-west; and, as a preliminary measure, Captain Phipps (afterwards Lord Mulgrave) was despatched towards the North Pole, to ascertain how far navigation was practicable in that quarter. After struggling obstinately with innumerable difficulties and dangers, arising from the quantity of ice that beset him, he was obliged to return, after having penetrated to the Latitude of 80° 30', or within nine degrees and a half of the Terrestrial Pole.

"The hope of finding a passage between the Atlantic and Pacific Oceans was not, however, abandoned; and consultations were held by Lord Sandwich with Sir Hugh Palliser and other experienced officers, relative to the plan which should be adopted in the expedition, and to the choice of a commander. Captain Cook had earned, by his eminent services, the privilege of honourable repose; and no one thought of imposing on him, for the third time, the dangers and hardships of a voyage of discovery round the world: but being invited to dine with Lord Sandwich, in order that he might lend the light of his valuable experience to the various particulars under discussion, he was so fired with the observations that were made on the benefits likely to redound to science, to navigation, and the intercourse of mankind, from the projected expedition, that he voluntarily offered to take the command of it himself. This proposal was too much in accordance with the wishes of Lord Sandwich to be rejected through motives of mere delicacy; and Captain Cook was appointed accordingly to the command of the expedition, in February 1776. The Act of Parliament, passed in 1745, which secured a reward of £20,000 to ships *belonging to any of his Majesty's subjects*, which should make the proposed discovery, was now also amended so as to include ships *belonging to his Majesty*, and proceeding in *any direction*, for the old Act referred only to ships which should find a passage through Hudson's Bay; whereas Cook was directed by his instructions to proceed into the Pacific Ocean, and to commence his researches on the north-west coast of America, in the Latitude of 65°, and not to lose time in exploring rivers or inlets until he had reached that latitude."

COOK'S THIRD VOYAGE.[1]

BOOK I.

TRANSACTIONS FROM THE BEGINNING OF THE VOYAGE TILL OUR DEPARTURE FROM NEW ZEALAND.

CHAPTER I.

HAVING, on the 9th day of February 1776, received a commission to command his Majesty's sloop the Resolution, I went on board the next day, hoisted the pendant, and began to enter men. At the same time the

---

[1] The account of this voyage was originally published in 1784, in three quarto volumes, the first and second being written by Cook himself, the third by Captain King, who had sailed as one of the Resolution's lieutenants, but returned to England in command of the Discovery. The title was as follows: "A Voyage to the Pacific Ocean; undertaken by the command of His Majesty, for making Discoveries in the Northern Hemisphere, to determine the Position and Extent of the West Side of North America, its Distance from Asia, and the Practicability of a Northern Passage to Europe. Performed under the direction of Captains Cook, Clerke, and Gore, in His Majesty's Ships the Resolution and Discovery, in the

Discovery, of 300 tons burthen, was purchased into the service, and the command of her given to Captain Clerke, who had been my second lieutenant on board the Resolution in my second voyage round the world, from which we had lately returned. These two ships were at this time in the dock at Deptford, under the hands

Years 1776, 1777, 1778, 1779, and 1780. Published by Order of the Lords Commissioners of the Admiralty." In the portion of the work specially ascribed to Captain Cook, however, there are many valuable contributions from the pen of Mr Anderson, surgeon of the Resolution, usually on the physical features and natural products of the countries visited, the habits, ethnography, and language of the inhabitants, &c. In more than one instance the original editor of the book—Dr Douglas, Bishop of Salisbury, who, at the request of Lord Sandwich, undertook that task—preferred Mr Anderson's notes of actual incidents to Cook's own story; and not without wisdom, as any one will admit who reads the surgeon's account of the dances and entertainments shown off before the white strangers at Haapee (B. II., Ch. V.), and at Tongataboo (B. II., Ch. VII.). Necessities of space have compelled the omission of many passages directly ascribed to Mr Anderson by Cook himself; but in every case these are scientific and technical in their character, and the lapse of a century has given us abundant light on many matters which at the time of Cook's last voyage were but imperfectly known, or subjects of crude and vague speculation. Dr Douglas prefixed to the voyage an elaborate introductory treatise on the possibility of finding a north-east passage from the Pacific to the Atlantic Ocean, and also enriched the volumes with many learned notes, comparatively few of which have been retained in the present edition, as, dealing with matters of controversy long since settled, and with records of travel all but totally forgotten, they could only confuse the reader.

of the shipwrights, being ordered to be equipped to make further discoveries in the Pacific Ocean, under my direction.

On the 9th of March the Resolution was hauled out of dock into the river, where we completed her rigging, and took on board the stores and provisions requisite for a voyage of such duration. Both ships, indeed, were supplied with as much of every necessary article as we could conveniently stow, and with the best of every kind that could be procured. And besides this, everything that had been found by the experience acquired during our former extensive voyages to be of any utility in preserving the health of seamen, was supplied in abundance.[1]

It was our intention to have sailed to Long Reach on the 6th of May, when a pilot came on board to carry us thither; but it was the 29th before the wind would permit us to move, and the 30th before we arrived at that station, where our artillery, powder, shot, and other ordnance stores were received. While we lay in Long Reach thus employed, the Earl of Sandwich, Sir Hugh Palliser, and others of the Board of Admiralty, as the last mark of the very great attention they had all along shown to this equipment, paid us a visit on the 8th of June, to examine whether everything had been completed conformably to their intentions and orders, and to the satisfaction of all who were to embark in the voyage. They and several other noblemen and gentlemen, their friends, honoured me with their company at dinner on that day; and on their coming on board, and also on their going ashore, we saluted them with seventeen guns, and three cheers.

With the benevolent view of conveying some permanent benefit to the inhabitants of Otaheite, and of the

---

[1] Contrast the excellence of Cook's equipment and the perfect success of his arrangements for securing the health of his ships' companies, with the wretched plight in which Anson left port thirty-six years before, and the miserable fate of his crews.

other islands in the Pacific Ocean, whom we might happen to visit, his Majesty having commanded some useful animals to be carried out, we took on board, on the 10th, a bull, two cows, with their calves, and some sheep, with hay and corn for their subsistence, intending to add to these other useful animals when I should arrive at the Cape of Good Hope. I was also, from the same laudable motives, furnished with a sufficient quantity of such of our European garden seeds as could not fail to be a valuable present to our newly-discovered islands, by adding fresh supplies of food to their own vegetable productions. Many other articles calculated to improve the condition of our friends in the other hemisphere in various ways, were at the same time delivered to us by order of the Board of Admiralty. And both ships were provided with a proper assortment of iron tools and trinkets, as the means of enabling us to traffic, and to cultivate a friendly intercourse with the inhabitants of such new countries as we might be fortunate enough to meet with.

The same humane attention was extended to our own wants. Some additional clothing, adapted to a cold climate, was ordered for our crews; and nothing was denied to us that could be supposed in the least conducive to health, or even to convenience. Nor did the extraordinary care of those at the head of the naval department stop here. They were equally solicitous to afford us every assistance towards rendering our voyage of public utility. Accordingly, we received on board, next day, several astronomical and nautical instruments, which the Board of Longitude intrusted to me and to Mr King, my second lieutenant; we having engaged to that Board to make all the necessary observations during the voyage for the improvement of astronomy and navigation, and, by our joint labours, to supply the place of a professed observator.

Mr Anderson, my surgeon, who, to skill in his immediate profession, added great proficiency in natural history, was as willing as he was well qualified to describe everything in that branch of science which should occur worthy of notice. As he had already visited the South Sea islands in the same ship, and been of singular service by enabling me to enrich my relation of that voyage with various useful remarks on men and things, I reasonably expected to derive considerable assistance from him, in recording our new proceedings. I had several young men amongst my sea-officers, who, under my direction, could be usefully employed in constructing charts, in taking views of the coasts and headlands near which we should pass, and in drawing plans of the bays and harbours in which we should anchor.

Every preparation being now completed, I received an order to proceed to Plymouth, and to take the Discovery under my command. I accordingly gave Captain Clerke two orders; one to put himself under my command, and the other to carry his ship round to Plymouth. On the 15th, the Resolution sailed from Long Reach, with the Discovery in company, and the same evening they anchored at the Nore. Next day the Discovery proceeded in obedience to my order; but the Resolution was ordered to remain at the Nore till I should join her, being at this time in London.

As we were to touch at Otaheite and the Society Islands in our way to the intended scene of our fresh operations, it had been determined not to omit this opportunity (the only one ever likely to happen) of carrying Omai back to his native country.

Omai left London with a mixture of regret and satisfaction. When we talked about England, and about those who, during his stay, had honoured him with their protection or friendship, I could observe that his spirits were sensibly affected, and that it was with difficulty he could refrain from tears. But the instant the conversation turned to his own islands, his eyes began to sparkle with joy. He was deeply impressed with a sense of the good treatment he had met with in England, and entertained the highest ideas of the country and of the people. But the pleasing prospect he now had before him of returning home, loaded with what he well knew would be esteemed invaluable treasures there, and the flattering hope which the possession of these gave him of attaining to a distinguished superiority amongst his countrymen, were considerations which operated by degrees to suppress every uneasy sensation; and he seemed to be quite happy when he got on board the ship. He was furnished by his Majesty with an ample provision of every article which, during our intercourse with his country, we had observed to be in any estimation there, either as useful or as ornamental. He had, besides, received many presents of the same nature from Lord Sandwich, Mr[1] Banks, and several other gentlemen and ladies of his acquaintance. In short, every method had been employed, both during his abode in England, and at his departure, to make him the instrument of conveying to the inhabitants of the islands of the Pacific Ocean the most exalted opinion of the greatness and generosity of the British nation.

On the 25th, about noon, we weighed anchor, and made sail for the Downs, through the Queen's Channel, with a gentle breeze at NW. by W. At nine in the evening we anchored, with the North Foreland bearing S. by E., and Margate Point SW. by S. Next morning, at 2 o'clock, we weighed and stood round the Foreland. At 8 o'clock the same morning, we anchored in the Downs. Two boats had been built for us at Deal, and I immediately sent on shore for them. I was told that many people had assembled there to see Omai; but, to their great disappointment, he did not land. Having received the boats on board, and a light breeze at SSE. springing up, we got under sail the next day at 2 o'clock in the afternoon. But the breeze soon died away, and we were obliged to anchor again till 10 o'clock at night. We then weighed, with the wind at east, and proceeded down the Channel. On the 30th, at 3 o'clock in the afternoon, we anchored in Plymouth Sound, where the Discovery had arrived only three days before. I saluted Admiral Amherst, whose flag was flying on board the Ocean, with thirteen guns, and he returned the compliment with eleven. It was the first object of our care, on arriving at Plymouth, to replace the water and provisions that we had expended, and to receive on board a supply of port wine. This was the employment which occupied us on the 1st and 2d of July.

It could not but occur to us as a singular and affecting circumstance, that at the very instant of our departure upon a voyage, the object of which was to benefit Europe by making fresh discoveries in North America, there should be the unhappy necessity of employing others of his Majesty's ships, and of conveying numerous bodies of land forces, to secure the obedience of those parts of that continent which had been discovered and settled by our countrymen in the last century. On the 6th, his Majesty's ships Diamond, Ambuscade, and Unicorn, with a fleet of transports, consisting of sixty-two sail, bound to America, with the last division of the Hessian troops, and some horse,[2] were forced into the Sound by a strong north-west wind. On the 8th, I received by express, my instructions for the voyage, and an order to proceed to the Cape of Good Hope with the Resolution. I was also directed to leave an order for Captain Clerke to follow us, as soon as he should join his ship; he being, at this time, detained in London.

The Resolution was fitted out with the same complement of officers and men she had before;[3] and the Discovery's establishment varied from that of the Adventure, in the single instance of her having no marine

---

[1] Afterwards Sir Joseph.

[2] To reinforce Sir William Howe, then confronting General Washington, near New York.

[3] In setting out on the second voyage in 1772.

officer on board. This arrangement was to be finally completed at Plymouth ; and, on the 9th, we received the party of marines allotted for our voyage. Colonel Bell, who commanded the division at this port, gave me such men for the detachment as I had reason to be satisfied with. And the supernumerary seamen, occasioned by this reinforcement, being turned over into the Ocean man-of-war, our several complements remained fixed, as represented in the following table :

RESOLUTION.			DISCOVERY.	
Officers and Men.	No.	*Officers' Names.*	No.	*Officers' Names.*
Captain, . .	1	James Cook. . .	1	Charles Clerke.
Lieutenants, . .	3	John Gore. . .	2	James Burney.
		James King. . .		John Rickman.
		John Williamson. .		
Master, . .	1	William Bligh.[1]	1	Thomas Edgar.
Boatswain, . .	1	William Ewin. .	1	Eneas Atkins.
Carpenter. . .	1	James Clevely. .	1	Peter Reynolds.
Gunner, . .	1	Robert Anderson. .	1	William Peckover.
Surgeon, . .	1	William Anderson.	1	John Law.
Master's Mates, .	3	. . . .	2	
Midshipmen, .	6	. . . .	4	
Surgeon's Mates, .	2	. . . .	2	
Captain's Clerk, .	1	. . . .	1	
Master at Arms, .	1	. . . .	1	
Corporal, . .	1	. . . .		
Armourer, . .	1	. . . .	1	
Ditto Mate, . .	1	. . . .	1	
Sailmaker, . .	1	. . . .	1	
Ditto Mate, . .	1	. . . .	1	
Boatswain's Mates,	3	. . . .	2	
Carpenter's Ditto, .	3	. . . .	2	
Gunner's Ditto, .	2	. . . .	1	
Carpenter's Crew, .	4	. . . .	4	
Cook, . . .	1	. . . .	1	
Ditto Mate, . .	1	. . . .		
Quarter-Masters, .	6	. . . .	4	
Able Seamen, .	45	. . . .	33	
		Marines.		
Lieutenant, . .	1	Molesworth Philips.		
Sergeant, . .	1	. . . .	1	
Corporals, . .	2	. . . .	1	
Drummer, . .	1	. . . .	1	
Privates, . .	15	. . . .	8	
Total,	112		80	

[1] Afterwards captain of the Bounty, famous for his voyage of nearly 4000 miles in an open boat, into which he and twenty of his crew had been forced after the mutiny on board that vessel.

On the 10th, the commissioner and pay-clerks came on board, and paid the officers and crew up to the 30th of last month. The petty officers and seamen had, besides, two months' wages in advance. Such indulgence to the latter, is no more than what is customary in the navy. But the payment of what was due to the superior officers was humanely ordered by the Admiralty, in consideration of our peculiar situation, that we might be better able to defray the very great expense of furnishing ourselves with a stock of necessaries for a voyage which, probably, would be of unusual duration, and to regions where no supply could be expected.

Nothing now obstructing my departure but a contrary wind, which blew strong at SW., in the morning of the 11th, I delivered into the hands of Mr Burney, first lieutenant of the Discovery, Captain Clerke's sailing orders, a copy of which I also left with the officer commanding his Majesty's ships at Plymouth, to be delivered to the captain immediately on his arrival. In the afternoon, the wind moderating, we weighed with ebb, and got farther out, beyond all the shipping in the Sound, where, after making an unsuccessful attempt to get to sea, we were detained most of the following day, which was employed in receiving on board a supply of water ; and, by the same vessel that brought it, all the empty casks were returned. We weighed again at eight in the evening, and stood out of the Sound, with a gentle breeze at NW. by W.

CHAPTER II.

We had not been long out of Plymouth Sound before the wind came more westerly, and blew fresh, so that we were obliged to ply[1] down the Channel ; and it was not till the 14th,

at eight in the evening, that we were off the Lizard. On the 16th, at noon, St Agnes's Lighthouse, on the Isles of Scilly, bore NW. by W., distant seven or eight miles. On the 17th[2] and 18th we were off Ushant. With a strong gale at S. on the 19th, we stood to the westward till 8 o'clock in the morning, when, the wind shifting to the W. and NW., we tacked and stretched to the southward. At this time we saw nine sail of large ships, which we judged to be French men-of-war. They took no particular notice of us, nor we of them. At 10 o'clock in the morning of the 22d, we saw Cape Ortegal. After two days of calm weather we passed Cape Finisterre, on the afternoon of the 24th, with a fine gale at NNE. On the 30th, at six minutes and thirty-eight seconds past 10 o'clock at night, apparent time, I observed with a night telescope the moon totally eclipsed. By the ephemeris,[3] the same happened at Greenwich at nine minutes past 11 o'clock, the difference being one hour, two minutes, and twenty-two seconds, or $15° 35' 30''$ of Longitude. No other observation could be made on this eclipse, as the moon was hid behind the clouds the greater part of the time ; and, in particular, when the beginning and end of total darkness and the end of the eclipse happened.

Finding that we had not hay and corn sufficient for the subsistence of the stock of animals on board till our arrival at the Cape of Good Hope, I determined to touch at Teneriffe to get a supply of these and of the usual refreshments for ourselves, thinking that island, for such purposes, better adapted than Madeira. At four in the afternoon of the 31st we saw Teneriffe, and steered for the eastern part. At

------

[1] To "ply," in nautical terminology, is to boat to windward, or sail against the direction of the wind by alternate tacks.

[2] It appears from Captain Cook's log-book that he began his judicious operations for preserving the health of his crew very early in the voyage. On the 17th the ship was smoked between decks with gunpowder. The spare sails also were then well aired.— *Note in Original Edition.*

[3] Nautical almanac.

nine, being near it, we hauled up, and stood off and on during the night. At daylight on the morning of the 1st of August we sailed round the east point of the island, and about 8 o'clock anchored on the SE. side of it, in the road of Santa Cruz, in twenty-three fathoms water, the bottom sand and ooze.

No sooner had we anchored than we were visited by the master of the port, who satisfied himself with asking the ship's name. Upon his leaving us, 1 sent an officer ashore to present my respects to the Governor, and to ask his leave to take in water, and to purchase such articles as we were in want of. All this he granted with the greatest politeness, and soon after sent an officer on board to compliment me on my arrival. In the afternoon I waited upon him in person, accompanied by some of my officers; and, before I returned to my ship, bespoke some corn and straw for the live stock; ordered a quantity of wine from Mr M'Carrick, the contractor; and made an agreement with the master of a Spanish boat to supply us with water, as I found that we could not do it ourselves.

Were we to judge from the appearance of the country in the neighbourhood of Santa Cruz, it might be concluded that Teneriffe is a barren spot, insufficient to maintain even its own inhabitants. The ample supplies, however, which we received, convinced us that they had enough to spare for visitors. Besides wine, which is the chief produce of the island, beef may be had at a moderate price. The oxen are small and bony, and weigh about ninety pounds a quarter. The meat is but lean, and was, at present, sold for half a bit (threepence sterling) a pound. I, unadvisedly, bought the bullocks alive, and paid considerably more. Hogs, sheep, goats, and poultry, are likewise to be bought at the same moderate rate; and fruits are in great plenty. At this time we had grapes, figs, pears, mulberries, plantains, and musk melons. There is a variety of other fruits produced here, though not in season at this time. Their pumpkins, onions, and potatoes, are ex-

ceedingly good of their kind, and keep better at sea than any I ever before met with. The Indian corn, which is also their produce, cost me about three shillings and sixpence a bushel; and the fruits and roots were, in general, very cheap. They have not any plentiful supply of fish from the adjoining sea, but a very considerable fishery is carried on by their vessels upon the coast of Barbary, and the produce of it sells at a reasonable price. Upon the whole, I found Teneriffe to be a more eligible place than Madeira for ships bound on long voyages to touch at, though the wine of the latter, according to my taste, is as much superior to that of the former as strong beer is to small. To compensate for this, the difference of prices is considerable, for the best Teneriffe wine was now sold for twelve pounds a pipe, whereas a pipe of the best Madeira would have cost considerably more than double that sum.[1]

CHAPTER III.

HAVING completed our water, and got on board every other thing we wanted at Teneriffe, we weighed anchor on the 4th of August, and proceeded on our voyage, with a fine gale at NE. At 9 o'clock in the evening on the 10th,[2] we saw the Island of

----

[1] The remainder of this Chapter, which is omitted, is occupied with a technical account of observations for fixing the longitude of Teneriffe, and with a description, from the pen of Mr Anderson, the surgeon, of the natural features and products of the island.

[2] As a proof of Captain Cook's attention, both to the discipline and to the health of his ship's company, it may be worth while to observe here, that it appears from his log-book he exercised them at great guns and small arms, and cleared and smoked the ship below decks, twice in the interval between the 4th and the 10th of August.—*Note in Original Edition.*

Bonavista bearing S., distant little more than a league ; though, at this time, we thought ourselves much farther off ; but this proved a mistake. For, after hauling to the eastward till 12 o'clock, to clear the sunken rocks that lie about a league from the SE. point of the island, we found ourselves, at that time, close upon them, and did but just weather the breakers. Our situation, for a few minutes, was very alarming. I did not choose to sound, as that might have heightened the danger without any possibility of lessening it. As soon as we were clear of the rocks, we steered SSW. till daybreak next morning, and then hauled to the westward, to go between Bonavista and the Isle of Mayo ; intending to look into Port Praya for the Discovery, as I had told Captain Clerke that I should touch there, and did not know how soon he might sail after me. At one in the afternoon, we saw the rocks that lie on the SW. side of Bonavista, bearing SE., distant three or four leagues. Next morning at 6 o'clock the Isle of Mayo bore SSE., distant about five leagues. In this situation we sounded, and found ground at sixty fathoms. . . .

At 9 o'clock in the morning of the 13th, we arrived before Port Praya, in the Island of St Jago, where we saw two Dutch East India ships and a small brigantine at anchor. As the Discovery was not there, and we had expended but little water in our passage from Teneriffe, I did not think proper to go in, but stood to the southward. The day after we left the Cape de Verd Islands, we lost the NE. trade-wind ; but did not get that which blows from the SE. till the 30th, when we were in the Latitude of 2° N., and in the 25th degree of W. Longitude. During this interval, the wind was mostly in the SW. quarter. Sometimes it blew fresh, and in squalls ; but for the most part a gentle breeze. The calms were few, and of short duration. Between the Latitude of 12° and of 7° N., the weather was generally dark and gloomy, with frequent rains, which enabled us to save as much water as filled most of our empty casks.

These rains, and the close sultry weather accompanying them, too often bring on sickness in this passage. Every bad consequence, at least, is to be apprehended from them ; and commanders of ships cannot be too much upon their guard, by purifying the air between decks with fires and smoke, and by obliging the people to dry their clothes at every opportunity. These precautions were constantly observed on board the Resolution[1] and Discovery ; and we certainly profited by them, for we had now fewer sick than on either of my former voyages. We had, however, the mortification to find our ship exceedingly leaky in all her upper works. The hot and sultry weather we had just passed through had opened her seams, which had been badly calked at first, so wide, that they admitted the rain water through as it fell. There was hardly a man that could lie dry in his bed ; and the officers in the gun room were all driven out of their cabins, by the water that came through the sides. The sails in the sail-room got wet ; and before we had weather to dry them, many of them were much damaged, and a great expense of canvas and of time became necessary to make them in some degree serviceable. Having experienced the same defect in our sail-rooms on my late voyage, it had been represented to the yard officers, who undertook to remove it. But it did not appear to me that anything had been done to remedy the complaint. To repair these defects the calkers were set to work, as soon as we got into fair settled weather, to calk the decks and inside weather works of the

---

[1] The particulars are mentioned in his log-book. On the 14th of August, a fire was made in the well, to air the ship below. On the 15th, the spare sails were aired upon deck, and a fire made to air the sail-room. On the 17th, cleaned and smoked betwixt decks, and the bread-room aired with fires. On the 21st, cleaned and smoked betwixt decks ; and on the 22d, the men's bedding was spread on deck to air.—*Note in Original Edition.*

ship; for I would not trust them over the sides while we were at sea.

On the 1st of September[1] we crossed the Equator in the Longitude of 27° 38′ W., with a fine gale at SE. by S.; and notwithstanding my apprehensions of falling in with the coast of Brazil in stretching to the SW., I kept the ship a full point from the wind. However, I found my fears were ill grounded; for on drawing near that coast, we met with the wind more and more easterly; so that, by the time we were in the Latitude of 10° S., we could make a south-easterly course good. On the 8th, we were in the Latitude of 8° 57′ S.; which is a little to the southward of Cape St Augustine, on the coast of Brazil. Our longitude, deduced from a very great number of lunar observations, was 34° 16′ W.; and by the watch 34° 47′. The former is 1° 43′, and the latter 2° 14′ more westerly than the Island of Fernando de Noronha, the situation of which was pretty well determined during my late voyage. Hence I concluded that we could not now be farther from the continent than twenty or thirty leagues at most; and perhaps not much less, as we neither had soundings, nor any other signs of land.

We proceeded on our voyage, without meeting with anything of note, till the 6th of October. Being then in the Latitude of 35° 15′ S., Longitude 7° 45′ W., we met with light airs and calms by turns, for three days successively. We had, for some days before, seen albatrosses, pintadoes, and other petrels; and here we saw three penguins, which occasioned us to sound, but we found no ground with a line of 150 fathoms. We put a boat in the water, and shot a few birds; one of which was a black petrel, about the size of a crow, and, except as to the bill and feet, very like one. It had a few white feathers under the throat; and the under-side of the quill-feathers was of an ash-colour. All the other feathers were jet black, as also the bill and legs. On the 8th, in the evening, one of those birds which sailors call noddies settled on our rigging and was caught. It was something larger than an English blackbird, and nearly as black, except the upper part of the head, which was white, looking as if it were powdered; the whitest feathers growing out from the base of the upper bill, from which they gradually assumed a darker colour, to about the middle of the upper part of the neck, where the white shade was lost in the black, without being divided by any line. It was web-footed; had black legs and a black bill, which was long, and not unlike that of a curlew. It is said these birds never fly far from land. We knew of none nearer the station we were in, than Gough's or Richmond Island, from which our distance could not be less than 100 leagues. But it must be observed that the Atlantic Ocean, to the southward of this latitude, has been but little frequented; so that there may be more islands there than we are acquainted with.

This calm weather was succeeded by a fresh gale from the NW., which lasted two days. Then we had again variable light airs for about twenty-four hours; when the NW. wind returned, and blew with such strength that on the 17th we had sight of the Cape of Good Hope, and the next day anchored in Table Bay.

As soon as we had received the usual visit from the master attendant and the surgeon, I sent an officer to wait on Baron Plettenberg, the governor; and, on his return, saluted the garrison with thirteen guns, which compliment was returned with the same number. As soon as we had saluted, I went on shore, accompanied by some of my officers, and waited on the Governor, the lieutenant-gover-

---

[1] The afternoon, as appears from Mr Anderson's Journal, was spent in performing the old and ridiculous ceremony of ducking those who had not crossed the Equator before. Though Captain Cook did not suppress the custom, he thought it too trifling to deserve the least mention of it in his journal, or even in his log-book.

nor, the fiscal, and the commander of the troops. These gentlemen received me with the greatest civility; and the Governor, in particular, promised me every assistance that the place afforded. At the same time I obtained his leave to set up our observatory on any spot I should think most convenient; to pitch tents for the sailmakers and coopers; and to bring the cattle on shore, to graze near our encampment. Before I returned on board, I ordered soft bread, fresh meat, and greens to be provided every day for the ship's company. On the 22d, we set up the tents and observatory, and began to send the several articles out of the ship which I wanted on shore. This could not be done sooner, as the militia of the place were exercising on or near the ground which we were to occupy.

The next day, we began to observe equal altitudes of the sun, in order to ascertain the rate of the watch, or which is the same thing, to find whether it had altered its rate. These observations were continued every day, whenever the weather would permit, till the time of our departure drew near. But before this, the calkers had been set to work to calk the ship; and I had concerted measures for supplying both ships with such provisions as I should want. Bakers, likewise, had been ordered, immediately after our arrival, to bake such a quantity of bread as I thought would be requisite. As fast as the several articles destined for the Resolution were got ready, they were carried on board.

Nothing remarkable happened till the evening of the 31st, when it came on to blow excessively hard at SE., and continued for three days; during which time there was no communication between the ship and the shore. The Resolution was the only ship in the bay that rode out the gale without dragging her anchors. We felt its effects as sensibly on shore. Our tents and observatory were torn to pieces; and our astronomical quadrant narrowly escaped irreparable damage. On the 3d of November

the storm ceased, and the next day we resumed our different employments. In the morning of the 10th the Discovery arrived in the bay. Captain Clerke informed me that he had sailed from Plymouth on the 1st of August, and should have been with us here a week sooner if the late gale of wind had not blown him off the coast. Upon the whole, he was seven days longer in his passage from England than we had been. He had the misfortune to lose one of his marines, by falling overboard; but there had been no other mortality amongst his people, and they now arrived well and healthy. [Here the history of an excursion into the country, narrated by Mr Anderson, is omitted, with the exception of a passage describing a remarkable stone or rock.]

"In the afternoon we went to see a stone of a remarkable size, called by the inhabitants the Tower of Babylon, or the Pearl Diamond. It lies, or stands, upon the top of some low hills, at the foot of which our farm-house[1] was situated; and though the road to it is neither very steep nor rugged, we were above an hour and a half in walking to it. It is of an oblong shape, rounded on the top, and lies nearly south and north. The east and west sides are steep and almost perpendicular. The south end is likewise steep, and its greatest height is there; from whence it declines gently to the north part, by which we ascended to its top, and had an extensive view of the whole country. Its circumference, I think, must be at least half-a-mile; as it took us above half-an-hour to walk round it, including every allowance for the bad road and stopping a little. At its highest part, which is the south end, comparing it with a known object, it seems to equal the dome of St Paul's Church. It is one uninterrupted mass or stone, if we except some fissures, or rather impressions, not above three or four feet deep, and

---

[1] Where the party had their quarters on the previous night.

a vein which runs across near its north end. It is of that sort of stone called by mineralogists *Saxum conglutinatum*, and consists chiefly of pieces of coarse quartz and glimmer, held together by a clayey cement. But the vein which crosses it, though of the same materials, is much compacter. This vein is not above a foot broad or thick, and its surface is cut into little squares or oblongs, disposed obliquely, which makes it look like the remains of some artificial work. But I could not observe whether it penetrated far into the large rock, or was only superficial. In descending, we found at its foot a very rich black mould; and on the sides of the hills, some trees of a considerable size, natives of the place, which are a species of olea."

On the 23d, we got on board the observatory, clock, &c.[1]

CHAPTER IV.

AFTER the disaster which happened to our sheep,[2] it may be well supposed I did not trust those that remained long on shore, but got them and the other cattle on board as fast as possible. I also added to my original stock by purchasing two young bulls, two heifers, two young stone-horses, two mares, two rams, several ewes and goats, and some rabbits and poultry. All of them were intended for New Zealand, Otaheite, and the neighbouring islands, or any other places, in the course of our voyage, where there might be a prospect that the leaving any of them would be useful to posterity.

Towards the latter end of November

---

[1] The rest of the Chapter, omitted, consists of purely technical accounts of astronomical observations, and nautical remarks on the passage from England to the Cape, with regard to the currents and the variation.

[2] "Some dogs having got in amongst them, forced them out of the pen, killing four, and dispersing the rest."

the calkers had finished their work on board the Discovery, and she had received all her provisions and water. Of the former, both ships had a supply sufficient for two years and upwards. And every other article we could think of necessary for such a voyage, that could be had at the Cape, was procured, neither knowing when nor where we might come to a place where we could furnish ourselves so well. Having given Captain Clerke a copy of my instructions, and an order directing him how to proceed in case of separation, in the morning of the 30th we repaired on board. At five in the afternoon a breeze sprung up at SE., with which we weighed and stood out of the bay. At nine it fell calm, and we anchored between Penguin Island and the east shore, where we lay till 3 o'clock next morning. We then weighed and put to sea, with a light breeze at S.; but did not get clear of the land till the morning of the 3d [of December], when, with a fresh gale at WNW., we stood to the SE. to get more into the way of these winds.

On the 5th, a sudden squall of wind carried away the Resolution's mizzen-topmast. Having another to replace it, the loss was not felt, especially as it was a bad stick, and had often complained. On the 6th, in the evening, being then in the Latitude of 39° 14′ S., and in the Longitude of 23° 56′ E., we passed through several small spots of water of reddish colour. Some of this was taken up, and it was found to abound with a small animal, which the microscope discovered to be like a cray-fish, of a reddish hue. We continued our course to the SE., with a very strong gale from the westward, followed by a mountainous sea, which made the ship roll and tumble exceedingly, and gave us a great deal of trouble to preserve the cattle we had on board. Notwithstanding all our care, several goats, especially the males, died, and some sheep. This misfortune was, in a great measure, owing to the cold, which we now began most sensibly to feel.

On the 12th, at noon, we saw land extending from SE. by S. to SE. by E.

Upon a nearer approach we found it to be two islands. That which lies most to the south, and is also the largest, I judged to be about fifteen leagues in circuit, and to be in the Latitude of 46° 53' S., and in the Longitude of 37° 46' E. The most northerly one is about nine leagues in circuit, and lies in the Latitude of 46° 40' S., and in 38° 8' E. Longitude. The distance from the one to the other is about five leagues. We passed through this channel, at equal distance from both islands, and could not discover, with the assistance of our best glasses, either tree or shrub on either of them. They seemed to have a rocky and bold shore; and excepting the south-east parts, where the land is rather low and flat, a surface composed of barren mountains, which rise to a considerable height, and whose summits and sides were covered with snow, which in many places seemed to be of a considerable depth. The south-east parts had a much greater quantity on them than the rest, owing, probably, to the sun acting for a less space of time on these than on the north and north-west parts. The ground, where it was not hid by the snow, from the various shades it exhibited, may be supposed to be covered with moss, or, perhaps, such a coarse grass as is found in some parts of Falkland's Islands. On the north side of each of the islands is a detached rock; that near the south island is shaped like a tower, and seemed to be at some distance from the shore. As we passed along, a quantity of sea-weed was seen, and the colour of the water indicated soundings. But there was no appearance of an inlet, unless near the rock just mentioned; and that, from its smallness, did not promise a good anchoring-place. These two islands, as also four others which lie from nine to twelve degrees of longitude more to the east, and nearly in the same latitude, were discovered by Captains Marion du Fresne and Crozet, French navigators, in January 1772, on their passage in two ships from the Cape of Good Hope to the Philippine Islands. As they have no names

in the French chart of the southern hemisphere, which Captain Crozet communicated to me in 1775, I shall distinguish the two we now saw by calling them Prince Edward's Islands, after his Majesty's fourth son; and the other four by the name of Marion's and Crozet's Islands, to commemorate their discoverers.

We had now, for the most part, strong gales between the north and west, and but very indifferent weather, not better, indeed, than we generally have in England in the very depth of winter, though it was now the middle of summer in this hemisphere. Not discouraged, however, by this, after leaving Prince Edward's Islands I shaped our course to pass to the southward of the others that I might get into the latitude of the land discovered by Monsieur de Kerguelen. I had applied to the Chevalier de Borda, whom I found at Teneriffe,[1] requesting that if he knew anything of the island discovered by Monsieur de Kerguelen, between the Cape of Good Hope and New Holland, he would be so obliging as to communicate it to me. Accordingly, just before we sailed from Santa Cruz Bay, he sent me the following account of it, viz.: "That the pilot of the Boussole, who was in the voyage with Monsieur de Kerguelen, had given him the latitude and longitude of a little island, which Monsieur de Kerguelen called the Isle of Rendezvous, and which lies not far from the great island which he saw. Latitude of the little isle, by seven observations, 48° 26' S.; Longitude, by seven observations of the distance of the sun and moon, 64° 57' E. from Paris." I was very sorry I had not sooner known that there was on board the frigate at Teneriffe an officer who had been with Monsieur de Kerguelen, especially the pilot, because from him I might have obtained more interesting information about this land than the situation alone, of which I was not before entirely ignorant.

---

[1] In command of the French frigate La Boussole, riding in the road of Santa Cruz.

My instructions directing me to examine it, with a view to discover a good harbour, I proceeded in the search; and on the 16th, being then in the Latitude of 48° 45′ S., and in the Longitude of 52° E., we saw penguins and divers, and rock-weed floating in the sea. We continued to meet with more or less of these every day as we proceeded to the eastward; and on the 21st, in the Latitude of 48° 27′ S., and in the Longitude of 65° E., a very large seal was seen. We had now much foggy weather, and as we expected to fall in with the land every hour, our navigation became both tedious and dangerous. At length on the 24th, at 6 o'clock in the morning, as we were steering to the eastward—the fog clearing away a little—we saw land,[1] bearing SSE., which, upon a nearer approach, we found to be an island of considerable height, and about three leagues in circuit. Soon after we saw another of the same magnitude one league to the eastward; and between these two, in the direction of SE., some smaller ones. In the direction of S. by E. half E., from the east end of the first island, a third high island was seen. At times, as the fog broke away, we had the appearance of land over the small islands, and I had thoughts of steering for it by running in between them. But on drawing nearer, I found this would be a dangerous attempt while the weather continued foggy. For if there should be no passage, or if we should meet with any sudden danger, it would have been impossible for us to get off, the wind being right astern, and a prodigious sea running that broke on all the shores in a frightful surf. At the same time, seeing another island in the north-east direction, and not knowing but that there might be more, I judged it prudent to haul off

and wait for clearer weather lest we should get entangled amongst unknown lands in a thick fog. We did but just weather the island last mentioned. It is a high round rock, which was named Bligh's Cap. Perhaps this is the same that Monsieur de Kerguelen called the Isle of Rendezvous,[2] but I know nothing that can rendezvous at it but fowls of the air, for it is certainly inaccessible to every other animal.

At 11 o'clock the weather began to clear up, and we immediately tacked, and steered in for the land. At noon we had a pretty good observation, which enabled us to determine the latitude of Bligh's Cap, which is the northernmost island, to be 48° 29′ S., and its longitude 68° 40′ E. We passed it at 3 o'clock, standing to the SSE., with a fresh gale at W. Soon after we saw the land, of which we had a faint view in the morning; and at 4 o'clock it extended from SE. half E. to SW. by S., distant about four miles. The left extreme, which I judged to be the northern point of this land, called in the French chart of the southern hemisphere, Cape St Louis,[3] terminated in a perpendicular rock of a considerable height; and the right one (near which is a detached rock) in a high indented point. From this point the coast seemed to turn short round to the southward; for we could see no land to the westward of the direction in which it now bore to us, but the islands we had observed in the morning; the most southerly

---

[1] Captain Cook was not the original discoverer of these small islands which he now fell in with. It is certain that they had been seen and named by Kerguelen, on his second voyage, in December 1773.

[2] This isle, or rock, was the single point about which Captain Cook had received the least information at Teneriffe; and we may observe how sagacious he was in tracing it. Kerguelen's words are: "Isle de Reunion, qui n'est qu'une Roche, nous servoit de Rendezvous, ou de point de ralliement, et ressemble à un coin de mire."—*Note in Original Edition.*

[3] Cook is here declared by his editor to be in error; the northern point he here describes being really that to which the French had given the name of Cape François.

of them lying nearly west from the point, about two or three leagues distant. About the middle of the land there appeared to be an inlet, for which we steered; but, on approaching, found it was only a bending on the coast, and therefore bore up, to go round Cape St Louis. Soon after, land opened off the cape, in the direction of S. 53° E., and appeared to be a point at a considerable distance; for the trending of the coast from the cape was more southerly. We also saw several rocks and islands to the eastward of the above directions, the most distant of which was about seven leagues from the cape, bearing S. 88° E. We had no sooner got off the cape, than we observed the coast to the southward to be much indented by projecting points and bays; so that we now made sure of soon finding a good harbour. Accordingly, we had not run a mile farther, before we discovered one behind the cape, into which we began to ply; but after making one board, it fell calm, and we anchored at the entrance in forty-five fathoms water, the bottom black sand; as did the Discovery soon after. I immediately despatched Mr Bligh, the master, in a boat to sound the harbour; who, on his return, reported it to be safe and commodious, with good anchorage in every part, and great plenty of fresh water, seals, penguins, and other birds on the shore, but not a stick of wood. While we lay at anchor, we observed that the flood tide came from the SE., running two knots, at least, in an hour.

At daybreak in the morning of the 25th, we weighed with a gentle breeze at W., and having wrought into the harbour, to within a quarter of a mile of the sandy beach at its head, we anchored in eight fathoms water, the bottom a fine dark sand. The Discovery did not get in till 2 o'clock in the afternoon; when Captain Clerke informed me, that he had narrowly escaped being driven on the south point of the harbour, his anchor having started before they had time to shorten in the cable. This obliged them to set sail, and drag the anchor after them, till they had room to heave it up; and then they found one of its palms was broken off. As soon as we had anchored, I ordered all the boats to be hoisted out; the ship to be moored with a kedge anchor; and the water-casks to be got ready to send on shore. In the meantime I landed, to look for the most convenient spot where they might be filled, and to see what else the place afforded. I found the shore, in a manner, covered with penguins and other birds, and seals. These latter were not numerous, but so insensible of fear (which plainly indicated that they were unaccustomed to such visitors), that we killed as many as we chose, for the sake of their fat or blubber, to make oil for our lamps, and other uses. Fresh water was in no less plenty than were birds; for every gully afforded a large stream. But not a single tree or shrub, nor the least sign of any, was to be discovered, and but very little herbage of any sort. Before I returned to my ship, I ascended the first ridge of rocks, which rise in a kind of amphitheatre above one another. I was in hopes, by this means, of obtaining a view of the country; but before I reached the top, there came on so thick a fog, that I could hardly find my way down again. In the evening, we hauled the scine at the head of the harbour, but caught only half-a-dozen small fish. We had no better success next day, when we tried with hook and line. So that our only resource here, for fresh provisions, was birds, of which there was an inexhaustible store.

The morning of the 26th proved foggy, with rain. However, we went to work to fill water, and to cut grass for our cattle, which we found in small spots near the head of the harbour. The rain which fell swelled all the rivulets to such a degree, that the sides of the hills bounding the harbour seemed to be covered with a sheet of water. For the rain, as it fell, run into the fissures and crags of the rocks that composed the interior parts of the hills, and was precipitated down their sides in prodigious torrents. The people having wrought hard the two preceding days, and nearly completed our water, which we filled from a brook at the left corner of the beach, I allowed them the 27th as a day of rest, to celebrate Christmas. Upon this indulgence, many of them went on shore, and made excursions, in different directions, into the country, which they found barren and desolate in the highest degree. In the evening, one of them brought to me a quart bottle which he had found, fastened with some wire to a projecting rock on the north side of the harbour. This bottle contained a piece of parchment, on which was written the following inscription :

" Ludovico XV Galliarum
rege, et d.[1] de Boynes
regi a Secretis ad res
maritimas annis 1772 et
1733."

From this inscription, it is clear that we were not the first Europeans who had been in this harbour. I supposed it to be left by Monsieur de Boisguehenneu, who went on shore in a boat on the 13th of February 1772, the same day that Monsieur de Kerguelen discovered this land.[2] As a memorial of our having been in this harbour, I wrote on the other side of the parchment :

-----

[1] The (*d*), no doubt, is a contraction of the word Domino. The French Secretary of the Marine was then Monsieur de Boynes.

[2] The bottle and inscription were really left nearly two years later, in January 1774, when Kerguelen, on his second voyage, by M. de Rochegude, one of his officers, took possession of the country, with all the requisite formalities, in the name of the King of France. As the French ships had arrived on the coast in December 1773, it was natural that the inscription should refer to that year rather than the following, as barring possible claims by rival navigators.

" Naves Resolution
et Discovery
de Rege Magnæ Britanniæ,
Decembris 1776."

I then put it again into a bottle, together with a silver twopenny piece of 1772 ; and having covered the mouth of the bottle with a leaden cap, I placed it, the next morning, in a pile of stones erected for the purpose, upon a little eminence on the north shore of the harbour, and near to the place where it was first found ; in which position it cannot escape the notice of any European whom chance or design may bring into this port. Here I displayed the British flag, and named the place Christmas Harbour, from our having arrived in it on that festival.

After I had finished this business of the inscription, I went in my boat round the harbour, and landed in several places, to examine what the shore afforded, and particularly to look for drift wood. For although the land here was totally destitute of trees, this might not be the case in other parts ; and if there were any, the torrents would force some, or, at least, some branches, into the sea, which would afterward throw them upon the shores, as in all other countries where there is wood, and in many where there is none ; but throughout the whole extent of the harbour I found not a single piece. In the afternoon, I went upon Cape St Louis,[3] accompanied by Mr King, my second lieutenant. I was in hopes, from this elevation, to have had a view of the sea coast, and of the islands lying off it. But, when I got up, I found every distant object below me hid in a thick fog. The land on the same plain,[4] or of a greater height, was visible enough, and appeared naked and desolate in the highest degree, except some hills to the southward, which were covered with snow. When I got on board, I found the launch hoisted in, the ships unmoored, and ready to put to sea ;

-----

[3] Cape François.   [4] Level.

but our sailing was deferred till 5 o'clock the next morning, when we weighed anchor.

CHAPTER V.[1]

BEING desirous of getting the length of Cape George,[2] to be assured whether or no it was the most southerly point of the whole land, I continued to stretch to the south, under all the sail we could carry, till half-an-hour past 7 o'clock [December 30]; when, seeing no likelihood of accomplishing my design, as the wind had by this time shifted to WSW., the very direction in which we wanted to go, I took the advantage of the shifting of the wind, and stood away from the coast. At this time, Cape George bore S. 53° W., distant about seven leagues. A small island that lies off the pitch of the cape, was the only land we could see to the south of it; and we were further confirmed that there was no more in that quarter, by a SW. swell which we met as soon as we brought the cape to bear in this direction.

But we have still a stronger proof that no part of this land can extend much, if at all, to the southward of Cape George; and that is, Captain Furneaux's track in February 1773, after his separation from me during my late voyage. His log-book is now lying before me, and I find from it that he crossed the meridian of this land only about seventeen leagues to the southward of Cape George; a distance at which it may very well be seen in clear weather. This seems to have been the case when Captain Furneaux passed it. For his log-book makes no mention of fogs or hazy weather; on the contrary, it expressly tells us that, when in this situation, they had it in their power to make observations, both for latitude and longitude, on board his ship; so that, if this land extends farther south than Cape George, it would have been scarcely possible that he should have passed without seeing it.

From these circumstances we are able to determine, within a very few miles, the quantity of latitude that this land occupies, which does not much exceed one degree and a quarter. As to its extent from east to west, that still remains undecided. We only know, that no part of it can reach so far to the west as the meridian of 65°; because, in 1773, under that meridian, I searched for it in vain. The French discoverers, with some reason, imagined Cape St Louis to be the projecting point of a southern continent. The English have since proved that no such continent exists; and that the land in question is an island of no great extent,[3] which, from its sterility, I should, with great propriety, call the Island of Desolation, but that I would not rob Monsieur de Kerguelen of the honour of its bearing his name.[4] . . .

---

[1] This Chapter is almost entirely devoted to a minute account of Captain Cook's examination of the coast of Kerguelen's Land, and to Mr Anderson's observations on the natural products, the animals, the soil, &c., of that remote and unprofitable region. The present interest of these matters is so slight, that there is no loss in the omission of the Chapter, with the exception of a brief passage, in which Cook affirms the insularity of Kerguelen's Land, described at first by its discoverer as a magnificent continent.

[2] So called by Captain Cook in honour of the King; it is placed by him in Latitude 49° 54′ S., Longitude 70° 13′ E.

[3] Kerguelen concurs with Captain Cook as to this. However, he tells us, that he has reason to believe that it is about 200 leagues in circuit; and that he was acquainted with about fourscore leagues of its coast. "J'en connois environs quatre-vingt lieues des cotes; et j'ai lieu de croire, qu'elle a environ deux cents lieues de circuit."—*Note in Original Edition.*

[4] Cook's alternative title, amply

CHAPTER VI.

AFTER leaving Kerguelen's Land I steered E. by N., intending, in obedience to my instructions, to touch next at New Zealand, to recruit our water, to take in wood, and to make hay for the cattle. Their number by this time had been considerably diminished; two young bulls, one of the heifers, two rams, and several of the goats having of late died while we were employed in exploring this desolate coast. . . .

Thus far [to Jan. 3] we had fresh gales from the W. and SW., and tolerably clear weather. But now the wind veered to the N., where it continued eight days, and was attended with a thick fog. During this time, we ran above 300 leagues in the dark. Now and then the weather would clear up, and give us a sight of the sun; but this happened very seldom, and was always of short continuance. On the 7th, I hoisted out a boat, and sent an order to Captain Clerke, appointing Adventure Bay, in Van Diemen's Land, as our place of rendezvous, in case of separation before we arrived in the meridian of that land. But we were fortunate enough, amidst all this foggy weather, by frequently firing guns as signals, though we seldom saw each other, not to lose company.

On the 12th, being in the Latitude of 48° 40′ S., Longitude 110° 26′ E., the northerly winds ended in a calm; which, after a few hours, was succeeded by a wind from the southward. This, with rain, continued for twenty-four hours; when it freshened, and veered to the west and north-west, and brought on fair and clear weather. We continued our course to the eastward, without meeting with anything worthy of notice, till 4 o'clock in the morning of the 19th, when, in a sudden squall of wind, though the Discovery received no damage, our

justified by all that he and Mr Anderson observed, is · now commonly adopted in English maps.

fore-topmast went by the board, and carried the maintop-gallantmast with it. This occasioned some delay, as it took us up the whole day to clear the wreck, and to fit another topmast. The former was accomplished without losing any part of it, except a few fathoms of small rope. Not having a spare maintop-gallantmast on board, the foretop-gallantmast was converted into one for our immediate use.

On the 24th, at 3 o'clock in the morning, we discovered the coast of Van Diemen's Land, bearing N. half W. At 6 o'clock in the afternoon we sounded, and found sixty fathoms water, over a bottom of broken coral and shells. Soon after we had sight of land the westerly winds left us, and were succeeded by variable light airs and alternate calms, till the 26th at noon. At that time a breeze sprung up and freshened at SE., which put it in my power to carry into execution the design I had upon due consideration formed, of carrying the ships into Adventure Bay, where I might expect to get a supply of wood and of grass for the cattle; of both which articles we should, as I now found, have been in great want, if I had waited till our arrival in New Zealand. We therefore stood for the bay, and anchored in it at 4 o'clock in the afternoon, in twelve fathoms water. Our distance from the nearest shore was about three quarters of a mile. As soon as we had anchored, I ordered the boats to be hoisted out. In one of them I went myself, to look for the most commodious place for furnishing ourselves with the necessary supplies; and Captain Clerke went in his boat upon the same service. Wood and water we found in plenty, and in situations convenient enough, especially the first. But grass, of which we stood most in need, was scarce, and also very coarse. Necessity, however, obliged us to take such as we could get. Next morning early, I sent Lieutenant King to the east side of the bay with two parties, one to cut wood, and the other to cut grass, under the protection of the marines, whom I judged it prudent to land as a guard. For although, as yet, none of the natives had appeared, there could be no doubt that some were in our neighbourhood, as we had seen columns of smoke from the time of our approaching the coast; and some now was observed at no great distance up in the woods. I also sent the launch for water; and afterwards visited all the parties myself. In the evening, we drew the seine at the head of the bay, and, at one haul, caught a great quantity of fish. We should have got many more had not the net broken in drawing it ashore. Most of them were of that sort known to seamen by the name of elephant fish. After this every one repaired on board with what wood and grass we had cut, that we might be ready to sail whenever the wind should serve. This not happening next morning, the people were sent on shore again on the same duty as the day before. I also employed the carpenter, with part of his crew, to cut some spars for the use of the ship; and despatched Mr Roberts, one of the mates, in a small boat to survey the bay.

In the afternoon, we were agreeably surprised, at the place where we were cutting wood, with a visit from some of the natives—eight men and a boy. They approached us from the woods, without betraying any marks of fear, or rather with the greatest confidence imaginable; for none of them had any weapons, except one who held in his hand a stick about two feet long, and pointed at one end. They were quite naked, and wore no ornaments, unless we consider as such, and as a proof of their love of finery, some large punctures or ridges raised on different parts of their bodies, some in straight and others in curved lines. They were of the common stature, but rather slender. Their skin was black, and also their hair, which was as woolly as that of any native of Guinea; but they were not distinguished by remarkably thick lips, nor flat noses. On the contrary, their features were far from being disagreeable. They had pretty good eyes, and their teeth were tolerably even, but very dirty. Most

of them had their hair and beards smeared with a red ointment; and some had their faces also painted with the same composition. They received every present we made to them without the least appearance of satisfaction. When some bread was given, as soon as they understood that it was to be eaten, they either returned it or threw it away, without even tasting it. They also refused some elephant fish, both raw and dressed, which we offered to them. But upon giving some birds to them, they did not return these, and easily made us comprehend that they were fond of such food. I had brought two pigs ashore, with a view to leave them in the woods. The instant these came within their reach, they seized them, as a dog would have done, by the ears, and were for carrying them off immediately, with no other intention, as we could perceive, but to kill them.

Being desirous of knowing the use of the stick which one of our visitors carried in his hand, I made signs to them to show me, and so far succeeded, that one of them set up a piece of wood as a mark, and threw at it, at the distance of about twenty yards. But we had little reason to commend his dexterity, for after repeated trials, he was still very wide from the object. Omai, to show them how much superior our weapons were to theirs, then fired his musket at it; which alarmed them so much, that notwithstanding all we could do or say, they ran instantly into the woods. One of them was so frightened, that he let drop an axe and two knives that had been given to him. From us, however, they went to the place where some of the Discovery's people were employed in taking water into their boat. The officer of that party, not knowing that they had paid us so friendly a visit, nor what their intent might be, fired a musket in the air, which sent them off with the greatest precipitation.

Thus ended our first interview with the natives. Immediately after their final retreat, judging that their fears would prevent their remaining near enough to observe what was passing,

I ordered two pigs, being a boar and sow, to be carried about a mile within the woods, at the head of the bay. I saw them left there, by the side of a fresh-water brook. A young bull and a cow, and some sheep and goats were also at first intended to have been left by me, as an additional present to Van Diemen's Land. But I soon laid aside all thoughts of this, from a persuasion that the natives, incapable of entering into my views of improving their country, would destroy them. If ever they should meet with the pigs, I have no doubt this will be their fate. But as that race of animals soon becomes wild, and is fond of the thickest cover of the woods, there is great probability of their being preserved. An open place must have been chosen for the accommodation of the other cattle ; and in such a situation they could not possibly have remained concealed many days.

The morning of the 29th was ushered in with a dead calm, which continued all day, and effectually prevented our sailing. I therefore sent a party over to the east point of the bay to cut grass, having been informed that some of a superior quality grew there. Another party, to cut wood, was ordered to go to the usual place, and I accompanied them myself. We had observed several of the natives this morning sauntering along the shore, which assured us, that though their consternation had made them leave us so abruptly the day before, they were convinced that we intended them no mischief, and were desirous of renewing the intercourse. It was natural that I should wish to be present on the occasion. We had not been long landed before about twenty of them, men and boys, joined us, without expressing the least sign of fear or distrust. There was one of this company conspicuously deformed, and who was not more distinguishable by the hump upon his back than by the drollery of his gestures and the seeming humour of his speeches, which he was very fond of exhibiting, as we supposed, for our entertainment. But, unfortunately, we could not under-

stand him ; the language spoken here being wholly unintelligible to us. It appeared to me to be different from that spoken by the inhabitants of the more northern parts of this country whom I met with in my first voyage, which is not extraordinary, since those we now saw, and those we then visited, differ in many other respects.[1] Nor did they seem to be such miserable wretches as the natives whom Dampier mentions to have seen on its western coast. Some of our present group wore, loose round their necks, three or four folds of small cord made of the fur of some animal ; and others of them had a narrow slip of the kangaroo skin tied round their ancles. I gave to each of them a string of beads and a medal, which I thought they received with some satisfaction. They seemed to set no value on iron or on iron tools. They were even ignorant of the use of fish-hooks, if we might judge from their manner of looking at some of ours which we showed to them. We cannot, however, suppose it to be possible that a people who inhabit a sea coast, and who seem to derive no part of their sustenance from the productions of the ground, should not be acquainted with some mode of catching fish, although we did not happen to see any of them thus employed, nor observe any canoe or vessel in which they could go upon the water. Though they absolutely rejected the sort of fish that we offered to them, it was evident that shell-fish, at least, made a part of their food, from the many heaps of mussel-shells we saw in different parts near the shore, and about some deserted habitations near the head of the bay. These were little sheds or hovels built of sticks and covered with bark. We could also perceive evident signs of their some-

---

[1] The most striking difference seemed to be with regard to the texture of the hair. The natives whom Captain Cook met with at Endeavour River in 1769 are said by him to have naturally long and black hair, though it be universally cropped short.

times taking up their abode in the trunks of large trees, which had been hollowed out by fire most probably for this very purpose. In or near all these habitations, and wherever there was a heap of shells, there remained the marks of fire, an indubitable proof that they do not eat their food raw.

After staying about an hour with the wooding party and the natives, as I could now be pretty confident that the latter were not likely to give the former any disturbance, I left them, and went over to the grass-cutters on the east point of the bay, and found that they had met with a fine patch. Having seen the boats loaded, I left that party and returned on board to dinner, where, some time after, Lieutenant King arrived. From him I learned that I had but just left the shore when several women and children made their appearance, and were introduced to him by some of the men who attended them. He gave presents to all of them of such trifles as he had about him. These females wore a kangaroo skin (in the same shape as it came from the animal) tied over the shoulders and round the waist. But its only use seemed to be to support their children when carried on their backs, for it did not cover those parts which most nations conceal; being in all other respects as naked as the men, and as black, and their bodies marked with scars in the same manner. But in this they differed from the men, that though their hair was of the same colour and texture, some of them had their heads completely shorn or shaved; in others this operation had been performed only on one side, while the rest of them had all the upper part of the head shorn close, leaving a circle of hair all round, somewhat like the tonsure of the Romish ecclesiastics. Many of the children had fine features, and were thought pretty; but of the persons of the women, especially those advanced in years, a less favourable report was made. However, some of the gentlemen belonging to the Discovery, I was told, paid their

addresses, and made liberal offers of presents, which were rejected with great disdain; whether from a sense of virtue, or the fear of displeasing their men, I shall not pretend to determine. That this gallantry was not very agreeable to the latter, is certain; for an elderly man, as soon as he observed it, ordered all the women and children to retire, which they obeyed, though some of them showed a little reluctance.

This conduct of Europeans amongst savages to their women is highly blamable, as it creates a jealousy in their men that may be attended with consequences fatal to the success of the common enterprise, and to the whole body of adventurers, without advancing the private purpose of the individual, or enabling him to gain the object of his wishes. I believe it has been generally found, amongst uncivilised people, that where the women are easy of access the men are the first to offer them to strangers; and that, where this is not the case, neither the allurement of presents nor the opportunity of privacy, will be likely to have the desired effect. This observation, I am sure, will hold good throughout all the parts of the South Sea where I have been. Why, then, should men act so absurd a part as to risk their own safety, and that of all their companions, in pursuit of a gratification which they have no probability of obtaining?

In the afternoon I went again to the grass-cutters to forward their work. I found them then upon Penguin Island, where they had met with a plentiful crop of excellent grass. We laboured hard till sunset, and then repaired on board satisfied with the quantity we had collected, which I judged sufficient to last till our arrival in New Zealand. During our whole stay we had either calms or light airs from the eastward. Little or no time, therefore, was lost by my putting in at this place. For if I had kept the sea, we should not have been twenty leagues advanced farther on our voyage; and, short as our continuance was here, it has enabled me to add somewhat to the imperfect acquaintance that has hitherto been acquired with this part of the globe.[1]

CHAPTER VII.

At 8 o'clock in the morning of the 30th of January, a light breeze springing up at W., we weighed anchor, and put to sea from Adventure Bay. Soon after, the wind veered to the southward, and increased to a perfect storm. Its fury abated in the evening, when it veered to the E. and NE. We pursued our course to the eastward without meeting with anything worthy of note, till the night between the 6th and 7th of February, when a marine belonging to the Discovery fell overboard and was never seen afterward. This was the second misfortune of the kind that had happened to Captain Clerke since he left England.[1]

On the 10th, at four in the afternoon, we discovered the land of New Zealand. The part we saw proved to be Rocks Point, and bore SE. by S., about eight or nine leagues distant. After making the land, I steered for Cape Farewell, which at daybreak the next morning bore S. by W., distant about four leagues. At 8 o'clock it bore SW. by S., about five leagues distant; and in this situation, we had forty-five fathoms water over a sandy bottom. In rounding the Cape we had fifty fathoms, and the same sort of bottom. I now steered for Stephen's Island, which we came up with at 9 o'clock at night; and at ten next morning, anchored in our old station in Queen Charlotte's Sound. Unwilling to lose any time, our operations commenced that very afternoon, when we landed a number of empty watercasks, and began to clear a place where we might

set up the two observatories, and tents for the reception of a guard and of such of our people whose business might make it necessary for them to remain on shore.

We had not been long at anchor before several canoes, filled with natives, came alongside of the ships; but very few of them would venture on board, which appeared the more extraordinary, as I was well known to them all. There was one man in particular amongst them whom I had treated with remarkable kindness during the whole of my stay when I was last here. Yet now neither professions of friendship nor presents could prevail upon him to come into the ship. This shyness was to be accounted for only upon this supposition, that they were apprehensive we had revisited their country in order to revenge the death of Captain Furneaux's people. Seeing Omai on board my ship now, whom they must have remembered to have seen on board the Adventure when the melancholy affair happened, and whose first conversation with them, as they approached, generally turned on that subject, they must be well assured that I was no longer a stranger to it. I thought it necessary, therefore, to use every endeavour to assure them of the continuance of my friendship, and that I should not disturb them on that account. I do not know whether this had any weight with them; but certain it is, that they very soon laid aside all manner of restraint and distrust.

On the 13th we set up two tents, one from each ship, on the same spot where we had pitched them formerly. The observatories were at the same time erected; and Messrs King and Bayly began their operations immediately, to find the rate of the timekeeper, and to make other observations. The remainder of the empty water-casks were also sent on shore, with the cooper to trim and a sufficient number of sailors to fill them. Two men were appointed to brew spruce beer, and the carpenter and his crew were ordered to cut wood.

---

[1] Several pages of naturalistic and other observations on Van Diemen's Land, by Mr Anderson—valuable and novel in their day, but now devoid of interest—are here omitted.

A boat, with a party of men, under the direction of one of the mates, was sent to collect grass for our cattle; and the people that remained on board were employed in refitting the ship, and arranging the provisions. In this manner we were all profitably busied during our stay. For the protection of the party on shore, I appointed a guard of ten marines, and ordered arms for all the workmen; and Mr King and two or three petty officers, constantly remained with them. A boat was never sent to any considerable distance from the ships without being armed, and under the direction of such officers as I could depend upon, and who were well acquainted with the natives. During my former visits to this country, I had never taken some of these precautions; nor were they, I firmly believe, more necessary now than they had been formerly. But after the tragical fate of the Adventure's boat's crew in this sound, and of Captain Marion du Fresne, and of some of his people, in the Bay of Islands,[1] it was impossible totally to divest ourselves of all apprehension of experiencing a similar calamity.

If the natives entertained any suspicion of our revenging these acts of barbarity, they very soon laid it aside. For, during the course of this day, a great number of families came from different parts of the coast, and took up their residence close to us; so that there was not a spot in the cove where a hut could be put up, that was not occupied by them, except the place where we had fixed our little encampment. This they left us in quiet possession of; but they came and took away the ruins of some old huts that were there, as materials for their new erections. It is curious to observe with what facility they build these occasional places of abode. I have seen above twenty of them erected on a spot of ground that, not an hour before, was covered with shrubs and plants. They generally bring some part of the materials with them; the rest they find upon the premises. I was present when a number of people landed, and built one of these villages. The moment the canoes reached the shore, the men leaped out, and at once took possession of a piece of ground, by tearing up the plants and shrubs, or sticking up some part of the framing of a hut. They then returned to their canoes, and secured their weapons by setting them up against a tree, or placing them in such a position that they could be laid hold of in an instant. I took particular notice that no one neglected this precaution. While the men were employed in raising the huts, the women were not idle. Some were stationed to take care of the canoes; others to secure the provisions, and the few utensils in their possession; and the rest went to gather dry sticks, that a fire might be prepared for dressing their victuals. As to the children, I kept them, as also some of the more aged, sufficiently occupied in scrambling for beads, till I had emptied my pockets, and then I left them. These temporary habitations are abundantly sufficient to afford shelter from the wind and rain, which is the only purpose they are meant to answer. I observed that generally, if not always, the same tribe or family, though it were ever so large, associated and built together; so that we frequently saw a village, as well as their larger towns, divided into different districts by low pallisades, or some similar mode of separation.

The advantage we received from the natives coming to live with us was not inconsiderable. For every day, when the weather would permit, some of them went out to catch fish; and we generally got, by exchanges, a good share of the produce of their labours. This supply, and what our own nets and lines afforded us, was so ample, that we seldom were in want of fish. Nor was there any deficiency of other refreshments. Celery, scurvy-grass, and portable soup were boiled with the pease and wheat, for both ships' companies, every day during our whole stay; and they had spruce-

[1] In 1772.

beer for their drink, so that, if any of our people had contracted the seeds of the scurvy, such a regimen soon removed them. But the truth is, when we arrived here, there were only two invalids (and these on board the Resolution) upon the sick lists in both ships. Besides the natives who took up their abode close to us, we were occasionally visited by others of them whose residence was not far off, and by some who lived more remote. Their articles of commerce were curiosities, fish, and women. The two first always came to a good market; which the latter did not. The seamen had taken a kind of dislike to these people, and were either unwilling or afraid to associate with them; which produced this good effect, that I knew no instance of a man's quitting his station to go to their habitations.

Amongst our occasional visitors was a chief named Kahoora, who, as I was informed, headed the party that cut off Captain Furneaux's people, and himself killed Mr Rowe, the officer who commanded. To judge of the character of Kahoora, by what I heard from many of his countrymen, he seemed to be more feared than beloved amongst them. Not satisfied with telling me that he was a very bad man, some of them even importuned me to kill him; and, I believe, they were not a little surprised that I did not listen to them; for, according to their ideas of equity, this ought to have been done. But if I had followed the advice of all our pretended friends, I might have extirpated the whole race; for the people of each hamlet or village, by turns, applied to me to destroy the other. One would have almost thought it impossible that so striking a proof of the divided state in which this miserable people live could have been assigned. And yet I was sure that I did not misconceive the meaning of those who made these strange applications to me; for Omai, whose language was a dialect of their own, and perfectly understood all that they said, was our interpreter.

On the 15th, I made an excursion in my boat to look for grass, and visited the "hippah," or fortified village,[1] at the SW. point of Motuara, and the places where our gardens had been planted on that island. There were no people at the former; but the houses and pallisades had been rebuilt, and were now in a state of good repair; and there were other evident marks of its having been inhabited not long before.

When the Adventure arrived first at Queen Charlotte's Sound, in 1773, Mr Bayly fixed upon this place for making his observations; and he and the people with him, at their leisure hours, planted several spots with English garden seeds. Not the least vestige of these now remained. It is probable that they had been all rooted out to make room for buildings, when the village was re-inhabited; for at all the other gardens then planted by Captain Furneaux, although now wholly overrun with the weeds of the country, we found cabbages, onions, leeks, purslane, radishes, mustard, &c., and a few potatoes. These potatoes, which were first brought from the Cape of Good Hope, had been greatly improved by change of soil; and, with proper cultivation, would be superior to those produced in most other countries. Though the New Zealanders are fond of this root, it was evident that they had not taken the trouble to plant a single one (much less any other of the articles which we had introduced); and if it were not for the difficulty of clearing ground where potatoes had been once planted, there would not have been any now remaining.

On the 16th, at daybreak, I set out with a party of men, in five boats, to collect food for our cattle. Captain

---

[1] Of which a minute description is given in the account of Cook's first voyage, in Hawkesworth's Collection. The hippahs, or pahs, of New Zealand have become painfully familiar to English minds by the experiences of the late war in that colony.

Clerke, and several of the officers, Omai, and two of the natives, accompanied me. We proceeded about three leagues up the sound, and then landed on the east side, at a place where I had formerly been. Here we cut as much grass as loaded the two launches. As we returned down the sound, we visited Grass Cove, the memorable scene of the massacre of Captain Furneaux's people.

We stayed here till the evening, when, having loaded the rest of the boats with grass, celery, scurvy-grass, &c., we embarked to. return to the ships. We had prevailed upon Pedro to launch his canoe and accompany us; but we had scarcely put off from the shore, when the wind began to blow very hard at NW., which obliged him to put back. We proceeded ourselves, but it was with a good deal of difficulty that we could reach the ships, where some of the boats did not arrive till 1 o'clock the next morning; and it was fortunate that they got on board then, for it afterward blew a perfect storm, with abundance of rain, so that no manner of work could go forward that day. In the evening the gale ceased, and the wind having veered to the east, brought with it fair weather. The next day we resumed our works; the natives ventured out to catch fish; and Pedro, with all his family, came and took up his abode near us. This chief's proper name is Matahouah; the other being given him by some of my people during my last voyage, which I did not know till now. He was, however, equally well known amongst his countrymen by both names.

On the 20th, in the forenoon, we had another storm from the NW. Though this was not of so long continuance as the former, the gusts of wind from the hills were far more violent, insomuch that we were obliged to strike the yards and topmasts to the very utmost; and, even with all this precaution, it was with difficulty that we rode it out. These storms are very frequent here, and sometimes violent and troublesome.

The neighbouring mountains, which at these times are always loaded with vapours, not only increase the force of the wind, but alter its direction in such a manner, that no two blasts follow each other from the same quarter; and the nearer the shore, the more their effects are felt. The next day we were visited by a tribe or family consisting of about thirty persons, men, women, and children, who came from the upper part of the sound. I had never seen them before. The name of their chief was Tomatongeauooranuc, a man of about forty-five years of age, with a cheerful open countenance; and, indeed, the rest of his tribe were, in general, the handsomest of the New Zealand race I had ever met with. By this time more than two-thirds of the inhabitants of the sound had settled themselves about us. Great numbers of them daily frequented the ships and the encampment on shore; but the latter became by far the most favourite place of resort, while our people there were melting some seal blubber. No Greenlander was ever fonder of train oil than our friends here seem to be. They relished the very skimmings of the kettle and dregs of the casks; but a little of the pure stinking oil was a delicious feast, so eagerly desired, that I supposed it is seldom enjoyed.

Having got on board as much hay and grass as we judged sufficient to serve the cattle till our arrival at Otaheite, and having completed the wood and water of both ships, on the 23d we struck our tents, and carried everything off from the shore; and next morning we weighed anchor and stood out of the cove. But the wind not being very fair, and finding that the tide of ebb would be spent before we could get out of the sound, we cast anchor again a little without the Island Motuara, to wait for a more favourable opportunity of putting into the strait. While we were unmooring and getting under sail, Tomatongeauooranuc, Matahouah, and many more of the natives, came to take their leave of us, or rather to obtain, if they could, some additional present from us before we left them. These two chiefs became suitors to me for some goats and hogs. Accordingly, I gave to Matahouah two goats, a male and female with kid; and to Tomatongeauooranuc two pigs, a boar and a sow. They made me a promise not to kill them, though I must own I put no great faith in this. The animals which Captain Furneaux sent on shore here, and which soon after fell into the hands of the natives, I was now told were all dead; but I could get no intelligence about the fate of those I had left in West Bay, and in Cannibal Cove, when I was here in the course of my last voyage. However, all the natives whom I conversed with agreed that poultry are now to be met with wild in the woods behind Ship Cove; and I was afterward informed, by the two youths who went away with us, that Tiratou, a popular chief amongst them, had a great many cocks and hens in his separate possession, and one of the sows.

On my present arrival at this place, I fully intended to have left not only goats and hogs, but sheep, and a young bull, with two heifers, if I could have found either a chief powerful enough to protect and keep them, or a place where there might be a probability of their being concealed from those who would ignorantly attempt to destroy them. But neither the one nor the other presented itself to me. I could not learn that there remained in our neighbourhood any tribe whose numbers could secure to them a superiority of power over the rest of their countrymen. To have given the animals to any of the natives who possessed no such power, would not have answered the intention; for in a country like this, where no man's property is secure, they would soon have fallen a prey to different parties, and been either separated or killed; but most likely both. This was so evident, from what we had observed since our arrival, that I had resolved to leave no kind of animal, till Matahouah and the other

chief solicited me for the hogs and goats. As I could spare them, I let them go, to take their chance. I have, at different times, left in New Zealand no less than ten or a dozen hogs, besides those put on shore by Captain Furneaux. It will be a little extraordinary, therefore, if this race should not increase and be preserved here, either in a wild or in a domestic state, or in both.

We had not been long at anchor near Motuara before three or four canoes filled with natives came off to us from the south-east side of the sound, and a brisk trade was carried on with them for the curiosities of this place. In one of these canoes was Kahoora, whom I have already mentioned as the leader of the party who cut off the crew of the Adventure's boat. This was the third time he had visited us without betraying the smallest appearance of fear. I was ashore when he now arrived, but had got on board just as he was going away. Omai, who had returned with me, presently pointed him out and solicited me to shoot him. Not satisfied with this, he addressed himself to Kahoora, threatening to be his executioner if ever he presumed to visit us again. The New Zealander paid so little regard to these threats that he returned the next morning with his whole family—men, women, and children—to the number of twenty and upwards. Omai was the first who acquainted me with his being alongside the ship, and desired to know if he should ask him to come on board. I told him he might; and accordingly he introduced the chief into the cabin, saying, "There is Kahoora; kill him!" But, as if he had forgot his former threats, or were afraid that I should call upon him to perform them, he immediately retired. In a short time, however, he returned; and seeing the chief unhurt, he expostulated with me very earnestly, saying, "Why do you not kill him? You tell me if a man kills another in England that he is hanged for it. This man has killed ten, and yet you will not kill him, though many of his countrymen

desire it, and it would be very good."
Omai's arguments, though specious
enough, having no weight with me, I
desired him to ask the chief why he
had killed Captain Furneaux's people.
At this question, Kahoora folded his
arms, hung down his head, and looked
like one caught in a trap; and I firmly
believe he expected instant death.
But no sooner was he assured of his
safety than he became cheerful. He
did not, however, seem willing to give
me an answer to the question that
had been put to him till I had again
and again repeated my promise that
he should not be hurt. Then he ventured to tell us that one of his countrymen, having brought a stone
hatchet to barter, the man to whom
it was offered took it, and would
neither return it nor give anything
for it; on which the owner of it
snatched up the bread as an equivalent, and then the quarrel began.

The remainder of Kahoora's account
of this unhappy affair differed very
little from what we had before learned
from the rest of his countrymen. He
mentioned the narrow escape he had
during the fray, a musket being
levelled at him, which he avoided by
skulking behind the boat, and another
man who stood close to him was shot
dead. As soon as the musket was
discharged, he instantly seized the
opportunity to attack Mr Rowe, who
commanded the party, and who defended himself with his hanger (with
which he wounded Kahoora in the
arm), till he was overpowered by numbers. Mr Burney, who was sent by
Captain Furneaux the next day with
an armed party to look for his missing
people, upon discovering the horrid
proofs of their shocking fate, had fired
several volleys amongst the crowds of
natives who still remained assembled
on the spot, and were, probably, partaking of the detestable banquet. It
was natural to suppose that he had
not fired in vain, and that therefore
some of the murderers and devourers
of our unhappy countrymen had suffered under our just resentment.
Upon inquiry, however, into this
matter, not only from Kahoora, but

from others who had opportunities
of knowing, it appeared that our
supposition was groundless, and that
not one of the shots fired by Mr
Burney's people had taken effect so
as to kill or even to hurt a single
person.

It was evident that most of the
natives we had met with since our
arrival, as they knew I was fully acquainted with the history of the massacre, expected I should avenge it
with the death of Kahoora. And
many of them seemed not only to
wish it, but expressed their surprise
at my forbearance. As he could not
be ignorant of this, it was a matter of
wonder to me that he put himself so
often in my power. When he visited
us while the ships lay in the cove,
confiding in the number of his friends
that accompanied him, he might think
himself safe. But his two last visits
had been made under such circumstances that he could no longer rely
upon this. We were then at anchor
in the entrance of the sound, and at
some distance from any shore, so that
he could not have any assistance from
thence, nor flatter himself he could
have the means of making his escape
had I determined to detain him. And
yet, after his first fears on being in-
terrogated were over, he was so far
from entertaining any uneasy sensa-
tions, that on seeing a portrait of one
of his countrymen hanging up in the
cabin he desired to have his own por
trait drawn, and sat till Mr Webber
had finished it without marking the
least impatience. I must confess I
admired his courage, and was not a
little pleased to observe the extent of
the confidence he put in me. For he
placed his whole safety in the declarations I had uniformly made to those
who solicited his death; that I had
always been a friend to them all, and
would continue so, unless they gave
me cause to act otherwise; that as to
their inhuman treatment of our people,
I should think no more of it, the
transaction having happened long ago,
and when I was not present; but
that, if ever they made a second
attempt of that kind, they might

rest assured of feeling the weight of my resentment.

For some time before we arrived at New Zealand, Omai had expressed a desire to take one of the natives with him to his own country. We had not been there many days before he had an opportunity of being gratified in this, for a youth about seventeen or eighteen years of age, named Taweiharooa, offered to accompany him, and took up his residence on board. I paid little attention to this at first, imagining that he would leave us when we were about to depart, and after he had got what he could from Omai. At length, finding that he was fixed in his resolution to go with us, and having learned that he was the only son of a deceased chief; and that his mother, still living, was a woman much respected here, I was apprehensive that Omai had deceived him and his friends by giving them hopes and assurances of his being sent back. I therefore caused it to be made known to them all that if the young man went away with us he would never return. But this declaration seemed to make no sort of impression. The afternoon before we left the cove, Tiratoutou, his mother, came on board, to receive her last present from Omai. The same evening, she and Taweiharooa parted with all the marks of tender affection that might be expected between a parent and a child who were never to meet again. But she said she would cry no more; and, sure enough, she kept her word, for when she returned the next morning to take her last farewell of him, all the time she was on board she remained quite cheerful, and went away wholly unconcerned.

That Taweiharooa might be sent away in a manner becoming his birth, another youth was to have gone with him as a servant; and with this view, as we supposed, he remained on board till we were about to sail, when his friends took him ashore. However, his place was supplied next morning by another, a boy of about nine or ten years of age, named Kokoa. He was presented to me by his own father, who, I believe, would have parted with his dog with far less indifference. The very little clothing the boy had, he stripped him of, and left him as naked as he was born. It was to no purpose that I endeavoured to convince these people of the improbability, or rather of the impossibility, of these youths ever returning home. Not one, not even their nearest relations, seemed to trouble themselves about their future fate. Since this was the case, and I was well satisfied that the boys would be no losers by exchange of place, I the more readily gave my consent to their going.[1]

BOOK II.

FROM LEAVING NEW ZEALAND TO OUR ARRIVAL AT OTAHEITE, OR THE SOCIETY ISLANDS.

CHAPTER I.

ON the 25th, at 10 o'clock in the morning, a light breeze springing up at N.W. by W., we weighed, stood out of the sound, and made sail through the strait, with the Discovery in company. We had hardly got the length of Cape Tierawhitte, when the wind took us aback at SE. It continued in this quarter till 2 o'clock the next morning, when we had a few

---

[1] Omission is made of the remainder of this Chapter, and of Chapter VIII.—the latter entirely written by Mr Anderson—which are occupied with dissertations on the morals,

hours' calm. After which we had a breeze at N.; but here it fixed not long, before it veered to the E., and after that to the S. At length, on the 27th, at 8 o'clock in the morning, we took our departure from Cape Palliser. We had a fine gale, and I steered E. by N. We had no sooner lost sight of the land than our two New Zealand adventurers, the sea sickness they now experienced giving a turn to their reflections, repented heartily of the step they had taken. All the soothing encouragement we could think of availed but little. They wept, both in public and in private, and made their lamentations in a kind of song, which, as far as we could comprehend the meaning of the words, was expressive of their praises of their country and people, from which they were to be separated for ever. Thus they continued for many days, till their sea sickness wore off, and the tumult of their minds began to subside. Then these fits of lamentation became less and less frequent, and at length entirely ceased. Their native country and their friends were by degrees forgot, and they appeared to be as firmly attached to us as if they had been born amongst us.

On the 29th [of March], at ten in the morning, as we were standing to the NE., the Discovery made the signal of seeing land. We saw it from the masthead almost the same moment, bearing NE. by E. by compass. We soon discovered it to be an island of no great extent, and stood for it till sunset, when it bore NNE., distant about two or three leagues. The night was spent in standing off and on, and at daybreak the next morning I bore up for the lee or west side of the island, as neither anchorage nor landing appeared to be practicable on the south side, on account of a great surf which broke everywhere with violence against the shore, or against the reef that surrounded it.

---

manners, and customs, &c., &c., of the New Zealanders, but do not in any way relate to the actual transactions of the voyage.

We presently found that the island was inhabited, and saw several people on a point of the land we had passed, wading to the reef, where, as they found the ship leaving them quickly, they remained. But others, who soon appeared in different parts, followed her course, and sometimes several of them collected into small bodies, who made a shouting noise all together, nearly after the manner of the inhabitants of New Zealand. Between 7 and 8 o'clock, we were at the WNW. part of the island, and, being near the shore, we could perceive with our glasses that several of the natives, who appeared upon a sandy beach, were all armed with long spears and clubs, which they brandished in the air with signs of threatening, or as some on board interpreted their attitudes, with invitations to land. Most of them appeared naked, except having a sort of girdle, which, being brought up between the thighs, covered that part of the body. But some of them had pieces of cloth of different colours, white, striped, or chequered, which they wore as a garment, thrown about their shoulders. And almost all of them had a white wrapper about their heads, not much unlike a turban, or, in some instances, like a high conical cap. We could also perceive that they were of a tawny colour, and in general of a middling stature, but robust, and inclining to corpulence.

At this time, a small canoe was launched in a great hurry from the farther end of the beach, and a man getting into it, put off, as with a view to reach the ship. On perceiving this, I brought to, that we might receive the visit; but the man's resolution failing, he soon returned toward the beach, where, after some time, another man joined him in the canoe; and then they both paddled towards us. They stopped short, however, as if afraid to approach, until Omai, who addressed them in the Otaheite language, in some measure quieted their apprehensions. They then came near enough to take some beads and nails, which were tied to a piece of wood and thrown into the canoe. They seemed afraid to touch these things, and put the piece of wood aside without untying them. This, however, might arise from superstition; for Omai told us, that when they saw us offering them presents, they asked something for their "Eatooa," or god. He also, perhaps improperly, put the question to them, "Whether they ever ate human flesh?" which they answered in the negative, with a mixture of indignation and abhorrence. One of them, whose name was Mourooa, being asked how he came by a scar on his forehead, told us that it was the consequence of a wound he had got in fighting with the people of an island which lies to the north-eastward, who sometimes came to invade them. They afterward took hold of a rope. Still, however, they would not venture on board; but told Omai, who understood them pretty well, that their countrymen on shore had given them this caution, at the same time directing them to inquire from whence our ship came, and to learn the name of the captain. On our part, we inquired the name of the island, which they called "Mangya" or "Mangeea;" and sometimes added to it "Nooe, nai, naiwa." The name of their chief, they said, was Orooaeeka.

Mourooa was lusty and well made, but not very tall. His features were agreeable, and his disposition seemingly no less so; for he made several droll gesticulations, which indicated both good-nature and a share of humour. He also made others which seemed of a serious kind, and repeated some words with a devout air, before he ventured to lay hold of the rope at the ship's stern; which was probably to recommend himself to the protection of some divinity. His colour was nearly of the same cast with that common to the most southern Europeans. The other man was not so handsome. Both of them had strong, straight hair, of a jet colour, tied together on the crown of the head with a bit of cloth. They wore such girdles as we had perceived about those on shore, and we found they were a substance made from the *Morus papyri-*

fera, in the same manner as at the other islands of this ocean. It was glazed like the sort used by the natives of the Friendly Islands; but the cloth on their heads was white, like that which is found at Otaheite. They had on a kind of sandals, made of a grassy substance interwoven, which we also observed were worn by those who stood upon the beach, and, as we supposed, intended to defend their feet against the rough coral rock. Their beards were long; and the inside of their arms, from the shoulder to the elbow, and some other parts, were punctured or tattooed, after the manner of the inhabitants of almost all the other islands in the South Sea. The lobe of their ears was pierced, or rather slit, and to such a length, that one of them stuck there a knife and some beads which he had received from us; and the same person had two polished pearl shells, and a bunch of human hair, loosely twisted, hanging about his neck, which was the only ornament we observed. The canoe they came in (which was the only one we saw) was not above ten feet long, and very narrow; but both strong and neatly made. The forepart had a flat board fastened over it, and projecting out, to prevent the sea getting in on plunging, like the small "evaas" at Otaheite; but it had an upright stern, about five feet high, like some in New Zealand; and the upper end of this stern-post was forked. The lower part of the canoe was of white wood, but the upper was black; and their paddles made of wood of the same colour, not above three feet long, broad at one end, and blunted. They paddled either end of the canoe forward indifferently, and only turned about their faces to paddle the contrary way.

We now stood off and on, and as soon as the ships were in a proper station, about 10 o'clock I ordered two boats, one of them from the Discovery to sound the coast, and to endeavour to find a landing-place. With this view, I went in one of them myself, taking with me such articles to give the natives as I thought might serve to gain their goodwill. I had no sooner put off from the ship than the canoe, with the two men which had left us not long before, paddled towards my boat; and, having come alongside, Mourooa stepped into her, without being asked, and without a moment's hesitation. Omai, who was with me, was ordered to inquire of him where we could land, and he directed us to two different places. But I saw with regret that the attempt could not be made at either place, unless at the risk of having our boats filled with water, or even staved to pieces. Nor were we more fortunate in our search for anchorage, for we could find no bottom till within a cable's length of the breakers. There we met with from forty to twenty fathoms depth, over sharp coral rocks, so that anchoring would have been attended with much more danger than landing. Thus were we obliged to leave, unvisited, this fine island, which seemed capable of supplying all our wants.

The natives of Mangeea seem to resemble those of Otaheite and the Marquesas in the beauty of their persons more than any other nation I have seen in these seas; having a smooth skin, and not being muscular. Their general disposition also corresponds, as far as we had opportunities of judging, with that which distinguishes the first-mentioned people. For they are not only cheerful, but, as Mourooa showed us, are acquainted with all the lascivious gesticulations which the Otaheiteans practise in their dances. It may also be supposed that their method of living is similar; for, though the nature of the country prevented our seeing many of their habitations, we observed one house near the beach, which much resembled, in its mode of construction, those of Otaheite. It was pleasantly situated in a grove of trees, and appeared to be about thirty feet long, and seven or eight high, with an open end, which represented an ellipse divided transversely. Before it was spread something white on a few bushes, which we conjectured to be a fishing-net, and, to appearance, of a very delicate texture.

They salute strangers much after the manner of the New Zealanders, by joining noses; adding, however, the additional ceremony of taking the hand of the person to whom they are paying civilities, and rubbing it with a degree of force upon their nose and mouth.

CHAPTER II.

AFTER leaving Mangeea, on the afternoon of the 30th, we continued our course northward all that night, and till noon on the 31st, when we again saw land, in the direction of NE. by N., distant eight or ten leagues. Next morning at 8 o'clock, we had got abreast of its north end, within four leagues of it, but to leeward, and could now pronounce it to be an island, nearly of the same appearance and extent with that we had so lately left. At the same time, another island, but much smaller, was seen right ahead. We could have soon reached this; but the largest one had the preference, as most likely to furnish a supply of food for the cattle, of which we began to be in great want. With this view I determined to work up to it; but as there was but little wind, and that little was unfavourable, we were still two leagues to leeward at 8 o'clock the following morning. Soon after, I sent two armed boats from the Resolution, and one from the Discovery, under the command of Lieutenant Gore, to look for anchoring-ground and a landing-place. In the meantime, we plied up under the island with the ships.

Just as the boats were putting off, we observed several single canoes coming from the shore. They went first to the Discovery, she being the nearest ship. It was not long after when three of these canoes came alongside of the Resolution, each conducted by one man. They are long and narrow, and supported by outriggers. The stern is elevated about three or four feet, something like a ship's stern-post. The head is flat above, but prow-like below, and turns down at the extremity, like the end of a violin. Some knives, beads, and other trifles were conveyed to our visitors, and they gave us a few cocoa-nuts, upon our asking for them. But they did not part with them by way of exchange for what they had received from us. For they seemed to have no idea of bartering; nor did they appear to estimate any of our presents at a high rate. With a little persuasion, one of them made his canoe fast to the ship, and came on board, and the other two, encouraged by his example, soon followed him. Their whole behaviour marked that they were quite at their ease, and felt no sort of apprehension of our detaining or using them ill.

After their departure, another canoe arrived, conducted by a man who brought a bunch of plantains as a present to me; asking for me by name, having learned it from Omai, who was sent before us in the boat with Mr Gore. In return for this civility, I gave him an axe, and a piece of red cloth, and he paddled back to the shore well satisfied. I afterward understood from Omai, that this present had been sent from the king, or principal chief, of the island. Not long after, a double canoe, in which were twelve men, came toward us. As they drew near the ship, they recited some words in concert, by way of chorus, one of their number first standing up, and giving the word before each repetition. When they had finished their solemn chant, they came alongside, and asked for the chief. As soon as I showed myself, a pig and a few cocoa-nuts were conveyed up into the ship; and the principal person in the canoe made me an additional present of a piece of matting, as soon as he and his companions got on board.

Our visitors were conducted into the cabin, and to other parts of the ship. Some objects seemed to strike them with a degree of surprise; but nothing fixed their attention for a moment. They were afraid to come near the cows and horses; nor did they form the least conception of their nature. But the sheep and goats did not surpass the limits of their ideas; for they gave us to understand that they knew them to be birds. It will appear rather incredible that human ignorance could ever make so strange a mistake; there not being the most distant similitude between a sheep or goat and any winged animal. But these people seemed to know nothing of the existence of any other land-animals besides hogs, dogs, and birds. Our sheep and goats, they could see, were very different creatures from the two first, and therefore they inferred that they must belong to the latter class, in which they knew there is a considerable variety of species. I made a present to my new friend of what I thought might be most acceptable to him; but, on his going away, he seemed rather disappointed than pleased. I afterward understood that he was very desirous of obtaining a dog, of which animal this island could not boast, though its inhabitants knew that the race existed in other islands of their ocean. Captain Clerke had received the like present, with the same view, from another man, who met with from him the like disappointment.

The people in these canoes were in general of a middling size, and not unlike those of Mangeea; though several were of a blacker cast than any we saw there. Their hair was tied on the crown of the head, or flowing loose upon the shoulders; and though in some it was of a frizzling disposition, yet, for the most part, that, as well as the straight sort, was long. Their features were various, and some of the young men rather handsome. Like those of Mangeea, they had girdles of glazed cloth, or fine matting, the ends of which, being brought betwixt their thighs, covered the adjoining parts. Ornaments composed of a sort of broad grass, stained with red, and strung with berries of the night-shade, were worn about their necks. Their ears were bored, but not slit; and they were punctured upon the legs, from the knee to the heel, which made them appear as if they wore a kind of boots. They also resembled the inhabitants of Mangeea in the length of their beards, and like them wore a sort of sandals upon their feet. Their behaviour was frank and cheer-ful, with a great deal of good-nature.

At 3 o'clock in the afternoon, Mr Gore returned with the boat, and informed me that he had examined all the west side of the island, without finding a place where a boat could land or the ships could anchor, the shore being everywhere bounded by a steep coral rock, against which the sea broke in a dreadful surf. But as the natives seemed very friendly, and to express a degree of disappointment when they saw that our people failed in their attempts to land, Mr Gore was of opinion that, by means of Omai, who could best explain our request, they might be prevailed upon to bring off to the boats, beyond the surf, such articles as we most wanted; in particular, the stems of plantain trees, which make good food for the cattle. Having little or no wind, the delay of a day or two was not of any moment; and therefore I determined to try the experiment, and got everything ready against the next morning.

Soon after daybreak, we observed some canoes coming off to the ships, and one of them directed its course to the Resolution. In it was a hog, with some plantains and cocoa-nuts, for which the people who brought them demanded a dog from us, and refused every other thing that we offered in exchange. One of our gentlemen on board happened to have a dog and a bitch, which were great nuisances in the ship, and might have been disposed of on this occasion for a purpose of real utility, by propagating a race of so useful an animal in this island. But their owner had no such views in making them the companions of his voyage. However, to gratify these people, Omai parted with a favourite dog he had brought from England; and with this acquisition they departed highly satisfied. About 10 o'clock, I despatched Mr Gore with three boats, two from the Resolution and one from the Discovery, to try the experiment he had proposed. And, as I could confide in his diligence and ability, I left it entirely to himself to act as from circumstances he should judge to be most proper. Two of the natives, who had been on board, accompanied him, and Omai went with him in his boat as an interpreter. The ships being a full league from the island when the boats put off, and having but little wind, it was noon before we could work up to it. We then saw our three boats riding at their grapplings, just without the surf, and a prodigious number of the natives on the shore abreast of them. By this we concluded, that Mr Gore, and others of our people, had landed; and our impatience to know the event may be easily conceived. In order to observe their motions, and to be ready to give them such assistance as they might want and our respective situations would admit of, I kept as near the shore as was prudent. I was sensible, however, that the reef was as effectual a barrier between us and our friends who had landed, and put them as much beyond the reach of our protection, as if half the circumference of the globe had intervened; but the islanders, it was probable, did not know this so well as we did. Some of them, now and then, came off to the ships in their canoes, with a few cocoa-nuts, which they exchanged for whatever was offered to them, without seeming to give the preference to any particular article.

These occasional visits served to lessen my solicitude about our people who had landed. Though we could get no information from our visitors, yet their venturing on board seemed to imply, at least, that their countrymen on shore had not made an improper use of the confidence put in them. At length, a little before sunset, we had the satisfaction of seeing the boats put off. When they got on board, I found that Mr Gore himself, Omai, Mr Anderson, and Mr Burney, were the only persons who had landed. The transactions of the day were now fully reported to me by Mr Gore; but Mr Anderson's account of them being very particular, and including some remarks on the island and its inhabitants, I shall give it a place here, nearly in his own words.

"We rowed toward a small sandy beach, upon which, and upon the adjacent rocks, a great number of the natives had assembled, and came to an anchor within 100 yards of the reef, which extends about as far, or a little farther, from the shore. Several of the natives swam off, bringing cocoa-nuts; and Omai, with their countrymen, whom we had with us in the boats, made them sensible of our wish to land. But their attention was taken up for a little time by the dog, which had been carried from the ship, and was just brought on shore, round whom they flocked with great eagerness. Soon after, two canoes came off; and, to create a greater confidence in the islanders, we determined to go unarmed and run the hazard of being treated well or ill.

"Mr Burney, the first lieutenant of the Discovery, and I, went in one canoe a little time before the other; and our conductors, watching attentively the motions of the surf, landed us safely upon the reef. An islander took hold of each of us, obviously with an intention to support us in walking over the rugged rocks to the beach, where several of the others met us, holding the green boughs of a [species of mimosa in their hands, and saluted us by applying their noses to ours.

"We were conducted from the beach by our guides amidst a great crowd of people, who flocked with very eager curiosity to look at us, and would have prevented our proceeding had not some men, who seemed to have authority, dealt blows with little distinction amongst them to keep them off. We were then led up an avenue of cocoa-palms, and soon came to a number of men arranged in two rows, armed with clubs, which they held on their shoulders much in the manner we rest a musket. After walking a little way amongst these, we found a person who seemed a chief sitting on the ground cross-legged, cooling himself with a sort of triangular fan made from a leaf of the cocoa-palm, with a polished handle of black wood fixed to one corner. In his ears were large bunches of beautiful red feathers which pointed forward. But he had no other mark or ornament to distinguish him from the rest of the people, though they all obeyed him with the greatest alacrity. He either naturally had, or at this time put on, a serious but not severe countenance; and we were desired to salute him as he sat by some people who seemed of consequence.

"We proceeded still amongst the men armed with clubs, and came to a second chief, who sat fanning himself, and ornamented as the first. He was remarkable for his size and uncommon corpulence, though, to appearance, not above thirty years of age. In the same manner we were conducted to a third chief, who seemed older than the two former; and though not so fat as the second, was of a large size. He also was sitting, and adorned with red feathers; and after saluting him as we had done the others, he desired us both to sit down, which we were very willing to do, being pretty well fatigued with walking up, and with the excessive heat we felt amongst the vast crowd that surrounded us.

"In a few minutes the people were ordered to separate; and we saw, at the distance of thirty yards, about twenty young women ornamented as the chiefs, with red feathers, engaged in a dance, which they performed to a slow and serious air sung by them all. We got up and went forward to see them, and though we must have been strange objects to them, they continued their dance without paying the least attention to us. They seemed to be directed by a man who served as a prompter, and mentioned each motion they were to make. But they never changed the spot, as we do in dancing; and though their feet were not at rest, this exercise consisted more in moving the fingers very nimbly, at the same time holding their hands in a prone position near the face, and now and then also clapping them together. Their motions and song were performed in such exact concert that it should seem they had been taught with great care; and probably they were selected for this ceremony, as few of those whom we saw in the crowd equalled them in beauty. In general, they were rather stout than slender, with black hair flowing in ringlets down the neck, and of an olive complexion. Their features were rather fuller than what we allow to perfect beauties, and much alike; but their eyes were of a deep black, and each countenance expressed a degree of complacency and modesty peculiar to the sex in every part of the world, but perhaps more conspicuous here where Nature presented us with her productions in the fullest perfection, unbiassed in sentiment by custom, or unrestrained in manner by art. Their shape and limbs were elegantly formed; for, as their dress consisted only of a piece of glazed cloth fastened about the waist, and scarcely reaching so low as the knees, in many we had an opportunity of observing every part. This dance was not finished when we heard a noise as if some horses had been galloping toward us, and, on looking aside, we saw the people armed with clubs, who had been desired, as we supposed, to entertain us with the sight of their manner of fighting. This they now did, one party pursuing another who fled.

"As we supposed the ceremony of being introduced to the chiefs was at an end, we began to look about for Mr Gore and Omai; and, though the crowd would hardly suffer us to move, we at length found them coming up, as much incommoded by the number of people as we had been, and introduced in the same manner to the three chiefs, whose names were Otteroo, Taroa, and Fatouweera. Each of these expected a present, and Mr Gore gave them such things as he had brought with him from the ship for that purpose. After this, making use of Omai as his interpreter, he informed the chiefs with what intention we had come on shore; but was given to understand that he must wait till the next day, and then he should have what was wanted.

"They now seemed to take some pains to separate us from each other, and every one of us had his circle to surround and gaze at him. For my own part, I was at one time above an hour apart from my friends; and when I told the chief with whom I sat that I wanted to speak to Omai, he peremptorily refused my request. At the same time, I found the people began to steal several trifling things which I had in my pocket; and when I took the liberty of complaining to the chief of this treatment, he justified it. From these circumstances, I now entertained apprehensions that they might have formed the design of detaining us amongst them. They did not, indeed, seem to be of a disposition so savage as to make us anxious for the safety of our persons; but it was nevertheless vexing to think we had hazarded being detained by their curiosity. In this situation, I asked for something to eat, and they readily brought to me some cocoa-nuts, bread-fruit, and a sort of sour pudding, which was presented by a woman. And on my complaining much of the heat, occasioned by the crowd, the chief himself condescended to fan me, and gave me a small piece of cloth which he had round his waist.

"Mr Burney happening to come to the place where I was, I mentioned my suspicions to him; and, to put it to the test whether they were well founded, we attempted to get to the beach. But we were stopped when about half way by some men, who told us that we must go back to the place which we had left. On coming up, we found Omai entertaining the same apprehensions. But he had, as he fancied, an additional reason for being afraid, for he had observed that they had dug a hole in the ground for an oven, which they were now heating; and he could assign no other reason for this than that they meant to roast and eat us, as is practised by the inhabitants of New Zealand. Nay, he went so far as to ask them the question, at which they were greatly surprised, asking in return whether that was a custom with us. Mr Burney and I were rather angry that they should be thus suspected by him, there having as yet been no appearances in their conduct toward us of their being capable of such brutality.

"In this manner we were detained the greatest part of the day, being sometimes together, and sometimes separated, but always in a crowd, who, not satisfied with gazing at us, frequently desired us to uncover parts of our skin; the sight of which commonly produced a general murmur of admiration. At the same time, they did not omit these opportunities of rifling our pockets; and, at last, one of them snatched a small bayonet from Mr Gore, which hung in its sheath by his side. This was represented to the chief, who pretended to send some person in search of it. But, in all probability, he countenanced the theft; for, soon after, Omai had a dagger stolen from his side in the same manner, though he did not miss it immediately.

"Whether they observed any signs of uneasiness in us, or that they voluntarily repeated their emblems of friendship when we expressed a desire to go, I cannot tell; but, at this time, they brought some green boughs, and, sticking their ends in the ground, desired we might hold them as we sat. Upon our urging again the business we came upon, they gave us to understand that we must stay and eat with them; and a pig which we saw, soon after, lying near the oven, which they had prepared and heated, removed Omai's apprehensions of being put into it himself, and made us think it might be intended for our repast. The chief also promised to send some people to procure food for the cattle; but it was not till pretty late in the afternoon that we saw them return with a few plantain trees, which they carried to our boats.

"In the meantime, Mr Burney and I attempted again to go to the beach; but, when we arrived, found ourselves watched by people who, to appearance, had been placed there for this purpose. For when I tried to wade in upon the reef, one of them took hold of my clothes and dragged me back. I picked up some small pieces of coral, which they required me to throw down again; and, on my refusal, they made no scruple to take them forcibly from me. I had gathered some small plants, but these also I could not be permitted to retain. And they took a fan from Mr Burney, which he had received as a present on coming ashore. Omai said we had done wrong in taking up anything, for it was not the custom here to permit freedoms of that kind to strangers, till they had in some measure naturalised them to the country, by entertaining them with festivity for two or three days.

"Finding that the only method of procuring better treatment was to yield implicit obedience to their will, we went up again to the place we had left, and they now promised that we should have a canoe to carry us off to our boats, after we had eaten of a repast which had been prepared for us. Accordingly, the second chief, to whom we had been introduced in the morning, having seated himself upon a low broad stool of blackish, hard wood, tolerably polished, and directing the multitude to make a pretty large ring, made us sit down by him. A considerable number of cocoa-nuts were now brought, and, shortly after, a long green basket, with a sufficient quantity of baked plantains to have served a dozen persons. A piece of the young hog that had been dressed was then set before each of us, of which we were desired to eat. Our appetites, however, had failed from the fatigue of the day; and though we did eat a little to please them, it was without satisfaction to our-selves.

"It being now near sunset, we told them it was time to go on board. This they allowed, and sent down to the beach the remainder of the victuals that had been dressed, to be carried with us to the ships. But, before we set out, Omai was treated with a drink he had been used to in his own country, which, we observed, was made here, as at other islands in the South Sea, by chewing the root of a sort of pepper. We found a canoe ready to put us off to our boats, which the natives did with the same caution as when we landed. But even here their thievish disposition did not leave them. For a person of some consequence among them, who came with us, took an opportunity, just as they were pushing the canoe into the surf, to snatch a bag out of her, which I had with the greatest difficulty preserved all the day, there being in it a small pocket pistol which I was unwilling to part with. Perceiving him, I called out, express-ing as much displeasure as I could. On which he thought proper to return, and swim with the bag to the canoe; but denied he had stolen it, though detected in the very act. They put us on our boats, with the cocoa-nuts, plantains, and other provisions which they had brought; and we rowed to the ships, very well pleased that we had at last got out of the hands of our troublesome masters.

"We regretted much that our restrained situation gave us so little opportunity of making observations on the country. For, during the whole day, we were seldom 100 yards from the place where we were intro-duced to the chiefs on landing; and, consequently, were confined to the surrounding objects. The first thing that presented itself worthy of our notice was the number of people, which must have been at least 2000; for those who welcomed us on the shore bore no proportion to the multitude we found amongst the trees, on pro-ceeding a little way up. We could also observe that, except a few, those we had hitherto seen on board were of the lower class. For a great num-ber of those we now met with had a superior dignity in their air, and were of a much whiter cast. In general, they had the hair tied on the crown of the head, long, black, and of a most luxuriant growth. Many of the young men were perfect models in shape, of a complexion as delicate as that of the women, and, to appear-ance, of a disposition as amiable. Others, who were more advanced in years, were corpulent; and all had a remarkable smoothness of the skin. Their general dress was a piece of cloth, or mat, wrapped about the waist, and covering the parts which modesty conceals. But some had pieces of mats, most curiously varied with black and white, made into a sort of jacket without sleeves; and others wore conical caps of cocoa-nut coir, neatly interwoven with small beads, made of a shelly substance. Their ears were pierced, and in them they hung bits of the membranceous part of some plant, or stuck there an odoriferous flower, which seemed to be a species of *Gardenia*. Some, who were of a superior class, and also the chiefs, had two little balls, with a common base, made from the bone of some animal, which was hung round the neck, with a great many folds of small cord. And after the ceremony of introduction to the chiefs was over, they then appeared without their red feathers, which are certainly con-sidered here as a particular mark of distinction, for none but themselves, and the young women who danced, assumed them.

"Some of the men were punctured all over the sides and back in an uncommon manner; and some of the women had the same ornament on their legs. But this method was con-fined to those who seemed to be of a superior rank; and the men, in that case, were also generally distinguished by their size and corpulence, unless very young. The women of an ad-vanced age had their hair cropped short; many were cut in oblique lines all over the fore-part of the body; and some of the wounds, which formed rhomboidal figures, had been so lately inflicted, that the coagulated blood still remained in them.

"The wife of one of the chiefs appeared with her child laid in a piece of red cloth which had been presented to her husband, and seemed to carry it with great tenderness, suckling it much after the manner of our women. Another chief introduced his daughter, who was young and beautiful, but appeared with all the timidity natural to the sex; though she gazed on us with a kind of anxious concern that seemed to struggle with her fear, and to express her astonishment at so unusual a sight. Others advanced with more firmness, and, indeed, were less reserved than we expected; but behaved with a becoming modesty. We did not observe any personal deformities amongst either sex, except in a few who had scars of broad superficial ulcers remaining on the face and other parts. In proportion to the number of people assembled, there appeared not many old men or women, which may easily be accounted for by supposing that such as were in an advanced period of life might neither have the inclination nor the ability to come from the more distant parts of the island. On the other hand, the children were numerous; and both these and the men climbed the trees to look at us, when we were hid by the surrounding crowd.

"About a third part of the men were armed with clubs and spears; and, probably, these were only the persons who had come from a distance, as many of them had small baskets, mats, and other things, fastened to the ends of their weapons. The clubs were generally about six feet long, made of a hard black wood, lance-shaped at the end, but much broader, with the edge nicely scolloped, and the whole neatly polished. Others of them were narrower at the point, much shorter, and plain; and some were even so small as to be used with one hand. The spears were made of the same wood, simply pointed, and, in general, above twelve feet long; though some were so short that they seemed intended to be thrown as darts.

"The place where we were all the day was under the shade of various trees; in which they preserved their canoes from the sun. About eight or ten of them were here, all double ones; that is, two single ones fastened together (as is usual throughout the whole extent of the Pacific Ocean), by rafters lashed across. They were about twenty feet long, about four feet deep, and the sides rounded, with a plank raised upon them, which was fastened strongly by means of withes. Two of these canoes were most curiously stained or painted all over with black, in numberless small figures, as squares, triangles, &c., and excelled by far anything of that kind I had ever seen at any other island in this ocean. Our friends here, indeed, seemed to have exerted more skill in doing this, than in puncturing their own bodies. The paddles were about four feet long, nearly elliptical, but broader at the upper end than the middle. Near the same place was a hut or shed about thirty feet long and nine or ten high, in which, perhaps, these boats are built; but, at this time, it was empty."

Though the landing of our gentlemen proved the means of enriching my journal with the foregoing particulars, the principal object I had in view was, in a great measure, unattained; for the day was spent without getting any one thing from the island worth mentioning. The natives, however, were gratified with a sight they never before had, and, probably, will never have again. And mere curiosity seems to have been their chief motive for keeping the gentlemen under such restraint, and for using every art to prolong their continuance amongst them.

It has been mentioned, that Omai was sent upon this expedition; and, perhaps, his being Mr Gore's interpreter was not the only service he performed this day. He was asked by the natives a great many questions concerning us, our ships, our country, and the sort of arms we used ; and, according to the account he gave me, his answers were not a little upon the marvellous. As, for instance, he told them, that our country had ships as large as their island, on board which were instruments of war (describing our guns), of such dimensions, that several people might sit within them ; and that one of them was suffi-cient to crush the whole island at one shot. This led them to inquire of him what sort of guns we actually had in our two ships. He said that though they were but small in com-parison with those he had just de-scribed, yet, with such as they were, we could with the greatest ease, and at the distance the ships were from the shore, destroy the island and kill every soul in it. They persevered in their inquiries, to know by what means this could be done ; and Omai explained the matter as well as he could. He happened luckily to have a few cartridges in his pocket. These he produced ; the balls, and the gun-powder which was to set them in motion, were submitted to inspection : and, to supply the defects of his de-scription, an appeal was made to the senses of the spectators. It has been mentioned above, that one of the chiefs had ordered the multitude to form themselves into a circle. This furnished Omai with a convenient stage for his exhibition. In the centre of this amphitheatre, the in-considerable quantity of gunpowder collected from his cartridges was pro-perly disposed upon the ground, and, by means of a bit of burning wood from the oven where dinner was dress-ing, set on fire. The sudden blast and loud report, the mingled flame and smoke, that instantly succeeded, now filled the whole assembly with aston-ishment : they no longer doubted the tremendous power of our weapons, and gave full credit to all that Omai had said.

If it had not been for the terrible ideas they conceived of the guns of our ships from this specimen of their mode of operation, it was thought that they would have detained the gentlemen all night. For Omai as-sured them, that, if he and his com-panions did not return on board the same day, they might expect that I would fire upon the island. And as we stood in nearer the land in the evening than we had done any time before, of which position of the ships they were observed to take great notice, they probably thought we were medi-tating this formidable attack, and, therefore, suffered their guests to de-part ; under the expectation, however, of seeing them again on shore next morning. But I was too sensible of the risk they had already run to think of a repetition of the experiment.

This day, it seems, was destined to give Omai more occasions than one of being brought forward to bear a prin-cipal part in its transactions. The island, though never before visited by Europeans, actually happened to have other strangers residing in it ; and it was entirely owing to Omai's being one of Mr Gore's attendants, that this curious circumstance came to our knowledge. Scarcely had he been landed upon the beach, when he found amongst the crowd there assembled three of his own countrymen, natives of the Society Islands. At the dis-tance of about 200 leagues from those islands, an immense unknown ocean intervening, with such wretched sea-boats as their inhabitants are known to make use of, fit only for a passage where sight of land is scarcely ever lost, such a meeting, at such a place, so accidentally visited by us, may well be looked upon as one of those unexpected situations with which the writers of feigned adventures love to surprise their readers, and which, when they really happen in common life, deserve to be recorded for their singularity.

It may easily be guessed, with what mutual surprise and satisfaction Omai and his countrymen engaged in con-versation. Their story, as related by them, is an affecting one. About twenty persons in number of both sexes, had embarked on board a canoe at Otaheite, to cross over to the neighbouring island Ulietea. A violent contrary wind arising, they could neither reach the latter, nor get back to the former. Their intended passage being a very short one, their stock of provisions was scanty and soon exhausted. The hardships they suffered, while driven along by the storm they knew not whither, are not to be conceived. They passed many days without having anything to eat or drink. Their numbers gradually diminished, worn out by famine and fatigue. Four men only survived when the canoe overset; and then the perdition of this small remnant seemed inevitable. However, they kept hanging by the side of their vessel during some of the last days, till Providence brought them in sight of the people of this island, who immediately sent out canoes, took them off their wreck, and brought them ashore. Of the four who were thus saved, one was since dead. The other three, who lived to have this opportunity of giving an account of their almost miraculous transplantation, spoke highly of the kind treatment they here met with. And so well satisfied were they with their situation, that they refused the offer made to them by our gentlemen, at Omai's request, of giving them a passage on board our ships, to restore them to their native islands. The similarity of manners and language had more than naturalised them to this spot; and the fresh connections which they had here formed, and which it would have been painful to have broken off after such a length of time, sufficiently account for their declining to revisit the places of their birth. They had arrived upon this island at least twelve years ago. For I learned from Mr Anderson that he found they knew nothing of Captain Wallis's visit to Otaheite in 1765, nor of several other memorable occurrences, such as the conquest of Ulietea, by those of Bolabola, which had preceded the arrival of the Europeans. To Mr Anderson I am also indebted for their names, Orououte,

Otirreroa, and Tavee : the first, born at Matavai in Otaheite ; the second, at Ulietea ; and the third, at Huaheine.

The landing of our gentlemen on this island, though they failed in the object of it, cannot but be considered as a very fortunate circumstance. It has proved, as we have seen, the means of bringing to our knowledge a matter of fact not only very curious, but very instructive. The application of the above narrative is obvious. It will serve to explain, better than a thousand conjectures of speculative reasoners, how the detached parts of the earth, and, in particular, how the islands of the South Sea, may have been first peopled ; especially those that lie remote from any inhabited continent, or from each other.

This island is called Wateeoo by the natives. It lies in the Latitude of 20° 1′ S., and in the Longitude of 201° 45′ E., and is about six leagues in circumference. It is a beautiful spot, with a surface composed of hills and plains, and covered with verdure of many hues.

[Having failed in obtaining some effectual supply at Wateeoo, Captain Cook steered for the smaller neighbouring island previously observed, where his boats' crews succeeded in procuring about 100 cocoa-nuts for each ship, with a quantity of grass and leaves and branches of young cocoa-trees, &c., for the cattle. The island, which was only about three miles in circumference, and uninhabited, was called, by the natives of Wateeoo, generally Otakootaia, but sometimes Wenooa-ette, which signifies "little island." The navigators then steered northward for Harvey's Island, which had been discovered in 1773, during Cook's second voyage.]

CHAPTER III.

As we drew near it, at 8 o'clock [on the morning of the 6th April], we observed several canoes put off from the shore; and they came directly toward the ships. This was a sight that, indeed, surprised me, as no signs of inhabitants were seen when the island was first discovered, which might be owing to a pretty brisk wind that then blew, and prevented their canoes venturing out, as the ships passed to leeward, whereas now we were to windward. As we still kept on toward the island, six or seven of the canoes, all double ones, soon came near us. There were from three to six men in each of them. They stopped at the distance of about a stone's throw from the ship, and it was some time before Omai could prevail upon them to come alongside; but no entreaties could induce any of them to venture on board. Indeed, their disorderly and clamorous behaviour by no means indicated a disposition to trust us, or treat us well. We afterward learned that they had attempted to take some oars out of the Discovery's boat that lay alongside, and struck a man who endeavoured to prevent them. They also cut away, with a shell, a net with meat which hung over that ship's stern, and absolutely refused to restore it, though we afterwards purchased it from them. Those who were about our ship behaved in the same daring manner; for they made a sort of hook of a long stick, with which they endeavoured openly to rob us of several things; and at last actually got a frock belonging to one of our people, that was towing overboard. At the same time, they immediately showed a knowledge of bartering, and sold some fish they had (amongst which was an extraordinary flounder, spotted like porphyry, and a cream-coloured eel, spotted with black), for small nails, of which they were immoderately fond, and called them "goore." But, indeed, they caught, with the greatest avidity, bits of paper or anything else that was thrown to them; and if what was thrown fell into the sea they made no scruple to swim after it. These people seemed to differ as much in person as in disposition from the natives of Wateeoo, though the distance between the two islands is not very great. Their colour was of a deeper cast; and several had a fierce,

rugged aspect resembling the natives of New Zealand; but some were fairer. They had strong black hair, which in general they wore either hanging loose about the shoulders, or tied in a bunch on the crown of the head. Some, however, had it cropped pretty short; and in two or three of them it was of a brown or reddish colour. Their only covering was a narrow piece of mat, wrapt several times round the lower part of the body, and which passed between the thighs; but a fine cap of red feathers was seen lying in one of the canoes. The shell of a pearl oyster polished, and hung about the neck, was the only ornamental fashion that we observed amongst them; for not one of them had adopted that mode of ornament, so generally prevalent amongst the natives of this ocean, of puncturing or tattooing their bodies.

[Lieutenant King was sent, with two armed boats, to search for a suitable anchoring-ground or landing-place; but he returned with a completely unfavourable report, and further stated, that decided manifestations of hostility had been made by the natives. Captain Cook, therefore, thought it prudent to run no risks for the uncertain chance of finding the grass and water of which the ships were in need.]

Being thus disappointed at all the islands we had met with since our leaving New Zealand, and the unfavourable winds and other unforeseen circumstances having unavoidably retarded our progress so much, it was now impossible to think of doing anything this year in the high latitudes of the northern hemisphere, from which we were still at so great a distance, though the season for our operations there was already begun. In this situation it was absolutely necessary to pursue such measures as were most likely to preserve the cattle we had on board, in the first place; and, in the next place (which was still a more capital object), to save the stores and provisions of the ships that we might be better enabled to prosecute our northern discoveries, which could not now commence till a year later than was originally intended. If I had been so fortunate as to have procured a supply of water and of grass at any of the islands we had lately visited, it was my purpose to have stood back to the south till I had met with a westerly wind. But the certain consequence of doing this without such a supply would have been the loss of all the cattle before we could possibly reach Otaheite, without gaining any one advantage with regard to the great object of our voyage. I therefore determined to bear away for the Friendly Islands, where I was sure of meeting with abundance of everything I wanted ; and it being necessary to run in the night as well as in the day, I ordered Captain Clerke to keep about a league ahead of the Resolution. I used this precaution, because his ship could best claw off the land, and it was very possible we might fall in with some in our passage.

At daybreak in the morning of the 13th, we saw Palmerston Island, bearing W. by S., distant about five leagues. However, we did not get up with it till 8 o'clock the next morning. I then sent four boats, three from the Resolution and one from the Discovery, with an officer in each, to search the coast for the most convenient landing-place. For now we were under an absolute necessity of procuring from this island some food for the cattle, otherwise we must have lost them. What is comprehended under the name of Palmerston's Island is a group of small islets, of which there are, in the whole, nine or ten, lying in a circular direction, and connected together by a reef of coral rocks. The boats first examined the south-easternmost of the islets which compose this group; and, failing there, ran down to the second, where we had the satisfaction to see them land. I then bore down with the ships till abreast of the place, and there we kept standing off and on. For no bottom was to be found to anchor upon, which was not of much consequence, as the party who had landed from our boats were the only

human beings upon the island. There were no traces of inhabitants having ever been here, if we except a small piece of a canoe that was found upon the beach, which probably may have drifted from some other island. But, what is pretty extraordinary, we saw several small brown rats on this spot, a circumstance, perhaps, difficult to account for, unless we allow that they were imported in the canoe of which we saw the remains. After the boats were laden, I returned on board, leaving Mr Gore with a party to pass the night on shore, in order to be ready to go to work early the next morning.

[The next three days were spent in provisioning the ships from this and other islets of the group, where cocoa-trees and vegetation suitable for feeding the cattle abounded, but where water was not to be found—the islets being merely the heads or summits of coral rock. Twelve hundred cocoa-nuts were shipped and equally divided among the whole crew, while the fish and birds, which were caught in abundance, afforded a salutary and welcome relief from the monotony of ship-fare.]

After leaving Palmerston's Island I steered W. with a view to make the best of my way to Annamooka. We still continued to have variable winds, frequently between the N. and W., with squalls, some thunder, and much rain. During these showers, which were generally very copious, we saved a considerable quantity of water ; and finding that we could get a greater supply by the rain in one hour than we could get by distillation in a month, I laid aside the still as a thing attended with more trouble than profit. The heat, which had been great for about a month, became now much more disagreeable in this close rainy weather ; and, from the moisture attending it, threatened soon to be noxious, as the ships could not be kept dry, nor the scuttles open, for the sea. However, it is remarkable enough that though the only refreshment we had received since leaving the Cape of Good Hope was that at New Zealand, there was not as yet a single person on board sick, from the constant use of salt food or vicissitude of climate.

[Savage Island, which Cook had discovered in 1774, was passed in the night between the 24th and 25th of April; on the 28th, in the afternoon, Annamooka was sighted; but as night drew on, and the weather was squally and rainy, anchor was cast two leagues from the neighbouring isle of Komango.]

CHAPTER IV.

Soon after we had anchored, two canoes, the one with four and the other with three men, paddled toward us, and came alongside without the least hesitation. They brought some cocoa-nuts, bread-fruit, plantains, and sugar-cane, which they bartered with us for nails. One of the men came on board; and when these canoes had left us, another visited us, but did not stay long, as night was approaching. Komango, the island nearest to us, was at least five miles off, which shows the hazard these people would run in order to possess a few of our most trifling articles. Besides this supply from the shore, we caught this evening, with hooks and lines, a considerable quantity of fish. Next morning at 4 o'clock I sent Lieutenant King with two boats to Komango to procure refreshments, and at five made the signal to weigh, in order to ply up to Annamooka, the wind being unfavourable at NW.

It was no sooner daylight than we were visited by six or seven canoes from different islands, bringing with them, besides fruits and roots, two pigs, several fowls, some large wood-pigeons, small rails, and large violet-coloured coots. All these they exchanged with us for beads, nails, hatchets, &c. They had also other articles of commerce; such as pieces of their cloth, fish-hooks, small baskets, musical reeds, and some clubs, spears, and bows. But I ordered that no curiosities should be purchased till the ships should be supplied with provisions,

and leave given for that purpose. Knowing, also, from experience, that if all our people might trade with the natives according to their own caprice, perpetual quarrels would ensue, I ordered that particular persons should manage the traffic both on board and on shore, prohibiting all others to interfere. Before mid-day Mr King's boat returned with seven hogs, some fowls, a quantity of fruit and roots for ourselves, and some grass for the cattle. His party was very civilly treated at Komango. The inhabitants did not seem to be numerous; and their huts, which stood close to each other, within a plantain walk, were but indifferent. Not far from them was a pretty large pond of fresh water, tolerably good; but there was not any appearance of a stream. With Mr King came on board the chief of the island, named Tooboulangee, and another whose name was Taipa. They brought with them a hog as a present to me, and promised more the next day.

As soon as the boats were aboard, I stood for Annamooka; and the wind being scant, I intended to go between Annamooka-ette,[1] and the breakers to the SE. of it. But, on drawing near, we met with very irregular soundings, varying, every cast, ten or twelve fathoms. This obliged me to give up the design, and to go to the southward of all; which carried us to leeward, and made it necessary to spend the night under sail. It was very dark, and we had the wind from every direction, accompanied with heavy showers of rain. So that, at daylight the next morning, we found ourselves much farther off than we had been the evening before; and the little wind that now blew was right in our teeth.

We continued to ply all day to very little purpose, and in the evening anchored. Tooboulangee and Taipa kept their promise, and brought off to me some hogs. Several others were also procured by bartering from different canoes that followed us, and

----

[1] That is, Little Annamooka.

as much fruit as we could well manage. It was remarkable that during the whole day our visitors from the islands would hardly part with any of their commodities to anybody but me. Captain Clerke did not get above one or two hogs.

At 4 o'clock next morning I ordered a boat to be hoisted out, and sent the master to sound the SW. side of Annamooka. In the meantime the ships were got under sail, and wrought up to the island. When the master returned, he reported that he had sounded between Great and Little Annamooka, where he found ten and twelve fathoms' depth of water, the bottom coral sand; that the place was very well sheltered from all winds; but that there was no fresh water to be found, except at some distance inland, and even there little of it was to be got, and that little not good. For this reason only, and it was a very sufficient one, I determined to anchor on the north side of the island, where, during my last voyage, I had found a place fit both for watering and landing. It was not above a league distant, and yet we did not reach it till 5 o'clock in the afternoon, being considerably retarded by the great number of canoes that continually crowded round the ships, bringing to us abundant supplies of the produce of their island. Amongst these canoes there were some double ones, with a large sail, that carried between forty and fifty men each. These sailed round us, apparently with the same case as if we had been at anchor. There were several women in the canoes, who were, perhaps, incited by curiosity to visit us; though, at the same time, they bartered as eagerly as the men, and used the paddle with equal labour and dexterity. I came to an anchor in eighteen fathoms water, the bottom coarse coral sand; the island extending from E. to SW., and the W. point of the westernmost cove SE., about three-quarters of a mile distant. Thus I resumed the very same station which I had occupied when I visited Annamooka three years before; and, probably, almost in the same place where Tasman, the first discoverer of this and some of the neighbouring islands, anchored in 1643.[1]

Finding that we had quite exhausted the island of almost every article of food that it afforded, I employed the 11th in moving off from the shore the horses, observatories, and other things that we had landed, as also the party of marines who had mounted guard at our station, intending to sail as soon as the Discovery should have recovered her best bower anchor. The 12th and the 13th were spent in attempting the recovery of Captain Clerke's anchor, which, after much trouble, was happily accomplished; and on the 14th, in the morning, we got under sail and left Annamooka.

To the north and north-east of Annamooka, and in the direct tract to Hapaee, whither we were now bound, the sea is sprinkled with a great number of small isles. Amidst the shoals and rocks adjoining to this group, I could not be assured that there was a free or safe passage for such large ships as ours; though the natives sailed through the intervals in their canoes. For this substantial reason, when we weighed anchor from Annamooka I thought it necessary to go to the westward of the above islands, and steered NNW. toward Kao and Toofoa, the two most westerly islands in sight, and remarkable for their great height. Feenou and his attendants remained on board the Resolution till near noon, when he went into the large sailing canoe which had brought him from Tongataboo, and stood in amongst the clus-

---

[1] Captain Cook, accompanied by Captain Clerke, went ashore here to fix a place for their observatories, when Loobu, the chief of the island, showed them every attention and civility. On the 6th they were visited by a chief from Tongataboo, whose name was Feenou, who was fond of associating with them, and who often dined on board.

ter of islands above mentioned, of which we were now almost abreast; and a tide or current from the westward had set us, since our sailing in the morning, much over toward them. They lie scattered at unequal distances, and are, in general, nearly as high as Annamooka; but only from two or three miles to half-a-mile in length, and some of them scarcely so much. They have either steep rocky shores, like Annamooka, or reddish cliffs; but some have sandy beaches extending almost their whole length. Most of them are entirely clothed with trees, amongst which are many cocoa-palms; and each forms a prospect like a beautiful garden placed in the sea. To heighten this, the serene weather we now had contributed very much; and the whole might supply the imagination with an idea of some fairy-land realised.

At 4 o'clock in the afternoon, being the length of Kotoo, the westernmost of the above cluster of small islands, we steered to the north, leaving Toofoa and Kao on our larboard, keeping along the west side of a reef of rocks which lie to the westward of Kotoo, till we came to their northern extremity, round which we hauled in for the island. It was our intention to have anchored for the night; but it came upon us before we could find a place in less than fifty-five fathoms water; and rather than come to in this depth I chose to spend the night under sail. We had in the afternoon been within two leagues of Toofoa, the smoke of which we saw several times in the day. The Friendly Islanders have some superstitious notions about the volcano upon it, which they call "Kollofeea," and say it is an "Otooa," or divinity. According to their account, it sometimes throws up very large stones; and they compare the crater to the size of a small islet, which has never ceased smoking in their memory; nor have they any tradition that it ever did. We sometimes saw the smoke rising from the centre of the island, while we were at Annamooka, though at the distance of at least ten

leagues. Toofoa, we were told, is but thinly inhabited, but the water upon it is good.

At day-break the next morning, being then not far from Kao, which is a vast rock of a conic figure, we steered to the east, for the passage between the islands Footooha and Hafaiva, with a gentle breeze at SE. About 10 o'clock Feenou came on board, and remained with us all day. He brought with him two hogs and a quantity of fruit; and, in the course of the day, several canoes, from the different islands round us, came to barter quantities of the latter article, which was very acceptable, as our stock was nearly expended. After passing Footooha, we met with a reef of rocks; and, as there was but little wind, it cost us some trouble to keep clear of them. This reef lies between Footooha and Neeneeva, which is a small low isle, in the direction of ENE. from Footooha, at the distance of seven or eight miles. Being past the reef of rocks just mentioned, we hauled up for Neeneeva, in hopes of finding anchorage; but were again disappointed, and obliged to spend the night, making short boards.[1] For, although we had land in every direction, the sea was unfathomable. In the course of this night we could plainly see flames issuing from the volcano upon Toofoa, though to no great height.

At daybreak in the morning of the 16th, with a gentle breeze at SE., we steered NE. for Hapaee, which was now in sight; and we could judge it to be low land, from the trees only appearing above the water. About 9 o'clock we could see it plainly, forming three islands, nearly of an equal size; and soon after, a fourth to the southward of these, as large as the others. Each seemed to be about six or seven miles long, and of a similar height and appearance. The northernmost of them is called Haanno, the next Foa, the third Lefooga, and the southernmost Hoolaiva; but all four are included by

---

[1] Tacks.

the natives under the general name Hapaee.

The wind scanting upon us, we could not fetch the land; so that we were forced to ply to windward. In doing this, we once passed over some coral rocks on which we had only six fathoms water; but the moment we were over them, found no ground with eighty fathoms of line. We got up with the northernmost of these isles by sunset; and there found ourselves in the very same distress, for want of anchorage, that we had experienced the two preceding evenings; so that we had another night to spend under sail, with land and breakers in every direction. Towards the evening Feenou, who had been on board all day, went forward to Hapaee, and took Omai in the canoe with him. He did not forget our disagreeable situation, and kept up a good fire all night by way of a land-mark. As soon as the daylight returned, being then close in with Foa, we saw it was joined to Haanno by a reef running even with the surface of the sea from the one island to the other. I now despatched a boat to look for anchorage. A proper place was soon found, and we came to abreast of a reef, being that which joins Lefooga to Foa (in the same manner that Foa is joined to Haanno), having twenty-four fathoms' depth of water. We lay before a creek in the reef, which made it convenient landing at all times; and we were not above three-quarters of a mile from the shore.

CHAPTER V.

By the time we had anchored, the ships were filled with the natives, and surrounded by a multitude of canoes filled also with them. They brought from the shore hogs, fowls, fruit, and roots, which they exchanged for hatchets, knives, nails, beads, and cloth. Feenou and Omai having come on board, after it was light, in order to introduce me to the people of the island, I soon ac-

companied them on shore for that purpose, landing at the north part of Lefooga, a little to the right of the ships' station.

The chief conducted me to a house, or rather a hut, situated close to the sea-beach, which I had seen brought thither but a few minutes before for our reception. In this Feenou, Omai, and myself, were seated. The other chiefs and the multitude composed a circle on the outside, fronting us, and they also sat down. I was then asked, "How long I intended to stay?" On my saying, "Five days," Taipa was ordered to come and sit by me, and proclaim this to the people. He then harangued them, in a speech mostly dictated by Feenou. The purport of it, as I learned from Omai, was that they were all, both old and young, to look upon me as a friend, who intended to remain with them a few days; that, during my stay, they must not steal anything, nor molest me any other way; and that it was expected they should bring hogs, fowls, fruit, &c., to the ships, where they would receive in exchange for them such and such things which he enumerated. Soon after Taipa had finished this address to the assembly, Feenou left us. Taipa then took occasion to signify to me, that it was necessary I should make a present to the chief of the island, whose name was Earoupa. I was not unprepared for this; and gave him such articles as far exceeded his expectation. My liberality to him brought upon me demands of the same kind from two chiefs of other isles who were present and from Taipa himself. When Feenou returned, which was immediately after I had made the last of these presents, he pretended to be angry with Taipa for suffering me to give away so much; but I looked upon this as a mere *finesse*, being confident that he acted in concert with the others. He now took his seat again and ordered Earoupa to sit by him and to harangue the people as Taipa had done, and to the same purpose; dictating as before, the heads of the speech.

These ceremonies being performed, the chief, at my request, conducted me to three stagnant pools of fresh water, as he was pleased to call it; and, indeed, in one of these the water was tolerable, and the situation not inconvenient for filling our casks. After viewing the watering-place, we returned to our former station, where I found a baked hog and some yams, smoking hot, ready to be carried on board for my dinner. I invited Feenou and his friends to partake of it, and we embarked for the ship; but none but himself sat down with us at the table. After dinner I conducted them on shore; and before I returned on board, the chief gave me a fine large turtle and a quantity of yams. Our supply of provisions was copious, for in the course of the day we got, by barter alongside the ship, about twenty small hogs, besides fruit and roots. I was told that on my first landing in the morning, a man came off to the ships, and ordered every one of the natives to go on shore. Probably, this was done with a view to have the whole body of inhabitants present at the ceremony of my reception; for when that was over, multitudes of them returned again to the ships.

Next morning early, Feenou and Omai, who scarcely ever quitted the chief, and now slept on shore, came on board. The object of the visit was to require my presence upon the island. After some time I accompanied them, and, upon landing, was conducted to the same place where I had been seated the day before, where I saw a large concourse of people already assembled. I guessed that something more than ordinary was in agitation, but could not tell what, nor could Omai inform me. I had not been long seated, before near a hundred of the natives appeared in sight, and advanced, laden with yams, bread-fruit, plantains, cocoanuts, and sugar-canes. They deposited their burdens in two heaps, or piles, upon our left, being the side they came from. Soon after arrived a number of others from the right,

bearing the same kind of articles; which were collected into two piles upon that side. To these were tied two pigs and six fowls; and to those upon the left, six pigs and two turtles. Earoupa seated himself before the several articles upon the left, and another chief before those upon the right; they being, as I judged, the two chiefs who had collected them by order of Feenou, who seemed to be as implicitly obeyed here as he had been at Annamooka, and, in consequence of his commanding superiority over the chiefs of Hapaee, had laid this tax upon them for the present occasion.

As soon as this munificent collection of provisions was laid down in order, and disposed to the best advantage, the bearers of it joined the multitude, who formed a large circle round the whole. Presently after, a number of men entered this circle, or area, before us, armed with clubs made of the green branches of the cocoa-nut tree. These paraded about for a few minutes, and then retired, the one half to one side, and the other half to the other side; seating themselves before the spectators. Soon after, they successively entered the lists, and entertained us with single combats. One champion, rising up and stepping forward from one side, challenged those of the other side, by expressive gestures more than by words, to send one of their body to oppose him. If the challenge was accepted, which was generally the case, the combatants put themselves in proper attitudes, and then began the engagement, which continued till one or other owned himself conquered, or till their weapons were broken. As soon as each combat was over, the victor squatted himself down facing the chief, then rose up and retired. At the same time, some old men, who seemed to sit as judges, gave their plaudit in a few words, and the multitude, especially those on the side to which the victor belonged, celebrated the glory he had acquired, in two or three huzzas.

This entertainment was, now and then, suspended for a few minutes. During these intervals there were both wrestling and boxing matches. The first were performed in the same manner as at Otaheite; and the second differed very little from the method practised in England. But what struck us with most surprise was to see a couple of lusty wenches step forth and begin boxing without the least ceremony, and with as much art as the men. This contest, however, did not last above half-a-minute before one of them gave it up. The conquering heroine received the same applause from the spectators which they bestowed upon the successful combatants of the other sex. We expressed some dislike at this part of the entertainment; which, however, did not prevent two other females from entering the lists. They seemed to be girls of spirit, and would certainly have given each other a good drubbing, if two old women had not interfered to part them. All these combats were exhibited in the midst of at least 3000 people, and were conducted with the greatest good humour on all sides; though some of the champions, women as well as men, received blows which, doubtless, they must have felt for some time after.

As soon as these diversions were ended, the chief told me that the heaps of provisions on our right hand were a present to Omai; and that those on our left hand, being about two-thirds of the whole quantity, were given to me. He added, that I might take them on board whenever it was convenient; but that there would be no occasion to set any of our people as guards over them, as I might be assured that not a single cocoa-nut would be taken away by the natives. So it proved; for I left everything behind, and returned to the ship to dinner, carrying the chief with me; and when the provisions were removed on board in the afternoon, not a single article was missing. There was as much as loaded four boats; and I could not but be struck with the munificence of Fee-

nou, for this present far exceeded any I had ever received from any of the sovereigns of the various islands I had visited in the Pacific Ocean. I lost no time in convincing my friend that I was not insensible of his liberality; for, before he quitted my ship, I bestowed upon him such of our commodities as I guessed were most valuable in his estimation. And the return I made was so much to his satisfaction that, as soon as he got on shore, he left me still indebted to him by sending me a fresh present, consisting of two large hogs, a considerable quantity of cloth, and some yams.

Feenou had expressed a desire to see the marines go through their military exercise. As I was desirous to gratify his curiosity, I ordered them all ashore from both ships in the morning of the 20th. After they had performed various evolutions, and fired several volleys, with which the numerous body of spectators seemed well pleased, the chief entertained us in his turn with an exhibition which, as was acknowledged by us all, was performed with a dexterity and exactness far surpassing the specimen we had given of our military manœuvres. It was a kind of a dance so entirely different from anything I had ever seen, that I fear I can give no description that will convey any tolerable idea of it, to my readers. It was performed by men; and 105 persons bore their parts in it. Each of them had in his hand an instrument neatly made, shaped somewhat like a paddle, of two feet and a half in length, with a small handle and a thin blade; so that they were very light. With these instruments they made many and various flourishes, each of which was accompanied with a different attitude of the body or a different movement. At first the performers ranged themselves in three lines; and, by various evolutions, each man changed his station in such a manner that those who had been in the rear came into the front. Nor did they remain long in the same position; but these changes were made by pretty quick transitions. At one time they extended themselves in one line; they then formed into a semicircle; and, lastly, into two square columns. While this last movement was executing, one of them advanced, and performed an antic dance before me; with which the whole ended.

The musical instruments consisted of two drums, or rather two hollow logs of wood, from which some varied notes were produced by beating on them with two sticks. It did not, however, appear to me that the dancers were much assisted or directed by these sounds, but by a chorus of vocal music, in which all the performers joined at the same time. Their song was not destitute of pleasing melody; and all their corresponding motions were executed with so much skill, that the numerous body of dancers seemed to act as if they were one great machine. It was the opinion of every one of us that such a performance would have met with universal applause on a European theatre; and it so far exceeded any attempt we had made to entertain them, that they seemed to pique themselves upon the superiority they had over us. As to our musical instruments, they held none of them in the least esteem, except the drum; and even that they did not think equal to their own. Our French horns, in particular, seemed to be held in great contempt; for neither here, nor at any other of· the islands, would they pay the smallest attention to them.

In order to give them a more favourable opinion of English amusements, and to leave their minds fully impressed with the deepest sense of our superior attainments, I directed some fireworks to be got ready; and, after it was dark, played them off in the presence of Feenou, the other chiefs, and a vast concourse of their people. Some of the preparations we found damaged; but others of them were in excellent order, and succeeded so perfectly as to answer the end I had in view. Our water and sky rockets,

in particular, pleased 'and astonished them beyond all conception; and the scale was now turned in our favour. This, however, seemed only to furnish them with an additional motive to proceed to fresh exertions of their very singular dexterity; and our fireworks were no sooner ended, than a succession of dances, which Feenou had got ready for our entertainment, began. As[1] a prelude to them, a band of music, or chorus of eighteen men, seated themselves before us, in the centre of the circle composed by the numerous spectators, the area of which was to be the scene of the exhibitions. Four or five of this band had pieces of large bamboo, from three to five or six feet long, each managed by one man, who held it nearly in a vertical position, the upper end open but the other end closed by one of the joints. With this close end, the performers kept constantly striking the ground, though slowly, thus producing different notes, according to the different lengths of the instruments, but all of them of the hollow or bass sort; to counteract which, a person kept striking quickly with two sticks a piece of the same substance, split, and laid along the ground, and by that means furnishing a tone as acute as those produced by the others were grave. The rest of the band, as well as those who performed upon the bamboos, sung a slow and soft air, which so tempered the harsher notes of the above instruments, that no bystander, however accustomed to hear the most perfect and varied modulation of sweet sounds, could avoid confessing the vast power and pleasing effect of this simple harmony.

The concert having continued about a quarter of an hour, twenty women entered the circle. Most of them had upon their heads garlands of the crimson flowers of the China rose, or others; and many of them had ornamented their

---

[1] Mr Anderson's account of the night dances, being much fuller than Captain Cook's, was adopted by the editor of the original edition.

persons with leaves of trees, cut with a great deal of nicety about the edges. They made a circle round the chorus turning their faces toward it, and began by singing a soft air, to which responses were made by the chorus in the same tone ; and these were repeated alternately. All this while, the women accompanied their song with several very graceful motions of their hands toward their faces, and in other directions at the same time, making constantly a step forward, and then back again, with one foot, while the other was fixed. They then turned their faces to the assembly, sung some time, and retreated slowly in a body to that part of the circle which was opposite the hut where the principal spectators sat. After this, one of them advanced from each side, meeting and passing each other in the front, and continuing their progress round, till they came to the rest. On which, two advanced from each side, two of whom also passed each other, and returned as the former ; but the other two remained ; and to these came one, from each side, by intervals, till the whole number had again formed a circle about the chorus. Their manner of dancing was now changed to a quicker measure, in which they made a kind of half turn by leaping, and clapped their hands, and snapped their fingers, repeating some words in conjunction with the chorus. Towards the end, as the quickness of the music increased, their gestures and attitudes were varied with wonderful vigour and dexterity ; and some of their motions, perhaps, would with us be reckoned rather indecent. Though this part of the performance, most probably, was not meant to convey any wanton ideas, but merely to display the astonishing variety of their movements.

To this grand female ballet succeeded one performed by fifteen men. Some of them were old ; but their age seemed to have abated little of their agility or ardour for the dance. They were disposed in a sort of circle, divided at the front, with their faces not turned out toward the assembly, nor inward to the chorus ; but one

half of their circle faced forward as they had advanced, and the other half in a contrary direction. They sometimes sung slowly in concert with the chorus ; and while thus employed, they also made several very fine motions with their hands, but different from those made by the women, at the same time inclining the body to either side alternately, by raising one leg, which was stretched outward, and resting on the other ; the arm of the same side being also stretched fully upward. At other times, they recited sentences in a musical tone, which were answered by the chorus ; and at intervals increased the measure of the dance, by clapping the hands, and quickening the motions of the feet, which, however, were never varied. At the end, the rapidity of the music and of the dancing increased so much, that it was scarcely possible to distinguish the different movements ; though one might suppose the actors were now almost tired, as their performance had lasted near half-an-hour.

After a considerable interval, another act, as we may call it, began. Twelve men now advanced, who placed themselves in double rows fronting each other, but on opposite sides of the circle ; and on one side a man was stationed, who, as if he had been a prompter, repeated several sentences, to which the twelve new performers and the chorus replied. They then sung slowly, and afterwards danced and sung more quickly, for about a quarter of an hour, after the manner of the dancers whom they had succeeded. Soon after they had finished, nine women exhibited themselves, and sat down fronting the hut where the chief was. A man then rose, and struck the first of these women on the back with both fists joined. He proceeded, in the same manner, to the second and third ; but when he came to the fourth, whether from accident or design I cannot tell, instead of the back, he struck her on the breast. Upon this, a person rose instantly from the crowd, who brought him to the ground with a blow on the head ; and he was carried off without the least noise or disorder. But this did not save the other five women from so odd a discipline, or perhaps necessary ceremony; for a person succeeded him, who treated them in the same manner. Their disgrace did not end here; for when they danced, they had the mortification to find their performance twice disapproved of, and were obliged to repeat it. This dance did not differ much from that of the first women, except in this one circumstance, that the present set sometimes raised the body upon one leg, by a sort of double motion, and then upon the other alternately, in which attitude they kept snapping their fingers; and at the end they repeated with great agility the brisk movements in which the former group of female dancers had shown themselves so expert.

In a little time, a person entered unexpectedly, and said something in a ludicrous way about the fireworks that had been exhibited, which extorted a burst of laughter from the multitude. After this, we had a dance composed of the men who attended or had followed Fecuou. They formed a double circle (*i.e.*, one within another) of twenty-four each, round the chorus, and began a gentle soothing song, with corresponding motions of the hands and head. This lasted a considerable time, and then changed to a much quicker measure, during which they repeated sentences, either in conjunction with the chorus, or in answer to some spoken by that band. They then retreated to the back part of the circle, as the women had done, and again advanced, on each side, in a triple row, till they formed a semicircle, which was done very slowly, by inclining the body on one leg, and advancing the other a little way, as they put it down. They accompanied this with such a soft air as they had sung at the beginning; but soon changed it to repeat sentences in a harsher tone, at the same time quickening the dance very much, till they finished with a general shout and clap of the hands. The same was repeated several times; but, at last, they formed a double circle as at the beginning, danced, and repeated very quickly, and finally closed with several very dexterous transpositions of the two circles.

The entertainments of this memorable night concluded with a dance, in which the principal people present exhibited. It resembled the immediately preceding one in some respects, having the same number of performers, who began nearly in the same way; but their ending at each interval was different. For they increased their motions to a prodigious quickness, shaking their heads from shoulder to shoulder with such force, that a spectator, unaccustomed to the sight, would suppose that they ran a risk of dislocating their necks. This was attended with a smart clapping of the hands, and a kind of savage "Holla!" or shriek, not unlike what is sometimes practised in the comic dances on our European theatres. They formed the triple semicircle, as the preceding dancers had done; and a person, who advanced at the head on one side of the semicircle, began by repeating something in a truly musical recitative, which was delivered with an air so graceful as might put to the blush our most applauded performers. He was answered in the same manner by the person at the head of the opposite party. This being repeated several times, the whole body on one side joined in the responses to the whole corresponding body on the opposite side, as the semicircle advanced to the front; and they finished by singing and dancing as they had begun.

These two last dances were performed with so much spirit, and so great exactness, that they met with universal approbation. The native spectators, who, no doubt, were perfect judges whether the several performances were properly executed, could not withhold their applauses at some particular parts; and even a stranger, who never saw the diversion before, felt similar satisfaction at the same instant. For though, through the whole, the most strict concert was observed, some of the gestures were so expressive, that it might be said they spoke the language that accompanied them ; if we allow that there is any connection between motion and sound. At the same time, it should be observed that though the music of the chorus and that of the dancers corresponded, constant practice in these favourite amusements of our friends seems to have a great share in effecting the exact time they keep in their performances. For we observed, that if any of them happened accidentally to be interrupted, they never found the smallest difficulty in recovering the proper place of the dance or song. And their perfect discipline was in no instance more remarkable than in the sudden transitions they so dexterously made from the ruder exertions, and harsh sounds, to the softest arts and gentlest movements.

The place where the dances were performed was an open space amongst the trees, just by the sea, with lights at small intervals placed round the inside of the circle. The concourse of people was pretty large, though not equal to the number assembled in the forenoon when the marines exercised. At that time, some of our gentlemen guessed there might be present about 5000 persons; others thought there were more; but they who reckoned that there were fewer probably came nearer to the truth.

CHAPTER VI.

CURIOSITY on both sides being now sufficiently gratified by the exhibition of the various entertainments I have described, I began to have time to look about me. Accordingly, next day [May 21st], I took a walk into the Island of Lefooga, of which I was desirous to obtain some knowledge. I found it to be in some respects superior to Annamooka. The plantations were both more numerous and more extensive. In many places, indeed, towards the sea, especially on the east side, the country is still waste, owing perhaps to the sandy soil; as it is

much lower than Anuamooka and its surrounding isles. But towards the middle of the island the soil is better, and the marks of considerable population and of improved cultivation were very conspicuous. For we met here with very large plantations, enclosed in such a manner, that the fences running parallel to each other, form fine spacious public roads, that would appear ornamental in countries where rural conveniences have been carried to the greatest perfection. We observed large spots covered with the paper mulberry-trees; and the plantations in general were well stocked with such roots and fruits as are the natural produce of the island. To these I made some addition, by sowing the seeds of Indian corn, melons, pumpkins, and the like. At one place was a house, four or five times as large as those of the common sort, with a large area of grass before it; and I take it for granted the people resort thither on certain public occasions. Near the landing-place we saw a mount, two or three feet high, covered with gravel; and on it stood four or five small huts, in which, the natives told us, the bodies of some of their principal people had been interred.

In my walk on the 25th I happened to step into a house where a woman was dressing the eyes of a young child, who seemed blind; the eyes being much inflamed, and a thin film spread over them. The instruments she used were two slender wooden probes, with which she had brushed the eyes so as to make them bleed. It seems worth mentioning, that the natives of these islands should attempt an operation of this sort; though I entered the house too late to describe exactly how this female oculist employed the wretched tools she had to work with. I was fortunate enough to see a different operation going on in the same house, of which I can give a tolerable account. I found there another woman shaving a child's head with a shark's tooth stuck into the end of a piece of stick. I observed that she first wet the hair with a rag dipped in water, applying her instrument to that part which she had previously soaked. The operation seemed to give no pain to the child; although the hair was taken off as close as if one of our razors had been employed. Encouraged by what I now saw, I soon after tried one of these singular instruments upon myself, and found it to be an excellent succedaneum. However, the men of these islands have recourse to another contrivance when they shave their beards. The operation is performed with two shells; one of which they place under a small part of the beard, and with the other, applied above, they scrape that part off. In this manner they are able to shave very close. The process is, indeed, rather tedious, but not painful; and there are men amongst them who seem to profess this trade. It was as common, while we were here, to see our sailors go ashore to have their beards scraped off, after the fashion of Hapaee, as it was to see their chiefs come on board to be shaved by our barbers.

Finding that little or nothing of the produce of the island was now brought to the ships, I resolved to change our station, and to await Feenou's return from Vavaoo in some other convenient anchoring-place, where refreshments might still be met with. Accordingly, in the forenoon of the 26th we got under sail, and stood to the southward along the reef of the island. At half-past two in the afternoon, I hauled into a bay that lies between the south end of Lefooga and the north end of Hoolaiva, and there anchored in seventeen fathoms water. The Discovery did not get to an anchor till sunset. She had touched upon one of the shoals, but backed off again without receiving any damage. The place where we now anchored is much better sheltered than that which we had lately come from; but between the two is another anchoring station much better than either. Lefooga and Hoolaiva are divided from each other by a reef of coral rocks, which is dry at low water; so that one may walk at that time from the one to the other without wetting a foot. Some

of our gentlemen, who landed in the latter island, did not find the least mark of cultivation or habitation upon it; except a single hut, the residence of a man employed to catch fish and turtle.

At daybreak on the 27th, I made the signal to weigh; and as I intended to attempt a passage to Annamooka in my way to Tongataboo by the south-west amongst the intervening islands, I sent the master in a boat to sound before the ships. But before we could get under sail, the wind became unsettled; which made it unsafe to attempt a passage this way till we were better acquainted with it. I therefore lay fast, and made the signal for the master to return, and afterward sent him and the master of the Discovery, each in a boat, with instructions to examine the channels as far as they could, allowing themselves time to get back to the ships before the close of the day.[1]

At daybreak on the 29th, I weighed with a fine breeze at ENE., and stood to the westward, with a view to return to Annamooka by the track we had already experienced. We were followed by several sailing canoes, in one of which was the King. As soon as he got on board the Resolution, he inquired for his brother and the others who had remained with us all night. It now appeared that they had stayed without his leave, for he gave them in a very few words such a reprimand as brought tears from their eyes; and yet they were men not less than thirty years of age. He was, however, soon

---

[1] While lying here they received a visit from Poulaho, the real king of Tongataboo, who brought two fat hogs on board as a present, but which are described as not so fat as himself. He endeavoured to convince them that he and not Feenou was the king. Early in the morning of the last day of their stay, he brought a present to Captain Cook of one of their native caps, which was covered with the tail feathers of tropic birds, and highly prized even amongst themselves.

reconciled to their making a longer stay; for on quitting us he left his brother and five of his attendants on board. We had also the company of a chief, just then arrived from Tonga-taboo, whose name was Tooboueitoa. The moment he arrived he sent his canoe away, and declared that he and five more who came with him would sleep on board; so that I had now my cabin filled with visitors. This, indeed, was some inconvenience; but I bore with it more willingly, as they brought plenty of provisions with them as presents to me; for which they always had suitable returns. About 1 o'clock in the afternoon the easterly wind was succeeded by a fresh breeze at SSE. Our course now being SSW., or more southerly, we were obliged to ply to windward, and did but just fetch the north side of Footooha by 8 o'clock, where we spent the night, making short boards. The next morning we plied up to Lofanga, where, according to the information of our friends, there was anchorage. It was 1 o'clock in the afternoon before we got soundings, under the lee or north-west side, in forty fathoms water, near half-a-mile from the shore; but the bank was steep and the bottom rocky, and a chain of breakers lay to leeward. All these circumstances being against us, I stretched away for Kotoo, with the expectation of finding better anchoring ground under that island. But so much time had been spent in plying up to Lofanga, that it was dark before we reached the other; and, finding no place to anchor in, the night was spent as the preceding one.

At daybreak on the 31st, I stood for the channel which is between Kotoo and the reef of rocks that lies to the westward of it; but on drawing near I found the wind too scant to lead us through. I therefore bore up on the outside of the reef, and stretched to the SW. till near noon, when, perceiving that we made no progress to windward, and being apprehensive of losing the islands with so many of the natives on board, I tacked and stood back, intending to wait till some more favourable opportunity.

We did but just fetch in with Footooha, between which and Kotoo we spent the night under reefed topsails and foresail. The wind blew fresh, and by squalls, with rain; and we were not without apprehensions of danger. I kept the deck till midnight, when I left it to the master, with such directions as I thought would keep the ships clear of the shoals and rocks that lay round us. But after making a trip to the north, and standing back again to the south, our ship, by a small shift of the wind, fetched farther to the windward than was expected. By this means she was very near running full upon a low sandy isle, called Pootoo Pootooa, surrounded with breakers. It happened very fortunately that the people had just been ordered upon the deck, to put the ship about, and the most of them were at their stations, so that the necessary movements were not only executed with judgment, but also with alertness, and this alone saved us from destruction. The Discovery, being astern, was out of danger. Such hazardous situations are the unavoidable companions of the man who goes upon a voyage of discovery.

This circumstance frightened our passengers so much, that they expressed a strong desire to get ashore. Accordingly, as soon as daylight returned, I hoisted out a boat, and ordered the officer who commanded her, after landing them at Kotoo, to sound along the reef that spits off from that island, for anchorage. For I was full as much tired as they could be with beating about amongst the surrounding isles and shoals, and determined to get to an anchor somewhere or other if possible. While the boat was absent, we attempted to turn the ships through the channel between the sandy isle and the reef of Kotoo, in expectation of finding a moderate depth of water behind them to anchor in. But meeting with a tide or current against us, we were obliged to desist, and anchor in fifty fathoms water, with the sandy isle bearing E. by N., one mile distant. We lay here till the 4th. While in this station we were several times visited by the King, by Tooboueitoa, and by people from the neighbouring islands, who came off to trade with us, though the wind blew very fresh most of the time. The master was now sent to sound the channels between the islands that lie to the eastward; and I landed on Kotoo, to examine it, in the forenoon of the 2d [of June]. This island is scarcely accessible by boats, on account of coral reefs that surround it. It is not more than a mile and a half or two miles long, and not so broad. The NW. end of it is low, like the islands of Hapaee; but it rises suddenly in the middle, and terminates in reddish clayey cliffs, at the SE. end, about thirty feet high. The soil in that quarter is of the same sort as in the cliffs; but in the other parts it is a loose, black mould. It produces the same fruits and roots which we found at the other islands, is tolerably cultivated, but thinly inhabited. While I was walking all over it, our people were employed in cutting some grass for the cattle; and we planted some melon seeds, with which the natives seemed much pleased, and enclosed them with branches. On our return to the boat, we passed by two or three ponds of dirty water, which was more or less brackish in each of them; and saw one of their burying-places, which was much neater than those that were met with at Hapaee.

On the 4th, at seven in the morning, we weighed, and, with a fresh gale at ESE. stood away for Annamooka, where we anchored next morning nearly in the same station which we had so lately occupied. I went on shore soon after, and found the inhabitants very busy in their plantations, digging up yams to bring to market; and in the course of the day about 200 of them had assembled on the beach, and traded with as much eagerness as during our late visit. Their stock appeared to have been recruited much, though we had returned so soon; but instead of bread-fruit, which was the only article we could purchase on our first arrival,

nothing was to be seen now but yams and a few plantains. This shows the quick succession of the seasons, at least of the different vegetables produced here at the several times of the year. It appeared also that they had been very busy while we were absent in cultivating; for we now saw several large plantain fields in places which we had so lately seen lying waste. The yams were now in the greatest perfection; and we procured a good quantity in exchanges for pieces of iron. These people, in the absence of Toobou, whom we left behind us at Kotoo with Poulaho and other chiefs, seemed to be under little subordination. For we could not perceive this day that one man assumed more authority than another. Before I returned on board, I visited the several places where I had sown melon seeds, and had the mortification to find that most of them were destroyed by a small ant; but some pine-apple plants, which I had also left, were in a thriving state.

About noon next day Feenou arrived from Vavaoo. He told us that several canoes, laden with hogs and other provisions, which had sailed with him from that island, had been lost, owing to the late blowing weather; and that everybody on board them had perished. This melancholy tale did not seem to affect any of his countrymen who heard it; and as to ourselves, we were by this time too well acquainted with his character to give much credit to such a story. The truth probably was, that he had not been able to procure at Vavaoo the supplies which he expected, or, if he got any there, that he had left them at Hapaee, which lay in his way back, and where he could not but receive intelligence that Poulaho had been with us, who therefore, he knew, would as his superior have all the merit and reward of procuring them, though he had not any share of the trouble. The invention of this loss at sea was, however, well imagined. For there had lately been very blowing weather, insomuch that the King and other chiefs, who had followed us from Hapaee to Kotoo, had been left there, not caring to venture to sea when we did; but desired I might wait for them at Annamooka, which was the reason of my anchoring there this second time, and of my not proceeding directly to Tongataboo.

The following morning, Poulaho and the other chiefs who had been windbound with him arrived. I happened, at this time to be ashore in company with Feenou, who now seemed to be sensible of the impropriety of his conduct in assuming a character that did not belong to him. For he not only acknowledged Poulaho to be King of Tongataboo and the other isles, but affected to insist much on it, which no doubt was with a view to make amends for his former presumption. I left him to visit this greater man, whom I found sitting with a few people before him. But, every one hastening to pay court to him, the circle increased pretty fast. I was very desirous of observing Feenou's behaviour on this occasion; and had the most convincing proof of his inferiority, for he placed himself amongst the rest that sat before Poulaho as attendants on his majesty. He seemed at first rather abashed, as some of us were present who had been used to see him act a different part; but he soon recovered himself. Some little conversation passed between these two chiefs, which none of us understood; nor were we satisfied with Omai's interpretation of it. We were, however, by this time sufficiently undeceived as to Feenou's rank. Both he and Poulaho went on board with me to dinner; but only the latter sat at table. Feenou, having made his obeisance in the usual way, saluting his sovereign's foot with his head and hands, retired out of the cabin. The King had before told us that this would happen; and it now appeared that Feenou could not even eat nor drink in his royal presence.

At 8 o'clock next morning we weighed and steered for Tongataboo, having a gentle breeze at NE. About fourteen or fifteen sailing vessels belonging to the natives set out without us; but every one of them outrun the ships considerably. Feenou was to have taken his passage in the Resolution, but preferred his own canoe, and put two men on board to conduct us to the best anchorage. We steered S. by W. by compass. We continued the same course till 2 o'clock next morning, when, seeing some lights ahead, and not knowing whether they were on shore or on board the canoes, we hauled the wind, and made a short trip each way till daybreak. We then resumed our course to the S. by W.; and, presently after, saw several small islands before us, and Eooa and Tongataboo beyond them. We had at this time twenty-five fathoms water, over a bottom of broken coral and sand. The depth gradually decreased as we drew near the isles above mentioned, which lie ranged along the NE. side of Tongataboo. By the direction of our pilots we steered for the middle of it, and for the widest space between the small isles which we were to pass, having our boats ahead employed in sounding. We were, insensibly, drawn upon a large flat, upon which lay innumerable coral rocks, of different depths below the surface of the water. Notwithstanding all our care and attention to keep the ship clear of them, we could not prevent her from striking on one of these rocks. Nor did the Discovery, though behind us, escape any better. Fortunately neither of the ships stuck fast, nor received any damage. We could not get back without increasing the danger, as we had come in almost before the wind. Nor could we cast anchor but with the certainty of having our cables instantly cut in two by the rocks. We had no other resource but to proceed. To this, indeed, we were encouraged, not only by being told, but by seeing, that there was deeper water between us and the shore. However, that we might be better informed, the moment we found a spot where we could drop the anchor clear of rocks, we came to, and sent the masters, with the boats, to sound.

Soon after we had anchored, which was about noon, several of the inhabitants of Tongataboo came off in their canoes to the ships. These, as well as our pilots, assured us that we should find deep water farther in, and a bottom free from rocks. They were not mistaken, for about 4 o'clock the boats made the signal for having found good anchorage. Upon this we weighed and stood in till dark, and then anchored in nine fathoms, having a fine, clear, sandy bottom. During the night we had some showers of rain; but towards the morning the wind shifted to the S. and SE., and brought on fair weather. At daybreak we weighed, and, working in to the shore, met with no obstructions but such as were visible and easily avoided. While we were plying up to the harbour, to which the natives directed us, the King kept sailing round us in his canoe. There were at the same time a great many small canoes about the ships. Two of these, which could not get out of the way of his royal vessel, he run quite over, with as little concern as if they had been bits of wood. Amongst many others who came on board the Resolution was Otago, who had been so useful to me when I visited Tongataboo during my last voyage; and one Toobou, who at that time had attached himself to Captain Furneaux. Each of them brought a hog and some yams as a testimony of his friendship; and I was not wanting on my part in making a suitable return. At length, about two in the afternoon, we arrived at our intended station. It was a very snug place, formed by the shore of Tongataboo on the SE., and two small islands on the E. and NE. Here we anchored in ten fathoms water, over a bottom of oozy sand, distant from the shore one-third of a mile.

CHAPTER VII.

Soon after we had anchored, having first dined, I landed, accompanied by Omai and some of the officers. We found the King waiting for us upon the beach. He immediately conducted us to a small neat house, situated a little within the skirts of the woods, with a fine large area before it. This house, he told me, was at my service during our stay at the island, and a better situation we could not wish for.

We had not been long in the house before a pretty large circle of the natives were assembled before us and seated upon the area. A root of the "kava" plant being brought and laid down before the King, he ordered it to be split into pieces and distributed to several people of both sexes, who began the operation of chewing it; and a bowl of their favourite liquor was soon prepared. In the meantime a baked hog, and two baskets of baked yams, were produced, and afterward divided into ten portions. These portions were then given to certain people present, but how many were to share in each I could not tell. One of them, I observed, was bestowed upon the King's brother; and one remained undisposed of, which I judged was for the King himself, as it was a choice bit. The liquor was next served out, but Poulaho seemed to give no directions about it. The first cup was brought to him, which he ordered to be given to one who sat near him. The second was also brought to him, and this he kept. The third was given to me, but their manner of brewing having quenched my thirst, it became Omai's property. The rest of the liquor was distributed to different people by direction of the man who had the management of it. One of the cups being carried to the King's brother, he retired with this and with his mess of victuals. Some others also quitted the circle with their portions; and the reason was, they could neither eat nor drink in the royal presence; but there were others present of a much inferior rank of both sexes, who did both. Soon after, most of them withdrew, carrying with them what they had not eaten of their share of the feast. I observed that not a fourth part of the company had tasted either the victuals or the drink—those who partook of the former I supposed to be of the King's household. The servants, who distributed the baked meat and the "kava," always delivered it out of their hand sitting, not only to the King, but to every other person. It is worthy of remark, though this was the first time of our landing, and a great many people were present who had never seen us before, yet no one was troublesome; but the greatest good order was preserved throughout the whole assembly.

Before I returned on board I went in search of a watering-place, and was conducted to some ponds, or, rather, holes, containing fresh water, as they were pleased to call it. The contents of one of these, indeed, were tolerable; but it was at some distance inland, and the supply to be got from it was very inconsiderable. Being informed that the little island of Pangimodoo, near which the ships lay, could better furnish this necessary article, I went over to it next morning, and was so fortunate as to find there a small pool that had rather fresher water than any we had met with amongst these islands. The pool being very dirty, I ordered it to be cleaned, and here it was that we watered the ships. As I intended to make some stay at Tongataboo, we pitched a tent in the forenoon just by the house which Poulaho had assigned for our use. The horses, cattle, and sheep, were afterwards landed, and a party of marines, with their officer, stationed there as a guard. The observatory was then set up at a small distance from the other tent, and Mr King resided on shore to attend the observations, and to superintend the several operations necessary to be conducted there; for the sails were carried thither to be repaired; a party was employed in cutting wood for fuel and plank for the use of the ships; and the gunners of both were ordered to remain upon the spot to conduct the traffic with the natives, who thronged from every part of the island with hogs, yams, cocoa-nuts, and other articles of their produce. In a short time our land-post was like a fair, and the ships were so crowded with visitors that we had hardly room to stir upon the decks. [On hearing that there were other great men on the island whom they had not seen, with some little difficulty they were introduced to Marecwagee and old Toobou, whom they entertained for an hour with a performance on two French horns and a drum. This visit old Toobou returned next morning by coming on board ship, when he received a considerable present from Captain Clerke.]

Toward noon [on the 4th] Poulaho returned from the place where we had left him two days before, and brought with him his son, a youth about twelve years of age. I had his company at dinner, but the son, though present, was not allowed to sit down with him. It was very convenient to have him for my guest; for when he was present, which was generally the case while we stayed here, every other native was excluded from the table, and but few of them would remain in the cabin. Whereas, if by chance it happened that neither he nor Feenou was on board, the inferior chiefs would be very importunate to be of our dining party, or to be admitted into the cabin at that time; and then we were so crowded that we could not sit down to a meal with any satisfaction. The King was very soon reconciled to our manner of cookery. But still I believe he dined thus frequently with me more for the sake of what we gave him to drink than for what we set before him to eat. For he had taken a liking to our wine, could empty his bottle as well as most men, and was as cheerful over it. He now fixed his residence at the house, or "malaee," by our tent; and there he entertained our people this evening with a dance. To the surprise of everybody the unwieldy Poulaho endeavoured to vie with others in that active amusement.

In the morning of the 15th I received a message from old Toobou that he wanted to see me ashore.

Accordingly Omai and I went to wait upon him. We found him, like an ancient patriarch, seated under the shade of a tree, with a large piece of a cloth made in the island spread out at full length before him, and a number of respectable-looking people sitting round it. He desired us to place ourselves by him, and then he told Omai that the cloth, together with a piece of red feathers and about a dozen cocoa-nuts, were his present to me. I thanked him for the favour, and desired he would go on board with me, as I had nothing on shore to give him in return. Omai now left me, being sent for by Poulaho; and soon after Feenou came and acquainted me that young Fatrafaihe, Poulaho's son, desired to see me. I obeyed the summons, and found the prince and Omai sitting under a large canopy of the finer sort of cloth, with a piece of the coarser sort spread under them and before them that was seventy-six yards long and seven and a half broad. On one side was a large old boar, and on the other side a heap of cocoa-nuts. A number of people were seated round the cloth, and amongst them I observed Mareewagee and others of the first rank. I was desired to sit down by the prince, and then Omai informed me that he had been instructed by the King to tell me that, as he and I were friends, he hoped his son might be joined in this friendship, and that, as a token of my consent, I would accept of his present. I very readily agreed to the proposal; and it being now dinner-time, I invited them all on board.

Accordingly the young prince, Mareewagee, old Toobou, three or four inferior chiefs, and two respectable old ladies of the first rank, accompanied me. Mareewagee was dressed in a new piece of cloth, on the skirts of which were fixed six pretty large patches of red feathers. This dress seemed to have been made on purpose for this visit, for as soon as he got on board he put it off and presented it to me, having, I guess, heard that it would be acceptable on account of the feathers. Every one of my visitors received from me such presents as I had reason to believe they were highly satisfied with. When dinner came upon table, not one of them would sit down, or eat a bit of anything that was served up. On expressing my surprise at this, they were all "taboo," as they said, which word has a very comprehensive meaning, but in general signifies that a thing is forbidden. Why they were laid under such restraints at present was not explained. Dinner being over, and having gratified their curiosity by showing to them every part of the ship, I then conducted them ashore. As soon as the boat reached the beach, Feenou and some others instantly stepped out. Young Fatrafaihe following them, was called back by Marcewagee, who now paid the heir-apparent the same obeisance, and in the same manner, that I had seen it paid to the King. And when old Toobou and one of the old ladies had shown him the same marks of respect, he was suffered to land. This ceremony being over, the old people stepped from my boat into a canoe that was waiting to carry them to their place of abode.

I was not sorry to be present on this occasion, as I was thus furnished with the most unequivocal proofs of the supreme dignity of Poulaho and his son over the other principal chiefs. Indeed by this time I had acquired some certain information about the relative situations of the several great men whose names have been so often mentioned. I now knew that Mareewagee and old Toobou were brothers. Both of them were men of great property in the island, and seemed to be in high estimation with the people; the former, in particular, had the very honourable appellation given to him, by everybody, of "Motooa Tonga;" that is to say, Father of Tonga, or of his country. The nature of his relationship to the King was also no longer a secret to us; for we now understood that he was his father-in-law, Poulaho having married one of his daughters, by whom he had this son; so that Mareewagee was the prince's grandfather. Peulaho's appearance having satisfied us that we had been under a mistake in considering Feenou as the sovereign of these islands, we had been at first much puzzled about his real rank; but that was by this time ascertained, Feenou was one of Mareewagee's sons, and Tooboueitoa was another.

On my landing I found the King in the house adjoining to our tent, along with our people who resided on shore. The moment I got to him, he bestowed upon me a present of a large hog and a quantity of yams. About the dusk of the evening a number of men came, and, having sat down in a round group, began to sing in concert with the music of bamboo drums, which were placed in the centre. There were three long ones and two short. With these they struck the ground endwise, as before described.[1] There were two others which lay on the ground side by side, and one of them was split or shivered; on these a man kept beating with two small sticks. They sung three songs while I stayed, and I was told that after I left them the entertainment lasted till 10 o'clock. They burnt the leaves of the "wharra" palm for a light; which is the only thing I ever saw them make use of for this purpose.

On the 16th in the morning, after visiting the several works now carrying on ashore, Mr Gore and I took a walk into the country; in the course of which nothing remarkable appeared but our having opportunities of seeing the whole process of making cloth, which is the principal manufacture of these islands, as well as of many others in this ocean. In the narrative of my first voyage, a minute description is given of these operations as performed at Otaheite; but the process here differing in some particulars, it may be worth while to give the following account of it:

The manufacturers, who are females, take the slender stalks or trunks of the paper-mulberry, which they cultivate for that purpose, and which seldom grows more than six or seven feet in height and about four fingers in thickness. From these they strip the bark, and scrape off the outer rind with a mussel-shell. The bark is then rolled up to take off the convexity which it had round the stalk, and macerated in water for some time (they say a night). After this, it is laid across the trunk of a small tree squared, and beaten with a square wooden instrument, about a foot long, full of coarse grooves on all sides; but sometimes with one that is plain. According to the size of the bark, a piece is soon produced; but the operation is often repeated by another hand, or it is folded several times and beaten longer, which seems rather intended to close than to divide its texture. When this is sufficiently effected, it is spread out to dry; the pieces being from four to six or more feet in length, and half as broad. They are then given to another person, who joins the pieces, by smearing part of them over with the viscous juice of a berry called "to-oo," which serves as a glue. Having been thus lengthened, they are laid over a large piece of wood, with a kind of stamp, made of a fibrous substance pretty closely interwoven, placed beneath. They then take a bit of cloth, and dip it in a juice expressed from the bark of a tree called "kokka," which they rub briskly upon the piece that is making. This at once leaves a dull brown colour and a dry gloss upon its surface; the stamp at the same time making a slight impression, that answers no other purpose that I could see but to make the several pieces that are glued together stick a little more firmly. In this manner they proceed, joining and staining by degrees, till they produce a piece of cloth of such length and breadth as they want; generally leaving a border of a foot broad at the sides, and longer at the ends, unstained. Throughout the whole, if any parts of the original pieces are too thin, or have holes, which is often the case, they glue spare bits

---

[1] In the account of the festivities at Hapaee, *ante*, Chapter V.

upon them till they become of an equal thickness. When they want to produce a black colour, they mix the soot procured from an oily nut called "dooe dooe," with the juice of the "kokka," in different quantities, according to the proposed depth of the tinge. They say that the black sort of cloth, which is most commonly glazed, makes a cold dress, but the other a warm one; and, to obtain strength in both they are always careful to join the small pieces length-wise, which makes it impossible to tear the cloth in any direction but one.

On our return from the country we met with Feenou, and took him and another young chief on board to dinner. When our fare was set upon the table, neither of them would eat a bit; saying that they were "taboo avy." But after inquiring how the victuals had been dressed, having found that no "avy" (water) had been used in cooking a pig and some yams, they both sat down and made a very hearty meal; and, on being assured that there was no water in the wine, they drank of it also. From this we conjectured that on some account or another they were at this time forbidden to use water; or, which was more probable, they did not like the water we made use of, it being taken up out of one of their bathing places. This was not the only time of our meeting with people that were "taboo avy;" but for what reason we never could tell with any degree of certainty.

Next day, the 17th, was fixed upon by Marcewagee for giving a grand "Haiva," or entertainment, to which we were all invited. For this purpose a large space had been cleared before the temporary hut of this chief near our post, as an area where the per-formances were to be exhibited. In the morning great multitudes of the natives came in from the country, every one carrying a pole about six feet long upon his shoulder; and at each end of every pole a yam was suspended. These yams and poles were deposited on each side of the area, so as to form two large heaps, decorated with different sorts of small fish, and piled up to the greatest advantage. They were Mareewagee's present to Captain Clerke and me; and it was hard to say whether the wood for fuel or the yams for food were of most value to us. As for the fish, they might serve to please the sight, but were very offensive to the smell; part of them having been kept two or three days, to be presented to us on this occasion. Everything being thus prepared, about 11 o'clock they began to exhibit various dances, which they call "mai." The music[1] consisted at first of seventy men as a chorus, who sat down; and amidst them were placed three instruments which we called drums, though very unlike them. They are large cylindrical pieces of wood, or trunks of trees, from three to four feet long, some twice as thick as an ordinary-sized man, and some smaller, hol-lowed entirely out, but close at both ends, and open only by a chink about three inches broad running almost the whole length of the drums; by which opening the rest of the wood is certainly hollowed, though the opera-tion must be difficult. This instru-ment is called "naffa;" and with the chink turned toward them, they sit and beat strongly upon it with two cylindrical pieces of hard wood about a foot long and as thick as the wrist; by which means they produce a rude though loud and powerful sound. They vary the strength and rate of their beating at different parts of the dance; and also change the tones, by beating in the middle or near the end of their drum.

The first dance consisted of four ranks of twenty-four men each, hold-ing in their hands a little, thin, light wooden instrument, above two feet long, and in shape not unlike a small oblong paddle. With these, which

---

[1] Mr Anderson's description of the entertainments of this day, being much fuller than Captain Cook's, has been adopted, as on a former occa-sion.

are called "pagge," they made a great many different motions; such as pointing them towards the ground on one side, at the same time inclining their bodies that way, from which they were shifted to the opposite side in the same manner; then passing them quickly from one hand to the other, and twirling them about very dexterously, with a variety of other manœuvres, all which were accompanied by corresponding attitudes of the body. Their motions were at first slow, but quickened as the drums beat faster; and they recited sentences in a musical tone the whole time, which were answered by the chorus; but at the end of a short space they all joined, and finished with a shout. After ceasing about two or three minutes, they began as before, and continued, with short intervals, above a quarter of an hour, when, the rear rank dividing, shifted themselves very slowly round each end, and meeting in the front, formed the first rank, the whole number continuing to recite the sentences as before. The other ranks did the same successively, till that which at first was the front became the rear; and the evolution continued in the same manner till the last rank regained its first situation. They then began a much quicker dance (though slow at first), and sang for about ten minutes, when the whole body divided into two parts, retreated a little, and then approached, forming a sort of circular figure, which finished the dance, the drums being removed, and the chorus going off the field at the same time.

The second dance had only two drums, with forty men for a chorus; and the dancers, or rather actors, consisted of two ranks, the foremost having seventeen and the other fifteen persons. Feenou was at their head, or in the middle of the front rank, which is the principal place in these cases. They danced and recited sentences, with some very short intervals, for about half-an-hour, sometimes quickly, sometimes more slowly, but with such a degree of exactness as if all the motions were made by one man, which did them great credit. Near the close, the back rank divided, came round, and took the place of the front, which again resumed its situation, as in the first dance; and when they finished, the drums and chorus, as before, went off.

Three drums (which at least took two, and sometimes three, men to carry them) were now brought in, and seventy men sat down as a chorus to the third dance. This consisted of two ranks of sixteen persons each, with young Toobou at their head, who was richly ornamented with a sort of garment covered with red feathers. These danced, sang, and twirled the "pagge" as before, but in general much quicker, and performed so well that they had the constant applauses of the spectators. A motion that met with particular approbation was one in which they held the face aside as if ashamed, and the "pagge" before it. The back rank closed before the front one, and that again resumed its place, as in the two former dances; but then they began again, formed a triple row, divided, retreated to each end of the area, and left the greatest part of the ground clear. At that instant two men entered very hastily, and exercised the clubs which they use in battle. They did this by first twirling them in their hands and making circular strokes before them with great force and quickness, but so skilfully managed that though standing quite close they never interfered. They shifted their clubs from hand to hand with great dexterity; and after continuing a little time, kneeled and made different motions, tossing the clubs up in the air, which they caught as they fell, and then went off as hastily as they entered. Their heads were covered with pieces of white cloth tied at the crown almost like a nightcap, with a wreath of foliage round the forehead; but they had only very small pieces of white cloth tied about their waists, probably that they might be cool and free from every encumbrance or weight. A person with a spear, dressed like the former, then came in, and in the same hasty manner, looking about eagerly as if in search of somebody to throw it at. He then ran hastily to one side of the crowd in the front, and put himself in a threatening attitude, as if he meant to strike with his spear at one of them, bending the knee a little, and trembling as it were with rage. He continued in this manner only a few seconds, when he moved to the other side, and having stood in the same posture there for the same short time, retreated from the ground as fast as when he made his appearance. The dancers, who had divided into two parties, kept repeating something slowly all this while, and now advanced and joined again, ending with universal applause. It should seem that this dance was considered as one of their capital performances, if we might judge from some of the principal people being engaged in it. For one of the drums was beat by Futtafaihe, the brother of Poulaho; another by Feenou; and the third, which did not belong to the chorus, by Mareewagee himself, at the entrance of his hut.

The last dance had forty men and two drums as a chorus. It consisted of sixty men who had not danced before, disposed in three rows, having twenty-four in front. But before they began we were entertained with a pretty long preliminary harangue, in which the whole body made responses to a single person who spoke. They recited sentences (perhaps verses) alternately with the chorus, and made many motions with the "pagge," in a very brisk mode, which were all applauded with "mareeai" and "fy-fogge," words expressing two different degrees of praise. They divided into two bodies, with their backs to each other, formed again, shifted their ranks as in the other dances, divided and retreated, making room for two champions, who exercised their clubs as before; and after them two others, the dancers all the time reciting slowly in turn with the chorus, after which they advanced and finished These dances, if they can properly be called so, lasted from 11 till near 3

o'clock; and though they were doubtless intended particularly either in honour of us, or to show a specimen of their dexterity, vast numbers of their own people attended as spectators. Their numbers could not be computed exactly, on account of the inequality of the ground; but by reckoning the inner circle, and the number in depth, which was between twenty and thirty in many places, we supposed that there must be near 4000. At the same time there were round the trading place at the tent and straggling about, at least as many more; and some of us computed that at this time there were not less than 10,000 or 12,000 people in our neighbourhood—that is, within the compass of a quarter of a mile,—drawn together for the most part by mere curiosity.

At night we were entertained with the "bomai," or night dances, on a space before Feenou's temporary habitation. They lasted about three hours, in which time we had about twelve of them performed, much after the same manner as those at Hapaee. But in two, that were performed by women, a number of men came and formed a circle within theirs; and in another, consisting of twenty-four men, there were a number of motions with the hands that we had not seen before, and were highly applauded. The music was also once changed in the course of the night, and in one of the dances Feenou appeared, at the head of fifty men who had performed at Hapaee, and he was well dressed with linen, a large piece of gauze, and some little pictures hung round his neck. But it was evident, after the diversions were closed, that we had put these poor people, or rather that they had put themselves, to much inconvenience; for being drawn together on this uninhabited part of their island, numbers of them were obliged to lie down and sleep under the bushes, by the side of a tree, or of a canoe—nay, many either lay down in the open air, which they are not fond of, or walked about all the night. The whole of this entertainment was conducted with far better order than could have been expected in so large an assembly. Amongst such a multitude there must be a number of ill-disposed people, and we hourly experienced it. All our care and attention did not prevent their plundering us in every quarter, and that in the most daring and insolent manner. There was hardly anything that they did not attempt to steal; and yet, as the crowd was always so great, I would not allow the sentries to fire, lest the innocent should suffer for the guilty. They once, at noon-day, ventured to aim at taking an anchor from off the Discovery's bows, and they would certainly have suc-ceeded if the fluke had not hooked one of the chain plates in lowering down the ship's side, from which they could not disengage it by hand, and tackles were things they were unacquainted with. The only act of violence they were guilty of was the breaking the shoulder-bone of one of our goats, so that she died soon after. This loss fell upon themselves, as she was one of those that I intended to leave upon the island; but of this the person who did it was ignorant.

Early in the morning of the 18th, an incident happened that strongly marked one of their customs. A man got out of a canoe into the quarter-gallery of the Resolution, and stole from thence a pewter basin. He was discovered, pursued, and brought alongside the ship. On this occasion three old women who were in the canoe made loud lamentations over the prisoner, beating their breasts and faces in a most violent manner with the inside of their fists, and all this was done without shedding a tear. This mode of expressing grief is what occasions the mark which almost all this people bear on the face over the cheek-bones. The repeated blows which they inflict upon this part abrade the skin, and make even the blood flow out in a considerable quantity; and when the wounds are recent they look as if a hollow circle had been burned in. On many occa-sions they actually cut this part of the face with an instrument, in the same manner as the people of Otaheite cut their heads.

This day I bestowed on Mareewa-gee some presents in return for those we had received from him the day be-fore; and as the entertainments which he had then exhibited for our amuse-ment called upon us to make some exhibition in our way, I ordered the party of marines to go through their exercise on the spot where his dances had been performed, and in the even-ing played off some fireworks at the same place. Poulaho,· with all the principal chiefs, and a great number of people of all denominations, were present. The platoon firing, which was executed tolerably well, seemed to give them pleasure; but they were lost in astonishment when they be-held our water rockets. They paid but little attention to the fife and drum, or French horns, that played during the intervals. The King sat behind everybody, because no one is allowed to sit behind him, and, that his view might not be obstructed, nobody sat immediately before him; but a lane, as it were, was made by the people from him quite down to the space allotted for the fireworks.

In expectation of this evening show, the circle of natives about our tent being pretty large, they engaged the greatest part of the afternoon in box-ing and wrestling; the first of which exercises they call "fangatooa" and the second "fooboo." When any of them chooses to wrestle, he gets up from one side of the ring, and crosses the ground in a sort of measured pace, clapping smartly on the elbow joint of one arm, which is bent, and pro-duces a hollow sound; that is reck-oned the challenge. If no person comes out from the opposite side to engage him, he returns in the same manner and sits down; but sometimes stands clapping in the midst of the ground to provoke some one to come out. If an opponent appear, they come together with marks of the greatest good-nature, generally smil-ing, and taking time to adjust the piece of cloth which is fastened round the waist.   They then lay hold of each other by this girdle, with a hand on each side; and he who succeeds in drawing his antagonist to him, immediately tries to lift him upon his breast and throw him upon his back; and if he be able to turn round with him two or three times in that position before he throws him, his dexterity never fails of procuring plaudits from the spectators.   If they be more equally matched, they close soon, and endeavour to throw each other by entwining their legs, or lifting each other from the ground, in which struggles they show a prodigious exertion of strength, every muscle, as it were, being ready to burst with straining.   When one is thrown, he immediately quits the field; but the victor sits down for a few seconds, then gets up and goes to the side he came from, who proclaim the victory aloud, in a sentence delivered slowly and in a musical cadence.   After sitting a short space, he rises again and challenges, when sometimes several antagonists make their appearance; but he has the privilege of choosing which of them he pleases to wrestle with, and has likewise the preference of challenging again, if he should throw his adversary, until he himself be vanquished; and then the opposite side sing the song of victory in favour of their champion.   It also often happens that five or six rise from each side and challenge together, in which case it is common to see three or four couple engaged on the field at once.   But it is astonishing to see what temper they preserve in this exercise, for we observed no instances of their leaving the spot with the least displeasure in their countenances.   When they find that they are so equally matched as not to be likely to throw each other, they leave off by mutual consent.   And if the fall of one is not fair, or if it does not appear very clearly who has had the advantage, both sides sing the victory, and then they engage again. But no person who has been vanquished can engage with his conqueror a second time.

The boxers advance sideways, changing the side at every pace, with one arm stretched fully out before, the other behind, and holding a piece of cord in one hand, which they wrap firmly about it when they find an antagonist, or else have done so before they enter.   This I imagine they do to prevent dislocation of the hand or fingers.   Their blows are directed chiefly to the head, but sometimes to the sides, and are dealt out with great activity.   They shift sides, and box equally well with both hands.   But one of their favourite and most dexterous blows is to turn round on their heel just as they have struck their antagonist, and to give him another very smart one with the other hand backward.   The boxing matches seldom last long, and the parties either leave off together, or one acknowledges his being beaten.   But they never sing the song of victory in these cases, unless one strikes his adversary to the ground, which shows, that of the two, wrestling is their most approved diversion.   Not only boys engage in both the exercises, but frequently little girls box very obstinately for a short time.   In all which cases it does not appear that they ever consider it as the smallest disgrace to be vanquished; and the person overcome sits down with as much indifference as if he had never entered the lists.   Some of our people ventured to contend with them in both exercises, but were always worsted, except in a few instances, where it appeared that the fear they were in of offending us contributed more to the victory than the superiority of the person they engaged.

The cattle which we had brought, and which were all on shore, however carefully guarded, I was sensible, ran no small risk, when I considered the thievish disposition of many of the natives, and their dexterity in appropriating to themselves by stealth what they saw no prospect of obtaining by fair means.   For this reason I thought it prudent to declare my intention of leaving behind me some of our animals, and even to make a distribution of them previously to my departure. With this view, in the evening of the 19th, I assembled all the chiefs before our house, and my intended presents to them were marked out. To Poulaho, the King, I gave a young English bull and cow; to Mareewagee, a Cape ram and two ewes; and to Feenou a horse and a mare. As my design to make such a distribution had been made known the day before, most of the people in the neighbourhood were then present. I instructed Omai to tell them that there were no such animals within many mouths' sail of their island; that we had brought them for their use from that immense distance, at a vast trouble and expense; that therefore they must be careful not to kill any of them till they had multiplied to a numerous race; and lastly, that they and their children ought to remember that they had received them from the men of "Britane." He also explained to them their several uses, and what else was necessary for them to know, or rather as far as he knew; for Omai was not very well versed in such things himself. As I intended that the above presents should remain with the other cattle till we were ready to sail, I desired each of the chiefs to send a man or two to look after their respective animals along with my people, in order that they might be better acquainted with them, and with the manner of treating them. The King and Feenou did so, but neither Mareewagee, nor any other person for him, took the least notice of the sheep afterwards; nor did old Toobou attend at this meeting, though he was invited, and was in the neighbourhood. I had meant to give him the goats, viz., a ram and two ewes, which, as he was so indifferent about them, I added to the King's share.

It soon appeared that some were dissatisfied with this allotment of our animals; for early next morning one of our kids and two turkey cocks were missing. I could not be so simple as to suppose that this was merely an accidental loss; and I was determined to have them again. The first step I took was to seize on three canoes that happened to be alongside the ships. I then went ashore, and having found the King, his brother, Feenou, and some other chiefs, in the house that we occupied, I immediately put a guard over them, and gave them to understand that they must remain under restraint till not only the kid and the turkeys, but the other things that had been stolen from us, at different times, were restored. They concealed, as well as they could, their feelings on finding themselves prisoners; and having assured me that everything should be restored as I desired, sat down to drink their "kava," seemingly much at their ease. It was not long before an axe and an iron wedge were brought to me. In the meantime some armed natives began to gather behind the house; but on a part of our guard marching against them they dispersed, and I advised the chiefs to give orders that no more should appear. Such orders were accordingly given by them, and they were obeyed. On asking them to go aboard with me to dinner, they readily consented. But some having afterward objected to the King's going, he instantly rose up and declared he would be the first man. Accordingly we came on board. I kept them there till near 4 o'clock, when I conducted them ashore, and soon after the kid and one of the turkey cocks were brought back. The other, they said, should be restored the next morning. I believed this would happen, and released both them and the canoes.

After the chiefs had left us, I walked out with Omai to observe how the people about us fared, for this was the time of their meals. I found that in general they were at short commons. Nor is this to be wondered at, since most of the yams and other provisions which they brought with them were sold to us; and they never thought of returning to their own habitations while they could find any sort of subsistence in our neighbourhood. Our station was upon an uncultivated point of land, so that there were none of the islanders who, properly, resided within half-a-mile of us. But even at this distance, the multitude of strangers being so great, one might have expected that every house would have been much crowded. It was quite otherwise. The families residing there were as much left to themselves as if there had not been a supernumerary visitor near them. All the strangers lived in little temporary sheds, or under trees and bushes; and the cocoa-trees were stripped of their branches to erect habitations for the chiefs. In this walk we met with about half-a-dozen women in one place at supper. Two of the company, I observed, being fed by the others, on our asking the reason they said "taboo mattee." On further inquiry we found that one of them had two months before washed the dead corpse of a chief, and that on this account she was not to handle any food for five months. The other had performed the same office to the corpse of another person of inferior rank, and was now under the same restriction, but not for so long a time. At another place hard by we saw another woman fed, and we learned that she had assisted in washing the corpse of the above-mentioned chief.

Early the next morning the King came on board to invite me to an entertainment which he proposed to give the same day. He had already been under the barber's hands, his head being all besmeared with red pigment in order to redden his hair, which was naturally of a dark brown colour. After breakfast I attended him to the shore, and we found his people very busy, in two places in the front of our area, fixing in an upright and square position, thus [⠶], four very long posts near two feet from each other. The space between the posts was afterwards filled up with yams, and as they went on filling it, they fastened pieces of sticks across from post to post at the distance of about every four feet, to prevent the posts from separating by the weight of the enclosed yams, and also to get up by. When the yams had reached the top of the first posts, they fastened others to them, and so continued till each pile was the height of thirty feet or upwards. On the top of one they placed two baked hogs, and on the top of the other a living one; and another they tied by the legs halfway up. It was matter of curiosity to observe with what facility and despatch these two piles were raised. Had our seamen been ordered to execute such a work, they would have sworn that it could not be performed without carpenters; and the carpenters would have called to their aid a dozen different sorts of tools, and have expended at least a hundredweight of nails; and after all it would have employed them as many days as it did these people hours. But seamen, like most other amphibious animals, are always the most helpless on land. After they had completed these two piles, they made several other heaps of yams and bread-fruit on each side of the area, to which were added a turtle and a large quantity of excellent fish. All this, with a piece of cloth, a mat, and some red feathers, was the King's present to me; and he seemed to pique himself on exceeding, as he really did, Feenou's liberality which I experienced at Hapaee.

About 1 o'clock they began the "mai," or dances, the first of which was almost a copy of the first that was exhibited at Mareewagee's entertainment. The second was conducted by Captain Furneaux's Toobou, who, as we mentioned, had also danced there; and in this four or five women were introduced, who went through the several parts with as much exactness as the men. Towards the end, the performers divided to leave room for two champions, who exercised their clubs, as described on a former occasion. And in the third dance, which was the last now presented, two more men with their clubs displayed their dexterity. The dances were succeeded by wrestling and boxing, and one man entered the lists with a sort of club made from the stem of a cocoa-leaf, which is firm and heavy, but could find no antagonist to engage him at so rough a sport. At night we had the "bomai" repeated, in which Poulaho himself danced, dressed in English manufacture. But neither these nor the dances in the daytime were so considerable, nor carried on with so much spirit, as Feenou's or Mareewagee's; and therefore there is less occasion to be more particular in our description of them.

In order to be present the whole time, I dined ashore. The King sat down with us, but he neither ate nor drank. I found that this was owing to the presence of a female whom, at his desire, I had admitted to the dining party, and who, as we afterwards understood, had superior rank to himself. As soon as this great personage had dined, she stepped up to the King, who put his hands to her feet, and then she retired. He immediately dipped his fingers into a glass of wine, and then received the obeisance of all her followers. This was the single instance we ever observed of his paying this mark of reverence to any person. At the King's desire I ordered some fireworks to be played off in the evening, but unfortunately being damaged, this exhibition did not answer expectation.

———

CHAPTER VIII.

As no more entertainments were to be expected on either side, and the curiosity of the populace was by this time pretty well satisfied, on the day after Poulaho's "Haiva," most of them left us. We still, however, had thieves about us; and, encouraged by the negligence of our own people, we had continual instances of their depredations. Some of the officers belonging to both ships, who had made an excursion into the interior parts of the island without my leave, and indeed without my knowledge, returned this evening, after an absence of two days. They had taken with them their muskets, with the necessary ammunition, and several small articles of the favourite commodities;

all which the natives had the dexterity to steal from them in the course of their expedition. This affair was likely to be attended with inconvenient consequences. For our plundered travellers, upon their return, without consulting me, employed Omai to complain to the King of the treatment they had met with. He, not knowing what step I should take, and, from what had already happened, fearing lest I might lay him again under restraint, went off early the next morning. His example was followed by Feenou; so that we had not a chief of any authority remaining in our neighbourhood. I was very much displeased at this, and reprimanded Omai for having presumed to meddle. This reprimand put him upon his metal to bring his friend Feenou back; and he succeeded in the negotiation, having this powerful argument to urge, that he might depend upon my using no violent measures to oblige the natives to restore what had been taken from the gentlemen. Feenou, trusting to this declaration, returned toward the evening; and, encouraged by his reception, Poulaho favoured us with his company the day after.

Both these chiefs, upon this occasion, very justly observed to me that if any of my people at any time wanted to go into the country, they ought to be acquainted with it; in which case they would send proper people along with them, and then they would be answerable for their safety. And I am convinced from experience that, by taking this very reasonable precaution, a man and his property may be as safe among these islanders as in other parts of the more civilised world. Though I gave myself no trouble about the recovery of the things stolen upon this occasion, most of them, through Feenou's interposition, were recovered, except one musket and a few other articles of inferior value. By this time also we had recovered the turkey cock and most of the tools and other matters that had been stolen from our workmen. We had now recruited the ships with wood and water; we had finished the repairs of our sails; and had little more to expect from the inhabitants of the produce of their island. However, as an eclipse of the sun was to happen upon the 5th of the next month, I resolved to defer sailing till that time had elapsed, in order to have a chance of observing it. Having therefore some days of leisure before me, a party of us, accompanied by Poulaho, set out early next morning in a boat, for Mooa, the village where he and the other great men usually reside. As we rowed up the inlet, we met with fourteen canoes fishing in company, in one of which was Poulaho's son. In each canoe was a triangular net, extended between two poles, at the lower end of which was a cod[1] to receive and secure the fish. They had already caught some fine mullets, and they put about a dozen into our boat. I desired to see their method of fishing, which they readily complied with. A shoal of fish was supposed to be upon one of the banks, which they instantly enclosed in a long net like a seine or set-net. This the fishers, one getting into the water out of each boat, surrounded with the triangular nets in their hands; with which they scooped the fish out of the seine, or caught them as they attempted to leap over it. They showed us the whole process of this operation (which seemed to be a sure one), by throwing in some of the fish they had already caught, for at this time there happened to be none upon the bank that was enclosed.

Leaving the prince and his fishing party, we proceeded to the bottom of the bay, and landed where we had done before on our fruitless errand to see Mareewagee. As soon as we got on shore, the King desired Omai to tell me that I need be under no apprehensions about the boat or anything in her, for not a single article would be touched by any one; and we afterward found this to be the case. We were immediately conducted to one of Poulaho's houses not far off,

and near the public one, or "malaee," in which we had been, when we first visited Mooa. This, though pretty large, seemed to be his private habitation, and was situated within a plantation. The King took his seat at one end of the house, and the people who came to visit him sat down, as they arrived, in a semicircle at the other end. The first thing done was to prepare a bowl of "kava," and to order some yams to be baked for us. While these were getting ready, some of us, accompanied by a few of the King's attendants, and Omai as our interpreter, walked out to take a view of a "fiatooka," or burying-place, which we had observed to be almost close by the house, and was much more extensive, and seemingly of more consequence, than any we had seen at the other islands. We were told that it belonged to the King. It consisted of three pretty large houses, situated upon a rising ground, or rather just by the brink of it, with a small one at some distance, all ranged longitudinally. The middle house of the three first was by much the largest, and placed in a square, twenty-four paces by twenty-eight, raised about three feet. The other houses were placed on little mounts raised artificially to the same height. The floors of these houses, as also the tops of the mounts round them, were covered with loose, fine pebbles, and the whole was enclosed by large flat stones of hard coral rock, properly hewn, placed on their edges; one of which stones measured twelve feet in length, two in breadth, and above one in thickness. One of the houses, contrary to what we had seen before, was open on one side; and within it were two rude wooden busts of men, one near the entrance and the other farther in. On inquiring of the natives who had followed us to the ground, but durst not enter here, what these images were intended for, they made us as sensible as we could wish, that they were merely memorials of some chiefs who had been buried there, and not the representations of any deity. Such monuments,

---

[1] A bag, or pocket.

it should seem, are seldom raised; for these had probably been erected several ages ago. We were told that the dead had been buried in each of these houses; but no marks of this appeared. In one of them was the carved head of an Otaheite canoe, which had been driven ashore on their coast, and deposited here. At the foot of the rising ground was a large area or grass plot, with different trees planted about it; amongst which were several of those called "etoa," very large. These, as they resemble the cypress, had a fine effect in such a place. There was also a row of low palms near one of the houses, and behind it a ditch in which lay a great number of old baskets.

After dinner, or rather after we had refreshed ourselves with some provisions which we had brought with us from our ship, we made an excursion into the country, taking a pretty large circuit, attended by one of the King's ministers. Our train was not great, as he would not suffer the rabble to follow us. He also obliged all those whom we met upon our progress to sit down till we had passed; which is a mark of respect due only to their sovereigns. We found by far the greatest part of the country cultivated, and planted with various sorts of productions; and most of these plantations were fenced round. Some spots, where plantations had been formerly, now produced nothing, lying fallow; and there were places that had never been touched, but lay in a state of nature; and yet even these were useful in affording them timber, as they were generally covered with trees. We met with several large uninhabited houses, which, we were told, belonged to the King. There were many public and well-beaten roads, and abundance of foot-paths leading to every part of the island. The roads being good and the country level, travelling was very easy. It is remarkable that when we were on the most elevated parts, at least 100 feet above the level of the sea, we often met with the same coral rock which is found at the shore, pro-

jecting above the surface, and perforated and cut into all those inequalities which are usually seen in rocks that lie within the wash of the tide. And yet these very spots, with hardly any soil upon them, were covered with luxuriant vegetation. We were conducted to several little pools and to some springs of water; but in general they were either stinking or brackish, though recommended to us by the natives as excellent. The former were mostly inland, the latter near the shore of the bay and below high-water mark; so that tolerable water could be taken up from them only when the tide was out.

When we returned from our walk, which was not till the dusk of the evening, our supper was ready. It consisted of a baked hog, some fish, and yams, all excellently well cooked after the method of these islands. As there was nothing to amuse us after supper, we followed the custom of the country, and lay down to sleep, our beds being mats spread upon the floor, and cloth to cover us. The King, who had made himself very happy with some wine and brandy which we had brought, slept in the same house, as well as several others of the natives. Long before daybreak he and they all rose, and sat conversing by moonlight. The conversation, as might well be guessed, turned wholly upon us, the King entertaining his company with an account of what he had seen or remarked. As soon as it was day, they dispersed, some one way and some another; but it was not long before they all returned, and with them several more of their countrymen. They now began to prepare a bowl of "kava;" and leaving them so employed, I went to pay a visit to Toobou, Captain Furneaux's friend, who had a house hard by, which for size and neatness was exceeded by few in the place. As I had left the others, so I found here a company preparing a morning draught. This chief made a present to me of a living hog, a baked one, a quantity of yams, and a large piece of cloth. When I returned to the King, I found him and his circle of attendants drinking the second bowl of "kava." That being emptied, he told Omai that he was going presently to perform a mourning ceremony, called "tooge," on account of a son who had been dead some time, and he desired us to accompany him. We were glad of the opportunity, expecting to see somewhat new or curious.

The first thing the chief did was to step out of the house, attended by two old women, and put on a new suit of clothes, or rather a new piece of cloth, and over it an old ragged mat that might have served his great-grandfather on some such occasion. His servants, or those who attended him, were all dressed in the same manner, excepting that none of their mats could vie in antiquity with that of their master. Thus equipped, we marched off, preceded by about eight or ten persons, all in the above habits of ceremony, each of them besides having a small green bough about his neck. Poulaho held his bough in his hand till we drew near the place of rendezvous, when he also put it about his neck. We now entered a small enclosure, in which was a neat house, and we found one man sitting before it. As the company entered, they pulled off the green branches from round their necks and threw them away. The King having first seated himself, the others sat down before him in the usual manner. The circle increased, by others dropping in, to the number of 100 or upwards, mostly old men, all dressed as above described. The company being completely assembled, a large root of "kava," brought by one of the King's servants, was produced, and a bowl which contained four or five gallons. Several persons now began to chew the root, and this bowl was made brim-full of liquor. While it was preparing, others were employed in making drinking-cups of plantain leaves. The first cup that was filled was presented to the King, and he ordered it to be given to another person. The second was also brought to him, which he drank, and the third was offered to

me. Afterward, as each cup was filled, the man who filled it asked who was to have it. Another then named the person, and to him it was carried. As the bowl grew low, the man who distributed the liquor seemed rather at a loss to whom cups of it should be next sent, and frequently consulted those who sat near him. This mode of distribution continued while any liquor remained, and though not half the company had a share, yet no one seemed dissatisfied. About half-a-dozen cups served for all, and each, as it was emptied, was thrown down upon the ground, where the servants picked it up and carried it to be filled again. During the whole time the chief and his circle sat, as was usually the case, with a great deal of gravity, hardly speaking a word to each other. We had long waited in expectation each moment of seeing the mourning ceremony begin, when, soon after the "kava" was drank out, to our great surprise and disappointment they all rose up and dispersed, and Poulaho told us he was now ready to attend us to the ships. If this was a mourning ceremony, it was a strange one. Perhaps it was the second, third, or fourth mourning; or, which was not very uncommon, Omai might have misunderstood what Poulaho said to him. For, excepting the change of dress and the putting the green bough round their necks, nothing seemed to have passed at this meeting but what we saw them practise too frequently every day.

As soon as this mourning ceremony was over, we left Mooa and set out to return to the ships. While we rowed down the lagoon or inlet, we met with two canoes coming in from fishing. Poulaho ordered them to be called alongside our boat, and took from them every fish and shell they had got. He afterwards stopped two other canoes and searched them, but they had nothing. Why this was done I cannot say, for we had plenty of provisions in the boat. Some of this fish he gave to me, and his servants sold the rest on board the ship. As we proceeded down the inlet we overtook a large sailing canoe. Every person on board her that was upon his legs when we came up sat down till we had passed, even the man who steered, though he could not manage the helm except in a standing posture.

When we got on board the ship I found that everything had been quiet during my absence, not a theft having been committed, of which Feenou and Futtafaihe, the King's brother, who had undertaken the management of his countrymen, boasted not a little. This shows what power the chiefs have when they have the will to execute it, which we were seldom to expect, since whatever was stolen from us generally, if not always, was conveyed to them. The good conduct of the natives was of short duration, for the next day six or eight of them assaulted some of our people who were sawing planks. They were fired upon by the sentry, and one was supposed to be wounded and three others taken. These I kept confined till night, and did not dismiss them without punishment. After this they behaved with a little more circumspection, and gave us much less trouble. This change of behaviour was certainly occasioned by the man being wounded, for before they had only been told of the effect of firearms, but now they had felt it. The repeated insolence of the natives had induced me to order the muskets of the sentries to be loaded with small shot, and to authorise them to fire on particular occasions. I took it for granted, therefore, that this man had only been wounded with small shot. But Mr King and Mr Anderson, in an excursion into the country, met with him, and found indubitable marks of his having been wounded, but not dangerously, with a musket ball. I never could find out how this musket happened to be charged with ball, and there were people enough ready to swear that its contents were only small shot.[1]

I had prolonged my stay at this island on account of the approaching eclipse; but on the 2d of July, on looking at the micrometer belonging to the Board of Longitude, I found some of the rack-work broken, and the instrument useless till repaired, which there was not time to do before it was intended to be used. Preparing now for our departure, I got on board this day all the cattle, poultry, and other animals, except such as were destined to remain. I had designed to leave a turkey cock and hen; but having now only two of each undisposed of, one of the hens, through the ignorance of one of my people, was strangled, and died upon the spot. I had brought three turkey hens to these islands. One was killed as above mentioned; and the other by a useless dog belonging to one of the officers. These two accidents put it out of my power to leave a pair here, and at the same time to carry the breed to Otaheite, for which island they were originally intended. I was sorry afterwards that I did not give the preference to Tongataboo, as the present would have been of more value there than at Otaheite; for the natives of the former island, I am persuaded, would have taken more pains to multiply the breed. The next day we took up our anchor, and moved the ships behind Pangimodoo, that we might be ready to take the advantage of the first favourable wind to get through the narrows. The King, who was one of our company this day at dinner, I observed took particular notice of the plates. This occasioned me to make him an offer of one, either of pewter or of earthenware. He chose the first, and then began to tell us the several uses to which he intended to apply it. Two of them are so extraordinary that I cannot omit mentioning them. He said that, whenever he should have occasion to visit any of the other islands, he would leave this plate behind him at Tongataboo, as a sort of representa-

____

[1] Mr Anderson's account of the excursion just mentioned, containing little or nothing new, is omitted.

tive in his absence, that the people might pay it the same obeisance they do to himself in person. He was asked what had been usually employed for this purpose before he got this plate; and we had the satisfaction of learning from him that this singular honour had hitherto been conferred on a wooden bowl in which he washed his hands. The other extraordinary use to which he meant to apply it, in the room of his wooden bowl, was to discover a thief. He said that when anything was stolen, and the thief could not be found out, the people were all assembled together before him, when he washed his hands in water in this vessel; after which it was cleaned, and then the whole multitude advanced, one after another, and touched it in the same manner that they touch his foot when they pay him obeisance. If the guilty person touched it, he died immediately upon the spot, not by violence, but by the hand of Providence; and if any one refused to touch it, his refusal was a clear proof that he was the man.

In the morning of the 5th, the day of the eclipse, the weather was dark and cloudy, with showers of rain, so that we had little hopes of an observation. About 9 o'clock the sun broke out at intervals for about half-an-hour; after which it was totally obscured till within a minute or two of the beginning of the eclipse. We were all at our telescopes, viz., Mr Bayly, Mr King, Captain Clerke, Mr Bligh, and myself. I lost the observation by not having a dark glass at hand suitable to the clouds that were continually passing over the sun; and Mr Bligh had not got the sun into the field of his telescope; so that the commencement of the eclipse was only observed by the other three gentlemen, and by them, with an uncertainty of several seconds, as follows:

	Ho.	Min.	Sec.
By Mr Bayly, at	11	46	23½
Mr King, at	11	46	28
Capt. Clerke, at	11	47	5
Apparent time.			

Mr Bayly and Mr King observed with the achromatic telescopes belonging to the Board of Longitude, of equal magnifying powers; and Captain Clerke observed with one of the reflectors. The sun appeared at intervals till about the middle of the eclipse; after which it was seen no more during the day, so that the end could not be observed. The disappointment was of little consequence, since the longitude was more than sufficiently determined, independently of this eclipse, by lunar observations. As soon as we knew the eclipse to be over, we packed up the instruments, took down the observatories, and sent everything on board that had not been already removed. As none of the natives had taken the least notice or care of the three sheep allotted to Mareewagee, I ordered them to be carried back to the ships. I was apprehensive that if I had left them here they run great risk of being destroyed by dogs. That animal did not exist upon this island when I first visited it in 1773; but I now found they had got a good many, partly from the breed then left by myself, and partly from some imported since that time from an island not very remote, called Feejee. The dogs, however, at present had not found their way into any of the Friendly Islands except Tongataboo; and none but the chiefs there had as yet got possession of any.[1]

———

CHAPTER IX.

We were now ready to sail; but the wind being easterly, we had not sufficient daylight to turn through the narrows, either with the morning or with the evening flood; the one falling out too early, and the other too late. So that, without a leading wind, we were under a necessity of waiting two or three days. I took

---

[1] The remainder of the Chapter, taken up by Mr Anderson's notes on the physical formation and features and natural products of Tongataboo or Amsterdam Island, is omitted

the opportunity of this delay to be present at a public solemnity to which the King had invited us when we went last to visit him, and which, he had informed us, was to be performed on the 8th. With a view to this, he and all the people of note quitted our neighbourhood on the 7th, and repaired to Mooa, where the solemnity was to be exhibited. A party of us followed them the next morning. We understood from what Poulaho had said to us that his son and heir was now to be initiated into certain privileges; amongst which was that of eating with his father, an honour he had not as yet been admitted to.

We arrived at Mooa about 8 o'clock, and found the King with a large circle of attendants sitting before him, within an enclosure so small and dirty as to excite my wonder that any such could be found in that neighbourhood. They were intent upon their usual morning occupation, in preparing a bowl of "kava." As this was no liquor for us, we walked out to visit some of our friends, and to observe what preparations might be making for the ceremony which was soon to begin. About 10 o'clock, the people began to assemble in a large area which is before the "malaee," or great house, to which we had been conducted the first time we visited Mooa. At the end of a road that opens into this area stood some men with spears and clubs, who kept constantly reciting or chanting short sentences in a mournful tone, which conveyed some idea of distress, and as if they called for something. This was continued about an hour; and in the meantime many people came down the road, each of them bringing a yam tied to the middle of a pole, which they laid down before the persons who continued repeating the sentences. While this was going on, the King and prince arrived, and seated themselves upon the area; and we were desired to sit down by them, but to pull off our hats, and to untie our hair. The bearers of the yams being all come in, each pole was taken up between two men, who carried it over their shoulders. After forming themselves into companies of ten or twelve persons each, they marched across the place with a quick pace; each company headed by a man bearing a club or spear, and guarded on the right by several others armed with different weapons. A man carrying a living pigeon on a perch closed the rear of the procession, in which about 250 persons walked.

Omai was desired by me to ask the chief to what place the yams were to be thus carried with so much solemnity. But, as he seemed unwilling to give us the information we wanted, two or three of us followed the procession, contrary to his inclination. We found that they stopped before a "morai" or "fiatooka" of one house, standing upon a mount, which was hardly a quarter of a mile from the place where they first assembled. Here we observed them depositing the yams, and making them up into bundles; but for what purpose we could not learn. And as our presence seemed to give them uneasiness, we left them and returned to Poulaho, who told us we might amuse ourselves by walking about, as nothing would be done for some time. The fear of losing any part of the ceremony prevented our being long absent. When we returned to the King, he desired me to order the boat's crew not to stir from the boat; for as everything would very soon be "taboo," if any of our people, or of their own, should be found walking about, they would be knocked down with clubs, nay, "mateed," that is, killed. He also acquainted us that we could not be present at the ceremony; but that we should be conducted to a place where we might see everything that passed. Objections were made to our dress. We were told that to qualify us to be present it was necessary that we should be naked as low as the breast, with our hats off and our hair untied. Omai offered to conform to these requisites, and began to strip; other objections were then started, so that the exclusion was given to him equally with ourselves.

I did not much like this restriction, and therefore stole out to see what might now be going forward. I found very few people stirring, except those dressed to attend the ceremony; some of whom had in their hands small poles about four feet long, and to the under-part of these were fastened two or three other sticks, not bigger than one's finger, and about six inches in length. These men were going toward the "morai" just mentioned. I took the same road, and was several times stopped by them, all crying out "taboo." However, I went forward without much regarding them, till I came in sight of the "morai," and of the people who were sitting before it. I was now urged very strongly to go back; and not knowing what might be the consequence of a refusal, I complied. I had observed that the people who carried the poles passed this "morai," or what I may as well call temple; and guessing from this circumstance that something was transacting beyond it which might be worth looking at, I had thoughts of advancing, by making a round, for this purpose; but I was so closely watched by three men that I could not put my design in execution. In order to shake these fellows off, I returned to the "malaee" where I had left the King, and from thence made an elopement a second time; but I instantly met the same three men, so that it seemed as if they had been ordered to watch my motions. I paid no regard to what they said or did, till I came within sight of the King's principal "fiatooka" or "morai," which I have already described,[1] before which a great number of men were sitting, being the same persons whom I had just before seen pass by the other "morai," from which this was but a little distant. Observing that I could watch the proceedings of this company from the King's plantation, I repaired thither, very much to the satisfaction of those who attended me.

---

[1] In the Chapter immediately preceding.

As soon as I got in, I acquainted the gentlemen who had come with me from the ships with what I had seen; and we took a proper station to watch the result. The number of people at the "fiatooka" continued to increase for some time; and at length we could see them quit their sitting posture and march off in procession. They walked in pairs, one after another, every pair carrying between them one of the small poles above mentioned, on their shoulders. We were told that the small pieces of sticks fastened to the poles were yams; so that probably they were meant to represent this root emblematically. The hindmost man of each couple, for the most part, placed one of his hands to the middle of the pole, as if without this additional support it were not strong enough to carry the weight that hung to it, and under which they all seemed to bend as they walked. This procession consisted of 108 pairs, and all or most of them men of rank. They came close by the fence behind which we stood; so that we had a full view of them. Having waited here till they had all passed, we then repaired to Poulaho's house, and saw him going out. We could not be allowed to follow him; but were forthwith conducted to the place allotted to us, which was behind a fence adjoining to the area of the "fiatooka" where the yams had been deposited in the forenoon. As we were not the only people who were excluded from being publicly present at this ceremony, but allowed to peep from behind the curtain, we had a good deal of company; and I observed that all the other enclosures round the place were filled with people. And yet all imaginable care seemed to be taken that they should see as little as possible; for the fences had not only been repaired that morning, but in many places raised higher than common, so that the tallest man could not look over them. To remedy this defect in our station, we took the liberty to cut holes in the fence with our knives; and by this means we could see pretty distinctly everything that was transacting on the other side.

On our arrival at our station, we found two or three hundred people sitting on the grass near the end of the road that opened into the area of the "morai;" and the number continually increased by others joining them. At length arrived a few men carrying some small poles, and branches or leaves of the cocoa-nut tree; upon their first appearance an old man seated himself in the road, and with his face toward them, pronounced a long oration in a serious tone. He then retired back, and the others advancing to the middle of the area, began to erect a small shed, employing for that purpose the materials above mentioned. When they had finished their work, they all squatted down for a moment before it, then rose up and retired to the rest of the company. Soon after came Poulaho's son, preceded by four or five men, and they seated themselves a little aside from the shed, and rather behind it. After them appeared twelve or fourteen women of the first rank, walking slowly in pairs, each pair carrying between them a narrow piece of white cloth extended, about two or three yards in length. These marched up to the prince, squatted down before him, and, having wrapped some of the pieces of the cloth they had brought, round his body, they rose up and retired in the same order to some distance on his left, and there seated themselves. Poulaho himself soon made his appearance, preceded by four men, who walked two and two abreast, and sat down on his son's left hand, about twenty paces from him. The young prince then quitting his first position, went and sat down under the shed with his attendants; and a considerable number more placed themselves on the grass before this royal canopy. The prince himself sat facing the people, with his back to the "morai." This being done, three companies of ten or a dozen men in each started up from amongst the large crowd, a

little after each other, and running hastily to the opposite side of the area, sat down for a few seconds; after which they returned in the same manner to their former stations. To them succeeded two men, each of whom held a small green branch in his hand, who got up and approached the prince, sitting down for a few seconds, three different times as they advanced; and then, turning their backs, retired in the same manner, inclining their branches to each other as they sat. In a little time two more repeated this ceremony.

The grand procession which I had seen march off from the other "morai" now began to come in. To judge of the circuit they had made, from the time they had been absent, it must have been pretty large. As they entered the area they marched up to the right of the shed, and, having prostrated themselves on the grass, deposited their pretended burthens (the poles above mentioned), and faced round to the prince. They then rose up and retired in the same order, closing their hands, which they held before them, with the most serious aspect, and seated themselves along the front of the area. During all the time that this numerous band were coming in and depositing their poles, three men who sat under the shed with the prince continued pronouncing separate sentences in a melancholy tone. After this a profound silence ensued for a little time, and then a man, who sat in the front of the area, began an oration (or prayer), during which, at several different times, he went and broke one of the poles which had been brought in by those who had walked in procession. When he had ended, the people sitting before the shed separated to make a lane through which the prince and his attendants passed, and the assembly broke up. Some of our party, satisfied with what they had already seen, now returned to the ships; but I and two or three more of the officers remained at Mooa to see the conclusion of the solemnity, which was not to be till the next day, being desirous of omitting no opportunity which might afford any information about the religious or the political institutions of this people. The small sticks or poles which had been brought into the area by those who walked in procession, being left lying on the ground after the crowd had dispersed, I went and examined them. I found that to the middle of each two or three small sticks were tied, as has been related. Yet we had been repeatedly told by the natives who stood near us that they were young yams, insomuch that some of our gentlemen believed them rather than their own eyes. As I had the demonstration of my senses to satisfy me that they were not real yams, it is clear that we ought to have understood that they were only the artificial representations of these roots.

Our supper was got ready about 7 o'clock. It consisted of fish and yams. We might have had pork also; but we did not choose to kill a large hog which the King had given to us for that purpose. He supped with us, and drank pretty freely of brandy and water; so that he went to bed with a sufficient dose. We passed the night in the same house with him and several of his attendants. About 1 or 2 o'clock in the morning they waked and conversed for about an hour, and then went to sleep again. All but Poulaho himself rose at day-break, and went I know not whither. Soon after, a woman, one of those who generally attended upon the chief, came in and inquired where he was. I pointed him out to her, and she immediately sat down by him, and began the same operation which Mr Anderson had seen practised upon Futtafaihe, tapping or beating gently with her clenched fists on his thighs. This, instead of prolonging his sleep as was intended, had the contrary effect; however, though he awaked, he continued to lie down. Omai and I now went to visit the prince, who had parted from us early in the evening. For he did not lodge with the King, but in apartments of his own, or at least such as had been allotted to

him, at some distance from his father's house. We found him with a circle of boys, or youths, about his own age, sitting before him; and an old woman and an old man, who seemed to have the care of him, sitting behind. There were others, both men and women, employed about their necessary affairs in different departments, who probably belonged to his household.

From the prince we returned to the King. By this time he had got up, and had a crowded circle before him, composed chiefly of old men. While a large bowl of "kava" was preparing, a baked hog and yams, smoking hot, were brought in, the greatest part of which fell to our share, and was very acceptable to the boat's crew; for these people eat very little in the morning, especially the "kava" drinkers. I afterward walked out and visited several other chiefs; and found that all of them were taking their morning draught, or had already taken it. Returning to the King, I found him asleep in a small retired hut, with two women tapping on his breech. About 11 o'clock he arose again; and then some fish and yams, which tasted as if they had been stewed in cocoa-nut milk, were brought to him. Of these he ate a large portion, and lay down once more to sleep. I now left him, and carried to the prince a present of cloth, beads, and other articles, which I had brought with me from the ship for the purpose. There was a sufficient quantity of cloth to make him a complete suit; and he was immediately decked out with it. Proud of his dress, he first went to show himself to his father, and then conducted me to his mother; with whom were about ten or a dozen other women of a respectable appearance. Here the prince changed his apparel, and made me a present of two pieces of the cloth manufactured in the island. By this time it was past noon, when by appointment I repaired to the palace to dinner. Several of our gentlemen had returned this morning from the ships; and we were all invited to the feast, which was presently served up, and consisted of two pigs and yams. I roused the drowsy monarch to partake of what he had provided for our entertainment. In the meantime two mullets and some shell-fish were brought to him, as I supposed, for his separate portion. But he joined it to our fare, sat down with us, and made a hearty meal.

When dinner was over, we were told that the ceremony would soon begin, and were strictly enjoined not to walk out. I had resolved, however, to peep no longer from behind the curtain, but to mix with the actors themselves if possible. With this view I stole out from the plantation, and walked toward the "morai," the scene of the solemnity. I was several times desired to go back by people whom I met; but I paid no regard to them, and they suffered me to pass on. When I arrived at the "morai," I found a number of men seated on the side of the area, on each side of the road that leads up to it. A few were sitting on the opposite side of the area, and two men in the middle of it, with their faces turned to the "morai." When I got into the midst of the first company, I was desired to sit down, which I accordingly did. Where I sat there were lying a number of small bundles or parcels, composed of cocoa-nut leaves, and tied to sticks made into the form of hand-barrows. All the information I could get about them was that they were "taboo." Our number kept continually increasing; every one coming from the same quarter. From time to time, one or another of the company turned himself to those who were coming to join us, and made a short speech; in which I could remark that the word "arakee," that is, King, was generally mentioned. One man said something that produced bursts of hearty laughter from all the crowd; others of the speakers met with public applause. I was several times desired to leave the place; and at last, when they found that I would not stir, after some seeming consultation they

applied to me to uncover my shoulders as theirs were. With this request I complied, and then they seemed to be no longer uneasy at my presence.

I sat a full hour without anything more going forward, beside what I have mentioned. At length the prince, the women, and the King all came in, as they had done the day before. The prince being placed under the shed, after his father's arrival, two men, each carrying a piece of mat, came repeating something seriously, and put them about him. The assembled people now began their operations; and first three companies ran backwards and forwards across the area, as described in the account of the proceedings of the former day. Soon after, the two men who sat in the middle of the area made a short speech or prayer; and then the whole body amongst whom I had my place started up, and ran and seated themselves before the shed under which the prince and three or four men were sitting. I was now partly under the management of one of the company, who seemed very assiduous to serve me. By his means I was placed in such a situation, that if I had been allowed to make use of my eyes, nothing that passed could have escaped me. But it was necessary to sit with down-cast looks, and demure as maids. Soon after, the procession came in, as on the day before; each two persons bearing on their shoulders a pole, round the middle of which a cocoa-nut leaf was plaited. These were deposited with ceremonies similar to those observed on the preceding day. This first procession was followed by a second; the men composing which brought baskets such as are usually employed by this people to carry provisions in, and made of palm leaves. These were followed by a third procession, in which were brought different kinds of small fish, each fixed at the end of a forked stick. The baskets were carried up to an old man, whom I took to be the chief priest, and who sat on the prince's right hand, without the shed. He held each in his hand, while he made a short speech or prayer; then laid it down and called for another, repeating the same words as before; and thus he went through the whole number of baskets. The fish were presented, one by one, on the forked sticks, as they came in, to two men who sat on the left, and who till now held green branches in their hands. The first fish they laid down on their right, and the second on their left. When the third was presented, a stout-looking man who sat behind the other two reached his arm over between them and made a snatch at it; as also did the other two at the very same time. Thus they seemed to contend for every fish that was presented; but as there were two hands against one, besides the advantage of situation, the man behind got nothing but pieces; for he never quitted his hold till the fish was torn out of his hand, and what little remained in it he shook out behind him. The others laid what they got on the right and left alternately. At length, either by accident or design, the man behind got possession of a whole fish without either of the other two so much as touching it. At this the word "Mareeai," which signifies "Very good!" or "Well done!" was uttered in a low voice throughout the whole crowd. It seemed that he had performed now all that was expected from him, for he made no attempt upon the few fish that came after. These fish, as also the baskets, were all delivered, by the persons who brought them in, sitting; and in the same order and manner the small poles, which the first procession carried, had been laid upon the ground.

The last procession being closed, there was some speaking or praying by different persons. Then on some signal being given, we all started up, ran several paces to the left, and sat down with our backs to the prince and the few who remained with him. I was desired not to look behind me. However, neither this injunction, nor the remembrance of Lot's wife, discouraged me from facing about. I now saw that the prince had turned his face to the "morai:" but this last movement had brought so many people between him and me, that I could not perceive what was doing. I was afterward assured that at this very time the prince was admitted to the high honour of eating with his father, which till now had never been permitted to him; a piece of roasted yam being presented to each of them for this purpose. This was the more probable, as we had been told beforehand that this was to happen during the solemnity; and as all the people turned their backs to them at this time, which they always do when their monarch eats. After some little time we all faced about, and formed a semicircle before the prince, leaving a large open space between us. Presently there appeared some men coming toward us, two and two, bearing large sticks or poles upon their shoulders, making a noise that might be called singing, and waving their hands as they advanced. When they had got close up to us, they made a show of walking very fast, without proceeding a single step. Immediately after, three or four men started up from the crowd, with large sticks in their hands, who ran toward those newcomers. The latter instantly threw down the poles from their shoulders and scampered off; and the others attacked the poles, and, having beat them most unmercifully, returned to their places. As the pole-bearers ran off, they gave the challenge that is usual here in wrestling; and not long after, a number of stout fellows came from the same quarter, repeating the challenge as they advanced. These were opposed by a party who came from the opposite side almost at the same instant. The two parties paraded about the area for a few minutes, and then retired each to their own side. After this there were wrestling and boxing matches for about half-an-hour. Then two men seated themselves before the prince, and made speeches addressed, as I thought, entirely to him. With this the solemnity ended, and the whole assembly broke up.

I now went and examined the several baskets which had been presented ; a curiosity that I was not allowed before to indulge, because everything was then "taboo." But the solemnity being now over, they became simply what I found them to be, empty baskets. So that whatever they were supposed to contain was emblematically represented. And so indeed was every other thing which had been brought in procession except the fish. We endeavoured in vain to find out the meaning, not only of the ceremony in general, which is called " Natche," but of its different parts. We seldom got any other answer to our inquiries, but "Taboo ;" a word which, I have before observed, is applied to many other things. But as the prince was evidently the principal person concerned in it ; and as we had been told by the King, ten days before the celebration of the " Natche," that the people would bring in yams for him and his son to eat together ; and as he even described some part of the ceremony, we concluded from what he had then said, and from what we now saw, that an oath of allegiance, if I may so express myself, or solemn promise, was on this occasion made to the prince, as the immediate successor to the regal dignity, to stand by him and to furnish him with the several articles that were here emblematically represented. That seems the more probable, as all the principal people of the island whom we had ever seen assisted in the processions. But be this as it may, the whole was conducted with a great deal of mysterious solemnity ; and that there was a mixture of religion in the institution was evident not only from the place where it was performed, but from the manner of performing it. Our dress and deportment had never been called in question upon any former occasion whatever. Now it was expected that we should be uncovered as low as the waist ; that our hair should be loose and flowing over our shoulders ; that we should like themselves sit cross-legged, and at times in the most humble posture, with down-cast eyes and hands locked together : all which requisites were most devoutly observed by the whole assembly. And, lastly, every one was excluded from the solemnity but the principal people and those who assisted in the celebration. All these circumstances were to me a sufficient testimony that upon this occasion they considered themselves as acting under the immediate inspection of a Supreme Being. The present "Natche" may be considered, from the above account of it, as merely figurative. For the small quantity of yams which we saw the first day could not be intended- as a general contribution ; and indeed we were given to understand that they were a portion consecrated to the " Otooa," or divinity. But we were informed that in about three months there would be performed, on the same account, a far more important and grander solemnity ; on which occasion not only the tribute of Tongataboo, but that of Hapaeo, Vavaoo, and of all the other islands, would be brought to the chief, and confirmed more awfully by sacrificing ten human victims from amongst the inferior sort of people. A horrid solemnity indeed ! which is a most significant instance of the influence of gloomy and ignorant superstition over the minds of one of the most benevolent and humane nations upon earth. On inquiring into the reasons of so barbarous a practice, they only said that it was a necessary part of the " Natche ; " and that if they omitted it the deity would certainly destroy their king.

Before the assembly broke up, the day was far spent ; and as we were at some distance from the ships, and had an intricate navigation to go through, we were in haste to set out from Mooa. When I took leave of Poulaho, he pressed me much to stay till the next day, to be present at a funeral ceremony. The wife of Mareewagee, who was mother-in-law to the King, had lately died ; and her corpse had, on account of the " Natche," been carried on board a canoe that lay in the lagoon. Poulaho told me that as soon as he had paid the last offices to her he would attend me to Eooa ; but, if I did not wait, that he would follow me thither. I understood at the same time, that if it had not been for the death of this woman most of the chiefs would have accompanied us to that island, where, it seems, all of them have possessions. I would gladly have waited to see this ceremony also, had not the tide been now favourable for the ships to get through the narrows. The wind, besides, which, for several days past had been very boisterous, was now moderate and settled ; and to have lost this opportunity might have detained us a fortnight longer. But, what was decisive against my waiting, we understood that the funeral ceremonies would last five days ; which was too long a time, as the ships lay in such a situation that I could not get to sea at pleasure. I however, assured the King that if we did not sail I should certainly visit him again the next day. And so we all took leave of him, and set out for the ships, where we arrived about 8 o'clock in the evening.

I had forgot to mention that Omai was present at this second day's ceremony as well as myself; but we were not together, nor did I know that he was there till it was almost over. He afterwards told me that as soon as the King saw that I had stolen out from the plantation, he sent several people one after another to desire me to come back. Probably these messengers were not admitted to the place where I was ; for I saw nothing of them. At last intelligence was brought to the chief that I had actually stripped in conformity to their custom ; and then he told Omai that he might be present also, if he would comply with all the necessary forms. Omai had no objection, as nothing was required of him but to conform to the custom of his own country. Accordingly he was furnished with a proper dress, and appeared at the ceremony as one of the natives. It is likely that one reason of our being excluded at first was an apprehension that we would not submit to the requisites to qualify us to assist.

While I was attending the "Natche" at Mooa, I ordered the horses, bull and cow, and goats, to be brought thither, thinking that they would be safer there, under the eyes of the chiefs, than at a place that would be in a manner deserted the moment after our departure. Besides the above-mentioned animals, we left with our friends here a young boar and three young sows of the English breed. They were exceedingly desirous of them, judging, no doubt, that they would greatly improve their own breed, which is rather small. Feenou also got from us two rabbits, a buck, and a doe; and before we sailed we were told that young ones had been already produced. If the cattle succeed, of which I make no doubt, it will be a vast acquisition to these islands ; and as Tongataboo is a fine level country, the horses cannot but be useful.

[Weighing anchor on the morning of the 10th, the ships got with some difficulty through the channel, and did not weather the east end of Tongataboo before 10 o'clock next night. On the morning of the 12th they anchored off Middleburg Island, called by the natives Eooa, or English Road—the name Cook had given to his station in 1773.]

We had no sooner anchored than Taoofa the chief[1] and several other natives visited us on board, and seemed to rejoice much at our arrival. In a little time I went ashore with him in search of fresh water, the procuring of which was the chief object that brought me to Eooa. I had been told at Tongataboo that there was here a stream running from the hills into the sea, but this was not the case now. I was first conducted to a brackish spring, between low and high water mark amongst rocks in the cove where we landed, and where no one would ever have thought of looking for what we wanted. However, I be-

---

[1] In the account of Captain Cook's former voyage, he calls the only chief he then met with at this place Tioony.—*Note in Original Edition.*

lieve the water of this spring might be good, were it possible to take it up before the tide mixes with it. Finding that we did not like this, our friends took us a little way into the island, where in a deep chasm we found very good water, which, at the expense of some time and trouble, might be conveyed down to the shore by means of spouts or troughs that could be made with plantain leaves and the stem of the tree. But rather than undertake that tedious task I resolved to rest contented with the supply the ships had got at Tongataboo. Before I returned on board I set on foot a trade for hogs and yams. Of the former we could procure but few, but of the latter plenty. I put ashore at this island the ram and two ewes of the Cape of Good Hope breed of sheep, entrusting them to the care of Taoofa, who seemed proud of his charge. It was fortunate, perhaps, that Mareewagee, to whom I had given them, as before mentioned, slighted the present. Eooa, not having as yet got any dogs upon it, seems to be a properer place than Tongataboo for the rearing of sheep. As we lay at anchor, this island bore a very different aspect from any we had lately seen, and formed a most beautiful landscape. It is higher than any we had passed since leaving New Zealand (as Kao may justly be reckoned an immense rock), and from its top, which is almost flat, declines very gently toward the sea. As the other isles of this cluster are level, the eye can discover nothing but the trees that cover them ; but here the land, rising gently upward, presents us with an extensive prospect, where groves of trees are only interspersed at irregular distances in beautiful disorder, and the rest covered with grass. Near the shore, again, it is quite shaded with various trees, amongst which are the habitations of the natives ; and to the right of our station was one of the most extensive groves of cocoa-palms we had ever seen. . . .

Soon after we weighed, and with a light breeze at SE. stood out to sea ;

and then Taoofa and a few other natives that were in the ship left us. On heaving up the anchor, we found that the cable had suffered considerably by the rocks, so that the bottom in this road is not to be depended upon. Besides this, we experienced that a prodigious swell rolls in there from the SW. We had not been long under sail before we observed a sailing canoe coming from Tongataboo, and entering the creek before which we had anchored. Some hours after, a small canoe, conducted by four men, came off to us, for as we had but little wind, we were still at no great distance from the land. These men told us that the sailing canoe which we had seen arrive from Tongataboo had brought orders to the people of Eooa to furnish us with a certain number of hogs, and that in two days the King and other chiefs would be with us. They therefore desired we would return to our former station. There was no reason to doubt the truth of what these men told us. Two of them had actually come from Tongataboo in the sailing canoe, and they had no view in coming off to us but to give this intelligence. However, as we were now clear of the land, it was not a sufficient inducement to bring me back, especially as we had already on board a stock of fresh provisions sufficient in all probability to last during our passage to Otaheite. Besides Taoofa's present, we had got a good quantity of yams at Eooa in exchange chiefly for small nails. Our supply of hogs was also considerably increased there, though doubtless we should have got many more if the chiefs of Tongataboo had been with us, whose property they mostly were. At the approach of night these men, finding that we would not return, left us, as also some others who had come off in two canoes with a few cocoa-nuts and shaddocks to exchange them for what they could get; the eagerness of these people to get into their possession more of our commodities inducing them to follow the ships out to sea, and to continue their intercourse with us to the last moment.

CHAPTER X.[1]

Thus we took leave of the Friendly Islands and their inhabitants, after a stay of between two and three months, during which time we lived together in the most cordial friendship. Some accidental differences, it is true, now and then happened, owing to their great propensity to thieving, but too often encouraged by the negligence of our own people. But these differences were never attended with any fatal consequences, to prevent which all my measures were directed; and I believe few on board our ships left our friends here without some regret. The time employed amongst them was not thrown away. We expended very little of our sea provisions, subsisting in general upon the produce of the islands while we stayed, and carrying away with us a quantity of refreshments sufficient to last till our arrival at another station, where we could depend upon a fresh supply. I was not sorry, besides, to have had an opportunity of bettering the condition of these good people, by leaving the useful animals before mentioned among them; and at the same time those designed for Otaheite received fresh strength in the pastures of Tongataboo. Upon the whole, therefore, the advantages we received by touching here were very great; and I had the additional satisfaction to reflect that they were received without retarding one moment the prosecution of the great object of our voyage; the season for proceeding to the north being, as

---

[1] This, and the subsequent Chapter of Book II., devoted to an account of the Friendly Isles and their inhabitants, although obstructing not a little the course of Cook's narrative, have been retained with some unimportant or desirable omissions, condensations, and as giving, mainly from his own pen and his own observation, a lively picture of one of the great Australasian communities which he first unveiled to the knowledge of the world.

has been already observed, lost before I took the resolution of bearing away for these islands. But besides the immediate advantages which both the natives of the Friendly Islands and ourselves received by this visit, future navigators from Europe, if any such should ever tread our steps, will profit by the knowledge I acquired of the geography of this part of the Pacific Ocean; and the more philosophical reader, who loves to view human nature in new situations, and to speculate on singular but faithful representations of the persons, the customs, the arts, the religion, the government, and the language of uncultivated man in remote and fresh discovered quarters of the globe, will perhaps find matter of amusement, if not of instruction, in the information which I have been enabled to convey to him concerning the inhabitants of this archipelago. I shall suspend my narrative of the progress of the voyage, while I faithfully relate what I had opportunities of collecting on these several topics.

[Best articles for traffic at Friendly Islands: iron, tools, and nails of all kinds, red cloth, linen, looking-glasses, and beads—useful and ornamental commodities not always swaying the market with equal power, though the useful have generally the preference. In exchange may be procured hogs, fowl, fish, yams, bread-fruit, plantains, cocoa-nuts, sugar-cane, and everything that can be got at the Society Islands, though not all of equally good quality. Good water is scarce, but indifferent may be had on all the islands.]

Under the denomination of Friendly Islands we must include not only the group at Hapaee which I visited, but also all those islands that have been discovered nearly under the same meridian to the north, as well as some others that have never been seen hitherto by any European navigators, but are under the dominion of Tongataboo, which, though not the largest, is the capital and seat of government. According to the information that we received there, this archipelago is very extensive. Above 150 islands were reckoned up to us by the natives, who made use of bits of leaves to ascertain their number ; and Mr Anderson, with his usual diligence, even procured all their names. Fifteen of them are said to be high or hilly, such as Toofoa and Eooa ; and thirty-five of them large. Of these only three were seen this voyage : Hapaee (which is considered by the natives as one island), Tongataboo, and Eooa ; of the size of the unexplored thirty-two nothing more can be mentioned but that they must be all larger than Annamooka, which those from whom we had our information ranked amongst the smaller isles. Some, or indeed several, of this latter denomination are mere spots without inhabitants.[1]

I have not the least doubt that Prince William's Islands, discovered and so named by Tasman, are included in the foregoing list. For while we lay at Hapaee, one of the natives told me that three or four days' sail from thence to the NW. there was a cluster of small islands consisting of upwards of forty. This situation corresponds very well with that assigned, in the accounts we have of Tasman's voyage, to his Prince William's Islands.[2]

We have also very good authority to believe that Keppel's and Boscawen's Islands, two of Captain Wallis's discoveries in 1765, are comprehended in our list ; and that they are not only well known to these people, but are under the same sovereign. The following information

seemed to me decisive as to this. Upon my inquiring one day of Poulaho, the King, in what manner the inhabitants of Tongataboo had acquired the knowledge of iron, and from what quarter they had procured a small iron tool which I had seen amongst them when I first visited their island during my former voyage, he informed me that they had received this iron from an island which he called Neeootabootaboo. Carrying my inquiries further, I then desired to know whether he had ever been informed from whom the people of Neeootabootaboo had got it. I found him perfectly acquainted with its history. He said that one of these islanders sold a club for five nails to a ship which had touched there, and that these five nails afterwards were sent to Tongataboo. He added that this was the first iron known amongst them ; so that what Tasman left of that metal must have been worn out and forgotten long ago. I was very particular in my inquiries about the situation, size, and form of the island ; expressing my desire to know when this ship had touched there, how long she stayed, and whether any more were in company. The leading facts appeared to be fresh in his memory. He said that there was but one ship ; that she did not come to an anchor, but left the island after her boat had been on shore. And from many circumstances which he mentioned, it could not be many years since this had happened. According to his information, there are two islands near each other, which he himself had been at. The one he described as high and peaked like Kao, and he called it Kootahee ; the other, where the people of the ship landed, called Neeootabootaboo, he represented as much lower. He added that the natives of both are the same sort of people with those of Tongataboo, built their canoes in the same manner, that their islands had hogs and fowls, and in general the same vegetable productions. The ship so pointedly referred to in this conversation could be no other than

***

[1] Follows in the original a list of ninety-five islands of the group, mentioned by the inhabitants of the islands which Cook visited ; but we mercifully spare the reader the infliction of the soft but unwieldy polysyllables.

[2] Tasman saw eighteen or twenty of these small islands, every one of which was surrounded with sands, shoals, and rocks. They are also called, in some charts, Heemskirk's Banks.—*Note in Original Edition.*

the Dolphin; the only single ship from Europe, as far as we have ever learned, that had touched of late years at any island in this part of the Pacific Ocean prior to my former visit to the Friendly Islands.[1]

But the most considerable islands in this neighbourhood that we now heard of (and we heard a great deal about them) are Hamoa, Vavaoo, and Feejee. Each of these was represented to us as larger than Tongataboo. No European that we know of has as yet seen any one of them. Tasman, indeed, lays down in his chart an island nearly in the situation where I suppose Vavaoo to be; that is, about the Latitude of 19°. But then that island is there marked as a very small one; whereas Vavaoo, according to the united testimony of all our friends at Tongataboo, exceeds the size of their own island, and has high mountains. I should certainly have visited it, and have accompanied Feenou from Hapaee, if he had not then discouraged me by representing it to be very inconsiderable and without any harbour. But Poulaho, the King, afterwards assured me that it was a large island, and that it not only produced everything in common with Tongataboo, but had the peculiar advantage of possessing several streams of fresh water, with as good a harbour as that which we found at his capital island. He offered to attend me if I would visit it; adding that if I did not find everything agreeing with his representation, I might kill him. I had not the least doubt of the truth of his

---

[1] See Captain Wallis's voyage, in Hawkesworth's Collection. Captain Wallis there calls both these islands high ones. But the superior height of one of them may be inferred from his saying that it appears like a sugarloaf. This strongly marks its resemblance to Kao. From comparing Poulaho's intelligence to Captain Cook, with Captain Wallis's account, it seems to be past all doubt that Boscawen's Island is our Kootahee, and Keppel's Island our Neeootabootaboo.—*Note in Original Edition.*

intelligence; and was satisfied that Feenou, from some interested view, attempted to deceive me.

Hamoa, which is also under the dominion of Tongataboo, lies two days' sail NW. from Vavaoo. It was described to me as the largest of all their islands, as affording harbours and good water, and as producing in abundance every article of refreshment found at the places we visited. Poulaho himself frequently resides there. It should seem that the people of this island are in high estimation at Tongataboo, for we were told that some of the songs and dances with which we were entertained had been copied from theirs, and we saw some houses said to be built after their fashion.

Feejee, as we were told, lies three days' sail from Tongataboo in the direction of NW. by W. It was described to us as a high but very fruitful island, abounding with hogs, dogs, fowls, and all kinds of fruit and roots that are found in any of the others, and as much larger than Tongataboo, to the dominion of which, as was represented to us, it is not subject, as the other islands of this archipelago are. On the contrary, Feejee and Tongataboo frequently make war upon each other; and it appeared from several circumstances that the inhabitants of the latter are much afraid of this enemy. They used to express their sense of their own inferiority to the Feejee men by bending their body forward, and covering the face with their hands. And it is no wonder that they should be under this dread, for those of Feejee are formidable on account of the dexterity with which they use their bows and slings, but much more so on account of the savage practice to which they are addicted, like those of New Zealand, of eating their enemies whom they kill in battle. We were satisfied that this was not a misrepresentation; for we met with several Feejee people at Tongataboo, and on inquiring of them they did not deny the charge.

Now that I am again led to speak

of cannibals, let me ask those who maintain that the want of food first brings men to feed on human flesh, What is it that induceth the Feejee people to keep it up in the midst of plenty? This practice is detested very much by those of Tongataboo, who cultivate the friendship of their savage neighbours of Feejee apparently out of fear, though they sometimes venture to skirmish with them on their own ground, and carry off red feathers as their booty, which are in great plenty there, and, as has been frequently mentioned, are in great estimation amongst our Friendly Islanders. When the two islands are at peace, the intercourse between them seems to be pretty frequent, though they have doubtless been but lately known to each other, or we may suppose that Tongataboo and its adjoining islands would have been supplied before this with a breed of dogs which abound at Fœejee, and had not been introduced at Tongataboo so late as 1773, when I first visited it. The natives of Feejee whom we met with here were of a colour that was a full shade darker than that of the inhabitants of the Friendly Islands in general. One of them had his left ear slit, and the lobe was so distended that it almost reached his shoulder, which singularity I had met with at other islands of the South Sea during my second voyage. It appeared to me that the Fœejee men whom we now saw were much respected here, not only perhaps from the power and cruel manner of their nation's going to war, but also from their ingenuity. For they seem to excel the inhabitants of Tongataboo in that respect, if we might judge from several specimens of their skill in workmanship which we saw, such as clubs and spears, which were carved in a very masterly manner, cloth beautifully chequered, variegated mats, earthen pots, and some other articles, all which had a cast of superiority in the execution.

I have mentioned that Feejee lies three days' sail from Tongataboo, because these people have no other method of measuring the distance from island to island but by expressing the time required to make the voyage in one of their canoes. In order to ascertain this with some precision, or at least to form some judgment how far these canoes can sail in a moderate gale in any given time, I went on board one of them when under sail, and by several trials with the log found that she went seven knots or miles in an hour, close-hauled in a gentle gale. From this I judge that they will sail on a medium, with such breezes as generally blow in their sea, about seven or eight miles in an hour. But the length of each day is not to be reckoned at twenty-four hours, for when they spoke of one day's sail, they mean no more than from the morning to the evening of the same day—that is, ten or twelve hours at most; and two days' sail with them signifies from the morning of the first day to the evening of the second; and so for any other number of days. In these navigations the sun is their guide by day, and the stars by night. When these are obscured they have recourse to the points from whence the winds and the waves come upon the vessel. If during the obscuration both the wind and the waves should shift (which, within the limits of the trade-wind, seldom happens at any other time), they are then bewildered, frequently miss their intended port, and are never heard of more. The history of Omai's countrymen, who were driven to Wateeoo, leads us to infer that those not heard of are not always lost.

Of all the harbours and anchoring places I have met with amongst these islands, that of Tongataboo is by far the best, not only on account of its great security, but of its capacity, and of the goodness of its bottom. Although Tongataboo has the best harbour, Annamooka furnishes the best water, and yet it cannot be called good. However, by digging holes near the side of the pond we can get what may be called tolerable. This island, too, is the best situated for drawing refreshments from all the others, as being nearly in the centre of the whole group.

It may be expected that after spending between two and three months amongst the [natives] I should be enabled to give a tolerably satisfactory account of their customs, opinions, and institutions, both civil and religious, especially as we had a person on board who might be supposed qualified to act the part of an interpreter, by understanding their language and others. But poor Omai was very deficient; for unless the object or thing we wanted to inquire about was actually before us, we found it difficult to gain a tolerable knowledge of it from information only, without falling into a hundred mistakes, and to such mistakes Omai was more liable than we were; for having no curiosity, he never gave himself the trouble to make remarks for himself; and when he was disposed to explain matters to us, his ideas appeared to be so limited, and perhaps so different from ours, that his accounts were often so confused as to perplex instead of instructing us. Add to this, that it was very rare that we found amongst the natives a person who united the ability and the inclination to give us the information we wanted; and we found that most of them hated to be troubled with what they probably thought idle questions. Our situation at Tongataboo, where we remained the longest, was likewise unfavourable. It was in a part of the country where there were few inhabitants except fishers. It was always holiday with our visitors, as well as with those we visited; so that we had but few opportunities of observing what was really the domestic way of living of the natives. Under these disadvantages it is not surprising that we should not be able to bring away with us satisfactory accounts of many things; but some of us endeavoured to remedy those disadvantages by diligent observation; and I am indebted to Mr Anderson for a considerable share of what follows in this and in the following Chapter.

The natives of the Friendly Islands seldom exceed the common stature (though we have measured some who were above six feet), but are very strong and well made, especially as to their limbs. They are generally broad about the shoulders, and though the muscular disposition of the men, which seems a consequence of much action, rather conveys the appearance of strength than of beauty, there are several to be seen who are really handsome. Their features are very various, insomuch that it is scarcely possible to fix on any general likeness by which to characterise them, unless it be a fulness at the point of the nose, which is very common. But, on the other hand, we met with hundreds of truly European faces, and many genuine Roman noses amongst them. Their eyes and teeth are good, but the last neither so remarkably white nor so well set as is often found amongst Indian nations, though, to balance that, few of them have any uncommon thickness about the lips, a defect as frequent as the other perfection. The women are not so much distinguished from the men by their features as by their general form, which is for the most part destitute of that strong fleshy firmness that appears in the latter. Though the features of some are so delicate as not only to be a true index of their sex, but to lay claim to a considerable share of beauty and expression, the rule is by no means so general as in many other countries. But at the same time this is frequently the most exceptionable part, for the bodies and limbs of most of the females are well proportioned, and some absolutely perfect models of a beautiful figure. But the most remarkable distinction in the women is the uncommon smallness and delicacy of their fingers, which may be put in competition with the finest in Europe.

The general colour is a cast deeper than the copper brown, but several of the men and women have a true olive complexion; and some of the last are even a great deal fairer, which is probably the effect of being less exposed to the sun, as a tendency to corpulence in a few of the principal people seems to be the consequence of a more indolent life. It is also amongst the last that a soft clear skin is most frequently observed. Amongst the bulk of the people the skin is more commonly of a dull hue, with some degree of roughness, especially the parts that are not covered, which perhaps may be occasioned by some cutaneous disease. We saw a man and boy at Hapaee, and a child at Annamooka, perfectly white. Such have been found amongst all black nations, but I apprehend that their colour is rather a disease than a natural phenomenon. There are, nevertheless, upon the whole, few natural defects or deformities to be found amongst them, though we saw two or three with their feet bent inward, and some afflicted with a sort of blindness occasioned by a disease of the cornea. Neither are they exempt from some other diseases, the most common of which is the tetter, or ring-worm, that seems to affect almost one-half of them, and leaves whitish serpentine marks everywhere behind it. But this is of less consequence than another disease which is very frequent, and appears on every part of the body in large broad ulcers with thick white edges, discharging a thin, clear matter, some of which had a very virulent appearance, particularly those on the face, which were shocking to look at. And yet we met with some who seemed to be cured of it, and others in a fair way of being cured; but this was not effected without the loss of the nose, or of the best part of it. As we know for a certainty[1] (and the fact is acknowledged by themselves) that the people of these islands were subject to this loathsome disease before the English first visited them, notwithstanding the similarity of

symptoms, it cannot be the effect of the venereal contagion, unless we adopt a supposition, which I could wish had sufficient foundation in truth, that the venereal disorder was not introduced here from Europe by our ships in 1773. It assuredly was now found to exist amongst them, for we had not been long there before some of our people received the infection; and I had the mortification to learn from thence that all the care I took when I first visited these islands to prevent this dreadful disease from being communicated to their inhabitants had proved ineffectual. What is extraordinary, they do not seem to regard it much; and as we saw few signs of its destroying effects, probably the climate and the way of living of these people greatly abate its virulence. [Two other diseases are frequent amongst them.] But in other respects they may be considered as uncommonly healthy, not a single person having been seen during our stay confined to the house by sickness of any kind. On the contrary, their strength and activity are every way answerable to their muscular appearance; and they exert both in their usual employment and in their diversions, in such a manner that there can be no doubt of their being as yet little debilitated by the numerous diseases that are the consequence of indolence and an unnatural method of life. The graceful air and firm step with which these people walk are not the least obvious proof of their personal accomplishments. They consider this as a thing so natural or so necessary to be acquired that nothing used to excite their laughter sooner than to see us frequently stumbling upon the roots of trees or other inequalities of the ground.

Their countenances very remarkably express the abundant mildness or good-nature which they possess, and are entirely free from that savage keenness which marks nations in a barbarous state. One would indeed be apt to fancy that they had been bred up under the severest restrictions to acquire an aspect so settled,

---

[1] Captain Cook, in the account of his Second Voyage, gives a particular account of meeting with a person afflicted with this disease at Annamooka on his landing there in 1773.

and such a command of their passions, as well as steadiness in conduct. But they are at the same time frank, cheerful, and good-humoured, though sometimes in the presence of their chiefs they put on a degree of gravity and such a serious air as becomes stiff and awkward, and has an appearance of reserve. Their peaceable disposition is sufficiently evinced from the friendly reception all strangers have met with who have visited them. Instead of offering to attack them openly or clandestinely, as has been the case with most of the inhabitants of these seas, they have never appeared in the smallest degree hostile; but on the contrary, like the most civilised people, have courted an intercourse with their visitors by bartering, which is the only medium that unites all nations in a sort of friendship. They understand barter (which they call "fukkatou") so perfectly that at first we imagined they might have acquired this knowledge of it by commercial intercourse with the neighbouring islands, but we were afterward assured that they had little or no traffic except with Feejee, from which they get the red feathers and the few other articles mentioned before. Perhaps no nation in the world traffic with more honesty and less distrust. We could always safely permit them to examine our goods, and to hand them about one to another; and they put the same confidence in us. If either party repented of the bargain, the goods were re-exchanged with mutual consent and good-humour. Upon the whole, they seem possessed of many of the most excellent qualities that adorn the human mind, such as industry, ingenuity, perseverance, affability, and perhaps other virtues which our short stay with them might prevent our observing. The only defect sullying their character that we know of is a propensity to thieving, to which we found those of all ages and both sexes addicted, and to an uncommon degree.

Their hair is in general straight, thick, and strong, though a few have it bushy or frizzled. The natural colour, I believe, almost without exception, is black; but the greatest part of the men and some of the women have it stained of a brown or purple colour, and a few of an orange cast. The first colour is produced by applying a sort of plaster of burned coral mixed with water; the second by the raspings of a reddish wood, which is made up with water into a poultice and laid over the hair; and the third is, I believe, the effect of turmeric root. When I first visited these islands I thought it had been a universal custom for both men and women to wear the hair short, but during our present longer stay we saw a great many exceptions. Indeed they are so whimsical in their fashions of wearing it that it is hard to tell which is most in vogue. Some have it cut off one side of the head, while that on the other side remains long; some have only a portion of it cut short or perhaps shaved; others have it entirely cut off except a single lock, which is left commonly on one side; or it is suffered to grow to its full length without any of these mutilations. The women in general wear it short. The men have their beards cut short, and both men and women strip the hair from their arm-pits. The operation by which this is performed has been already described.[1] The men are stained from about the middle of the belly to about half way down the thighs with a deep blue colour. This is done with a flat bone instrument cut full of fine teeth, which, being dipped in the staining mixture prepared from the juice of the "dooe dooe," is struck into the skin with a bit of stick, and by that means indelible marks are made. In this manner they trace lines and figures, which in some are very elegant, both from the variety and from the arrangement. The women have only a few small lines or spots thus imprinted on the inside of their hands. Their kings, as a mark of distinction, are exempted from this custom, as also from inflict-

---

[1] In Chapter VI. of this Book.

'ng on themselves any of those bloody marks of mourning which shall be mentioned in another place.

The dress of both men and women is the same, and consists of a piece of cloth or matting (but mostly the former), about two yards wide and two and a half long; at least, so long as to go once and a half round the waist, to which it is confined by a girdle or cord. It is double before, and hangs down like a petticoat as low as the middle of the leg. The upper part of the garment above the girdle is plaited into several folds, so that when unfolded there is cloth sufficient to draw up and wrap round the shoulders; which is very seldom done. This, as to form, is the general dress; but large pieces of cloth and fine matting are worn only by the superior people. The inferior sort are satisfied with small pieces, and very often wear nothing but a covering made of leaves of plants, or the "maro," which is a narrow piece of cloth or matting like a sash. This they pass between the thighs and wrap round the waist; but the use of it is chiefly confined to the men. In their great "Haivas," or entertainments, they have various dresses made for the purpose, but the form is always the same, and the richest dresses are covered more or less with red feathers. On what particular occasion their chiefs wear their large red feather-caps 1 could not learn. Both men and women sometimes shade their faces from the sun with little bonnets made of various materials. As the clothing, so are the ornaments worn by those of both sexes the same. The most common of these are necklaces made of the fruit of the *Pandanus* and various sweet-smelling flowers, which go under the general name of "kabulla." Others are composed of small shells, the wing and leg-bones of birds, sharks' teeth, and other things; all which hang loose upon the breast. In the same manner they often wear a mother-of-pearl shell neatly polished, or a ring of the same substance carved, on the upper part of the arm; rings of tortoise-shell on the fingers; and a number of these joined together as bracelets on the wrists. The lobes of the ears (though most frequently only one) are perforated with two holes, in which they wear cylindrical bits of ivory about three inches long, introduced at one hole and brought out of the other, or bits of reed of the same size filled with a yellow pigment. This seems to be a fine powder of turmeric, with which the women rub themselves all over in the same manner as our ladies use their dry rouge upon the cheeks.

Nothing appears to give them greater pleasure than personal cleanliness; to produce which they frequently bathe in the ponds, which seem to serve no other purpose. Though the water in most of them stinks intolerably, they prefer them to the sea; and they are so sensible that salt water hurts their skin, that when necessity obliges them to bathe in the sea they commonly have some cocoa-nut shells filled with fresh water poured over them to wash it off. They are immoderately fond of cocoanut oil for the same reason; a great quantity of which they not only pour upon their head and shoulders, but rub the body all over briskly with a smaller quantity. And none but those who have seen this practice can easily conceive how the appearance of the skin is improved by it. This oil, however, is not to be procured by every one, and the inferior sort of people doubtless appear less smooth for want of it.

CHAPTER XI.

THEIR domestic life is of that middle kind, neither so laborious as to be disagreeable, nor so vacant as to suffer them to degenerate into indolence. Nature has done so much for their country that the first can hardly occur, and their disposition seems to be a pretty good bar to the last. By this happy combination of circumstances their necessary labour seems to yield in its turn to their recreations in such a manner, that the latter are never interrupted by the thoughts of being obliged to recur to the former, till satiety makes them wish for such a transition.

The employment of the women is of the easy kind, and for the most part such as may be executed in the house. The manufacturing their cloth is wholly consigned to their care. Having already described the process, I shall only add that they have this cloth of different degrees of fineness. The coarser sort, of which they make very large pieces, does not receive the impression of any pattern. Of the finer sort they have some that is striped and chequered, and of other patterns differently coloured. But how these colours are laid on I cannot say, as I never saw any of this sort made. The cloth in general will resist water for some time, but that which has the strongest glaze will resist longest. The manufacture next in consequence, and also within the department of the women, is that of their mats, which excel everything I have seen at any other place both as to their texture and their beauty. In particular, many of them are so superior to those made at Otaheite, that they are not a bad article to carry thither by way of trade. Of these mats they have seven or eight different sorts for the purposes of wearing or sleeping upon, and many are merely ornamental. The last are chiefly made from the tough, membraneous part of the stock of the plantain tree; those that they wear, from the *Pandanus*, cultivated for that purpose, and never suffered to shoot into a trunk; and the coarser sort, which they sleep upon, from a plant called "evarra." There are many other articles of less note that employ the spare time of their females, as combs, of which they make vast numbers, little baskets made of the same substance as the mats, and others of the fibrous cocoa-nut husk, either plain or interwoven with small beads, but all finished with such neatness and taste in the disposition of the various parts, that a stranger cannot

help admiring their assiduity and dexterity.

The province allotted to the men is, as might be expected, far more laborious and extensive than that of the women. Agriculture, architecture, boat-building, fishing, and other things that relate to navigation, are the objects of their care. Cultivated roots and fruits being their principal support, this requires their constant attention to agriculture, which they pursue very diligently, and seem to have brought almost to as great perfection as circumstances will permit. The large extent of the plantain fields has been taken notice of already; and the same may be said of the yams, these two together being at least as ten to one with respect to all the other articles. In planting both these, they dig small holes for their reception, and afterwards root up the surrounding grass, which in this hot country is quickly deprived of its vegetating power, and, soon rotting, becomes a good manure. The instruments they use for this purpose, which they call "hooo," are nothing more than pickets or stakes of different lengths, according to the depth they have to dig. These are flattened and sharpened to an edge at one end, and the largest have a short piece fixed transversely for pressing it into the ground with the foot. With these, though they are not more than from two to four inches broad, they dig and plant ground of many acres in extent. In planting the plantains and yams they observe so much exactness, that whichever way you look the rows present themselves regular and complete.

The cocoa-nut and bread-fruit trees are scattered about without any order, and seem to give them no trouble after they have attained a certain height. The same may be said of another large tree, which produces great numbers of a large, roundish, compressed nut, called "eeefee;" and of a smaller tree that bears a rounded oval nut two inches long, with two or three triangular kernels, tough and insipid, called "mabba," most frequently planted near their houses. The "kappe" is, commonly, regularly planted, and in pretty large spots; but the "mawhaha" is interspersed amongst other things, as the "jeejee" and yams are: the last of which I have frequently seen in the interspaces of the plantain trees at their common distance. Sugar-cane is commonly in small spots, crowded closely together; and the mulberry, of which the cloth is made, though without order, has sufficient room allowed for it, and is kept very clean. The only other plant that they cultivate for their manufactures is the *Pandanus*, which is generally planted in a row close together at the sides of the other fields; and they consider it as a thing so distinct in this state, that they have a different name for it, which shows that they are very sensible of the great changes brought about by cultivation.

It is remarkable that these people, who in many things show much taste and ingenuity, should show little of either in building their houses; though the defect is rather in the design than in the execution. Those of the lower people are poor huts, scarcely sufficient to defend them from the weather, and very small. Those of the better sort are larger and more comfortable; but not what one might expect. The dimensions of one of a middling size are about thirty feet long, twenty broad, and twelve high. Their house is, properly speaking, a thatched roof or shed, supported by posts and rafters disposed in a very judicious manner. The floor is raised with earth smoothed, and covered with strong, thick matting, and kept very clean. The most of them are closed on the weather side (and some more than two-thirds round) with strong mats, or with branches of the cocoa-nut tree plaited or woven into each other. These they fix up edgewise, reaching from the eaves to the ground, and thus they answer the purpose of a wall. A thick, strong mat, about two and one-half or three feet broad, bent into the form of a semicircle, and set upon its edge with the ends

touching the side of the house, in shape resembling the fender of a fire-hearth, encloses a space for the master and mistress of the family to sleep in. The lady, indeed, spends most of her time during the day within it. The rest of the family sleep upon the floor wherever they please to lie down; the unmarried men and women apart from each other. Or, if the family be large, there are small huts adjoining to which the servants retire in the night; so that privacy is as much observed here as one could expect. They have mats made on purpose for sleeping on; and the clothes that they wear in the day serve for their covering in the night. Their whole furniture consists of a bowl or two, in which they make "kava;" a few gourds, cocoa-nut shells, some small wooden stools which serve them for pillows, and, perhaps, a large stool for the chief or master of the family to sit upon. The only probable reason I can assign for their neglect of ornamental architecture in the construction of their houses, is their being fond of living much in the open air. Indeed, they seem to consider their houses, within which they seldom eat, as of little use but to sleep in and to retire to in bad weather. And the lower sort of people, who spend a great part of their time in close attendance upon the chiefs, can have little use for their own houses but in the last case.

They make amends for the defects of their houses by their great attention to and dexterity in naval architecture, if I may be allowed to give it that name. But I refer to the narrative of my last voyage for an account of their canoes, and their manner of building and navigating them. The only tools which they use to construct these boats are hatchets, or rather thick adzes, of a smooth black stone that abounds at Toofoa; augers made of sharks' teeth fixed on small handles; and rasps of a rough skin of a fish, fastened on flat pieces of wood, thinner on one side, which also have handles. The labour and time employed in finishing their canoes, which are the most perfect of their mechanical productions, will account for their being very careful of them. For they are built and preserved under sheds; or they cover the decked part of them with cocoa-leaves when they are hauled on shore, to prevent their being hurt by the sun. The same tools are all they have for other works, if we except different shells, which they use as knives. But there are few of their productions that require these, unless it be some of their weapons; the other articles being chiefly their fishing materials, and cordage. The cordage is made from the fibres of the cocoa-nut husk, which, though not more than nine or ten inches long, they plait, about the size of a quill or less, to any length that they please, and roll it up in balls, from which the larger ropes are made by twisting several of these together. The lines that they fish with are as strong and even as the best cord we make, resembling it almost in every respect. The other fishing implements are large and small hooks. The last are composed entirely of pearl-shell, but the first are only covered with it on the back, and the points of both commonly of tortoise-shell; those of the small being plain and the others barbed. With the large ones they catch bonitos and albicores, by putting them to a bamboo rod twelve or fourteen feet long, with a line of the same length, which rests in a notch of a piece of wood fixed in the stern of the canoe for that purpose, and is dragged on the surface of the sea as she rows along, without any other bait than a tuft of flaxy stuff near the point. They have also great numbers of pretty small seines, some of which are of a very delicate texture. These they use to catch fish with in the holes on the reefs when the tide ebbs.

The other manual employments consist chiefly in making musical reeds, flutes, warlike weapons, and stools or rather pillows to sleep on. The reeds have eight, nine, or ten pieces placed parallel to each other, but not in any regular progression, having the longest sometimes in the middle, and several of the same length; so that I have seen none with more than six notes; and they seem incapable of playing any music on them that is distinguishable by our ears. The flutes are a joint of bamboo, close at both ends, with a hole near each, and four others; two of which, and one of the first only, are used in playing. They apply the thumb of the left hand to close the left nostril, and blow into the hole at one end with the other. The middle finger of the left hand is applied to the first hole on the left, and the forefinger of the right to the lowest hole on that side. In this manner, though the notes are only three, they produce a pleasing yet simple music, which they vary much more than one would think possible with so imperfect an instrument. Their being accustomed to a music which consists of so few notes is perhaps the reason why they do not seem to relish any of ours, which is so complex. But they can taste what is more deficient than their own; for we observed that they used to be well pleased with hearing the chant of our two young New Zealanders, which consisted rather in mere strength than in melody of expression. The weapons which they make are clubs of different sorts (in the ornamenting of which they spend much time), spears, and darts. They have also bows and arrows; but these seemed to be designed only for amusement, such as shooting at birds, and not for military purposes. The stools are about two feet long, but only four or five inches high, and near four broad, bending downward in the middle, with four strong legs and circular feet; the whole made of one piece of black or brown wood, neatly polished and sometimes inlaid with bits of ivory. They also inlay the handles of flyflaps with ivory, after being neatly carved; and they shape bones into small figures of men, birds, and other things, which must be very difficult, as their carving instrument is only a shark's tooth.

Yams, plantains, and cocoa-nuts, compose the greatest part of their vegetable diet. Of their animal food, the chief articles are hogs, fowls, fish, and all sorts of shell-fish; but the lower people eat rats. The two first vegetable articles, with bread-fruit, are what may be called the basis of their food at different times of the year, with fish and shell-fish; for hogs, fowls, and turtle, seem only to be occasional dainties reserved for their chiefs. The intervals between the seasons of these vegetable productions must be sometimes considerable, as they prepare a sort of artificial bread from plantains, which they put under ground before ripe, and suffer them to remain till they ferment, when they are taken out and made up into small balls; but so sour and indifferent, that they often said our bread was preferable, though somewhat musty. Their food is, generally, dressed by baking, in the same manner as at Otaheite; and they have the art of making from different kinds of fruit several dishes which most of us esteemed very good. I never saw them make use of any kind of sauce; nor drink anything at their meals but water or the juice of the cocoanut; for the "kava" is only their morning draught. I cannot say that they are cleanly either in their cookery or manner of eating. The generality of them will lay their victuals upon the first leaf they meet with, however dirty it may be; but when food is served up to the chiefs it is commonly laid upon green plantain leaves. When the King made a meal, he was for the most part attended upon by three or four persons. One cut large pieces of the joint or of the fish; another divided it into mouthfuls; and others stood by with cocoanuts and whatever else he might want. I never saw a large company sit down to what we should call a sociable meal, by eating from the same dish. The food, be what it will, is always divided into portions, each to serve a certain number; these portions are again subdivided; so that one seldom sees above two or three persons eating together. The women are not excluded from eating with the men, but there are certain ranks or orders amongst them that can neither eat nor drink together. This distinction begins with the King, but where it ends I cannot say. They seem to have no set time for meals; though it should be observed that during our stay amongst them their domestic economy was much disturbed by their constant attention to us. As far as we could remark, those of the superior rank only drink "kava" in the forenoon, and the others eat perhaps a bit of yam; but we commonly saw all of them eat something in the afternoon. It is probable that the practice of making a meal in the night is pretty common; and their rest being thus interrupted they frequently sleep in the day. They go to bed as soon as it is dark, and rise with the dawn in the morning.

They are very fond of associating together, so that it is common to find several houses empty, and the owners of them convened in some other one, or rather upon a convenient spot in the neighbourhood where they recreate themselves by conversing and other amusements. Their private diversions are chiefly singing, dancing, and music performed by the women. When two or three women sing in concert, and snap their fingers, it is called "oobai;" but when there is a greater number they divide into several parties, each of which sings on a different key, which makes a very agreeable music, and is called "heeva" or "haiva." In the same manner, they vary the music of their flutes, by playing on those of a different size; but their dancing is much the same as when they perform publicly. The dancing of the men (if it is to be called dancing), although it does not consist much in moving the feet as we do, has a thousand different motions with the hands to which we are entire strangers; and they are performed with an ease and grace which are not to be described nor even conceived but by those who have seen them. But I need add nothing to what has been already said on this subject in the account of the incidents that happened during our stay at the islands.

Whether their marriages be made lasting by any kind of solemn contract, we could not determine with precision; but it is certain, that the bulk of the people satisfied themselves with one wife. The chiefs, however, have commonly several women; though some of us were of opinion that there was only one that was looked upon as the mistress of the family. As female chastity at first sight seemed to be held in no great estimation, we expected to have found frequent breaches of their conjugal fidelity; but we did them great injustice. I do not know that a single instance happened during our whole stay. Neither are those of the better sort that are unmarried more free of their favours. It is true, there was no want of those of a different character; and perhaps such are more frequently met with here in proportion to the number of people, than in many other countries. But it appeared to me that the most, if not all of them, were of the lowest class; and such of them as permitted familiarities to our people were prostitutes by profession.

Nothing can be a greater proof of the humanity of these people than the concern they show for the dead. To use a common expression, their mourning is not in words but deeds. For, besides the " tooge " mentioned before, and burnt circles and scars, they beat the teeth with stones, strike a shark's tooth into the head until the blood flows in streams, and thrust spears into the inner part of the thigh, into their sides below the arm-pits, and through the cheeks into the mouth. All these operations convey an idea of such rigorous discipline as must require either an uncommon degree of affection, or the grossest superstition, to exact. I will not say that the last has no share in it; for sometimes it is so universal that many could not have any knowledge of the person for whom the concern is expressed. Thus we saw the people of Tongataboo mourning the death of a

chief at Vavaoo; and other similar instances occurred during our stay. It should be observed, however, that the more painful operations are only practised on account of the death of those most nearly connected with the mourners. When a person dies, he is buried, after being wrapped up in mats and cloth, much after our manner. The chiefs seem to have the " fiatookas " appropriated to them as their burial-places; but the common people are interred in no particular spot. What part of the mourning ceremony follows immediately after is uncertain; but that there is something besides the general one, which is continued for a considerable length of time, we could infer from being informed that the funeral of Mareewagee's wife, as mentioned before, was to be attended with ceremonies that were to last five days, in which all the principal people were to commemorate her.

Their long and general mourning proves that they consider death as a very great evil. And this is confirmed by a very odd custom which they practise to avert it. When I first visited these islands, during my last voyage, I observed that many of the inhabitants had one or both of their little fingers cut off; and we could not then receive any satisfactory account of the reason of this mutilation. But we now learned that this operation is performed when they labour under some grievous disease and think themselves in danger of dying. They suppose that the Deity will accept of the little finger as a sort of sacrifice efficacious enough to procure the recovery of their health. They cut it off with one of their stone hatchets. There was scarcely one in ten of them whom we did not find thus mutilated in one or both hands; which has a disagreeable effect, especially as they sometimes cut so close that they encroach upon the bone of the hand which joins to the amputated finger.[1]

---

[1] It may be proper to mention here, on the authority of Captain King, that

From the rigid severity with which some of these mourning and religious ceremonies are executed, one would expect to find that they meant thereby to secure to themselves felicity beyond the grave; but their principal object relates to things merely temporal, for they seem to have little conception of future punishment for faults committed in this life. They believe, however, that they are justly punished upon earth; and consequently use every method to render their Divinities propitious. The Supreme Author of most things they call "Kallafootonga," who, they say, is a female residing in the sky and directing the thunder, wind, rain, and in general all the changes of weather. They believe that when she is angry with them the productions of the earth are blasted; that many things are destroyed by lightning; and that they themselves are afflicted with sickness and death, as well as their hogs and other animals. When this anger abates, they suppose that everything is restored to its natural order; and it should seem that they have a great reliance on the efficacy of their endeavours to appease their offended Divinity. They also admit a plurality of deities, though all inferior to "Kallafootonga." Amongst them they mention "Toofooa-boolootoo," god of the clouds and fog; "Talleteboo," and some others, residing in the heavens. The first in rank and power, who has the government of the sea and its productions, is called "Futtafaihe," or, as it was sometimes pronounced, "Footafooa," who, they say, is a male, and has for his wife "Fykavakajeea;" and here, as in heaven, there are several inferior potentates, such as "Vahaa-fonooa," "Tareeava," "Mattaba," "Evaroo," and others. The same religious system, however, does not extend all over the cluster of the Friendly Isles;

for the supreme god of Hapaee, for instance, is called "Alo Alo;" and other isles have two or three of different names. But their notions of the power and other attributes of these beings are so very absurd, that they suppose they have no further concern with them after death.

They have, however, very proper sentiments about the immateriality and the immortality of the soul. They call it life, the living principle, or, what is more agreeable to their notions of it, an "Otooa;" that is, a divinity or invisible being. They say that immediately upon death the souls of their chiefs separate from their bodies, and go to a place called "Boolootoo," the chief or god of which is "Gooleho." This "Gooleho" seems to be a personification of death; for they used to say to us, "You and the men of Feejee" (by this junction meaning to pay a compliment expressive of their confession of our superiority over themselves) "are also subject to the power and dominion of 'Gooleho.'" His country, the general receptacle of the dead, according to their mythology, was never seen by any person; yet it seems they know that it lies to the westward of Feejee, and that they who are once transported thither live for ever, or, to use their own expression, are not subject to death again, but feast upon all the favourite products of their own country, with which this everlasting abode is supposed to abound. As to the souls of the lower sort of people, they undergo a sort of transmigration; or, as they say, are eaten up by a bird called "Ioata," which walks upon their graves for that purpose.

I think I may venture to assert that they do not worship anything that is the work of their own hands, or any visible part of the creation. They do not make offerings of hogs, dogs, and fruit, as at Otaheite, unless it be emblematically, for their "morais" were perfectly free from everything of the kind. But that they offer real human sacrifices is with me beyond a doubt. Their "morais" or "fiatookas" (for they are called by

---

it is common for the inferior people to cut off a joint of their little finger, on account of the sickness of the chiefs to whom they belong.—*Note in Original Edition.*

both names, but mostly by the latter) are, as at Otaheite and many other parts of the world, burying-grounds and places of worship, though some of them seemed to be only appropriated to the first purpose, but these were small, and in every other respect inferior to the others.

Of the nature of their government we know no more than the general outline. A subordination is established among them that resembles the feudal system of our progenitors in Europe. But of its subdivisions, of the constituent parts, and in what manner they are connected so as to form a body politic, I confess myself totally ignorant. Some of them told us that the power of the King is unlimited, and that the life and property of the subject is at his disposal. But the few circumstances that fell under our observation rather contradicted than confirmed the idea of a despotic government. Mareewagee, old Toobou, and Feenou, acted each like petty sovereigns, and frequently thwarted the measures of the King, of which he often complained. Neither was his court more splendid than those of the two first, who are the most powerful chiefs in the islands; and next to them Fecnou, Marcewagee's son, seemed to stand highest in authority. But however independent on the despotic power of the King the great men may be, we saw instances enough to prove that the lower order of people have no property nor safety for their persons but at the will of the chiefs to whom they respectively belong.

Tongataboo is divided into many districts, of above thirty of which we learned the names. Each of these has its particular chief, who decides differences and distributes justice within his own district. But we could not form any satisfactory judgment about the extent of their power in general, or their mode of proportioning punishments to crimes. Most of these chiefs have possessions in other islands, whence they draw supplies. At least we know this is so with respect to the King, who at certain established times receives the product of his distant domains at Tongataboo, which is not only the principal place of his residence, but seemingly of all the people of consequence amongst these isles. Its inhabitants in common conversation call it the Land of Chiefs, while the subordinate isles are distinguished by the appellation of Lands of Servants. These chiefs are by the people styled not only Lords of the Earth, but of the Sun and Sky; and the King's family assume the name of Futtafaihe, from the god so called, who is probably their tutelary patron and perhaps their common ancestor. The Sovereign's peculiar earthly title is, however, simply "Tooee Tonga."

There is a decorum observed in the presence of their principal men, and particularly of their King, that is truly admirable. Whenever he sits down, whether it be in a house or without, all the attendants seat themselves at the same time in a semicircle before him, leaving always a convenient space between him and them, into which no one attempts to come unless he has some particular business. Neither is any one allowed to pass or sit behind him, nor even near him, without his order or permission; so that our having been indulged with this privilege was a significant proof of the great respect that was paid us. When any one wants to speak with the King, he advances and sits down before him, delivers what he has to say in a few words; and, having received his answer, retires again to the circle. But if the King speaks to any one, that person answers from his seat, unless he is to receive some order, in which case he gets up from his place and sits down before the chief with his legs across, which is a posture to which they are so much accustomed that any other mode of sitting is disagreeable to them.[1] To speak to the King standing would be accounted here as a striking mark of rudeness,

---

[1] This is peculiar to the men, the women always sitting with both legs thrown a little on one side.

as it would be with us for one to sit down and put on his hat when he addresses himself to his superior, and that superior on his feet and uncovered.

It does not indeed appear that any of the most civilised nations have ever exceeded this people in the great order observed on all occasions, in ready compliance with the commands of their chiefs, and in the harmony that subsists throughout all ranks, and unites them as if they were all one man, informed with and directed by the same principle. Such a behaviour is remarkably obvious whenever it is requisite that their chief should harangue any body of them collected together, which is frequently done. The most profound silence and attention are observed during the harangue, even to a much greater degree than is practised amongst us on the most interesting and serious deliberations of our most respectable assemblies. And whatever might have been the subject of the speech delivered, we never saw an instance when any individual present showed signs of his being displeased, or indicated the least inclination to dispute the declared will of a person who had a right to command. Nay, such is the force of these verbal laws, as I may call them, that I have seen one of their chiefs express his being astonished at a person's having acted contrary to such orders, though it appeared that the poor man could not possibly have been informed in time to have observed them.

Though some of the more potent chiefs may vie with the King in point of actual possessions, they fall very short in rank and in certain marks of respect which the collective body have agreed to pay the monarch. It is a particular privilege annexed to his sovereignty not to be punctured nor circumcised as all his subjects are. Whenever he walks out, every one whom he meets must sit down till he has passed. No one is allowed to be over his head; on the contrary, all must come under his feet, for there cannot be a greater outward mark of submission than that which is paid to the Sovereign and other great people of these islands by their inferiors. The method is this: the person who is to pay obeisance squats down before the chief, and bows the head to the sole of his foot, which when he sits is so placed that it can be easily come at; and having tapped or touched it with the under and upper side of the fingers of both hands, he rises up and retires. It should seem that the King cannot refuse any one who chooses to pay him this homage, which is called "moe moea," for the common people would frequently take it into their heads to do it when he was walking; and he was always obliged to stop and hold up one of his feet behind him till they had performed the ceremony. This to a heavy unwieldy man like Poulaho must be attended with some trouble and pain; and I have sometimes seen him make a run, though very unable, to get out of the way or to reach a place where he might conveniently sit down. The hands, after this application of them to the chief's feet, are in some cases rendered useless for a time, for until they be washed they must not touch any kind of food. This interdiction, in a country where water is so scarce, would seem to be attended with some inconvenience; but they are never at a loss for a succedaneum, and a piece of any juicy plant, which they can easily procure immediately, being rubbed upon them, this serves for the purpose of purification as well as washing them with water. When the hands are in this state they call it "taboo rema." "Taboo," in general, signifies forbidden; and "rema" is their word for hand.

When the "taboo" is incurred by paying obeisance to a great personage, it is thus easily washed off. But in some other cases it must necessarily continue for a certain time. We have frequently seen women who have been "taboo rema" fed by others. At the expiration of the time, the interdicted person washes herself in one of their baths, which are dirty holes, for the most part, of brackish water. She then waits upon the King, and, after making her obeisance in the usual way, lays hold of his foot and applies it to her breast, shoulders, and other parts of her body. He then embraces her on each shoulder, after which she retires purified from her uncleanness. I do not know that it is always necessary to come to the King for this purpose, though Omai assured me it was. If this be so, it may be one reason why he is for the most part travelling from island to island. I saw this ceremony performed by him two or three times, and once by Feenou to one of his own women; but as Omai was not then with me I could not ask the occasion. "Taboo," as I have before observed, is a word of an extensive signification. Human sacrifices are called "tangata taboo;" and when anything is forbidden to be eaten or made use of, they say that it is "taboo." They tell us that if the King should happen to go into a house belonging to a subject, that house would be "taboo," and could never more be inhabited by the owner, so that wherever he travels there are particular houses for his reception. Old Toobou at this time presided over the "taboo," that is, if Omai comprehended the matter rightly, he and his deputies inspected all the produce of the island, taking care that every man should cultivate and plant his quota, and ordering what should be eaten and what not. By this wise regulation they effectually guard against a famine, a sufficient quantity of ground is employed in raising provisions, and every article thus raised is secured from unnecessary waste.

By another prudent regulation in their government, they have an officer over the police, or something like it. This department when we were amongst them was administered by Feenou; whose business, we were told, it was to punish all offenders, whether against the State or against individuals. He was also generalissimo, and commanded the warriors when called out upon service; but by all accounts this is very seldom. The King frequently took some pains to inform us of Feenou's office; and, among other things, told us that if he himself should become a bad man, Feenou would kill him. What I understood by this expression of being a bad man was, that if he did not govern according to law or custom, Feenou would be ordered by the other great men, or by the people at large, to put him to death. There should seem to be no doubt that a sovereign thus liable to be controlled and punished for an abuse of power, cannot be called a despotic monarch. When we consider the number of islands that compose this little state, and the distance at which some of them lie from the seat of government, attempts to throw off the yoke and to acquire independency, it should seem, might be apprehended. But they tell us that this never happens. One reason why they are not thus disturbed by domestic quarrels may be this, that all the powerful chiefs, as we have already mentioned, reside at Tongataboo. They also secure the independence of the other islands by the celerity of their operations; for if at any time a troublesome and popular man should start up in any of them, Feenou, or whoever holds his office, is immediately despatched thither to kill him. By this means they crush a rebellion in its very infancy.

The orders or classes amongst their chiefs, or those who call themselves such, seemed to be almost as numerous as amongst us; but there are few in comparison that are lords of large districts of territory, the rest holding their lands under those principal barons, as they may be called. I was, indeed, told that when a man of property dies, everything he leaves behind him falls to the King; but that it is usual to give it to the eldest son of the deceased, with an obligation to make a provision out of it for the rest of the children. It is not the custom here, as at Otaheite, for the son, the moment he is born, to take from the father the homage and title, but he succeeds to them at his decease; so that their form of government is not only monarchical but hereditary.

The order of succession to the crown has not been of late interrupted; for we know from a particular circumstance that the Futtafaihes (Poulaho being only an addition to distinguish the King from the rest of his family) have reigned in a direct line for at least 135 years. Upon inquiring whether any account had been preserved amongst them of the arrival of Tasman's ships, we found that this history had been handed down to them from their ancestors with an accuracy which marks that oral tradition may sometimes be depended upon. For they described the two ships as resembling ours; mentioning the place where they had anchored; their having stayed but a few days; and their moving from that station to Annamooka. And, by way of informing us how long ago this had happened, they told us the name of the Futtafaihe who was then king, and of those who had succeeded, down to Poulaho, who is the fifth since that period; the first being an old man at the time of the arrival of the ships.

From what has been said of the present King, it would be natural to suppose that he had the highest rank of any person in the islands. But to our great surprise we found it is not so; for Latoolibooloo, the person who was pointed out to me as King when I first visited Tongataboo, and three women, are in some respects superior to Poulaho himself. On our inquiring who these extraordinary personages were whom they distinguish by the name and title of "Tammaha," we were told that the late King, Poulaho's father, had a sister of equal rank, and older than himself; that she, by a man who came from the island of Feejee, had a son and two daughters; and that these three persons, as well as their mother, rank above Futtafaihe, the King. We endeavoured in vain to trace the reason of this singular pre-eminence of the "Tammahas;" for we could learn nothing besides this account of their pedigree. The mother, and one of the daughters, called Tooeela-kaipa, live at Vavaoo. Latoolibooloo, the son, and the other daughter, whose name is Moungoula - kaipa, reside at Tongataboo. The latter is the woman who is mentioned to have dined with me on the 21st of June.[1] This gave occasion to our discovering her superiority over the King, who would not eat in her presence, though she made no scruple to do so before him, and received from him the customary obeisance by touching her foot. We never had an opportunity of seeing him pay this mark of respect to Latoolibooloo; but we have observed him leave off eating, and have his victuals put aside, when the latter came into the same house. Latoolibooloo assumed the privilege of taking anything from the people, even if it belonged to the King; and yet, in the ceremony called "Natche," he assisted only in the same manner as the other principal men. He was looked upon by his countrymen as a madman; and many of his actions seemed to confirm this judgment. At Eooa they showed me a good deal of land said to belong to him; and I saw there a son of his, a child whom they distinguished by the same title as his father. The son of the greatest prince in Europe could not be more humoured and caressed than this little "Tammaha" was.[2]

---

[1] In Chapter VII. of this Book, *ante*, p. 135.

[2] The remainder of the Chapter is omitted; it is taken up with linguistic speculations, and lists of similar words current at the Friendly Islands and Otaheite; and with a technical record of the nautical and astronomical observations made during the sojourn at Tongataboo.

BOOK III.

TRANSACTIONS AT OTAHEITE, AND THE SOCIETY ISLANDS; AND PROSECUTION OF THE VOYAGE TO THE COAST OF NORTH AMERICA.

CHAPTER I.

HAVING taken our final leave of the Friendly Islands, I now resume my narrative of the voyage. In the evening of the 17th of July, at 8 o'clock, the body of Eooa bore NE. by N., distant three or four leagues. The wind was now at E., and blew a fresh gale. With it I stood to the S. till half-an-hour past 6 o'clock the next morning, when a sudden squall from the same direction took our ship aback; and before the sails could be trimmed on the other tack, the mainsail and top-gallant sails were much torn. The wind kept between the SW. and SE. on the 19th and 20th; afterward it veered to the ENE., and N. The night between the 20th and 21st an eclipse of the moon was observed. I continued to stretch to the ESE., with the wind at NE. and N., without meeting with anything worthy of note till 7 o'clock in the evening of the 29th, when we had a sudden and very heavy squall of wind from the N. At this time we were under single reefed topsails, courses, and stay-sails. Two of the latter were blown to pieces; and it was with difficulty that we saved the other sails. After this squall, we observed several lights moving about on board the Discovery, by which we concluded that something had given way; and the next morning we saw that her main-topmast had been lost. Both wind and weather continued very unsettled till noon this day, when the latter cleared up, and the former settled in the NW. quarter. At this time we were in the Latitude of 28° 6′ S., and our Longitude was 198° 23′ E. Here we saw some pintado birds, being the first since we left the land.

On the 31st at noon Captain Clerke made a signal to speak with me. By the return of the boat which I sent on board his ship, he informed me that the head of the mainmast had been discovered to be sprung in such a manner as to render the rigging of another topmast very dangerous, and that therefore he must rig something lighter in its place. He also informed me that he had lost his maintop-gallantyard, and that he neither had another nor a spar to make one on board. The Resolution's spritsail and topsail-yard, which I sent him, supplied this want. The next day we got up a jury topmast, on which he set a mizzen topsail, and this enabled him to keep way with the Resolution. The wind was fixed in the western board—that is, from the N. round by the W. to S., and I steered E. and NE., without meeting with anything remarkable, till 11 o'clock in the morning of the 8th of August, when the land was seen bearing NNE. nine or ten leagues distant. At first it appeared in detached hills, like so many separate islands, but as we drew nearer we found that they were all connected, and belonged to one and the same island. I steered directly for it, with a fine gale at SE. by S., and at half-past 6 o'clock in the afternoon it extended from N. by E. to NNE. three-quarters E., distant three or four leagues.

The night was spent standing off and on, and at daybreak the next morning I steered for the NW., or leeside of the island; and as we stood round its S. or SW. part, we saw it everywhere guarded by a reef of coral rock, extending in some places a full mile from the land, and a high surf beating upon it. Some thought that they saw land to the southward of this island, but as that was to the windward it was left undetermined.

As we drew near we saw people on several parts of the coast, walking or running along shore, and in a little time after we had reached the leeside of the island we saw them launch two canoes, into which above a dozen men got, and paddled toward us. I now shortened sail, as well to give these canoes time to come up with us, as to sound for anchorage. At the distance of about half-a-mile from the reef we found from forty to thirty-five fathoms water, over a bottom of fine sand. Nearer in, the bottom was strewed with coral rocks. The canoes having advanced to about the distance of a pistol-shot from the ship, there stopped. Omai was employed, as he usually had been on such occasions, to use all his eloquence to prevail upon the men in them to come nearer, but no entreaties could induce them to trust themselves within our reach. They kept eagerly pointing to the shore with their paddles, and calling to us to go thither; and several of their countrymen who stood upon the beach held up something white, which we considered also as an invitation to land. We could very well have done this, as there was good anchorage without the reef, and a break or opening in it, from whence the canoes had come out, which had no surf upon it, and where, if there was not water for the ships, there was more than sufficient for the boats. But I did not think proper to risk losing the advantage of a fair wind for the sake of examining an island that appeared to be of little consequence. We stood in no need of refreshments, if I had been sure of meeting with them there; and having already been so unexpectedly delayed in my progress to the Society Islands, I was desirous of avoiding every possibility of further retardment. For this reason, after making several unsuccessful attempts to induce these people to come alongside, I made sail to the north, and left them, but not without getting from them during their vicinity to our ship the name of their island, which they called Toobouai. It is situated in the Latitude of 22° 15′ S.,

and in 210° 37′ E. Longitude. Its greatest extent in any direction, exclusive of the reef is not above five or six miles.

After leaving this island, I steered to the N. with a fresh gale at E. by S., and at daybreak in the morning of the 12th we saw the island of Maitea. Soon after Otaheite made its appearance, and at noon it extended from SW. by W. to WNW., the point of Oheitepeha Bay, bearing W., about four leagues distant. I steered for this bay, intending to anchor there, in order to draw what refreshments I could from the SE. part of the island before I went down to Matavai, from the neighbourhood of which station I expected my principal supply. We had a fresh gale easterly till 2 o'clock in the afternoon, when, being about a league from the bay, the wind suddenly died away, and was succeeded by baffling light airs from every direction, and calms by turns. This lasted about two hours; then we had sudden squalls, with rain, from the east. These carried us before the bay, where we got a breeze from the land, and attempted in vain to work in, to gain the anchoring place; so that at last, about 9 o'clock, we were obliged to stand out and to spend the night at sea.

When we first drew near the island several canoes came off to the ship, each conducted by two or three men. But as they were common fellows, Omai took no particular notice of them, nor they of him. They did not even seem to perceive that he was one of their countrymen, although they conversed with him for some time. At length a chief whom I had known before, named Ootee, and Omai's brother-in-law, who chanced to be now at this corner of the island, and three or four more persons, all of whom knew Omai before he embarked with Captain Furneaux, came on board. Yet there was nothing either tender or striking in their meeting. On the contrary, there seemed to be a perfect indifference on both sides, till Omai, having taken his brother down into the cabin, opened the drawer where he kept his red feathers, and gave him a few. This being presently known amongst the rest of the natives upon deck, the face of affairs was entirely turned, and Ootee, who would hardly speak to Omai before, now begged that they might be "tayos,"[1] and exchange names. Omai accepted of the honour, and confirmed it with a present of red feathers, and Ootee, by way of return, sent ashore for. a hog. But it was evident to every one of us that it was not the man, but his property, they were in love with. Had he not shown them his treasure of red feathers, which is the commodity in greatest estimation at the island, I question much whether they would have bestowed even a cocoa-nut upon him. Such was Omai's first reception among his countrymen. I own I never expected it would be otherwise, but still I was in hopes that the valuable cargo of presents with which the liberality of his friends in England had loaded him would be the means of raising him into consequence, and of making him respected and even courted by the first persons throughout the extent of the Society Islands. This could not but have happened had he conducted himself with any degree of prudence. But instead of it, I am sorry to say that he paid too little regard to the repeated advice of those who wished him well, and suffered himself to be duped by every designing knave.

From the natives who came off to us in the course of this day we learned that two ships had twice been in Oheitepeha Bay since my last visit to this island, in 1774, and that they had left animals there such as we had on board. But on further inquiry we found they were only hogs, dogs, goats, one bull, and the male of some other animal, which from the imperfect description now given us we could not find out. They told us that these ships had come from a place called "Reema," by which we guessed that

Lima, the capital of Peru, was meant, and that these late visitors were Spaniards. We were informed that the first time they came they built a house, and left four men behind them —viz., two priests, a boy or servant, and a fourth person, called Mateema, who was much spoken of at this time, carrying away with them when they sailed four of the natives; that in about ten months the same two ships returned, bringing back two of the islanders, the other two having died at Lima; and that after a short stay they took away their own people, but that the house which they had built was left standing.

The important news of red feathers being on board our ships having been conveyed on shore by Omai's friends, day had no sooner begun to break next morning than we were surrounded by a multitude of canoes crowded with people, bringing hogs and fruit to market. At first, a quantity of feathers not greater than what might be got from a tom-tit would purchase a hog of forty or fifty pounds weight. But as almost everybody in the ships was possessed of some of this precious article in trade, it fell in its value above 500 per cent. before night. However, even then the balance was much in our favour; and red feathers continued to preserve their superiority over every other commodity. Some of the natives would not part with a hog unless they received an axe in exchange; but nails, and beads, and other trinkets, which during our former voyages had so great a run at this island, were now so much despised that few would deign so much as to look at them.

There being but little wind all the morning, it was 9 o'clock before we could get to an anchor in the bay, where we moored with two bowers. Soon after we had anchored, Omai's sister came on board to see him. I was happy to observe that, much to the honour of them both, their meeting was marked with expressions of the tenderest affection, easier to be conceived than to be described. This moving scene having closed, and the

---

[1] Friends.

ship being properly moored, Omai and I went ashore. My first object was to pay a visit to a man whom my friend represented as a very extraordinary personage indeed, for he said that he was the god of Bolabola. We found him seated under one of those small awnings which they usually carry in their larger canoes. He was an elderly man, and had lost the use of his limbs, so that he was carried from place to place upon a hand-barrow. Some called him "Olla" or "Orra," which is the name of the god of Bolabola; but his own proper name was Etary. From Omai's account of this person I expected to have seen some religious adoration paid to him; but excepting some plantain trees that lay before him and upon the awning under which he sat, I could observe nothing by which he might be distinguished from their other chiefs. Omai presented to him a tuft of red feathers tied to the end of a small stick; but, after a little conversation on indifferent matters with this Bolabola man, his attention was drawn to an old woman, the sister of his mother. She was already at his feet, and had bedewed them plentifully with tears of joy.

I left him with the old lady, in the midst of a number of people who had gathered round him, and went to take a view of the house said to be built by the strangers who had lately been here. I found it standing at a small distance from the beach. The wooden materials of which it was composed seemed to have been brought hither ready prepared, to be set up occasionally; for all the planks were numbered. It was divided into two small rooms; and in the inner one were a bedstead, a table, a bench, some old hats, and other trifles, of which the natives seemed to be very careful, as also of the house itself, which had suffered no hurt from the weather, a shed having been built over it. There were scuttles all around which served as air holes; and perhaps they were also meant to fire from with muskets, if ever this should be found necessary. At a little distance from the front stood a wooden cross, on the transverse part of which was cut the following inscription:

" Christus vincit."

And on the perpendicular part (which confirmed our conjecture that the two ships were Spanish):

" Carolus III. Imperat. 1774."

On the other side of tho post I preserved the memory of the prior visits of the English by inscribing:

" Georgius Tertius Rex,
Annis 1767,
1769, 1773, 1774, & 1777."

The natives pointed out to us, near the foot of the cross, the grave of the Commodore of the two ships, who had died here while they lay in the bay the first time. His name, as they pronounced it, was Oreede. Whatever the intentions of the Spaniards in visiting this island might be, they seemed to have taken great pains to ingratiate themselves with the inhabitants; who upon every occasion mentioned them with the strongest expressions of esteem and veneration.

I met with no chief of any considerable note on this occasion excepting the extraordinary personage above described. Waheiadooa, the sovereign of Tiaraboo (as this part of the island is called), was now absent; and I afterwards found that he was not the same person, though of the same name, with the chief whom I had seen here during my last voyage, but his brother, a boy of about ten years of age, who had succeeded upon the death of the elder Waheiadooa, about twenty months before our arrival. We also learned that the celebrated Oberea was dead, but that Otoo and all our other friends were living. When I returned from viewing the house and cross erected by the Spaniards, I found Omai holding forth to a large company; and it was with some difficulty that he could be got away to accompany me on board, where I had an important affair to settle.

On our landing [on the 17th] we first visited Etary, who, carried on a hand-barrow, attended us to a large house, where he was set down, and we seated ourselves on each side of him. I caused a piece of Tongataboo cloth to be spread out before us, on which I laid the presents I intended to make. Presently the young chief came, attended by his mother and several principal men, who all seated themselves at the other end of the cloth, facing us. Then a man who sat by me made a speech, consisting of short and separate sentences, part of which was dictated by those about him. He was answered by one from the opposite side, near the chief. Etary spoke next, then Omai; and both of them were answered from the same quarter. These orations were entirely about my arrival, and connections with them. The person who spoke last told me, amongst other things, that the men of "Reema," that is, the Spaniards, had desired them not to suffer me to come into Oheitepeha Bay if I should return any more to the island, for that it belonged to them; but that they were so far from paying any regard to this request, that he was authorised now to make a formal surrender of the province of Tiaraboo to me, and everything in it; which marks very plainly that these people are no strangers to the policy of accommodating themselves to present circumstances. At length the young chief was directed by his attendants to come and embrace me; and by way of confirming this treaty of friendship we exchanged names. The ceremony being closed, he and his friends accompanied me on board to dinner.

Omai had prepared a "maro," composed of red and yellow feathers, which he intended for Otoo, the King of the whole island; and, considering where we were, it was a present of very great value. I said all that I could to persuade him not to produce it now, wishing him to keep it on board till an opportunity should offer of presenting it to Otoo with his own hands. But he had too good an opinion of the honesty and fidelity of his countrymen to take my advice. Nothing

would serve him but to carry it ashore on this occasion, and to give it to Waheiadooa, to be by him forwarded to Otoo, in order to its being added to the royal "maro." He thought by this management that he should oblige both chiefs; whereas he highly disobliged the one whose favour was of the most consequence to him, without gaining any reward from the other. What I had foreseen happened; for Waheiadooa kept the "maro" for himself, and only sent to Otoo a very small piece of feathers, not the twentieth part of what belonged to the magnificent present. On the 19th this young chief made me a present of ten or a dozen hogs, a quantity of fruit, and some cloth. In the evening we played off some fireworks, which both astonished and entertained the numerous spectators.

This day some of our gentlemen in their walks found what they were pleased to call a Roman Catholic chapel. Indeed, from their account, this was not to be doubted, for they described the altar and every other constituent part of such a place of worship. However, as they mentioned at the same time that two men who had the care of it would not suffer them to go in, I thought that they might be mistaken, and had the curiosity to pay a visit to it myself. The supposed chapel proved to be a "toopapaoo," in which the remains of the late Waheiadooa lay as it were in state. It was in a pretty large house, which was enclosed with a low palisade. The "toopapaoo" was uncommonly neat, and resembled one of those little houses, or awnings, belonging to their large canoes. Perhaps it had originally been employed for that purpose. It was covered, and hung round with cloth and mats of different colours so as to have a pretty effect. There was one piece of scarlet broad-cloth four or five yards in length conspicuous among the other ornaments, which no doubt had been a present from the Spaniards. This cloth, and a few tassels of feathers which our gentlemen supposed to be silk, suggested to them the idea of a chapel; for whatever else was wanting to create a resemblance, their imagination supplied; and if they had not previously known that there had been Spaniards lately here they could not possibly have made the mistake. Small offerings of fruit and roots seemed to be daily made at this shrine, as some pieces were quite fresh. These were deposited upon a "whatta," or altar, which stood without the palisades; and within these we were not permitted to enter. Two men constantly attended night and day, not only to watch over the place, but also to dress and undress the "toopapaoo." For when I first went to survey it, the cloth and its appendages were all rolled up; but at my request the two attendants hung it out in order, first dressing themselves in clean white robes. They told me that the chief had been dead twenty months.

Having taken in a fresh supply of water, and finished all our other necessary operations, on the 22d I brought off the cattle and sheep which had been put on shore here to graze, and made ready for sea. In the morning of the 23d, while the ships were unmooring, Omai and I landed to take leave of the young chief. While we were with him, one of those enthusiastic persons whom they call "Eatooas," from a persuasion that they are possessed with the spirit of the Divinity, came and stood before us. He had all the appearance of a man not in his right senses, and his only dress was a large quantity of plantain leaves wrapped round his waist. He spoke in a low squeaking voice so as hardly to be understood, at least not by me. But Omai said that he comprehended him perfectly, and that he was advising Waheiadooa not to go with me to Matavai, an expedition which I had never heard he intended, nor had I ever made such a proposal to him. The "Eatooa" also foretold that the ships would not get to Matavai that day. But in this he was mistaken, though appearances now rather favoured his prediction, there not being a breath of wind in any direction. While he was prophe-

sying, there fell a very heavy shower of rain, which made every one run for shelter but himself, who seemed not to regard it. He remained squeaking by us about half-an-hour, and then retired. No one paid any attention to what he uttered, though some laughed at him. I asked the chief what he was, whether an "Earee" or a "Towtow," and the answer I received was, that he was "taato eno," that is, a bad man. And yet, notwithstanding this, and the little notice any of the natives seemed to take of the mad prophet, superstition has so far got the better of their reason that they firmly believe such persons to be possessed with the spirit of the "Eatooa." Omai seemed to be very well instructed about them. He said that during the fits that came upon them they knew nobody, not even their most intimate acquaintances; and that if any one of them happens to be a man of property he will very often give away every movable he is possessed of if his friends do not put them out of his reach; and when he recovers, will inquire what had become of those very things which he had but just before distributed, not seeming to have the least remembrance of what he had done while the fit was upon him.

As soon as I got on board a light breeze springing up at E., we got under sail and steered for Matavai Bay, where the Resolution anchored the same evening. But the Discovery did not get in till the next morning, so that half of the man's prophecy was fulfilled.

CHAPTER II.

About 9 o'clock in the morning, Otoo, the King of the whole island, attended by a great number of canoes full of people, came from Oparre, his place of residence; and having landed on Matavai Point, sent a message on board expressing his desire to see me there. Accordingly I landed, accompanied by Omai and some of the officers. We found a prodigious number of people assembled on this occasion, and in the midst of them was the King, attended by his father, his two brothers, and three sisters. I went up first and saluted him, being followed by Omai, who kneeled and embraced his legs. He had prepared himself for this ceremony by dressing himself in his very best suit of clothes, and behaved with a great deal of respect and modesty. Nevertheless, very little notice was taken of him. Perhaps envy had some share in producing this cold reception. He made the chief a present of a large piece of red feathers and about two or three yards of gold cloth ; and I gave him a suit of fine linen, a gold-laced hat, some tools, and, what was of more value than all the other articles, a quantity of red feathers and one of the bonnets in use at the Friendly Islands.

After the hurry of this visit was over, the King and the whole royal family accompanied me on board, followed by several canoes laden with all kinds of provisions, in quantity sufficient to have served the companies of both ships for a week. Each of the family owned, or pretended to own, a part, so that I had a present from every one of them ; and every one of them had a separate present in return from me, which was the great object in view. Soon after, the King's mother, who had not been present at the first interview, came on board, bringing with her a quantity of provisions and cloth, which she divided between me and Omai. For although he was but little noticed at first by his countrymen, they no sooner gained the knowledge of his riches than they began to court his friendship. I encouraged this as much as I could, for it was my wish to fix him with Otoo. As I intended to leave all my European animals at this island, I thought he would be able to give some instruction about the management of them and about their use. Besides, I knew and saw that the farther he was from his native island he would be the better respected. But

unfortunately poor Omai rejected my advice, and conducted himself in so imprudent a manner that he soon lost the friendship of Otoo, and of every other person of note in Otaheite. He associated with none but vagabonds and strangers, whose sole views were to plunder him ; and if I had not interfered they would not have left him a single article worth the carrying from the island. This necessarily drew upon him the ill-will of the principal chiefs, who found that they could not procure from any one in the ships such valuable presents as Omai bestowed on the lowest of the people, his companions.

As soon as we had dined, a party of us accompanied Otoo to Oparre, taking with us the poultry with which we were to stock the island. They consisted of a peacock and hen (which Lord Bessborough was so kind as to send me for this purpose a few days before I left London), a turkey cock and hen, one gander and three geese, a drake and four ducks. All these I left at Oparre in the possession of Otoo ; and the geese and ducks began to breed before we sailed. We found there a gander which the natives told us was the same that Captain Wallis had given to Oberea ten years before, several goats, and the Spanish bull, which they kept tied to a tree near Otoo's house. I never saw a finer animal of his kind. He was now the property of Etary, and had been brought from Oheitepeha to this place in order to be shipped for Bolabola. But it passes my comprehension how they can contrive to carry him in one of their canoes. If we had not arrived, it would have been of little consequence who had the property of him, as without a cow he could be of no use, and none had been left with him. Though the natives told us that there were cows on board the Spanish ships, and that they took them away with them, I cannot believe this, and should rather suppose that they had died in the passage from Lima. The next day I sent the three cows that I had on board to this bull ; and the bull which

I had brought, the horse and mare, and sheep, I put ashore at Matavai. Having thus disposed of these passengers, I found myself lightened of a very heavy burthen. The trouble and vexation that attended the bringing of this living cargo thus far is hardly to be conceived; but the satisfaction that I felt in having been so fortunate as to fulfil his Majesty's humane design in sending such valuable animals to supply the wants of two worthy nations, sufficiently recompensed me for the many anxious hours I had passed before this subordinate object of my voyage could be carried into execution.

As I intended to make some stay here, we set up the two observatories on Matavai Point. Adjoining to them two tents were pitched for the reception of a guard, and of such people as it might be necessary to leave on shore in different departments. At this station I entrusted the command to Mr King, who, at the same time, attended the observations for ascertaining the going of the time-keeper and other purposes. During our stay various necessary operations employed the crews of both ships. The Discovery's mainmast was carried ashore and made as good as ever. Our sails and water-casks were repaired; the ships were calked; and the rigging all overhauled. We also inspected all the bread that we had on board in casks, and had the satisfaction to find that but little of it was damaged. On the 26th I had a piece of ground cleared for a garden, and planted it with several articles, very few of which I believe the natives will ever look after. Some melons, potatoes, and two pine-apple plants were in a fair way of succeeding before we left the place. I had brought from the Friendly Islands several shaddock trees. These I also planted here, and they can hardly fail of success, unless their growth should be checked by the same premature curiosity which destroyed a vine planted by the Spaniards at Oheitepeha. A number of the natives got together to taste the first fruit it bore; but as the grapes were still sour they considered it as little better than poison, and it was unanimously determined to tread it under foot. In that state Omai found it by chance, and was overjoyed at the discovery; for he had a full confidence that if he had but grapes he could easily make wine. Accordingly he had several slips cut from off the tree to carry away with him, and we pruned and put in order the remains of it. Probably grown wise by Omai's instructions, they may now suffer the fruit to grow to perfection, and not pass so hasty a sentence upon it again.

We had not been eight-and-forty hours at anchor in Matavai Bay before we were visited by our old friends whose names are recorded in the account of my last voyage. Not one of them came empty-handed, so that we had more provisions than we knew what to do with. What was still more, we were under no apprehensions of exhausting the island, which presented to our eyes every mark of the most exuberant plenty in every article of refreshment. Soon after our arrival here, one of the natives whom the Spaniards had carried with them to Lima paid us a visit; but in his external appearance he was not distinguishable from the rest of his countrymen. However, he had not forgot some Spanish words which he had acquired, though he pronounced them badly. Amongst them the most frequent were "Si, Señor;" and when a stranger was introduced to him he did not fail to rise up and accost him as well as he could. We also found here the young man whom we called Oedidee, but whose real name is Heete-heete. I had carried him from Ulietea in 1773, and brought him back in 1774, after he had visited the Friendly Islands, New Zealand, Easter Island, and the Marquesas, and been on board my ship in that extensive navigation about seven months. He was at least as tenacious of his good breeding as the man who had been at Lima, and "Yes, Sir," or "If you please, Sir," were as frequently repeated by him as "Si,

Señor" was by the other. Heete-heete, who is a native of Bolabola, had arrived in Otaheite about three months before, with no other intention that we could learn than to gratify his curiosity, or perhaps some other favourite passion, which are very often the only object of the pursuit of other travelling gentlemen. It was evident, however, that he preferred the modes and even garb of his countrymen to ours; for though I gave him some clothes which our Admiralty Board had been pleased to send for his use (to which I added a chest of tools and a few other articles as a present from myself), he declined wearing them after a few days. This instance, and that of the person who had been at Lima, may be urged as a proof of the strong propensity natural to man of returning to habits acquired at an early age, and only interrupted by accident. And perhaps it may be concluded that even Omai, who had imbibed almost the whole English manners, will in a very short time after our leaving him, like Oedidee and the visitor of Lima, return to his own native garments.

In the morning of the 27th a man came from Oheitepeha, and told us that two Spanish ships had anchored in that bay the night before; and in confirmation of this intelligence he produced a piece of coarse blue cloth, which he said he got out of one of the ships, and which, indeed, to appearance was almost quite new. He added that Mateema was in one of the ships, and that they were to come down to Matavai in a day or two. Some other circumstances which he mentioned with the foregoing ones, gave the story so much the air of truth, that I despatched Lieutenant Williamson in a boat to look into Oheitepeha Bay; and in the meantime I put the ships into a proper posture of defence. For though England and Spain were in peace when I left Europe, for aught I knew a different scene might by this time have opened. However, on further inquiry we had reason to think that the fellow who brought the intelli-gence had imposed upon us; and this was put beyond all doubt when Mr Williamson returned next day, who made his report to me that he had been at Oheitepcha, and found that no ships were there now, and that none had been there since we left it The people of this part of the island where we now were, indeed, told us from the beginning that it was a fiction invented by those of Tiaraboo. But what view they could have we were at a loss to conceive, unless they supposed that the report would have some effect in making us quit the island, and by that means deprive the people of Otaheite-nooe of the advantages they might reap from our ships continuing there; the inhabitants of the two parts of the island being inveterate enemies to each other.

From the time of our arrival at Matavai the weather had been very unsettled, with more or less rain every day, till the 29th; before which we were not able to get equal altitudes of the sun for ascertaining the going of the time-keeper. The same cause also retarded the calking and other necessary repairs of the ships. In the evening of this day the natives made a precipitate retreat both from on board the ships and from our station on shore, for what reason we could not at first learn, though in general we guessed it arose from their knowing that some theft had been committed, and apprehending punishment on that account. At length I understood what had happened. One of the surgeon's mates had been in the country to purchase curiosities, and had taken with him four hatchets for that purpose. Having employed one of the natives to carry them for him, the fellow took an opportunity to run off with so valuable a prize. This was the cause of the sudden flight, in which Otoo himself and his whole family had joined; and it was with difficulty that I stopped them, after following them two or three miles. As I had resolved to take no measures for the recovery of the hatchets, in order to put my people upon their guard against such negligence for the future, I found no difficulty in bringing the natives back and in restoring everything to its usual tranquillity.

Hitherto the attention of Otoo and his people had been confined to us; but next morning a new scene of business opened by the arrival of some messengers from Eimeo or (as it is much oftener called by the natives) Morea,[1] with intelligence that the people in that island were in arms, and that Otoo's partisans there had been worsted and obliged to retreat to the mountains. The quarrel between the two islands, which commenced in 1774, had, it seems, partly subsisted ever since. . . .

On the arrival of these messengers, all the chiefs who happened to be at Matavai assembled at Otoo's house, where I actually was at the time, and had the honour to be admitted into their council. One of the messengers opened the business of the assembly in a speech of considerable length; but I understood little of it besides its general purport, which was to explain the situation of affairs in Eimeo, and to excite the assembled chiefs of Otaheite to arm on the occasion. This opinion was combated by others who were against commencing hostilities; and the debate was carried on with great order, no more than one man speaking at a time. At last they became very noisy, and I expected that our meeting would have ended like a Polish Diet. But the contending great men cooled as fast as they grew warm, and order was soon restored. At length the party for war prevailed, and it was determined that a strong force should be sent to assist their friends in Eimeo. But this resolution was far from being unanimous. Otoo during the whole debate remained silent, except that now and then he addressed a word or two to the speakers. Those of the council who were for prosecuting the war applied to me for my assistance; and all of them wanted to know what

part I would take. Omai was sent for to be my interpreter; but as he could not be found I was obliged to speak for myself, and told them, as well as I could, that as I was not thoroughly acquainted with the dispute, and as the people of Eimeo had never offended me, I could not think myself at liberty to engage in hostilities against them. With this declaration they either were or seemed satisfied. The assembly then broke up; but before I left them Otoo desired me to come to him in the afternoon, and to bring Omai with me. Accordingly, a party of us waited upon him at the appointed time, and we were conducted by him to his father, in whose presence the dispute with Eimeo was again talked over. Being very desirous of devising some method to bring about an accommodation, I sounded the old chief on that head; but we found him deaf to any such proposal, and fully determined to prosecute the war. He repeated the solicitations which I had already resisted about giving them my assistance. On our inquiring into the cause of the war, we were told, that some years ago a brother of Waheiadooa, of Tiaraboo, was sent to Eimeo, at the request of Maheine, a popular chief of that island, to be their king; but that he had not been there a week before Maheine, having caused him to be killed, set up for himself, in opposition to Tierataboonooe, his sister's son, who became the lawful heir, or else had been pitched upon by the people of Otaheite to succeed to the government on the death of the other.

Towha, who is a relation of Otoo and chief of the district of Tettaha, a man of much weight in the island, and who had been commander-in-chief of the armament fitted out against Eimeo in 1774, happened not to be at Matavai at this time, and consequently was not present at any of these consultations. It, however, appeared that he was no stranger to what was transacted, and that he entered with more spirit into the affair than any other chief. For early in the morning of the 1st of September a

---

[1] Morea, according to Dr Forster, is a district in Eimeo.

messenger arrived from him to acquaint Otoo that he had killed a man to be sacrificed to "Eatooa," to implore the assistance of the god against Eimeo. This act of worship was to be performed at the great "morai" at Attahooroo, and Otoo's presence, it seems, was absolutely necessary on that solemn occasion. That the offering of human sacrifices is part of the religious institutions of this island had been mentioned by M. de Bougainville on the authority of the native whom he carried with him to France. During my last visit to Otaheite, and while I had opportunities of conversing with Omai on the subject, I had satisfied myself that there was too much reason to admit that such a practice, however inconsistent with the general humanity of the people, was here adopted. But as this was one of those extraordinary facts about which many are apt to retain doubts unless the relater himself has had ocular proofs to confirm what he had heard from others, I thought this a good opportunity of obtaining the highest evidence of its certainty by being present myself at the solemnity, and accordingly proposed to Otoo that I might be allowed to accompany him. To this he readily consented, and we immediately set out in my boat, with my old friend Potatou, Mr Anderson, and Mr Webber, Omai following in a canoe. In our way we landed upon a little island which lies off Tettaha, where we found Towha and his retinue. After some little conversation between the two chiefs on the subject of the war, Towha addressed himself to me, asking my assistance. When I excused myself, he seemed angry; thinking it strange that I, who had always declared myself to be the friend of their island, would not now go and fight against its enemies. Before we parted, he gave to Otoo two or three red feathers tied up in a tuft, and a lean, half-starved dog was put into a canoe that was to accompany us. We then embarked again, taking on board a priest who was to assist at the solemnity.

As soon as we landed at Attahooroo, which was about 2 o'clock in the afternoon, Otoo expressed his desire that the seamen might be ordered to remain in the boat; and that Mr Anderson, Mr Webber, and myself, might take off our hats as soon as we should come to the "morai," to which we immediately proceeded, attended by a great many men and some boys, but not one woman. We found four priests and their attendants or assistants waiting for us. The dead body, or sacrifice, was in a small canoe that lay on the beach, and partly in the wash of the sea, fronting the "morai." Two of the priests, with some of their attendants, were sitting by the canoe; the others at the "morai." Our company stopped about twenty or thirty paces from the priests. Here Otoo placed himself; we and a few others standing by him, while the bulk of the people remained at a greater distance.

The ceremonies now began. One of the priest's attendants brought a young plantain tree and laid it down before Otoo. Another approached with a small tuft of red feathers, twisted on some fibres of the cocoanut husk, with which he touched one of the King's feet, and then retired with it to his companions. One of the priests seated at the "morai," facing those who were upon the beach, now began a long prayer, and at certain times sent down young plantain trees, which were laid upon the sacrifice. During this prayer, a man who stood by the officiating priest held in his hands two bundles, seemingly of cloth. In one of them, as we afterward found, was the royal "maro," and the other, if I may be allowed the expression, was the ark of the "Eatooa." As soon as the prayer was ended, the priests at the "morai," with their attendants, went and sat down by those upon the beach, carrying with them the two bundles. Here they renewed their prayers, during which the plantain trees were taken one by one, at different times, from off the sacrifice, which was partly wrapped up in cocoa leaves and small branches. It was now taken out of the canoe, and laid upon the beach, with the feet to the sea. The priests placed themselves around it, some sitting and others standing, and one or more of them repeated sentences for about ten minutes. The dead body was now uncovered, by removing the leaves and branches, and laid in a parallel direction with the sea-shore. One of the priests then, standing at the feet of it, pronounced a long prayer, in which he was at times joined by the others, each holding in his hand a tuft of red feathers. In the course of this prayer, some hair was pulled off the head of the sacrifice, and the left eye taken out ; both which were presented to Otoo, wrapped up in a green leaf. He did not, however, touch it, but gave to the man who presented it the tuft of feathers which he had received from Towha. This, with the hair and eye, was carried back to the priests. Soon after, Otoo sent to them another piece of feathers, which he had given me in the morning to keep in my pocket. During some part of this last ceremony, a kingfisher making a noise in the trees, Otoo turned to me, saying, "That is the 'Eatooa,'" and seemed to look upon it to be a good omen.

The body was then carried a little way, with its head toward the 'morai," and laid under a tree; near which were fixed three broad thin pieces of wood differently but rudely carved. The bundles of cloth were laid on a part of the "morai;" and the tufts of red feathers were placed at the feet of the sacrifice, round which the priests took their stations; and we were now allowed to go as near as we pleased. He who seemed to be the chief priest sat at a small distance, and spoke for a quarter of an hour, but with different tones and gestures ; so that he seemed often to expostulate with the dead person, to whom he constantly addressed himself ; and sometimes asked several questions, seemingly with respect to the propriety of his having been killed. At other times he made several demands, as if the deceased either now had power himself, or interest with the Divinity, to engage him to comply with such requests. Amongst which, we understood, he asked him to deliver Eimeo, Maheine its chief, the hogs, women, and other things of the island, into their hands ; which was, indeed, the express intention of the sacrifice. He then chanted a prayer, which lasted half-an-hour, in a whining, melancholy tone, accompanied by two other priests ; in which Potatou and some others joined. In the course of this prayer some more hair was plucked by a priest from the head of the corpse, and put upon one of the bundles. After this the chief priest prayed alone, holding in his hand the feathers which came from Towha. When he had finished, he gave them to another, who prayed in like manner. Then all the tufts of feathers were laid upon the bundles of cloth ; which closed the ceremony at this place.

The corpse was then carried up to the most conspicuous part of the "morai," with the feathers, the two bundles of cloth, and the drums ; the last of which beat slowly. The feathers and bundles were laid against the pile of stones, and the corpse at the foot of them. The priests, having again seated themselves round it, renewed their prayers ; while some of the attendants dug a hole about two feet deep, into which they threw the unhappy victim, and covered it with earth and stones. While they were putting him into the grave, a boy squeaked aloud, and Omai said to me that it was the "Eatooa." During this time, a fire having been made, the dog before mentioned was produced, and killed by twisting his neck and suffocating him. The hair was singed off, and the entrails taken out and thrown into the fire, where they were left to consume. But the heart, liver, and kidneys were only roasted by being laid on the stones for a few minutes ; and the body of the dog, after being besmeared with the blood which had been collected in a cocoa-nut shell and dried over the fire, was, with the liver, &c., carried and laid down before the priests, who sat praying round the grave. They continued their ejaculations over the dog for some time, while two men, at intervals, beat on two drums very loud; and a boy screamed, as before, in a loud, shrill voice three different times. This, as we were told, was to invite the "Eatooa" to feast on the banquet that they had prepared for him. As soon as the priests had ended their prayers, the carcase of the dog, with what belonged to it, were laid on a "whatta," or scaffold, about six feet high, that stood close by, on which lay the remains of two other dogs and of two pigs which had lately been sacrificed and at this time emitted an intolerable stench. This kept us at a greater distance than would otherwise have been required of us. For after the victim was removed from the seaside toward the "morai," we were allowed to approach as near as we pleased. Indeed, after that, neither seriousness nor attention were much observed by the spectators. When the dog was put upon the "whatta," the priests and attendants gave a kind of shout, which closed the ceremonies for the present. The day being now also closed, we were conducted to a house belonging to Potatou, where we were entertained and lodged for the night. We had been told that the religious rites were to be renewed in the morning; and I would not leave the place, while anything remained to be seen.

Being unwilling to lose any part of the solemnity, some of us repaired to the scene of action pretty early, but found nothing going forward. However, soon after, a pig was sacrificed and laid upon the same "whatta" with the others. About 8 o'clock, Otoo took us again to the "morai," where the priests and a great number of men were by this time assembled. The two bundles occupied the place in which we had seen them deposited the preceding evening; the two drums stood in the front of the "morai," but somewhat nearer it than before; and the priests were beyond them. Otoo placed himself between the two drums, and desired me to stand by him. The ceremony began as usual

with bringing a young plantain-tree and laying it down at the King's feet. After this a prayer was repeated by the priests, who held in their hands several tufts of red feathers, and also a plume of ostrich feathers, which I had given to Otoo on my first arrival, and which had been consecrated to this use. When the priests had made an end of the prayer, they changed their station, placing themselves between us and the "morai;" and one of them—the same person who had acted the principal part the day before—began another prayer, which lasted about half-an-hour. During the continuance of this, the tufts of feathers were one by one carried and laid upon the ark of the "Eatooa."

Some little time after, four pigs were produced; one of which was immediately killed, and the others were taken to a sty hard by, probably reserved for some future occasion of sacrifice. One of the bundles was now untied, and it was found, as I have before observed, to contain the "maro," with which these people invest their kings; and which seems to answer in some degree to the European ensigns of royalty. It was carefully taken out of the cloth in which it had been wrapped up, and spread at full length upon the ground before the priests. It is a girdle about five yards long and fifteen inches broad; and from its name seems to be put on in the same manner as is the common "maro," or piece of cloth, used by these people to wrap round the waist. It was ornamented with red and yellow feathers, but mostly with the latter, taken from a dove found upon the island. The one end was bordered with eight pieces, each about the size and shape of a horse-shoe, having their edges fringed with black feathers. The other end was forked, and the points were of different lengths. The feathers were in square compartments, ranged in two rows, and otherwise so disposed as to produce a pleasing effect. They had been first pasted or fixed upon some of their own country cloth, and then sewed to the upper end of the pendant which Captain Wallis had displayed, and left flying ashore, the first time that he landed at Matavai. This was what they told us; and we had no reason to doubt it, as we could easily trace the remains of an English pendant. About six or eight inches square of the "maro" was unornamented; there being no feathers upon that space, except a few that had been sent by Waheiadooa, as already mentioned. The priests made a long prayer relative to this part of the ceremony, and, if I mistook not, they called it the prayer of the "maro." When it was finished, the badge of royalty was carefully folded up, put into the cloth, and deposited again upon the "morai." The other bundle which I have distinguished by the name of the ark, was next opened at one end; but we were not allowed to go near enough to examine its mysterious contents. The information we received was, that the "Eatooa" to whom they had been sacrificing, and whose name is "Ooro," was concealed in it; or rather what is supposed to represent him. This sacred repository is made of the twisted fibres of the husk of the cocoa-nut, shaped somewhat like a large fid, or sugar-loaf—that is, roundish, with one end much thicker than the other. We had very often got small ones from different people, but never knew their use before.

By this time the pig that had been killed was cleaned, and the entrails taken out. These happened to have a considerable share of those convulsive motions which often appear in different parts after an animal is killed; and this was considered by the spectators as a very favourable omen to the expedition on account of which the sacrifices had been offered. After being exposed for some time, that those who choose might examine their appearances, the entrails were carried to the priests and laid down before them. While one of the number prayed, another inspected the entrails more narrowly, and kept turning them gently with a stick.[1]

When they had been sufficiently examined, they were thrown into the fire and left to consume. The sacrificed pig, and its liver, &c., were now put upon the "whatta" where the dog had been deposited the day before; then all the feathers, except the ostrich plume, were enclosed with the "Eatooa" in the ark; and the solemnity finally closed. Four double canoes lay upon the beach before the place of sacrifice all the morning. On the fore-part of each of these was fixed a small platform covered with palm-leaves tied in mysterious knots; and this also is called a "morai." Some cocoa-nuts, plantains, pieces of bread-fruit, fish, and other things, lay upon each of these naval "morais." We were told that they belonged to the "Eatooa;" and that they were to attend the fleet designed to go against Eimeo.

The unhappy victim offered to the object of their worship upon this occasion seemed to be a middle-aged man, and, as we were told, was a towtow—that is, one of the lowest class of the people. But, after all my inquiries, I could not learn that he had been pitched upon on account of any particular crime committed by him meriting death. It is certain, however, that they generally make choice of such guilty persons for their sacrifice; or else of common low fellows, who stroll about from place to place and from island to island without having any fixed abode or any visible way of getting an honest livelihood; of which description of men enough are to be met with at these islands. Having had an opportunity of examining the appearance of the body of the poor sufferer now offered up, I could observe that it was bloody about the head and face, and a good deal bruised upon the right temple, which marked the manner of his being

---

[1] There is a grotesque analogy between these South Sea soothsayers and the Roman "haruspices," whose never highly-honoured craft it was to draw omens of good or ill from the entrails of victims slain in the same sort of interrogatory sacrifice.

killed. And we were told that he had been privately knocked on the head with a stone. Those who are devoted to suffer, in order to perform this bloody act of worship, are never apprized of their fate till the blow is given that puts an end to their existence. Whenever any one of the great chiefs thinks a human sacrifice necessary on any particular emergency, he pitches upon the victim. Some of his trusty servants are then sent, who fall upon him suddenly and put him to death with a club or by stoning him. The King is next acquainted with it, whose presence at the solemn rites that follow is, as I was told, absolutely necessary; and indeed on the present occasion we could observe that Otoo bore a principal part. The solemnity itself is called "Poore Eree," or chief's prayer; and the victim, who is offered up, "Taata-taboo," or consecrated man. This is the only instance where we have heard the word "taboo" used at this island, where it seems to have the same mysterious signification as at Tonga; though it is there applied to all cases where things are not to be touched. But at Otaheite the word "raa" serves the same purpose, and is full as extensive in its meaning.

The "morai" (which, undoubtedly, is a place of worship, sacrifice, and burial, at the same time) where the sacrifice was now offered, is that where the supreme chief of the whole island is always buried, and is appropriated to his family and some of the principal people. It differs little from the common ones except in extent. Its principal part is a large, oblong pile of stones, lying loosely upon each other, about twelve or fourteen feet high, contracted towards the top, with a square area on each side loosely paved with pebble stones, under which the bones of the chiefs are buried. At a little distance from the end nearest the sea is the place where the sacrifices are offered; which, for a considerable extent, is also loosely paved. There is here a very large scaffold, or "whatta," on which the offerings of fruits and other vegetables are laid.

But the animals are deposited on a smaller one, already mentioned, and the human sacrifices are buried under different parts of the pavement. There are several other relics which ignorant superstition had scattered about this place; such as small stones, raised in different parts of the pavement, some with bits of cloth tied round them, others covered with it; and upon the side of the large pile which fronts the area are placed a great many pieces of carved wood, which are supposed to be sometimes the residence of their divinities, and consequently held sacred. But one place, more particular than the rest, is a heap of stones, at one end of the large "whatta," before which the sacrifice was offered, with a kind of platform at one side. On this are laid the skulls of all the human sacrifices, which are taken up after they have been several months under ground. Just above them are placed a great number of the pieces of wood; and it was also here where the "maro" and the other bundles supposed to contain the god "Ooro" (and which I call the ark) were laid during the ceremony, a circumstance which denotes its agreement with the altar of other nations.

It is much to be regretted that a practice so horrid in its own nature, and so destructive of that inviolable right of self-preservation which every one is born with, should be found still existing; and (such is the power of superstition to counteract the first principles of humanity!) existing amongst a people in many other respects emerged from the brutal manners of savage life. What is still worse, it is probable that these bloody rites of worship are prevalent throughout all the wide extended islands of the Pacific Ocean. The similarity of customs and language which our late voyages have enabled us to trace between the most distant of these islands, makes it not unlikely that some of the most important articles of their religious institutions should agree. And, indeed, we have the most authentic information that human sacrifices continue to be offered at the

Friendly Islands.   When I described the "Natche" at Tongataboo, I mentioned that, on the approaching sequel of that festival, we had been told that ten men were to be sacrificed. This may give us an idea of the extent of this religious massacre in that island. And though we should suppose that never more than one person is sacrificed on any single occasion at Otaheite, it is more than probable that these occasions happen so frequently as to make a shocking waste of the human race; for I counted no less than forty-nine skulls of former victims lying before the "morai" where we saw one more added to the number. And as none of those skulls had as yet suffered any considerable change from the weather, it may hence be inferred that no great length of time had elapsed since at least this considerable number of unhappy wretches had been offered upon this altar of blood.

The custom, though no consideration can make it cease to be abominable, might be thought less detrimental in some respects if it served to impress any awe for the Divinity, or reverence for religion, upon the minds of the multitude.   But this is so far from being the case, that though a great number of people had assembled at the "morai" on this occasion, they did not seem to show any proper reverence for what was doing or saying during the celebration of the rites. And Omai happening to arrive after they had begun, many of the spectators flocked round him and were engaged the remainder of the time in making him relate some of his adventures, which they listened to with great attention, regardless of the solemn offices performing by their priests.   Indeed, the priests themselves, except the one who chiefly repeated the prayers, either from their being familiarised to such objects, or from want of confidence in the efficacy of their institutions, observed very little of that solemnity which is necessary to give to religious performances their due weight.   Their dress was only an ordinary one; they conversed together without scruple; and the only

attempt made by them to preserve any appearance of decency was by exerting their authority to prevent the people from coming upon the very spot where the ceremonies were performed, and to suffer us as strangers to advance a little forward.   They were, however, very candid in their answers to any questions that were put to them concerning the institution; and particularly on being asked what the intention of it was.   They said that it was an old custom, and was agreeable to their god, who delighted in, or in other words came and fed upon, the sacrifices; in consequence of which he complied with their petitions.   Upon its being objected that he could not feed on these, as he was neither seen to do it, nor were the bodies of the animals quickly consumed; and that as to the human victim they prevented his feeding on him by burying him: to all this they answered, that he came in the night, but invisibly; and fed only on the soul or immaterial part, which according to their doctrine remains about the place of sacrifice until the body of the victim be entirely wasted by putrefaction.

It were much to be wished that this deluded people may learn to entertain the same horror of murdering their fellow-creatures, in order to furnish such an invisible banquet to their god, as they now have of feeding corporeally on human flesh themselves.   And yet we have great reason to believe that there was a time when they were cannibals.   We were told (and indeed partly saw it) that it is a necessary ceremony, when a poor wretch is sacrificed, for the priest to take out the left eye.   This he presents to the king, holding it to his mouth, which he desires him to open; but instead of putting it in, immediately withdraws it.   This they call "eating the man," or "food for the chief;" and perhaps we may observe here some traces of former times, when the dead body was really feasted upon.   But, not to insist upon this, it is certain that human sacrifices are not the only barbarous custom we find still prevailing amongst this benevolent, humane people. For besides cutting out the jaw-bones of their enemies slain in battle, which they carry about as trophies, they in some measure offer their dead bodies as a sacrifice to the "Eatooa." Soon after a battle in which they have been victors, they collect all the dead that have fallen into their hands, and bring them to the "morai," where with a great deal of ceremony they dig a hole and bury them all in it, as so many offerings to the gods; but their skulls are never after taken up.

Their own great chiefs that fall in battle are treated in a different manner. We were informed that their late King Tootaha, Tubourai-tamaide, and another chief who fell with them in the battle, fought with those of Tiaraboo, and were brought to this "morai," at Attahooroo. There their bowels were cut out by the priests before the great altar; and the bodies afterward buried in three different places, which were pointed out to us, in the great pile of stones that compose the most conspicuous part of this "morai." And their common men who also fell in this battle were all buried in one hole at the foot of the pile. This Omai, who was present, told me was done the day after the battle, with much pomp and cere-mony, and in the midst of a great concourse of people, as a thanksgiving offering to the "Eatooa," for the victory they had obtained; while the vanquished had taken refuge in the mountains. There they remained a week or ten days, till the fury of the victors was over, and a treaty set on foot by which it was agreed that Otoo should be declared King of the whole island; and the solemnity of invest-ing him with the "maro" was per-formed at the same "morai," with great pomp, in the presence of all the principal men of the country.

CHAPTER III.

THE close of the very singular scene exhibited at the "morai," which I have faithfully described in the last Chapter, leaving us no other business in Attahooroo, we embarked about noon in order to return to Matavai, and in our way visited Towha, who had remained on the little island where we met him the day before. Some conversation passed between Otoo and him on the present posture of public affairs, and then the latter solicited me once more to join them in their war against Eimeo. By my positive refusal I entirely lost the good graces of this chief. . . .

On the 14th, a party of us dined ashore with Omai, who gave excellent fare, consisting of fish, fowls, pork, and puddings. After dinner, I attended Otoo, who had been one of the party, back to his house, where I found all his servants very busy getting a quantity of provisions ready for me. Amongst other articles there was a large hog, which they killed in my presence. The entrails were divided into eleven portions, in such a man-ner that each of them contained a bit of everything. These portions were distributed to the servants, and some dressed theirs in the same oven with the hog, while others carried off un-dressed what had come to their share. There was also a large pudding, the whole process in making which I saw. It was composed of bread-fruit, ripe plantains, taro, and palm, or *Pan-danus*, nuts, each rasped, scraped, or beat up fine, and baked by itself. A quantity of juice expressed from cocoa-nut kernels was put into a large tray or wooden vessel. The other articles, hot from the oven, were de-posited in this vessel, and a few hot stones were also put in, to make the contents simmer. Three or four men made use of sticks to stir the several ingredients, till they were incorpo-rated one with another, and the juice of the cocoa-nut was turned to oil; so that the whole mass at last became of the consistency of a hasty-pudding. Some of these puddings are excellent, and few that we make in England equal them. I seldom or never dined without one when I could get it, which was not always the case. Otoo's hog being baked, and the pudding which I have described being made, they, together with two living hogs and a quantity of bread-fruit and cocoa-nuts, were put into a canoe and sent on board my ship, followed by myself and all the royal family.

The following evening, a young ram of the Cape breed, that had been lambed, and with great care brought up on board the ship, was killed by a dog. Incidents are of more or less consequence, as connected with situation. In our present situation, desirous as I was to propagate this useful race amongst these islands, the loss of the ram was a serious misfortune, as it was the only one I had of that breed, and I had only one of the English breed left. And in the evening of the 7th we played off some fireworks before a great concourse of people.

The next day a party of us dined with our former shipmate, Oedidee, on fish and pork. The hog weighed about thirty pounds; and it may be worth mentioning that it was alive, dressed, and brought upon the table within the hour. We had but just dined, when Otoo came and asked me if my belly was full? On my answering in the affirmative, he said, "Then come along with me." I accordingly went with him to his father's, where I found some people employed in dressing two girls with a prodigious quantity of fine cloth, after a very singular fashion. The one end of each piece of cloth, of which there was a good many, was held up over the heads of the girls, while the remainder was wrapped round their bodies, under the arm-pits. Then the upper ends were let fall, and hung down in folds to the ground over the other, so as to bear some resemblance to a circular hoop-petticoat. Afterwards, round the outside of all, were wrapped several pieces of differently coloured cloth, which considerably increased the size; so that it was not less than five or six yards in circuit, and the weight of this singular attire was as much as the poor girls could support. To each were hung two "taames," or breast-plates, by way of enriching the whole, and giving it a picturesque appearance. Thus equipped, they were conducted on board the ship, together with several hogs and a quantity of fruit, which, with the cloth, was a present to me from Otoo's father. Persons of either sex dressed in this manner are called "atee;" but I believe it is never practised except when large presents of cloth are to be made. At least I never saw it practised upon any other occasion, nor, indeed, had I ever such a present before; but both Captain Clerke and I had cloth given to us afterwards thus wrapped round the bearers. The next day I had a present of five hogs and some fruit from Otoo, and one hog and some fruit from each of his sisters. Nor were other provisions wanting. For two or three days great quantities of mackerel had been caught by the natives, within the reef, in seines; some of which they brought to the ships and tents, and sold.

Otoo was not more attentive to supply our wants by a succession of presents, than he was to contribute to our amusement by a succession of diversions. A party of us having gone down to Oparre on the 10th, he treated us with what may be called a play. His three sisters were the actresses; and the dresses they appeared in were new and elegant, that is, more so than we had usually met with at any of these islands. But the principal object I had in view this day in going to Oparre was to take a view of an embalmed corpse, which some of our gentlemen had happened to meet with at that place, near the residence of Otoo. On inquiry I found it to be the remains of Tee, a chief well known to me when I was at this island during my last voyage. It was lying in a "toopapaoo," more elegantly constructed than their common ones, and in all respects similar to that lately seen by us at Oheitepeha, in which the remains of Waheiadooa are deposited, embalmed in the same manner. When we arrived at the place, the body was under cover and wrapped up in cloth within the "toopapaoo;" but at my desire the man who had the care of it brought it out and laid it upon a kind of bier, in such a manner that we had as full a view of it as we could wish; but we were not allowed to go within the pales that enclosed the "toopapaoo." After he had thus exhibited the corpse, he hung the place with mats and cloth, so disposed as to produce a very pretty effect. We found the body not only entire in every part, but what surprised us much more, was that putrefaction seemed scarcely to be begun, as there was not the least disagreeable smell proceeding from it, though the climate is one of the hottest, and Tee had been dead above four months. The only remarkable alteration that had happened was a shrinking of the muscular parts of the eyes; but the hair and nails were in their original state, and still adhered firmly; and the several joints were quite pliable, or in that kind of relaxed state which happens to persons who faint suddenly. Such were Mr Anderson's remarks to me, who also told me, that on his inquiring into the method of effecting this preservation of their dead bodies, he had been informed that soon after their death they are disembowelled by drawing the intestines and other viscera out at the anus, and the whole cavity is then filled or stuffed with cloth introduced through the same part; that when any moisture appeared on the skin it was carefully dried up, and the bodies afterward rubbed all over with a large quantity of perfumed cocoa-nut oil, which being frequently repeated, preserved them a great many months, but at last they gradually moulder away. This was the information Mr Anderson received; for my own part I could not learn any more about their mode of operation than what Omai told me, who said that they made use of the juice of a plant which grows amongst the mountains; of cocoa-nut oil; and of frequent washing with sea-water. I was also told that the bodies of all their great men who died a natural

death are preserved in this manner; and that they expose them to public view for a considerable time after. At first they are laid out every day when it does not rain, afterwards the intervals become greater and greater, and at last they are seldom to be seen.

In the evening we returned from Oparee, where we left Otoo and all the royal family; and I saw none of them till the 12th, when all but the chief himself paid me a visit. He, as they told me, was gone to Attabooroo to assist this day at another human sacrifice which the chief of Tiaraboo had sent thither to be offered up at the "morai." This second instance within the course of a few days was too melancholy a proof how numerous the victims of this bloody superstition are amongst this humane people. I would have been present at this sacrifice too had I known of it in time, for now it was too late. From the very same cause I missed being present at a public transaction which had passed at Oparre the preceding day, when Otoo, with all the solemnities observed on such occasions, restored to the friends and followers of the late King Tootaha the lands and possessions which had been withheld from them ever since his death. Probably the new sacrifice was the concluding ceremony of what may be called the reversal of attainder.

The following evening Otoo returned from exercising this most disagreeable of all his duties as Sovereign; and the next day, being now honoured with his company, Captain Clerke and I, mounted on horseback, took a ride round the plain of Matavai, to the very great surprise of a great train of people who attended on the occasion, gazing upon us with as much astonishment as if we had been Centaurs. Omai, indeed, had once or twice before this attempted to get on horseback, but he had as often been thrown off before he could contrive to seat himself; so that this was the first time they had seen anybody ride a horse. What Captain Clerke and I began was after this repeated every day while we stayed, by one or another of our people, and yet the curiosity of the natives continued still unabated. They were exceedingly delighted with these animals, after they had seen the use that was made of them; and as far as I could judge they conveyed to them a better idea of the greatness of other nations than all the other novelties put together that their European visitors had carried amongst them. Both the horse and mare were in good case, and looked extremely well.

The next day, Etary or Olla, the god of Bolabola, who had for several days past been in the neighbourhood of Matavai, removed to Oparre, attended by several sailing canoes. We were told that Otoo did not approve of his being so near our station, where his people could more easily invade our property. I must do Otoo the justice to say that he took every method prudence could suggest to prevent thefts and robberies; and it was more owing to his regulations than to our circumspection that so few were committed. He had taken care to erect a little house or two on the other side of the river behind our post, and two others close to our tents on the bank between the river and the sea. In all these places some of his own people constantly kept watch, and his father generally resided on Matavai Point, so that we were in a manner surrounded by them. Thus stationed, they not only guarded us in the night from thieves, but could observe everything that passed in the day, and were ready to collect contributions from such girls as had private connections with our people, which was generally done every morning. So that the measures adopted by him to secure our safety at the same time served the more essential purpose of enlarging his own profits. Otoo informing me that his presence was necessary at Oparre, where he was to give audience to the great personage from Bolabola, and asking me to accompany him, I readily consented in hopes of meeting with something worth our notice. Accordingly I went with him in the morning of the

16th, attended by Mr Anderson. Nothing, however, occurred on this occasion that was either interesting or curious. We saw Etary and his followers present some coarse cloth and hogs to Otoo, and each article was delivered with some ceremony and a set speech. After this, they and some other chiefs held a consultation about the expedition to Eimeo. Etary at first seemed to disapprove of it, but at last his objections were overruled. Indeed it appeared next day that it was too late to deliberate about this measure; and that Towha, Potatou, and another chief had already gone upon the expedition, with the fleet of Attahooroo. For a messenger arrived in the evening with intelligence that they had reached Eimeo, and that there had been some skirmishes without much loss or advantage on either side.

In the morning of the 18th Mr Anderson, myself, and Omai went again with Otoo to Oparre, and took with us the sheep which I intended to leave upon the island; consisting of an English ram and ewe and three Cape ewes, all which I gave to Otoo. As all the three cows had taken the bull, I thought I might venture to divide them and carry some to Ulietea. With this view I had them brought before us, and proposed to Etary that if he would leave his bull with Otoo, he should have mine and one of the three cows, adding that I would carry them for him to Ulietea; for I was afraid to remove the Spanish bull, lest some accident should happen to him, as he was a bulky, spirited beast. To this proposal of mine Etary at first made some objections, but at last agreed to it, partly through the persuasion of Omai. However, just as the cattle were putting into the boat, one of Etary's followers valiantly opposed any exchange whatever being made. Finding this, and suspecting that Etary had only consented to the proposed arrangement for the present moment to please me, and that after I was gone he might take away his bull, and then Otoo would not have one, I thought it best to drop the idea of an exchange, as it could not be made with the mutual consent of both parties, and finally determined to leave them all with Otoo, strictly enjoining him never to suffer them to be removed from Oparre, not even the Spanish bull, nor any of the sheep, till he should get a stock of young ones, which he might then dispose of to his friends, and send to the neighbouring islands.

This being settled, we left Etary and his party to ruminate upon their folly, and attended Otoo to another place hard by, where we found the servants of a chief whose name I forgot to ask, waiting with a hog, a pig, and a dog, as a present from their master to the Sovereign. These were delivered with the usual ceremonies, and with an harangue in form in which the speaker in his master's name inquired after the health of Otoo and of all the principal people about him. This compliment was echoed back in the name of Otoo by one of his ministers, and then the dispute with Eimeo was discussed, with many arguments for and against it. The deputies of this chief were for prosecuting the war with vigour, and advised Otoo to offer a human sacrifice. On the other hand, a chief who was in constant attendance on Otoo's person opposed it, seemingly with great strength of argument. This confirmed me in the opinion that Otoo himself never entered heartily into the spirit of this war. He now received repeated messages from Towha strongly soliciting him to hasten to his assistance. We were told that his fleet was in a manner surrounded by that of Mahcine, but that neither the one nor the other durst hazard an engagement.

After dining with Otoo, we returned to Matavai, leaving him at Oparre. This day, and also the 19th, we were very sparingly supplied with fruit. Otoo hearing of this, he and his brother, who had attached himself to Captain Clerke, came from Oparre between 9 and 10 o'clock in the evening with a large supply for both ships. This marked his humane attention

more strongly than anything he had hitherto done for us. The next day all the royal family came with presents, so that our wants were not only relieved, but we had more provisions than we could consume.

Having got all our water on board, the ships being calked, the rigging overhauled, and everything put in order, I began to think of leaving the island, that I might have sufficient time to spare for visiting others in this neighbourhood. With this view we removed from the shore our observatories and instruments, and bent the sails. Early the next morning Otoo came on board to acquaint me that all the war canoes of Matavai and of the three other districts adjoining were going to Oparre to join those belonging to that part of the island, and that there would be a general review there. Soon after the squadron of Matavai was all in motion, and, after parading a while about the bay, assembled ashore near the middle of it. I now went in my boat to take a view of them. Of those with stages on which they fight, or what they call their war-canoes, there were about sixty, with near as many more of a smaller size. I was ready to have attended them to Oparre, but soon after a resolution was taken by the chiefs that they should not move till the next day. I looked upon this to be a fortunate delay, as it afforded me a good opportunity to get some insight into their manner of fighting. With this view I expressed my wish to Otoo that he would order some of them to go through the necessary manœuvres. Two were accordingly ordered out into the bay, in one of which Otoo, Mr King, and myself embarked, and Omai went on board the other. When we had got sufficient sea-room, we faced and advanced upon each other, and retreated by turns, as quick as our rowers could paddle. During this, the warriors on the stages flourished their weapons, and played a hundred antic tricks, which could answer no other end, in my judgment, than to work up their passions and prepare them for fighting.

Otoo stood by the side of our stage, and gave the necessary orders when to advance and when to retreat. In this great judgment and a quick eye combined together seemed requisite to seize every advantage that might offer, and to avoid giving any advantage to the adversary. At last, after advancing and retreating from each other at least a dozen times, the two canoes closed, head to head or stage to stage; and after a short conflict the troops on our stage were supposed to be all killed, and we were boarded by Omai and his associates. At that very instant Otoo and all our paddlers leaped overboard, as if reduced to the necessity of endeavouring to save their lives by swimming.

If Omai's information is to be depended upon, their naval engagements are not always conducted in this manner. He told me that they sometimes begin with lashing the two vessels together, head to head, and then fight till all the warriors are killed on one side or the other. But this close combat, I apprehend, is never practised but when they are determined to conquer or die. Indeed, one or the other must happen, for all agree that they never give quarter, unless it be to reserve their prisoners for a more cruel death the next day. The power and strength of these islands lie entirely in their navies. I never heard of a general engagement on land, and all their decisive battles are fought on the water. If the time and place of conflict are fixed upon by both parties, the preceding day and night are spent in diversions and feasting. Toward morning they launch the canoes, put everything in order, and with the day begins the battle, the fate of which generally decides the dispute. The vanquished save themselves by a precipitate flight, and such as reach the shore fly with their friends to the mountains, for the victors, while their fury lasts, spare neither the aged, women, nor children. The next day they assemble at the "morai," to return thanks to the "Eatooa" for the victory, and to offer up the slain as sacrifices, and the prisoners also if they have any. After this a treaty is set on foot, and the conquerors for the most part obtain their own terms, by which particular districts of land, and sometimes whole islands, change their owners. Omai told us that he was once taken a prisoner by the men of Bolabola, and carried to that island, where he and some others would have been put to death the next day if they had not found means to escape in the night.

As soon as this mock-fight was over, Omai put on his suit of armour, mounted a stage in one of the canoes, and was paddled all along the shore of the bay, so that every one had a full view of him. His coat of mail did not draw the attention of his countrymen so much as might have been expected. Some of them, indeed, had seen a part of it before; and there were others, again, who had taken such a dislike to Omai, from his imprudent conduct at this place, that they would hardly look at anything, however singular, that was exhibited by him.

CHAPTER IV.

EARLY in the morning of the 22d, Otoo and his father came on board to know when I proposed sailing. For having been informed that there was a good harbour at Eimeo, I had told them that I should visit that island on my way to Huaheine; and they were desirous of taking a passage with me, and of their fleet sailing at the time to reinforce Towha. As I was ready to take my departure, I left it to them to name the day; and the Wednesday following was fixed upon, when I was to take on board Otoo, his father, mother, and in short the whole family. These points being settled, I proposed setting out immediately for Oparre, where all the fleet fitted out for the expedition was to assemble this day and to be reviewed.

I had but just time to get into my boat when news was brought that Towha had concluded a treaty with

Maheine, and had returned with his fleet to Attahooroo. This unexpected event made all further proceedings in the military way quite unnecessary; and the war-canoes, instead of rendez-vousing at Oparre, were ordered home to their respective districts. This alteration, however, did not hinder me from following Otoo to Oparre, accompanied by Mr King and Omai. Soon after our arrival, and while dinner was preparing, a messenger arrived from Eimeo and related the conditions of the peace, or rather of the truce, it being only for a limited time. The terms were disadvantageous to Ota-heite, and much blame was thrown upon Otoo, whose delay in sending reinforcements had obliged Towha to submit to a disgraceful accommoda-tion. It was even currently reported that Towha, resenting his not being supported, had declared that as soon as I could leave the island he would join his forces to those of Tiaraboo, and attack Otoo at Matavai or Oparre. This called upon me to declare in the most public manner that I was deter-mined to espouse the interest of my friend against any such combination, and that whoever presumed to attack him should feel the weight of my heavy displeasure when I returned again to their island. My declaration probably had the desired effect, and if Towha had any such hostile intention at first, we soon heard no more of the report. Whappai, Otoo's father, highly dis-approved of the peace, and blamed Towha very much for concluding it. This sensible old man wisely judged that my going down with them to Eimeo must have been of singular service to their cause, though I should take no other part whatever in the quarrel. And it was upon this that he built his arguments, and main-tained that Otoo had acted properly by waiting for me, though this had prevented his giving assistance to Towha so soon as he expected.

Our debates at Oparre on this sub-ject were hardly ended before a mes-senger arrived from Towha, desiring Otoo's attendance the next day at the "morai" in Attahooroo, to give thanks to the gods for the peace he had concluded; at least such was Omai's account to me of the object of this solemnity. I was asked to go, but being much out of order was ob-liged to decline. Desirous, however, of knowing what ceremonies might be observed on so memorable an occasion, I sent Mr King and Omai, and returned on board my ship, attended by Otoo's mother, his three sisters, and eight more women. At first I thought that this numerous train of females came into my boat with no other view than to get a passage to Matavai. But when we arrived at the ship they told me they intended passing the night on board for the express purpose of undertaking the cure of the disorder I complained of, which was a pain of the rheumatic kind extending from the hip to the foot. I accepted the friendly offer, had a bed spread for them upon the cabin floor, and sub-mitted myself to their directions. I was desired to lay myself down amongst them. Then as many of them as could get round me began to squeeze me with both hands from head to foot, but more particularly on the parts where the pain was lodged, till they made my bones crack and my flesh became a perfect mummy. In short, after undergoing this discipline about a quarter of an hour, I was glad to get away from them. How-ever, the operation gave me immediate relief, which encouraged me to submit to another rubbing-down before I went to bed; and it was so effectual that I found myself pretty easy all the night after. My female physicians repeated their prescription the next morning before they went ashore, and again in the evening when they re-turned on board, after which I found the pains entirely removed; and the cure being perfected. they took their leave of me the following morning. This they call "romee," an operation which in my opinion far exceeds the flesh-brush, or anything of the kind that we make use of externally. It is universally practised amongst these islanders, being sometimes performed by the men, but more generally by the women. If at any time one appears languid and tired, and sits down by any one of them, they immediately begin to practise the "romee" upon his legs; and I have always found it to have an exceeding good effect. . . .

[On the 27th] I accompanied Otoo to Oparre; and before I left it I looked at the cattle and poultry which I had consigned to my friend's care at that place. Everything was in a promising way, and properly attended to. Two of the geese and two of the ducks were sitting; but the pea and turkey hens had not begun to lay. I got from Otoo four goats, two of which I intended to leave at Ulietea, where none had as yet been introduced; and the other two I proposed to reserve for the use of any other islands I might meet with in my passage to the north.

Our friend Omai got one good thing at this island for the many good things he gave away. This was a very fine double sailing canoe, completely equipped, and fit for the sea. Some time before I had made up for him a suit of English colours; but he thought these too valuable to be used at this time, and patched up a parcel of colours, such as flags and pendants, to the number of ten or a dozen, which he spread on different parts of this vessel all at the same time, and drew together as many people to look at her as a man-of-war would, dressed, in a European port. These streamers of Omai were a mixture of English, French, Spanish, and Dutch, which were all the European colours that he had seen. When I was last at this island, I gave to Otoo an English jack and pendant, and to Towha a pendant; which I now found they had preserved with the greatest care. Omai had also provided himself with a good stock of cloth and cocoa-nut oil, which are not only in greater plenty, but much better, at Otaheite than at any of the Society Islands, insomuch that they are articles of trade. Omai would not have behaved so inconsistently, and so much unlike himself as he did in many instances,

but for his sister and brother-in-law, who, together with a few more of their acquaintance, engrossed him entirely to themselves, with no other view than to strip him of everything he had got. And they would undoubtedly have succeeded in their scheme, if I had not put a stop to it in time, by taking the most useful articles of his property into my possession. But even this would not have saved Omai from ruin, if I had suffered these relations of his to have gone with or to have followed us to his intended place of settlement, Huaheine. This they had intended, but I disappointed their further views of plunder by forbidding them to show themselves in that island while I remained in the neighbourhood; and they knew me too well not to comply.

On the 28th Otoo came on board, and informed me that he had got a canoe, which he desired I would take with me, and carry home as a present from him to the "Earee rahie no Pretane;" it being the only thing, he said, that he could send worth his Majesty's acceptance. I was not a little pleased with Otoo for this mark of his gratitude. It was a thought entirely his own, not one of us having given him the least hint about it; and it showed that he fully understood to whom he was indebted for the most valuable presents that he had received. At first I thought that this canoe had been a model of one of their vessels of war; but I soon found that it was a small "ivahah," about sixteen feet long. It was double, and seemed to have been built for the purpose; and was decorated with all those pieces of carved work which they usually fix upon their canoes. As it was too large for me to take on board, I could only thank him for his good intention; but it would have pleased him much better if his present could have been accepted.

We were detained here some days longer than I expected, by light breezes from the west, and calms, by turns; so that we could not get out of the bay. During this time the ships were crowded with our friends, and surrounded by a multitude of canoes; for not one would leave the place till we were gone. At length, at 3 o'clock in the afternoon of the 29th the wind came at east, and we weighed anchor. As soon as the ships were under sail, at the request of Otoo, and to gratify the curiosity of his people, I fired seven guns loaded with shot; after which all our friends, except him and two or three more, left us with such marks of affection and grief as sufficiently showed how much they regretted our departure. Otoo being desirous of seeing the ship sail, I made a stretch out to sea and then in again; when he also bid us farewell and went ashore in his canoe. The frequent visits we have lately paid to this island seem to have created a full persuasion that the intercourse will not be discontinued. It was strictly enjoined to me by Otoo to request, in his name, the "Earee rahie no Pretane" to send him by the next ships red feathers and the birds that produce them, axes, half-a-dozen muskets, with powder and shot; and by no means to forget horses.

I have occasionally mentioned my receiving considerable presents from Otoo and the rest of the family, without specifying what returns I made. It is customary for these people, when they make a present, to let us know what they expect in return; and we find it necessary to gratify them; so that what we get by way of present comes dearer than what we get by barter. But as we were sometimes pressed by occasional scar 'ty, we could have recourse to our f ends for a present or supply who. we could not get our wants relieved by any other method; and therefore, upon the whole, this way of traffic was full as advantageous to us as to the natives. For the most part, I paid for each separate article as I received it, except in my intercourse with Otoo. His presents generally came so fast upon me, that no account was kept between us. Whatever he asked for that I could spare, he had whenever he asked for it; and I always found him moderate in his demands.

If I could have prevailed upon Omai to fix himself at Otaheite, I should not have left it so soon as I did. For there was not a probability of our being better or cheaper supplied with refreshments at any other place than we continued to be here even at the time of our leaving it. Besides, such a cordial friendship and confidence subsisted between us and the inhabitants as could hardly be expected any where else; and it was a little extraordinary that this friendly intercourse had never once been suspended by any untoward accident, nor had there been a theft committed that deserves to be mentioned. Not that I believe their morals in this respect to be much mended, but am rather of opinion that their regularity of conduct was owing to the fear the chiefs were under of interrupting a traffic which they might consider as the means of securing to themselves a more considerable share of our commodities than could have been got by plunder or pilfering. Indeed, this point I settled at the first interview with their chiefs after my arrival. For observing the great plenty that was in the island, and the eagerness of the natives to possess our various articles of trade, I resolved to make the most of these two favourable circumstances, and explained myself in the most decisive terms that I would not suffer them to rob us as they had done upon many former occasions. In this Omai was of great use, as I instructed him to point out to them the good consequences of their honest conduct, and the fatal mischiefs they must expect to suffer by deviating from it. It is not always in the power of the chiefs to prevent robberies; they are frequently robbed themselves, and complain of it as a great evil. Otoo left the most valuable things he had from me in my possession till the day before we sailed; and the reason he gave for it was that they were nowhere so safe. Since the bringing-in of new riches, the inducements to pilfering must have increased. The chiefs, sensible of this, are now extremely desirous of chests. They seemed to set much value upon a few the Spaniards had left amongst them; and they were continually asking us for some. I had one made for Otoo, the dimensions of which, according to his own directions, were eight feet in length, five in breadth, and about three in depth. Locks and bolts were not a sufficient security; but it must be large enough for two people to sleep upon, by way of guarding it in the night.

It will appear a little extraordinary that we, who had a smattering of their language, and Omai besides for an interpreter, could never get any clear account of the time when the Spaniards arrived, how long they stayed, and when they departed. The more we inquired into this matter, the more we were convinced of the inability of most of these people to remember or note the time when past events happened; especially if it exceeded ten or twenty months. It, however, appeared by the date of the inscription upon the cross, and by the information we received from the most intelligent of the natives, that two ships arrived at Oheitepeha in 1774, soon after I left Matavai, which was in May the same year. They brought with them the house and live stock before mentioned. Some said that after landing these things, and some men, they sailed in quest of me and returned in about ten days. But I have some doubt of the truth of this, as they were never seen either at Huaheine or at Ulietea. The live stock they left here consisted of one bull, some goats, hogs, and dogs, and the male of some other animal; which we afterward found to be a ram, and at this time was at Bolabola, whither the bull was also to have been transported. The hogs are of a · large kind, have already greatly improved the breed originally found by us upon the island, and at the time of our late arrival were very numerous. Goats are also in tolerable plenty, there being hardly a chief of any note that has not some. As to the dogs that the Spaniards put ashore, which are of two or three sorts, I think they

would have done the island a great deal more service if they had hanged them all, instead of leaving them upon it. It was to one of them that my young ram fell a victim.

When these ships left the islands four Spaniards remained behind. Two were priests, one a servant, and the fourth made himself very popular among the natives, who distinguish him by the name of Mateema. He seems to have been a person who had studied their language, or at least to have spoken it so as to be understood; and to have taken uncommon pains to impress the minds of the islanders with the most exalted ideas of the greatness of the Spanish nation, and to make them think meanly of the English. He even went so far as to assure them that we no longer existed as an independent nation; that "Pretane" was only a small island which they (the Spaniards) had entirely destroyed; and for me, that they had met with me at sea, and with a few shot had sent my ship and every soul in her to the bottom, so that my visiting Otaheite at this time was of course very unexpected. All this and many other improbable falsehoods did this Spaniard make these people believe. If Spain had no other views in this expedition but to depreciate the English they had better have kept their ships at home; for my returning again to Otaheite was considered as a complete confutation of all that Mateema had said.

With what design the priests stayed we can only guess. If it was to convert the natives to the Catholic faith, they have not succeeded in any one instance. But it does not appear that they ever attempted it; for, if the natives are to be believed, they never conversed with them either on this or on any other subject. The priests resided constantly in the house at Oheitepeha; but Mateema roved about, visiting most parts of the island. At length, after he and his companions had stayed ten months, two ships came to Oheitepeha, took them on board, and sailed again in five days. This hasty departure shows that whatever design the Spaniards might have had upon this island, they had now laid it aside. And yet, as I was informed by Otoo and many others, before they went away they would have the natives believe that they still meant to return, and to bring with them houses, all kinds of animals, and men and women who were to settle, live, and die on the island. Otoo, when he told me this, added that if the Spaniards should return he would not let them come to Matavai Fort, which, he said, was ours. It was easy to see that the idea pleased him, little thinking that the completion of it would at once deprive him of his kingdom and the people of their liberties. This shows with what facility a settlement might be made at Otaheite; which, grateful as I am for repeated good offices, I hope will never happen. Our occasional visits may in some respects have benefited its inhabitants; but a permanent establishment amongst them conducted as most European establishments amongst Indian nations have unfortunately been, would, I fear, give them just cause to lament that our ships had ever found them out. Indeed, it is very unlikely that any measure of this kind should ever be seriously thought of, as it can neither serve the purposes of public ambition nor of private avarice; and without such inducements I may pronounce that it will never be undertaken.

I have already mentioned the visit that I had from one of the two natives of this island who had been carried by the Spaniards to Lima. I never saw him afterward; which I rather wondered at, as I had received him with uncommon civility. I believe, however, that Omai had kept him at a distance from me by some rough usage, jealous that there should be another traveller upon the island who might vie with himself. Our touching at Teneriffe was a fortunate circumstance for Omai, as he prided himself in having visited a place belonging to Spain as well as this man.

I did not meet with the other who had returned from Lima; but Captain Clerke, who had seen him, spoke of him as a low fellow, and as a little out of his senses. His own countrymen, I found, agreed in the same account of him. In short, these two adventurers seemed to be held in no esteem. They had not, indeed, been so fortunate as to return home with such valuable acquisitions of property as we had bestowed upon Omai, and with the advantages he reaped from his voyage to England, it must be his own fault if he should sink into the same state of insignificance.

CHAPTER V.

As I did not give up my design of touching at Eimeo, at daybreak in the morning of the 30th, after leaving Otaheite, I stood for the north end of the island; the harbour which I wished to examine being at that part of it. Omai, in his canoe, having arrived there long before us, had taken some necessary measures to show us the place. However, we were not without pilots, having several men of Otaheite on board, and not a few women. Not caring to trust entirely to these guides, I sent two boats to examine the harbour; and 'on their making the signal for safe anchorage, we stood in with the ships, and anchored close up to the head of the inlet, in ten fathoms water. We had no sooner anchored than the ships were crowded with the inhabitants, whom curiosity alone brought on board; for they had nothing with them for the purposes of barter. But the next morning this deficiency was supplied; several canoes then arriving from more distant parts, which brought with them abundance of bread-fruit, cocoa-nuts, and a few hogs. These they exchanged for hatchets, nails, and beads; for red feathers were not so much sought after here as at Otaheite. The ship being a good deal pestered with rats, I hauled her within thirty yards of the shore, as near as the depth of water would allow, and made a path for them to get to the land, by fastening hawsers to the trees. It is said that this experiment has sometimes succeeded, but I believe we got clear of very few, if any, of the numerous tribe that haunted us.

In the morning of the 2d, Maheine, the chief of the island, paid me a visit. He approached the ship with great caution, and it required some persuasion to get him on board. Probably he was under some apprehensions of mischief from us as friends of the Otaheiteans; these people not being able to comprehend how we can be friends with any one without adopting at the same time his cause against his enemies. Maheine was accompanied by his wife, who, as I was informed, is sister to Oamo of Otaheite, of whose death we had an account while we were at this island. I made presents to both of them, of such things as they seemed to set the highest value upon; and after a stay of about half-an-hour they went away. Not long after, they returned with a large hog, which they meant as a return for my present, but I made them another present to the full value of it. After this they paid a visit to Captain Clerke.

This chief, who, with a few followers, has made himself in a manner independent of Otaheite, is between forty and fifty years old. He is bald-headed, which is rather an uncommon appearance in these islands at that age. He wore a kind of turban, and seemed ashamed to show his head; but whether they themselves considered this deficiency of hair as a mark of disgrace, or whether they entertained a notion of our considering it as such, I cannot say. We judged that the latter supposition was the truth, from this circumstance, that they had seen us shave the head of one of their people whom we had caught stealing. They therefore concluded that this was the punishment usually inflicted by us upon all thieves; and one or two of our gentlemen, whose heads were not overbur-

thened with hair, we could observe, lay under violent suspicions of being "tetos." In the evening, Omai and I mounted on horseback, and took a ride along the shore to the eastward. Our train was not very numerous, as Omai had forbid the natives to follow us, and many complied, the fear of giving offence getting the better of their curiosity. Towha had stationed his fleet in this harbour, and though the war lasted but a few days, the marks of its devastation were everywhere to be seen. The trees were stripped of their fruit, and all the houses in the neighbourhood had been pulled down or burned.

[On the morning of the 6th they had intended putting off to sea, when they were prevented by first one and then another of their goats being stolen. One of them was recovered without much difficulty, the other was only restored to them after a threatening message had been sent to the chief Maheine, and a number of their canoes had been burned.]

About 9 o'clock [on the 11th] we weighed with a breeze down the harbour, but it proved so faint and variable that it was noon before we got out to sea, when I steered for Huaheine, attended by Omai in his canoe. He did not depend entirely upon his own judgment, but had got on board a pilot. I observed that they shaped as direct a course for the island as I could do. At Eimeo we abundantly supplied the ships with firewood. We had not taken in any at Otaheite, where the procuring this article would have been very inconvenient, there not being a tree at Matavai but what is useful to the inhabitants. We also got here good store of refreshments, both in hogs and vegetables, that is, bread-fruit and cocoa-nuts, little else being in season. I do not know that there is any difference between the produce of this island and of Otaheite; but there is a very striking difference in their women, that I can by no means account for. Those of Eimeo are of low stature, have a dark hue, and, in general, forbidding features. If we met with a fine woman amongst them, we were sure, upon inquiry, to find that she had come from some other island.

CHAPTER VI.

HAVING left Eimeo, with a gentle breeze and fine weather, at daybreak the next morning we saw Huaheine extending from SW. by W. half W. to W. by N. At noon we anchored at the north entrance of Owharre harbour, which is on the west side of the island. The whole afternoon was spent in warping the ships into a proper berth and mooring. Omai entered the harbour just before us in his canoe, but did not land. Nor did he take much notice of any of his countrymen, though many crowded to see him; but far more of them came off to the ships, insomuch that we could hardly work on account of their numbers. Our passengers presently acquainted them with what we had done at Eimeo, and multiplied the number of houses and canoes that we had destroyed by ten at least. I was not sorry for this exaggerated account, as I saw that it made a great impression upon all who heard it, so that I had hopes it would induce the inhabitants of this island to behave better to us than they had done during my former visits. While I was at Otaheite I had learned that my old friend Oree was no longer the chief of Huaheine; and that at this time he resided at Ulietea. Indeed, he never had been more than regent during the minority of Taireetareea, the present "Earee rahie;" but he did not give up the regency till he was forced. His two sons, Opoony and Towha, were the first who paid me a visit, coming on board before the ship was well in the harbour, and bringing a present with them.

Our arrival brought all the principal people of the island to our ships on the next morning, being the 13th. This was just what I wished, as it was high time to think of settling Omai; and the presence of these chiefs, I guessed, would enable me to do it in the most satisfactory manner. He now seemed to have an inclination to establish himself at Ulietea; and if he and I could have agreed about the mode of bringing that plan to bear, I should have had no objection to adopt it. His father had been dispossessed by the men of Bolabola, when they conquered Ulietea, of some land in that island; and I made no doubt of being able to get it restored to the son in an amicable manner. For that purpose it was necessary that he should be upon good terms with those who now were masters of the island; but he was too great a patriot to listen to any such thing, and was vain enough to suppose that I would reinstate him in his forfeited lands by force. This made it impossible to fix him at Ulietea, and pointed out to me Huaheine as the proper place. I therefore resolved to avail myself of the presence of the chief men of the island, and to make this proposal to them.

After the hurry of the morning was over, we got ready to pay a formal visit to Taireetareea, meaning then to introduce his business. Omai dressed himself very properly on the occasion, and prepared a handsome present for the chief himself, and another for his "Eatooa." Indeed, after he had got clear of the gang that surrounded him at Otaheite, he behaved with such prudence as to gain respect. Our landing drew most of our visitors from the ships, and they, as well as those that were on shore, assembled in a large house. The concourse of people on this occasion was very great; and amongst them there appeared to be a greater proportion of personable men and women than we had ever seen in one assembly at any of these new islands. Not only the bulk of the people seemed in general much stouter and fairer than those of Otaheite, but there was also a much greater number of men who appeared to be of consequence, in proportion to the extent of the island; most of whom had exactly the corpulent appearance of the chiefs of Wateeo.

We waited some time for Taireetareea, as I would do nothing till the "Earee rahie" came; but when he appeared I found that his presence might have been dispensed with, as he was not above eight or ten years of age. Omai, who stood at a little distance from this circle of great men, began with making his offering to the gods, consisting of red feathers, cloth, &c. Then followed another offering, which was to be given to the gods by the chief, and after that several other small pieces and tufts of red feathers were presented. Each article was laid before one of the company, who, I understood, was a priest, and was delivered with a set speech or prayer, spoken by one of Omai's friends who sat by him, but mostly dictated by himself. In these prayers he did not forget his friends in England, nor those who had brought him safe back. The "Earee rahie no Pretane," Lord Sandwich, "Toote," "Tatee,"[1] were mentioned in every one of them. When Omai's offerings and prayers were finished, the priest took each article, in the same order in which it had been laid before him, and after repeating a prayer, sent it to the "morai," which, as Omai told us, was at a great distance, otherwise the offerings would have been made there.

These religious ceremonies having been performed, Omai sat down by me, and we entered upon business by giving the young chief my present, and receiving his in return; and, all things considered, they were liberal enough on both sides. Some arrangements were next agreed upon as to the manner of carrying on the intercourse betwixt us; and I pointed out the mischievous consequences that would attend their robbing us as they had done during my former visits. Omai's establishment was then proposed to the assembled chiefs. He acquainted them "that he had been carried by us into our country, where he was well received by the great King and his 'Earees,' and treated with every mark of regard and affec-

---

[1] Cooke and Clerke.

tion while he stayed amongst us; that he had been brought back again, enriched by our liberality with a variety of articles which would prove very useful to his countrymen; and that, besides the two horses which were to remain with him, several other new and valuable animals had been left at Otaheite, which would soon multiply and furnish a sufficient number for the use of all the islands in the neighbourhood. He then signified to them that it was my earnest request, in return for all my friendly offices, that they would give him a piece of land to build a house upon, and to raise provisions for himself and servants, adding that if this could not be obtained for him in Huaheine, either by gift or by purchase, I was determined to carry him to Ulietea and fix him there."

Perhaps I have here made a better speech for my friend than he actually delivered, but these were the topics I dictated to him. I observed that what he concluded with, about carrying him to Ulietea, seemed to meet with the approbation of all the chiefs, and I instantly saw the reason. Omai had, as I have already mentioned, vainly flattered himself that I meant to use force in restoring him to his father's lands in Ulietea, and he had talked idly and without any authority from me on this subject to some of the present assembly, who dreamed of nothing less than a hostile invasion of Ulietea, and of being assisted by me to drive the Bolabola men out of that island. It was of consequence, therefore, that I should undeceive them; and in order to this I signified in the most peremptory manner that I neither would assist them in such an enterprise, nor suffer it to be put in execution while I was in their seas; and that if Omai fixed himself in Ulietea, he must be introduced as a friend, and not forced upon the Bolabola men as their conqueror.

This declaration gave a new turn to the sentiments of the council. One of the chiefs immediately expressed himself to this effect: "That the whole island of Huaheine, and everything in it, were mine, and that therefore I might give what portion of it I pleased to my friend." Omai, who like the rest of his countrymen seldom sees things beyond the present moment, was greatly pleased to hear this, thinking, no doubt, that I should be very liberal and give him enough. But to offer what it would have been improper to accept, I considered as offering nothing at all; and therefore I now desired that they would not only assign the particular spot, but also the exact quantity of land which they would allot for the settlement. Upon this some chiefs who had already left the assembly were sent for, and after a short consultation among themselves, my request was granted by general consent, and the ground immediately pitched upon adjoining to the house where our meeting was held. The extent, along the shore of the harbour, was about 200 yards, and its depth to the foot of the hill somewhat more; but a proportional part of the hill was included in the grant. This business being settled to the satisfaction of all parties, I set up a tent ashore, established a post, and erected the observatories. The carpenters of both ships were also set to work to build a small house for Omai, in which he might secure the European commodities that were his property. At the same time some hands were employed in making a garden for his use, planting shaddocks, vines, pine-apples, melons, and the seeds of several other vegetable articles; all of which I had the satisfaction of observing to be in a flourishing state before I left the island.

Omai now began seriously to attend to his own affairs, and repented heartily of his ill-judged prodigality while at Otaheite. He found at Huaheine a brother, a sister, and a brother-in-law, the sister being married; but these did not plunder him as he had lately been by his other relations. I was sorry, however, to discover that though they were too honest to do him any injury, they were of too little consequence in the island to do him any positive good.

They had neither authority nor influence to protect his person or his property; and in that helpless situation I had reason to apprehend that he ran great risk of being stripped of everything he had got from us as soon as he should cease to have us within his reach to enforce the good behaviour of his countrymen by an immediate appeal to our irresistible power. A man who is richer than his neighbours is sure to be envied by numbers who wish to see him brought down to their own level. But in countries where civilisation, law, and religion impose their restraints, the rich have a reasonable ground of security. And, besides, there being in all such communities a diffusion of property, no single individual need fear that the efforts of all the poorer sort can ever be united to injure him, exclusively of others who are equally the objects of envy. It was very different with Omai. He was to live amongst those who are strangers, in a great measure, to any other principle of action besides the immediate impulse of their natural feelings. But what was his principal danger, he was to be placed in the very singular situation of being the only rich man in the community to which he was to belong; and having, by a fortunate connection with us, got into his possession an accumulated quantity of a species of treasure which none of his countrymen could create by any art or industry of their own, while all coveted a share of this envied wealth, it was natural to apprehend that all would be ready to join in attempting to strip its sole proprietor. To prevent this, if possible, I desired him to make a proper distribution of some of his movables to two or three of the principal chiefs, who, being thus gratified themselves, might be induced to take him under their patronage and protect him from the injuries of others. He promised to follow my advice; and I heard with satisfaction before I sailed that this very prudent step had been taken. Not trusting, however, entirely to the operation of gratitude, I had recourse to the more forcible motive of intimidation. With this view I took every opportunity of notifying to the inhabitants that it was my intention to return to their island again, after being absent the usual time, and that if I did not find Omai in the same state of security in which I was now to leave him, all those whom I should then discover to have been his enemies might expect to feel the weight of my resentment. This threatening declaration will probably have no inconsiderable effect; for our successive visits of late years have taught these people to believe that our ships are to return at certain periods; and while they continue to be impressed with such a notion, which I thought it a fair stratagem to confirm, Omai has some prospect of being permitted to thrive upon his new plantation.[1]

While we lay in this harbour we carried ashore the bread remaining in the bread-room to clear it of vermin. The number of cockroaches that infested the ship at this time is incredible. The damage they did us was very considerable, and every method devised by us to destroy them proved ineffectual. These animals, which at first were a nuisance like all other insects, had now become a real pest, and so destructive that few things were free from their ravages. If food of any kind was exposed only for a few minutes, it was covered with them; and they soon pierced it full of holes resembling a honeycomb. They were particularly destructive to birds which had been stuffed and preserved as curiosities, and, what was worse, were uncommonly fond of ink, so that the writing on the labels fastened to different articles was quite eaten out; and the only thing that preserved books from them was the closeness of the binding, which prevented these devourers getting between the leaves. According to Mr Anderson's observations, they were of two sorts, the *Blatta orientalis* and *germanica*.

The first of these had been carried home in the ship from her former voyage, where they withstood the severity of the hard winter in 1776, though she was in dock all the time. The others had only made their appearance since our leaving New Zealand, but had increased so fast, that they now not only did all the mischief mentioned above, but had even got amongst the rigging, so that when a sail was loosened thousands of them fell upon the decks. The *orientales*, though in infinite numbers, scarcely came out but in the night, when they made everything in the cabins seem as if in motion from the particular noise in crawling about. And, besides their disagreeable appearance, they did great mischief to our bread, which was so bespattered with their excrement that it would have been badly relished by delicate feeders.

The intercourse of trade and friendly offices was carried on between us and the natives without being disturbed by any one accident till the evening of the 22d, when a man found means to get into Mr Bayly's observatory, and to carry off a sextant unobserved. As soon as I was made acquainted with the theft, I went ashore and got Omai to apply to the chiefs to procure restitution. He did so, but they took no steps toward it, being more attentive to a "haiva" that was then acting, till I ordered the performers of the exhibition to desist. They were now convinced that I was in earnest, and began to make some inquiry after the thief, who was sitting in the midst of them quite unconcerned, insomuch that I was in great doubt of his being the guilty person, especially as he denied it. Omai, however, assuring me that he was the man, I sent him on board the ship and there confined him. This raised a general ferment amongst the assembled natives, and the whole body fled in spite of all my endeavours to stop them. Having employed Omai to examine the prisoner, with some difficulty he was brought to confess where he had laid the sextant; but as it was now dark he could not find

---

[1] See Note at end of Chapter on the subsequent fortunes of Omai.

it till daylight the next morning, when it was brought back unhurt. After this the natives recovered from their fright and began to gather about us as usual. And as to the thief, he appearing to be a hardened scoundrel, I punished him more severely than I had done any culprit before. Besides having his head and beard shaved, I ordered both his ears to be cut off, and then dismissed him.

This, however, did not deter him from giving us further trouble; for, in the night between the 24th and 25th, a general alarm was spread, occasioned as was said by one of our goats being stolen by this very man. On examination we found that all was safe in that quarter. Probably the goats were so well guarded that he could not put his design in execution. But his hostilities had succeeded against another object, and it appeared that he had destroyed and carried off several vines and cabbage-plants in Omai's grounds; and he publicly threatened to kill him and to burn his house as soon as we should leave the island. To prevent the fellow's doing me and Omai any more mischief, I had him seized and confined on board the ship with a view of carrying him off the island; and it seemed to give general satisfaction to the chiefs that I meant thus to dispose of him. He was from Bolabola, but there were too many of the natives here ready to assist him in any of his designs whenever he should think of executing them. I had always met with more troublesome people in Huaheine than in any other of the neighbouring islands; and it was only fear, and the want of opportunities, that induced them to behave better now. Anarchy seemed to prevail amongst them. Their nominal Sovereign, the "Earee rabie," as I have before observed, was but a child; and I did not find that there was any one man, or set of men, who managed the government for him; so that whenever any misunderstanding happened between us, I never knew with sufficient precision where to make application in order to bring about an accommodation or to procure

redress. The young chief's mother would, indeed, sometimes exert herself; but I did not perceive that she had greater authority than many others.

Omai's house being nearly finished, many of his movables were carried ashore on the 26th. Amongst a variety of other useless articles was a box of toys, which when exposed to public view seemed greatly to please the gazing multitude. But as to his pots, kettles, dishes, plates, drinking-mugs, glasses, and the whole train of our domestic accommodations, hardly any one of his countrymen would so much as look at them. Omai himself now began to think that they were of no manner of use to him; that a baked hog was more savoury food than a boiled one; that a plantain-leaf made as good a dish or plate as pewter; and that a cocoa-nut shell was as convenient a goblet as a black-jack. And therefore he very wisely disposed of as many of these articles of English furniture for the kitchen and pantry as he could find purchasers for amongst the people of the ships, receiving from them in return hatchets and other iron tools, which had a more intrinsic value in this part of the world, and added more to his distinguishing superiority over those with whom he was to pass the remainder of his days. In the long list of the presents bestowed upon him in England fireworks had not been forgotten. Some of these we exhibited in the evening of the 28th before a great concourse of people, who beheld them with a mixture of pleasure and fear. What remained after the evening's entertainment were put in order and left with Omai, agreeably to their original destination. Perhaps we need not lament it as a serious misfortune that the far greater share of this part of his cargo had been already expended in exhibitions at other islands, or rendered useless by being kept so long.

Between midnight and four in the morning of the 30th the Bolabola man whom I had in confinement found means to make his escape out of the ship. He carried with him the shackle of the bilbo-bolt that was about his leg, which was taken from him as soon as he got on shore by one of the chiefs, and given to Omai, who came on board very early in the morning to acquaint me that his mortal enemy was again let loose upon him. Upon inquiry it appeared that not only the sentry placed over the prisoner, but the whole watch upon the quarter-deck where he was confined, had laid themselves down to sleep. He seized the opportunity to take the key of the irons out of the binnacle-drawer, where he had seen it put, and set himself at liberty. This escape convinced me that my people had been very remiss in their night-duty, which made it necessary to punish those who were now in fault, and to establish some new regulations to prevent the like negligence for the future. I was not a little pleased to hear afterwards that the fellow who escaped had transported himself to Ulietea, in this seconding my views of putting him a second time in irons.

As soon as Omai was settled in his new habitation I began to think of leaving the island, and got everything off from the shore this evening except the horse and mare, and a goat big with kid, which were left in the possession of our friend, with whom we were now finally to part. I also gave him a boar and two sows of the English breed, and he had got a sow or two of his own. The horse covered the mare while we were at Otaheite, so that I consider the introduction of a breed of horses into these islands as likely to have succeeded by this valuable present. The history of Omai will perhaps interest a very numerous class of readers more than any other occurrence of a voyage, the objects of which do not in general promise much entertainment. Every circumstance, therefore, which may serve to convey a satisfactory account of the exact situation in which he was left will be thought worth preserving; and the following particulars are added to complete the view of his domestic establishment. He had picked up at Otaheite four or five "Toutous;" the

two New Zealand youths remained with him; and his brother and some others joined him at Huaheine, so that his family consisted already of eight or ten persons, if that can be called a family to which not a single female as yet belonged, nor, I doubt, was likely to belong, unless its master became less volatile. At present Omai did not seem at all disposed to take unto himself a wife. The house which we erected for him was twenty-four feet by eighteen, and ten feet high. It was composed of boards, the spoils of our military operations at Eimeo; and in building it, as few nails as possible were used, that there might be no inducement, from the love of iron, to pull it down. It was settled that immediately after our departure he should begin to build a large house after the fashion of his country, one end of which was to be brought over that which we had erected, so as to enclose it entirely for greater security. In this work some of the chiefs promised to assist him; and if the intended building should cover the ground which he marked out, it will be as large as most upon the island. His European weapons consisted of a musket, bayonet, and cartouche-box; a fowling-piece; two pair of pistols; and two or three swords or cutlasses. The possession of these made him quite happy, which was my only view in giving him such presents. For I was always of opinion that he would have been happier without fire-arms, and other European weapons, than with them; as such implements of war, in the hands of one whose prudent use of them I had some grounds for mistrusting, would rather increase his dangers than establish his superiority. After he had got on shore everything that belonged to him, and was settled in his house, he had most of the officers of both ships two or three times to dinner; and his table was always well supplied with the very best provisions that the island produced.

Before I sailed, I had the following inscription cut upon the outside of his house:

"*Georgius Tertius Rex,* 2 *Novembris,*
1777.

Naves { *Resolution, Jac. Cook, Pr.*
       { *Discovery, Car. Clerke, Pr.*"

On the 2d of November, at four in the afternoon, I took the advantage of a breeze which then sprung up at E., and sailed out of the harbour. Most of our friends remained on board till the ships were under sail; when, to gratify their curiosity, I ordered five guns to be fired. They then all took their leave, except Omai, who remained till we were at sea. We had come to sail by a hawser fastened to the shore. In casting the ship it parted, being cut by the rocks, and the outer end was left behind, as those who cast it off, did not perceive that it was broken; so that it became necessary to send a boat to bring it on board. In this boat Omai went ashore, after taking a very affectionate farewell of all the officers. He sustained himself with a manly resolution till he came to me. Then his utmost efforts to conceal his tears failed; and Mr King, who went in the boat, told me that he wept all the time in going ashore.

It was no small satisfaction to reflect that we had brought him safe back to the very spot from which he was taken. And yet such is the strange nature of human affairs, that it is probable we left him in a less desirable situation than he was in before his connection with us. I do not by this mean that, because he has tasted the sweets of civilised life, he must become more miserable from being obliged to abandon all thoughts of continuing them. I confine myself to this single disagreeable circumstance, that the advantages he received from us have placed him in a more hazardous situation with respect to his personal safety. Omai, from being much caressed in England, lost sight of his original condition, and never considered in what manner his acquisitions either of knowledge or of riches would be estimated by his countrymen at his return; which were the only things he could have

to recommend him to them now more than before, and on which he could build either his future greatness or happiness. He seemed even to have mistaken their genius in this respect, and, in some measure to have forgotten their customs; otherwise he must have known the extreme difficulty there would be in getting himself admitted as a person of rank, where there is perhaps no instance of a man's being raised from an inferior station by the greatest merit. Rank seems to be the very foundation of all distinction here, and of its attendant, power; and so pertinaciously or rather blindly adhered to, that unless a person has some degree of it, he will certainly be despised and hated if he assumes the appearance of exercising any authority. This was really the case in some measure with Omai; though his countrymen were pretty cautious of expressing their sentiments while we remained among them. Had he made a proper use of the presents he brought with him from England, this, with the knowledge he had acquired by travelling so far, might have enabled him to form the most useful connections. But we have given too many instances, in the course of our narrative, of his childish inattention to this obvious means of advancing his interest. His schemes seemed to be of a higher though ridiculous nature; indeed I might say meaner; for revenge, rather than a desire of becoming great, appeared to actuate him from the beginning. This, however, may be excused if we consider that it is common to his countrymen. His father was doubtless a man of considerable property in Ulietea when that island was conquered by those of Bolabola; and, with many others, sought refuge in Huaheine, where he died and left Omai with some other children, who by that means became totally dependent. In this situation he was taken up by Captain Furneaux and carried to England. Whether he really expected, from his treatment there, that any assistance would be given him against the enemies of his father and his country, or whether he imagined that his own personal courage and superiority of knowledge would be sufficient to dispossess the conquerors of Ulietea, is uncertain; but from the beginning of the voyage this was his constant theme. He would not listen to our remonstrances on so wild a determination; but flew into a passion if more moderate and reasonable counsels were proposed for his advantage. Nay, so infatuated and attached to his favourite scheme was he, that he affected to believe these people would certainly quit the conquered island as soon as they should hear of his arrival at Otaheite. As we advanced, however, on our voyage, he became more sensible of his error; and by the time we reached the Friendly Islands had even such apprehensions of his reception at home, that, as I have mentioned in my journal, he would fain have stayed behind at Tongataboo under Feenou's protection. At these islands he squandered away much of his European treasure very unnecessarily; and he was equally imprudent, as I also took notice of above, at Tiaraboo, where he could have no view of making friends, as he had not any intention of remaining there. At Matavai he continued the same inconsiderate behaviour till I absolutely put a stop to his profusion; and he formed such improper connections there, that Otoo, who was at first much disposed to countenance him, afterward openly expressed his dislike of him on account of his conduct. It was not, however, too late to recover his favour; and he might have settled to great advantage in Otaheite, as he had formerly lived several years there, and was now a good deal noticed by Towha, whose valuable present of a very large double canoe we have seen above. The objection to admitting him to some rank would have also been much lessened if he had fixed at Otaheite; as a native will always find it more difficult to accomplish such a change of state amongst his countrymen, than a stranger, who naturally claims respect. But Omai remained undetermined to the last,

and would not, I believe, have adopted my plan of settlement in Huaheine, if I had not so explicitly refused to employ force in restoring him to his father's possessions. Whether the remains of his European wealth, which after all his improvident waste was still considerable, will be more prudently administered by him, or whether the steps I took to insure him protection in Huaheine shall have proved effectual, must be left to the decision of future navigators of this ocean; with whom it cannot but be a principal object of curiosity to trace the future fortunes of our traveller. At present I can only conjecture that his greatest danger will arise from the very impolitic declarations of his antipathy to the inhabitants of Bolabola. For these people, from a principle of jealousy, will no doubt endeavour to render him obnoxious to those of Huaheine, as they are at peace with that island at present, and may easily effect their designs, many of them living there. This is a circumstance which, of all others, he might the most easily have avoided. For they were not only free from any aversion to him, but the person mentioned before, whom we found at Tiaraboo as an ambassador, priest, or god, absolutely offered to reinstate him in the property that was formerly his father's. But he refused this peremptorily; and to the very last continued determined to take the first opportunity that offered of satisfying his revenge in battle. To this, I guess, he is not a little spurred by the coat of mail he brought from England; clothed in which, and in possession of some fire-arms, he fancies that he shall be invincible.

Whatever faults belonged to Omai's character, they were more than overbalanced by his great good-nature and docile disposition. During the whole time he was with me I very seldom had reason to be seriously displeased with his general conduct. His grateful heart always retained the highest sense of the favours he had received in England; nor will he ever forget those who honoured him with their protection and friendship during his stay there. He had a tolerable share of understanding, but wanted application and perseverance to exert it; so that his knowledge of things was very general, and in many instances imperfect. He was not a man of much observation. There were many useful arts, as well as elegant amusements, amongst the people of the Friendly Islands, which he might have conveyed to his own; where they probably would have been readily adopted as being so much in their own way. But I never found that he used the least endeavour to make himself master of any one. This kind of indifference is, indeed, the characteristic foible of his nation. Europeans have visited them at times for these ten years past, yet we could not discover the slightest trace of any attempt to profit by this intercourse; nor have they hitherto copied after us in any one thing. We are not, therefore, to expect that Omai will be able to introduce many of our arts and customs among them, or much improve those to which they have been long habituated. I am confident, however, that he will endeavour to bring to perfection the various fruits and vegetables we planted, which will be no small acquisition. But the greatest benefit these islands are likely to receive from Omai's travels will be in the animals that have been left upon them; which probably they never would have got had he not come to England. When these multiply, of which I think there is little doubt, Otaheite and the Society Islands will equal, if not exceed, any place in the known world for provisions.

Omai's return, and the substantial proofs he brought back with him of our liberality, encouraged many to offer themselves as volunteers to attend me to "Pretane." I took every opportunity of expressing my determination to reject all such applications. But notwithstanding this, Omai, who was very ambitious of remaining the only great traveller, being afraid lest I might be prevailed upon to put others in a situation of rivalling him, fre-

quently put me in mind that Lord Sandwich had told him no others of his countrymen were to come to England. If there had been the most distant probability of any ship being again sent to New Zealand, I would have brought the two youths of that country home with me, as both of them were very desirous of continuing with us. Tiarooa, the eldest, was an exceedingly well disposed young man, with strong natural sense, and capable of receiving any instruction. He seemed to be fully sensible of the inferiority of his own country to these islands, and resigned himself, though perhaps with reluctance, to end his days in ease and plenty in Huaheine. But the other was so strongly attached to us, that he was taken out of the ship and carried ashore by force. He was a witty, smart boy, and on that account much noticed on board.[1]

CHAPTER VII.

The boat that carried Omai ashore, never to join us again, having returned to the ship with the remainder of the

---

[1] "Omai did not live long to enjoy his good fortune; it does not appear that he had any reason to complain of the rapacity or covetousness of his neighbours. The numerous articles of European manufacture which were in his possession rendered his house a splendid museum of curiosities in the eyes of a South Sea islander; and it is possible that his pride felt gratified in being thus able to minister to their wonder and admiration. He conducted himself prudently, and gained the esteem of his neighbours by the affability with which he recounted his voyages and adventures. About two years and a half after Captain Cook's departure, Omai died a natural death; nor did the New Zealanders survive him long enough to furnish European navigators with an ampler account of the influence which his experience and observations abroad may have exerted on his countrymen."

hawser, we hoisted her in and immediately stood over for Ulietea, where I intended to touch next. At 10 o'clock at night we brought to till four the next morning, when we made sail round the south end of the island for the harbour of Ohamaneno. We met with calms and light airs of wind from different directions by turns, so that at noon we were still a league from the entrance of the harbour. While we were thus detained, my old friend Oreo, chief of the island, with his son, and Pootoe, his son-in-law, came off to visit us. . . .

Though we had separated from Omai, we were still near enough to have intelligence of his proceeding; and I had desired to hear from him. Accordingly, about a fortnight after our arrival at Ulietea he sent two of his people in a canoe, who brought me the satisfactory intelligence that he remained undisturbed by the people of the island, and that everything went well with him, except that his goat had died in kidding. He accompanied this intelligence with a request that I would send him another goat and two axes. Being happy to have this additional opportunity of serving him, the messengers were sent back to Huaheine on the 18th with the axes, and two kids, male and female, which were spared for him out of the Discovery.

The next day I delivered to Captain Clerke instructions how to proceed in case of being separated from me after leaving these islands; and it may not be improper to give them a place here.

"By Captain James Cook, Commander of His Majesty's Sloop the Resolution.

"Whereas the passage from the Society Islands to the northern coast of America is of considerable length both in distance and in time, and as a part of it must be performed in the very depth of winter, when gales of wind and bad weather must be expected, and may possibly occasion a separation, you are to take all imaginable care to prevent this. But if, notwithstanding all our endeavours to keep company, you should be separated from me, you are first to look for me where you last saw me. Not seeing me in five days, you are to proceed (as directed by the instructions of their Lordships, a copy of which you have already received) for the coast of New Albion, endeavouring to fall in with it in the Latitude of 45°.

"In that latitude, and at a convenient distance from the land, you are to cruise for me ten days. Not seeing me in that time, you are to put into the first convenient port, in or to the north of that latitude, to recruit your wood and water, and to procure refreshments.

"During your stay in port, you are constantly to keep a good lookout for me. It will be necessary, therefore, to make choice of a station situated as near the sea-coast as is possible, the better to enable you to see me when I shall appear in the offing.

"If I do not join you before the 1st of next April, you are to put to sea, and proceed northward to the Latitude 56°; in which latitude, and at a convenient distance from the coast, never exceeding fifteen leagues, you are to cruise for me till the 10th of May.

"Not seeing me in that time, you are to proceed northward, and endeavour to find a passage into the Atlantic Ocean, through Hudson's or Baffin's Bays, as directed by the above-mentioned instructions.

"But if you should fail in finding a passage through either of the said bays, or by any other way, as the season of the year may render it unsafe for you to remain in high latitudes, you are to repair to the harbour of St Peter and St Paul in Kamtschatka, in order to refresh your people and to pass the winter.

"But nevertheless if you find that you cannot procure the necessary refreshments at the said port, you are at liberty to go where you shall judge most proper; taking care, before you depart, to leave with the governor an account of your intended destination, to be delivered to me upon my arrival; and in the spring of the ensuing year,

1779, you are to repair back to the above-mentioned port, endeavouring to be there by the 10th of May, or sooner.

"If, on your arrival, you receive no orders from, or account of me, so as to justify your pursuing any other measures than what are pointed out in the before-mentioned instructions, your future proceedings are to be governed by them.

"You are also to comply with such parts of said instructions as have not been executed, and are not contrary to these orders. And in case of your inability, by sickness or otherwise, to carry these and the instructions of their Lordships into execution, you are to be careful to leave them with the next officer in command, who is hereby required to execute them in the best manner he can.

"Given under my hand, on board the Resolution, at Ulietea, the 18th day of November 1777.

"J. Cook.

"*To Captain Charles Clerke, Commander of His Majesty's Sloop the Discovery.*"

While we lay moored to the shore, we heeled, and scrubbed both sides of the bottoms of the ships. At the same time, we fixed some tin plates under the binds; first taking off the old sheathing, and putting in a piece unfilled, over which the plates were nailed. These plates I had from the ingenious Mr Pelham, Secretary to the Commissioners for Victualling his Majesty's Navy, with a view of trying whether tin would answer the same end as copper on the bottoms of ships.

On the 24th in the morning I was informed that a midshipman and a seaman, both belonging to the Discovery, were missing. Soon after, we learned from the natives that they went away in a canoe the preceding evening, and were at this time at the other end of the island. As the midshipman was known to have expressed a desire to remain at these islands, it seemed pretty certain that he and his companion had gone off with this intention, and Captain Clerke set out in quest of them with two armed boats and a party of marines. His expedition proved fruitless, for he returned in the evening without having got any certain intelligence where they were. From the conduct of the natives, Captain Clerke seemed to think that they intended to conceal the deserters, and with that view had amused him with false information the whole day, and directed him to search for them in places where they were not to be found. The captain judged right, for the next morning we were told that our runaways were at Otaha. As these two were not the only persons in the ships who wished to end their days at these favourite islands, in order to put a stop to any further desertion it was necessary to get them back at all events, and that the natives might be convinced that I was in earnest, I resolved to go after them myself, having observed, from repeated instances, that they seldom offered to deceive me with false information. Accordingly I set out the next morning with two armed boats, being accompanied by the chief himself. I proceeded, as he directed, without stopping anywhere till we came to the middle of the east side of Otaha. There we put ashore; and Oreo despatched a man before us with orders to seize the deserters and keep them till we should arrive with the boats. But when we got to the place where we expected to find them, we were told that they had quitted this island and gone over to Bolabola the day before. I did not think proper to follow them thither, but returned to the ships, fully determined, however, to have recourse to a measure which I guessed would oblige the natives to bring them back.

Soon after daybreak the chief, his son, daughter, and son-in-law came on board the Resolution. The three last I resolved to detain till the two deserters should be brought back. With this view Captain Clerke invited them to go on board his ship; and, as soon as they arrived there, confined them in his cabin. The chief was with me when the news reached him. He immediately acquainted me with it, supposing that this step had been taken without my knowledge and consequently without my approbation. I instantly undeceived him; and then he began to have apprehensions as to his own situation, and his looks expressed the utmost perturbation of mind. But I soon made him easy as to this, by telling him that he was at liberty to leave the ship whenever he pleased, and to take such measures as he should judge best calculated to get our two men back; that if he succeeded, his friends on board the Discovery should be delivered up; if not, that I was determined to carry them away with me. I added that his own conduct, as well as that of many of his people, in not only assisting these two men to escape, but in being even at this very time assiduous in enticing others to follow them, would justify any step I could take to put a stop to such proceedings.

This explanation of the motives upon which I acted, and which we found means to make Oreo and his people who were present fully comprehend, seemed to recover them in a great measure from that general consternation into which they were at first thrown. But, if relieved from apprehensions about their own safety, they continued under the deepest concern for those who were prisoners. Many of them went under the Discovery's stern in canoes to bewail their captivity; which they did with long and loud exclamations. "Poedooa!" for so the chief's daughter was called, resounded from every quarter, and the women seemed to vie with each other in mourning her fate with more significant expressions of their grief than tears and cries, for there were many bloody heads upon the occasion. Oreo himself did not give way to unavailing lamentations, but instantly began his exertions to recover our deserters by dispatching a canoe to Bolabola with a message to Opoony, the Sovereign of that island,

acquainting him with what had happened, and requesting him to seize the two fugitives and send them back. The messenger, who was no less a man than the father of Pootoe, Oreo's son-in-law, before he set out came to receive my commands. I strictly enjoined him not to return without the deserters; and to tell Opoony from me that if they had left Bolabola he must send canoes to bring them back; for I suspected that they would not long remain in one place.

The consequence, however, of the prisoners was so great that the natives did not think proper to trust to the return of our people for their release; or at least their impatience was so great, that it hurried them to make an attempt which might have involved them in still greater distress had it not been fortunately prevented. Between 5 and 6 o'clock in the evening I observed that all their canoes in and about the harbour, began to move off as if some sudden panic had seized them. I was ashore, abreast of the ship at the time, and inquired in vain to find out the cause; till our people called to us from the Discovery, and told us that a party of the natives had seized Captain Clerke and Mr Gore, who had walked out a little way from the ships. Struck with the boldness of this plan of retaliation, which seemed to counteract me so effectually in my own way, there was no time to deliberate. I instantly ordered the people to arm, and in less than five minutes a strong party under the command of Mr King was sent to rescue our two gentlemen. At the same time two armed boats, and a party under Mr Williamson, went after the flying canoes to cut off their retreat to the shore. These several detachments were hardly out of sight before an account arrived that we had been misinformed; upon which I sent and called them all in.

It was evident, however, from several corroborating circumstances, that the design of seizing Captain Clerke had really been in agitation amongst the natives; nay, they made no secret in speaking of it the next day. But their first and great plan of operations was to have laid hold of me. It was my custom every evening to bathe in the fresh water. Very often I went alone, and always without arms. Expecting to go as usual this evening, they had determined to seize me, and Captain Clerke too, if he had accompanied me. But I had, after confining Oreo's family, thought it prudent to avoid putting myself in their power ; and had cautioned Captain Clerke and the officers not to go far from the ships. In the course of the afternoon the chief asked me three several times if I would not go to the bathing-place ; and when he found at last that I could not be prevailed upon, he went off with the rest of his people, in spite of all I could do or say to stop him. But as I had no suspicion at this time of their design, I imagined that some sudden fright had seized them, which would as usual soon be over. Finding themselves disappointed as to me, they fixed on those who were more in their power. It was fortunate for all parties that they did not succeed, and not less fortunate that no mischief was done on the occasion. For not a musket was fired, except two or three to stop the canoes. To that firing, perhaps, Messrs Clerke and Gore owed their safety;[1] for at that very instant a party of the natives armed with clubs were advancing toward them ; and on hearing the report of the muskets they dispersed. This conspiracy, as it may be called, was first discovered by a girl whom one of the officers had brought from Huaheine. She, overhearing some of the Ulieteans say that they would seize Captain Clerke and Mr Gore, ran to acquaint the first of our people that

she met with. Those who were charged with the execution of the design threatened to kill her, as soon as we should leave the island, for disappointing them. Being aware of this, we contrived that her friends should come some days after, and take her out of the ship to convey her to a place of safety, where she might lie concealed till they should have an opportunity of sending her back to Huaheine.

On the 27th our observatories were taken down, and everything we had ashore carried on board ; the moorings of the ships were cast off ; and we transported them a little way down the harbour, where they came to an anchor again. Toward the afternoon the natives began to shake off their fears, gathering round and on board the ships as usual ; and the awkward transaction of the day before seemed to be forgotten on both sides. The following night the wind blew in hard squalls from S. to E., attended with heavy showers of rain. In one of the squalls the cable by which the Resolution was riding, parted just without the hawse. We had another anchor ready to let go ; so that the ship was presently brought up again. In the afternoon the wind became moderate, and we hooked the end of the best small bower cable and got it again into the hawse.

Oreo, the chief, being uneasy, as well as myself, that no account had been received from Bolabola, set out this evening for that island, and desired me to follow down the next day with the ships. This was my intention, but the wind which kept us in the harbour brought Oreo back from Bolabola with the two deserters. They had reached Otaha the same night they deserted ; but finding it impossible to get to any of the islands to the eastward (which was their intention) for want of wind, they had proceeded to Bolabola, and from thence to the small island Toobaee, where they were taken by the father of Pootoe, in consequence of the first message sent to Opoony. As soon as they were on board, the three pri-

---

[1] Perhaps they owed their safety principally to Captain Clerke's walking with a pistol in his hand, which he once fired. This circumstance is omitted both in Captain Cook's and in Mr Anderson's journal, but is here mentioned on the authority of Captain King.—*Note in Original Edition.*

soners were released. Thus ended an affair which had given me much trouble and vexation. Nor would I have exerted myself so resolutely on the occasion but for the reason before mentioued, and to save the son of a brother officer from being lost to his country. The wind continued constantly between the N. and W., and confined us in the harbour till 8 o'clock in the morning of the 7th of December, when we took the advantage of a light breeze which then sprung up at NE., and with the assistance of all the boats got out to sea, with the Discovery in company.

During the last week we had been visited by people from all parts of the island, who furnished us with a large stock of hogs and green plantains; so that the time we lay wind-bound in the harbour was not entirely lost, green plantains being an excellent substitute for bread, as they will keep good a fortnight or three weeks. Besides this supply of provisions we also completed our wood and water. The inhabitants of Ulietea seemed in general smaller and blacker than those of the other neighbouring islands, and appeared also less orderly, which perhaps may be considered as the consequence of their having become subject to the natives of Bolabola. Oreo, their chief, is only a sort of deputy of the Sovereign of that island, and the conquest seems to have lessened the number of subordinate chiefs resident among them; so that they are less immediately under the inspection of those whose interest it is to enforce due obedience to authority. Ulietea, though now reduced to this humiliating state, was formerly, as we were told, the most eminent of this cluster of islands, and probably the first seat of government; for they say that the present royal family of Otaheite is descended from that which reigned here before the late revolution. Ooroo, the dethroned monarch of Ulietea, was still alive when we were at Huaheine, where he resides, a royal wanderer, furnishing in his person an instauce of the instability of power, but what is more remarkable, of the respect paid by these people to particular families, and to the customs which have once conferred sovereignty; for they suffer Ooroo to preserve all the ensigns which they appropriate to majesty, though he has lost his dominions.

We saw a similar instance of this while we were at Ulietea. One of the occasional visitors I now had was my old friend Oree, the late chief of Huaheine. He still preserved his consequence, came always at the head of a numerous body of attendants, and was always provided with such presents as were very acceptable. This chief looked much better now than I had ever seen him during either of my former voyages.[1] I could account for his improving in health as he grew older only from his drinking less copiously of the "ava" in his present station as a private gentleman than he had been accustomed to do when he was regent.

CHAPTER VIII.

As soon as we had got clear of the harbour we took leave of Ulietea and steered for Bolabola. The chief, if not sole, object I had in view by visiting that island was to procure from its monarch, Opoony, one of the anchors which M. de Bougainville had lost at Otaheite. This having afterwards been taken up by the natives there, had as they informed me been sent by them as a present to that chief. My desire to get possession of it did not arise from our being in want of anchors. But having expended all the hatchets and other iron tools which we had brought from England in purchasing refreshments, we were now reduced to the necessity of creating a fresh assortment of trad-

---

[1] Captain Cook had seen Oree in 1769, when he commanded the Endeavour; also twice during his second voyage in 1772.—*Note in Original Edition.*

ing articles by fabricating them out of the spare iron we had on board; and in such conversions, and in the occasional uses of the ships, great part of that had been already expended. I thought that M. de Bougainville's anchor would supply our want of this useful material, and I made no doubt that I should be able to tempt Opoony to part with it.

Oreo, and six or eight men more from Ulietea, took a passage with us to Bolabola. Indeed, most of the natives in general, except the chief himself, would have gladly taken a passage with us to England. At sunset, being the length of the south point of Bolabola, we shortened sail, and spent the night making short boards. At daybreak on the 8th we made sail for the harbour, which is on the west side of the island. The wind was scant, so that we had to ply up, and it was 9 o'clock before we got near enough to send away a boat to sound the entrance; for I had thoughts of running the ships in and anchoring for a day or two. When the boat returned, the master, who was in her, reported that though at the entrance of the harbour the bottom was rocky, there was good ground within, and the depth of water twenty-seven and twenty-five fathoms, and that there was room to turn the ships in, the channel being one-third of a mile broad. In consequence of this report we attempted to work the ships in; but the tide as well as the wind being against us, after making two or three trips I found that it could not be done till the tide should turn in our favour. Upon this I gave up the design of carrying the ships into the harbour, and having ordered the boats to be got ready, I embarked in one of them, accompanied by Oreo and his companions, and was rowed in for the island.

We landed where the natives directed us, and soon after I was introduced to Opoony, in the midst of a great concourse of people. Having no time to lose, as soon as the necessary formality of compliments was ever I asked the chief to give me the anchor, and produced the present I had prepared for him, consisting of a linen night-gown, a shirt, some gauze handkerchiefs, a looking-glass, some beads and other toys, and six axes. At the sight of these last there was a general outcry. I could only guess the cause by Opoony's absolutely refusing to receive my present till I should get the anchor. He ordered three men to go and deliver it to me, and, as I understood, I was to send by them what I thought proper in return. With these messengers we set out in our boats for an island lying at the north side of the entrance into the harbour, where the anchor had been deposited. I found it to be neither so large nor so perfect as I expected. It had originally weighed 700 pounds, according to the mark that was upon it; but the ring, with part of the shank, and the two points, were now wanting. I was no longer at a loss to guess the reason of Opoony's refusing my present; he doubtless thought that it so much exceeded the value of the anchor in its present state that I should be displeased when I saw it. Be this as it may, I took the anchor as I found it, and sent him every article of the present that I at first intended. Having thus completed my negotiation, I returned on board, and having hoisted in the boats, made sail from the island to the north.

While the boats were hoisting in, some of the natives came off in three or four canoes to see the ships, as they said. They brought with them a few cocoa-nuts and one pig, which was the only one we got at the island. I make no doubt, however, that if we had stayed till the next day we should have been plentifully supplied with provisions; and I think the natives would feel themselves disappointed when they found that we were gone. But as we had already a very good stock both of hogs and of fruit on board, and very little of anything left to purchase more, I could have no inducement to defer any longer the prosecution of our voyage. [An account is here omitted of the circumstances attending the conquest of Ulietea and Otaha by the people of Bolabola—those two islands remaining under the sway of King Opoony, while Huaheine, which had also been conquered, thanks to the aid of the Otaheiteans, regained and retained their independence.   The reader will recall Omai's rancour against the Bolabolans, through whose predominance in the contest he lost his patrimony in Ulietea.]

Ever since the conquest of Ulietea and Otaha, the Bolabola men have been considered by their neighbours as invincible; and such is the extent of their fame, that even at Otaheite, which is almost out of their reach, if they are not dreaded, they are at least respected for their valour.   It is said that they never fly in battle, and that they always beat an equal number of the other islanders.   But, besides these advantages, their neighbours seem to ascribe a great deal to the superiority of their god, who, they believed, detained us at Ulietea by contrary winds, as being unwilling that we should visit an island under his special protection.   How high the Bolabola men are now in estimation at Otaheite may be inferred from M. de Bougainville's anchor having been conveyed to them.   To the same cause we must ascribe the intention of transporting to their island the Spanish bull.   And they had already got possession of a third. European curiosity, the male of another animal, brought to Otaheite by the Spaniards. We had been much puzzled by the imperfect description of the natives to guess what this could be; but Captain Clerke's deserters, when brought back from Bolabola, told me that the animal had been there shown to them, and that it was a ram.   It seldom happens but that some good arises out of evil; and if our two men had not deserted I should not have known this.   In consequence of their information, at the same time that I landed to meet Opoony, I carried ashore a ewe which we had brought from the Cape of Good Hope; and I hope that by this present I have laid the found-

ation for a breed of sheep at Bolabola.   I also left at Ulietea, under the care of Oreo, an English boar and sow and two goats; so that not only Otaheite, but all the neighbouring islands will in a few years have their race of hogs considerably improved, and probably be stocked with all the valuable animals which have been transported hither by their European visitors.

When once this comes to pass, no part of the world will equal these islands in variety and abundance of refreshments for navigators.   Indeed, even in their present state I know no place that excels them.   After repeated trials in the course of several voyages, we find when they are not disturbed by intestine broils, but live in amity with one another, which has been the case for some years past, that their productions are in the greatest plenty, and particularly the most valuable of all their articles, their hogs.   If we had had a larger assortment of goods and a sufficient quantity of salt on board, I make no doubt that we might have salted as much pork as would have served both ships near twelve months.   But our visiting the Friendly Islands, and our long stay at Otaheite and the neighbourhood, quite exhausted our trading commodities, particularly our axes, with which alone hogs in general were to be purchased; and we had hardly salt enough to cure fifteen puncheons of meat.   Of these, five were added to our stock of provisions at the Friendly Islands, and the other ten at Otaheite.   Captain Clerke also salted a proportionable quantity for his ship.

Perhaps the frequent visits Europeans have lately made to these islanders may be one great inducement to their keeping a large stock of hogs, as they have had experience enough to know that whenever we come they may be sure of getting from us what they esteem a valuable consideration for them.   At Otaheite they expect the return of the Spaniards every day; and they will look for the English two or three years hence not only there, but at the other islands.   It is to no purpose to tell them that you will not return. They think you must, though not one of them knows or will give himself the trouble to inquire the reason of your coming. I own I cannot avoid expressing it as my real opinion, that it would have been far better for these poor people never to have known our superiority in the accommodations and arts that make life comfortable, than after once knowing it to be again left and abandoned to their original incapacity of improvement. Indeed, they cannot be restored to that happy mediocrity in which they lived before we discovered them, if the intercourse between us should be discontinued. It seems to me that it has become in a manner incumbent on the Europeans to visit them once in three or four years, in order to supply them with those conveniences which we have introduced among them and have given them a predilection for. The want of such occasional supplies will probably be very heavily felt by them, when it may be too late to go back to their old, less perfect contrivances which they now despise and have discontinued since the introduction of ours. For by the time that the iron tools of which they are now possessed are worn out, they will have almost lost the knowledge of their own. A stone hatchet is at present as rare a thing amongst them as an iron one was eight years ago, and a chisel of bone or stone is not to be seen. Spike-nails have supplied the place of the last; and they are weak enough to fancy that they have got an inexhaustible store of them, for these were not now at all sought after. Sometimes, however, nails much smaller than a spike would still be taken in exchange for fruit. Knives happened at present to be in great esteem at Ulietea, and axes and hatchets remained unrivalled by any other of our commodities at all the islands. With respect to articles of mere ornament, these people are as changeable as any of the polished nations of Europe; so that what pleases their fancy while a fashion is in vogue may be rejected when another whim has supplanted it. But our iron tools are so strikingly useful that they will, we may confidently pronounce, continue to prize them highly, and be completely miserable if, neither possessing the materials nor trained up to the art of fabricating them, they should cease to receive supplies of what may now be considered as having become necessary to their comfortable existence.[1]

CHAPTER IX.[2]

PERHAPS there is scarcely a spot in the universe that affords a more luxuriant prospect than the south-east part of Otaheite. The hills are high and steep, and in many places craggy; but they are covered to the very summits with trees and shrubs, in such a manner that the spectator can scarcely help thinking that the very rocks possess the property of producing and supporting their verdant clothing. The flat land which bounds those hills toward the sea, and the interjacent valleys, also teem with various productions, that grow with the most exuberant vigour, and at once fill the mind of the beholder with the idea that no place upon earth can outdo this in the strength and beauty of vegetation. Nature has been no less liberal in distributing rivulets, which are found in every valley, and, as they approach the sea, often divide into two or three branches, fertilising the flat lands through which they run. The habitations of the natives are scattered without order upon the flats, and many of them appearing

---

[1] The rest of the Chapter, chiefly consisting of the record of astronomical and nautical observations, is omitted.

[2] This Chapter, contributed by Mr Anderson's pen, has been considerably curtailed by omission of the more uninteresting technical, naturalistic, linguistic, and professional passages.

toward the shore presented a delightful scene viewed from our ships, especially as the sea, within the reef which bounds the coast, is perfectly still, and affords a safe navigation at all times for the inhabitants, who are often seen paddling their canoes indolently along, in passing from place to place, or in going to fish. On viewing these charming scenes, I have often regretted my inability to transmit to those who have had no opportunity of seeing them such a description as might in some measure convey an impression similar to what must be felt by every one who has been fortunate enough to be upon the spot. It is doubtless the natural fertility of the country, combined with the mildness and serenity of the climate, that renders the natives so careless in their cultivation that in many places, though overflowing with the richest productions, the smallest traces of it cannot be observed.

The products of the island are not so remarkable for their variety as great abundance; and curiosities of any kind are not numerous. Amongst these we may reckon a pond or lake of fresh water, at the top of one of the highest mountains, to go to and to return from which takes three or four days. It is remarkable for its depth, and has eels of an enormous size in it, which are sometimes caught by the natives, who go upon this water in little floats of two or three wild plantain trees fastened together. This is esteemed one of the greatest natural curiosities of the country, insomuch that travellers who come from the other islands are commonly asked, amongst the first things, by their friends at their return, if they have seen it. There is also a sort of water, of which there is only one small pond upon the island, as far distant as the lake, and to appearance very good, with a yellow sediment at the bottom; but it has a bad taste, and proves fatal to those who drink any quantity, or makes them break out in blotches if they bathe in it.

Nothing could make a stronger impression at first sight, on our arrival here, than the remarkable contrast between the robust make and dark colour of the people of Tongataboo, and a sort of delicacy and whiteness which distinguish the inhabitants of Otaheite. It was even some time before that difference could preponderate in favour of the Otaheiteans; and then only, perhaps, because we became accustomed to them, the marks which had recommended the others began to be forgotten. Their women, however, struck us as superior in every respect, and as possessing all those delicate characteristics which distinguish them from the other sex in many countries. The beard, which the men here wear long, and the hair, which is not cut so short as is the fashion at Tongataboo, made also a great difference; and we could not help thinking that on every occasion they showed a greater degree of timidity and fickleness. The muscular appearance so common amongst the Friendly Islanders, and which seems a consequence of their being accustomed to much action, is lost here, where the superior fertility of their country enables the inhabitants to lead a more indolent life; and its place is supplied by a plumpness and smoothness of the skin, which, though perhaps more consonant with our ideas of beauty, is no real advantage, as it seems attended with a kind of languor in all their motions, not observable in the others. This observation is fully verified in their boxing and wrestling, which may be called little better than the feeble efforts of children, if compared to the vigour with which these exercises are performed at the Friendly Islands.

Personal endowments being in great esteem amongst them, they have recourse to several methods of improving them, according to their notions of beauty. In particular, it is a practice, especially amongst the "Erreoes," or unmarried men of some consequence, to undergo a kind of physical operation to render them fair. This is done by remaining a month or two in the house, during which time they wear a great quantity of clothes, and eat nothing but bread-fruit, to which they ascribe a remarkable property in whitening them. They also speak as if their corpulence and colour at other times depended upon their food, as they are obliged, from the change of seasons, to use different sorts at different times. Their common diet is made up of at least nine-tenths of vegetable food; and I believe more particularly the "mahee," or fermented bread-fruit, which enters almost every meal, has a remarkable effect upon them, preventing a costive habit, and producing a very sensible coolness about them, which could not be perceived in us who fed on animal food. And it is perhaps owing to this temperate course of life that they have so few diseases among them. They only reckon five or six, which might be called chronic or national disorders; amongst which are the dropsy, and the "fefai," or indolent swellings before mentioned as frequent at Tonga-taboo. But this was before the arrival of the Europeans; for we have added to this short catalogue a disease which abundantly supplies the place of all the others, and is now almost universal. For this they seem to have no effectual remedy.

Their behaviour on all occasions seems to indicate a great ·openness and generosity of disposition. Omai, indeed, who as their countryman should be supposed rather willing to conceal any of their defects, has often said that they are sometimes cruel in punishing their enemies. According to his representation, they torment them very deliberately, at one time tearing out small pieces of flesh from different parts, at another taking out the eyes, then cutting of the nose, and lastly killing them by opening the belly. But this only happens on particular occasions. If cheerfulness argues a conscious innocence, one would suppose that their life is seldom sullied by crimes. This, however, I rather impute to their feelings, which, though lively, seem in no case permanent; for I never saw them in any misfortune labour under the ap-

pearance of anxiety after the critical moment was past. Neither does care ever seem to wrinkle their brow. On the contrary, even the approach of death does not appear to alter their usual vivacity. I have seen them when brought to the brink of the grave by disease, and when preparing to go to battle, but in neither case ever observed their countenances overclouded with melancholy, or serious reflection. Such a disposition leads them to direct all their aims only to what can give them pleasure and ease. Their amusements all tend to excite and continue their amorous passions; and their songs, of which they are immoderately fond, answer the same purpose. . But as a constant succession of sensual enjoyments must cloy, we found that they frequently varied them to more refined subjects, and had much pleasure in chanting their triumphs in war and their occupations in peace, their travels to other islands and adventures there, and the peculiar beauties and superior advantages of their own island over the rest, or of different parts of it over other less favourable districts. This marks that they receive great delight from music; and though they rather expressed a dislike to our complicated compositions, yet were they always delighted with the more melodious sounds produced singly on our instruments, as approaching nearer to the simplicity of their own.

Neither are they strangers to the soothing effects produced by particular sorts of motion, which in some cases seem to allay any perturbation of mind with as much success as music. Of this I met with a remarkable instance. For on walking one day about Matavai Point, where our tents were erected, I saw a man paddling in a small canoe so quickly, and looking about him with such eagerness on each side, as to command all my attention. At first I imagined that he had stolen something from one of the ships, and was pursued; but, on waiting patiently, saw him repeat his amusement. He went out from the shore till he was near the place where the swell begins to take its rise; and, watching its first motion very attentively, paddled before it with great quickness, till he found that it overlooked him, and had acquired sufficient force to carry his canoe before it without passing underneath. He then sat motionless, and was carried along at the same swift rate as the wave, till it landed him upon the beach. Then he started out, emptied his canoe, and went in search of another swell. I could not help concluding that this man felt the most supreme pleasure while he was driven on so fast and so smoothly, by the sea; especially as, though the tents and ships were so near, he did not seem in the least to envy or even to take any notice of the crowds of his countrymen collected to view them as objects which were rare and curious. During my stay, two or three of the natives came up, who seemed to share his felicity, and always called out when there was an appearance of a favourable swell, as he sometimes missed it by his back being turned, and looking about for it. By them I understood that this exercise, which is called "choroee," was frequent amongst them; and they have probably more amusements of this sort which afford them at least as much pleasure as skating, which is the only one of ours with whose effects I could compare it.

The language of Otaheite abounds with beautiful and figurative expressions which, were it perfectly known, would, I have no doubt, put it upon a level with many of the languages that are most in esteem for their warmth and bold images. For instance, the Otaheiteans express their notions of death very emphatically by saying "that the soul goes into darkness," or rather "into night." And if you seem to entertain any doubt in asking the question, "If such a person is their mother?" they immediately reply with surprise, "Yes, the mother that bore me." They have one expression, that corresponds exactly with the phraseology of the Scriptures, where we read of the

"yearning of the bowels." They use it on all occasions when the passions give them uneasiness; as they constantly refer pain from grief, anxious desire, and other affections, to the bowels as its seat; where they likewise suppose all operations of the mind are performed. Their language admits of that inverted arrangement of words which so much distinguishes the Latin and Greek from most of our modern European tongues, whose imperfections require a more orderly construction, to prevent ambiguities. It is so copious that for the breadfruit alone, in its different states, they have above twenty names; as many for the "taro" root; and about ten for the cocoa-nut. Add to this, that besides the common dialect they often expostulate in a kind of stanza or recitative, which is answered in the same manner.

Their arts are few and simple; yet, if we may credit them, they perform cures in surgery which our extensive knowledge in that branch has not as yet enabled us to imitate. In simple fractures they bind them up with splints; but if part of the substance of the bone be lost, they insert a piece of wood between the fractured ends, made hollow like the deficient part. In five or six days the "rapaoo," or surgeon, inspects the wound, and finds the wood partly covered with the growing flesh. In as many more days it is generally entirely covered; after which, when the patient has acquired some strength, he bathes in the water, and recovers. We know that wounds will heal over leaden bullets; and sometimes, though rarely, over other extraneous bodies. But what makes me entertain some doubt of the truth of so extraordinary skill as in the above instance is, that in other cases which fell under my own observation they are far from being so dexterous. I have seen the stump of an arm, which was taken off after being shattered by a fall from a tree, that bore no marks of skilful operation, though some allowance be made for their defective instruments. And I met a man going about with a dislocated shoulder, some months after the accident, from their being ignorant of a method to reduce it; though this be considered as one of the simplest operations of our surgery. They know that fractures or luxations of the spine are mortal, but not fractures of the skull; and they likewise know from experience in what parts of the body wounds prove fatal. They have sometimes pointed out those inflicted by spears, which, if made in the direction they mentioned, would certainly have been pronounced deadly by us; and yet these people have recovered. Their physical knowledge seems more confined; and that, probably, because their diseases are fewer than their accidents.

The times of eating at Otaheite are very frequent. Their first meal, or (as it may rather be called) their last, as they go to sleep after it, is about 2 o'clock in the morning; and the next is at eight. At eleven they dine; and again, as Omai expressed it, at two and at five; and sup at eight. In this article of domestic life they have adopted some customs which are exceedingly whimsical. The women, for instance, have not only the mortification of being obliged to eat by themselves, and in a different part of the house from the men; but, by a strange kind of policy, are excluded from a share of most of the better sorts of food. They dare not taste turtle, nor fish of the tunny kind, which is much esteemed, nor some particular sorts of the best plantains; and it is very seldom that even those of the first rank are suffered to eat pork. The children of each sex also eat apart, and the women generally serve up their own victuals; for they would certainly starve before any grown man would do them such an office. In this, as well as in some other customs relative to their eating, there is a mysterious conduct which we could never thoroughly comprehend. When we inquired into the reasons of it, we could get no other answer but that it is right and necessary it should be so.

In other customs respecting the females there seems to be no such obscurity; especially as to their connections with the men. If a young man and woman, from mutual choice, cohabit, the man gives the father of the girl such things as are necessary in common life, as hogs, cloth, or canoes, in proportion to the time they are together; and if he thinks that he has not been sufficiently paid for his daughter, he makes no scruple of forcing her to leave her friend and to cohabit with another person who may be more liberal. The man, on his part, is always at liberty to make a new choice; but, should his consort become pregnant, he may kill the child, and after that either continue his connection with the mother or leave her. But if he should adopt the child, and suffer it to live, the parties are then considered as in the married state, and they commonly live together ever after. However, it is thought no crime in the man to join a more youthful partner to his first wife, and to live with both. The custom of changing their connections is, however, much more general than this last; and it is a thing so common that they speak of it with great indifference. The "Erreoes,"[1] are only those of the better sort who from their fickleness, and their possessing the means of purchasing a succession of fresh connections, are constantly roaming about, and, from having no particular attachment, seldom adopt the more settled method mentioned above. And so agreeable is this licentious plan of life to their disposition, that the most beautiful of both sexes thus

---

[1] Otherwise spelt "Arreoys." In the Original Edition there is a long and learned note at this point, the only part of which really pertinent is the citation of Father le Gobien's "History of the Ladrone Islands," where he describes a similar society under the substantially identical designation of "Urritoes." His words are: "Les Urritoes sont parmi eux les jeunes gens qui vivent avec des maîtresses, sans vouloir s'engager dans les liens du mariage."

commonly spend their youthful days, habituated to the practice of enormities which would disgrace the most savage tribes, but are peculiarly shocking amongst a people whose general character, in other respects, has evident traces of the prevalence of humane and tender feelings. When an "Erreoe" woman is delivered of a child, a piece of cloth dipped in water is applied to the mouth and nose, which suffocates it. As in such a life their women must contribute a very large share of its happiness, it is rather surprising, besides the humiliating restraints they are laid under with regard to food, to find them often treated with a degree of harshness, or rather brutality, which one would scarcely suppose a man would bestow on an object for whom he had the least affection. Nothing, however, is more common than to see the men beat them without mercy; and unless this treatment is the effect of jealousy, which both sexes at least pretend to be sometimes infected with, it will be difficult to admit this as the motive, as I have seen several instances where the women have preferred personal beauty to interest. Though I must own, that even in these cases they seem scarcely susceptible of those delicate sentiments that are the result of mutual affection; and I believe that there is less Platonic love in Otaheite than in any other country.

Their religious system is extensive, and in many instances singular; but few of the common people have a perfect knowledge of it, that being confined chiefly to their priests, who are pretty numerous. They do not seem to pay any respect to one god as possessing pre-eminence, but believe in a plurality of divinities who are all very powerful; and in this case, as different parts of the island, and the other islands in the neighbourhood, have different ones, the inhabitants of each no doubt think that they have chosen the most eminent, or at least one who is invested with power sufficient to protect them and to supply all their wants. If he should not answer their expectations, they think

it no impiety to change; as very lately happened in Tiaraboo, where in the room of the two divinities formerly honoured there, Oraa,[1] god of Bolabola, has been adopted, I should suppose because he is the protector of a people who have been victorious in war; and as, since they have made this change, they have been very successful themselves against the inhabitants of "Otaheite-nooe," they impute it entirely to "Oraa," who, as they literally say, fights their battles.

Their assiduity in serving their gods is remarkably conspicuous. Not only the "whattas," or offering places of the "morais," are commonly loaded with fruit and animals; but there are few houses where you do not meet with a small place of the same sort near them. Many of them are so rigidly scrupulous, that they will not begin a meal without first laying aside a morsel for the "Eatooa;" and we had an opportunity during this voyage of seeing their superstitious zeal carried to a most pernicious height, in the instance of human sacrifices, the occasions of offering which I doubt are too frequent. Perhaps they have recourse to them when misfortunes occur; for they asked if one of our men who happened to be confined when we were detained by a contrary wind was "taboo."[2] Their prayers are also very frequent, which they chant much after the manner of the songs in their festive entertainments. And the women, as in other cases, are also obliged to show their inferiority in religious observances; for it is required of them that they should partly uncover themselves as they pass the "morais," or take a considerable circuit to avoid them. Though they have no notion that their god must always be conferring benefits, without sometimes forgetting them, or suffer-

---

[1] We have here an instance of the same word being differently pronounced by the people. Captain Cook speaks of Olla as the Bolabola god.

[2] That is, if he had been killed for a sacrifice.

ing evil to befall them, they seem to regard this less than the attempts of some more inauspicious being to hurt them. They tell us that "Etee" is an evil spirit, who sometimes does them mischief, and to whom, as well as to their god, they make offerings. But the mischiefs they apprehend from any superior invincible beings are confined to things merely temporal.

They believe the soul to be both immaterial and immortal. They say that it keeps fluttering about the lips during the pangs of death ; and that then it ascends and mixes with, or as they express it, is eaten by the deity. In this state it remains for some time, after which it departs to a certain place destined for the reception of the souls of men, where it exists in eternal night, or, as they sometimes say, in twilight or dawn. They have no idea of any permanent punishment after death for crimes that they have committed on earth ; for the souls of good and bad men are eaten indiscriminately by God. But they certainly consider this coalition with the Deity as a kind of purification necessary to be undergone before they enter a state of bliss. For, according to their doctrine, if a man refrain from all connection with women some months before death, he passes immediately into his eternal mansion without such a previous union, as if already, by this abstinence, he were pure enough to be exempted from the general lot. They are, however, far from entertaining those sublime conceptions of happiness which our religion and, indeed, reason give us room to expect hereafter. The only great privilege they seem to think they shall acquire by death is immortality ; for they speak of spirits being in some measure not totally divested of those passions which actuated them when combined with material vehicles. Thus if souls who were formerly enemies should meet, they have many conflicts, though, it should seem, to no purpose, as they are accounted invulnerable in this invisible state. There is a similar reasoning with regard to the meeting of man and wife. If the husband dies first the soul of his wife is known to him on its arrival in the land of spirits. They resume their former acquaintance in a spacious house called "tourooa," where the souls of the deceased assemble to recreate themselves with the gods. She then retires with him to his separate habitation, where they remain for ever, and have an offspring, which, however, is entirely spiritual, as they are neither married, nor are their embraces supposed to be the same as with corporeal beings.

Some of their notions about the Deity are extravagantly absurd. They believe that he is subject to the power of those very spirits to whom he has given existence ; and that, in their turn, they frequently eat or devour him, though he possess the power of re-creating himself. They, doubtless, use this mode of expression, as they seem incapable of conversing about immaterial things without constantly referring to material objects to convey their meaning. And in this manner they continue the account, by saying that in the "tourooa" the deity inquires if they intend or not to destroy him ; and that he is not able to alter their determination. This is known to the inhabitants on earth, as well as to the spirits ; for when the moon is in its wane it is said that they are then devouring their "Eatooa;" and that, as it increases, he is renewing himself. And to this accident not only the inferior but the most eminent gods are liable. They also believe that there are other places for the reception of souls at death. Thus those who are drowned in the sea remain there, where they think that there is a fine country, houses, and everything that can make them happy. But what is more singular, they maintain that not only all other animals, but trees, fruit, and even stones, have souls, which at death, or upon being consumed or broken, ascend to the divinity, with whom they first mix, and afterward pass into the mansion allotted to each.

They imagine that their punctual performance of religious offices procures for them every temporal blessing. And as they believe that the animating and powerful influence of the divine spirit is everywhere diffused, it is no wonder that they join to this many superstitious opinions about its operations. Accordingly, they believe that sudden deaths and all other accidents are affected by the immediate action of some divinity. If a man only stumble against a stone and hurt his toe, they impute it to an "Eatooa;" so that they may be literally said, agreeably to their system, to tread enchanted ground. They are startled in the night on approaching a "toopapaoo," where the dead are exposed, in the same manner that many of our ignorant and superstitious people are with the apprehensions of ghosts and at the sight of a churchyard; and they have an equal confidence in dreams, which they suppose to be communications either from their god or from the spirits of their departed friends, enabling those favoured with them to foretell future events; but this kind of knowledge is confined to particular people. Omai pretended to have this gift. He told us that the soul of his father had intimated to him in a dream, on the 26th of July 1776, that he should go on shore at some place within three days; but he was unfortunate in this first attempt to persuade us that he was a prophet, for it was the 1st of August before we got into Teucriffe. Amongst them, however, the dreamers possess a reputation little inferior to that of their inspired priests and priestesses, whose predictions they implicitly believe, and are determined by them in all undertakings of consequence. They also in some degree maintain our old doctrine of planetary influence; at least they are sometimes regulated in their public counsels by certain appearances of the moon; particularly when lying horizontally, or much inclined on the convex part, on its first appearance after the change, they are encouraged to engage in war with confidence of success.

They have traditions concerning the creation, which, as might be expected, are complex and clouded with obscurity. They say that a goddess having a lump or mass of earth suspended in a cord gave it a swing, and scattered about pieces of land, thus constituting Otaheite and the neighbouring islands, which were all peopled by a man and woman originally fixed at Otaheite. This, however, only respects their own immediate creation, for they have notions of a universal one before this, and of lands of which they have now no other knowledge than what is mentioned in the tradition. Their most remote account reaches to Tatooma and Tapuppa, male and female stones or rocks, who support the congeries of land and water, or our globe, underneath. These produced Totorro, who was killed and divided into land.; and after him Otaia and Oroo were begotten, who were afterward married, and produced first land and then a race of gods. Otaia is killed, and Oroo marries a god, her son, called Teorraha, whom she orders to create more land, the animals, and all sorts of food upon the earth; as also the sky, which is supported by men called Teeferei. The spots observed in the moon are supposed to be groves of a sort of trees which once grew in Otaheite, and, being destroyed by some accident, their seeds were carried up thither by doves, where they now flourish.

They have also many legends both religious and historical, one of which latter, relative to the practice of eating human flesh, I shall give the substance of as a specimen of their method. A long time since there lived in Otaheite two men called "Taheeai," the only name they yet have for cannibals. None knew whence they came, or in what manner they arrived at the island. Their habitation was in the mountains, whence they used to issue and kill many of the natives, whom they afterward devoured, and by that means prevented the progress of population. Two brothers, determined to rid their country of such a formidable enemy, used a stratagem for their destruction with success. These still lived farther upward than the "Taheeai," and in such a situation that they could speak with them without greatly hazarding their own safety. They invited them to accept of an entertainment that should be provided for them, to which these readily consented. The brothers then taking some stones, heated them in a fire, and thrusting them into pieces of "mahee," desired one of the "Taheeai" to open his mouth. On which one of these pieces was dropped in, and some water poured down, which made a boiling or hissing noise in quenching the stone, and killed him. They entreated the other to do the same, but he declined it, representing the consequences of his companion's eating. However, they assured him that the food was excellent, and its effects only temporary, for that the other would soon recover. His credulity was such that he swallowed the bait, and shared the fate of the first. The natives then cut them in pieces, which they buried; and conferred the government of the island on the brothers as a reward for delivering them from such monsters. Their residence was in the district called Whapaeenoo, and to this day there remains a bread-fruit tree once the property of the "Taheeai." They had also a woman who lived with them, and had two teeth of a prodigious size. After they were killed, she lived at the Island Otaha, and when dead was ranked amongst their deities. She did not eat human flesh as the men, but, from the size of her teeth, the natives still call any animal that has a fierce appearance, or is represented with large tusks, "Taheeai."

From some circumstances, I have been led to think that the natives of these isles were formerly cannibals. Upon asking Omai he denied it stoutly, yet mentioned a fact within his own knowledge which almost confirms such an opinion. When the people of Bolabola one time defeated those of Huaheine, a great number of his kinsmen were slain. But one of his relations had afterwards an opportunity of revenging himself, when the Bolabola men were worsted in their turn; and, cutting a piece out of the thigh of one of his enemies, he broiled and ate it. I have also frequently considered the offering of the person's eye who is sacrificed, to the chief, as a vestige of a custom which once really existed to a greater extent, and is still commemorated by this emblematical ceremony. . . .

Besides the cluster of high islands from Mataia to Mourooa inclusive, the people of Otaheite are acquainted with a low uninhabited island, which they name Mopeeha, and seems to be Howe's Island, laid down to the westward of Mourooa in our late charts of this ocean. To this the inhabitants of the most leeward islands sometimes go. There are also several low islands to the north-eastward of Otaheite, which they have sometimes visited, but not constantly, and are said to be only at the distance of two days' sail with a fair wind. They were thus named to me: Mataeeva, Oanaa, Taboohoe, Awehee, Kaoora, Orootooa, Otavaoo (where are large pearls). The inhabitants of these isles come more frequently to Otaheite and the other neighbouring high islands, from whose natives they differ in being of a darker colour, with a fiercer aspect, and differently punctured. I was informed that at Mataeeva, and others of them, it is a custom for the men to give their daughters to strangers who arrive amongst them; but the pairs must be five nights lying near each other without presuming to proceed further. On the sixth evening the father of the young woman treats his guest with food, and informs his daughter that she must that night receive him as her husband. The stranger, however, must not offer to express the least dislike, though the bed-fellow allotted to him should be ever so disagreeable; for this is considered as an unpardonable affront, and is punished with death. Forty men of Bolabola who, incited by curiosity, had roamed as far as Mataeeva in a canoe, were treated in this manner, one of them having incautiously mentioned his dislike of the woman who fell to his lot in the hearing of a boy, who informed her father. In consequence of this, the Mataeevans fell upon them; but these warlike people killed three times their own number, though with the loss of all their party, except five. These hid themselves in the woods and took an opportunity, when the others were burying their dead, to enter some houses, where, having provided themselves with victuals and water, they carried them on board a canoe, in which they made their escape; and after passing Mataia, at which they would not touch, at last arrived safe at Eimeo. The Bolabolans, however, were sensible enough that their travellers had been to blame; for a canoe from Mataeeva arriving sometime after at Bolabola, so far were they from retaliating upon them for the death of their countrymen that they acknowledged that they had deserved their fate, and treated their visitors kindly.

These low isles are, doubtless, the farthest navigation which those of Otaheite and the Society Islands perform at present. It seems to be a groundless supposition made by M. de Bougainville that they made voyages of the prodigious extent[1] he mentions, for I found that it is reckoned a sort of prodigy that a canoe once driven by a storm from Otaheite should have fallen in with Mopeeha, or Howe's Island, though so near and directly to leeward. The knowledge they have of other distant islands is no doubt traditional, and has been communicated to them by the natives of those islands driven accidentally upon their coasts, who, besides giving them the names, could easily inform them of the direction in which the places lie from whence they came, and of the number of days they had been upon the sea. In this manner it may be supposed that the natives of Wateeoo have increased their catalogue by the addition of Otaheite and

____

[1] In Bougainville's "Voyage autour du Monde" we are told that these people sometimes navigate to the distance of more than 300 leagues.

its neighbouring isles from the people we met with there, and also of the other islands these had heard of.

____

CHAPTER X.

AFTER leaving Bolabola I steered to the northward, close hauled, with the wind between NE. and E. Though seventeen months had now elapsed since our departure from England, during which we had not upon the whole been unprofitably employed, I was sensible that, with regard to the principal object of my instructions, our voyage was at this time only beginning, and therefore my attention to every circumstance that might contribute toward our safety and our ultimate success was now to be called forth anew. With this view I had examined into the state of our provisions at the last islands; and as soon as I had left them and got beyond the extent of my former discoveries, I ordered a survey to be taken of all the boatswain's and carpenter's stores that were in the ships, that I might be fully informed of the quantity, state, and condition of every article, and by that means know how to use them to the greatest advantage.

Before I sailed from the Society Islands, I lost no opportunity of inquiring of the inhabitants if there were any islands in a north or northwest direction from them, but I did not find that they knew of any. Nor did we meet with anything that indicated the vicinity of land till we came to about the Latitude of 8° S., where we began to see birds, such as boobies, tropic and man-of-war birds, tern, and some other sorts. At this time our longitude was 205° E. Mendana, in his first voyage in 1568, discovered an island which he named Isla de Jesus in Latitude 6° 45′ S., and 1450 leagues from Callao, which is 200° E. Longitude from Greenwich. We crossed this latitude near 100 leagues to the eastward of this longitude, and saw there many of the above-mentioned birds, which are seldom known to go very far from land. In the night between the 22d and 23d we crossed the Line, in the Longitude of 203° 15′ E.

On the 24th, about half-an-hour after daybreak, land was discovered, bearing NE. by E. half E. Upon a nearer approach it was found to be one of those low islands so common in this ocean, that is, a narrow bank of land enclosing the sea within. A few cocoa-nut trees were seen in two or three places, but in general the land had a very barren appearance. At noon it extended from NE. by E. to S. by E. half E., about four miles distant. The wind was at ESE., so that we were under a necessity of making a few boards to get up to the lee or W. side, where we found from forty to twenty and fourteen fathoms water, over a bottom of fine sand—the least depth about half-a-mile from the breakers, and the greatest about one mile. The meeting with soundings determined me to anchor, with a view to try to get some turtle; for the island seemed to be a likely place to meet with them, and to be without inhabitants. Accordingly we dropped anchor in thirty fathoms, and then a boat was despatched to examine whether it was practicable to land, of which I had some doubt, as the sea broke in a dreadful surf all along the shore. When the boat returned, the officer whom I had entrusted with this examination reported to me that he could see no place where a boat could land, but that there was great abundance of fish in the shoal water without the breakers.

In the morning of the 27th the pinnace and cutter, under the command of Mr King, were sent to the south-east part of the island, within the lagoon, and the small cutter to the northward, where I had been the day before—both parties being ordered upon the same service, to catch turtle. Captain Clerke having had some of his people on shore all night, they had been so fortunate as to turn between forty and fifty on the sand, which were brought on board with all expedition this day; and in the afternoon the party I had sent northward returned with six. They were sent back again, and remained there till we left the island, having in general pretty good success. On the 28th I landed, in company with Mr Bayly, on the island which lies between the two channels into the lagoon, to prepare the telescopes for observing the approaching eclipse of the sun, which was one great inducement to my anchoring here. About noon Mr King returned with one boat and eight turtles, leaving seven behind to be brought by the other boat, whose people were employed in catching more; and in the evening the same boat was sent with water and provisions for them. Mr Williamson now went to superintend this duty in the room of Mr King, who remained on board to attend the observation of the eclipse. The next day Mr Williamson despatched the two boats back to the ship laden with turtle. At the same time he sent me a message desiring that the boats might be ordered round by sea, as he had found a landing-place on the south-east side of the island, where most of the turtle were caught; so that by sending the boats thither the trouble would be saved of carrying them over the land to the inside of the lagoon, as had been hitherto done. The boats were accordingly despatched to the place which he pointed out.

On the morning of the 30th, the day when the eclipse was to happen, Mr King, Mr Bayly, and myself went ashore on the small island above mentioned, to attend the observation. The sky was overcast till past 9 o'clock, when the clouds about the sun dispersed long enough to take its altitude, to rectify the time by the watch we made use of. After this it was again obscured till about thirty minutes past nine, and then we found that the eclipse was begun. We now fixed the micrometers to the telescopes, and observed or measured the uneclipsed part of the sun's disc. At these observations I continued about three-quarters of an hour before the end, when I left off, being in fact unable to continue them longer on account of the great heat of the sun, increased by the reflection from the sand. The sun was clouded at times; but it was clear when the eclipse ended, the time of which was observed as follows :

	Ho.	Min.	Sec.
By Mr Bayly, at .	0	26	3
Mr King, .	0	26	1
Myself, .	0	25	37

Apparent time P.M.

Mr Bayly and I observed with the large achromatic telescopes, and Mr King with a reflector. As Mr Bayly's telescope and mine were of the same magnifying power, I ought not to have differed so much from him as I did. Perhaps it was in part, if not wholly, owing to a protuberance in the moon which escaped my notice, but was seen by both the other gentlemen. . . .

Having some cocoa-nuts and yams on board in a state of vegetation, I ordered them to be planted on the little island where we had observed the eclipse, and some melon-seeds were sown in another place. I also left on the little island a bottle containing this inscription :

"*Georgius Tertius Rex*, 31 *Decembris* 1777.

Naves { *Resolution, Jac. Cook, Pr.* { *Discovery, Car. Clerke, Pr.*"

On the 1st of January 1778, I sent boats to bring on board all our parties from the land, and the turtle they had caught. Before this was completed it was late in the afternoon, so that I did not think proper to sail till next morning. We got at this island, to both ships, about 300 turtle, weighing one with another about 90 or 100 pounds. They were all of the green kind, and perhaps as good as any in the world. We also caught with hook and line as much fish as we could consume during our stay. They consisted principally of cavallies of different sizes, large and small snappers, and a few of two sorts of rock-fish, one with numerous spots

of blue, and the other with whitish streaks scattered about. . . .

As we kept our Christmas here, I called this discovery Christmas Island. I judge it to be about fifteen or twenty leagues in circumference.[1] It seemed to be of a semicircular form, or like the moon in the last quarter, the two horns being the north and south points.

Christmas Island, like most others in this ocean, is bounded by a reef of coral rocks, which extends but a little way from the shore. Farther out than this reef, on the west side, is a bank of sand extending a mile into the sea. On this bank is good anchorage in any depth between eighteen and thirty fathoms. In less than the first-mentioned depth the reef would be too near; and in more than the last the edge of the bank would not be at a sufficient distance. During the time we lay here, the wind blew constantly a fresh gale at E. or E. by S., except one or two days. We had always a great swell from the northward, which broke upon the reef, in a prodigious surf. We had found this swell before we came to the island; and it continued for some days after we left it.

CHAPTER XI.

On the 2d of January at daybreak we weighed anchor and resumed our course to the N., having fine weather. We continued to see birds every day, of the sorts last mentioned, sometimes in greater numbers than others, and between the latitude of 10° and 11° we saw several turtle. All these are looked upon as signs of the vicinity of land. However, we discovered none till daybreak in the morning of the 18th, when an island made its appearance bearing NE. by E., and soon after we saw more land bearing N. and entirely detached

---

[1] It lies, according to Cook's observations, in 1° 59′ N. Latitude, and 202° 30′ E. Longitude.

from the former. Both had the appearance of being high land. We had now light airs and calms by turns; so that at sunset we were not less than nine or ten leagues from the nearest land.

On the 19th at sunrise the island first seen bore E. several leagues distant. This being directly to windward, which prevented our getting near it, I stood for the other, which we could reach; and not long after discovered a third island in the direction of WNW., as far distant as land could be seen. We had now a fine breeze at E. by N.; and I steered for the east end of the second island. At this time we were in some doubt whether or no the land before us was inhabited; but this doubt was soon cleared up by seeing some canoes coming off from the shore toward the ships. I immediately brought to, to give them time to join us. They had from three to six men each, and on their approach we were agreeably surprised to find that they spoke the language of Otaheite and of the other islands we had lately visited. It required but very little address to get them to come alongside; but no entreaties could prevail upon any of them to come on board. I tied some brass medals to a rope and gave them to those in one of the canoes, who in return tied some small mackerel to the rope as an equivalent. This was repeated, and some small nails or bits of iron, which they valued more than any other article, were given them. For these they exchanged more fish, and a sweet potato; a sure sign that they had some notion of bartering, or at least of returning one present for another. They had nothing else in their canoes except some large gourd shells, and a kind of fishing-net; but one of them offered for sale the piece of stuff that he wore round his waist after the manner of the other islands. These people were of a brown colour, and though of the common size, were stoutly made. There was little difference in the cast of their colour, but a considerable variation in their features; some of their visages not being very

unlike those of Europeans. The hair of most of them was cropped pretty short; others had it flowing loose; and with a few it was tied in a bunch on the crown of the head. In all it seemed to be naturally black; but most of them had stained it, as is the practice of the Friendly Islanders, with some stuff which gave it a brown or burnt colour. In general they wore their beards. They had no ornaments about their persons, nor did we observe that their ears were perforated; but some were punctured on the hands, or near the groin, though in a small degree; and the bits of cloth which they wore were curiously stained with red, black, and white colours. They seemed very mild, and had no arms of any kind, if we except some small stones which they had evidently brought for their own defence; and these they threw overboard when they found that they were not wanted. [Finding no proper anchoring-place at the eastern extreme of the island, they bore away to the middle of the NW. side, where they stood off in five fathoms, over a sandy bottom. The natives who afterwards came on board showed great ignorance of everything European, and proved themselves to be great thieves.]

While the boats were occupied in examining the coast, we stood on and off with the ships, waiting for their return. About noon Mr Williamson came back and reported that he had seen a large pond behind a beach near one of the villages, which the natives told him contained fresh water, and that there was anchoring-ground before it. He also reported that he had attempted to land in another place, but was prevented by the natives, who, coming down to the boats in great numbers, attempted to take away the oars, muskets, and in short everything that they could lay hold of, and pressed so thick upon him that he was obliged to fire, by which one man was killed. But this unhappy circumstance I did not know till after we had left the island, so that all my measures were directed as if nothing of the kind had happened. Mr Williamson told me that after the man fell, his countrymen took him up, carried him off, and then retired from the boat; but still they made signals for our people to land, which he declined. It did not appear to Mr Williamson that the natives had any design to kill or even to hurt any of his party; but they seemed excited by mere curiosity, to get from them what they had, being at the same time ready to give in return anything of their own. After the boats were on board, I despatched one of them to lie in the best anchoring-ground; and as soon as she had got to this station, I bore down with the ships, and anchored in twenty-five fathoms water. The Discovery anchored to the eastward of us, farther from the land. The ships being thus stationed between 3 and 4 o'clock, I went ashore with three armed boats and twelve marines, to examine the water, and to try the disposition of the inhabitants, several hundreds of whom were assembled on a sandy beach before the village; behind it was a narrow valley, the bottom of which was occupied by the piece of water.

The very instant I leaped on shore, the collected body of the natives all fell flat upon their faces, and remained in that very humble posture till by expressive signs I prevailed upon them to rise. They then brought a great many small pigs, which they presented to me, with plantain-trees, using much the same ceremonies that we had seen practised on such occasions at the Society and other islands, and a long prayer being spoken by a single person, in which others of the assembly sometimes joined. I expressed my acceptance of their proffered friendship, by giving them in return such presents as I had brought with me from the ship for that purpose. When this introductory business was finished, I stationed a guard upon the beach, and got some of the natives to conduct me to the water; which proved to be very good, and in a proper situation for our purpose. It was so considerable that it may be

called a lake, and it extended farther up the country than we could see. Having satisfied myself about this very essential point, and about the peaceable disposition of the natives, I returned on board, and then gave orders that everything should be in readiness for landing and filling our water-casks in the morning; when I went ashore with the people employed in that service, having a party of marines with us for a guard, who were stationed on the beach.

As soon as we landed, a trade was set on foot for hogs and potatoes, which the people of the island gave us in exchange for nails and pieces of iron formed into something like chisels. We met with no obstruction in watering; on the contrary, the natives assisted our men in rolling the casks to and from the pool, and readily performed whatever we required. Everything thus going on to my satisfaction, and considering my presence on the spot unnecessary, I left the command to Mr Williamson, who had landed with me, and made an excursion into the country up the valley, accompanied by Mr Anderson and Mr Webber; the former of whom was as well qualified to describe with the pen as the latter was to represent with his pencil everything we might meet with worthy of observation. A numerous train of natives followed us; and one of them, whom I had distinguished for his activity in keeping the rest in order, I made choice of as our guide. This man from time to time proclaimed our approach; and every one whom we met fell prostrate upon the ground and remained in that position till we had passed. This, as I afterward understood, is the mode of paying their respect to their own great chiefs. As we ranged down the coast from the east in the ships, we had observed at every village one or more elevated white objects, like pyramids or rather obelisks; and one of these, which I guessed to be at least fifty feet high, was very conspicuous from the ship's anchoring station, and seemed to be at no great distance up this valley. To have a nearer inspec tion of it was the principal object of my walk. Our guide perfectly understood that we wished to be conducted to it; but it happened to be so placed that we could not get at it, being separated from us by the pool of water. However, there being another of the same kind within our reach, about half-a-mile off upon our side of the valley, we set out to visit that. The moment we got to it we saw that it stood in a burying-ground, or "morai," the resemblance of which in many respects to those we were so well acquainted with at other islands in this ocean, and particularly Otaheite, could not but strike us; and we also soon found that the several parts that compose it were called by the same names. It was an oblong space, of considerable extent, surrounded by a wall of stone about four feet high. The space enclosed was loosely paved with smaller stones; and at one end of it stood what I call the pyramid, but in the language of the island is named "henananoo;" which appeared evidently to be an exact model of the larger one observed by us from the ships. It was about four feet square at the base, and about twenty feet high. The four sides were composed of small poles interwoven with twigs and branches, thus forming an indifferent wicker-work, hollow or open within from bottom to top. It seemed to be rather in a ruinous state; but there were sufficient remaining marks to show that it had originally been covered with a thin, light, grey cloth, which these people, it should seem, consecrate to religious purposes; as we could see a good deal of it hanging in different parts of the "morai," and some of it had been forced upon me when I first landed. On each side of the pyramid were long pieces of wicker-work called "hereanee," in the same ruinous condition; with two slender poles, inclining to each other, at one corner, where some plantains were laid upon a board fixed at the height of five or six feet. This they called "herairemy," and informed us that the fruit was an offering to their god, which makes it agree exactly

with the "whatta" of Otaheite. Before the "henananoo" were a few pieces of wood carved into something like human figures, which, with a stone near two feet high, covered with pieces of cloth called "hoho," and consecrated to "Tongarooa," who is the god of these people, still more and more reminded us of what we used to meet with in the "morais" of the islands we had lately left. Adjoining to these, on the outside of the "morai," was a small shed no bigger than a dog-kennel, which they called "hareepahoo;" and before it was a grave, where, as we were told, the remains of a woman lay.

On the farther side of the area of the "morai" stood a house or shed about forty feet long, ten broad in the middle, each end being narrower, and about ten feet high. This, which though much longer was lower than their common dwelling-places, we were informed was called "hemanaa." The entrance into it was at the middle of the side which was in the "morai." On the farther side of this house, opposite the entrance, stood two wooden images, cut out of one piece, with pedestals, in all about three feet high; neither very indifferently designed nor executed. These were said to be "Eatooa no Veheina," or representations of goddesses. On the head of one of them was a carved helmet not unlike those worn by the ancient warriors, and on that of the other a cylindrical cap, resembling the head-dress at Otaheite, called "tomou;" and both of them had pieces of cloth tied about the loins, and hanging a considerable way down. At the side of each was also a piece of carved wood, with bits of the cloth hung on them in the same manner; and between or before the pedestals lay a quantity of fern in a heap. It was obvious that this had been deposited there piece by piece and at different times; for there was of it in all states, from what was quite decayed to what was still fresh and green.

In the middle of the house, and before the two images, was an oblong space enclosed by a low edging of stone, and covered with shreds of the cloth so often mentioned. This on inquiry we found was the grave of seven chiefs, whose names were enumerated, and the place was called Heneene. We had met already with so many striking instances of resemblance between the burying-place we were now visiting and those of islands we had lately come from in the South Pacific, that we had little doubt in our minds that the resemblance existed also in the ceremonies practised here, and particularly in the horrid one of offering human sacrifices. Our suspicions were too soon confirmed by direct evidence. For on coming out of the house, just on one side of the entrance, we saw a small square place, and another still less near it; and on asking what these were, our guide immediately informed us that in the one was buried a man who had been sacrificed; a "Taata ("Tanata" or "Tangata," in this country) taboo" ("tafoo," as here pronounced); and in the other a hog which had also been made an offering to the divinity. At a little distance from these, near the middle of the "morai," were three more of these square enclosed places, with two pieces of carved wood at each, and upon them a heap of fern. These we were told were the graves of three chiefs; and before them was an oblong enclosed space to which our conductor also gave the name of "Tangata-taboo;" telling us, so explicitly that we could not mistake his meaning, that three human sacrifices had been buried there, that is, one at the funeral of each chief. It was with most sincere concern that I could trace on such undoubted evidence the prevalence of these bloody rites throughout this immense ocean, amongst people disjoined by such a distance, and even ignorant of each other's existence, though so strongly marked as originally of the same nation. It was no small addition to this concern to reflect that every appearance led us to believe the barbarous practice was very general here. The island seemed to abound with such places of sacrifice as this which we were now visiting, and which appeared to be one of the most incon-

siderable of them; being far less conspicuous than several others which we had seen as we sailed along the coast, and particularly than that on the opposite side of the water in this valley; the white "henananao," or pyramid, of which, we were now almost sure, derived its colour only from pieces of the consecrated cloth laid over it. In several parts within the enclosure of this burying-ground were planted trees of the *Cordia sebestina*, some of the *Morinda citrifolia*, and several plants of the "etee," or "jejee," of Tonga-taboo, with the leaves of which the "hemanaa was thatched;" and as I observed that this plant was not made use of in thatching their dwelling-houses, probably it is reserved entirely for religious purposes.

Our road to and from the "morai" which I have described lay through the plantations. The greatest part of the ground was quite flat, with ditches full of water intersecting different parts, and roads that seemed artificially raised to some height. The interspaces were in general planted with "taro," which grows here with great strength, as the fields are sunk below the common level so as to contain the water necessary to nourish the roots. This water probably comes from the same source which supplies the large pool from which we filled our casks. On the drier spaces were several spots where the cloth-mulberry was planted in regular rows, also growing vigorously, and kept very clean. The cocoa-trees were not in so thriving a state, and were all low; but the plantain-trees made a better appearance, though they were not large. In general, the trees round this village, and which were seen at many of those which we passed before we anchored, are the *Cordia sebestina*, but of a more diminutive size than the product of the southern isles. The greatest part of the village stands near the beach, and consists of above sixty houses there; but perhaps about forty more stand scattered about farther up the country towards the burying-place. . . .

At 7 o'clock on the 23d, a breeze of wind springing up at NE., I took up the anchors with a view of removing the ship farther out. The moment that the last anchor was up, the wind veered to the E., which made it necessary to set all the sail we could in order to clear the shore; so that before we had tolerable sea-room we were driven some distance to leeward. We made a stretch off with a view to regain the road; but having very little wind, and a strong current against us, I found that this was not to be effected. I therefore despatched Messrs King and Williamson ashore with three boats for water, and to trade for refreshments. At the same time I sent an order to Captain Clerke to put to sea after me, if he should see that I could not recover the road. Being in hopes of finding one, or perhaps a harbour, at the west end of the island, I was the less anxious about getting back to my former station. But as I had sent the boats thither, we kept to windward as much as possible; notwithstanding which, at noon we were three leagues to leeward. As we drew near the west end of the island, we found the coast to round gradually to the north-east, without forming a creek or cove to shelter a vessel from the force of the swell which rolled in from the north, and broke upon the shore in a prodigious surf; so that all hopes of finding a harbour here vanished.

Several canoes came off in the morning, and followed us as we stood out to sea, bartering their roots and other articles. Being very averse to believe these people to be cannibals, notwithstanding the suspicious circumstance which had happened the day before, we took occasion now to make some more inquiries about this. A small wooden instrument, beset with sharks' teeth, had been purchased; and from its resemblance to the saw or knife used by the New Zealanders to disect the bodies of their enemies, it was suspected to have the same use here. One of the natives being asked about this, immediately gave the name of the instrument, and told us that it was used to cut out the fleshy part of the belly when any person was killed.

This explained and confirmed the circumstance above mentioned of the person pointing to his belly. The man, however, from whom we had this information, being asked if his countrymen eat the part thus cut out, denied it strongly; but, upon the question being repeated, showed some degree of fear and swam to his canoe. Just before he reached it, he made signs as he had done before, expressive of the use of the instrument. And an old man, who sat foremost in the canoe, being then asked whether they ate the flesh, answered in the affirmative, and laughed, seemingly at the simplicity of such a question. He affirmed the fact on being asked again; and also said it was excellent food, or, as he expressed it, "savoury eating." At 7 o'clock in the evening the boats returned, with two tons of water, a few hogs, a quantity of plantains, and some roots. Mr King informed me that a great number of the inhabitants were at the watering or landing-place. He supposed that they had come from all parts of the island. They had brought with them a great many fine fat hogs to barter; but my people had not commodities with them equal to the purchase. This, however, was no great loss, for we had already got as many on board as we could well manage for immediate use; and wanting the materials we could not have salted them. Mr King also told me that a great deal of rain had fallen ashore, whereas out at sea we had only a few showers; and that the surf had run so high that it was with great difficulty our men landed and got back into the boats.

We had light airs and calms by turns, with showers of rain, all night; and at daybreak in the morning of the 24th we found that the currents had carried the ship to the NW. and N.; so that the west end of the island, upon which we had been, called Atooi by the natives, bore E. one league distant; another island, called Oreehoua, W. by S.; and the high land of a third island, called Oneeheow, from SW. by W. to WSW. Soon after, a breeze sprang up at N.; and as I expected that this would bring the Discovery to sea, I steered for Oneeheow, in order to take a nearer view of it, and to anchor there if I should find a convenient place. I continued to steer for it till past 11 o'clock, at which time we were about two leagues from it. But not seeing the Discovery, and being doubtful whether they could see us, I was fearful lest some ill consequence might attend our separating so far. I therefore gave up the design of visiting Oneeheow for the present, and stood back to Atooi, with an intent to anchor again in the road to complete our water. At 2 o'clock in the afternoon the northerly wind died away, and was succeeded by variable light airs and calms that continued till eleven at night, with which we stretched to the SE. till daybreak in the morning of the 25th, when we tacked and stood in for Atooi road, which bore about N. from us; and soon after we were joined by the Discovery. We fetched in with the land about two leagues to leeward of the road, which, though so near, we never could recover; for what we gained at one time we lost at another, so that by the morning of the 29th the currents had carried us westward within three leagues of Oneeheow. Being tired with plying so unsuccessfully, I gave up all thoughts of getting back to Atooi, and came to the resolution of trying whether we could not procure what we wanted at the other island, which was within our reach. With this view I sent the master in a boat to sound the coast, to look out for a landing-place, and, if he should find one, to examine if fresh water could be conveniently got in its neighbourhood. To give him time to execute his commission, we followed under an easy sail with the ships. At 10 o'clock the master returned, and reported that he had landed in one place but could find no fresh water; and that there was anchorage all along the coast. Seeing a village a little farther to leeward, and some of the islanders who had come off to the ships informing us that fresh water might be got there, I ran down and came to an anchor before it, in twenty-six fathoms water, about three-quarters of a mile from the shore.

Six or seven canoes had come off to us before we anchored, bringing some small pigs and potatoes, and a good many yams and mats. The people in them resembled those of Atooi, and seemed to be equally well acquainted with the use of iron, which they asked for also by the names of "hamaite" and "toe;" parting readily with all their commodities for pieces of this precious metal. Several more canoes soon reached the ships after they had anchored, but the natives in these seemed to have no other object than to pay us a formal visit. Many of them came readily on board, crouching down upon the deck, and not quitting that humble posture till they were desired to get up. They had brought several females with them, who remained alongside in the canoes, behaving with far less modesty than their countrywomen of Atooi; and at times all joining in a song not remarkable for its melody, though performed in very exact concert by beating time upon their breasts with their hands. The men who had come on board did not stay long; and before they departed some of them requested our permission to lay down on the deck locks of their hair. These visitors furnished us with an opportunity of agitating again this day the curious inquiry whether they were cannibals, and the subject did not take its rise from any questions of ours, but from a circumstance that seemed to remove all ambiguity. One of the islanders who wanted to get in at the gun-room port was refused, and at the same time asked whether, if he should come in, we would kill and eat him, accompanying this question with signs so expressive that there could be no doubt about his meaning. This gave a proper opening to retort the question as to this practice; and a person behind the other in the canoe, who paid great attention to what was passing, immediately answered that if we were killed on shore they would certainly eat us. He spoke with so little emotion that it appeared plainly to be his meaning that they would not destroy us for that purpose, but that their eating us would be the consequence of our being at enmity with them. I have availed myself of Mr Anderson's collections for the decision of this matter, and I am sorry to say that I cannot see the least reason to hesitate in pronouncing it to be certain that the horrid banquet of human flesh is as much relished here amidst plenty as it is in New Zealand.

In the afternoon I sent Lieutenant Gore with three armed boats to look for the most convenient landing-place, and when on shore to search for fresh water. In the evening he returned, having landed at the village above mentioned, and acquainted me that he had been conducted to a well half-a-mile up the country; but by his account, the quantity of water it contained was too inconsiderable for our purpose, and the road leading to it exceedingly bad. On the 30th I sent Mr Gore ashore again, with a guard of marines and a party, to trade with the natives for refreshments. I intended to have followed soon after, and went from the ship with that design. But the surf had increased so much by this time that I was fearful, if I got ashore, I should not be able to get off again. This really happened to our people who had landed with Mr Gore, the communication between them and the ships by our own boats being soon stopped. In the evening they made a signal for the boats, which were sent accordingly; and not long after they returned with a few yams and some salt. A tolerable quantity of both had been procured in the course of the day, but the surf was so great that the greatest part of both these articles had been lost in conveying them to the boats. The officer and twenty men, deterred by the danger of coming off, were left ashore all night; and by this unfortunate circumstance the very thing happened which, as I have already mentioned, I wished so heartily to prevent, and vainly imagined I had effectually guarded against. The violence of the surf, which our own boats could not act against, did not hinder the natives from coming off to the ships in their canoes. They brought refreshments with them, which were purchased in exchange for nails and pieces of iron hoops; and I distributed a good many pieces of ribbon and some buttons as bracelets amongst the women in the canoes. One of the men had the figure of a lizard punctured upon his breast, and upon those of others were the figures of men badly imitated. These visitors informed us that there was no chief, or "Hairee," of this island, but that it was subject to Teneooneoo, a chief of Atooi; which island, they said, was not governed by a single chief, but that there were many to whom they paid the honour of "moe," or prostration; and among others they named Otaeaio and Terarotoa. Amongst other things which these people now brought off was a small drum, almost like those of Otaheite.

About 10 or 11 o'clock at night the wind veered to the south, and the sky seemed to forebode a storm. With such appearances, thinking that we were rather too near the shore, I ordered the anchors to be taken up; and having carried the ships into forty-two fathoms, came to again in that safer station. The precaution, however, proved to be unnecessary, for the wind soon after veered to NNE., from which quarter it blew a fresh gale, with squalls, attended with very heavy showers of rain. This weather continued all the next day, and the sea ran so high that we had no manner of communication with our party on shore; and even the natives themselves durst not venture out to the ships in their canoes. In the evening I sent the master in a boat up to the south-east head or point of the island to try if he could land under it. He returned with a favourable report; but it was too late now to send for our party till the next morning, and thus they had another night to improve their intercourse with the natives. Encouraged by the master's report, I sent a boat to the south-east point as soon as daylight returned with an order to Mr Gore if he could not embark his people from the spot where they now were to march them up to the point. As the boat could not get to the beach, one of the crew swam ashore and carried the order. On the return of the boat, I went myself with the pinnace and launch up to the point to bring the party on board, taking with me a ram-goat and two ewes, a boar and sow pig of the English breed, and the seeds of melons, pumpkins, and onions, being very desirous of benefiting these poor people by furnishing them with some additional articles of food. I landed with the greatest ease under the west side of the point, and found my party already there, with some of the natives in company. To one of them whom Mr Gore had observed assuming some command over the rest, I gave the goats, pigs, and seeds. I should have left these well-intended presents at Atooi had we not been so unexpectedly driven from it.

The habitations of the natives were thinly scattered about, and it was supposed that there could not be more than 500 people upon the island, as the greatest part were seen at the marketing-place of our party, and few found about the houses by those who walked up the country. They had an opportunity of observing the method of living amongst the natives, and it appeared to be decent and cleanly. They did not, however, see any instance of the men and women eating together; and the latter seemed generally associated in companies by themselves. It was found that they burned here the oily nuts of the "dooe dooe" for lights in the night, as at Otaheite; and that they baked their hogs in ovens, but, contrary to the practice of the Society and Friendly Islands, split their carcases through their whole length. They met with a positive proof of the existence of the "taboo" (or, as they pronounce it, the "tafoo"), for one woman fed another who was under that interdiction. They also observed some other mysterious ceremonies, one of which was performed by a woman, who took a small pig and threw it into the surf, till it was drowned, and then tied up a bundle of wood, which she also disposed of in the same manner. The same woman at another time beat with a stick upon a man's shoulders, who sat down for that purpose. A particular veneration seemed to be paid here to owls, which they have very tame; and it was observed to be a pretty general practice amongst them to pull out one of their teeth,[1] for which odd custom, when asked the reason, the only answer that could be got was, that it was "teeha," which was also the reason assigned for another of their practices, the giving a lock of their hair.

After the water-casks had been filled and conveyed into the boat, and we had purchased from the natives a few roots, a little salt, and some salted fish, I returned on board with all the people, intending to visit the island the next day. But about 7 o'clock in the evening the anchor of the Resolution started, and she drove off the bank. As we had a whole cable out, it was some time before the anchor was at the bows, and then we had the launch to hoist up alongside before we could make sail. By this unlucky accident we found ourselves at daybreak next morning three leagues to the leeward of our last station; and foreseeing that it would require more time to recover it than I chose to spend, I made the signal for the Discovery to weigh and join us. This was done

---

[1] It is very remarkable that in this custom, which one would think is so unnatural as not to be adopted by two different tribes originally unconnected, the people of this island, and Dampier's natives on the west side of New Holland, at such an immense distance should be found to agree.—*Note in Original Edition.* Dampier, in his Sixteenth Chapter (*ante*, p. 254), says of the New Hollanders: "The two fore teeth of their upper jaw are wanting in all of them, men and women, old and young; whether they draw them out, I know not."

about noon, and we immediately stood away to the northward in prosecution of our voyage. Thus after spending more time about these islands than was necessary to have answered all our purposes, we were obliged to leave them before we had completed our water and got from them such a quantity of refreshments as their inhabitants were both able and willing to have supplied us with. But as it was, our ship procured from them provisions sufficient for three weeks at least; and Captain Clerke, more fortunate than us, got of their vegetable productions a supply that lasted his people upward of two months. The observations I was enabled to make, combined with those of Mr Anderson, who was a very useful assistant on all such occasions, will furnish materials for the next Chapter.

CHAPTER XII.

It is worthy of observation that the islands in the Pacific Ocean which our late voyages have added to the geography of the globe have been generally found lying in groups or clusters, the single intermediate islands as yet discovered being few in proportion to the others, though probably there are many more of them still unknown, which serve as steps between the several clusters. Of what number this newly discovered archipelago consists must be left for future investigation. We saw five of them, whose names, as given to us by the natives, are Woahoo, Atooi, Oneeheow, Oreehoua, and Tahoora. The last is a small elevated island, lying four or five leagues from the south-east point of Oneeheow, in the direction of S. 69° W. We were told that it abounds with birds, which are its only inhabitants. We also got some information of the existence of a low uninhabited island in the neighbourhood, whose name is Tammata-papa. Besides these six, which we can distinguish by their names, it appeared that the inhabitants of those with whom we had intercourse were acquainted with some other islands both to the eastward and westward. I named the whole group the Sandwich Islands, in honour of the Earl of Sandwich. Those that I saw are situated between the Latitude of 21° 30' and 22° 15' N., and between the Longitude of 199° 20' and 201° 30' E.

Of Woahoo, the most easterly of these islands seen by us, which lies in the Latitude of 21° 36', we could get no other intelligence but that it is high land and is inhabited.

We had opportunities of knowing some particulars about Oneeheow, which have been mentioned already. It lies several leagues to the westward of our anchoring-place at Atooi, and is not above fifteen leagues in circuit. Its chief vegetable produce is yams, if we may judge from what was brought to us by the natives. They have salt, which they call "patai," and is produced in salt-ponds. With it they cure both fish and pork, and some salt fish which we got from them kept very well and were found to be very good. This island is mostly low land, except the part facing Atooi, which rises directly from the sea to a good height, as does also the south-east point of it, which terminates in a round hill. It was on the west side of this point where our ships anchored.

Of Oreehoua we know nothing more than that it is a small elevated island lying close to the north side of Oneeheow.

Atooi, which is the largest, being the principal scene of our operations, I shall now proceed to lay before my readers what information I was able to collect about it, either from actual observation while on shore, or from conversation with its inhabitants, who were perpetually on board the ships while we lay at anchor, and who in general could be tolerably well understood by those of us who had acquired an acquaintance with the dialects of the South Pacific islands. It is, however, to be regretted that we should have been obliged so soon to leave a place which, as far as our opportunities of knowing reached, seemed to be highly worthy of a more accurate examination.

Atooi, from what we saw of it, is at least ten leagues in length from east to west, from whence its circuit may nearly be guessed, though it appears to be much broader at the east than at the west point, if we may judge from the double range of hills which appeared there. The road or anchoring-place which we occupied is on the south-west side of the island, about six miles from the west end, before a village which has the name of Wymoa.

The land, as to its general appearance, does not in the least resemble any of the islands we have hitherto visited within the tropic, on the south side of the Equator, if we except its hills near the centre, which are high, but slope gently to the sea or lower lands. Though it be destitute of the delightful borders of Otaheite, and of the luxuriant plains of Tongataboo, covered with trees, which at once afford a friendly shelter from the scorching sun, and an enchanting prospect to the eye, and food for the natives, which may be truly said to drop from the trees into their mouths, without the laborious task of rearing; though I say Atooi be destitute of these advantages, its possessing a greater quantity of gently-rising land renders it in some measure superior to the above favourite islands, as being more capable of improvement. The height of the land within, the quantity of clouds which we saw, during the whole time we stayed, hanging over it, and frequently on the other parts, seems to put it beyond all doubt that there is a sufficient supply of water, and that there are some running streams which we did not see, especially in the deep valleys, at the entrance of which the villages commonly stand. From the wooded part to the sea, the ground is covered with an excellent sort of grass, about two feet high, which grows sometimes in tufts, and, though not very thick at the place where we were, seemed capable of being converted into plen-

tiful crops of fine hay. But not even a shrub grows naturally on this extensive space.

In the break, or narrow valley, through which we had our road to the "morai," the soil is of a brownish black colour, somewhat loose; but as we advanced upon the high ground it changed to a reddish brown, more stiff and clayey, though at this time brittle from its dryness. It is most probably the same all over the cultivated parts; for what adhered to most of the potatoes bought by us, which no doubt came from very different spots, was of this sort. Its quality, however, may be better understood from its products than from its appearance. For the vale, or moist ground, produces "taro" of a much larger size than any we had ever seen; and the higher ground furnishes sweet potatoes, that often weigh ten, and sometimes twelve or fourteen pounds, very few being under two or three.

The temperature of the climate may be easily guessed from the situation of the island. Were we to judge of it from our experience, it might be said to be very variable; for, according to the generally received opinion, it was now the season of the year when the weather is supposed to be most settled, the sun being at his greatest annual distance. The heat was at this time very moderate; and few of those inconveniences which many tropical countries are subject to, either from heat or moisture, seem to be experienced here, as the habitations of the natives are quite close; and they salt both fish and pork, which keep well, contrary to what has usually been observed to be the case when this operation is attempted in hot countries. Neither did we find any dews of consequence, which may in some measure be accounted for by the lower part of the country being destitute of trees. . . .

The inhabitants are of a middling stature, firmly made, with some exceptions neither remarkable for a beautiful shape, nor for striking features, which rather express an openness and good-nature, than a keen, intelligent disposition. Their visage, especially amongst the women, is sometimes round, but others have it long; nor can we say that they are distinguished as a nation by any general cast of countenance. Their colour is nearly of a nut brown; and it may be difficult to make a nearer comparison, if we take in all the different hues of that colour; but some individuals are darker. The women have been already mentioned as being little more delicate than the men in their formation; and I may say that, with a very few exceptions, they have little claim to those peculiarities that distinguish the sex in other countries. There is, indeed, a more remarkable equality in the size, colour, and figure of both sexes than in most places I have visited. However, upon the whole, they are far from being ugly, and appear to have few natural deformities of any kind. Their skin is not very soft nor shining, perhaps for want of oiling, which is practised at the Southern Islands; but their eyes and teeth are in general very tolerable. The hair, for the greatest part, is straight, though in some frizzling; and though its natural colour be commonly black, it is stained as at the Friendly and other islands. We saw but few instances of corpulence, and these oftener among the women than the men; but it was chiefly amongst the latter that personal defects were observed, though, if any of them can claim a share of beauty, it was most conspicuous amongst the young men. They are vigorous, active, and most expert swimmers, leaving their canoes upon the most trifling occasion, diving under them, and swimming to others, though at a great distance. It was very common to see women, with infants at the breast, when the surf was so high that they could not land in the canoes, leap overboard, and, without endangering their little ones, swim to the shore through a sea that looked dreadful.

They seem to be blest with a frank, cheerful disposition; and were I to draw any comparisons, I should say that they are equally free from the fickle levity which distinguishes the natives of Otaheite, and the sedate cast observable amongst many of those of Tongataboo. They seem to live very sociably in their intercourse with one another; and except the propensity to thieving, which seems innate in most of the people we have visited in this ocean, they were exceedingly friendly to us. And it does their sensibility no little credit, without flattering ourselves, that when they saw the various articles of our European manufacture, they could not help expressing their surprise, by a mixture of joy and concern that seemed to apply the case as a lesson of humility to themselves; and on all occasions they appeared deeply impressed with a consciousness of their own inferiority, a behaviour which equally exempts their national character from the preposterous pride of the more polished Japanese, and of the ruder Greenlander. It was a pleasure to observe with how much affection the women managed their infants, and how readily the men lent their assistance to such a tender office, thus sufficiently distinguishing themselves from those savages, who esteem a wife and child as things rather necessary than desirable or worthy of their notice.

From the numbers which we saw collected at every village as we sailed past, it may be supposed that the inhabitants of this island are pretty numerous. Any computation that we make can be only conjectural. But, that some notion may be formed which shall not greatly err on either side, I should suppose that, including the straggling houses there might be upon the whole island, sixty such villages as that before which we anchored; and that, allowing five persons to each house, there would be in every village 500, or 30,000 upon the island. This number is certainly not exaggerated, for we had sometimes 3000 persons at least upon the beach, when it could not be supposed that above a tenth part of the inhabitants were present.

The common dress both of the

women and of the men has been already described. The first have often much larger pieces of cloth wrapped round them, reaching from just below the breasts to the hams, or lower ; and several were seen with pieces thrown loosely about the shoulders, which covered the greatest part of the body ; but the children, when very young, are quite naked. They wear nothing upon the head, but the hair in both sexes is cut in different forms ; and the general fashion, especially among the women, is to have it long before, and short behind. The men often had it cut or shaved on each side, in such a manner that the remaining part in some measure resembles the crest of their caps or helmets formerly described. Both sexes, however, seem very careless about their hair, and have nothing like combs to dress it with. Instances of wearing it in a singular manner were sometimes met with among the men, who twist it into a number of separate parcels, like the tails of a wig, each about the thickness of a finger, though the greatest part of these, which are so long that they reach far down the back, we observed were artificially fixed upon the head over their own hair.

It is remarkable that, contrary to the general practice of the islands we had hitherto discovered in the Pacific Ocean, the people of the Sandwich Islands have not their ears perforated, nor have they the least idea of wearing ornaments in them. Both sexes, nevertheless, adorn themselves with necklaces made of bunches of small black cord, like our hat-string, often above a hundred-fold, exactly like those of Wateeoo, only that instead of the two little balls, on the middle before, they fix a small bit of wood, stone, or shell, about two inches long, with a broad hook, turning forward at its lower part, well polished. They have likewise necklaces of many strings of very small shells, or of the dried flowers of the Indian mallow ; and sometimes a small human image of bone, about three inches long, neatly polished, is hung round the neck.

The women also wear bracelets of a single shell, pieces of black wood with bits of ivory interspersed, and well polished, fixed by a string drawn very close through them ; or others of hogs' teeth, laid parallel to each other, with the concave part outward, and the points cut off, fastened together as the former ; some of which, made only of large boars' tusks, are very elegant. The men sometimes wear plumes of the tropic birds' feathers stuck in their heads, or those of cocks fastened round neat polished sticks two feet long, commonly decorated at the lower part with "oora ;" and, for the same purpose, the skin of a white dog's tail is sewed over a stick, with its tuft at the end. They also frequently wear on the head a kind of ornament of a finger's thickness or more, covered with red and yellow feathers, curiously varied, and tied behind ; and on the arm, above the elbow, a kind of broad shell-work grounded upon net-work. The men are frequently punctured, though not in any particular part, as the Otaheiteans and those of Tonga-taboo. Sometimes there are a few marks upon their hands or arms, and near the groin ; but frequently we could observe none at all, though a few individuals had more of this sort of ornament than we had usually seen at other places, and ingeniously executed in a great variety of lines and figures on the arms and forepart of the body, on which latter some of them had the figure of the " taame," or breastplate of Otaheite, though we did not meet with the thing itself amongst them.

Though they seem to have adopted the mode of living in villages, there is no appearance of defence or fortification near any of them ; and the houses are scattered about without any order either with respect to their distances from each other, or their position in any particular direction. Neither is there any proportion as to their size ; some being large and commodious, from forty to fifty feet long and twenty or thirty broad, while others of them are mere hovels. Their figure is not unlike oblong corn or hay stacks; or perhaps a better idea may be conceived of them if we suppose the roof of a barn placed on the ground in such a manner as to form a high, acute ridge, with two very low sides hardly discernible at a distance. The gable at each end, corresponding to the sides, makes these habitations perfectly close all round; and they are well thatched with long grass, which is laid on slender poles, disposed with some regularity. The entrance is made indifferently in the end or side, and is an oblong hole so low that one must rather creep than walk in, and is often shut up by a board of planks fastened together, which serves as a door, but having no hinges, must be removed occasionally. No light enters the house but by this opening; and though such close habitations may afford a comfortable retreat in bad weather, they seem but ill-adapted to the warmth of the climate. They are, however, kept remarkably clean, and their floors are covered with a large quantity of dried grass, over which they spread mats to sit and sleep upon. At one end stands a kind of bench about three feet high, on which their household utensils are placed. The catalogue is not long. It consists of gourd-shells, which they convert into vessels that serve as bottles to hold water, and as baskets to contain their victuals and other things, with covers of the same; and of a few wooden bowls and trenchers of different sizes. Judging from what we saw growing, and from what was brought to market, there can be no doubt that the greatest part of their vegetable food consists of sweet potatoes, "taro," and plantains, and that bread-fruit and yams are rather to be esteemed rarities. Of animal food they can be in no want, as they have abundance of hogs, which run without restraint about the houses; and if they eat dogs, which is not improbable, their stock of these seemed to be very considerable. The great number of fishing-hooks found among them showed that they derive no in-

considerable supply of animal food from the sea. But it should seem, from their practice of salting fish, that the openness of their coast often interrupts the business of catching them; as it may be naturally supposed that no set of people would ever think of preserving quantities of food artificially if they could depend upon a daily regular supply of it in its fresh state. This sort of reasoning, however, will not account for their custom of salting their pork as well as their fish, which are preserved in gourd-shells. The salt, of which they use a great quantity for this purpose, is of a red colour, not very coarse, and seems to be much the same with what our stragglers found at Christmas Island. It has its colour, doubtless, from a mixture of the mud at the bottom of the part where it is formed; for some of it that had adhered in lumps was of a sufficient whiteness and purity.

They bake their vegetable food with heated stones as at the Southern Islands; and from the vast quantity which we saw dressed at one time, we suspected that the whole village, or at least a considerable number of people, joined in the use of a common oven. We did not see them dress any animal food at this island, but Mr Gore's party, as already mentioned, had an opportunity of satisfying themselves that it was dressed in Oneeheow in the same sort of ovens, which leaves no doubt of this being also the practice in Atooi, especially as we met with no utensil there that could be applied to the purpose of stewing or boiling. The only artificial dish we met with was a "taro" pudding, which, though a disagreeable mess from its sourness, was greedily devoured by the natives. They eat off a kind of wooden plates or trenchers; and the women, as far as we could judge from one instance, if restrained from feeding at the same dish with the men, as at Otaheite, are at least permitted to eat in the same place near them.

Their amusements seem pretty various, for during our stay several were discovered. The dances at which they use the feathered cloaks and caps were not seen; but from the motions which they made with their hands on other occasions when they sang, we could form some judgment that they are in some degree at least similar to those we had met with at the Southern Islands, though not executed so skilfully. Neither had they amongst them either flutes or reeds; and the only two musical instruments which we observed were of an exceedingly rude kind. One of them does not produce a melody exceeding that of a child's rattle. It consists of what may be called a conic cap inverted, but scarcely hollowed at the base above a foot high, made of a coarse sedge-like plant; the upper part of which and the edges are ornamented with beautiful red feathers, and to the point or lower part is fixed a gourd-shell larger than the fist. Into this is put something to rattle, which is done by holding the instrument by the small part, and shaking or rather moving it from place to place briskly, either to different sides, or backward and forward just before the face, striking the breast with the other hand at the same time. The other musical instrument (if either of them deserve that name) was a hollow vessel of wood like a platter, combined with the use of two sticks, on which one of our gentlemen saw a man performing. He held one of the sticks, about two feet long, as we do a fiddle, with one hand, and struck it with the other, which was smaller and resembled a drumstick, in a quicker or slower measure; at the same time beating with his foot upon the hollow vessel that lay inverted upon the ground, and thus producing a tune that was by no means disagreeable. This music was accompanied by the vocal performance of some women, whose song had a pleasing and tender effect. We observed great numbers of small polished rods about four or five feet long, somewhat thicker than the rammer of a musket, with a tuft of long white dogs' hair fixed on the small end. These are probably used in their diversions. We saw a person take one of them in his hand, and, holding it up, give a smart stroke till he brought it into a horizontal position, striking with the foot on the same side upon the ground, and with his other hand beating his breast at the same time. They play at bowls with pieces of whetstone of about a pound weight, shaped somewhat like a small cheese, but rounded at the sides and edges, which are very nicely polished; and they have other bowls of the same sort, made of a heavy reddish brown clay, neatly glazed over with a composition of the same colour, or of a coarse, dark grey slate. They also use, in the manner that we throw quoits, small, flat, rounded pieces of the writing slate, of the diameter of the bowls, but scarcely a quarter of an inch thick, also well polished. From these circumstances one would be induced to think that their games are rather trials of skill than of strength.

In everything manufactured by these people there appears to be an uncommon degree of neatness and ingenuity. Their cloth, which is the principal manufacture, is made from the *Morus papyrifera*, and doubtless in the same manner as at Otaheite and Tongataboo; for we bought some of the grooved sticks with which it is beaten. Its texture, however, though thicker, is rather inferior to that of the cloth of either of the other places; but in colouring or staining it the people of Atooi display a superiority of taste, by the endless variation of figures which they execute. One would suppose, on seeing a number of their pieces, that they had borrowed their patterns from some mercer's shop in which the most elegant productions of China and Europe are collected; besides some original patterns of their own. Their colours, indeed, except the red, are not very bright; but the regularity of the figures and stripes is truly surprising, for, as far as we knew, they have nothing like stamps or prints to make the impressions. In what manner they produce their colours we had not opportunities of learning; but besides the party-coloured sorts they have some pieces of plain white cloth, and others of a single colour, particularly dark brown and light blue. In general, the pieces which they brought to us were about two feet broad, and four or five feet long, being the form and quantity that they use for their common dress or "maro;" and even these we sometimes found were composed of pieces sewed together, an art which we did not find to the southward, but is strongly though not very neatly performed here. There is also a particular sort that is thin, much resembling oil-cloth; and which is actually either oiled or soaked in some kind of varnish, and seems to resist the action of water pretty well. They fabricate a great many white mats, which are strong, with many red stripes, rhombuses, and other figures interwoven on one side, and often pretty large. These, probably, make a part of their dress occasionally; for they put them on their backs when they offered them for sale. But they make others coarser, plain and strong, which they spread over their floors to sleep upon.

They stain their gourd-shells prettily with undulated lines, triangles, and other figures of a black colour, instances of which we saw practised at New Zealand. And they seem to possess the art of varnishing; for some of these stained gourd-shells are covered with a kind of lacquer; and on other occasions they use a strong size, or gluey substance, to fasten their things together. Their wooden dishes and bowls, out of which they drink their "ava," are of the "etooa" tree, or *cordia*, as neat as if made in our turning-lathe, and perhaps better polished. And amongst their articles of handicraft may be reckoned small square fans of mat or wicker-work, with handles tapering from them of the same, or of wood, which are neatly wrought with small cords of hair and fibres of the cocoa-nut coir intermixed. The great variety of fishing-hooks are ingeniously made; some of bone, others of wood pointed with bone, and many of pearl shell. Of the last,

some are like a sort that we saw at Tongataboo; and others simply curved, as the common sort at Otaheite, as well as the wooden ones. The bones are mostly small, and composed of two pieces; and all the different sorts have a barb, either on the inside like ours, or on the outside opposite the same part; but others have both, the outer one being farthest from the point. Of this last sort one was procured, nine inches long, of a single piece of bone, which doubtless belonged to some large fish. The elegant form and polish of this could not certainly be outdone by any European artist, even if he should add all his knowledge in design to the number and convenience of his tools. They polish their stones by constant friction with pumice-stone in water; and such of their working instruments or tools as I saw resembled those of the Southern Islands. Their hatchets, or rather adzes, were exactly of the same pattern, and either made of the same sort of blackish stone or of a clay-coloured one. They have also little instruments made of a single shark's tooth, some of which are fixed to the forepart of a dog's jaw-bone, and others to a thin wooden handle of the same shape; and at the other end there is a bit of string fastened through a small perforation. These serve as knives occasionally, and are perhaps used in carving.

The only iron tools, or rather bits of iron, seen amongst them, and which they had before our arrival, were a piece of iron hoop about two inches long, fitted into a wooden handle;[1] and another edge-tool which our people guessed to be made of the point of a broad-sword. Their having the actual possession of these, and their so generally knowing the use of this metal, inclined some on board to think that we had not been the first European visitors of these islands. But it seems to me that the very great surprise expressed by them on seeing our ships, and their total ignorance of the use of

---

[1] Captain King purchased this, and brought it to England.

fire-arms, cannot be reconciled with such a notion.   There are many ways by which such people may get pieces of iron, or acquire the knowledge of the existence of such a metal, without ever having had an immediate connection with nations that use it.   It can hardly be doubted that it was unknown to all the inhabitants of this sea before Magellan led the way into it; for no discoverer, immediately after his voyage, ever found any of this metal in their possession, though in the course of our late voyages it has been observed that the use of it was known at several islands to which no former European ships had ever, as far as we know, found their way.   At all the places where Mendana[1] touched in his two voyages, it must have been seen and left; and this would extend the knowledge of it, no doubt, to all the various islands with which those whom he had visited had any immediate intercourse.   It might even be carried farther; and where specimens of this article could not be procured, descriptions might in some measure serve to make it known when afterward seen.   The next voyage to the southward of the Line in which any intercourse was had with the natives of this ocean was that of Quiros, who landed at Sagittaria, the Island of Handsome People, and Tierra del Espiritu Santo,[2] at all which places, and at those with whom they had any communication, it must of consequence have been made known.   To him succeeded in this navigation Le Maire and Schouten,[3] whose connections with the natives commenced much farther to the eastward, and ended at Cocos and Horn Islands.   It was not surprising that when I visited Tongataboo in 1773 I should find a bit of iron there, as we knew that Tasman had visited it before me;[4] but let us suppose that he had never discovered the Friendly Islands, our finding iron amongst them would have occasioned much speculation, though we have mentioned before[5] the method by which they had gained a renewal of their knowledge of this metal, which confirms my hypothesis.   For Neeootabootaboo, or Boscawen's Island, where Captain Wallis's ships left it, and from whence Poulaho received it, lies some degrees to the north-west of Tongataboo.   It is well known that Roggewein lost one of his ships on the Pernicious Islands,[6] which from their situation are probably not unknown to, though not frequently visited by, the inhabitants of Otaheite and the Society Islands.   It is equally certain that these last people had a knowledge of iron, and purchased it with the greatest avidity, when Captain Wallis discovered Otaheite; and this knowledge could only have been acquired through the mediation of those neighbouring islands where it had been originally left.   Indeed they acknowledge that this was actually the case; and they have told us since that they held it in such estimation before Captain Wallis's arrival, that a chief of Otaheite, who had got two nails into his possession, received no small emolument by letting out the use of these to his neighbours for the purpose of boring holes when their own methods failed or were thought too tedious.   The men of the Society

---

[1] An enterprising Spanish navigator, who in the latter half of the sixteenth century undertook two voyages, in the first of which he discovered the Salomon Islands, and in the second the Marquesas and Queen Charlotte's Islands, &c.

[2] Quiros sailed from Callao at the end of 1605, in command of four ships, to plant a Spanish colony in Santa Cruz, discovered by Mendana.   Sagittaria is supposed to be Otaheite; Tierra del Espiritu Santo, which Quiros sanguinely mistook for part of the long-sought Southern Continent, is the group now better known by the name Cook gave it, that of New Hebrides.

[3] 1615-1617.

[4] In 1643.

[5] *Ante*, Book II., Chapter X., p. 151.

[6] Believed to be the Palliser's Isles of English maps.   The wreck happened in 1722.

Islands, whom we found at Wateeoo, had been driven thither long after the knowledge and use of iron had been introduced amongst their country-men ; and though probably they had no specimen of it with them, they would naturally and with ease com-municate at that island their know-ledge of this valuable material by description. From the people of Wateeoo, again, those of Hervey's Island might derive that desire to possess some of it, of which we had proofs during our short intercourse with them. . . .

The very short and imperfect inter-course which we had with the natives put it out of our power to form any accurate judgment of the mode of government established amongst them, but from the general resemblance of customs, and particularly from what we observed of the honours paid to their chiefs, it seems reasonable to believe that it is of the same nature with that which prevails throughout all the islands we had hitherto visited, and probably their wars amongst themselves are equally frequent. This indeed, might be inferred from the number of weapons which we found them possessed of, and from the ex-cellent order these were kept in. But we had direct proof of the fact from their own confession, and as we under-stood these wars are between the differ-ent districts of their own island, as well as between it and their neighbours at Oneeheow and Orrehoua. We need scarcely assign any other cause besides this to account for the appearance, already mentioned, of their population bearing no proportion to the extent of their ground capable of cultivation.

Besides their spears or lances, made of a fine chesnut-coloured wood beauti-fully polished, some of which are barbed at one end and flattened to a point at the other, they have a sort of weapon which we had never seen before, and not mentioned by any navigator as used by the natives of the South Sea. It is somewhat like a dagger, in general about a foot and a half long, sharpened at one or both ends, and secured to the hand by a string. Its use is to stab at close fight, and it seems well adapted to the purpose. Some of these may be called double daggers, having a handle in the middle, with which they are better enabled to strike different ways. They have also bows and arrows ; but both from their appar-ent scarcity and their slender make it may almost be presumed that they never use them in battle. The knife or saw formerly mentioned, with which they dissect the dead bodies, may also be ranked amongst their weapons, as they both strike and cut with it when closely engaged. It is a small flat wooden instrument of an oblong shape, about a foot long, rounded at the corners, with a handle almost like one sort of the "patoos" of New Zealand ; but its edges are entirely surrounded with sharks' teeth strongly fixed to it, and point-ing outward, having commonly a hole in the handle through which passes a long string which is wrapped several times round the wrist. We also sus-pected that they use slings on some occasions ; for we got some pieces of the *hæmatites* or blood-stone, artifici-ally made of an oval shape, divided longitudinally, with a narrow groove in the middle of the convex part. To this the person who had one of them applied a cord of no great thickness, but would not part with it, though he had no objection to part with the stone ; which must prove fatal when thrown with any force as it weighed a pound. We likewise saw some oval pieces of whetstone well polished, but somewhat pointed toward each end, nearly resembling in shape some stones which we had seen at New Caledonia in 1774, and used there in their slings.

What we could learn of their relig-ious institutions, and the manner of disposing of their dead, which may properly be considered as closely con-nected, has been already mentioned. And as nothing more strongly points out the affinity between the manners of these people and of the Friendly and Society Islands, I must just mention some other circumstances to place this in a strong point of view; and at the same time to show how a few of the infinite modifications of which a few leading principles are capable, may distinguish any particular nation. The people of Tongataboo inter their dead in a very decent manner, and they also inter their human sacrifices; but they do not offer or expose any other animal or even vegetable to their gods, as far as we know. Those of Otaheite do not inter their dead, but expose them to waste by time and putrefaction though the bones are afterward buried; and as this is the case, it is very remarkable that they should inter the entire bodies of their human sacrifices. They also offer other animals and vegetables to their gods, but are by no means attentive to the state of the sacred places where those solemn rites are performed; most of their "morais" being in a ruinous condition and bearing evident marks of neglect. The people of Atooi, again, inter both their common dead and human sacrifices as at Tongataboo; but they resemble those of Otaheite in the slovenly state of their religious places, and in offering vegetables and animals to their gods. .The "taboo" also prevails in Atooi in its full extent, and seemingly with much more rigour than even at Tongataboo. For the people here always asked, with great eagerness and signs of fear to offend, whether any particular thing which they desired to see, or we were unwilling to show, was "taboo," or, as they pronounced the word, "tafoo." The "maia raa," or forbidden articles, at the Society Islands, though doubtless the same thing, did not seem to be so strictly observed by them, except with respect to the dead, about whom we thought them more superstitious than any of the others were. But these are circumstances with which we are not as yet sufficiently acquainted to be decisive about; and I shall only just observe, to show the similitude in other matters connected with religion, that the priests or "tahounas" here, are as numerous as at the other islands, if we may judge from our being able, during our stay, to distinguish several saying their "poore" or prayer.

But whatever resemblance we might discover, in the general manners of the people of Atooi, to those of Otaheite, these of course were less striking than the coincidence of language. Indeed, the languages of both places may be said to be almost word for word the same. It is true that we sometimes remarked particular words to be pronounced exactly as we had found at New Zealand and the Friendly Islands; but though all the four dialects are indisputably the same, these people in general have neither the strong guttural pronunciation of the former, nor a less degree of it which also distinguishes the latter; and they have not only adopted the soft mode of the Otaheiteans in avoiding harsh sounds, but the whole idiom of their language, using not only the same affixes and suffixes to their words, but the same measure and cadence in their songs, though in a manner somewhat less agreeable. There seems indeed, at first hearing, some disagreement to the ear of a stranger; but it ought to be considered that the people of Otaheite, from their frequent connections with the English, had learned in some measure to adapt themselves to our scanty knowledge of their language, by using not only the most common but even corrupted expressions in conversation with us; whereas when they conversed among themselves, and used the several parts necessary to propriety of speech, they were scarcely at all understood by those amongst us who had made the greatest proficiency in their vocabulary.

How shall we account for this nation's having spread itself in so many detached islands so widely disjoined from each other in every quarter of the Pacific Ocean? We find it from New Zealand in the south as far as the Sandwich Islands to the north; and, in another direction, from Easter Island to the Hebrides, that is, over an extent of sixty degrees of latitude or 1200 leagues north and south, and eighty-three degrees of longitude or 1660 leagues east and west. How much farther in either direction its colonies reach, is not known; but what we know already, in consequence of this and our former voyage, warrants our pronouncing it to be, though perhaps not the most numerous, certainly by far the most extensive nation upon earth.

Had the Sandwich Islands been discovered at an early period by the Spaniards, there is little doubt that they would have taken advantage of so excellent a situation, and have made use of Atooi or some other of the islands as a refreshing-place for the ships that sail annually from Acapulco for Manilla. They lie almost midway between the first place and Guam, one of the Ladrones, which is at present their only port in traversing this vast ocean; and it would not have been a week's sail out of their common route to have touched at them, which could have been done without running the least hazard of losing the passage, as they are sufficiently within the verge of the easterly trade-wind. An acquaintance with the Sandwich Islands would have been equally favourable to our Buccaneers, who used sometimes to pass from the coast of America to the Ladrones with a stock of food and water scarcely sufficient to preserve life.[1] Here they might always have found plenty, and have been within a month's sure sail of the very part of California which the Manilla ship is obliged to make,[2] or else have returned to the coast of America, thoroughly refitted, after an absence of two months. How happy would Lord Anson have been, and what hardships would he have avoided, if he had known that there was a group of islands half way between America and Tinian, where all his wants could

have been effectually supplied, and in describing which the elegant historian of that voyage would have presented his reader with a more agreeable picture than I have been able to draw in this Chapter![3]

CHAPTER XIII.

AFTER the Discovery had joined us, we stood away to the northward, close hauled, with a gentle gale from the east. On the 7th, being in the Latitude of 29° N., and in the Longitude of 200° E., the wind veered to SE. This enabled us to steer NE. and E., which course we continued till the 12th, when the wind had veered round by the S. and W. to NE. and ENE. I then tacked and stood to the northward, our Latitude being 30° N., and our Longitude 206° 15' E. Notwithstanding our advanced latitude, and its being the winter season, we had only begun for a few days past to feel a sensation of cold in the mornings and evenings. This is a sign of the equal and lasting influence of the sun's heat at all seasons to 30° on each side the Line. The disproportion is known to become very great after that. This must be attributed almost entirely to the direction of the rays of the sun, independent of the bare distance, which is by no means equal to the effect.

On the 19th, being now in the Latitude of 37° N., and in the Longitude of 206° E., the wind veered to SE.; and I was enabled again to steer to the E., inclining to the N.

---

[1] Witness Dampier's description of the weary and perilous passage.

[2] Cape San Lucas, the southernmost point.

[3] With all deference to Mr Walter, the Narrator of Anson's voyage—or to Captain Cook's self-humbling estimate of his own performance, we think most will prefer the plain unvarnished tale, full of new and interesting facts, told by the unlettered sailor to the eloquent flourishes of the Centurion's Chaplain, whose glowing descriptions of Tinian were sadly discredited by the subsequent experience and report of practical, prosaic men.

We had on the 25th reached the Latitude of 42° 30′ and the Longitude of 219°, and then we began to meet with the rock-weed mentioned by the writer of Lord Anson's voyage, under the name of sea-leek, which the Manilla ships generally fall in with. Now and then a piece of wood also appeared; but if we had not known that the Continent of North America was not far distant, we might, from the few signs of the vicinity of land hitherto met with, have concluded that there was none within some thousand leagues of us. We had hardly seen a bird or any other oceanic animal since we left the Sandwich Islands.

On the 1st of March, our Latitude being now 44° 49′ N., and our Longitude 228° E., we had one calm day. This was succeeded by a wind from the north, with which I stood to the east, close hauled, in order to make the land. According to the charts, it ought not to have been far from us. It was remarkable that we should still be attended with such moderate and mild weather so far to the northward, and so near the coast of an extensive continent, at this time of the year. The present season either must be uncommon for its mildness, or we can assign no reason why Sir Francis Drake should have met with such severe cold about this latitude in the month of June.[2] Viscaino, indeed, who was near the same place in the depth of winter,[3] says little of the

cold, and speaks of a ridge of snowy mountains somewhere on the coast as a thing rather remarkable. Our seeing so few birds in comparison of what we met with in the same latitudes to the south of the Line, is another singular circumstance, which must either proceed from a scarcity of the different sorts or from a deficiency of places to rest upon. From hence we may conclude that beyond 40° in the southern hemisphere the species are much more numerous, and the isles where they inhabit also more plentifully scattered about than anywhere between the coast of California and Japan in or near that latitude.

During a calm on the morning of the 2d, some parts of the sea seemed covered with a kind of slime, and some small sea animals were swimming about, the most conspicuous of which were of the gelatinous or *Medusa* kind, almost globular; and another sort smaller, that had a white or shining appearance, and were very numerous. Some of these last were taken up and put into a glass cup with some salt water, in which they appeared like small scales or bits of silver when at rest in a prone situation. When they began to swim about, which they did with equal ease upon their back, sides, or belly, they emitted the brightest colours of the most precious gems, according to their position with respect to the light. Sometimes they appeared quite pellucid, at other times assuming various tints of blue, from a pale sapphirine to a deep violet colour, which were frequently mixed with a ruby or opaline redness, and glowed with a strength sufficient to illuminate the vessel and water. These colours appeared most vivid when the glass was held to a strong light, and mostly vanished on the subsiding of the animals to the bottom, when they had a brownish cast. But with candle light the colour was chiefly a beautiful pale green, tinged with a burnished glass; and in the dark it had a faint

---

[2] Cook even understates the case against his own experience, for it was only in the Latitude of 38° 30′ N. that Drake found the "convenient and fit harbour," where he continued from the 17th of June till the 23d day of July 1579, "during all which time we were constantly visited with like nipping colds as we had never felt before"—more intense than some of his people had felt at Wardhys, in 72°, not at the height of summer, but at the end of it. See *ante*, pp. 73, 75.

[3] Sent from Acapulco in May 1602 to search the Californian coast for a secure harbour in which the galleons

might find refuge. The settlement and fortification of Monterey was the result.

appearance of glowing fire. They proved to be a new species of *Oniscus*, and from their properties were by Mr Anderson (to whom we owe this account of them) called *Oniscus fulgens*, being probably an animal which has a share in producing some sorts of that lucid appearance often observed near ships at sea in the night. On the same day two large birds settled on the water near the ship. One of these was the *Procellaria maxima* (the "quebrantahuesos"[1]), and the other, which was little more than half the size, seemed to be of the albatross kind. The upper part of the wings and tip of the tail were black, with the rest white; the bill yellowish; upon the whole not unlike the sea-gull, though larger.

On the 6th at noon, being in the Latitude of 44° 10′ N. and the Longitude of 234½° E., we saw two sails and several whales; and at daybreak the next morning the long-looked-for coast of New Albion[2] was seen, extending from NE. to SE., distant ten or twelve leagues. At noon our Latitude was 44° 33′ N. and our Longitude 235° 20′ E.; and the land extended from NE. half N. to SE. by S., about eight leagues distant. In this situation we had seventy-three fathoms water over a muddy bottom, and about a league farther off found ninety fathoms. The land appeared to be of a moderate height, diversified with hills and valleys, and almost everywhere covered with wood. There was, however, no very striking object on any part of it except one hill, whose elevated summit was flat. This bore east from us at noon. At the northern extreme the land formed a point, which I called Cape Foulweather, from the very bad weather that we soon after met with. I judge

it to lie in the Latitude of 44° 55′ N. and in the Longitude of 235° 54′ E.

We had variable light airs and calms till 8 o'clock in the evening, when a breeze sprung up at SW. With it I stood to the NW. under an easy sail, waiting for daylight to range along the coast. But at four next morning the wind shifted to NW., and blew in squalls, with rain. Our course was NE. till near 10 o'clock, when, finding that I could make no progress on this tack, and seeing nothing like a harbour, I tacked and stood off SW. At this time Cape Foulweather bore NE. by N., about eight leagues distant. Towards noon the wind veered more to the W., and the weather became fair and clear, so that we were enabled to make lunar observations. Having reduced all those that we had made since the 19th of last month to the present ones, by the time-keeper, amounting in the whole to seventy-two sets, their mean result determined the Longitude to be 235° 15′ 26″ E., which was 14′ 11″ less than what the time-keeper gave. This longitude is made use of for settling that of the coast, and I have not a doubt of its being within a very few miles of the truth.

Our difficulties now began to increase. In the evening the wind came to the NW., blowing in squalls, with hail and sleet; and the weather being thick and hazy, I stood out to sea till near noon the next day, when I tacked and stood in again for the land, which made its appearance at two in the afternoon, bearing ENE. The wind and weather continued the same, but in the evening the former veered more to the W., and the latter grew worse, which made it necessary to tack and stand off till four the next morning, when I ventured to stand in again. At four in the afternoon we saw the land, which at six extended from NE. half E. to SE. by S., about eight leagues distant. In this situation we tacked and sounded, but a line of 160 fathoms did not reach the ground. I stood off till midnight, then stood in again; and at half-past six we were within three

---

[1] The Spanish name for the sea-eagle, or osprey; literally, "the bone-breaker;" Latin, "ossifrago," so called from the great strength of its beak.

[2] This part of the west side of North America was so named by Sir Francis Drake in 1579.

leagues of the land, which extended from N. by E. half E. to S. half E., each extreme about seven leagues distant. Seeing no signs of a harbour, and the weather being still unsettled, I tacked and stretched off SW., having then fifty-five fathoms of water over a muddy bottom.

That part of the land which we were so near when we tacked is of a moderate height, though in some places it rises higher within. It was diversified with a great many rising grounds and small hills, many of which were entirely covered with tall straight trees, and others, which were lower, and grew in spots like coppices; but the interspaces and sides of many of the rising grounds were clear. The whole, though it might make an agreeable summer prospect, had now an uncomfortable appearance, as the bare grounds toward the coast were all covered with snow, which seemed to be of a considerable depth between the little hills and rising grounds, and in several places towards the sea might easily have been mistaken at a distance for white cliffs. The snow on the rising grounds was thinner spread, and farther inland there was no appearance of any; from whence we might perhaps conclude that what we saw towards the sea had fallen during the night, which was colder than any we had experienced since our arrival on the coast, and we had sometimes a kind of sleet. The coast seemed everywhere almost straight, without any opening or inlet; and it appeared to terminate in a kind of white sandy beach, though some on board thought that appearance was owing to the snow. Each extreme of the land that was now before us seemed to shoot out into a point. The northern one was the same which we had first seen on the 7th, and on that account I called it Cape Perpetua. It lies in the Latitude of 44° 6′ N. and in the Longitude of 235° 52′ E. The southern extreme before us I named Cape Gregory.[1] Its Latitude is 43°

30′ N. and its Longitude 235° 57′ E., It is a remarkable point, the land of it rising almost directly from the sea to a tolerable height, while that on each side of it is low.

I continued standing off till one in the afternoon. Then I tacked and stood in, hoping to have the wind off from the land in the night. But in this I was mistaken; for at 5 o'clock it began to veer to the W. and SW., which obliged me, once more, to stand out to sea. At this time Cape Perpetua bore NE. by N.; and the farthest land we could see to the south of Cape Gregory bore S. by E., perhaps ten or twelve leagues distant. If I am right in this estimation, its Latitude will be 43° 10′ N. and its Longitude 235° 55′ E., which is nearly the situation of Cape Blanco discovered or seen by Martin d'Aguilar on the 19th of January 1603. It is worth observing that in the very latitude where we now were geographers have been pleased to place a large entrance or strait, the discovery of which they take upon them to ascribe to the same navigator; whereas nothing more is mentioned in the account of his voyage than his having seen, in this situation, a large river which he would have entered, but was prevented by the currents.

The wind, as I have observed, had veered to the SW. in the evening; but it was very unsettled, and blew in squalls, with snow showers. In one of these, at midnight, it shifted at once to WNW., and soon increased to a very hard gale, with heavy squalls, attended with sleet or snow. There was no choice now; and we were obliged to stretch to the southward in order to get clear of the coast. This was done under courses and two close-reefed topsails, being rather more sail than the ships could safely bear; but it was necessary to carry it to avoid the more pressing danger of being forced on shore. This gale continued till 8 o'clock in the morning of the 13th; when it abated, and I stood in again

---

[1] In the English calendar the 7th of March is distinguished by the name of Perpetua M., and the 12th by that of Gregory B.

for the land. We had been forced a considerable way backward; for at the time of our tacking we were in the Latitude of 42° 45′ and in the Longitude of 233° 30′. The wind continued at W. and NW., storms, moderate weather, and calms, succeeding each other by turns till the morning of the 21st; when, after a few hours' calm, a breeze sprung up at SW. This bringing with it fair weather, I steered NE. in order to fall in with the land beyond that part of it where we had already so unprofitably been tossed about for the last fortnight. In the evening the wind veered to the westward; and at 8 o'clock the next morning we saw the land, extending from NE. to E. nine leagues distant. At this time we were in the Latitude of 47° 5′ N. and in the Longitude of 235° 10′ E.

I continued to stand to the north with a fine breeze at W. and WNW., till near 7 o'clock in the evening, when I tacked to wait for daylight. At this time we were in forty-eight fathoms water, and about four leagues from the land, which extended from N. to SE. half E., and a small round hill, which had the appearance of being an island, bore N. three-quarters E., distant six or seven leagues, as I guessed; it appears to be of a tolerable height, and was but just to be seen from the deck. Between this island or rock, and the northern extreme of the land, there appeared to be a small opening, which flattered us with the hopes of finding a harbour. These hopes lessened as we drew nearer, and at last we had some reason to think that the opening was closed by low land. On this account I called the point of land to the north of it Cape Flattery. It lies in the Latitude of 48° 15′ N., and in the Longitude of 235° 3′ E. There is a round hill of a moderate height over it, and all the land upon this part of the coast is of a moderate and pretty equal height, well covered with wood, and had a very pleasant and fertile appearance. It is in this very latitude where we now were, that geographers have placed the pretended Strait of Juan de Fuca. We saw nothing like it, nor is there the least probability that ever any such thing existed.[1] I stood off to the southward till night, when I tacked and steered to the NW. with a gentle breeze at SW., intending to stand in for the land as soon as daylight should appear. But by that time we were reduced to two courses and close-reefed topsails, having a very hard gale, with rain, right on shore; so that, instead of running in for the land, I was glad to get an offing, or to keep that which we had already got. The SW. wind was, however, but of short continuance, for in the evening it veered again to the W. Thus we had perpetually strong W. and NW. winds to encounter. Sometimes in an evening the wind would become moderate and veer to the southward; but this was always a sure prelude to a storm, which blew the hardest at SSE., and was attended with rain and sleet. It seldom lasted above four or six hours before it was succeeded by another gale from the NW., which generally brought with it fair weather. It was by the means of these southerly blasts that we were enabled to get to the NW. at all.

At length, at 9 o'clock in the morning of the 29th, as we were

---

[1] Cook here lent himself too readily to the undiscriminating condemnation of the romancing Cephalonian's marvellous tales about a strait or channel which he entered in this latitude, emerging after a prolonged navigation, into the Atlantic. There is now little doubt that Juan de Fuca really discovered, and partly explored the Strait that bears his name, and that Cook credulously, and with quite unusual lack of enterprise passed lightly by. At all events, the channel bears at this day the name of the Greco-Spanish navigator; and the recent arbitration (1872) by the German Emperor on the San Juan dispute with America has rendered its name not quite pleasantly familiar to many English folk who never heard of it before.

standing to the NE., we again saw the land, which, at noon, extended from NW. by W. to ESE., the nearest part about six leagues distant. Our Latitude was now 49° 29′ N., and our Longitude 232° 29′ E. The appearance of the country differed much from that of the parts which we had before seen, being full of high mountains, whose summits were covered with snow. But the valleys between them, and the grounds on the sea coast, high as well as low, were covered to a considerable breadth with high, straight trees, that formed a beautiful prospect as of one vast forest. The SE. extreme of the land formed a low point, off which are many breakers, occasioned by sunken rocks. On this account it was called Point Breakers. It lies in the Latitude of 49° 15′ N., and in the Longitude of 233° 20′ E., and the other extreme in about the Latitude of 50° and the Longitude of 232°. I named this last Woody Point. It projects pretty much out to the SW., and is high land. Between these two points the shore forms a large bay, which I called Hope Bay, hoping from the appearance of the land to find in it a good harbour. The event proved that we were not mistaken.

As we drew nearer the coast, we perceived the appearance of two inlets; one in the NW., and the other in the NE. corner of the bay. As I could not fetch the former, I bore up to the latter, and passed some breakers or sunken rocks that lay a league or more from the shore. We had nineteen and twenty fathoms water half-a-league without them; but as soon as we had passed them, the depth increased to thirty, forty, and fifty fathoms, with a sandy bottom; and farther in we found no bottom with the greatest length of line. Notwithstanding appearances, we were not yet sure that there were any inlets; but, as we were in a deep bay, I resolved to anchor, with a view to endeavour to get some water, of which by this time we were in great want. At length, as we advanced, the existence of the inlet was no longer doubtful. At 5 o'clock we reached the west point of it, where we were becalmed for some time. While in this situation I ordered all the boats to be hoisted out to tow the ships in. But this was hardly done before a fresh breeze sprung up again at NW., with which we were enabled to stretch up into an arm of the inlet that was observed by us to run in to the northeast. There we were again becalmed, and obliged to anchor in eighty-five fathoms water, and so near the shore as to reach it with a hawser. The wind failed the Discovery before she got within the arm, where she anchored, and found only seventy fathoms.

We no sooner drew near the inlet than we found the coast to be inhabited; and at the place where we were first becalmed three canoes came off to the ship. In one of these were two men, in another six, and in the third ten. Having come pretty near us, a person in one of the two last stood up and made a long harangue, inviting us to land, as we guessed by his gestures. At the same time he kept strewing handfuls of feathers towards us;[1] and some of his companions threw handfuls of red dust or powder in the same manner. The person who played the orator wore the skin of some animal, and held in each hand something which rattled as he kept shaking it. After tiring himself with his repeated exhortations, of which we did not understand a word, he was quiet; and then others took it by turns to say something, though they acted their part neither so long nor with so much vehemence as the other. We observed that two or three had their hair quite strewed over with small white feathers, and others had large ones stuck into different parts of the head. After the tumultuous noise had ceased, they lay at a little distance from the ship, and conversed with each other in a very easy manner; nor did they seem

---

[1] The natives of this coast twelve degrees farther south, also brought feathers as presents to Sir Francis Drake on his arrival.

to show the least surprise or distrust. Some of them now and then got up and said something after the manner of their first harangues; and one sung a very agreeable air, with a degree of softness and melody which we could not have expected, the word "haela" being often repeated as the burden of the song. The breeze which soon after sprung up bringing us nearer to the shore, the canoes began to come off in greater numbers; and we had at one time thirty-two of them near the ship, carrying from three to seven or eight persons each, both men and women. Several of these stood up in their canoes haranguing and making gestures after the manner of our first visitors. One canoe was remarkable for a singular head, which had a bird's eye and bill of an enormous size painted on it; and a person who was in it, who seemed to be a chief, was no less remarkable for his uncommon appearance, having many feathers hanging from his head, and being painted in an extraordinary manner.[1] He held in his hand a carved bird of wood, as large as a pigeon, with which he rattled as the person first mentioned had done; and was no less vociferous in his harangue, which was attended with some expressive gestures.

Though our visitors behaved very peaceably, and could not be suspected of any hostile intention, we could not prevail upon any of them to come on board. They showed great readiness, however, to part with anything they had, and took from us whatever we offered them in exchange; but were more desirous of iron than of any other of our articles of commerce, appearing to be perfectly acquainted with the use of that metal. Many of the canoes followed us to our anchoring-place; and a group of about ten or a dozen of them remained alongside the Resolution most part of the night.

These circumstances gave us a reasonable ground of hope that we should find this a comfortable station to supply all our wants, and to make us forget the hardships and delays experienced during a constant succession of adverse winds and boisterous weather almost ever since our arrival upon the coast of America.

BOOK IV.

TRANSACTIONS AMONGST THE NATIVES OF NORTH AMERICA; DISCOVERIES ALONG THAT COAST, AND THE EASTERN EXTREMITY OF ASIA, NORTHWARD TO ICY CAPE; AND RETURN SOUTHWARD TO THE SANDWICH ISLANDS.

CHAPTER I.

The ships having happily found so excellent shelter in an inlet, the coasts of which appeared to be inhabited by a race of people whose inoffensive behaviour promised a friendly intercourse, the next morning, after coming to anchor, I lost no time in endeavouring to find a commodious harbour where we might station ourselves during our continuance in the sound. Accordingly I sent three armed boats under the command of Mr King upon this service; and soon after, I went myself in a small boat on the same search. I had very little trouble in finding what we wanted. On the north-west of the arm we were

---

[1] Viscaino met with natives on the coast of California, while he was in the harbour of San Diego, who were painted or besmeared with black and white, and had their heads loaded with feathers.

now in, and not far from the ships, I met with a convenient snug cove well suited to our purpose. Mr King was equally successful; for he returned about noon with an account of a still better harbour which he had seen and examined, lying on the north-west side of the land. But as it would have required more time to carry the ships thither than to the cove where I had been, which was immediately within our reach, this reason operated to determine my choice in favour of the latter situation. But being apprehensive that we should not be able to transport our ships to it, and to moor them properly, before night came on, I thought it best to remain where we were till next morning; and that no time might be lost, I employed the remainder of the day to some useful purposes, ordering the sails to be unbent, the top-masts to be struck, and the fore-mast of the Resolution to be unrigged, in order to fix a new bib, one of the old ones being decayed.

A great many canoes filled with the natives were about the ships all day, and a trade commenced betwixt us and them which was carried on with the strictest honesty on both sides. The articles which they offered to sale were skins of various animals, such as bears, wolves, foxes, deer, racoons, polecats, martens, and in particular of the sea otters, which are found at the islands east of Kamtschatka. Besides the skins in their native shape, they also brought garments made of them, and another sort of clothing made of the bark of a tree, or some plant like hemp; weapons, such as bows, arrows, and spears; fish-hooks, and instruments of various kinds; wooden visors of many different monstrous figures; a sort of woollen stuff, or blanketing; bags filled with red ochre, pieces of carved work, beads, and several other little ornaments of thin brass and iron, shaped like a horse-shoe, which they hang at their noses, and several chisels or pieces of iron fixed to handles; from their possessing which metals, we could infer that they had either been visited before by some civilised nation, or had connection with tribes on their continent who had communication with them. But the most extraordinary of all the articles which they brought to the ships for sale were human skulls and hands, not yet quite stripped of the flesh, which they made our people plainly understand they had eaten; and indeed some of them had evident marks that they had been upon the fire. We had but too much reason to suspect from this circumstance that the horrid practice of feeding on their enemies is as prevalent here as we had found it to be at New Zealand and other South Sea Islands. For the various articles which they brought they took in exchange knives, chisels, pieces of iron and tin, nails, looking-glasses, buttons, or any kind of metal. Glass beads they were not fond of, and cloth of every sort they rejected.

We employed the next day in hauling our ships into the cove, where they were moored head and stern, fastening our hawsers to the trees on shore. On heaving up the anchor of the Resolution we found, notwithstanding the great depth of water in which it was let go, that there were rocks at the bottom. These had done some considerable damage to the cable, and the hawsers that were carried out to warp the ship into the cove also got foul of rocks, from which it appeared that the whole bottom was strewn with them. The ship being again very leaky in her upper works, I ordered the carpenters to go to work to calk her, and to repair such other defects as on examination we might discover.

The fame of our arrival brought a great concourse of the natives to our ships in the course of this day. We counted above 100 canoes at one time, which might be supposed to contain at an average five persons each, for few of them had less than three on board, great numbers had seven, eight, or nine, and one was manned with no less than seventeen. Amongst these visitors many now favoured us with their company for the first time, which we could guess from their approaching the ships with their orations and other ceremonies. If they had any distrust or fear of us at first, they now appeared to have laid it aside, for they came on board the ships and mixed with our people with the greatest freedom. We soon discovered by this nearer intercourse that they were as light-fingered as any of our friends in the islands we had visited in the course of the voyage. And they were far more dangerous thieves, for possessing sharp iron instruments, they could cut a hook from a tackle, or any other piece of iron from a rope, the instant that our backs were turned. A large hook weighing between twenty and thirty pounds, several smaller ones, and other articles of iron, were lost in this manner ; and as to our boats, they stripped them of every bit of iron that was worth carrying away, though we had always men left in them as a guard. They were dextrous enough in effecting their purposes, for one fellow would contrive to amuse the boat-keeper at one end of a boat, while another was pulling out the iron-work at the other. If we missed a thing immediately after it had been stolen we found little difficulty in detecting the thief, as they were ready enough to impeach one another. But the guilty person generally relinquished his prize with reluctance, and sometimes we found it necessary to have recourse to force.

The ships being securely moored, we began our other necessary business the next day. The observatories were carried ashore and placed upon an elevated rock on one side of the cove close to the Resolution. A party of men, with an officer, was sent to cut wood and to clear a place for the conveniency of watering. Others were employed to brew spruce-beer, as pine-trees abounded here. The forge was also set up to make the iron-work wanting for the repairs of the fore-mast. But, besides one of the bibs being defective, the larboard trestle-tree and one of the cross-trees were sprung. . . .

After a fortnight's bad weather, the 19th proving a fair day, we availed ourselves of it to get up the top-masts and yards, and to get up the rigging. And having now finished most of our heavy work, I set out the next morning to take a view of the sound. I first went to the west point, where I found a large village, and before it a very snug harbour, in which was from nine to four fathoms water over a bottom of fine sand. The people of this village, who were numerous, and to most of whom I was well known, received me very courteously; every one pressing me to go into his house, or, rather, his apartment, for several families live under the same roof. I did not decline the invitations, and my hospitable friends whom I visited spread a mat for me to sit upon, and showed me every other mark of civility. In most of the houses were women at work making dresses of the plant or bark before mentioned, which they executed exactly in the same manner that the New Zealanders manufacture their cloth. Others were occupied in opening sardines. I had seen a large quantity of them brought on shore from canoes. and divided by measure amongst several people, who carried them up to their houses, where the operation of curing them by smoke-drying is performed. They hang them on small rods at first about a foot from the fire, afterward they remove them higher and higher to make room for others, till the rods on which the fish hang reach the top of the house. When they are completely dried, they are taken down and packed close in bales, which they cover with mats. Thus they are kept till wanted, and they are not a disagreeable article of food. Cod and other large fish are also cured in the same manner by them, though they sometimes dry these in the open air without fire.

From this village I proceeded up the west side of the sound. For about three miles I found the shore covered with small islands, which are so situated as to form several convenient harbours, having various depths of water from thirty to seven fathoms, with a good bottom. Two leagues within the sound on this west side there runs in an arm in the direction of NNW.; and two miles farther is another nearly in the same direction, with a pretty large island before it. I had no time to examine either of these arms, but have reason to believe that they do not extend far inland, as the water was no more than brackish at their entrances. A mile above the second arm I found the remains of a village. The logs or framings of the houses were standing, but the boards that had composed their sides and roofs did not exist. Before this village were some large fishing weirs, but I saw nobody attending them. These weirs were composed of pieces of wicker-work made of small rods, some closer than others, according to the size of the fish intended to be caught in them. These pieces of wicker-work (some of whose superficies are at least twenty feet by twelve) are fixed up edgewise in shallow water by strong poles or pickets that stand firm in the ground. Behind this ruined village is a plain of a few miles' extent, covered with the largest pine-trees that I ever saw. This was the more remarkable as the elevated ground on most other parts of this west side of the sound was rather naked.

From this place I crossed over to the other, or east side of the sound, passing an arm of it that runs in NNE., to appearance not far. I now found, what I had before conjectured, that the land under which the ships lay was an island, and that there were many smaller ones lying scattered in the sound on the west side of it. Opposite the north end of our large island, upon the mainland, I observed a village, and there I landed. The inhabitants of it were not so polite as those of the other I had just visited. But this cold reception seemed in a great measure, if not entirely, owing to one surly chief, who would not let me enter their houses, following me wherever I went; and several times by expressive signs marking his impatience that I should be gone. I attempted in vain to soothe him by presents, but though

he did not refuse them, they did not alter his behaviour. Some of the young women, better pleased with us than was their inhospitable chief, dressed themselves expeditiously in their best apparel; and, assembling in a body, welcomed us to their village by joining in a song which was far from harsh or disagreeable. The day being now far spent, I proceeded for the ships round the north end of the large island, meeting in my way with several canoes laden with sardines which had been just caught somewhere in the east corner of the sound. When I got on board, I was informed that while I was absent the ships had been visited by some strangers in two or three large canoes, who by signs made our people understand that they had come from the south-east beyond the bay. They brought several skins, garments, and other articles, which they bartered. But, what was most singular, two silver table-spoons were purchased from them, which, from their peculiar shape, we supposed to be of Spanish manufacture. One of these strangers wore them round his neck by way of ornament. These visitors also appeared to be more plentifully supplied with iron than the inhabitants of the sound.

The mizzen-mast being finished, it was got in and rigged on the 21st; and the carpenters were set to work to make a new fore-topmast to replace the one that had been carried away some time before. Next morning, about 8 o'clock, we were visited by a number of strangers in twelve or fourteen canoes. They came into the cove from the southward, and as soon as they had turned the point of it, they stopped and lay drawn up in a body above half-an-hour about 200 or 300 yards from the ships. At first we thought that they were afraid to come nearer, but we were mistaken in this, and they were only preparing an introductory ceremony. On advancing toward the ships, they all stood up in their canoes and began to sing. Some of their songs, in which the whole body joined, were in a slow and others in quicker time; and they accompanied their notes with the most regular motions of their hands, or beating in concert with their paddles on the sides of the canoes, and making other very expressive gestures. At the end of each song they remained silent a few seconds, and then began again, sometimes pronouncing the word "hooee!" forcibly, as a chorus. After entertaining us with this specimen of their music, which we listened to with admiration for above half-an-hour, they came alongside the ships and bartered what they had to dispose of. Some of our old friends of the sound were now found to be amongst them, and they took the whole management of the traffic between us and the strangers, much to the advantage of the latter.

Our attendance on these visitors being finished, Captain Clerke and I went in the forenoon with two boats to the village at the west point of the sound. When I was there the day before, I had observed that plenty of grass grew near it ; and it was necessary to lay in a quantity of this as food for the few goats and sheep which were still left on board. The inhabitants received us with the same demonstrations of friendship which I had experienced before ; and the moment we landed I ordered some of my people to begin their operation of cutting. I had not the least imagination that the natives could make any objection to our furnishing ourselves with what seemed to be of no use to them, but was necessary for us. However, I was mistaken ; for, the moment that our men began to cut, some of the inhabitants interposed, and would not permit them to proceed, saying they must "makook," that is, must first buy it. I was now in one of the houses, but as soon as I heard of this I went to the field, where I found about a dozen of the natives, each of whom laid claim to some part of the grass that grew in this place. I bargained with them for it, and having completed the purchase, thought we were now at liberty to cut wherever we pleased. But here again it appeared that I was under a mis-

take, for the liberal manner in which I had paid the first pretended proprietors brought fresh demands upon me from others ; so that there did not seem to be a single blade of grass, that had not a separate owner, and so many of them were to be satisfied that I very soon emptied my pockets. When they found that I really had nothing more to give, their importunities ceased, and we were permitted to cut wherever we pleased, and as much as we choose to carry away.

Here I must observe that I have nowhere in my several voyages met with any uncivilised nation or tribe who had such strict notions of their having a right to the exclusive property of everything that their country produces, as the inhabitants of this sound. At first they wanted our people to pay for the wood and water that they carried on board ; and had I been upon the spot when these demands were made, I should certainly have complied with them. Our workmen in my absence thought differently, for they took but little notice of such claims ; and the natives, when they found that we were determined to pay nothing, at last ceased to apply. But they made a merit of necessity ; and frequently afterwards took occasion to remind us that they had given us wood and water out of friendship.[1]

When we had completed all our operations at this village, the natives and we parted very good friends, and we got back to the ships in the afternoon.

The three following days were employed in getting ready to put to sea ; the sails were bent ; the observatories and instruments, brewing vessels, and other things were moved from the shore ; some small spars for different

---

[1] Similar to the behaviour of the natives of Nootka on this occasion was that of another tribe of Indians farther north, in Latitude 57° 18′, to the Spaniards who had preceded Captain Cook only three years, in a voyage to explore the coast of America northward of California.

uses, and pieces of timber which might be occasionally sawn into boards were prepared and put on board; and both ships were cleared and put into a sailing condition. Everything being now ready, in the morning of the 26th I intended to have put to sea; but both wind and tide being against us, was obliged to wait till noon, when the south-west wind was succeeded by a calm, and, the tide turning in our favour, we cast off the moorings, and with our boats towed the ships out of the cove. After this we had variable light airs and calms till four in the afternoon, when a breeze sprung up northerly, with very thick hazy weather. The mercury in the barometer fell unusually low; and we had every other forerunner of an approaching storm, which we had reason to expect would be from the southward. This made me hesitate a little, as night was at hand, whether I should venture to sail, or wait till the next morning. But my anxious impatience to proceed upon the voyage, and the fear of losing this opportunity of getting out of the sound, making a greater impression on my mind than any apprehension of immediate danger, I determined to put to sea at all events.

Our friends the natives attended us till we were almost out of the sound; some on board the ships and others in their canoes. One of their chiefs, who had some time before attached himself to me, was amongst the last who left us. Having before he went bestowed upon him a small present, I received in return a beaver-skin of much greater value. This called upon me to make some addition to my present, which pleased him so much that he insisted upon my acceptance of the beaver-skin cloak which he then wore, and of which I knew he was particularly fond. Struck with this instance of generosity, and desirous that he should be no sufferer by his friendship to me, I presented to him a new broadsword with a brass hilt; the possession of which made him completely happy. He, and also many others of his countrymen, im-

portuned us much to pay them another visit; and by way of encouragement promised to lay in a good stock of skins. I make no doubt that whoever comes after me to this place will find the natives prepared accordingly, with no inconsiderable supply of an article of trade which, they could observe, we were eager to possess, and which we found could bo purchased to great advantage.

Such particulars about the country and its inhabitants as came to our knowledge during our short stay, and have not been mentioned in the course of the narrative, will furnish materials for the two following Chapters.

CHAPTER II.

On my arrival in this inlet I had honoured it with the name of King George's Sound, but I afterwards found that it is called Nootka by the natives. The entrance is situated in the east corner of Hope Bay, in the Latitude of 49° 33′ N. and in the Longitude of 233° 12′ E. The east coast of that bay, all the way from Breakers Point to the entrance of the sound, is covered by a chain of sunken rocks that seemed to extend some distance from the shore; and near the sound are some islands and rocks above water. We enter this sound between two rocky points that lie ESE. and WNW. from each other, distant between three and four miles. Within these points the sound widens considerably, and extends in to the northward four leagues at least, exclusive of the several branches towards its bottom, the termination of which we had not an opportunity to ascertain. But from the circumstance of finding that the water freshened where our boats crossed their entrance, it is probable that they had almost reached its utmost limits. And this probability is increased by the hills that bounded it toward the land, being covered with thick snow, when those toward the sea, or where we lay, had not a speck remaining on them, though in general they were much higher. In the middle of the sound are a number of islands of various sizes. The depth of water in the middle of the sound, and even close home to some parts of its shore, is from forty-seven to ninety fathoms, and perhaps more. The harbours and anchoring-places within its circuit are numerous, but we had no time to survey them. The cove in which our ships lay is on the east side of the sound and on the east side of the largest of the islands. It is covered from the sea, but has little else to recommend it, being exposed to the south-east winds, which we found to blow with great violence; and the devastation they make sometimes was apparent in many places.

The land bordering upon the sea-coast is of a middling height and level, but within the sound it rises almost everywhere into steep hills, which agree in their general formation, ending in round or blunted tops, with some sharp though not very prominent ridges on their sides. Some of these hills may be reckoned high, while others of them are of a very moderate height; but even the highest are entirely covered to their tops with the thickest woods, as well as every flat part toward the sea. There are sometimes spots upon the sides of some of the hills which are bare, but they are few in comparison of the whole, though they sufficiently point out the general rocky disposition of these hills. Properly speaking, they have no soil upon them except a kind of compost produced from rotten mosses and trees of the depth of two feet or more. Their foundations are therefore to be considered as nothing more than stupendous rocks of a whitish or grey cast where they have been exposed to the weather; but when broken they appeared to be of a bluish-grey colour, like that universal sort which were found at Kerguelen's Land. The rocky shores are a continued mass of this, and the little coves in the sound have beaches composed of fragments of it, with a few other pebbles. All these coves are furnished with a great quantity of fallen wood lying in them, which is carried in by the tide, and with rills of fresh water sufficient for the use of a ship, which seem to be supplied entirely from the rains and fogs that hover about the tops of the hills. For few springs can be expected in so rocky a country, and the fresh water found farther up the sound most probably arose from the melting of the snow, there being no room to suspect that any large river falls into the sound, either from strangers coming down it or from any other circumstance. The water of these rills is perfectly clear, and dissolves soap easily.

The weather during our stay corresponded pretty nearly with that which we had experienced off the coast. That is, when the wind was anywhere between N. and W. the weather was fine and clear; but if to the S. of W. hazy, with rain. The climate, as far as we had any experience of it, is infinitely milder than that on the east coast of America under the same parallel of latitude. The mercury in the thermometer never even in the night fell lower than 42°, and very often in the day it rose to 60°. No such thing as frost was perceived in any of the low ground, on the contrary, vegetation had made a considerable progress, for I met with grass that was already above a foot long.

The trees which chiefly compose the woods are the Canadian pine, white cypress, *Cypressus thyoides*, the wild pine, with two or three other sorts of pine less common. The first two make up almost two-thirds of the whole, and at a distance might be mistaken for the same tree, as they both run up into pointed spire-like tops; but they are easily distinguished on coming nearer from their colour, the cypress being of a much paler green, or shade, than the other. The trees in general grow with great vigour, and are all of a large size. There is but little variety of other vegetable productions, though doubtless several had not yet sprung up at the early season when we visited the place; and many more might be hid from the narrow sphere of our researches. About the rocks and verge of the woods we found strawberry plants, some raspberry, currant, and gooseberry bushes, which were all in a most flourishing state, with a few small black alder-trees. There are likewise a species of sow-thistle, goose-grass, some crow's-foot, which has a very fine crimson flower; and two sorts of *Anthericum*, one with a large orange flower, and the other with a blue one. We also found in these situations some wild rose-bushes which were just budding; a great quantity of young leeks with triangular leaves; a small sort of grass; and some water-cresses, which grow about the sides of the rills; besides great abundance of *Andromeda*. Within the woods, besides two sorts of underwood shrubs unknown to us, are mosses and ferns. Of the first of which are seven or eight different sorts, of the last not above three or four; and the species of both are mostly such as are common to Europe and America.

The account that we can give of the quadrupeds is taken from the skins which the natives brought to sell, and these were often so mutilated with respect to the distinguishing parts, such as the paws, tails, and heads, that it was impossible even to guess at the animals to which they belonged, though others were so perfect, or at least so well known, that they left no room to doubt about them.

Of these the most common were bears, deer, foxes, and wolves. The bear-skins were in great numbers, few of them very large, but in general of a shining black colour. The deer-skins were scarcer, and they seem to belong to that sort called the fallow-deer by the historians of Carolina, though Mr Pennant[1] thinks it quite a different species from ours, and distin-

guishes it by the name of Virginian deer. The foxes are in great plenty, and of several varieties; some of their skins being quite yellow, with a black tip to the tail; others of a deep or reddish yellow intermixed with black; and a third sort of a whitish grey or ash-colour, also intermixed with black. Our people used to apply the name of fox or wolf indiscriminately when the skins were so mutilated as to leave room for a doubt; but we got at last an entire wolf-skin with the head on, and it was grey. Besides the common sort of marten, the pine-marten is also here, and another, whose skin is of a lighter brown colour than either, with coarser hair; but is not so common, and is perhaps only a mere variety arising from age or some other accidental circumstance. The ermine is also found at this place, but is rare and small; nor is the hair remarkably fine, though the animal appeared to be perfectly white; and squirrels are of the common sort, but the latter is rather smaller than ours, and has a deeper rusty colour running along the back.

We were clear as to the existence of all the animals already mentioned, but there are two others besides which we could not distinguish with sufficient certainty. Of the first of these we saw none of the skins but what were dressed or tanned like leather. The natives wear them on some occasions, and from the size as well as thickness they were generally concluded to belong to the elk or moose-deer, though some of them perhaps might belong to the buffalo. The other animal, which seems by no means rare, was guessed to be a species of the wild cat or lynx. The length of the skins without the head, which none of them had, was about two feet two inches. They are covered with a very fine wool or fur of a very light brown or whitish yellow colour, intermixed with long hairs, which on the back, where they are shortest, are blackish; on the sides, where they are longer, of a silver white; and on the belly, where they are longest, of the colour of the wool; but the whitish or

---

[1] The celebrated naturalist and antiquary, whose "British Zoology," "History of Quadrupeds," "Arctic Zoology," &c., are less remembered and relished at this day than his Tours in Scotland and in Wales, and his "Account of London."

silver hairs are often so predominant that the whole animal acquires a cast of that kind. The tail is only three inches long, and has a black tip. The whole skin being by the natives called "wanshee," that most probably is their name for this animal. Hogs, dogs, and goats have not as yet found their way to this place. Nor do the natives seem to have any knowledge of our brown rats, to which, when they saw one on board the ships, they applied the name they give to squirrels. And though they called our goats "eineetla," this most probably is their name for a young deer or fawn.

The sea-animals seen off the coast were whales, porpoises, and seals. The last of these seem only of the common sort, judging from the skins which we saw here; their colour being either silvery, yellowish, plain, or spotted with black. The porpoise is the *Phocœna*. I have chosen to refer to this class the sea-otter, as living mostly in the water. It might have been sufficient to have mentioned that this animal abounds here, as it is fully described in different books taken from the accounts of the Russian adventurers in their expeditions eastward from Kamtschatka, if there had not been a small difference in one that we saw. We for some time entertained doubts whether the many skins which the natives brought really belonged to this animal, as our only reason for being of that opinion was founded on the size, colour, and fineness of the fur; till a short while before our departure, when a whole one that had been just killed was purchased from some strangers who came to barter. It was rather young, weighing only twenty-five pounds; of a shining or glossy black colour; but many of the hairs being tipt with white, gave it a greyish cast at first sight. The face, throat, and breast were of a yellowish white or very light brown colour, which in many of the skins extended the whole length of the belly. It had six cutting-teeth in each jaw; two of those of the lower jaw being very minute, and placed

without at the base of the two middle ones. In these circumstances it seems to disagree with those found by the Russians, and also in not having the outer toes of the hind feet skirted with a membrane. There seemed also a greater variety in the colour of the skins than is mentioned by the describers of the Russian sea-otters. These changes of colour certainly take place at the different gradations of life. The very young ones had brown hair, which was coarse, with very little fur underneath, but those of the size of the entire animal which came into our possession had a considerable quantity of that substance; and both in that colour and state the sea-otters seem to remain till they have attained their full growth. After that they lose their black colour, and assume a deep brown or sooty colour; but have then a greater quantity of very fine fur and scarcely any long hairs. Others, which we suspected to be still older, were of a chestnut brown; and a few skins were seen that had even acquired a perfectly yellow colour. The fur of these animals, as mentioned in the Russian accounts, is certainly softer and finer than that of any others we know of, and therefore the discovery of this part of the continent of North America, where so valuable an article of commerce may be met with, cannot be a matter of indifference.

Birds in general are not only rare as to the different species, but very scarce as to numbers, and these few are so shy, that in all probability they are continually harassed by the natives, perhaps to eat them as food, certainly to get possession of their feathers, which they use as ornaments. Those which frequent the woods are crows and ravens, not at all different from our English ones; a bluish jay or magpie; common wrens, which are the only singing bird that we hear; the Canadian or migrating thrush; and a considerable number of brown eagles with white heads and tails, which, though they seem principally to frequent the coast, come into the sound in bad weather and sometimes perch upon the trees. Amongst some other birds of which the natives either brought fragments or dried skins, we could distinguish a small species of hawk, a heron, and the *Alcyon* or large-crested American kingfisher. There are also some which, I believe, are not mentioned, or at least vary very considerably from the accounts given of them by any writers who have treated professedly on this part of natural history. The first two of these are species of woodpeckers; one less than a thrush, of a black colour above, with white spots on the wings, a crimson head, neck, and breast, and a yellowish, olive-coloured belly, from which last circumstance it might perhaps not improperly be called the yellow-bellied woodpecker. The other is a larger and much more elegant bird, of a dusky brown colour on the upper part, richly waved with black, except about the head, the belly of a reddish cast, with round black spots, a black spot on the breast, and the under side of the wings and tail of a plain scarlet colour, though blackish above; with a crimson streak running from the angle of the mouth a little down the neck on each side. The third and fourth are a small bird of the finch kind, about the size of a linnet, of a dark dusky colour, whitish below, with a black head and neck and white bill, and a sand-piper of the size of a small pigeon, of a dusky brown colour, and white below except the throat and breast, with a broad white band across the wings. There are also humming-birds; which yet seem to differ from the numerous sorts of this delicate animal already known, unless they be a mere variety of the *Trochilus colubris* of Linnæus. These perhaps inhabit more to the southward, and spread northward as the season advances, because we saw none at first, though near the time of our departure the natives brought them to the ships in great numbers. The birds which frequent the waters and the shores, are not more numerous than the others. The "quebrantahuesos" [or ospreys], gulls, and shags, were seen off the coast; and the last two also frequent the sound. They are of the common sorts, the shags being our cormorant or water-crow. We saw two sorts of wild ducks; one black, with a white head, which were in considerable flocks; the other white, with a red bill, but of a larger size; and the greater "lumme," or diver, found in our northern countries. There were also seen, once or twice, some swans flying across the sound to the northward, but we knew nothing of their haunts. On the shores, besides the sand-piper described above, we found another about the size of a lark, which bears a great affinity to the "burre;" and a plover differing very little from our common sea-lark.

Fish are more plentiful in quantity than birds, though the variety is not very great; and yet from several circumstances it is probable that even the variety is considerably increased at certain seasons. The principal sorts, which we found in great numbers, are the common herring, but scarcely exceeding seven inches in length; a smaller sort, which is the same with the anchovy or sardine, though rather larger; a white or silver-coloured bream, and another of a gold-brown colour, with many narrow longitudinal blue stripes. The herrings and sardines, doubtless, come in large shoals, and only at stated seasons, as is common with that sort of fish. The bream of both sorts may be reckoned the next to these in quantity; and the full-grown ones weighed at least a pound. The other fish, which are all scarce, are a small brown kind of "sculpin," such as is found on the coast of Norway; another of a brownish red cast; frost fish; a large one somewhat resembling the bullhead, with a tough skin destitute of scales; and now and then, towards the time of our leaving the sound, the natives brought a small brownish cod spotted with white, and a red fish of the same size, which some of our people said they had seen in the Straits of Magellan; besides another differing little from the hake. There are also considerable numbers of those fish called the *Chimæræ*, or little sea-wolves, by some, which is akin to and about the size of the "pezegallo" or elephant-fish. Sharks likewise sometimes frequent the sound, for the natives have some of their teeth in their possession; and we saw some pieces of ray or skate which seemed to have been pretty large. The other marine animals that ought to be mentioned here are a small cruciated *Medusa* or blubber; star-fish which differ somewhat from the common ones; two small sorts of crabs, and two others which the natives brought, one of them of a thick, tough, gelatinous consistence, and the other a sort of membranaceous tube or pipe; both which are probably taken from the rocks. And we also purchased from them once a very large cuttle-fish. There is abundance of large mussels about the rocks; many sea-ears; and we often saw shells of pretty large plain *Chamæ*. The smaller sorts are some *Trochi* of two species; a curious *Murex*, rugged wilks, and a snail, all which are probably peculiar to this place; at least I do not recollect to have seen them in any country near the same latitude in either hemisphere. There are besides these some small plain cockles, limpets; and some strangers who came into the sound, wore necklaces of a small bluish volute, or *Panamæ*. Many of the mussels are a span in length, and some having pretty large pearls, which, however, are both badly shaped and coloured. We may conclude that there is red coral in the sound or somewhere upon the coast; some thick pieces or branches having been seen in the canoes of the natives.

The only animals of the reptile kind observed here, and found in the woods, were brown snakes two feet long, with whitish stripes on the back and sides, which are harmless, as we often saw the natives carry them alive in their hands; and brownish water-lizards, with a tail exactly like that of an eel, which frequented the small standing pools about the rocks. The insect tribe seem to be more numerous. For though the season which is peculiarly

fitted to their appearing abroad was only beginning, we saw four or five different sorts of butterflies, none of which were uncommon; a good many humble bees; some of our common gooseberry moths; two or three sorts of flies; a few beetles; and some mosquitoes, which probably may be more numerous and troublesome, in a country so full of wood, during the summer, though at this time they did little mischief.

As to the mineral substances in this country, though we found both iron and copper here, there is little reason to believe that either of them belong to the place. Neither were the ores of any metal seen, if we except a coarse, red, earthy or ochry substance used by the natives in painting themselves, which probably may contain a little iron, with a white and black pigment used for the same purpose. But we did not procure specimens of them, and therefore cannot positively determine what are their component parts. Besides the stone or rock that constitutes the mountains and shores, which sometimes contains pieces of very coarse quartz, we found amongst the natives things made of a hard black granite, though not remarkably compact or fine grained; a greyish whetstone; the common oil-stone of our carpenters, in coarser and finer pieces; and some black bits which are little inferior to the hone-stone. The natives also use the transparent leafy "glimmer," or muscovy glass; a brown leafy or martial sort; and they sometimes brought to us pieces of rock crystal, tolerably transparent. The first two are probably found near the spot, as they seemed to be in considerable quantities; but the latter seems to be brought from a greater distance, or is very scarce, for our visitors always parted with it reluctantly. Some of the pieces were octangular, and had the appearance of being formed into that shape by art.

The persons of the natives are in general under the common stature, but not slender in proportion, being commonly pretty full or plump, though not muscular. Neither doth the soft fleshiness seem ever to swell into corpulence; and many of the older people are rather spare or lean. The visage of most of them is round and full, and sometimes also broad, with large prominent cheeks; and above these the face is frequently much depressed, or seems fallen in quite across between the temples; the nose also flattening at its base, with pretty wide nostrils and a rounded point. The forehead rather low; the eyes small, black, and rather languishing than sparkling; the mouth round, with large round thickish lips; the teeth tolerably equal and well set, but not remarkably white. They have either no beards at all, which was most commonly the case, or a small thin one upon the point of the chin, which does not arise from any natural defect of hair on that part, but from plucking it out more or less; for some of them, and particularly the old men, have not only considerable beards all over the chin, but whiskers or moustaches both on the upper lip and running from thence towards the lower jaw obliquely downward. Their eyebrows are also scanty, and always narrow; but the hair of the head is in great abundance, very coarse and strong, and without a single exception black, straight, and lank, or hanging down over the shoulders. The neck is short; the arms and body have no particular mark of beauty or elegance in their formation, but are rather clumsy; and the limbs in all are very small in proportion to the other parts, and crooked or ill made, with large feet badly shaped, and projecting ankles. This last defect seems in a great measure to arise from their sitting so much on their hams or knees, both in their canoes and houses.

Their colour we could never positively determine, as their bodies were incrusted with paint and dirt, though in particular cases, when these were well rubbed off, the whiteness of the skin appeared almost to equal that of Europeans, though rather of that pale effete cast which distinguishes those of our southern nations. Their children, whose skins had never been stained with paint, also equalled ours in whiteness. During their youth some of them have no disagreeable look, if compared to the generality of the people; but this seems to be entirely owing to the particular animation attending that period of life, for after attaining a certain age there is hardly any distinction. Upon the whole, a very remarkable sameness seems to characterise the countenances of the whole nation; a dull phlegmatic want of expression, with very little variation, being strongly marked in all of them. The women are nearly of the same size, colour, and form with the men, from whom it is not easy to distinguish them, as they possess no natural delicacies sufficient to render their persons agreeable; and hardly any one was seen, even amongst those who were in the prime of life, who had the least pretensions to be called handsome.

Their common dress is a flaxen garment, or mantle, ornamented on the upper edge by a narrow strip of fur, and at the lower edge by fringes or tassels. It passes under the left arm, and is tied over the right shoulder by a string before and one behind, near its middle, by which means both arms are free; and it hangs evenly, covering the left side, but leaving the right open, except from the loose part of the edges falling upon it, unless when the mantle is fastened by a girdle (of coarse matting or woollen) round the waist, which is often done. Over this, which reaches below the knees, is worn a small cloak of the same substance, likewise fringed at the lower part. In shape this resembles a round dish-cover, being quite close except in the middle, where there is a hole just large enough to admit the head; and then, resting upon the shoulders, it covers the arms to the elbows and the body as far as the waist. Their head is covered with a cap of the figure of a truncated cone, or like a flower-pot, made of fine matting, having the top frequently ornamented with a round or pointed knob or a bunch of leathern tassels; and there is a string that passes under the chin to prevent its blowing off. Besides the above dress, which is common to both sexes, the men frequently throw over their other garments the skin of a bear, wolf, or sea-otter, with the hair outward, and tie it as a cloak near the upper part, wearing it sometimes before and sometimes behind. In rainy weather they throw a coarse mat about their shoulders. They have also woollen garments, which, however, are little in use. The hair is commonly worn hanging down loose; but some, when they have no cap, tie it in a bunch on the crown of the head. Their dress upon the whole is convenient, and would by no means be inelegant were it kept clean. But as they rub their bodies constantly over with a red paint of a clayey or coarse ochry substance mixed with oil, their garments by this means contract a rancid offensive smell and a greasy nastiness. So that they make a very wretched dirty appearance; and what is still worse, their heads and their garments swarm with vermin, which, so depraved is their taste for cleanliness, we used to see them pick off with great composure and eat.

Though their bodies are always covered with red paint, their faces are often stained with a black, a bright red, or a white colour, by way of ornament. The last of these gives them a ghastly, disgusting aspect. They also strew the brown martial mica upon the paint, which makes it glitter. The ears of many of them are perforated in the lobe, where they make a pretty large hole, and two others higher up on the outer edge. In these holes they hang bits of bone, quills fixed upon a leathern thong, small shells, bunches of woollen tassels, or pieces of thin copper, which our beads could never supplant. The *septum* of the nose in many is also perforated, through which they draw a piece of soft cord; and others wear at the same place small thin pieces of iron, brass, or copper, shaped almost like a horseshoe, the narrow opening of which receives the *septum* so as that the two points may gently pinch it, and the ornament thus hangs over the upper lip. The rings of our brass buttons, which they eagerly purchased, were appropriated to this use. About their wrists they wear bracelets or bunches of white bugle beads, made of a conic shelly substance; bunches of thongs with tassels; or a broad, black, shining, horny substance, of one piece. And about their ankles they also frequently wear many folds of leathern thongs, or the sinews of animals twisted to a considerable thickness.

Thus far of their ordinary dress and ornaments; but they have some that seem to be used only on extraordinary occasions, either when they exhibit themselves as strangers, in visits of ceremony, or when they go to war. Amongst the first may be considered the skins of animals, such as wolves or bears, tied on in the usual manner, but ornamented at the edges with broad borders of fur, or of the woollen stuff manufactured by them, ingeniously wrought with various figures. These are worn either separately or over their other common garments. On such occasions the most common headdress is a quantity of withe, or half-beaten bark, wrapped about the head, which at the same time has various large feathers, particularly those of eagles, stuck in it, or is entirely covered, or we may say powdered, with small white feathers. The face, at the same time, is variously painted, having its upper and lower parts of different colours, the strokes appearing like fresh gashes; or it is besmeared with a kind of tallow, mixed with paint, which is afterward formed into a great variety of regular figures, and appears like carved work. Sometimes, again, the hair is separated into small parcels, which are tied at intervals of about two inches, to the end, with thread; and others tie it together behind, after our manner, and stick branches of the *Cypressus thyoides* in it. Thus dressed, they have a truly savage and incongruous appearance; but this is much heightened when they assume what may be called their monstrous decorations. These consist of an endless variety of carved wooden masks or visors applied on the face, or to the upper part of the head or forehead. Some of these resemble human faces, furnished with hair, beards, and eye-brows; others, the heads of birds, particularly of eagles and "quebrantahuesos;" and many, the heads of land and sea animals, such as wolves, deer, porpoises, and others. But in general these representations much exceed the natural size; and they are painted, and often strewed with pieces of the foliaceous mica, which makes them glitter, and serves to augment their enormous deformity. They even exceed this sometimes, and fix on the same part of the head large pieces of carved work, resembling the prow of a canoe, painted in the same manner, and projecting to a considerable distance. So fond are they of these disguises, that I have seen one of them put his head into a tin kettle he had got from us, for want of another sort of mask. Whether they use these extravagant masquerade ornaments on any particular religious occasion or diversion; or whether they be put on to intimidate their enemies when they go to battle, by their monstrous appearance, or as decoys when they go to hunt animals, is uncertain. But it may be concluded that if travellers or voyagers in an ignorant and credulous age, when many unnatural or marvellous things were supposed to exist, had seen a number of people decorated in this manner, without being able to approach so near as to be undeceived, they would readily have believed, and in their relations, would have attempted to make others believe, that there existed a race of beings partaking of the nature of man and beast; more especially when, besides the heads of animals on the human shoulders, they might have seen the whole bodies of their men-monsters covered with quadrupeds' skins.

The only dress amongst the people of Nootka observed by us that seems peculiarly adapted to war, is a thick leathern mantle doubled, which from its size appears to be the skin of an elk or buffalo tanned. This they fasten on in the common manner; and it is so contrived that it may reach up and cover the breast quite to the throat, falling at the same time almost to the heels. It is sometimes ingeniously painted in different compartments, and is not only sufficiently strong to resist arrows, but, as they informed us by signs, even spears cannot pierce it, so that it may be considered as their coat of mail or most complete defensive armour. Upon the same occasion they sometimes wear a kind of leathern cloak, covered with rows of dried hoofs of deer disposed horizontally, appended by leathern thongs covered with quills; which when they move make a loud rattling noise, almost equal to that of many small bells. It seems doubtful, however, whether this part of their garb be intended to strike terror in war, or only is to be considered as belonging to their eccentric ornaments on ceremonious occasions, for we saw one of their musical entertainments conducted by a man dressed in this sort of cloak, with his mask on, and shaking his rattle.

Though these people cannot be viewed without a kind of horror when equipped in such extravagant dresses, yet when divested of them and beheld in their common habit and actions, they have not the least appearance of ferocity in their countenances; and seem on the contrary, as observed already, to be of a quiet, phlegmatic, and inactive disposition, destitute in some measure of that degree of animation and vivacity that would render them agreeable as social beings. If they are not reserved, they are far from being loquacious; but their gravity is perhaps rather a consequence of the disposition just mentioned than of any conviction of its propriety, or the effect of any particular mode of education. For even in the greatest paroxysms of their rage they seem unable to express it sufficiently, either with warmth of language or significancy of gestures. Their orations, which are made either when engaged in any altercation or dispute, or to explain their sentiments publicly on other occasions, seem little more than short sentences, or rather single words, forcibly repeated and constantly in one tone and degree of strength, accompanied only with a single gesture, which they use at every sentence, jerking their whole body a little forward by bending the knees, their arms hanging down by their sides at the same time.

Though there be but too much reason, from their bringing to sale human skulls and bones, to infer that they treat their enemies with a degree of brutal cruelty, this circumstance rather marks a general agreement of character with that of almost every tribe of uncivilised man in every age and in every part of the globe, than that they are to be reproached with any charge of peculiar inhumanity. We had no reason to judge unfavourably of their disposition in this respect. They seem to be a docile, courteous, good-natured people; but, notwithstanding the predominant phlegm of their tempers, quick in resenting what they look upon as an injury, and, like most other passionate people, as soon forgetting it. I never found that these fits of passion went further than the parties immediately concerned; the spectators not troubling themselves about the quarrel, whether it was with any of us or amongst their own body, and preserving as much indifference as if they had not known anything about it. I have often seen one of them rave and scold, without any of his countrymen paying the least attention to his agitation, and when none of us could trace the cause or the object of his displeasure. In such cases they never discover the least symptom of timidity, but seem determined at all events to punish the insult. For even with respect to us they never appeared to be under the least apprehension of our superiority; but, when any difference happened, were just as ready to avenge the wrong as amongst themselves.

Their other passions, especially their curiosity, appear in some measure to lie dormant. For few expressed any desire to see or examine things wholly unknown to them, and which, to those truly possessed of that passion, would have appeared astonishing. They were always contented to procure the articles they knew and wanted, regarding everything else with great indifference; nor did our persons, apparel, and manners, so different from their own, or even the extraordinary size and construction of our ships, seem to excite admiration or even engage attention. One cause of this may be their indolence, which seems considerable. But on the other hand they are certainly not wholly unsusceptible of the tender passions, if we may judge from their being so fond of music, which is mostly of the grave or serious but truly pathetic sort. They keep the exactest concert in their songs, which are often sung by great numbers together, as those already mentioned with which they used to entertain us in their canoes. These are generally slow and solemn; but the music is not of that confined sort found amongst many rude nations, for the variations are very numerous and expressive, and the cadence or melody powerfully soothing. Besides their full concerts, sonnets of the same grave cast were frequently sung by single performers, who keep time by striking the hand against the thigh. However, the music was sometimes varied from its predominant solemnity of air, and there were instances of stanzas being sung in a more gay and lively strain, and even with a degree of humour.

The only instruments of music (if such they may be called) which I saw amongst them were a rattle, and a small whistle, about an inch long, incapable of any variation, from having but one hole. They use the rattle when they sing; but upon what occasions they use the whistle I know not, unless it be when they dress themselves like particular animals, and endeavour to imitate their howl or cry. I once saw one of them dressed in a wolf-skin, with the head over his own, and imitating that animal by making a squeaking noise with one of these whistles, which he had in his mouth. The rattles are for the most part made in the shape of a bird, with a few pebbles in the belly; and the tail is the handle. They have others, however, that bear rather more resemblance to a child's rattle.

In trafficking with us, some of them would betray a knavish disposition, and carry off our goods without making any return. But in general it was otherwise; and we had abundant reason to commend the fairness of their conduct. However, their eagerness to possess iron and brass, and indeed any kind of metal, was so great, that few of them could resist the temptation to steal it whenever an opportunity offered. The inhabitants of the South Sea Islands, as appears from a variety of instances in the course of this voyage, rather than be idle, would steal anything that they could lay their hands upon, without ever considering whether it could be of use to them or no. The novelty of the object with them was a sufficient motive for endeavouring by any indirect means to get possession of it; which marked that in such cases they were rather actuated by a childish curiosity than by a dishonest disposition, regardless of the modes of supplying real wants. The inhabitants of Nootka, who invaded our property, cannot have such apology made for them. They were thieves in the strictest sense of the word; for they pilfered nothing from us but what they knew could be converted to the purposes of private utility, and had a real value according to their estimation of things. And it was lucky for us that nothing was thought valuable by them but the single articles of our metals. Linen and such like things were perfectly secure from their depredations; and we could safely leave them hanging out ashore all night without watching. The same principle which prompted our Nootka friends to pilfer from us, it was natural to suppose, would produce a similar conduct in their intercourse with each other. And accordingly we had abundant reason to believe, that stealing is much practised amongst them, and that it chiefly gives rise to their quarrels, of which we saw more than one instance.

———

CHAPTER III.

The two towns or villages mentioned in the course of my Journal seem to be the only inhabited parts of the sound. The number of inhabitants in both might be pretty exactly computed from the canoes that were about the ships the second day after our arrival. They amounted to about a hundred, which, at a very moderate allowance, must upon an average have held five persons each. But as there were scarcely any women, very old men, children, or youths amongst them at that time, I think it will rather be rating the number of the inhabitants of the two towns too low if we suppose they could be less than four times the number of our visitors, that is, 2000 in the whole.

The village at the entrance of the sound stands on the side of a rising ground, which has a pretty steep ascent from the beach to the verge of the wood, in which space it is situated. The houses are disposed in three ranges or rows, rising gradually behind each other, the largest being that in front, and the others less; besides a few straggling or single ones at each end. These ranges are interrupted or disjoined at irregular distances by narrow paths or lanes that pass upward; but those which run in the direction of the houses between the rows are much broader. Though there be some appearance of regularity in this disposition, there is none in the single houses; for each of the divisions made by the paths may be considered either as one house or as many, there being no regular or complete separation either without or within to distinguish them by. They are built of very long and broad planks, resting upon the edges of each other, fastened or tied by withes of pine-bark here and there, and have only slender posts, or rather poles, at considerable distances on the outside, to which they are also tied; but within are some larger poles placed aslant. The height of the sides and ends of these habitations is seven or eight feet; but the back part is a little higher, by which means the planks that compose the roof slant forward, and are laid on loose so as to be moved about, either to be put close to exclude the rain, or in fair weather to be separated to let in the light and carry out the smoke. They are, however, upon the whole, miserable dwellings, and constructed with little care or ingenuity. For though the side planks be made to fit pretty closely in some places, in others they are quite open; and there are no regular doors into them, the only way of entrance being either by a hole, where the unequal length of the planks has accidentally left an open-ing; or in some cases planks are made to pass a little beyond each other, or overlap, about two feet asunder, and the entrance is in this space. There are also holes or win-dows in the sides of the houses to look out at, but without any regu-larity of shape or disposition; and these have bits of mat hung before them to prevent the rain getting in.

On the inside one may frequently see from one end to the other of these ranges of building without interrup-tion. For though in general there be the rudiments, or rather vestiges, of separations on each side for the accommodation of different families, they are such as do not intercept the sight; and often consist of no more than pieces of plank running from the side toward the middle of the house, so that, if they were com-plete, the whole might be compared to a long stable, with a double range of stalls, and a broad passage in the middle. Close to the sides, in each of these parts, is a little bench of boards, raised five or six inches higher than the rest of the floor, and covered with mats, on which the family sit and sleep. These benches are commonly

seven or eight feet long, and four or five broad. In the middle of the floor, between them, is the fireplace, which has neither hearth nor chimney. In one house, which was in the end of a middle range, almost quite separated from the rest by a high close parti-tion, and the most regular as to de-sign of any that I saw, there were four of these benches, each of which held a single family at a corner, but without any separation by boards; and the middle part of the house ap-peared common to them all.

Their furniture consists chiefly of a great number of chests and boxes of all sizes, which are generally piled upon each other close to the sides or ends of the house, and contain their spare garments, skins, masks, and other things which they set a value upon. Some of these are double, or one covers the other as a lid; others have a lid fastened with thongs; and some of the very large ones have a square hole or scuttle cut in the upper part, by which the things are put in and taken out. They are often painted black, studded with the teeth of differ-ent animals, or carved with a kind of frieze-work, and figures of birds or animals, as decorations. Their other domestic utensils are mostly square and oblong pails or buckets to hold water and other things; round wooden cups and bowls, and small shallow wooden troughs about two feet long, out of which they eat their food; and baskets of twigs, bags of matting, &c. Their fishing implements and other things also lie or hang up in different parts of the house, but without the least order, so that the whole is a complete scene of confusion; and the only places that do not partake of this confusion are the sleeping-benches, that have nothing on them but the mats, which are also cleaner or of a finer sort than those they commonly have to sit on in their boats. The nastiness and stench of their houses are, however, at least equal to the confusion. For as they dry their fish within doors, they also gut them there; which, with their bones and fragments thrown down at meals, and the addition of other sorts of filth, lie every-where in heaps, and are, I believe, never carried away till it becomes troublesome from their size to walk over them. In a word, their houses are as filthy as hog-sties; everything in and about them stinking of fish, train-oil, and smoke.

But amidst all the filth and confusion that are found in the houses, many of them are decorated with images. These are nothing more than the trunks of very large trees, four or five feet high, set up singly or by pairs at the upper end of the apartment, with the front carved into a human face, the arms and hands cut out upon the sides, and variously painted; so that the whole is a truly monstrous figure. The general name of these images is "klumma;" and the names of two particular ones, which stood abreast of each other, three or four feet asunder, in one of the houses, were "Natchkoa" and "Matseeta." A mat, by way of curtain, for the most part hung before them, which the natives were not willing at all times to remove; and when they did unveil them they seemed to speak of them in a very mysterious manner. It should seem that they are at times accustomed to make offerings to them; if we can draw this inference from their desiring us, as we interpreted their signs, to give something to these images when they drew aside the mats that covered them. It was natural from these circumstances for us to think that they were representatives of their gods, or symbols of some religious or superstitious object; and yet we had proofs of the little real estimation they were in, for with a small quantity of iron or brass I could have purchased all the gods (if their images were such) in the place. I did not see one that was not offered to me; and I actually got two or three of the very smallest sort.

The chief employment of the men seems to be that of fishing, and killing land or sea animals, for the sustenance of their families, for we saw few of them doing anything in the houses;

whereas the women were occupied in manufacturing their flaxen or woollen garments, and in preparing the sardines for drying, which they also carry up from the beach in twig-baskets after the men have brought them in their canoes. The women are also sent in the small canoes to gather mussels and other shell-fish, and perhaps on some other occasions; for they manage these with as much dexterity as the men, who, when in the canoes with them, seem to pay little attention to their sex by offering to relieve them from the labour of the paddle, nor indeed do they treat them with any particular respect or tenderness in other situations. The young men appeared to be the most indolent or idle set in this community; for they were either sitting about in scattered companies to bask themselves in the sun, or lay wallowing in the sand upon the beach like a number of hogs, for the same purpose, without any covering. But this disregard of decency was confined to the men. The women were always properly clothed, and behaved with the utmost propriety, justly deserving all commendation for a bashfulness and modesty becoming their sex; but more meritorious in them as the men seem to have no sense of shame. It is impossible, however, that we should have been able to observe the exact mode of their domestic life and employments from a single visit (as the first was quite transitory) of a few hours. For it may be easily supposed that on such an occasion most of the labour of all the inhabitants of the village would cease upon our arrival, and an interruption be given even to the usual manner of appearing in their houses during their more remiss or sociable hours, when left to themselves. We were much better enabled to form some judgment of their disposition, and in some measure even of their method of living, from the frequent visits so many of them paid us at our ships in their canoes; in which, it should seem, they spend a great deal of time, at least in the summer season. For we observed that they not only eat and sleep frequently in them, but strip off their clothes and lay themselves along to bask in the sun, in the same manner as we had seen practised at their village. Their canoes of the larger sort are, indeed, sufficiently spacious for that purpose, and perfectly dry; so that, under shelter of a skin, they are, except in rainy weather, much more comfortable habitations than their houses.

Though their food, strictly speaking, may be said to consist of everything animal or vegetable that they can procure, the quantity of the latter bears an exceedingly small proportion to that of the former. Their greatest reliance seems to be upon the sea as affording fish, mussels, and smaller shell-fish, and sea-animals. Of the first the principal are herrings and sardines, the two species of bream formerly mentioned, and small cod. But the herrings and sardines are not only eaten fresh in their season, but likewise serve as stores which, after being dried and smoked, are preserved by being sewed up in mats, so as to form large bales three or four feet square. It seems that the herrings also supply them with another grand resource for food, which is a vast quantity of roe, very curiously prepared. It is strewed upon, or, as it were, incrustated about small branches of the Canadian pine. They also prepare it upon a long narrow sea-grass which grows plentifully upon the rocks under water. This caviare, if it may be so called, is kept in baskets or bags of mat, and used occasionally, being first dipped in water. It may be considered as the winter bread of these people, and has no disagreeable taste. They also eat the roe of some other fish, which from the size of its grains must be very large, but it has a rancid taste and smell. It does not appear that they prepare any other fish in this manner to preserve them for any length of time. For though they split and dry a few of the bream and *Chimaræ,* which are pretty plentiful, they do not smoke them as the herrings and sardines.

The next article on which they seem to depend for a large proportion of their food is the large mussel, great abundance of which are found in the sound. These are roasted in their shells, then stuck upon long wooden skewers and taken off occasionally as wanted, being eaten without any other preparation, though they often dip them in oil as a sauce. The other marine productions, such as the smaller shell-fish, though they contribute to increase the general stock, are by no means to be looked upon as a standing or material article of their food when compared to those just mentioned. Of the sea-animals the most common that we saw in use amongst them as food is the porpoise, the fat or rind of which, as well as the flesh, they cut in large pieces, and having dried them as they do the herrings, eat them without any further preparation. They also prepare a sort of broth from this animal in its fresh state in a singular manner, putting pieces of it in a square wooden vessel or bucket with water, and then throwing heated stones into it. This operation they repeat till they think the contents are sufficiently stewed or seethed. They put in the fresh and take out the other stones with a cleft stick, which serves as tongs, the vessel being always placed near the fire for that purpose. This is a pretty common dish amongst them, and from its appearance seems to be strong nourishing food. The oil which they procure from these and other sea-animals is also used by them in great quantities, both supping it alone with a large scoop or spoon made of horn, or mixing it with other food as sauce. It may also be presumed that they feed upon other sea-animals, such as seals, sea-otters, and whales; not only from the skins of the two first being frequent amongst them, but from the great number of implements of all sorts intended to destroy these different animals, which clearly points out their dependence upon them. Though perhaps they do not catch them in great plenty at all seasons, which seemed to be the case while we lay there, as no great number of fresh skins or pieces of the flesh were seen. The same might perhaps be said of the land-animals, which, though doubtless the natives sometimes kill them, appeared to be scarce at this time, as we did not see a single piece of the flesh belonging to any of them; and though their skins be. in tolerable plenty, it is probable that many of these are procured by traffic from other tribes. Upon the whole, it seems plain from a variety of circumstances that these people procure almost all their animal food from the sea, if we except a few birds, of which the gulls or sea-fowl, which they shoot with their arrows, are the most material.

As the Canadian pine-branches and sea-grass on which the fish-roe is strewed may be considered as their only winter vegetables, so as the spring advances they make use of several others as they come in season. The most common of these which we observed were two sorts of liliaceous roots, one simply tunicated, the other granulated upon its surface, called "mahkatte" and "koohquoppa," which have a mild sweetish taste, and are mucilaginous and eaten raw. The next which they have in great quantities is a root called "aheita," resembling in taste our liquorice, and another fern root whose leaves were not yet disclosed. They also eat raw another small, sweetish, insipid root about the thickness of sarsaparilla, but we were ignorant of the plant to which it belongs; and also of another root, which is very large and palmated, which we saw them dig up near the village and afterward eat it. It is also probable that as the season advances they have many others which we did not see. For though there be no appearance of cultivation amongst them, there are great quantities of alder, gooseberry, and currant-bushes, whose fruit they may eat in their natural state, as we have seen them eat the leaves of the last, and of the lilies, just as they were plucked from the plant. It must, however, be observed that one of the conditions which they seem to require in all food is, that it should be of the bland or less acrid kind; for they would not eat the leek or garlic, though they brought vast quantities to sell when they understood we were fond of it. Indeed they seemed to have no relish for any of our food; and when offered spirituous liquors, they rejected them as something unnatural and disgusting to the palate.

Though they sometimes eat small marine-animals, in their fresh state, raw, it is their common practice to roast or broil their food; for they are quite ignorant of our method of boiling, unless we allow that of preparing their porpoise broth is such; and indeed their vessels, being all of wood, are quite insufficient for this purpose. Their manner of eating is exactly consonant to the nastiness of their houses and persons; for the troughs and platters in which they put their food appear never to have been washed from the time they were first made, and the dirty remains of a former meal are only swept away by the succeeding one. They also tear everything solid or tough to pieces with their hands and teeth; for though they make use of their knives to cut off the larger portions, they have not as yet thought of reducing these to smaller pieces and mouthfuls by the same means, though obviously more convenient and cleanly. But they seem to have no idea of cleanliness; for they eat the roots which they dig from the ground without so much as shaking off the soil that adheres to them. We are uncertain if they have any set time for meals; for we have seen them eat at all hours in their canoes. And yet, from seeing several messes of the porpoise broth preparing towards noon, when we visited the village, I should suspect that they make a principal meal about that time.

Their weapons are bows and arrows, slings, spears, short truncheons of bone somewhat like the "patoo patoo" of New Zealand, and a small pick-axe not unlike the common American tomahawk. The spear has generally a long point made of bone. . Some of the arrows are pointed with iron; but most commonly their points were of indented bone. The tomahawk is a stone, six or eight inches long, pointed at one end, and the other end fixed into a handle of wood. This handle resembles the head and neck of the human figure; and the stone is fixed in the mouth, so as to represent an enormously large tongue. To make the resemblance still stronger, human hair is also fixed to it. This weapon they call "taaweesh" or "tsuskeeah." They have another stone weapon called "seeaik," nine inches or a foot long, with a square point. From the number of stone weapons and others, we might almost conclude that it is their custom to engage in close fight; and we had too convincing proofs that their wars are both frequent and bloody, from the vast number of human skulls which they brought to sell.

Their manufactures and mechanic arts are far more extensive and ingenious, whether we regard the design or the execution, than could have been expected from the natural disposition of the people and the little progress that civilisation has made amongst them in other respects. The flaxen and woollen garments with which they cover themselves must necessarily engage their first care, and are the most material of those that can be ranked under the head of manufactures. The former of these are made of the bark of a pine-tree, beat into a hempen state. It is not spun, but after being properly prepared is spread upon a stick which is fastened across to two others that stand upright. It is disposed in such a manner that the manufacturer, who sits on her hams at this simple machine, knots it across with small plaited threads at the distance of half-an-inch from each other. Though by this method it be not so close or firm as cloth that is woven, the bunches between the knots make it sufficiently impervious to the air, by filling the interstices; and it has the additional advantage of being softer and more pliable. The woollen garments, though probably manufactured in the same manner, have the

strongest resemblance to woven cloth. But the various figures which are very artificially inserted in them destroy the supposition of their being wrought in a loom; it being extremely unlikely that these people should be so dexterous as to be able to finish such a complex work unless immediately by their hands. They are of different degrees of fineness; some resembling our coarsest rugs or blankets, and others almost equal to our finest sorts, or even softer, and certainly warmer. The wool of which they are made seems to be taken from animals, as the fox and brown lynx, the last of which is by far the finest sort, and in its natural state differs little from the colour of our coarser wools; but the hair with which the animal is also covered being intermixed, its appearance when wrought is somewhat different. The ornamental parts or figures in these garments, which are disposed with great taste, are commonly of a different colour, being dyed chiefly either of a deep brown or of a yellow; the last of which, when it is new, equals the best in our carpets as to brightness.

To their taste or design in working figures upon their garments, corresponds their fondness for carving in everything they make of wood. Nothing is without a kind of friezework or the figure of some animal upon it; but the most general representation is that of the human face, which is often cut out upon birds, and the other monstrous figures mentioned before, and even upon their stone and their bone weapons. The general design of all these things is perfectly sufficient to convey a knowledge of the object they are intended to represent; but the carving is not executed with the nicety that a dexterous artist would bestow even upon an indifferent design. The same, however, cannot be said of many of the human masks and heads, where they show themselves to be ingenious sculptors. They not only preserve with exactness the general character of their own faces, but finish the more minute parts with a degree of accuracy in proportion and neatness in execution. The strong propensity of this people to works of this sort is remarkable, in a vast variety of particulars. Small whole human figures; representations of birds, fish, and land and sea animals; models of their household utensils, and of their canoes, were found amongst them in great abundance.

The imitative arts being nearly allied, no wonder that to their skill in working figures in their garments and carving them in wood, they should add that of drawing them in colours. We have sometimes seen the whole process of their whale-fishery painted on the caps they wear. This, though rudely executed, serves at least to show that though there be no appearance of the knowledge of letters amongst them, they have some notion of a method of commemorating and representing actions in a lasting way, independently of what may be recorded in their songs and traditions. They have also other figures painted on some of their things; but it is doubtful if they ought to be considered as symbols that have certain established significations, or only the mere creation of fancy and caprice.

Their canoes are of a simple structure, but, to appearance, well calculated for every useful purpose. Even the largest, which carry twenty people or more, are formed of one tree. Many of them are forty feet long, seven broad, and about three deep. From the middle towards each end they become gradually narrower, the after-part or stern ending abruptly or perpendicularly, with a small knob on the top; but the forepart is lengthened out, stretching forwards and upwards, ending in a notched point, or prow, considerably higher than the sides of the canoe, which run nearly in a straight line. For the most part they are without any ornament, but some have a little carving, and are decorated by setting seals' teeth on the surface, like studs; as is the practice on their masks and weapons. A few have likewise a kind of additional head or prow, like a large cutwater, which is painted with the figure of some animal. They have no seats, nor any other supporters on the inside than several round sticks, little thicker than a cane, placed across at mid depth. They are very light, and their breadth and flatness enable them to swim firmly without an outrigger, which none of them have; a remarkable distinction between the navigation of all the American nations, and that of the Southern parts of the East Indies and the islands in the Pacific Ocean. Their paddles are small and light; the shape in some measure resembling that of a large leaf pointed at the bottom, broadest in the middle, and gradually losing itself in the shaft, the whole being about five feet long. They have acquired great dexterity in managing these paddles by constant use; for sails are no part of their art of navigation.

Their implements for fishing and hunting, which are both ingeniously contrived and well made, are nets, hooks and lines, harpoons, gigs, and an instrument like an oar. This last is about twenty feet long, four or five inches broad, and about half-an-inch thick. Each edge, for about two-thirds of its length (the other third being its handle), is set with sharp bone teeth about two inches long. Herrings and sardines, and such other small fish as come in shoals, are attacked with this instrument, which is struck into the shoal, and the fish are caught either upon or between the teeth. Their hooks are made of bone and wood, and rather inartificially; but the harpoon with which they strike the whales and lesser sea animals shows a great reach of contrivance. It is composed of a piece of bone, cut into two barbs, in which is fixed the oval blade of a large mussel shell, in which is the point of the instrument. To this are fastened about two or three fathoms of rope; and to throw this harpoon they use a shaft of about twelve or fifteen feet long, to which the line or rope is made fast, and to one end of which the harpoon is fixed, so as to separate from the shaft, and leave it floating upon the water as a buoy when the animal darts away with the harpoon.

We can say nothing as to the manner of their catching or killing land animals, unless we may suppose that they shoot the smaller sorts with their arrows, and engage bears or wolves and foxes with their spears. They have, indeed, several nets, which are probably applied to that purpose, as they frequently threw them over their heads, to show their use, when they brought them to us for sale. They also sometimes decoy animals by covering themselves with a skin, and running about upon all fours, which they do very nimbly, as appeared from the specimens of their skill which they exhibited to us, making a kind of noise or neighing at the same time; and on these occasions the masks, or carved heads, as well as the real dried heads, of the different animals are put on. As to the materials of which they make their various articles, it is to be observed that everything of the rope kind is formed either from thongs of skins and sinews of animals, or from the same flaxen substance of which their mantles are manufactured. The sinews often appeared to be of such a length, that it might be presumed they could be of no other animal than the whale. And the same may be said of the bones of which they make their weapons already mentioned; such as their bark-beating instruments, the points of their spears, and the barbs of their harpoons.

Their great dexterity in works of wood may in some measure be ascribed to the assistance they receive from iron tools. For as far as we know they use no other; at least we saw only one chisel of bone. And though originally their tools must have been of different materials, it is not improbable that many of their improvements have been made since they acquired a knowledge of that metal, which is now universally used in their various wooden works. The chisel and the knife are the only forms, as far as we saw, that iron assumes amongst them. The chisel is a long flat piece fitted into a handle of wood. A stone serves for a mallet, and a piece of fish skin for a polisher. I have seen some of these chisels that were eight

or ten inches long, and three or four inches broad; but in general they were smaller. The knives are of various sizes; some very large; and their blades are crooked, somewhat like our pruning-knife, but the edge is on the back or convex part. Most of them that we saw were about the breadth and thickness of an iron hoop; and their singular form marks that they are not of European make. Probably they are imitations of their own original instruments used for the same purposes. They sharpen these iron tools upon a coarse slate whetstone, and likewise keep the whole instrument constantly bright.

Iron, which they call "seekemaile" (which name they also give to tin and all white metals), being familiar to these people, it was very natural for us to speculate about the mode of its being conveyed to them. Upon our arrival in the sound they immediately discovered a knowledge of traffic and an inclination for it, and we were convinced afterwards that they had not received this knowledge from a cursory interview with any strangers; but, from their method, it seemed to be an established practice of which they were fond, and in which they were also well skilled. With whom they carry on this traffic, may perhaps admit of some doubt. For though we found amongst them things doubtless of European manufacture, or at least derived from some civilised nation, such as iron and brass, it by no means appears that they receive them immediately from these nations. For we never observed the least sign of their having seen ships like ours before, nor of their having traded with such people. Many circumstances serve to prove this almost beyond a doubt. They were earnest in their inquiries, by signs, on our arrival, if we meant to settle amongst them, and if we came as friends; signifying, at the same time, that they gave the wood and water freely, from friendship. This not only proves that they considered the place as entirely their property, without fearing any superiority; but the inquiry would have been an unnatural one, on a supposition that any ships had been here before, had trafficked and supplied themselves with wood and water, and had then departed; for in that case they might reasonably expect we would do the same. They indeed expressed no marks of surprise at seeing our ships. But this, as I observed before, may be imputed to their natural indolence of temper and want of curiosity. Nor were they even startled at the report of a musket; till one day, upon their endeavouring to make us sensible that their arrows and spears could not penetrate the hide dresses, one of our gentlemen shot a musket ball through one of them folded six times. At this they were so much staggered that they plainly discovered their ignorance of the effect of fire-arms. This was very often confirmed afterwards, when we used them at their village and other places to shoot birds, the manner of which plainly confounded them; and our explanations of the use of shot and ball were received with the most significant marks of their having no previous ideas on this matter.

Some accounts of a Spanish voyage to this coast in 1774 or 1775 had reached England before I sailed, but the foregoing circumstances sufficiently prove that these ships had not been at Nootka.[1] Besides this, it was evident that iron was too common here, was in too many hands, and the uses of it were too well known for them to have had the first knowledge of it so very lately, or indeed at any earlier period, by an accidental supply from a ship. Doubtless, from the general use they make of this metal, it may be supposed to come from some constant source by way of traffic, and that not of a very late date, for they are as dexterous in using their tools as the longest practice can make them. The most probable way, therefore, by which we can suppose that they get their iron, is by trading for it with other Indian tribes, who either have immediate communication with European settlements upon the continent, or receive it perhaps through several intermediate nations. The same might be said of the brass and copper found amongst them. Whether these things be introduced by way of Hudson's Bay and Canada from the Indians who deal with our traders, and so successively across from one tribe to the other, or whether they be brought from the north-western parts of Mexico in the same manner, perhaps cannot be easily determined. But it should seem that not only the rude materials, but some articles in their manufactured state, find their way hither. The brass ornaments for noses, in particular, are so neatly made that I am doubtful whether the Indians are capable of fabricating them. The materials certainly are European, as no American tribes have been found who knew the method of making brass; though copper has been commonly met with, and from its softness might be fashioned into any shape, and also polished. If our traders to Hudson's Bay and Canada do not use such articles in their traffic with the natives, they must have been introduced at Nootka from the quarter of Mexico, whence no doubt the two silver table-spoons met with here were originally derived. It is most probable, however, that the Spaniards are not such eager traders, nor have formed such extensive connections with the tribes north of Mexico as to supply them with quantities of iron, from which they can spare so much to the people here.[2]

---

[1] We now know that Captain Cook's conjecture was well founded. It appears from the Journal of this Voyage, already referred to, that the Spaniards had intercourse with the natives of this coast only in three places—in Latitude 41° 7′, in Latitude 47° 21′, and in Latitude 57° 18′. So that they were not within two degrees of Nootka; and it is most probable that the people there never heard of these Spanish ships.—*Note in Original Edition.*

---

[2] Though the two silver table-spoons found at Nootka Sound most probably came from the Spaniards in the south,

Of the political and religious institutions established amongst them, it cannot be supposed that we should learn much. This we could observe, that there are such men as chiefs who are distinguished by the name or title of "acweek," and to whom the others are in some measure subordinate. But I should guess the authority of each of these great men extends no further than the family to which he belongs, and who own him as their head. These "acweeks" were not always elderly men, from which I concluded that this title came to them by inheritance. I saw nothing that could give the least insight into their notions of religion besides the figures before mentioned, called by them "klumma." Most probably these were idols; but as they frequently mentioned the word "acweek" when they spoke of them, we may perhaps be authorised to suppose that they are the images of some of their ancestors, whom they venerate as divinities. But all this is mere conjecture, for we saw no act of religious homage paid to them, nor could we gain any information, as we had learned little more of the language than to ask the names of things, without being able to hold any conversation with the natives that might instruct us as to their institutions and traditions.

CHAPTER IV.

HAVING put to sea on the evening of the 26th, as before related, with strong signs of an approaching storm, these signs did not deceive us. We were hardly out of the sound before the wind in an instant shifted from NE.

there seem to be sufficient grounds for believing that the regular supply of iron comes from a different quarter. It is remarkable that the Spaniards, in 1775, found at Puerto de la Trinidad, in Latitude 41° 7', arrows pointed with copper or iron, which they understood were procured from the north. *—Note in Original Edition.*

to SE. by E. and increased to a strong gale, with squalls and rain, and so dark a sky that we could not see the length of the ship. Being apprehensive, from the experience I had since our arrival on this coast, of the wind veering more to the S., which would put us in danger of a lee-shore, we got the tacks on board, and stretched off to the SW. under all the sail the ships could bear. Fortunately the wind veered no farther southerly than SE., so that at daylight the next morning we were quite clear of the coast.

The Discovery being at some distance astern, I brought to till she came up, and then bore away, steering NW., in which direction I supposed the coast to lie. The wind was at SE., blew very hard and in squalls, with thick hazy weather. At half-past one in the afternoon it blew a perfect hurricane, so that I judged it highly dangerous to run any longer before it, and therefore brought the ships to with their heads to the S. under the foresails and mizzen staysails. At this time the Resolution sprung a leak, which at first alarmed us not a little. It was found to be under the starboard buttock, where from the bread-room we could both hear and see the water rush in; and, as we then thought, two feet under water. But in this we were happily mistaken, for it was afterwards found to be even with the water-line, if not above it, when the ship was upright. It was no sooner discovered than the fish-room was found to be full of water, and the casks in it afloat; but this was in a great measure owing to the water not finding its way to the pumps through the coals that lay in the bottom of the room. For after the water was baled out, which employed us till midnight, and had found its way directly from the leak to the pumps, it appeared that one pump kept it under, which gave us no small satisfaction. In the evening the wind veered to the S., and its fury in some degree ceased. On this we set the mainsail and two topsails close-reefed, and stretched to the westward. But at 11 o'clock the gale again increased, and obliged us to take in the topsails, till 5 o'clock the next morning, when the storm began to abate, so that we could bear to set them again.

The weather now began to clear up, and being able to see several leagues round us, I steered more to the northward. At noon the Latitude, by observation, was 50° 1', Longitude 229° 26'.[1] I now steered NW. by N. with a fresh gale at SSE. and fair weather. But at nine in the evening it began again to blow hard, and in squalls, with rain. With such weather, and the wind between SSE. and SW., I continued the same course till the 30th at four in the morning, when I steered N. by W. in order to make the land. I regretted very much indeed that I could not do it sooner, for this obvious reason, that we were now passing the place where geographers have placed the pretended strait of Admiral de Fonte.[2] For my own part I give no credit to such vague and improbable stories that carry their own confutation along with them. Nevertheless I was very desirous of keeping the American coast aboard in order to clear up this point beyond dispute. But it would have been highly imprudent in me to have engaged with the land in weather so exceedingly tempestuous, or to have lost the advantage of a fair wind by waiting for better weather. This same day at noon we were in the

---

[1] As in the remaining part of this Book, the latitude and longitude are very frequently set down, the former being invariably north and the latter east, the constant repetition of the two words north and east has been omitted.

[2] Cook was in fact at this time passing the mouth of Dixon's Channel, between Queen Charlotte's Island and the Prince of Wales's Archipelago, a genuine examination of which, and of the numerous channels near, may have given the foundation for the ridiculous fables told in his name in 1708, nearly seventy years after the alleged date of his voyage, by a "sensational" literary hack in London.

Latitude of 53° 22', and in the Longitude of 225° 14'.

The next morning, being the 1st of May, seeing nothing of the land, I steered north-easterly, with a fresh breeze at SSE. and S., with squalls and showers of rain and hail. Our Latitude at noon was 54° 43', and our Longitude 224° 44'. At seven in the evening, being in the Latitude of 55° 20', we got sight of the land, extending from NNE. to E. or E. by S, about twelve or fourteen leagues distant. An hour after, I steered N. by W.; and at four the next morning the coast was seen from N. by W. to SE., the nearest part about six leagues distant. At this time the northern point of an inlet, or what appeared to be one, bore E. by S. It lies in the Latitude of 56°; and from it to the northward the coast seemed to be much broken, forming bays and harbours every two or three leagues, or else appearances much deceived us. At 6 o'clock, drawing nearer the land, I steered NW. by N., this being the direction of the coast, having a fresh gale at SE., with some showers of hail, snow, and sleet. Between 11 and 12 o'clock we passed a group of small islands lying under the mainland, in the Latitude of 56° 48', and off, or rather to the northward of, the south point of a large bay. An arm of this bay, in the northern part of it, seemed to extend in towards the north, behind a round elevated mountain that lies between it and the sea. This mountain I called Mount Edgcumbe; and the point of land that shoots out from it Cape Edgcumbe. The latter lies in the Latitude of 57° 3', and in the Longitude of 224° 7'; and at noon it bore N. 20°, W. six leagues distant. The land, except in some places close to the sea, is all of a considerable height, and hilly; but Mount Edgcumbe far out-tops all the other hills. It was wholly covered with snow, as were also all the other elevated hills; but the lower ones, and the flatter spots bordering upon the sea were free from it, and covered with wood.

As we advanced to the north, we

found the coast from Cape Edgcumbe to trend to north and north-easterly for six or seven leagues, and there form a large bay. In the entrance of that bay are some islands, for which reason I named it the Bay of Islands. It lies in the Latitude of 57° 20',[1] and seemed to branch into several arms, one of which turned to the south, and may probably communicate with the bay on the east side of Cape Edgcumbe, and make the land of that cape an island.

At half-an-hour past four in the morning on the 3d, Mount Edgcumbe bore S. 54° E.; a large inlet N. 50° E., distant six leagues; and the most advanced point of the land to the NW., lying under a very high peaked mountain, which obtained the name of Mount Fairweather, bore N. 32° W. The inlet was named Cross Sound, as being first seen on that day so marked in our Calendar. It appeared to branch in several arms, the largest of which turned to the northward. The south-east point of this sound is a high promontory, which obtained the name of Cross Cape. It lies in the Latitude of 57° 57', and its Longitude is 223° 21'. At noon it bore SE.; and the point under the peaked mountain, which was called Cape Fairweather, N. by W. quarter W., distant thirteen leagues.

Here the NE. wind left us, and was succeeded by light breezes from the NW., which lasted for several days. I stood to the SW. and WSW. till 8 o'clock the next morning, when we tacked and stood towards the shore. At noon the Latitude was 58° 22', and the Longitude 220° 45'. Mount Fairweather, the peaked mountain over the cape of the same name, bore N. 63° E.; the shore under it twelve leagues distant. This mountain, which lies in the Latitude of

58° 52', and in the Longitude of 222°, and five leagues inland, is the highest of a chain, or rather a ridge, of mountains that rise at the NW. entrance of Cross Sound, and extend to the NW. in a parallel direction with the coast. These mountains were wholly covered with snow, from the highest summit down to the sea-coast, some few places excepted, where we could perceive trees rising, as it were, out of the sea; and which, therefore, we supposed grew on low land, or on islands bordering upon the shore of the continent. At five in the afternoon our Latitude being then 58° 53', and our Longitude 220° 52', the summit of an elevated mountain appeared above the horizon, bearing N. 26° W., and, as was afterward found, forty leagues distant. We supposed it to be Behring's Mount St Elias; and it stands by that name in our chart. This day we saw several whales, seals, and porpoises; many gulls, and several flocks of birds, which had a black ring about the head, the tip of the tail, and upper part of the wings, with a black band, and the rest bluish above and white below. We also saw a brownish duck, with a black or deep blue head and neck, sitting upon the water.

Having but light winds, with some calms, we advanced slowly; so that, on the 6th, at noon, we were only in the Latitude of 59° 8', and in the Longitude of 220° 19'. Mount Fairweather bore S. 63° E., and Mount St Elias N. 30° W.; the nearest land about eight leagues distant. In the direction of N. 47° E. from this station, there was the appearance of a bay, and an island off the south point of it, that was covered with wood. It is here where I suppose Commodore Behring to have anchored. Behind the bay (which I shall distinguish by the name of Behring's Bay, in honour of its discoverer), or rather to the south of it, the chain of mountains before mentioned is interrupted by a plain of a few leagues' extent, beyond which the sight was unlimited; so that there is either a level country or water behind it. In the afternoon,

---

[1] It should seem that in this very bay the Spaniards in 1775 found their port which they call De los Remedios. The Latitude is exactly the same; and their Journal mentions its being protected by a long ridge of high islands.—*Note in Original Edition.*

having a few hours' calm, I took this opportunity to sound, and found twenty fathoms water over a muddy bottom. The calm was succeeded by a light breeze from the north, with which we stood to the westward; and at noon the next day we were in the Latitude of 59° 27', and the Longitude of 219° 7'.

We now found the coast to trend very much to the west, inclining hardly anything to the north; and as we had the wind mostly from the westward, and but little of it, our progress was slow. On the 9th, at noon, the Latitude was 59° 30', and the Longitude 217°. In this situation the nearest land was nine leagues distant, and Mount St Elias bore N. 30° E., nineteen leagues distant. This mountain lies twelve leagues inland, in the Latitude of 60° 27', and in the Longitude of 219°. It belongs to a ridge of exceedingly high mountains, that may be reckoned a continuation of the former, as they are only divided from them by the plain above mentioned. They extend as far to the west as the Longitude of 217°, where, although they do not end, they lose much of their height, and become more broken and divided.

At noon on the 10th our Latitude was 59° 51', and our Longitude 215° 56', being no more than three leagues from the coast of the continent, which extended from E. half N. to NW. half W., as far as the eye could reach. To the westward of this last direction was an island that extended from N. 52° W. to S. 85° W., distant six leagues. A point shoots out from the main toward the NE. end of the island, bearing at this time N. 30° W., five or six leagues distant. This point I named Cape Suckling. The point of the cape is low; but within it is a tolerably high hill, which is disjoined from the mountains by low land, so that at a distance the cape looks like an island. On the north side of Cape Suckling is a bay that appeared to be of some extent, and to be covered from most winds. To this bay I had some thoughts of going to stop our leak, as all our endeavours to do it at sea had proved ineffectual. With this view I steered for the Cape; but as we had only variable light breezes we approached it slowly. However, before night we were near enough to see some low land spitting out from the cape to the NW., so as to cover the east part of the bay from the south wind. We also saw some small islands in the bay, and elevated rocks between the cape and the north-east end of the island. But still there appeared to be a passage on both sides of these rocks; and I continued steering for them all night, having from forty-three to twenty-seven fathoms water, over a muddy bottom.

At 4 o'clock next morning, the wind, which had been mostly at NE., shifted to N. This being against us, I gave up the design of going within the island or into the bay, as neither could be done without loss of time. I therefore bore up for the west end of the island. The wind blew faint, and at 10 o'clock it fell calm. Being not far from the island, I went in a boat, and landed upon it with a view of seeing what lay on the other side; but finding it farther to the hills than I expected, and the way being steep and woody, I was obliged to drop the design. At the foot of a tree, on a little eminence not far from the shore, I left a bottle with a paper in it on which were inscribed the names of the ships and the date of our discovery; and along with it I enclosed two silver twopenny pieces of his Majesty's coin, of the date 1772. These, with many others, were furnished me by the Rev. Dr Kaye;[1] and as a mark of my esteem and regard for that gentleman I named the island, after him, Kaye's Island. It is eleven or twelve leagues in length in the direction of NE. and SW., but its breadth is not above a league or a league and a half in any part of it. The SW. point, which lies in the Latitude of 59° 49' and the Longitude of 216° 58', is very remarkable, being

---

[1] Then Sub-almoner and Chaplain to his Majesty, afterwards Dean of Lincoln.

a naked rock elevated considerably above the land within it. There is also an elevated rock lying off it, which from some points of view appears like a ruined castle. Towards the sea the island terminates in a kind of bare sloping cliffs, with a beach, only a few paces across to their foot, of large pebble stones, intermixed in some places with a brownish clayey sand which the sea seems to deposit after rolling in, having been washed down from the higher parts by the rivulets or torrents. The cliffs are composed of a bluish stone or rock, in a soft or mouldering state, except in a few places. There are parts of the shore interrupted by small valleys and gullies. In each of these a rivulet or torrent rushes down with considerable impetuosity, though it may be supposed that they are only furnished from the snow, and last no longer than till it is all melted. These valleys are filled with pine-trees, which grow down close to the entrance, but only to about half-way up the higher or middle part of the island. The woody part also begins everywhere immediately above the cliffs, and is continued to the same height with the former, so that the island is covered as it were with a broad girdle of wood spread upon its side, included between the top of the cliffy shore and the higher parts in the centre. The trees, however, are far from being of an uncommon growth, few appearing to be larger than one might grasp round with his arms, and about forty or fifty feet high; so that the only purpose they could answer for shipping would be to make top-gallant-masts and other small things. How far we may judge of the size of the trees which grow on the neighbouring continent it may be difficult to determine. But it was observed that none larger than those we saw growing lay upon the beach amongst the drift-wood. The pine-trees seemed all of one sort, and there was neither the Canadian pine nor cypress to be seen. But there were a few which appeared to be the alder, that were but small, and had not yet shot forth their leaves. Upon the edges of the cliffs, and on some sloping ground, the surface was covered with a kind of turf about half-a-foot thick, which seemed composed of the common moss, and the top or upper part of the island had almost the same appearance as to colour, but whatever covered it seemed to be thicker. I found amongst the trees some currant and hawberry bushes, a small yellow-flowered violet, and the leaves of some other plants not yet in flower, particularly one which Mr Anderson supposed to be the *Heracleum* of Linnæus, the sweet herb which Steller, who attended Behring, imagined the Americans here dress for food in the same manner as the natives of Kamtschatka.

We saw flying about the wood a crow, two or three of the white-headed eagles mentioned at Nootka, and another sort full as large, which appeared also of the same colour, or blacker, and had only a white breast. In the passage from the ship to the shore we saw a great many fowls sitting upon the water, or flying about in flocks or pairs; the chief of which were a few "quebrantahuesos," divers, ducks or large petrels, gulls, shags, and burres. The divers were of two sorts: one very large, of a black colour, with a white breast and belly; the other smaller, and with a longer and more pointed bill, which seemed to be the common guillemot. The ducks were also of two sorts, one brownish, with a black or deep blue head and neck, and perhaps the stone duck described by Steller. The others fly in larger flocks, but are smaller than these, and are of a dirty black colour. The gulls were of the common sort, and those which fly in flocks. The shags were large and black with a white spot behind the wings as they flew, but probably only the larger water cormorant. There was also a single bird seen flying about, to appearance of the gull kind, of a snowy white colour with black along part of the upper side of its wings. I owe all these remarks to Mr Anderson. At the place where we landed, a fox came from the verge of the wood, and eyed us with very little emotion, walking leisurely without any signs of fear. Ho was of a reddish-yellow colour, like some of the skins we bought at Nootka, but not of a large size. We also saw two or three little seals off shore, but no other animals or birds, nor the least signs of inhabitants having ever been upon the island. I returned on board at half-past two in the afternoon, and, with a light breeze easterly, steered for the SW. of the island, which we got round by 8 o'clock, and then stood for the westernmost land now in sight, which at this time bore NW. half N. On the NW. side of the NE. end of Kaye's Island lies another island, stretching SE. and NW. about three leagues, to within the same distance of the NW. boundary of the bay above mentioned, which is distinguished by the name of Comptroller's Bay.

Next morning at 4 o'clock Kaye's Island was still in sight, bearing E. quarter S. At this time we were about four or five leagues from the main; and the most western part in sight bore NW. half N. We had now a fresh gale at ESE; and as we advanced to the NW., we raised land more and more westerly, and at last to the southward of west; so that at noon, when the Latitude was 61° 11′ and the Longitude 213° 28′, the most advanced land bore from us SW. by W. half W. At the same time, the E. point of a large inlet bore WNW., three leagues distant. From Comptroller's Bay to this point, which I name Cape Hinchingbroke, the direction of the coast is nearly E. and W. Beyond this it seemed to incline to the southward; a direction so contrary to the modern charts founded upon the late Russian discoveries, that we had reason to expect that by the inlet before us we should find a passage to the N., and that the land to the W. and SW. was nothing but a group of islands. Add to this, that the wind was now at SE., and we were threatened with a fog and a storm; and I wanted to get into some place to stop the leak before we encountered

another gale. These reasons induced me to steer for the inlet, which we had no sooner reached than the weather became so foggy that we could not see a mile before us, and it became necessary to secure the ships in some place to wait for a clearer sky. With this view I hauled close under Cape Hinchingbroke, and anchored before a small cove a little within the cape, in eight fathoms water, a clayey bottom, and about a quarter of a mile from the shore.

The boats were then hoisted out, some to sound and others to fish. The seine was drawn in the cove, but without success, for it was torn. At some short intervals the fog cleared away and gave us a sight of the lands around us. The cape bore S. by W. half W., one league distant; the W. point of the inlet SW. by W., distant five leagues; and the land on that side extended as far as W. by N. Between this point and NW. by W. we could see no land; and what was in the last direction seemed to be at a great distance. The westernmost point we had in sight on the north shore bore NNW. half W., two leagues distant. Between this point and the shore under which we were at anchor, is a bay about three leagues deep; on the south-east side of which there are two or three coves such as that before which we had anchored, and in the middle some rocky islands. To these islands Mr Gore was sent in a boat, in hopes of shooting some eatable birds. But he had hardly got to them before about twenty natives made their appearance in two large canoes; on which he thought proper to return to the ships, and they followed him. They would not venture alongside, but kept at some distance, hallooing aloud, and alternately clasping and extending their arms; and in a short time began a kind of song, exactly after the manner of those at Nootka. Their heads were also powdered with feathers. One man held out a white garment, which we interpreted as a sign of friendship; and another stood up in the canoe, quite naked, for almost a quarter of an hour, with his arms stretched out like a cross and motionless. The canoes were not constructed of wood as at King George's or Nootka Sound. The frame only, being slender laths, was of that substance; the outside consisting of the skins of seals or of such like animals.[1] Though we returned all their signs of friendship, and by every expressive gesture tried to encourage them to come alongside, we could not prevail. Some of our people repeated several of the common words of the Nootka language, such as "seekemaile" and "mahook;"[2] but they did not seem to understand them. After receiving some presents which were thrown to them, they retired toward that part of the shore whence they came; giving us to understand by signs that they would visit us again the next morning. Two of them, however, each in a small canoe, waited upon us in the night; probably with a design to pilfer something, thinking we should be all asleep, for they retired as soon as they found themselves discovered.

During the night the wind was at SSE., blowing hard and in squalls, with rain and very thick weather. At 10 o'clock next morning the wind became more moderate, and the weather being somewhat clearer we got under sail, in order to look out for some snug place where we might search for and stop the leak; our present station being too much exposed for this purpose. At first I proposed to have gone up the bay before which we had anchored; but the clearness of the weather tempted me to steer to the northward, farther up the great inlet, as being all in our way. As soon as we had passed the north-west point of the bay above mentioned, we found the coast on that side to turn short to the east-

ward. I did not follow it, but continued our course to the north, for a point of land which we saw in that direction. The natives who visited us the preceding evening came off again in the morning, in five or six canoes, but not till we were under sail; and although they followed us for some time they could not get up with us. Before two in the afternoon the bad weather returned again, with so thick a haze that we could see no other land besides the point just mentioned, which we reached at half-past four, and found it to be a small island, lying about two miles from the adjacent coast, being a point of land on the east side of which we discovered a fine bay or rather harbour. To this we plied up under reefed topsails and courses. The wind blew strong at SE., and in excessively hard squalls, with rain. At intervals we could see land in every direction; but in general the weather was so foggy that we could see none but the shores of the bay into which we were plying. In passing the island the depth of water was twenty-six fathoms, with a muddy bottom. Soon after the depth increased to sixty and seventy fathoms, a rocky bottom; but in the entrance of the bay the depth was from thirty to six fathoms, the last very near the shore. At length, at 8 o'clock, the violence of the squalls obliged us to anchor in thirteen fathoms, before we had got so far into the bay as I intended; but we thought ourselves fortunate that we had already sufficiently secured ourselves at this hour, for the night was exceedingly stormy.

The weather, bad as it was, did not hinder three of the natives from paying us a visit. They came off in two canoes; two men in one, and one in the other, being the number each could carry. For they were built and constructed in the same manner with those of the Esquimaux; only in the one were two holes for two men to sit in, and in the other but one. Each of these men had a stick about three feet long, with the large feathers or wing of birds tied to it. These they frequently held up to us, with a view,

---

[1] Like the "oomyaks," or women's canoes, of the Greenlanders; as to which Dr Rae, of Arctic renown, has given such a pleasant description of his experiences, in "The Land of Desolation."

[2] "Iron" or metal; and "barter."

as we guessed, to express their pacific disposition. The treatment these men met with induced many more to visit us, between one and two the next morning, in both great and small canoes. Some ventured on board the ship, but not till some of our people had stepped into their boats. Amongst those who came on board was a good-looking middle-aged man, whom we afterward found to be the chief. He was clothed in a dress made of the sea-otter's skin, and had on his head such a cap as is worn by the people of King George's Sound, ornamented with sky-blue glass beads about the size of a large pea. He seemed to set a much higher value upon these than upon our white glass beads. Any sort of beads, however, appeared to be in high estimation with these people; and they readily gave whatever they had in exchange for them, even their fine sea-otter skins. But here I must observe that they set no more value upon these than upon other skins, which was also the case at King George's Sound till our people set a higher price upon them; and even after that the natives of both places would sooner part with a dress made of these than with one made of the skins of wildcats or of martins.

These people were also desirous of iron; but they wanted pieces eight or ten inches long at least, and of the breadth of three or four fingers; for they absolutely rejected small pieces. Consequently they got but little from us, iron having by this time become rather a scarce article. The points of some of their spears or lances were of that metal, others were of copper, and a few of bone, of which the points of their darts, arrows, &c., were composed. I could not prevail upon the chief to trust himself below the upper deck; nor did he and his companions remain long on board. But while we had their company it was necessary to watch them narrowly, as they soon betrayed a thievish disposition. At length, after being about three or four hours alongside the Resolution, they all left her and went to the Discovery; none having been there before except

one man, who, at this time came from her, and immediately returned thither in company with the rest. When I observed this, I thought this man had met with something there which he knew would please his countrymen better than what they met with at our ship. But in this I was mistaken, as will soon appear.

As soon as they were gone I sent a boat to sound the head of the bay. For as the wind was moderate I had thoughts of laying the ship ashore, if a convenient place could be found where I might begin our operations to stop the leak. It was not long before all the Americans left the Discovery, and, instead of returning to us, made their way toward our boat employed as above. The officer in her, seeing this, returned to the ship, and was followed by all the canoes. The boat's crew had no sooner come on board, leaving in her two of their number by way of a guard, than some of the Americans stepped into her. Some presented their spears before the two men; others cast loose the rope which fastened her to the ship; and the rest attempted to tow her away. But the instant they saw us preparing to oppose them they let her go, stepped out of her into canoes, and made signs to us to lay down our arms, having the appearance of being as perfectly unconcerned as if they had done nothing amiss. This, though rather a more daring attempt, was hardly equal to what they had meditated on board the Discovery. The man who came and carried all his countrymen from the Resolution to the other ship had first been on board of her; where, after looking down all the hatchways, and seeing nobody but the officer of the watch and one or two more, he no doubt thought they might plunder her with ease; especially as she lay at some distance from us. It was unquestionably with this view that they all repaired to her. Several of them, without any ceremony, went on board, drew their knives, made signs to the officer and people on deck to keep off, and began to look about them for plunder. The first thing they met with was the rudder of one of the boats, which they threw overboard to those of their party who had remained in the canoes. Before they had time to find another object that pleased their fancy, the crew were alarmed, and began to come upon deck armed with cutlasses. On seeing this, the whole company of plunderers sneaked off into their canoes with as much deliberation and indifference as they had given up the boat; and they were observed describing, to those who had not been on board, how much longer the knives of the ship's crew were than their own. It was at this time that my boat was on the sounding duty, which they must have seen, for they proceeded directly for her after their disappointment at the Discovery. I have not the least doubt that their visiting us so very early in the morning was with a view to plunder, on the supposition that they should find everybody asleep. May we not from these circumstances reasonably infer that these people are unacquainted with fire-arms! For certainly, if they had known anything of their effect, they never would have dared to attempt taking a boat from under a ship's guns in the face of above 100 men; for most of my people were looking at them at the very instant they made the attempt. However, after all these tricks, we had the good fortune to leave them as ignorant in this respect as we found them; for they neither heard nor saw a musket fired unless at birds.

Just as we were going to weigh the anchor to proceed farther up the bay, it began to blow and to rain as hard as before, so that we were obliged to veer away the cable again and lay fast. Towards the evening, finding that the gale did not moderate, and that it might be some time before an opportunity offered to get higher up, I came to a resolution to heel the ship where we were; and with this view moored her with a kedge-anchor and hawser. In heaving the anchor out of the boat, one of the seamen, either through ignorance or carelessness, or both, was carried overboard by the buoy-rope, and

followed the anchor to the bottom. It is remarkable that in this very critical situation he had presence of mind to disengage himself, and come up to the surface of the water, where he was taken up with one of his legs fractured in a dangerous manner. Early the next morning we gave the ship a good heel to port, in order to come at and stop the leak. On ripping off the sheathing, it was found to be in the seams, which were very open both in and under the wale; and in several places not a bit of oakum in them. While the carpenters were making good these defects, we filled all our empty water-casks at a stream hard by the ship. The wind was now moderate, but the weather was thick and hazy, with rain. The natives, who left us the preceding day, when the bad weather came on, paid us another visit this morning. Those who came first were in small canoes; others afterwards arrived in large boats, in one of which were twenty women and one man, besides children.

In the evening of the 16th the weather cleared up, and we then found ourselves surrounded on every side by land. Our station was on the east side of the sound, in a place which in the chart is distinguished by the name of Snug Corner Bay. And a very snug place it is. I went, accompanied by some of the officers, to view the head of it; and we found that it was sheltered from all winds, with a depth of water from seven to three fathoms over a muddy bottom. The land near the shore is low, part clear and part wooded. The clear ground was covered two or three feet thick with snow, but very little lay in the woods. The very summits of the neighbouring hills were covered with wood, but those farther inland seemed to be naked rocks buried in snow.

The leak being stopped, and the sheathing made good over it, at 4 o'clock in the morning of the 17th we weighed and steered to the northwestward, with a light breeze at ENE., thinking if there should be any passage to the north through this inlet that it must be in that direction. At length, about 1 o'clock, with the assistance of our boats, we got to an anchor under the eastern shore in thirteen fathoms water, and about four leagues to the north of our last station. In the morning the weather had been very hazy, but it afterwards cleared up so as to give us a distinct view of all the land round us, particularly to the northward, where it seemed to close. This left us but little hopes of finding a passage that way, or indeed in any other direction, without putting out again to sea.

To enable me to form a better judgment, I despatched Mr Gore with two armed boats to examine the northern arm, and the master with two other boats to examine another arm that seemed to take an easterly direction. Late in the evening they both returned. The master reported that the arm he had been sent to communicated with that from which he had last come, and that one side of it was only formed by a group of islands. Mr Gore informed me that he had seen the entrance of an arm which, he was of opinion, extended a long way to the north-east, and that probably by it a passage might be found. On the other hand, Mr Roberts, one of the mates whom I had sent with Mr Gore to sketch out the parts they had examined, was of opinion that they saw the head of this arm. The disagreement of these two opinions, and the circumstance already mentioned of the flood-tide entering the sound from the south, rendered the existence of a passage this way very doubtful. And as the wind in the morning had become favourable for getting out to sea, I resolved to spend no more time in searching for a passage in a place that promised so little success. Besides this, I considered that if the land on the west should prove to be islands, agreeably to the late Russian discoveries, we could not fail of getting far enough to the north, and that in good time, provided we did not lose the season in searching places where a passage was not only doubtful but improbable. We were now upwards of 520 leagues to the westward of any

part of Baffin's or of Hudson's Bay; and whatever passage there may be, it must be, or at least part of it must lie, to the north of Latitude 72°. Who could expect to find a passage or strait of such extent?[1]

"[To this wide inlet which he had entered, Cook gave] the name of Prince William's Sound, and here was surprised to find that the natives, in dress, language, and physical peculiarities, were exactly like the Esquimaux of Hudson's Bay. Beautiful skins were obtained in plenty from these people for a very moderate price. On proceeding to the north-west, a wide inlet was discovered, which some conjectured might be a strait communicating with the Northern Ocean. It was deemed, therefore, advisable to explore it ; but when the boats had proceeded as high as Lat. 61° 34', or about seventy leagues from the entrance, the inlet appeared to terminate in a small river. The ships now proceeded to the west, and doubled the great promontory of Alashka ; and, on the 9th of August, they reached the most westerly point of the American continent, distant only thirteen leagues from the opposite shores of Asia. To this headland Cook gave the name Cape Prince of Wales. Crossing the strait to the western shores, he anchored near the coast of the Tshuktzki, which he found to extend many degrees farther to the east than the position assigned to them in the maps of that day. He thus ascertained distinctly the width of the strait that separates Asia from America ; for though Behring had sailed through it before, he had not descried the shores of the latter continent, and, consequently, remained ignorant of the importance of his discoveries. Our navigators now pushed forward into the Northern Ocean, when they soon

---

[1] The synopsis of remainder of Chapter IV. to middle of Chapter IX., Book IV., in Original Edition, is given from "Maritime and Inland Discovery," in Lardner's "Cabinet Cyclopædia," vol. iii., pp. 80, 81.

fell in with ice, which gave them reason to suspect the impossibility of continuing their voyage much farther. At length, on the 18th of August, when after repeated struggles they had attained the Latitude of 70° 44', they saw the ice before them, extending as far as the eye could reach, forming a compact wall about six feet high : it was covered with a multitude of walruses or sea-horses, which though coarse food, were preferred by the seamen to salt provisions."

We now stood to the southward, and after running six leagues shoaled the water to seven fathoms ; but it soon deepened to nine fathoms. At this time the weather, which had been hazy, clearing up a little; we saw land extending from S. to SE. by E. about three or four miles distant. The eastern extreme forms a point which was much encumbered with ice ; for which reason it obtained the name of Icy Cape. Its latitude is 70° 29' and its longitude 198° 20'. The other extreme of the land was lost in the horizon, so that there can be no doubt of its being a continuation of the American continent. The Discovery being about a mile astern and to leeward, found less water than we did ; and tacking on that account, I was obliged to tack also to prevent separation. Our situation was now more and more critical. We were in shoal water, upon a lee shore, and the main body of the ice to windward, driving down upon us. It was evident that if we remained much longer between it and the land, it would force us ashore, unless it should happen to take the ground before us. It seemed nearly to join the land to leeward, and the only direction that was open was to the SW. After making a short board to the northward, I made the signal for the Discovery to tack, and tacked myself at the same time. The wind proved rather favourable; so that we lay up SW. and SW. by W.

At eight in the morning of the 19th, the wind veering back to W., I tacked to the northward ; and at noon the latitude was 70° 6' and the longitude 196° 42'. In this situation we had a good deal of drift-ice about us, and the main ice was about two leagues to the north. At half-past one we got in with the edge of it. It was not so compact as that which we had seen to the northward ; but it was too close, and in too large pieces, to attempt forcing the ships through it. On the ice lay a prodigious number of sea-horses;[1] and as we were in want of fresh provisions, the boats from each ship were sent to get some. By 7 o'clock in the evening we had received on board the Resolution nine of these animals, which till now we had supposed to be sea-cows ; so that we were not a little disappointed, especially some of the seamen, who for the novelty of the thing had been feasting their eyes for some days past. Nor would they have been disappointed now, nor have known the difference, if we had not happened to have one or two on board who had been in Greenland, and declared what animals these were, and that no one ever ate of them. But notwithstanding this we lived upon them as long as they lasted; and there were few on board who did not prefer them to our salt meat. The fat at first is as sweet as marrow, but in a few days it grows rancid, unless it be salted; in which state it will keep much longer. The lean flesh is coarse, black, and has rather a strong taste ; and the heart is nearly as well tasted as that of a bullock. The fat, when melted, yields a good deal of oil, which burns very well in lamps; and their hides, which are very thick, were very useful about our rigging. The teeth or tusks of most of them were at this time very small; even some of the largest and oldest of these animals had them not exceeding six inches in length. From this we concluded that they had lately shed their old teeth. They lie in herds of many hundreds upon the ice, huddling one over the other like swine ; and roar or bray very loud, so that in the night or in

---

[1] Walrus.

foggy weather they gave us notice of the vicinity of the ice before we could see it. We never found the whole herd asleep, some being always upon the watch. These, on the approach of the boat, would wake those next to them, and the alarm being thus gradually communicated, the whole herd would be awake presently. But they were seldom in a hurry to get away till after they had been once fired at. Then they would tumble one over the other into the sea in the utmost confusion; and if we did not at the first discharge kill those we fired at, we generally lost them, though mortally wounded. They did not appear to us to be that dangerous animal some authors have described, not even when attacked. They are rather more so to appearance than in reality. Vast numbers of them would follow and come close up to the boats; but the flash of a musket in the pan, or even the bare pointing of one at them, would send them down in an instant. The female will defend the young one to the very last, and at the expense of her own life, whether in the water or upon the ice. Nor will the young one quit the dam though she be dead; so that if you kill one you are sure of the other. The dam, when in the water, holds the young one between her fore-fins. Why they should be called sea-horses is hard to say, unless the word be a corruption of the Russian name "morse," for they have not the least resemblance of a horse. This is without doubt the same animal that is found in the Gulf of St Lawrence, and there called sea-cow. It is certainly more like a cow than a horse, but this likeness consists in nothing but the snout. In short, it is an animal like a seal, but incomparably larger. The dimensions and weight of one, which was none of the largest, were as follows:

		Ft.	In.
Length from the snout to the tail,	. . . . .	9	4
Length of the neck from the snout to the shoulder-bone,		2	6
Height of the shoulder,	.	5	0

			Ft.	In.
Length of the fins,	Fore,	.	2	4
	Hind,	.	2	6
Breadth of the fins,	Fore,	.	1	2½
	Hind,	.	2	0
Snout,	Breadth,	. .	0	5½
	Depth,	. . .	1	3
Circumference of the neck close to the ears,		.	2	7
Circumference of the body at the shoulder,		. .	7	10
Circumference near the hind fins,		. . .	5	6
From the snout to the eyes,		.	0	7

	Lb.
Weight of the carcase, without the head, skin, or entrails,	854
Head, ...	41½
Skin, ...	205

I could not find out what these animals feed upon. There was nothing in the maws of those we killed.

It is worth observing that for some days before this date we had frequently seen flocks of ducks flying to the southward. They were of two sorts, the one much larger than the other. The largest were of a brown colour; and of the small sort either the duck or drake was black and white, and the other brown. Some said they saw geese also. Does not this indicate that there must be land to the north where these birds find shelter in the proper season, to breed, and whence they were now returning to a warmer climate?

By the time we had got our sea-horses on board, we were in a manner surrounded with the ice, and had no way left to clear it but by standing to the southward; which was done till 3 o'clock next morning, with a gentle breeze westerly, and for the most part thick, foggy weather. The soundings were from twelve to fifteen fathoms. We then tacked and stood to the north till 10 o'clock, when, the wind veering to the northward, we directed our course to the WSW. and W. At two in the afternoon we fell in with the main ice, along the edge of which we kept; being partly directed by the roaring of the sea-horses, for we had a very thick fog. Thus we continued sailing till near midnight, when we got in amongst the loose ice, and heard the surge of the sea upon the main ice. The fog being very thick, and the wind easterly, I now hauled to the southward; and at 10 o'clock the next morning, the fog clearing away, we saw the continent of America, extending from S. by E. to E. by S.; and at noon from SW. half S. to E., the nearest part five leagues distant. At this time we were in the Latitude of 69° 32′ and in the Longitude of 195° 48′; and as the main ice was at no great distance from us, it is evident that it now covered a part of the sea which but a few days before had been clear, and that it extended farther to the south than where we first fell in with it. It must not be understood that I supposed any part of this ice which we had seen to be fixed; on the contrary, I am well assured that the whole was a movable mass.

Having but little wind, in the afternoon I sent the master in a boat to try if there was any current; but he found none. I continued to steer in for the American land until 8 o'clock, in order to get a nearer view of it, and to look for a harbour; but seeing nothing like one, I stood again to the north, with a light breeze westerly. At this time the coast extended from SW. to E.; the nearest part four or five leagues distant. The southern extreme seemed to form a point, which was named Cape Lisburne. It lies in the Latitude of 69° 5′ and in the Longitude of 194° 42′, and appeared to be pretty high land, even down to the sea. But there may be low land under it which we might not see, being not less than ten leagues from it. Everywhere else, as we advanced northward, we had found a low coast from which the land rises to a middle height. The coast now before us was without snow, except in one or two places, and had a greenish hue; but we could not perceive any wood upon it.

On the 22d the wind was southerly, and the weather mostly foggy, with some intervals of sunshine. At eight in the evening it fell calm, which continued till midnight, when we heard the surge of the sea against the ice, and had several loose pieces about us. A light breeze now sprang up at NE., and as the fog was very thick, I steered to the southward to clear the ice. At 8 o'clock next morning the fog dispersed, and I hauled to the westward. For finding that I could not get to the north near the coast on account of the ice, I resolved to try what could be done at a distance from it; and as the wind seemed to be settled at N. I thought it a good opportunity. As we advanced to the W., the water deepened gradually to twenty-eight fathoms, which was the most we had. With the northerly wind the air was raw, sharp, and cold; and we had fogs, sunshine, showers of snow and sleet, by turns. At ten in the morning of the 26th we fell in with the ice. At noon, it extended from NW. to E. by N., and appeared to be thick and compact. At this time we were by observation in the Latitude of 69° 36′, and in the Longitude of 184°, so that it now appeared we had no better prospect of getting to the north here than nearer the shore. I continued to stand to the westward till five in the afternoon, when we were in a manner embayed by the ice, which appeared high, and very close in the NW. and NE. quarters, with a great deal of loose ice about the edge of the main field. At this time we had baffling light winds, but it soon fixed at S., and increased to a fresh gale, with showers of rain. We got the tack aboard and stretched to the eastward, this being the only direction in which the sea was clear of ice.

At four in the morning of the 27th we tacked and stood to the W., and at seven in the evening we were close in with the edge of the ice, which lay ENE. and WSW., as far each way as the eye could reach. Having but little wind, I went with the boats to examine the state of the ice. I found it consisting of loose pieces of various extent, and so close together that I could hardly enter the outer edge with a boat; and it was as impossible for the ships to enter it as if it had been so many rocks. I took particular notice that it was all pure, transparent ice, except the upper surface, which was a little porous. It appeared to be entirely composed of frozen snow, and to have been all formed at sea. For setting aside the improbability, or rather impossibility, of such huge masses floating out of rivers in which there is hardly water for a boat, none of the productions of the land were found incorporated or fixed in it, which must have unavoidably been the case had it been formed in rivers either great or small. The pieces of ice that formed the outer edge of the field were from forty to fifty yards in extent to four or five ; and I judged that the larger pieces reached thirty feet or more under the surface of the water. It also appeared to me very improbable that this ice could have been the production of the preceding winter alone; I should suppose it rather to have been the production of a great many winters. Nor was it less improbable, according to my judgment, that the little that remained of the summer could destroy the tenth part of what now subsisted of this mass; for the sun had already exerted upon it the full influence of its rays. Indeed I am of opinion that the sun contributes very little toward reducing these great masses. For although that luminary is a considerable while above the horizon, it seldom shines out for more than a few hours at a time, and is not seen for several days in succession. It is the wind, or rather the waves raised by the wind, that bring down the bulk of these enormous masses, by grinding one piece against another, and by undermining and washing away those parts that lie exposed to the surge of the sea. This was evident from our observing that the upper surface of many pieces had been partly washed away, while the base or under part remained firm for several fathoms round that which appeared above water, exactly like a shoal round an elevated rock. We measured the depth of water upon one, and found it to be fifteen feet, so that the ships might have sailed over it. If I had not measured this depth I should not have believed that there was a sufficient weight of ice above the surface to have sunk the other so much below it. Thus it may happen that more ice is destroyed in one stormy season than is formed in several winters, and an endless accumulation is prevented. But that there is always a remaining store, every one who has been upon the spot will conclude, and none but closet-studying philosophers will dispute. A thick fog which came on while I was thus employed with the boats hastened me aboard rather sooner than I could have wished, with one sea-horse to each ship. We had killed more, but could not wait to bring them with us. The number of these animals on all the ice that we had seen is almost incredible. We spent the night standing off and on amongst the drift ice ; and at 9 o'clock the next morning, the fog having partly dispersed, boats from each ship were sent for seahorses. For by this time our people began to relish them, and those we had procured before were all consumed. At noon our Latitude was 69° 17', our Longitude 183°. At 2 o'clock, having got on board as much marine beef as was thought necessary, and the wind freshening at SSE., we took on board the boats and stretched to the SW. But not being able to weather the ice upon this tack, or to go through it, we made a board to the E. till 8 o'clock, then resumed our course to the SW., and before midnight were obliged to tack again on account of the ice. Soon after the wind shifted to the NW., blowing a stiff gale, and we stretched to the SW. close hauled.

In the morning of the 29th we saw the main ice to the northward, and not long after, land bearing SW. by W. Presently after this more land showed itself, bearing W. It showed itself in two hills like islands, but afterwards the whole appeared connected. As we approached the land, the depth of water decreased very fast, so that at noon, when we tacked, we had only eight fathoms, being three miles from the coast, which extended from S. 30° E. to N. 60° W. This last extreme terminated in a bluff point, being one of the hills above mentioned. The weather at this time was very hazy, with drizzling rain, but soon after it cleared, especially to the southward, westward, and northward. This enabled us to have a pretty good view of the coast, which in every respect is like the opposite one of America; that is, low land next the sea, with elevated land farther back. It was perfectly destitute of wood, and even snow, but was probably covered with a mossy substance that gave it a brownish cast. In the low ground lying between the high land and the sea was a lake extending to the SE. farther than we could see. As we stood off, the westernmost of the two hills before mentioned came open off the bluff point in the direction of NW. It had the appearance of being an island; but it might be joined to the other by low land, though we did not see it; and if so there is a two-fold point, with a bay between them. This point, which is steep and rocky, was named Cape North. Its situation is nearly in the Latitude of 68° 56', and in the Longitude of 180° 51'. The coast beyond it must take a very westerly direction, for we could see no land to the northward of it, though the horizon was there pretty clear. Being desirous of seeing more of the coast to the westward, we tacked again at 2 o'clock in the afternoon, thinking we could weather Cape North; but finding we could not, the wind freshening, a thick fog coming on with much snow, and being fearful of the ice coming down upon us, I gave up the design I had formed of plying to the westward, and stood off shore again.

The season was now so far advanced, and the time when the frost is expected to set in so near at hand, that I did not think it consistent with prudence to make any further attempts to find a passage into the Atlantic this year in any direction, so little was the prospect of succeeding. My attention was now directed toward finding out some place where we might supply ourselves with wood and water; and the object uppermost in my thoughts was how I should spend the winter so as to make some improvements in geography and navigation, and at the same time be in a condition to return to the north in further search of a passage the ensuing summer.

CHAPTER V.[1]

AFTER having stood off till we got into eighteen fathoms water, I bore up to the eastward along the coast, which by this time it was pretty certain could only be the continent of Asia. As the wind blew fresh, with a very heavy fall of snow and a thick mist, it was necessary to proceed with great caution. I therefore brought to for a few hours in the night.

At daybreak on the 30th we made sail, and steered such a course as I thought would bring us in with the land, being in a great measure guided by the lead; for the weather was as thick as ever, and it snowed incessantly. At ten we got sight of the coast, bearing SW. four miles distant, and presently after, having shoaled the water to seven fathoms, we hauled off. At this time a very low point or spit bore SSW. four miles distant, to the E. of which there appeared to be a narrow channel leading into some water that we saw over the point. Probably the lake before mentioned communicates here with the sea. At noon, the mist dispersing for a short interval, we had a tolerably good view of the coast, which extended from SE. to NW. by W. Some parts appeared higher than others, but in general it was very low, with high land farther up the country. The whole was now covered with snow, which had lately fallen, quite down to the sea. I continued to range along the coast at two leagues' distance till ten at night, when we hauled off; but we resumed our course

---

[1] Chapter X. in Original Edition.

next morning soon after daybreak, when we got sight of the coast again, extending from W. to SE. by S. At eight the eastern part bore S., and proved to be an island, which at noon bore SW. half S. four or five miles distant. It is about four or five miles in circuit, of a middling height, with a steep, rocky coast, situated about three leagues from the main, in the Latitude of 67° 45', and distinguished in the chart by the name of Burney's Island. The inland country hereabouts is full of hills, some of which are of a considerable height. The land was covered with snow, except a few spots upon the sea-coast, which still continued low, but less so than farther westward. For the two preceding days the main height of the mercury in the thermometer had been very little above the freezing point, and often below it; so that the water in the vessels upon the deck was frequently covered with a sheet of ice.

I continued to steer SSE., nearly in the direction of the coast, till five in the afternoon, when land was seen bearing S. 50° E., which we presently found to be a continuation of the coast, and hauled up for it. Being abreast of the eastern land at ten at night, and in doubts of weathering it, we tacked and made a board to the westward till past one the next morning, when we stood again to the E., and found that it was as much as we could do to keep our distance from the coast; the wind being exceedingly unsettled, varying continually from N. to NE. At half-an-hour past eight, the eastern extreme above mentioned bore S. by E. six or seven miles distant. At the same time a headland appeared in sight bearing E. by S. half S., and soon after we could trace the whole coast lying between them, and a small island at some distance from it. The coast seemed to form several rocky points, connected by a low shore, without the least appearance of a harbour. At some distance from the sea the low land appeared to swell into a number of hills. The highest of these were covered with snow, and in other respects the whole country seemed naked. At seven in the evening two points of land, at some distance beyond the eastern head, opened off it in the direction of S. 37° E. I was now well assured of what I had believed before, that this was the country of the Tschutski, or the north-east coast of Asia, and that thus far Behring proceeded in 1728; that is, to this head, which Muller says is called Serdze Kamen, on account of a rock upon it shaped like a heart. But I conceive that Mr Muller's knowledge of the geography of these parts is very imperfect. There are many elevated rocks upon this cape, and possibly some one or other of them may have the shape of a heart. It is a pretty lofty promontory, with a steep rocky cliff facing the sea, and lies in the Latitude of 67° 3', and in the Longitude of 188° 11'. To the eastward of it the coast is high and bold; but to the westward it is low, and trends NNW. and NW. by W., which is nearly its direction all the way to Cape North. The soundings are everywhere the same at the same distance from the shore, which is also the case on the opposite shore of America. The greatest depth we found in ranging along it was twenty-three fathoms. And in the night, or in foggy weather, the soundings are no bad guide in sailing along either of these shores.

At 8 o'clock in the morning of the 2d the most advanced land to the SE. bore S. 25° E., and from this point of view had the appearance of being an island. But the thick snow showers which succeeded one another pretty fast, and settled upon the land, hid great part of the coast at this time from our sight. Soon after, the sun, whose face we had not seen for near five days, broke out at intervals between the showers, and in some measure freed the coast from the fog, so that we had a sight of it, and found the whole to be connected. The wind still continued at N., the air was cold, and the mercury in the thermometer never rose above 35° and was sometimes as low as 30°. At noon, the observed Latitude was 66°

37'. We had now fair weather and sunshine; and as we ranged along the coast, at the distance of four miles, we saw several of the inhabitants, and some of their habitations, which looked like little hillocks of earth. In the evening we passed the Eastern Cape, or the point above mentioned, from which the coast changes its direction and trends SW. It is the same point of land which we had passed on the 11th of August. They who believed implicitly in Mr Stæhlin's map then thought it the east point of his island Alashka; but we had by this time satisfied ourselves that it is no other than the eastern promontory of Asia, and probably the proper Tschukotskoi Noss, though the promontory to which Behring gave that name is farther to the SW. It is a peninsula of considerable height, joined to the continent by a very low and, to appearance, narrow neck of land. It shows a steep rocky cliff next the sea, and off the very point are some rocks like spires. It is situated in the Latitude of 66° 6', and in the Longitude of 190° 22', and is distant, from Cape Prince of Wales, on the American coast, thirteen leagues, in the direction of N. 53° W. The land about this promontory is composed of hills and valleys. The former terminate at the sea in steep rocky points, and the latter in low shores. The hills seemed to be naked rocks, but the valleys had a greenish hue, but destitute of tree or shrub.[1]

After passing the cape, I steered SW. half W., for the northern point of St Laurence Bay, in which we had anchored on the 10th of last month. We reached it by 8 o'clock next morning, and saw some of the inha-

bitants at the place where I had seen them before, as well as several others on the opposite side of the bay. None of them, however, attempted to come off to us; which seemed a little extraordinary, as the weather was favourable enough, and those whom we had lately visited had no reason that I know of to dislike our company. These people must be the Tschutski; a nation that, at the time Mr Muller wrote, the Russians had not been able to conquer. And from the whole of their conduct with us it appears that they have not as yet brought them under subjection; though it is obvious that they must have a trade with the Russians, either directly or by means of some neighbouring nation, as we cannot otherwise account for their being in possession of the spontoons, in particular, of which we took notice.

This Bay of St Laurence[2] is at least five leagues broad at the entrance, and four leagues deep, narrowing toward the bottom, where it appeared to be tolerably well sheltered from the sea-winds, provided there be sufficient depth of water for ships. I did not wait to examine it, although I was very desirous of finding an harbour in those parts to which I might resort next spring. But I wanted one where wood might be got, and I knew that none was to be found here. From the south point of this bay, which lies in the Latitude of 65° 30', the coast trends W. by S. for about nine leagues, and there forms a deep bay or river; or else the land there is so low that we could not see it. At one in the afternoon, in the direction of our course, we saw what was first taken for a rock; but it proved to be a dead whale, which some natives of the Asiatic coast had killed and were tow-

---

[1] Deshniew's voyage in 1648, in quest of the Anadir River, is considered the only one before Cook's in which the north-eastern extremity of Asia was doubled. The Cossack navigator set out from the Kolima river in northern Siberia, and passed southwards through Behring's Straits—not then, of course, so named, or named at all—to the mouth of the Anadir.

[2] Captain Cook gives it this name, having anchored in it on St Laurence's day, August 10. It is remarkable that Behring sailed past this very place on the 10th of August 1728; on which account the neighbouring island was named by him after the same saint.—*Note in Original Edition.*

ing ashore. They seemed to conceal themselves behind the fish to avoid being seen by us. This was unnecessary; for we pursued our course without taking any notice of them.

At daybreak on the 4th I hauled to the NW., in order to get a nearer view of the inlet seen the preceding day; but the wind soon after veering to that direction I gave up the design, and, steering to the southward along the coast, passed two bays, each about two leagues deep. The northernmost lies before a hill which is remarkable by being rounder than any other upon the coast; and there is an island lying before the other. It may be doubted whether there be a sufficient depth for ships in either of these bays, as we always met with shoal water when we edged in for the shore. The country here is exceedingly hilly and naked. In several places on the low ground next the sea were the dwellings of the natives: and near all of them were erected stages of bones, such as before described. These may be seen at a great distance on account of their whiteness. At noon the Latitude was 64° 38′ and the Longitude 188° 15′; the southernmost point of the main in sight bore S. 48° W., and the nearest shore about three or four leagues distant. By this time the wind had veered again to the N., and blew a gentle breeze. The weather was clear, and the air cold. I did not follow the direction of the coast, as I found that it took [a westerly direction toward the Gulf of Anadir, into which I had no inducement to go, but steered to the southward, in order to get a sight of the Island of St Laurence, discovered by Behring; which accordingly showed itself, and at 8 o'clock in the evening it bore S. 20° E., by estimation, eleven leagues distant. At the same time the southernmost point of the mainland bore S. 83° W., distant twelve leagues. I take this point to be the point which Behring calls the East Point of Suchotski, or Cape Tschukotskoi; a name which he gave it, and with propriety, because it was from this part of the coast that the natives came off to him

who called themselves of the nation of the Tschutski. I make its Latitude to be 64° 13′ and its Longitude 186° 36′.

In justice to the memory of Behring, I must say that he has delineated the coast very well, and fixed the latitude and longitude of the points better than could be expected from the methods he had to go by. This judgment is not formed from Mr Muller's account of the voyage, or the chart prefixed to his book; but from Dr Campbell's account of it in his edition of Harris's Collection, and a map thereto annexed, which is both more circumstantial and accurate than that of Mr Muller. The more I was convinced of my being now upon the coast of Asia, the more I was at a loss to reconcile Mr Stæhlin's map of the New Northern Archipelago with my observations; and I had no way to account for the great difference, but by supposing that I had mistaken some part of what he calls the Island of Alashka for the American continent, and had missed the channel that separates them. Admitting even this, there would still have been a considerable difference. It was with me a matter of some consequence to clear up this point the present season, that I might have but one object in view the next. And, as these northern isles are represented by him as abounding with wood, I was in hopes, if I should find them, of getting a supply of that article, which we now began to be in great want of on board. With these views I steered over for the American coast, and at five in the afternoon the next day saw land bearing three-quarters E., which we took to be Anderson's Island or some other land near it, and therefore did not wait to examine it. On the 6th, at four in the morning, we got sight of the American coast near Sledge Island; and at six the same evening this island bore N. 6° E., ten leagues distant, and the easternmost land in sight N. 49° E. If any part of what I had supposed to be American coast could possibly be the Island of Alashka, it was that now before us; and in that case I must have missed the channel between it and the main, by steering to the west instead of the east after we first fell in with it. I was not, therefore, at a loss where to go in order to clear up these doubts.

At eight in the evening of the 7th we had got close in with the land, Sledge Island bearing N. 85° W., eight or nine leagues distant; and the eastern part of the coast N. 70° E., with high land in the direction of E. by N., seemingly at a great distance beyond the point. At this time we saw a light ashore, and two canoes filled with people coming off toward us. I brought to, that they might have time to come up. But it was to no purpose; for, resisting all the signs of friendship we could exhibit, they kept at a distance of a quarter of a mile, so that we left them and pursued our course along the coast. At one in the morning of the 8th, finding the water shoal pretty fast, we dropped anchor in ten fathoms, where we lay until daylight, and then resumed our course along the coast, which we found to trend E. and E. half S. At seven in the evening we were abreast of a point lying in the Latitude of 64° 21', and in the Longitude of 197°; beyond which the coast takes a more northerly direction. At eight this point, which obtained the name of Cape Darby, bore S. 62° W.; the northernmost land in sight, N. 32° E.; and the nearest shore three miles distant. In this situation we anchored in thirteen fathoms water, over a muddy bottom.

Next morning at daybreak we weighed and sailed along the coast. Two islands, as we supposed them to be, were at this time seen; the one bearing S. 70° E. and the other E. Soon after, we found ourselves upon a coast covered with wood; an agreeable sight, to which of late we had not been accustomed. As we advanced to the north, we raised land in the direction of NE. half N., which proved to be a continuation of the coast we were upon. We also saw high land over the islands, seemingly at a good distance beyond them. This was thought to be the continent, and the other land the Island of Alashka. But it was already doubtful whether we should find a passage between them; for the water shoaled insensibly as we advanced farther to the north. In this situation, two boats were sent to sound before the ships; and I ordered the Discovery to lead, keeping nearly in the mid-channel between the coast on our larboard and the northernmost island on our starboard. Thus we proceeded till three in the afternoon, when, having passed the island, we had not more than three fathoms and a half of water; and the Resolution at one time brought the mud up from the bottom. More water was not to be found in any part of the channel; for, with the ships and boats, we had tried it from side to side. I therefore thought it high time to return, especially as the wind was in such a quarter that we must ply back. But what I dreaded most was the wind increasing, and raising the sea into waves, so as to put the ships in danger of striking. At this time a headland on the west shore, which is distinguished by the name of Bald Head, bore N. by W., one league distant. The coast beyond it extended as far as NE. by N., where it seemed to end in a point, behind which the coast of the high land, seen over the islands, stretched itself; and some thought they could trace where it joined. On the west side of Bald Head the shore forms a bay, in the bottom of which is a low beach, where we saw a number of huts or habitations of the natives.

Having continued to ply back all night, by daybreak the next morning we had got into six fathoms water. At 9 o'clock, being about a league from the west shore, I took two boats and landed, attended by Mr King, to seek wood and water. We landed where the coast projects out into a bluff head, composed of perpendicular strata of a rock of a dark blue colour, mixed with quartz and glimmer. There joins to the beach a narrow border of land, now covered with long grass, where we met with some *Angel-*

ica. Beyond this the ground rises abruptly. At the top of this elevation we found a heath abounding with a variety of berries ; and farther on the country was level, and thinly covered with small spruce trees and birch and willows no bigger than broom stuff. We observed tracks of deer and foxes on the beach, on which also lay a great quantity of drift-wood ; and there was no want of fresh water. I returned on board with an intention to bring the ships to an anchor here ; but the wind then veering to NE., which blew rather on this shore, I stretched over to the opposite one in the expectation of finding wood there also, and anchored at 8 o'clock in the evening under the south end of the northernmost island. So we then supposed it to be ; but next morning we found it to be a peninsula, united to the continent by a low neck of land, on each side of which the coast forms a bay. We plied into the southernmost, and about noon anchored in five fathoms water, over a bottom of mud ; the point of the peninsula, which obtained the name of Cape Denbigh, bearing N. 68° W., three miles distant. Several people were seen upon the peninsula ; and one man came off in a small canoe. I gave him a knife and a few beads, with which he seemed well pleased. Having made signs to him to bring us something to eat, he immediately left us and paddled toward the shore. But meeting another man coming off, who happened to have two dried salmon, he got them from him, and on returning to the ship would give them to nobody but me. Some of our people thought that he asked for me under the name of "Capitane ;" but in this they were probably mistaken. He knew who had given him the knife and beads, but I do not see how he could know that I was the captain. Others of the natives soon after came off, and exchanged a few dry fish for such trifles as they could get or we had to give them. They were most desirous of knives ; and they had no dislike to tobacco.

After dinner Lieutenant Gore was sent to the peninsula, to see if wood and water were there to be got, or rather water, for the whole beach round the bay seemed to be covered with drift-wood. At the same time a boat was sent from each ship to sound round the bay ; and at three in the afternoon, the wind freshening at NE., we weighed in order to work farther in. But it was soon found to be impossible, on account of the shoals, which extended quite round the bay to the distance of two or three miles from the shore, as the officers who had been sent to sound reported. We therefore kept standing off and on with the ships, waiting for Mr Gore, who returned about 8 o'clock with the launch laden with wood. He reported that there was but little fresh water ; and that wood was difficult to be got at, by reason of the boats grounding at some distance from the beach. This being the case, I stood back to the other shore ; and at 8 o'clock the next morning sent all the boats and a party of men, with an officer, to get wood from the place where I had landed two days before. We continued for a while to stand on and off with the ships, but at length came to an anchor in one-fourth less than five fathoms, half-a-league from the coast, the south point of which bore S. 26° W., and Bald Head N. 60° E., nine leagues distant. Cape Denbigh bore S. 72° E., twenty-six miles distant ; and the island under the east shore, to the southward of Cape Denbigh, named Bessborough Island, S. 52° E., fifteen leagues distant.

As this was a very open road, and consequently not a safe station, I resolved not to wait to complete water, as that would require some time ; but only to supply the ships with wood, and then to go in search of a more convenient place for the other article. We took off the drift-wood that lay upon the beach ; and as the wind blew along shore the boats could sail both ways, which enabled us to make great despatch. In the afternoon I went ashore and walked a little into the country ; which, where there was no wood, was covered with heath and other plants, some of which produce berries in abundance. All the berries were ripe, the hurtle-berries[1] too much so ; and hardly a single plant was in flower. The underwood, such as birch, willows, and alders, rendered it very troublesome walking among the trees, which were all spruce, and none of them above six or eight inches in diameter. But we found some lying upon the beach more than twice this size. All the drift-wood in these northern parts was fir ; I saw not a stick of any other sort. Next day a family of the natives came near to the place where we were taking off wood. I know not how many there were at first ; but I saw only the husband, the wife, and their child, and a fourth person, who bore the human shape, and that was all ; for he was the most deformed cripple I had ever seen or heard of. The other man was almost blind, and neither he nor his wife were such good-looking people as we had sometimes seen amongst the natives of this coast. The under lips of both were bored ; and they had in their possession some such glass beads as I had met with before amongst their neighbours. But iron was their beloved article. For four knives, which we had made out of an old iron hoop, I got from them near 400 pounds weight of fish, which they had caught on this or the preceding day. Some were trout, and the rest were in size and taste somewhat between a mullet and a herring. I gave the child, who was a girl, a few beads ; on which the mother burst into tears, then the father, then the cripple, and at last, to complete the concert, the girl herself ; but this music continued not long. Before night we had got the ships amply supplied with wood, and had carried on board about twelve tons of water to each.

On the 14th a party of men were sent on shore to cut brooms, which we were in want of, and the branches of spruce trees for brewing beer. Towards noon everybody was taken on board ; for the wind freshening had raised such a surf on the beach that the boats could not continue to land without great difficulty. Some doubts being still entertained whether the coast we were now upon belonged to an island or the American continent, and the shallowness of the water putting it out of our power to determine this with our ships, I sent Lieutenant King with two boats under his command to make such searches as might leave no room for a variety of opinions on the subject. Next day the ships removed over to the bay which is on the south-east side of Cape Denbigh, where we anchored in the afternoon. Soon after, a few of the natives came off in their small canoes, and bartered some dried salmon for such trifles as our people had to give them.

At daybreak on the 16th, nine men, each in his canoe, paid us a visit. They approached the ship with some caution, and evidently came with no other view than to gratify their curiosity. They drew up abreast of each other under our stern, and gave us a song ; while one of their number beat upon a kind of drum, and another made a thousand antic motions with his hands and body. There was, however, nothing savage either in the song or in the gestures that accompanied it. None of us could perceive any difference between these people, either as to their size or features, and those whom we had met with on every other part of the coast, King George's Sound excepted. Their clothing, which consisted principally of deer-skins, was made after the same fashion ; and they observed the custom of boring their under lips, and fixing ornaments to them. The dwellings of these people were seated close to the beach. They consist simply of a sloping roof, without any side walls, composed of logs and covered with grass and earth. The floor is also laid with logs ; the entrance is at one end, the fireplace just within it, and a small hole is made near the door to let out the smoke.

After breakfast a party of men were sent to the peninsula for brooms and

---

[1] Whortle-berries, bilberries.

spruce. At the same time half the remainder of the people in each ship had leave to go and pick berries. These returned on board at noon, when the other half went on the same errand. The berries to be got here were wild currant-berries, partridge-berries, and heath-berries. I also went ashore myself and walked over part of the peninsula. In several places there was very good grass, and I hardly saw a spot on which some vegetable was not growing. The low land which connects this peninsula with the continent is full of narrow creeks, and abounds with ponds of water, some of which were already frozen over. There were a great many geese and bustards, but so shy that it was not possible to get within musket-shot of them. We also met with some snipes, and on the high ground were partridges of two sorts. Where there was any wood, mosquitoes were in plenty. Some of the officers, who travelled farther than I did, met with a few of the natives of both sexes, who treated them with civility. It appeared to me that this peninsula must have been an island in remote times ; for there were marks of the sea having flowed over the isthmus ; and even now it appeared to be kept out by a bank of sand, stones, and wood, thrown up by the waves. By this bank it was evident that the land was here encroaching upon the sea, and it was easy to trace its gradual formation.

About seven in the evening Mr King returned from his expedition, and reported that he proceeded with the boats about three or four leagues farther than the ships had been able to go ; that he then landed on the west side ; that, from the heights he could see the two coasts join, and the inlet to terminate in a small river or creek, before which were banks of sand or mud, and everywhere shoal water. The land, too, was low and swampy for some distance to the northward ; then it swelled into hills ; and the complete junction of those on each side of the inlet was easily traced. From the elevated spot on which Mr King surveyed the sound, he could distinguish many extensive valleys, with rivers running through them, well wooded, and bounded by hills of a gentle ascent and moderate height. One of these rivers to the north-west appeared to be considerable ; and from its direction he was inclined to think that it emptied itself into the sea at the head of the bay. Some of his people, who penetrated beyond this into the country, found the trees larger the farther they advanced. In honour of Sir Fletcher Norton,[1] Speaker of the House of Commons, and Mr King's near relation, I named this inlet Norton Sound. It extends to the northward as far as the Latitude of 64° 55'. The bay in which we were now at anchor lies on the south-east side of it, and is called by the natives Chacktoole. It is but an indifferent station, being exposed to the south and south-west winds ; nor is there a harbour in all this sound. But we were so fortunate as to have the wind from the north and north-east all the time, with remarkably fine weather.

Having now fully satisfied myself that Mr Stæhlin's map must be erroneous, and, having restored the American continent to that space which he had occupied with his imaginary island of Alashka, it was high time to think of leaving these northern regions and to retire to some place during the winter, where I might procure refreshments for my people, and a small supply of provisions. Petropaulowska, or the harbour of St Peter and St Paul, in Kamtschatka, did not appear likely to furnish either the one or the other for so large a number of men. I had, besides, other reasons for not repairing thither at this time. The first, on which all the others depended, was the great dislike I had to lie inactive for six or seven months, which would have been the necessary consequence of wintering in any of these northern parts. No place was so conveniently within our reach, where

---

[1] Afterwards Lord Grantley.

we could expect to have our wants supplied, as the Sandwich Islands; to them, therefore, I determined to proceed. But before this could be carried into execution, a supply of water was necessary. With this view I resolved to search the American coast for a harbour, by proceeding along it to the southward, and thus endeavour to connect the survey of this part of it with that lying immediately to the north of Cape Newenham. If I failed in finding a harbour there, my plan was then to proceed to Samganoodha, which was fixed upon as our place of rendezvous in case of separation.

·CHAPTER VI.

HAVING weighed on the 17th in the morning with a light breeze at E., we steered to the southward and attempted to pass within Bessborough Island; but though it lies six or seven miles from the continent, were prevented by meeting with shoal water. As we had but little wind all the day, it was dark before we passed the island, and the night was spent under an easy sail. We resumed our course at daybreak on the 18th, along the coast. At noon we had no more than five fathoms water. At this time the latitude was 63° 37'. Bessborough Island now bore N. 42° E.; the southernmost land in sight, which proved also to be an island, S. 66° W.; the passage between it and the main S. 40° W.; and the nearest land about two miles distant. I continued to steer for this passage until the boats, which were ahead, made the signal for having no more than three fathoms water. On this we hauled without the island, and made the signal for the Resolution's boat to keep between the ships and the shore.

This island, which obtained the name of Stuart's Island, lies in the Latitude of 63° 35', and seventeen leagues from Cape Denbigh in the direction of S. 27° W. It is six or seven leagues in circuit. Some parts of it are of a middling height; but in general it is low, with some rocks lying off the western part. The coast of the continent is for the most part low land, but we saw high land up the country. It forms a point, opposite the island, which was named Cape Stephens, and lies in Latitude 63° 33' and in Longitude 197° 41'. Some drift-wood was seen upon the shores both of the island and of the continent; but not a tree was perceived growing upon either. One might anchor upon occasion between the north-east side of this island and the continent, in a depth of five fathoms, sheltered from westerly, southerly, and easterly winds. But this station would be wholly exposed to the northerly winds, the land in that direction being at too great a distance to afford any security. Before we reached Stuart's Island, we passed two small islands lying between us and the main; and as we ranged along the coast several people appeared upon the shore, and by signs seemed to invite us to approach them. As soon as we were without the island, we steered S. by W. for the southernmost point of the continent in sight, till 8 o'clock in the evening, when, having shoaled the water from six fathoms to less than four, I tacked and stood to the northward into five fathoms, and then spent the night lying off and on. At the time we tacked, the southernmost point of land, the same which is mentioned above, and was named Point Shallow Water, bore S. half E. seven leagues distant.

We resumed our course to the southward at daybreak next morning, but shoal water obliged us to haul more to the westward. At length we got so far advanced upon the bank, that we could not hold a NNW. course, meeting sometimes with only four fathoms. The wind blowing fresh at ENE., it was high time to look for deep water, and to quit a coast upon which we could no longer navigate with any degree of safety. I therefore hauled the wind to the northward, and gradually deepened the water to eight fathoms. At the time we hauled the wind we were at least twelve leagues from the continent and nine to the westward of Stuart's Island. No land was seen to the southward of Point Shallow Water, which I judge to lie in the Latitude of 63°; so that between this latitude and Shoal Ness, in Latitude 60°, the coast is entirely unexplored. Probably it is accessible only to boats or very small vessels, or at least, if there be channels for larger vessels it would require some time to find them; and I am of opinion that they must be looked for near the coast. From the mast-head, the sea within us appeared to be chequered with shoals; the water was very much discoloured and muddy, and considerably fresher than at any of the places where we had lately anchored. From this I inferred that a considerable river runs into the sea in this unknown part.[1]

As soon as we got into eight fathoms water I steered to the westward, and afterwards more southerly, for the land discovered on the 5th, which at noon the next day bore SW. by W., ten or eleven leagues distant. At this time we had a fresh gale at N., with showers of hail and snow at intervals, and a pretty high sea; so that we got clear of the shoals but just in time. As I now found that the land before us lay too far to the westward to be Anderson's Island, I named it Clerke's Island. It lies in the Latitude of 63° 15', and in the Longitude of 190° 30'. It seemed to be a pretty large island, in which are four or more hills, all connected by low ground; so that at a distance it looks like a group of islands. Near its east part lies a small island remarkable by having upon it three elevated rocks. Not only the greater island

but this small spot was inhabited. We got up to the northern point of Clerke's Island about 6 o'clock, and having ranged along its coast till dark, brought to during the night. At daybreak next morning we stood in again for the coast, and continued to range along it in search of a harbour till noon, when, seeing no likelihood of succeeding, I left it and steered SSW. for the land which we had discovered on the 29th of July; having a fresh gale at N. with showers of sleet and snow. I remarked that as soon as we opened the channel which separates the two continents, cloudy weather with snow-showers immediately commenced; whereas all the time that we were in Norton Sound we had, with the same wind, clear weather. Might not this be occasioned by the mountains to the north of that place attracting the vapours and hindering them to proceed any farther?

At daybreak in the morning of the 23d the land above mentioned appeared in sight, bearing SW., six or seven leagues distant. From this point of view it resembled a group of islands; but it proved to be but one, of thirty miles in extent in the direction of NW. and SE., the SE. end being Cape Upright, already taken notice of. The island is but narrow, especially at the low necks of land that connect the hills. I afterward found that it was wholly unknown to the Russians; and therefore, considering it as a discovery of our own, I named it Gore's Island. It appeared to be barren, and without inhabitants; at least we saw none. Nor did we see so many birds about it as when we first discovered it. But we saw some sea-otters, an animal which we had not met with to the north of this latitude. Four leagues from Cape Upright, in the direction of S. 72° W., lies a small island whose elevated summit terminates in several pinnacle rocks. On this account it was named Pinnacle Island. At two in the afternoon, after passing Cape Upright, I steered SE. by S. for Samganoodha, with a gentle breeze

---

[1] In modern maps a large river named the Kwichpak, taking its rise far inland to the east and south-east, and debouching by several mouths into the sea north of Cape Romanzov, is marked just where Cook conjectured the existence of such a stream.

at NNW., being resolved to spend no more time in searching for a harbour amongst islands which I now began to suspect had no existence, at least not in the latitude and longitude where modern map-makers have thought proper to place them. In the evening of the 24th the wind veered to SW. and S., and increased to a fresh gale.

We continued to stretch to the eastward till 8 o'clock in the morning of the 25th, when, in the Latitude of 58° 32', and in the Longitude of 191° 10', we tacked and stood to the west; and soon after, the gale increasing, we were reduced to two courses and close-reefed maintop-sails. Not long after, the Resolution sprang a leak under the starboard buttock, which filled the spirit-room with water before it was discovered; and it was so considerable as to keep one pump constantly employed. We durst not put the ship upon the other tack for fear of getting upon the shoals that lie to the NW. of Cape Newenham; but continued standing to the west till six in the evening of the 26th, when we wore and stood to the eastward, and then the leak no longer troubled us. This proved that it was above the water line, which was no small satisfaction. The gale was now over, but the wind remained at S. and SW. for some days longer.

At length, on the 2d of October at daybreak, we saw the island of Oonalashka bearing SE. But as this was to us a new point of view, and the land was obscured by a thick haze, we were not sure of our situation till noon, when the observed latitude determined it. As all the harbours were alike to me provided they were equally safe and convenient, I hauled into a bay that lies ten miles to the westward of Samganoodha, known by the name of Egoochshac; but we found very deep water, so that we were glad to get out again. The natives, many of whom lived here, visited us at different times, bringing with them dried salmon and other fish, which they exchanged with the seamen for tobacco. But a few days before, every ounce of tobacco that was in the ship had been distributed among them; and the quantity was not half sufficient to answer their demands. Notwithstanding this, so improvident a creature is an English sailor, that they were as profuse in making their bargains as if we had now arrived at a port in Virginia; by which means, in less than eight-and-forty hours the value of this article of barter was lowered above 1000 per cent. At 1 o'clock in the afternoon of the 3d we anchored in Samganoodha harbour; and the next morning the carpenters of both ships were set to work to rip off the sheathing of and under the wale on the starboard side abaft. Many of the seams were found quite open, so that it was no wonder that so much water had found its way into the ship. While we lay here we cleared the fish and spirit rooms and the after-hold, disposing things in such a manner, that in case we should happen to have any more leaks of the same nature the water might find it way to the pumps. And besides this work, and completing our water, we cleared the forehold to the very bottom, and took in a quantity of ballast.

The vegetables which we had met with when we were here before were now mostly in a state of decay, so that we were but little benefited by the great quantities of berries everywhere found ashore. In order to avail ourselves as much as possible of this useful refreshment, one-third of the people by turns had leave to go and pick them. Considerable quantities of them were also procured from the natives. If there were any seeds of the scurvy in either ship, these berries, and the use of spruce beer, which [the crews] had to drink every other day, effectually eradicated them. We also got plenty of fish, at first mostly salmon, both fresh and dried, which the natives brought us. Some of the fresh salmon was in high perfection; but there was one sort, which we called hook-nosed, from the figure of its head, that was but indifferent. We drew the seine several times at the head of the bay, and caught a good many salmon-trout, and once a halibut that weighed 254 pounds. The fishery failing, we had recourse to hooks and lines. A boat was sent out every morning, and seldom returned without eight or ten halibut, which was more than sufficient to serve all our people. The halibut were excellent, and there were few who did not prefer them to salmon. Thus we not only procured a supply of fish for present consumption, but had some to carry with us to sea. This enabled us to make a considerable saving of our provisions, which was an object of no small importance.

On the 8th I received by the hands of an Oonalashka man, named Derramoushk, a very singular present, considering the place. It was a rye loaf, or rather a pie made in the form of a loaf, for it enclosed some salmon highly seasoned with pepper. This man had the like present for Captain Clerke, and a note for each of us written in a character which none of us could read. It was natural to suppose that this present was from some Russians now in our neighbourhood; and therefore we sent by the same hand, to these our unknown friends, a few bottles of rum, wine, and porter, which we thought would be as acceptable as anything we had beside; and we soon knew that in this we had not been mistaken. I also sent, along with Derramoushk, Corporal Lediard of the marines, an intelligent man, in order to gain some further information, with orders that if he met with any Russians he should endeavour to make them understand that we were English, the friends and allies of their nation.

On the 10th, Lediard returned with three Russian seamen or furriers, who with some others resided at Egoochshac, where they had a dwelling-house, some store-houses, and a sloop of about thirty tons burthen. One of these men was either master or mate of this vessel; another of them wrote a very good hand and understood figures; and they were all three well-behaved, intelligent men, and very ready to give me all the information I could desire. But for want of an interpreter we had some difficulty to understand each other. They appeared to have a thorough knowledge of the attempts that had been made by their countrymen to navigate the Frozen Ocean, and of the discoveries which had been made from Kamtschatka by Behring, Tscherikoff, and Spanberg. But they seemed to know no more of Lieutenant Syndo, or Synd, than his name. Nor had they the least idea what part of the world Mr Stæhlin's map referred to when it was laid before them. When I pointed out Kamtschatka and some other known places upon that map, they asked whether I had seen the islands there laid down; and on my answering in the negative, one of them put his finger upon a part of this map where a number of islands was represented, and said that he had cruised there for land but never could find any. I then laid before them my own chart, and found that they were strangers to every part of the American coast except what lies opposite this island. One of these men said that he had been with Behring in his American voyage, but he must then have been very young, for he had not now, at the distance of thirty-seven years, the appearance of being aged. Never was there greater respect paid to the memory of any distinguished person than by these men to that of Behring. The trade in which they are engaged is very beneficial; and its being undertaken and extended to the eastward of Kamtschatka was the immediate consequence of the second voyage of that able navigator, whose misfortunes proved to be the source of much private advantage to individuals and of public utility to the Russian nation. And yet, if his distresses had not accidentally carried him to die in the island which bears his name, and whence the miserable remnant of his ship's crew brought back sufficient specimens of its valuable furs, probably the Russians never would have undertaken any future voyages which could lead them to make discoveries in the sea towards the coast of America. Indeed, after his time Government seems to have paid less attention to this; and we owe what discoveries have been since made principally to the enterprising spirit of private traders, encouraged, however, by the superintending care of the Court of Petersburg. The three Russians having remained with me all night, visited Captain Clerke next morning, and then left us, very well satisfied with the reception they had met with, promising to return in a few days and to bring with them a chart of the islands lying between Oonalashka and Kamtschatka.

On the 15th, in the evening, while Mr Webber and I were at a village at a small distance from Samganoodha, a Russian landed there who, I found, was the principal person amongst his countrymen in this and the neighbouring islands. His name was Erasim Gregorioff Sin Ismyloff. He arrived in a canoe carrying three persons, attended by twenty or thirty other canoes, each conducted by one man. I took notice that the first thing they did after landing was to make a small tent for Ismyloff of materials which they brought with them, and then they made others for themselves of their canoes and paddles, which they covered with grass, so that the people of the village were at no trouble to find them lodging. Ismyloff, having invited us into his tent, set before us some dried salmon and berries, which, I was satisfied, was the best cheer he had. He appeared to be a sensible, intelligent man; and I felt no small mortification in not being able to converse with him unless by signs, assisted by figures and other characters, which, however, were a very great help. I desired to see him on board the next day, and accordingly he came, with all his attendants. Indeed he had moved into our neighbourhood for the express purpose of waiting upon us. I was in hopes to have had by him the chart which his three countrymen had promised, but I was disappointed. However, he assured me I should have it, and he kept his word. I found that he was very well acquainted with the geography of these parts, and with all the discoveries that had been made in them by the Russians. On seeing the modern maps, he at once pointed out their errors. He told me he had accompanied Lieutenant Syndo, or Synd, as he called him, in his expedition to the north; and, according to his account, they did not proceed farther than the Tschukotskoi Nos, or rather than the Bay of St Laurence, for he pointed on our chart to the very place where I landed. From thence, he said, they went to an island in Latitude 63°, upon which they did not land, nor could he tell me its name; but I should guess it to be the same to which I gave the name of Clerke's Island. To what place Synd went after that, or in what manner he spent the two years during which, as Ismyloff said, his researches lasted, he either could not, or would not, inform us. Perhaps he did not comprehend our inquiries about this; and yet in almost every other thing we could make him understand us. This created a suspicion that he had not really been in that expedition, notwithstanding his assertion.

Both Ismyloff and the others affirmed that they knew nothing of the continent of America to the northward, and that neither Lieutenant Synd nor any other Russian had ever seen it of late. They call it by the same name which Mr Stæhlin gives to his great island, that is, Alashka. Stachtan Nitada, as it is called in the modern maps, is a name quite unknown to these people, natives of the islands as well as Russians; but both of them know it by the name of America. From what we could gather from Ismyloff and his countrymen, the Russians have made several attempts to get a footing upon that part of this continent that lies contiguous to Oonalashka and the adjoining islands, but have always been repulsed by the natives, whom they describe as a very treacherous people. They mentioned two or three captains, or chief men, who had been murdered by them; and some of the Russians showed us wounds which they said they had received there. Some other information which we got from Ismyloff is worth recording, whether true or false. He told us that in the year 1773 an expedition had been made into the Frozen Sea in sledges over the ice to three large islands that lie opposite the mouth of the River Kolima. We were in some doubt whether he did not mean the same expedition of which Muller gives an account; and yet he wrote down the year and marked the islands on the chart. But a voyage which he himself had performed engaged our attention more than any other. He said that on the 12th of May 1771 he sailed from Bolscheretzk,[1] in a Russian vessel, to one of the Kurile Islands, named Mareekan, in the Latitude of 47°, where there is a harbour and a Russian settlement. From this island he proceeded to Japan, where he seems to have made but a short stay. For when the Japanese came to know that he and his companions were Christians, they made signs for them to be gone, but did not, so far as we could understand him, offer any insult or force. From Japan he got to Canton, and thence to France in a French ship. From France he travelled to St Petersburg, and was afterwards sent out again to Kamtschatka. What became of the vessel in which he first embarked, we could not learn, nor what was the principal object of the voyage. His not being able to speak one word of French made this story a little suspicious. He did not even know the name of any one of the most common things that must have been in use every day while he was on board the ship and in France. And yet he seemed clear as to the times of his arriving at the different places, and of his leaving them, which he put down in writing.

The next morning he would fain have made me a present of a sea-otter skin, which, he said, was worth eighty

roubles at Kamtschatka. However, I thought proper to decline it; but I accepted of some dried fish and several baskets of the lily, or "faranne" root. In the afternoon Mr Ismyloff, after dining with Captain Clerke, left us with all his retinue, promising to return in a few days. Accordingly on the 19th he made us another visit, and brought with him the charts before mentioned, which he allowed me to copy, and the contents of which furnish matter for the following observations.[2] There were two of them, both manuscripts, and bearing every mark of authenticity. The first comprehended the Penshinskian Sea,[3] the coast of Tartary as low as the Latitude of 41°, the Kurile Islands, and the peninsula of Kamtschatka. Since this map had been made, Wawseelee Irkeechoff, Captain of the Fleet, explored in 1758 the coast of Tartary, from Okotsk and the River Amoor to Japan, or 41° of Latitude. Mr Ismyloff also informed us that great part of the sea-coast of the peninsula of Kamtschatka had been corrected by himself, and described the instrument he made use of, which must have been a theodolite. He also informed us that there were only two harbours fit for shipping on all the east coast of Kamtschatka, viz., the Bay of Awatska, and the River Olutora, in the bottom of the gulf of the same name; that there was not a single harbour upon its west coast; and that Yamsk was the only one on all the west side of the Penshinskian Sea, except Okotsk, till we come to the River Amoor. The Kurile Islands afford only one harbour, and that is on the north-east side of Mareekan, in the Latitude of 47½°, where, as I have before observed, the Russians have a settlement. The second chart was to me the most interesting, for it comprehended all the discoveries made by the Russians to the eastward of Kamt-

---

[1] On the south-west coast of Kamtschatka, just across the peninsula from Petropaulovski on the south-east side.

[2] Considerably abridged, as now of comparatively slight value, having long ago been superseded by further research in those regions.

[3] The Sea of Okotsk.

schatka towards America, which, if we exclude the voyage of Behring and Tscherikoff, will amount to little or nothing. . . .

It appeared by the chart, as well as by the testimony of Ismyloff and the other Russians, that this[1] is as far as their countrymen have made any discoveries, or have extended themselves, since Behring's time. They all said that no Russians had settled themselves so far to the east as the place where the natives gave the note to Captain Clerke; which Mr Ismyloff, to whom I delivered it, on perusing it said had been written at Oomanak. It was, however, from him that we got the name of Kodiak,[2] the largest of Schumagin's Islands; for it had no name upon the chart produced by him. The names of all the other islands were taken from it, and we wrote them down as pronounced by him. He said they were all such as the natives themselves called their islands by; but, if so, some of the names seem to have been strangely altered. It is worth observing, that no names were put to the islands which Ismyloff told us were to be struck out of the chart; and I considered this as some confirmation that they were not in existence. I have already observed that the American continent is here called by the Russians, as well as by the islanders, Alashka; which name, though it properly belong only to the country adjoining to Ooneemak, is used by them when speaking of the American continent in general, which they know perfectly well to be a great land. This is all the information I got from these people relating to the geography of this part of the world; and I have reason to believe that this was all the information they were able to give. For they assured me over and over again that they knew of no other islands besides those which were laid down upon this chart;[3] and that no Russian had ever seen any part of the continent of America to the northward, except that which lies opposite the country of the Tschutskis.

Mr Ismyloff remained with us till the 21st in the evening, when he took his final leave. To his care I entrusted a letter to the Lords Commissioners of the Admiralty, in which was enclosed a chart of all the northern coasts I had visited. He said there would be an opportunity of sending it to Kamtschatka or Okotsk the ensuing spring; and that it would be at St Petersburg the following winter. He gave me a letter to Major Behm, Governor of Kamtschatka, who resides at Bolscheretsk; and another to the commanding officer at Petropaulowska. Mr Ismyloff seemed to have abilities that might entitle him to a higher station in life than that in which we found him. He was tolerably well versed in astronomy and in the most useful branches of the mathematics. I made him a present of a Hadley's octant; and though probably it was the first he had ever seen, he made himself acquainted in a very short time with most of the uses to which that instrument can be applied.

In the morning of the 22d we made an attempt to get to sea, with the wind at SE., which miscarried. The following afternoon we were visited by one Jacob Ivanovitch Soposnicoff, a Russian who commanded a boat or small vessel at Oomanak. This man had a great share of modesty, and would drink no strong liquor, of which the rest of his countrymen whom we had met with here were immoderately fond. He seemed to know more

---

[1] The Halibut Isles, and the Island of Ooneemak, forming—the latter especially—a westward continuation of the peninsula of Alashka; from which it is divided by a narrow and shallow channel, impracticable for ships.

[2] A Russian ship had been at Kodiack, in 1776; it lies south of the middle of the Alashkan peninsula, some distance westward from the entrance to Cook's inlet.

[3] They were Behring's Island, Copper Island, and the Aleutian chain, as far as the channel between Ooneemak and the peninsula of Alashka on the American mainland.

accurately what supplies could be got at the harbour of Petropaulowska, and the price of the different articles, than Mr Ismyloff. But, by all accounts, everything we should want at that place was very scarce and bore a high price. Flour, for instance, was from three to five roubles the pood;[1] and deer from three to five roubles each. This man told us that he was to be at Petropaulowska in May next; and, as I understood, was to have the charge of my letter. He seemed to be exceedingly desirous of having some token from me to carry to Major Behm; and to gratify him I sent a small spying-glass.

After we became acquainted with these Russians, some of our gentlemen at different times visited their settlement on the island; where they always met with a hearty welcome. This settlement consisted of a dwelling-house and two store-houses. And besides the Russians there was a number of the Kamtschadales and of the natives, as servants or slaves to the former. Some others of the natives, who seemed independent of the Russians, lived at the same place. Such of them as belonged to the Russians were all males; and they are taken, or perhaps purchased, from their parents when young. There were at this time about twenty of these, who could be looked upon in no other light than as children. They all live in the same house, the Russians at the upper end, the Kamtschadales in the middle, and the natives at the lower end; where is fixed a large boiler for preparing their food, which consists chiefly of what the sea produces, with the addition of wild roots and berries. There is little difference between the first and last table besides what is produced by cookery, in which the Russians have the art to make indifferent things palatable. I have eaten whale's flesh of their dressing which I thought very good; and they made a kind of pan-pudding of salmon roe, beaten up fine and fried, that is no bad succedaneum for bread. They may, now and then,

taste real bread, or have a dish in which flour is an ingredient; but this can only be an occasional luxury. If we except the juice of berries, which they sip at their meals, they have no other liquor besides pure water; and it seems to be very happy for them that they have nothing stronger. As the island supplies them with food, so it does in a great measure with clothing. This consists chiefly of skins, and is perhaps the best they could have. The upper garment is made like our waggoner's frock, and reaches as low as the knee. Besides this they wear a waistcoat or two, a pair of breeches, a fur cap, and a pair of boots, the soles and upper leathers of which are of Russian leather, but the legs are made of some kind of strong gut. Their two chiefs, Ismyloff and Ivanovitch, wore each a calico frock; and they, as well as some others, had skirts, which were of silk. These, perhaps, were the only part of their dress not made amongst themselves.

There are Russians settled upon all the principal islands between Oonalashka and Kamtschatka, for the sole purpose of collecting furs. Their great object is the sea-beaver or otter. I never heard them inquire after any other animal; though those whose skins are of inferior value are also made part of their cargoes. I never thought, to ask how long they have had a settlement upon Oonalashka and the neighbouring isles; but, to judge from the great subjection the natives are under, this cannot be of a very late date.[2] All these furriers are relieved from time to time by others. Those we met with arrived here from Okotsk in 1776, and are to return in 1781; so that their stay at the island will be four years at least.

It is now time to give some account of the native inhabitants. To all appearance they are the most peaceable, inoffensive people I ever met with, and as to honesty they might serve as a pattern to the most civilised

---

[1] Thirty-six pounds.

[2] The Russians began to frequent Oonalashka in 1762.

nation upon earth. But, from what I saw of their neighbours, with whom the Russians have no connection, I doubt whether this was their original disposition, and rather think that it has been the consequence of their present state of subjection. Indeed, if some of our gentlemen did not misunderstand the Russians, they had been obliged to make some severe examples before they could bring the islanders into any order. If there were severities inflicted at first, the best apology for them is that they have produced the happiest consequences ; and at present the greatest harmony subsists between the two nations. The natives have their own chiefs in each island, and seem to enjoy liberty and property unmolested. But whether or no they are tributaries to the Russians, we could never find out. There was some reason to think that they are.

These people are rather low of stature, but plump and well shaped, with rather short necks, swarthy chubby faces, black eyes, small beards, and long, straight, black hair ; which the men wear loose behind and cut before, but the women tie up in a bunch. Their dress has been occasionally mentioned. Both sexes wear the same in fashion ; the only difference is in the materials. The women's frock is made of sealskin, and that of the men of the skins of birds ; both reaching below the knee. This is the whole dress of the women. But over the frock the men wear another, made of gut, which resists water, and has a hood to it which draws over the head. Some of them wear boots ; and all of them have a kind of oval snouted cap, made of wood, with a rim to admit the head. The caps are dyed with green and other colours ; and round the upper part of the rim are stuck the long bristles of some sea-animal on which are strung glass beads, and on the front is a small image or two made of bone. They make use of no paint ; but the women puncture their faces slightly, and both men and women bore the under lip, to which they fix pieces of bone. But it is as uncommon at Oonalashka to see a man with this ornament, as to see a woman without it. Some fix beads to the upper lip, under the nostrils ; and all of them hang ornaments in their ears.

Their food consists of fish, sea-animals, birds, roots, and berries, and even of sea-weed. They dry large quantities of fish in summer, which they lay up in small huts for winter use, and probably they preserve roots and berries for the same time of scarcity. They eat almost everything raw. Boiling and broiling were the only methods of cookery that I saw them make use of ; and the first was probably learned from the Russians. Some have got little brass kettles ; and those who have not, make one of a flat stone, with sides of clay, not unlike a standing pie. I was once present when the chief of Oonalashka made his dinner off the raw head of a large halibut, just caught. Before any was given to the chief, two of his servants ate the gills, without any other dressing besides squeezing out the slime. This done, one of them cut off the head of the fish, took it to the sea, and washed it, then came with it, and sat down by the chief ; first pulling up some grass, upon a part of which the head was laid, and the rest was strewed before the chief. He then cut large pieces off the cheeks, and laid these within reach of the great man, who swallowed them with as much satisfaction as we should do raw oysters. When he had done, the remains of the head were cut in pieces and given to the attendants, who tore off the meat with their teeth, and gnawed the bones like so many dogs.

As these people use no paint, they are not so dirty in their persons as the savages who thus besmear themselves ; but they are full as lousy and filthy in their houses. Their method of building is as follows : They dig in the ground an oblong square pit, the length of which seldom exceeds fifty feet and the breadth twenty, but in general the dimensions are smaller. Over this excavation they form the roof, of wood which the sea throws ashore. This roof is covered first with grass, and then with earth, so that the outward appearance is like a dunghill. In the middle of the roof, towards each end, is left a square opening by which the light is admitted; one of these openings being for this purpose only, and the other being also used to go in and out by, with the help of a ladder, or rather a post with steps cut in it. In some houses there is another entrance below, but this is not common. Round the sides and ends of the huts the families (for several are lodged together) have their separate apartments, where they sleep and sit at work, not upon benches, but in a kind of a concave trench, which is dug all round the inside of the house, and covered with mats, so that this part is kept tolerably decent. But the middle of the house, which is common to all the families, is far otherwise. For although it be covered with dry grass, it is a receptacle for dirt of every kind, and the place for the urine trough, the stench of which is not mended by raw hides or leather being almost continually steeped in it. Behind and over the trench are placed the few effects they are possessed of, such as their clothing, mats, and skins. Their household furniture consists of bowls, spoons, buckets, piggins, or cans, matted baskets, and perhaps a Russian kettle or pot. All these utensils are very neatly made and well-formed; and yet we saw no other tools among them but the knife and the hatchet, that is, a small flat piece of iron made like an adze by fitting it into a crooked wooden handle. These were the only instruments we met with there made of iron. For although the Russians live amongst them, we found much less of this metal in their possession than we had met with in the possession of other tribes on the American continent who had never seen, nor perhaps had any intercourse with, the Russians. Probably a few beads, a little tobacco and snuff, purchase all they have to spare. There are few, if any of them,

that do not both smoke and chew tobacco, and take snuff; a luxury that bids fair to keep them always poor.

They did not seem to wish for more iron, or to want any other instruments except sewing needles, their own being made of bone. With these they not only sew their canoes and make their clothes, but also very curious embroidery. Instead of thread they use the fibres of sinews, which they split to the thickness which each sort of work requires. All sewing is performed by the women. They are the tailors, shoemakers, and boat-builders or boat-coverers, for the men most probably construct the frame of wood over which the skins are sewed. They make mats and baskets of grass that are both beautiful and strong. Indeed, there is a neatness and perfection in most of their work that shows they neither want ingenuity nor perseverance.

I saw not a fireplace in any one of their houses. They are lighted as well as heated by lamps, which are simple, and yet answer the purpose very well. They are made of a flat stone, hollowed on one side like a plate, and about the same size, or rather larger. In the hollow part they put the oil, mixed with a little dry grass, which serves the purpose of a wick. Both men and women frequently warm their bodies over one of these lamps, by placing it between their legs, under their garments, and sitting thus over it for a few minutes. They produce fire both by collision and by attrition; the former by striking two stones one against another, on one of which a good deal of brimstone is first rubbed. The latter method is with two pieces of wood, one of which is a stick of about eighteen inches in length, and the other a flat piece. The pointed end of the stick they press upon the other, whirling it nimbly round as a drill, thus producing fire in a few minutes. This method is common in many parts of the world. It is practised by the Kamtschadales, by these people, by the Greenlanders, by the Brazilians, by the Otaheiteans, by the New Hollanders, and probably by many other nations. Yet some learned and ingenious men have founded an argument on this custom to prove that this and that nation arc of the same extraction. But accidental agreements, in a few particular instances, will not authorise such a conclusion; nor will a disagreement either in manners or customs between two different nations of course prove that they are of different extraction. I could support this opinion by many instances besides the one just mentioned.

No such thing as an offensive or even defensive weapon was seen amongst the natives of Oonalashka. We cannot suppose that the Russians found them in such a defenceless state; it is more probable that, for their own security, they have disarmed them. Political reasons, too, may have induced the Russians not to allow these islanders to have any large canoes; for it is difficult to believe they had none such originally, as we found them amongst all their neighbours. However, we saw none here but one or two belonging to the Russians. The canoes made use of by the natives are the smallest we had anywhere seen upon the American coast, though built after the same manner, with some little difference in the construction. The stern of these terminates a little abruptly; the head is forked, the upper point of the fork projecting without the under one, which is even with the surface of the water. Why they should thus construct them is difficult to conceive, for the fork is apt to catch hold of everything that comes in the way, to prevent which they fix a piece of small stick from point to point. In other respects their canoes are built after the manner of those used by the Greenlanders and Esquimaux, the framing being of slender laths, and the covering of seal-skins. They are about twelve feet long, a foot and a half broad in the middle, and twelve or fourteen inches deep. Upon occa-

sion they can carry two persons; one of whom is stretched at full length in the canoe, and the other sits in the seat, or round hole, which is nearly in the middle. Round this hole is a rim or hoop of wood, about which is sewed gut skin, that can be drawn together or opened like a purse, with leathern thongs fitted to the outer edge. The man seats himself in this place, draws the skin tight round his body over his gut frock, and brings the ends of the thongs or purse-string over the shoulder to keep it in its place. The sleeves of his frock are tied round his wrists; and it being close round his neck, and the hood drawn over his head, where it is confined by his cap, water can scarcely penetrate either to his body or into the canoe. If any should, however, insinuate itself, the boatman carries a piece of sponge with which he dries it up. He uses the double-bladed paddle, which is held with both hands in the middle, striking the water with a quick regular motion, first on one side and then on the other. By this means the canoe is impelled at a great rate, and in a direction as straight as a line can be drawn. In sailing from Egoochshac to Samganoodha, two or three canoes kept way with the ship, though she was going at the rate of seven miles an hour. Their fishing and hunting implements lie ready upon their canoes, under straps fixed for the purpose. They are all made, in great perfection, of wood and bone, and differ very little from those used by the Greenlanders, as they are described by Crantz. The only difference is in the point of the missile dart, which in some we saw here is not above an inch long; whereas Crantz says, that those of the Greenlanders are a foot and a half in length. These people are very expert in striking fish, both in the sea and in rivers. They also make use of hooks and lines, nets and wears. The hooks are composed of bone, and the lines of sinews.

The fishes which are common to other northern seas are found here, such as whales, grampuses, porpoises, sword-fish, halibut, cod, salmon, trout, soles, flat-fish ; several other sorts of small fish ; and there may be many more that we had no opportunity of seeing. Halibut and salmon seem to be in the greatest plenty, and on them the inhabitants of these isles subsist chiefly, at least they were the only sort of fish, except a few cod, which we observed to be laid up for their winter store. To the north of 60° the sea is in a manner destitute of small fish of every kind, but then whales are more numerous. Seals, and that whole tribe of sea-animals, are not so numerous as in many other seas. Nor can this be thought strange, since there is hardly any part of the coast on either continent, nor any of the islands lying between them, that is not inhabited, and whose inhabitants hunt these animals for their food and clothing. Sea-horses are, indeed, in prodigious numbers about the ice ; and the sea-otter is, I believe, nowhere found but in this sea. We sometimes saw an animal with a head like a seal's, that blew after the manner of whales. It was larger than a seal, and its colour was white, with some dark spots. Probably this was the sea-cow or "manatee."

I think I may venture to assert, that sea and water fowls are neither in such numbers nor in such variety as with us in the northern parts of the Atlantic Ocean. There are some, however, here that I do not remember to have seen anywhere else, particularly the *Alca monochroa* of Steller, and a black and white duck, which I conceive to be different from the stone-duck described by Krasheninikoff.[1] All the other birds seen by us are mentioned by this author, except some that we met with near the ice ; and most if not all of these are described by Martin in his voyage to Greenland. It is a little extraordin-

ary that penguins, which are common in many parts of the world, should not be found in this sea. Albatrosses, too, are so very scarce that I cannot help thinking that this is not their proper climate. The few land-birds that we met with are the same with those in Europe ; but there may be many others which we had no opportunity of knowing. A very beautiful bird was shot in the woods at Norton Sound, which I am told is sometimes found in England, and known by the name of chatterer. Our people met with other small birds there, but in no great variety and abundance ; such as the woodpecker, the bullfinch, the yellow finch, and a small bird called a titmouse.

As our excursions and observations were confined wholly to the sea-coast, it is not to be expected that we could know much of the animals or vegetables of the country. Except mosquitoes, there are few other insects, nor reptiles that I saw, but lizards. There are no deer upon Oonalashka or upon any other of the islands. Nor have they any domestic animals, not even dogs. Foxes and weasels were the only quadrupeds we saw ; but they told us that they had hares also and the "marmottas"[2] mentioned by Krasheninikoff. Hence it is evident that the sea and rivers supply the greatest share of food to the inhabitants. They are also obliged to the sea for all the wood made use of for building and other necessary purposes ; for not a stick grows upon any of the islands nor upon the adjacent coast of the continent.

The learned tell us, that the seeds of plants are by various means conveyed from one part of the world to another ; even to islands in the midst of great oceans and far remote from any other land. How comes it to pass that there are no trees growing on this part of the continent of America, nor any other of the islands lying near it ? They are certainly as well situated for receiving seeds, by

---

[1] In his "Description of Kamtschatka," published in French at Amsterdam in 1770, and afterwards translated into English.

[2] Marmots.

all the various ways I have heard of, as any of those coasts that abound in wood. May not Nature have denied to some soil the power of raising trees without the assistance of art? As to the drift-wood upon the shores of the islands I have no doubt that it comes from America. For although there may be none on the neighbouring coast, enough may grow farther up the country, which torrents in the spring may break loose and bring down to the sea. And not a little may be conveyed from the woody coasts, though they lie at a greater distance.

There are a great variety of plants at Oonalashka, and most of them were in flower the latter end of June. Several of them are such as we find in Europe and in other parts of America, particularly in Newfoundland; and others of them, which are also met with in Kamtschatka, are eaten by the natives both there and here. The principal one is the "faranne," or lily root, which is about the size of a root of garlic, round, made up of a number of small cloves and grains like groats. When boiled it is somewhat like saloop; the taste is not disagreeable, and we found means to make some good dishes with it. It does not seem to be in great plenty, for we got none but what Ismyloff gave us. We must reckon amongst the food of the natives some other wild roots; the stalk of a plant resembling *Angelica;* and berries of several different sorts, such as bramble-berries, cran-berries, hurtle-berries, heath-berries, a small red berry which in Newfoundland is called partridge-berry; and another brown berry unknown to us. This has somewhat of the taste of a sloe, but is unlike it in every other respect. It is very astringent if eaten in any quantity. Brandy might be distilled from it. Captain Clerke attempted to preserve some, but they fermented and became as strong as if they had been steeped in spirits. There were a few other plants which we found serviceable, but are not made use of by either Russians or natives; such as wild purslain, peatops, a kind of scurvy-grass, cresses, and some others. All these we found very palatable dressed either in soups or in salads. On the low ground and in the valleys is plenty of grass, which grows very thick and to a great length. I am of opinion that cattle might subsist at Oonalashka all the year round without being housed. And the soil in many places seemed capable of producing grain, roots, and vegetables. But at present the Russian traders and the natives seem satisfied with what Nature brings forth.

Native sulphur was seen amongst the inhabitants of the island, but I had no opportunity of learning where they got it. We found also ochre, a stone that gives a purple colour, and another that gives a very good green. It may be doubted whether this last is known. In its natural state, it is of a greyish green colour, coarse and heavy. It easily dissolves in oil; but when put into water it entirely loses its properties. It seemed to be scarce in Oonalashka; but we were told that it was in greater plenty on the Island Oonemak. As to the stones about the shore and hills I saw nothing in them that was uncommon.

The people of Oonalashka bury their dead on the summits of hills, and raise a little hillock over the grave. In a walk into the country one of the natives who attended me pointed out several of these receptacles of the dead. There was one of them by the side of the road leading from the harbour to the village, over which was raised a heap of stones. It was observed that every one who passed it added one to it.[1] I saw in the country several stone hillocks that seemed to have been raised by art. Many of them were apparently of great antiquity. What their notions are of the Deity and of a

---

[1] It is almost superfluous to recall here the ancient Celtic practice, and modern Scottish proverb of "adding a stone to the cairn" of any one to whose memory honour was intended.

future state, I know not.   I am equally unacquainted with their diversions; nothing having been seen that could give us an insight into either.

They are remarkably cheerful and friendly amongst each other; and always behaved with great civility to us.   The Russians told us that they never had any connections with their women, because they were not Christians.   Our people were not so scrupulous; and some of them had reason to repent that the females of Oonalashka encouraged their addresses without any reserve, for their health suffered by a distemper that is not unknown here.   The natives of this island are also subject to the cancer, or a complaint like it, which those whom it attacks are very careful to conceal. They do not seem to be long-lived. I nowhere saw a person, man or woman, whom I could suppose to be sixty years of age; and but very few who appeared to be above fifty. Probably their hard way of living may be the means of shortening their days.

I have frequently had occasion to mention, from the time of our arrival in Prince William's Sound, how remarkably the natives on this northwest side of America resemble the Greenlanders and Esquimaux, in various particulars of person, dress, weapons, canoes, and the like.   However, I was much less struck with this than with the affinity which we found subsisting between the dialects of the Greenlanders and Esquimaux and those of Norton Sound and Oonalashka.   This appears from a table of corresponding words which I put together.   Enough is certain to warrant this judgment, that there is great reason to believe that all these nations are of the same extraction; and if so, there can be little doubt of there being a northern communication of some sort by sea between this west side of America and the east side through Baffin's Bay, which communication, however, may be effectually shut up against ships by ice and other impediments.   Such

at least was my opinion at this time.[1]

____

CHAPTER VII.

In the morning of Monday the 26th we put to sea from Samganoodha harbour, and, as the wind was southerly, stood away to the westward.   My intention was now to proceed to Sandwich Islands, there to spend a few of the winter months, in case we should meet with the necessary refreshments, and then to direct our course to Kamtschatka, so as to endeavour to be there by the middle of May the ensuing summer.   In consequence of this resolution, I gave Captain Clerke orders how to proceed in case of separation; appointing Sandwich Islands for the first place of rendezvous, and the harbour of Petropaulowska in Kamtschatka for the second.   Soon after we were out of the harbour, the wind veered to the SE. and ESE., which by the evening carried us as far as the western part of Oonalashka, where we got the wind at S.   With this we stretched to the westward till 7 o'clock the next morning, when we wore and stood to the E.   The wind by this time had increased in such a manner as to reduce us to our three courses. It blew in very heavy squalls, attended with rain, hail, and snow.

At 9 o'clock in the morning of the 28th, the Island of Oonalashka bore SE., four leagues distant.   We then wore and stood to the westward.   The strength of the gale was now over, and towards evening the little wind that blew insensibly veered round to the E., where it continued but a short time before it got to NE. and increased to a very hard gale with rain. I steered first to the southward; and as the wind inclined to the N. and NW., I steered more westerly.   On

____

[1] The justice of Captain Cook's inference has been amply demonstrated since his time by the success of those expeditions, the history of which is familiar to all.

the 29th, at half-past six in the morning, we saw land extending from E. by S. to S. by W., supposed to be the Island Amoghta. At eight, finding that we could not weather the island, as the wind had now veered to the westward, I gave over plying, and bore away for Oonalashka, with a view of going to the northward and eastward of that island, not daring to attempt a passage to the SE. of it in so hard a gale of wind. At the time we bore away, the land extended from E. by S. half S. to SSW., four leagues distant. The Longitude by the timekeeper was 191° 17′ and the Latitude 53° 38′. At 11 o'clock, as we were steering to the NE., we discovered an elevated rock, like a tower, bearing NNE. half E., four leagues distant. It lies in the Latitude of 53° 57′ and in the Longitude of 191° 2′. We must have passed very near it in the night. We could judge of its steepness from this circumstance, that the sea, which now ran very high, broke nowhere but against it. At three in the afternoon, after getting a sight of Oonalashka, we shortened sail and hauled the wind, not having time to get through the passage before night. At daybreak the next morning we bore away under courses and close-reefed topsails, having a very hard gale at WNW., with heavy squalls attended with snow. At noon we were in the middle of the strait between Oonalashka and Oonella, the harbour of Samganoodha bearing SSE., one league distant. At three in the afternoon, being through the strait and clear of the isles, Cape Providence bearing WSW., two or three leagues distant, we steered to the southward under double-reefed topsails and courses, with the wind at WNW., a strong gale and fair weather.

On Monday the 2d of November, the wind veered to the southward, and before night blew a violent storm, which obliged us to bring to. The Discovery fired several guns, which we answered, but without knowing on what occasion they were fired. At 8 o'clock we lost sight of her and did not see her again till eight the next morning. At ten she joined us; and as the height of the gale was now over, and the wind had veered back to WNW., we made sail and resumed our course to the southward. The 6th in the evening, being in the Latitude of 42° 12′ and in the Longitude of 201° 26′, the variation was 17° 15′ E. The next morning, our Latitude being 41° 20′ and our Longitude 202°, a shag or cormorant flew several times round the ship. As these birds are seldom if ever known to fly far out of sight of land, I judged that some was not far distant. However, we could see none. In the afternoon, there being but little wind, Captain Clerke came on board and informed me of a melancholy accident that happened on board his ship the second night after we left Samganoodha. The main-tack gave way, killed one man, and wounded the boatswain and two or three more. In addition to this misfortune, I now learned that on the evening of the 3d his sails and rigging received considerable damage; and that the guns which he fired were the signal to bring to.

On the 8th the wind was at N., a gentle breeze, with clear weather. On the 9th, in the Latitude of 39½°, we had eight hours' calm. This was succeeded by the wind from the S. attended with fair weather. Availing ourselves of this, as many of our people as could handle a needle were set to work to repair the sails; and the carpenters were employed to put the boats in order. On the 12th at noon, being then in the Latitude of 38° 14′ and in the Longitude of 206° 17′, the wind returned back to the northward; and on the 15th, in the Latitude of 33° 30′, it veered to the E. At this time we saw a tropic-bird and a dolphin; the first that we had observed during the passage. On the 17th the wind veered to the southward, where it continued till the afternoon of the 19th, when a squall of wind and rain brought it at once round by the W. to the N. This was in the Latitude of 32° 26′, and in the Longitude of 207° 30′. The wind presently increased to a very strong gale, attended with rain, so as to bring us under double-reefed topsails. In lowering down the main-topsail to reef it, the wind tore it quite out of the foot-rope; and it was split in several other parts. This sail had only been brought to the yard the day before, after having had a repair. The next morning we got another topsail to the yard. This gale proved to be the forerunner of the trade-wind, which in Latitude 25° veered to the E. and ESE. I continued to steer to the southward till daylight in the morning of the 25th, at which time we were in the Latitude of 20° 55′. I now spread the ships[1] and steered to the west. In the evening we joined, and at midnight brought to. At daybreak next morning land was seen extending from SSE. to W. We made sail and stood for it. At eight it extended from SE. half S. to W., the nearest part two leagues distant. It was supposed that we saw the extent of the land to the E., but not to the W. We were now satisfied that the group of the Sandwich Islands had been only imperfectly discovered; as those of them which we had visited in our progress northward all lie to the leeward of our present station.

In the country was an elevated saddle hill, whose summit appeared above the clouds. From this hill the land fell in a gentle slope, and terminated in a steep rocky coast, against which the sea broke in a dreadful surf. Finding that we could not weather the island, I bore up and ranged along the coast to the westward. It was not long before we saw people on several parts of the shore, and some houses and plantations. The country seemed to be both well wooded and watered, and running streams were seen falling into the sea in various places. As it was of the last importance to procure a supply of provisions at these islands, and experience having taught me that I could have no chance to succeed in this if a free trade

with the natives were to be allowed, that is, if it were left to every man's discretion to trade for what he pleased and in the manner he pleased; for this substantial reason I now published an order prohibiting all persons from trading except such as should bo appointed by me and Captain Clerke, and even these were enjoined to trade only for provisions and refreshments. Women were also forbidden to be admitted into the ships, except under certain restrictions. But the evil I meant to prevent by this regulation, I soon found had already got amongst them.

At noon the coast extended from S. 81° E. to N. 56° W.; a low flat, like an isthmus, bore S. 42° W.; the nearest shore three or four miles distant; the Latitude was 20° 59′, and the Longitude 203° 50′. Seeing some canoes coming off to us, I brought to. As soon as they got alongside, many of the people who conducted them came into the ship without the least hesitation. We found them to be of the same nation with the inhabitants of the islands more to leeward which we had already visited; and, if we did not mistake them, they knew of our having been there. Indeed, it rather appeared too evident, for these people had got amongst them the venereal distemper, and as yet I knew of no other way of its reaching them but by an intercourse with their neighbours since our leaving them. We got from our visitors a quantity of cuttle-fish for nails and pieces of iron. They brought very little fruit and roots, but told us that they had plenty of them on their island, as also hogs and fowls. In the evening, the horizon being clear to the westward, we judged the westernmost land in sight to be an island separated from that off which we now were. Having no doubt that the people would return to the ships next day with the produce of their country, I kept plying off all night, and in the morning stood close in shore. At first only a few of the natives visited us; but towards noon we had the company of a good many, who brought with them bread-fruit,

---

[1] To give the better chance of discovering the land, near which he knew that he had arrived.

potatoes, "taro" or eddy roots, a few plantains, and small pigs, all of which they exchanged for nails and iron tools. Indeed, we had nothing else to give them. We continued trading with them till 4 o'clock in the afternoon, when, having disposed of all their cargoes, and not seeming inclined to fetch more, we made sail and stood off shore. While we were lying to, though the wind blew fresh, I observed that the ships drifted to the east; consequently there must have been a current setting in that direction. This encouraged me to ply to windward, with a view to get round the east end of the island, and so have the whole leeside before us. In the afternoon of the 30th, being off the NE. end of the island, several canoes came off to the ships. Most of these belonged to a chief named Terreeoboo, who came in one of them. He made me a present of two or three small pigs, and we got by barter from the other people a little fruit. After a stay of about two hours they all left us, except six or eight of their company who chose to remain on board. A double sailing canoe came soon after to attend upon them, which we towed astern all night. In the evening we discovered another island to windward, which the natives call Owhyhee.[1] The name of that off which we had been for some days, we were also told, is Mowee.

On the 1st of December, at eight in the morning, Owhyhee extended from S. 22° E. to S. 12° W.; and Mowee from N. 41° to N. 83° W. Finding that we could fetch Owhyhee, I stood for it; and our visitors from Mowee, not choosing to accompany us, embarked in their canoe and went ashore. At seven in the evening we were close up with the north side of Owhyhee,

where we spent the night standing off and on. In the morning of the 2d we were surprised to see the summits of the mountains on Owhyhee covered with snow. They did not appear to be of any extraordinary height; and yet in some places the snow seemed to be of a considerable depth, and to have lain there some time. As we drew near the shore some of the natives came off to us. They were a little shy at first; but we soon enticed some of them on board, and at last prevailed upon them to return to the island and bring off what we wanted. Soon after these reached the shore, we had company enough, and few coming empty-handed, we got a tolerable supply of small pigs, fruit, and roots. We continued trading with them till six in the evening, when we made sail and stood off, with a view of plying to windward round the island. The current which I have mentioned as setting to the eastward had now ceased; for we gained but little by plying. On the 6th, in the evening, being about five leagues farther up the coast, and near the shore, we had some traffic with the natives. But as it had furnished only a trifling supply, I stood in again the next morning, when we had a considerable number of visitors; and we lay to, trading with them till two in the afternoon. By that time we had procured pork, fruit, and roots sufficient for four or five days. We then made sail and continued to ply to windward.

Having procured a quantity of sugar-cane, and having upon a trial made but a few days before found that a strong decoction of it produced a very palatable beer, I ordered some more to be brewed for our general use. But when the cask was now broached not one of my crew would even so much as taste it. As I had no motive in preparing this beverage but to save our spirit for a colder climate, I gave myself no trouble, either by exerting authority or by having recourse to persuasion, to prevail upon them to drink it, knowing that there was no danger of the scurvy so long as we could get a plentiful supply of other

---

[1] Better known as Hawaii; it is the largest of the group. Mowee is marked in the later maps as Maue Honolulu, the seat of government, is on the Island of Oahu, which in his former notice of the Sandwich Islands Cook merely mentions under the name of Woahoo (Book III., Chapter XII.).

vegetables.   But that I might not be disappointed in my views, I gave orders that no grog should be served in either ship.   I myself and the officers continued to make use of this sugar-cane beer whenever we could get materials for brewing it.   A few hops, of which we had some on board, improved it much.   It has the taste of new malt beer, and I believe no one will doubt of its being very wholesome.   And yet my inconsiderate crew alleged that it was injurious to their health.   They had no better reason to support a resolution which they took on our first arrival in King George's [Nootka] Sound, not to drink the spruce-beer made there.   But whether from a consideration that it was not the first time of their being required to use that liquor, or from some other reason, they did not attempt to carry their purpose into actual execution; and I had never heard of it till now, when they renewed their ignorant opposition to my best endeavours to serve them.   Every innovation whatever on board a ship, though ever so much to the advantage of seamen, is sure to meet with their highest disapprobation.   Both portable soup and sour krout[1] were at first condemned as stuff unfit for human beings.   Few commanders have introduced into their ships more novelties, as useful varieties of food and drink, than I have done.   Indeed few commanders have had the same opportunities of trying such experiments, or been driven to the same necessity of trying them.   It has, however, been in a great measure owing to various little deviations from established practice that I have been able to preserve my people, generally speaking, from that dreadful distemper the scurvy, which has perhaps

destroyed more of our sailors in their peaceful voyages than have fallen by the enemy in military expeditions.

I kept at some distance from the coast till the 13th, when I stood in again six leagues farther to windward than we had as yet reached; and after having some trade with the natives who visited us, returned to sea.   I should have got near the shore again on the 15th for a supply of fruit or roots, but the wind happening to be at SE. by S. and SSE., I thought this a good time to stretch to the eastward, in order to get round, or at least to get a sight of the south-east end of the island.   The wind continued at SE. by S. most part of the 16th.   It was variable between S. and E. on the 17th, and on the 18th it was continually veering from one quarter to another, blowing sometimes in hard squalls, and at other times calm, with thunder, lightning, and rain.   In the afternoon we had the wind westerly for a few hours, but in the evening it shifted to E. by S., and we stood to the southward close-hauled, under an easy sail, as the Discovery was at some distance astern.   At this time the south-east point of the island bore SW. by S., about five leagues distant; and I made no doubt that I should be able to weather it.   But at 1 o'clock next morning it fell calm, and we were left to the mercy of a north-easterly swell which impelled us fast toward the land; so that long before daybreak we saw lights upon the shore, which was not more than a league distant.   The night was dark, with thunder, lightning, and rain.

At 3 o'clock the calm was succeeded by a breeze from E. blowing in squalls, with rain.   We stood to the NE., thinking it the best tack to clear the coast; but if it had been daylight, we should have chosen the other.   At daybreak the coast was seen extending from N. by W. to SW. by W., a dreadful surf breaking upon the shore, which was not more than half-a-league distant.   It was evident that we had been in the most imminent danger.   Nor were we yet in safety, the wind veering more easterly, so that for some

---

[1] Cook on his second voyage took a quantity of this with him.   He describes it as cabbage cut small, to which is put a little salt, juniper-berries, and aniseed; it is then fermented, and close packed in casks, where it will keep a long time, retaining its virtues as a wholesome vegetable food and a great anti-scorbutic.

time we did but just keep our distance from the coast. What made our situation more alarming was the leach-rope of the main-topsail giving way, which was the occasion of the sail's being rent in two; and the two top-gallant-sails gave way in the same manner, though not half worn out. By taking a favourable opportunity, we soon got others to the yards, and then we left the land astern. The Discovery, by being at some distance to the north, was never near the land, nor did we see her till 8 o'clock.

As soon as daylight appeared the natives ashore displayed a white flag, which we conceived to be a signal of peace and friendship. Some of them ventured out after us, but the wind freshening, and it not being safe to wait, they were soon left astern. In the afternoon, after making another attempt to weather the eastern extreme, which failed, I gave it up and ran down to the Discovery. Indeed it was of no consequence to get round the island, for we had seen its extent to the south-east, which was the thing I aimed at; and according to the information which we had got from the natives, there is no other island to the windward of this. However, as we were so near the south end of it, and as the least shift of wind in our favour would serve to carry us round, I did not wholly give up the idea of weathering it, and therefore continued to ply. On the 20th at noon this south-east point bore S. three leagues distant, the snowy hills WNW., and we were about four miles from the nearest shore. In the afternoon some of the natives came in their canoes, bringing with them a few pigs and plantains. The latter were very acceptable, having had no vegetables for some days; but the supply we now received was so inconsiderable, being barely sufficient for one day, that I stood in again the next morning till within three or four miles of the land, where we were met by a number of canoes laden with provisions. We brought to and continued trading with the people in them till four in the afternoon, when, having got a pretty good supply, we made sail and stretched off to the northward.

I had never met with a behaviour so free from reserve and suspicion in my intercourse with any tribes of savages as we experienced in the people of this island. It was very common for them to send up into the ship the several articles they brought off for barter; afterwards they would come in themselves and make their bargains on the quarter-deck. The people of Otaheite, even after our repeated visits, do not care to put so much confidence in us. I infer from this that those of Owhyhee must be more faithful in their dealings with one another than the inhabitants of Otaheite are. For if little faith were observed amongst themselves they would not be so ready to trust strangers. It is also to be observed, to their honour, that they had never once attempted to cheat us in exchanges, nor to commit a theft. They understand trading as well as most people, and seemed to comprehend clearly the reason of our plying upon the coast. For though they brought off provisions in great plenty, particularly pigs, yet they kept up their price; and rather than dispose of them for less than they thought they were worth, would take them ashore again.

On the 22d, at eight in the morning, we tacked to the southward, with a fresh breeze at E. by N. At noon the Latitude was 20° 28′ 30″, and the snowy peak bore SW. half S. We had a good view of it the preceding day, and the quantity of snow seemed to have increased and to extend lower down the hill. I stood to the SE. till midnight, then tacked to the N. till four in the morning, when we returned to the SE. tack; and as the wind was at NE. by E., we had hopes of weathering the island. We should have succeeded if the wind had not died away and left us to the mercy of a great swell, which carried us fast toward the land, which was not two leagues distant. At length we got our head off, and some light puffs of wind, which came with showers of rain, put us out of danger. While we lay, as it were, becalmed, several of the islanders came off with hogs, fowls, fruit, and roots. Out of one canoe we got a goose, which was about the size of a Muscovy duck; its plumage was dark grey, and the bill and legs black.

At four in the afternoon, after purchasing everything that the natives had brought off, which was full as much as we had occasion for, we made sail and stretched to the N., with the wind at ENE. At midnight we tacked and stood to the SE. Upon a supposition that the Discovery would see us tack, the signal was omitted; but she did not see us, as we afterwards found, and continued standing to the N., for at daylight next morning she was not in sight. At this time, the weather being hazy, we could not see far, so that it was possible the Discovery might be following us; and being past the north-east part of the island I was tempted to stand on till, by the wind veering to NE., we could not weather the land upon the other tack. Consequently we could not stand to the N. to join or look for the Discovery. At noon we were by observation in the Latitude of 19° 55′ and in the Longitude of 205° 3′; the south-east point of the island bore S. by E. quarter E., six leagues distant; the other extreme bore N. 60° W., and we were two leagues from the nearest shore. At six in the evening the southernmost extreme of the island bore SW., the nearest shore seven or eight miles distant, so that we had now succeeded in getting to the windward of the island, which we had aimed at with so much perseverance. The Discovery, however, was not yet to be seen; but the wind, as we had it, being very favourable for her to follow us, I concluded that it would not be long before she joined us. I therefore kept cruising off this south-east point of the island, which lies in the Latitude of 19° 34′ and in the Longitude of 205° 6′, till I was satisfied that Captain Clerke could not join me here. I now conjectured that he had not been able to weather the north-east part of the island, and had

gone to leeward in order to meet me that way.

As I generally kept from five to ten leagues from the land, no canoes except one came off to us till the 28th, when we were visited by a dozen or fourteen. The people who conducted them brought, as usual, the produce of the island. I was very sorry that they had taken the trouble to come so far. For we could not trade with them, our old stock not being as yet consumed; and we had found by late experience that the hogs could not be kept alive, nor the roots preserved from putrefaction many days. However, I intended not to leave this part of the island before I got a supply, as it would not be easy to return to it again in case it should be found necessary. We began to be in want on the 30th, and I would have stood in near the shore but was prevented by a calm; but a breeze springing up at midnight from S. and SW., we were enabled to stand in for the land at daybreak. At 10 o'clock in the morning we were met by the islanders with fruit and roots, but in all the canoes were only three small pigs. Our not having bought those which had been lately brought off may be supposed to be the reason of this very scanty supply. We brought to for the purposes of trade, but soon after our marketing was interrupted by a very hard rain, and besides we were rather too far from the shore. Nor durst I go nearer, for I could not depend upon the wind's remaining where it was for a moment; the swell also being high, and setting obliquely upon the shore, against which it broke in a frightful surf. In the evening the weather mended, the night was clear, and it was spent in making short boards.

Before daybreak the atmosphere was again loaded with heavy clouds, and the New Year was ushered in with very hard rain, which continued at intervals till past 10 o'clock. The wind was southerly, a light breeze with some calms. When the rain ceased, the sky cleared and the breeze freshened. Being at this time about five miles from the land, several canoes arrived with fruit and roots, and at last some hogs were brought off. We lay to, trading with them, till 3 o'clock in the afternoon, when, having a tolerable supply, we made sail with a view of proceeding to the north-west or leeside of the island, to look for the Discovery. It was necessary, however, the wind being at S., to stretch first to the eastward, till midnight, when the wind came more favourable, and we went upon the other tack. For several days past both wind and weather had been exceedingly unsettled, and there fell a great deal of rain. The three following days were spent in running down the south-east side of the island. For during the nights we stood off and on, and part of each day was employed in lying to, in order to furnish an opportunity to the natives of trading with us. They sometimes came on board while we were five leagues from the shore; but whether from a fear of losing their goods in the sea, or from the uncertainty of the market, they never brought much with them. The principal article procured was salt, which was extremely good.

On the 5th, in the morning, we passed the south point of the island, which lies in the Latitude of 18° 54', and beyond it we found the coast to trend N. 60° W. On this point stands a pretty large village, the inhabitants of which thronged off to the ship with hogs and women. It was not possible to keep the latter from coming on board; and no women I ever met with were less reserved. Indeed it appeared to me that they visited us with no other view than to make a surrender of their persons. As I had now got a quantity of salt, I purchased no hogs but such as were fit for salting, refusing all that were under size. However we could seldom get any above fifty or sixty pounds weight. It was happy for us that we still had some vegetables on board, for we now received few such productions. Indeed this part of the country, from its appearance, did not seem capable of affording them. Marks of its having been laid waste by the

explosion of a volcano everywhere presented themselves; and though we had as yet seen nothing like one upon the island, the devastation that it had made in this neighbourhood was visible to the naked eye.[1] This part of the coast is sheltered from the reigning winds; but we could find no bottom to anchor upon, a line of 160 fathoms not reaching it, within the distance of half-a-mile from the shore. The islanders having all left us towards the evening, we ran a few miles down the coast, and then spent the night standing off and on.

The next morning the natives visited us again, bringing with them the same articles of commerce as before. Being now near the shore, I sent Mr Bligh, the master, in a boat to sound the coast, with orders to land and to look for fresh water. Upon his return he reported that at two cables' length from the shore he had found no soundings with a line of 160 fathoms; that when he landed he found no stream or spring, but only rain water deposited in holes upon the rocks, and even that was brackish from the spray of the sea; and that the surface of the country was entirely composed of slags and ashes, with a few plants here and there interspersed. Between ten and eleven we saw with pleasure the Discovery coming round the south point of the island; and at one in the afternoon she joined us. Captain Clerke then coming on board, informed me that he had cruised four or five days where we were separated, and then plied round the east side of the island; but that, meeting with unfavourable winds, he had been carried to some distance from the coast. He had one of the islanders on board all this time, who had remained there from choice, and had refused to quit the ship though opportunities had offered. Having spent the night standing off and on, we stood in again

---

[1] Several volcanoes are still active in the islands; and two of them, Morena Loa and Morena Kea, rise to the very respectable altitude of some 15,000 feet.

the next morning, and when we were about a league from the shore many of the natives visited us.

At daybreak on the 8th we found that the currents during the night, which we spent in plying, had carried us back considerably to windward; so that we were now off the south-west point of the island. There we brought to, in order to give the natives an opportunity of trading with us. We spent the night as usual, standing off and on. It happened that four men and ten women who had come on board the preceding day still remained with us. As I did not like the company of the latter, I stood inshore towards noon, principally with a view to get them out of the ship, and some canoes coming off I took that opportunity of sending away our guests. We had light airs from NW. and SW., and calms, till eleven in the morning of the 10th, when the wind freshened at WNW., which, with a strong current setting to the SE., so much retarded us that in the evening between 7 and 8 o'clock the south point of the island bore N. 10¼° W., four leagues distant. The south snowy hill now bore N. 1¼° E.

At four in the morning of the 11th, the wind having fixed at W., I stood in for the land in order to get some refreshments. As we drew near the shore the natives began to come off. We lay to, or stood on and off, trading with them all the day, but got a very scanty supply at last. Many canoes visited us whose people had not a single thing to barter, which convinced us that this part of the island must be very poor, and that we had already got all that they could spare. We spent the 12th plying off and on, with a fresh gale at W. A mile from the shore, and to the NE. of the south point of the island, having tried soundings, we found ground at fifty-five fathoms depth, the bottom a fine sand. At five in the evening we stood to the SW., with the wind at WNW., and soon after midnight we had a calm. At 8 o'clock next morning, having got a small breeze at SSE., we steered to the NNW. in for the land. Soon after, a few canoes came alongside with some hogs, but without any vegetables, which articles we most wanted. We had now made some progress; for at noon the south point of the island bore S. 86¼° E., the south-west point N. 13° W., the nearest shore two leagues distant, Latitude by observation 18° 56', and our Longitude by the timekeeper 203° 40'. We had got the length of the south-west point of the island in the evening; but the wind now veering to the westward and northward, during the night we lost all that we had gained. Next morning, being still off the south-west point of the island, some canoes came off, but they brought nothing that we were in want of. We had now neither fruit nor roots, and were under a necessity of making use of some of our sea provisions. At length some canoes from the northward brought us a small supply of hogs and roots.

We had variable light airs, next to a calm, the following day, till five in the afternoon, when a small breeze at ENE. springing up, we were at last enabled to steer along shore to the northward. The weather being fine, we had plenty of company this day, and abundance of everything. Many of our visitors remained with us on board all night, and we towed their canoes astern. At daybreak on the 16th, seeing the appearance of a bay, I sent Mr Bligh, with a boat from each ship, to examine it, being at this time three leagues off. Canoes now began to arrive from all parts, so that before 10 o'clock, there were not fewer than a thousand about the two ships, most of them crowded with people, and well laden with hogs and other productions of the island. We had the most satisfying proof of their friendly intentions, for we did not see a single person who had with him a weapon of any sort. Trade and curiosity alone had brought them off. Among such numbers as we had at times on board, it is no wonder that some should betray a thievish disposition. One of our visitors took out of the ship a boat's rudder. He was discovered, but too late to recover it. I thought this a good opportunity to show these people the use of fire-arms; and two or three muskets, and as many four-pounders were fired over the canoe which carried off the rudder. As it was not intended that any of the shot should take effect, the surrounding multitude of natives seemed rather more surprised than frightened. In the evening, Mr Bligh returned and reported that he had found a bay in which was good anchorage and fresh water, in a situation tolerably easy to be come at. Into this bay I resolved to carry the ships, there to refit and supply ourselves with every refreshment that the place could afford. As night approached, the greater part of our visitors retired to the shore; but numbers of them requested our permission to sleep on board. Curiosity was not the only motive, at least with some; for the next morning several things were missing, which determined me not to entertain so many another night.

At 11 o'clock in the forenoon we anchored in the bay (which is called by the natives Karakakooa),[1] in thirteen fathoms water, over a sandy bottom, and about a quarter of a mile from the north-east shore. In this situation the south point of the bay bore S. by W., and the north point W. half N. We moored with the stream anchor and cable to the northward, unbent the sails, and struck the yards and topmasts. The ships continued to be much crowded with natives, and were surrounded by a multitude of canoes. I had nowhere in the course of my voyages, seen so numerous a body of people assembled in one place. For besides those who

had come off to us in canoes, all the shore of the bay was covered with spectators, and many hundreds were swimming round the ships like shoals of fish. We could not but be struck with the singularity of this scene; and perhaps there were few on board who now lamented our having failed in our endeavours to find a northern passage homeward last summer. To this disappointment we owed our having it in our power to revisit the Sandwich Islands, and to enrich our voyage with a discovery which, though the last, seemed in many respects to be the most important that had hitherto been made by Europeans throughout the extent of the Pacific Ocean.[2]

---

[1] It lies on the west side of Owhyhee or Hawaii, near the southern extremity of the island.

[2] With these ardently confident expressions of hopefulness, and of most justifiable satisfaction in the past and prospective achievements of the voyage—so vividly in contrast with the calamity that imminently impended—Captain Cook's journal closes. The third volume of the Original Edition, written by Captain King, and consisting, with appendices, of between 500 and 600 pages (equal to at least 250 pages of the present edition), recounts in two books, V. and VI., the transactions on returning to the Sandwich Islands," and the " transactions during the second expedition to the north by the way of Kamtschatka; and on the return home by the way of Canton and the Cape of Good Hope." As the death of Captain Cook diminishes notably the interest of the voyage in its sequel, despite the elaborate and curious descriptions of Kamtschatka and the Kamtschadales—and as there is little or nothing in the homeward route, that has not been perhaps more vividly described in the narratives of the older navigators,—only that part of Captain King's volume is here given, which relates to the mournful events in Karakakooa Bay.

BOOK V.

CAPTAIN KING'S JOURNAL OF THE TRANSACTIONS ON RETURNING TO THE SANDWICH ISLANDS.

CHAPTER I.

KARAKAKOOA Bay is situated on the west side of the Island of Owhyhee, in a district called Akona. It is about a mile in depth, and bounded by two low points of land at the distance of half-a-league, and bearing SSE. and NNW. from each other. On the north point, which is flat and barren, stands the village of Kowrowa, and in the bottom of the bay, near a grove of tall cocoa-nut trees, there is another village of a more considerable size called Kakooa: between them runs a high rocky cliff, inaccessible from the sea shore. On the south side, the coast, for about a mile inland, has a rugged appearance; beyond which the country rises with a gradual ascent, and is overspread with cultivated enclosures and groves of cocoa-nut trees, where the habitations of the natives are scattered in great numbers. The shore all around the bay is covered with a black coral rock, which makes the landing very dangerous in rough weather; except at the village of Kakooa, where there is a fine sandy beach, with a " morai," or burying-place, at one extremity, and a small well of fresh water at the other. This bay appearing to Captain Cook a proper place to refit the ships, and lay in an additional supply of water and provisions, we moored on the north side, about a quarter of a mile from the shore, Kowrowa bearing NW.

As soon as the inhabitants perceived our intention of anchoring in the bay, they came off from the shore in astonishing numbers, and expressed their joy by singing and shouting and exhibiting a variety of wild and extravagant gestures. The sides, the decks, and rigging of both ships were soon completely covered with them; and a multitude of women and boys, who had not been able to get canoes, came swimming round us in shoals, many of whom, not finding room on board, remained the whole day playing in the water. Among the chiefs who came on board the Resolution was a young man called Pareea, whom we soon perceived to be a person of great authority. On presenting himself to Captain Cook, he told him that he was Jakanee[1] to the King of the island, who was at that time engaged on a military expedition at Mowee, and was expected to return within three or four days. A few presents from Captain Cook attached him entirely to our interests, and he became exceedingly useful to us in the management of his countrymen, as we had soon occasion to experience. For we had not been long at anchor when it was observed that the Discovery had such a number of people hanging on one side, as occasioned her to heel considerably; and that the men were unable to keep off the crowds which continued pressing into her. Captain Cook, being apprehensive that she might suffer some injury, pointed out the danger to Pareea, who immediately went to their assistance, cleared the ship of its incumbrances, and drove away the canoes that surrounded her.

The authority of the chiefs over the inferior people appeared from this incident to be of the most despotic kind. A similar instance of it happened the same day on board the Resolution, where the crowd being so

[1] We afterward met with several others of the same denomination; but whether it be an office, or some degree of affinity, we could never learn with certainty.—*Note in Original Edition.*

great as to impede the necessary business of the ship, we were obliged to have recourse to the assistance of Kaneena, another of their chiefs, who had likewise attached himself to Captain Cook. The inconvenience we laboured under being made known, he immediately ordered his countrymen to quit the vessel; and we were not a little surprised to see them jump overboard without a moment's hesitation, all except one man, who loitering behind and showing some unwillingness to obey, Kaneena took him up in his arms and threw him into the sea. Both these chiefs were men of strong and well-proportioned bodies, and of countenances remarkably pleasing. Kaneena especially was one of the finest men I ever saw. He was about six feet high, had regular and expressive features, with lively, dark eyes; his carriage was easy, firm, and graceful.

It has been already mentioned that during our long cruise off this island the inhabitants had always behaved with great fairness and honesty in their dealings, and had not shown the slightest propensity to theft; which appeared to us the more extraordinary, because those with whom we had hitherto held any intercourse were of the lowest rank, either servants or fisherman. We now found the case exceedingly altered. The immense crowd of islanders which blocked up every part of the ships, not only afforded frequent opportunity of pilfering without risk of discovery, but our inferiority in number held forth a prospect of escaping with impunity in case of detection. Another circumstance to which we attributed this alteration in their behaviour, was the presence and encouragement of their chiefs; for, generally tracing the booty into the possession of some men of consequence, we had the strongest reason to suspect that these depredations were committed at their instigation.

Soon after the Resolution had got into her station, our two friends, Pareea and Kaneena, brought on board a third chief named Koah, who, we were told, was a priest, and had been in his youth a distinguished warrior. He was a little old man, of an emaciated figure; his eyes exceedingly sore and red, and his body covered with a white leprous scurf, the effects of an immoderate use of the "ava." Being led into the cabin, he approached Captain Cook with great veneration, and threw over his shoulders a piece of red cloth which he had brought along with him. Then stepping a few paces back, he made an offering of a small pig which he held in his hand, whilst he pronounced a discourse that lasted for a considerable time. This ceremony was frequently repeated during our stay at Owhyhee, and appeared to us from many circumstances to be a sort of religious adoration. Their idols we found always arrayed with red cloth in the same manner as was done to Captain Cook; and a small pig was their usual offering to the "Eatooas." Their speeches, or prayers, were uttered, too, with a readiness and volubility that indicated them to be according to some formulary. When this ceremony was over, Koah dined with Captain Cook, eating plentifully of what was set before him; but, like the rest of the inhabitants of the islands in these seas, could scarcely be prevailed on to taste a second time our wine or spirits. In the evening, Captain Cook, attended by Mr Bayly and myself, accompanied him on shore. We landed at the beach, and were received by four men who carried wands tipped with dog's hair, and marched before us, pronouncing with a loud voice a short sentence, in which we could only distinguish the word "Orono."[1] The crowd which

---

[1] Captain Cook generally went by this name amongst the natives of Owhyhee; but we could never learn its precise meaning. Sometimes they applied it to an invisible being, who, they said, lived in the heavens. We also found that it was a title belonging to a personage of great rank and power in the island, who resembles pretty much the Delai Lama of the Tartars,

had been collected on the shore retired at our approach, and not a person was to be seen, except a few lying prostrate on the ground near the huts of the adjoining village.

Before I proceed to relate the adoration that was paid to Captain Cook, and the peculiar ceremonies with which he was received on this fatal island, it will be necessary to describe the "morai," situated, as I have already mentioned, at the south side of the beach at Kakooa. It was a square, solid pile of stones, about forty yards long, twenty broad, and fourteen in height. The top was flat and well-paved, and surrounded by a wooden rail, on which were fixed the sculls of the captives sacrificed on the death of their chiefs. In the centre of the area stood a ruinous old building of wood, connected with the rail on each side by a stone wall which divided the whole space into two parts. On the side next the country were five poles, upward of twenty feet high, supporting an irregular kind of scaffold; on the opposite side, towards the sea, stood two small houses with a covered communication.

We were conducted by Koah to the top of this pile by an easy ascent leading from the beach to the northwest corner of the area. At the entrance we saw two large wooden images, with features violently distorted, and a long piece of carved wood, of a conical form inverted, rising from the top of their heads; the rest was without form, and wrapped round with red cloth. We were here met by a tall young man with a long beard, who presented Captain Cook to the images, and after chanting a kind of hymn, in which he was joined by Koah, they led us to that end of the "morai" where the five poles were fixed. At the foot of them were twelve images ranged in a semicircular form, and before the middle figure stood a high stand or table, exactly resembling the "whatta" of Otaheite, on which lay a putrid hog,

and the Ecclesiastical Emperor of Japan.—*Note in Original Edition.*

and under it pieces of sugar-cane, cocoa-nuts, bread-fruit, plantains, and sweet potatoes. Koah having placed the Captain under this stand, took down the hog and held it toward him; and after having a second time addressed him in a long speech, pronounced with much vehemence and rapidity, he let it fall on the ground, and led him to the scaffolding, which they began to climb together, not without great risk of falling. At this time we saw, coming in solemn procession, at the entrance of the top of the "morai," ten men carrying a live hog and a large piece of red cloth. Being advanced a few paces, they stopped and · prostrated themselves; and Kaireekeea, the young man above mentioned, went to them, and receiving the cloth, carried it to Koah, who wrapped it round the Captain, and afterwards offered him the hog, which was brought by Kaireekeea, with the same ceremony.

Whilst Captain Cook was aloft in this awkward situation, swathed round with red cloth, and with difficulty keeping his hold amongst the pieces of rotten scaffolding, Kaireekeea and Koah began their office, chanting sometimes in concert, and sometimes alternately. This lasted a considerable time; at length Koah let the hog drop, when he and the Captain descended together. He then led him to the images before mentioned, and having said something to each in a sneering tone, snapping his fingers at them as he passed, he brought him to that in the centre, which, from its being covered with red cloth, appeared to be in greater estimation than the rest. Before this figure he prostrated himself, and kissed it, desiring Captain Cook to do the same, who suffered himself to be directed by Koah throughout the whole of this ceremony. We were now led back into the other division of the "morai," where there was a space ten or twelve feet square, sunk about three feet below the level of the area. Into this we descended, and Captain Cook was seated between two wooden idols, Koah supporting one of his arms, whilst I was desired to support the other. At this time arrived a second procession of natives, carrying a baked hog and a pudding, some bread-fruit, cocoa-nuts, and other vegetables. When they approached us, Kaireekeea put himself at their head, and presenting the pig to Captain Cook in the usual manner, began the same kind of chant as before, his companions making regular responses. We observed that after every response their parts became gradually shorter, till towards the close Kaireekeea's consisted of only two or three words, which the rest answered by the word "Orono."

When this offering was concluded, which lasted a quarter of an hour, the natives sat down fronting us, and began to cut up the baked hog, to peel the vegetables, and break the cocoa - nuts ; whilst others employed themselves in brewing the "ava," which is done by chewing it in the same manner as at the Friendly Islands. Kaireekeea then took part of the kernel of a cocoa-nut, which he chewed, and wrapping it in a piece of cloth, rubbed with it the Captain's face, head, hands, arms, and shoulders. The "ava" was then handed round, and after we had tasted it, Koah and Pareea began to pull the flesh of the hog in pieces, and to put it into our mouths. I had no great objection to being fed by Pareea, who was very cleanly in his person ; but Captain Cook, who was served by Koah, recollecting the putrid hog, could not swallow a morsel ; and his reluctance, as may be supposed, was not diminished, when the old man, according to his own mode of civility, had chewed it for him. When this last ceremony was finished, which Captain Cook put an end to as soon as he decently could, we quitted the "morai," after distributing amongst the people some pieces of iron and other trifles, with which they seemed highly gratified. The men with wands conducted us to the boats, repeating the same words as before. The people again retired, and the few that remained prostrated themselves as we passed along the shore. We immediately went on board, our minds full of what we had seen, and extremely well satisfied with the good dispositions of our new friends. The meaning of the various ceremonies with which we had been received, and which, on account of their novelty and singularity, have been related at length, can only be the subject of conjectures, and those uncertain and partial ; they were, however, without doubt, expressive of high respect on the part of the natives, and as far as related to the person of Captain Cook they seemed approaching to adoration.

The next morning I went on shore with a guard of eight marines, including the corporal and lieutenant, having orders to erect the observatory in such a situation as might best enable me to superintend and protect the waterers and the other working parties that were to be on shore. As we were viewing a spot conveniently situated for this purpose in the middle of the village, Pareea, who was always ready to show both his power and his goodwill, offered to pull down some houses that would have obstructed our observations. However, we thought it proper to decline this offer, and fixed on a field of sweet potatoes adjoining to the "morai," which was readily granted us ; and the priests, to prevent the intrusion of the natives, immediately consecrated the place by fixing their wands round the wall by which it was enclosed. This sort of religious interdiction they call "taboo," a word we heard often repeated during our stay amongst these islanders, and found to be of very powerful and extensive operation. It procured us even more privacy than we desired. No canoes ever presumed to land near us; the natives sat on the wall, but none offered to come within the tabooed space till he had obtained our permission. But though the men, at our request, would come across the field with provisions, yet not all our endeavours could prevail on the women to approach us. Presents were tried, but without effect; Pareea and Koah were tempted to bring them, but in vain; we were invariably answered that the "Eatooa" and Terreeoboo (which was the name of their King) would kill them. This circumstance afforded no small matter of amusement to our friends on board, where the crowds of people, and particularly of women, that continued to flock thither, obliged them almost every hour to clear the vessel in order to have room to do the necessary duties of the ship. On these occasions 200 or 300 women were frequently made to jump into the water at once, where they continued swimming and playing about till they could again procure admittance.

From the 19th to the 24th, when Pareea and Koah left us to attend Terreeoboo, who had landed on some other part of the island, nothing very material happened on board. The calkers were set to work on the sides of the ships, and the rigging was carefully overhauled and repaired. The salting of hogs for sea-store was also a constant and one of the principal objects of Captain Cook's attentions. It has generally been thought impracticable to cure the flesh of animals by salting in tropical climates, the progress of putrefaction being so rapid as not to allow time for the salt to take (as they express it) before the meat gets a taint, which prevents the effect of the pickle. We do not find that experiments relative to this subject have been made by the navigators of any nation before Captain Cook. In his first trials, which were made in 1774 during his second voyage to the Pacific Ocean, the success he met with, though very imperfect, was yet sufficient to convince him of the error of the received opinion. As the voyage in which he was now engaged was likely to be protracted a year beyond the time for which the ships had been victualled, he was under the necessity of providing by some such means for the subsistence of the crews, or of relinquishing the further prosecution of his discoveries. He therefore lost no opportunity of renewing his attempts, and the

event answered his most sanguine expectations.[1]

I shall now return to our transactions on shore at the observatory, where we had not been long settled before we discovered in our neighbourhood the habitations of a society of priests, whose regular attendance at the "morai" had excited our curiosity. Their huts stood round a pond of water, and were surrounded by a grove of cocoa-nut trees, which separated them from the beach and the rest of the village, and gave the place an air of religious retirement. On my acquainting Captain Cook with these circumstances, he resolved to pay them a visit. On his arrival at the beach he was conducted to a sacred building called Harre-no-Orono or the house of Orono, and seated before the entrance, at the foot of a wooden idol of the same kind with those on the "morai." I was here again made to support one of his arms, and after wrapping him in red cloth, Kaireekeea, accompanied by twelve priests, made an offering of a pig with the usual solemnities. The pig was then strangled, and a fire being kindled, it was thrown into the embers; and after the hair was singed off it was again presented, with a repetition of the chanting in the manner before described. The dead pig was then held for a short time under the Captain's nose, after which it was laid, with a cocoa-nut, at his feet, and the performers sat down. The "ava" was then brewed and handed round, a fat hog ready dressed was brought in, and we were fed as before.

During the rest of the time we remained in the bay, whenever Captain Cook came on shore he was attended by one of these priests, who went before him giving notice that

---

[1] After describing the process, King says: "I brought home with me some barrels of this pork which was pickled at Owhyhee in January 1779, and was tasted by several persons in England about Christmas 1780, and found perfectly sound and wholesome."

the "Orono" had landed, and ordering the people to prostrate themselves. The same person also constantly accompanied him on the water, standing in the bow of the boat with a wand in his hand, and giving notice of his approach to the natives who were in canoes, on which they immediately left off paddling and lay down on their faces till he had passed. Whenever he stopped at the observatory, Kaireekeea and his brethren immediately made their appearance with hogs, cocoa-nuts, bread-fruit, &c., and presented them with the usual solemnities. It was on these occasions that some of the inferior chiefs frequently requested to be permitted to make an offering to the "Orono." When this was granted, they presented the hog themselves, generally with evident marks of fear in their countenances, whilst Kaireekeea and the priests chanted their accustomed hymns. The civilities of this society were not, however, confined to mere ceremony and parade. Our party on shore received from them every day a constant supply of hogs and vegetables more than sufficient for our subsistence, and several canoes loaded with provisions were sent to the ships with the same punctuality. No return was ever demanded or even hinted at in the most distant manner. Their presents were made with a regularity more like the discharge of a religious duty than the effect of mere liberality; and when we inquired at whose charge all this munificence was displayed, we were told it was at the expense of a great man called Kaoo, the chief of the priests and grandfather to Kaireekeea, who was at that time absent attending the King of the island.

As everything relating to the character and behaviour of this people must be interesting to the reader on account of the tragedy that was afterwards acted here, it will be proper to acquaint him that we had not always so much reason to be satisfied with the conduct of the warrior chiefs, or "Earees," as with that of the priests. In all our dealings with the former we found them sufficiently attentive to their own interests; and besides their habit of stealing, which may admit of some excuse from the universality of the practice amongst the islanders of these seas, they made use of other artifices equally dishonourable. I shall only mention one instance, in which we discovered with regret our friend Koah to be a party principally concerned. As the chiefs who brought us presents of hogs were always sent back handsomely rewarded, we had generally a greater supply than we could make use of. On these occasions Koah, who never failed in his attendance on us, used to beg such as we did not want, and they were always given to him. It one day happened that a pig was presented us by a man whom Koah himself introduced as a chief who was desirous of paying his respects; and we recollected the pig to be the same that had been given to Koah just before. This leading us to suspect some trick, we found, on further inquiry, the pretended chief to be an ordinary person; and on connecting this with other circumstances, we had reason to suspect that it was not the first time we had been the dupes of the like imposition.

Things continued in this state till the 24th, when we were a good deal surprised to find that no canoes were suffered to put off from the shore, and that the natives kept close to their houses. After several hours' suspense, we learned that the bay was tabooed, and all intercourse with us interdicted, on account of the arrival of Terreeoboo. As we had not foreseen an accident of this sort, the crews of both ships were obliged to pass the day without their usual supply of vegetables. The next morning, therefore, they endeavoured both by threats and promises to induce the natives to come alongside; and as some of them were at last venturing to put off, a chief was observed attempting to drive them away. A musket was immediately fired over his head to make him desist, which had the desired effect, and refreshments were soon after purchased as usual. In the afternoon Terreeoboo arrived, and visited the ships in a private manner, attended only by one canoe in which were his wife and children. He stayed on board till near 10 o'clock, when he returned to the village of Kowrowa.

The next day about noon the King, in a large canoe attended by two others, set out from the village and paddled toward the ships in great state. Their appearance was grand and magnificent. In the first canoe were Terreeoboo and his chiefs, dressed in their rich feathered cloaks and helmets, and armed with long spears and daggers; in the second came the venerable Kaoo, the chief of the priests, and his brethren, with their idols displayed on red cloth. These idols were busts of a gigantic size, made of wicker-work, and curiously covered with small feathers of various colours wrought in the same manner with their cloaks. Their eyes were made of large pearl oysters, with a black nut fixed in the centre; their mouths were set with a double row of the fangs of dogs, and, together with the rest of their features, were strangely distorted. The third canoe was filled with hogs and various sorts of vegetables. As they went along the priests in the centre canoe sung their hymns with great solemnity; and after paddling round the ships, instead of going on board as was expected, they made toward the shore at the beach where we were stationed. As soon as I saw them approaching I ordered out our little guard to receive the King; and Captain Cook, perceiving that he was going on shore, followed him and arrived nearly at the same time. We conducted them into the tent, where they had scarcely been seated when the King rose up and in a very graceful manner threw over the Captain's shoulders the cloak he himself wore, put a feathered helmet on his head, and a curious fan into his hand. He also spread at his feet five or six other cloaks, all exceedingly beautiful and of the greatest value. His attendants then brought four very large hogs, with sugar-canes, cocoa-nuts, and bread-fruit; and this part of the ceremony was concluded by the King's

exchanging names with Captain Cook, which amongst all the islanders of the Pacific Ocean is esteemed the strongest pledge of friendship. A procession of priests, with a venerable old personage at their head, now appeared, followed by a long train of men leading large hogs, and others carrying plantains, sweet potatoes, &c. By the looks and gestures of Kaireekeea I immediately knew the old man to be the chief of the priests before mentioned, on whose bounty we had so long subsisted. He had a piece of red cloth in his hands, which he wrapped round Captain Cook's shoulders, and afterward presented him with a small pig in the usual form. A seat was then made for him next to the King, after which Kaireekeea and his followers began their ceremonies, Kaoo and the chiefs joining in the responses.

I was surprised to see in the person of this King the same infirm and emaciated old man that came on board the Resolution when we were off the north-east side of the Island of Mowee; and we soon discovered amongst his attendants most of the persons who at that time had remained with us all night. Of this number were the two younger sons of the King, the eldest of whom was sixteen years of age, and his nephew Maiha-Maiha, whom at first we had some difficulty in recollecting, his hair being plastered over with a dirty brown paste and powder which was no mean heightening to the most savage face I ever beheld. As soon as the formalities of the meeting were over, Captain Cook carried Terreeoboo, and as many chiefs as the pinnace could hold, on board the Resolution. They were received with every mark of respect that could be shown them; and Captain Cook, in return for the feathered cloak, put a linen shirt on the King, and girt his own hanger round him. The ancient Kaoo, and about half-a-dozen more old chiefs, remained on shore and took up their abode at the priests' houses. During all this time not a canoe was seen in the bay, and the natives either kept within their huts or lay prostrate on the ground. Before the King left the Resolution, Captain Cook obtained leave for the natives to come and trade with the ships as usual; but the women, for what reason we could not learn, still continued under the effects of the "taboo," that is, were forbidden to stir from home or to have any communication with us.

CHAPTER II.

The quiet and inoffensive behaviour of the natives having taken away every apprehension of danger, we did not hesitate to trust ourselves amongst them at all times and in all situations. The officers of both ships went daily up the country in small parties, or even singly, and frequently remained out the whole night. It would be endless to recount all the instances of kindness and civility which we received upon those occasions. Wherever we went the people flocked about us, eager to offer every assistance in their power, and highly gratified if their services were accepted. Various little arts were practised to attract our notice or to delay our departure. The boys and girls ran before as we walked through their villages, and stopped us at every opening where there was room to form a group for dancing. At one time we were invited to accept a draught of cocoa-nut milk or some other refreshment, under the shade of their huts; at another we were seated within a circle of young women, who exerted all their skill and agility to amuse us with songs and dances. The satisfaction we derived from their gentleness and hospitality was, however, frequently interrupted by that propensity to stealing which they have in common with all the other islanders of these seas. This circumstance was the more distressing as it sometimes obliged us to have recourse to acts of severity which we should willingly have avoided if the necessity of the case had not absolutely called for them. Some of their most expert swimmers were one day discovered under the ships drawing out the filling-nails of the sheathing, which they performed very dexterously by means of a short stick with a flint stone fixed in the end of it. To put a stop to this practice, which endangered the very existence of the vessels, we at first fired small shot at the offenders; but they easily got out of our reach by diving under the ship's bottom. It was therefore found necessary to make an example by flogging one of them on board the Discovery.

About this time a large party of gentlemen from both ships set out on an excursion into the interior parts of the country, with a view of examining its natural productions. [This] afforded Kaoo a fresh opportunity of showing his attention and generosity. For as soon as he was informed of their departure, he sent a large supply of provisions after them, together with orders that the inhabitants of the country through which they were to pass should give them every assistance in their power. And to complete the delicacy and disinterestedness of his conduct, even the people he employed could not be prevailed on to accept the smallest present. After remaining out six days our officers returned without having being able to penetrate above twenty miles into the island; partly from want of proper guides, and partly from the impracticability of the country.

The head of the Resolution's rudder being found exceedingly shaken, and most of the pintles either loose or broken, it was unhung and sent on shore, on the 27th in the morning, to undergo a thorough repair. At the same time the carpenters were sent into the country, under conduct of some of Kaoo's people, to cut planks for the head rail-work, which was also entirely decayed and rotten. On the 28th Captain Clerke, whose ill health confined him for the most part on board, paid Terreeoboo his first visit at his hut on shore. He was received with the same formalities as were observed with Captain Cook; and on his coming away, though the visit was quite unexpected, he received a present of thirty large hogs and as much fruit and roots as his crew could consume in a week.

As we had not yet seen anything of their sports or athletic exercises, the natives, at the request of some of our officers, entertained us this evening with a boxing-match. Though these games were much inferior, as well in point of solemnity and magnificence, as in the skill and powers of the combatants, to what we had seen exhibited at the Friendly Islands, yet as they differed in some particulars, it may not be improper to give a short account of them. We found a vast concourse of people assembled on a level spot of ground at a little distance from our tents. A long space was left vacant in the midst of them, at the upper end of which sat the judges, under three standards, from which hung slips of cloth of various colours, the skins of two wild geese, a few small birds, and bunches of feathers. When the sports were ready to begin, the signal was given by the judges, and immediately two combatants appeared. They came forward slowly, lifting up their feet very high behind, and drawing their hands along the soles. As they approached, they frequently eyed each other from head to foot in a contemptuous manner, casting several arch looks at the spectators, straining their muscles, and using a variety of affected gestures. Being advanced within reach of each other, they stood with both arms held out straight before their faces, at which part all their blows were aimed. They struck in what appeared to our eyes an awkward manner, with a full swing of the arm; made no attempt to parry, but eluded their adversary's attack by an inclination of the body or by retreating. The battle was quickly decided; for if either of them was knocked down, or even fell by accident, he was considered as vanquished, and the victor expressed his triumph by a variety of gestures, which usually excited, as was intended, a loud laugh among the spectators. He then waited for a second antagonist; and if again victorious, for a third, till he was at last in his turn defeated. A singular rule observed in these combats is, that whilst any two are preparing to fight, a third person may step in and choose either of them for his antagonist, when the other is obliged to withdraw. Sometimes three or four followed each other in this manner before the match was settled. When the combat proved longer than usual, or appeared too unequal, one of the chiefs generally stepped in and ended it by putting a stick between the combatants. The same good humour was preserved throughout which we before so much admired in the Friendly Islanders. As these games were given at our desire, we found it was universally expected that we should have borne our part in them; but our people, though much pressed by the natives, turned a deaf ear to their challenge, remembering full well the blows they got at the Friendly Islands.

This day died William Watman, a seaman of the gunner's crew; an event which I mention the more particularly as death had hitherto been very rare amongst us. He was an old man, and much respected on account of his attachment to Captain Cook. He had formerly served as a marine twenty-one years; after which he entered as a seaman on board the Resolution in 1772, and served with Captain Cook in his voyage towards the South Pole. At their return he was admitted into Greenwich Hospital, through the Captain's interest, at the same time with himself; and being resolved to follow throughout the fortunes of his benefactor, he also quitted it along with him on his being appointed to the command of the present expedition. During the voyage he had frequently been subject to slight fevers, and was a convalescent when we came into the bay, where being sent on shore for a few days he conceived himself perfectly recovered, and at his own desire returned on board; but the day following he had a paralytic stroke, which in two days more carried him off. At the request of the King of the island he was buried on the "morai," and the ceremony was performed with as much solemnity as our situation permitted. Old Kaoo and his brethren were spectators, and preserved the most profound silence and attention whilst the service was reading. When we began to fill up the grave, they approached it with great reverence, threw in a dead pig, some cocoa-nuts, and plantains; and for three nights afterwards they surrounded it, sacrificing hogs and performing their usual ceremonies of hymns and prayers, which continued till daybreak. At the head of the grave we erected a post, and nailed upon it a square piece of board, on which was inscribed the name of the deceased, his age, and the day of his death. This they promised not to remove; and we have no doubt but that it will be suffered to remain, as long as the frail materials of which it is made will permit.

The ships being in great want of fuel, the Captain desired me on the 2d of February to treat with the priests for the purchase of the rail that surrounded the top of the "morai." I must confess I had at first some doubt about the decency of this proposal, and was apprehensive that even the bare mention of it might be considered by them as a piece of shocking impiety. In this, however, I found myself mistaken. Not the smallest surprise was expressed at the application, and the wood was readily given, even without stipulating for anything in return. Whilst the sailors were taking it away, I observed one of them carrying off a carved image; and on further inquiry I found that they had conveyed to the boats the whole semicircle.[1] Though this was done in the presence of the natives, who had not shown any mark of resentment at it but had even assisted them in the removal, I thought it proper to speak to Kaoo on the subject, who appeared very indifferent about the matter, and only desired that we would restore the centre image I have mentioned

before, which he carried into one of the priest's houses.

Terreeoboo and his chiefs had for some days past been very inquisitive about the time of our departure. This circumstance had excited in me a great curiosity to know what opinion this people had formed of us, and what were their ideas respecting the cause and objects of our voyage. I took some pains to satisfy myself on these points, but could never learn anything further than that they imagined we came from some country where provisions had failed, and that our visit to them was merely for the purpose of filling our bellies. Indeed, the meagre appearance of some of our crew, the hearty appetites with which we sat down to their fresh provisions, and our great anxiety to purchase and carry off as much as we were able, led them naturally enough to such a conclusion. To these may be added a circumstance which puzzled them exceedingly—our having no women with us, together with our quiet conduct and unwarlike appearance. It was ridiculous enough to see them stroking the sides and patting the bellies of the sailors (who were certainly much improved in the sleekness of their looks during our short stay in the island), and telling them, partly by signs and partly by words, that it was time for them to go; but if they would come again the next bread-fruit season they should be better able to supply their wants. We had now been sixteen days in the bay, and if our enormous consumption of hogs and vegetables be considered, it need not be wondered that they should wish to see us take our leave.[2] It is

---

[1] Of twelve images, described in the preceding Chapter.

[2] It is shrewdly enough suggested, in a note in Kerr's Collection (vol. xvi., page 439), that the subsequent unexpected return of the ships to Karakakooa Bay may have alarmed the natives for the security of their own sustenance until the next season of plenty, and in a certain measure predisposed them to deal with the strangers in a less friendly, trustful, and respectful way.

very probable, however, that Terreeoboo had no other view in his inquiries at present than a desire of making sufficient preparation for dismissing us with presents suitable to the respect and kindness with which he had received us. For on our telling him we should leave the island on the next day but one, we observed that a sort of proclamation was immediately made through the villages to require the people to bring in their hogs and vegetables for the King to present to the " Orono " on his departure.

We were this day much diverted at the beach by the buffooneries of one of the natives. He held in his hand an instrument of the sort described [in Book III., Chapter XII.[1]]; some bits of sea-weed were tied round his neck; and round each leg a piece of strong netting about nine inches deep, on which a great number of dogs' teeth were loosely fastened in rows. His style of dancing was entirely burlesque, and accompanied with strange grimaces and pantomimical distortions of the face, which, though at times inexpressibly ridiculous, yet on the whole were without much meaning or expression. In the evening we were again entertained with wrestling and boxing-matches, and we displayed in return the few fireworks we had left. Nothing could be better calculated to excite the admiration of these islanders, and to impress them with an idea of our great superiority, than an exhibition of this kind. Captain Cook has already described the extraordinary effects of that which was made at Hapaee; and though the present was in every respect infinitely inferior, yet the astonishment of the natives was not less.

I have before mentioned that the carpenters from both ships had been sent up the country to cut planks for the head-rail work of the Resolution. This was the third day since their departure, and having received no intelligence from them, we began to be very anxious for their safety. We were communicating our apprehensions to old Kaoo, who appeared as much concerned as ourselves, and were concerting measures with him for sending after them, when they arrived all safe. They had been obliged to go farther into the country than was expected before they met with trees fit for their purpose, and it was this circumstance, together with the badness of the roads, and the difficulty of bringing back the timber, which had detained them so long. They spoke in high terms of their guides, who both supplied them with provisions, and guarded their tools with the utmost fidelity.

The next day being fixed for our departure, Terreeoboo invited Captain Cook and myself to attend him on the 3d to the place where Kaoo resided. On our arrival we found the ground covered with parcels of cloth, a vast quantity of red and yellow feathers tied to the fibres of cocoa-nut husks, and a great number of hatchets, and other pieces of iron-ware that had been got in barter from us. At a little distance from these lay an immense quantity of vegetables of every kind, and near them was a large herd of hogs. At first we imagined the whole to be intended as a present for us, till Kaireekeea informed me that it was a gift or tribute from the people of that district to the King, and accordingly, as soon as we were seated, they brought all the bundles and laid them severally at Terreeoboo's feet, spreading out the cloth and displaying the feathers and iron-ware before him. The King seemed much pleased with this mark of their duty, and having selected about a third part of the iron-ware, the same proportion of feathers, and a few pieces of cloth, these were set aside by themselves; and the remainder of the cloth, together with all the hogs and vegetables, were afterwards presented to Captain Cook and myself. We were astonished at the value and magnitude of this present, which far exceeded everything of the kind we had seen either at the Friendly or Society Islands. Boats were immediately sent to carry them on board, the large hogs

---

were picked out to be salted for sea-store, and upwards of thirty smaller pigs and the vegetables were divided between the two crews.

The same day we quitted the "morai" and got the tents and astronomical instruments on board. The charm of the taboo was now removed; and we had no sooner left the place than the natives rushed in and searched eagerly about in expectation of finding something of value that we might have left behind. As I happened to remain the last on shore, and waited for the return of the boat, several came crowding about me; and having made me sit down by them, began to lament our separation. It was, indeed, not without difficulty I was able to quit them. And here I hope I may be permitted to relate a trifling occurrence in which I was principally concerned. Having had the command of the party on shore during the whole time we were in the bay, I had an opportunity of becoming better acquainted with the natives, and of being better known to them, than those whose duty required them to be generally on board. As I had every reason to be satisfied with their kindness in general, so I cannot too often nor too particularly mention the unbounded and constant friendship of their priests. On my part, I spared no endeavours to conciliate their affections and gain their esteem; and I had the good fortune to succeed so far, that when the time of our departure was made known I was strongly solicited to remain behind, not without offers of the most flattering kind. When I excused myself by saying that Captain Cook would not give his consent, they proposed that I should retire into the mountains, where, they said, they would conceal me till after the departure of the ships; and on my further assuring them that the Captain would not leave the bay without me, Terreeoboo and Kaoo waited upon Captain Cook, whose son they supposed I was, with a formal request that I might be left behind. The Captain, to avoid giving a positive refusal to an offer so

kindly intended, told them that he could not part with me at that time, but that he should return to the island next year, and would then endeavour to settle the matter to their satisfaction.

Early in the morning of the 4th we unmoored and sailed out of the bay, with the Discovery in company, and were followed by a great number of canoes. Captain Cook's design was to finish the survey of Owhyhee before he visited the other islands, in hopes of meeting with a road better sheltered than the bay we had just left; and in case of not succeeding here, he purposed to take a view of the south-east part of Mowee, where the natives informed us we should find an excellent harbour. We had calm weather all this and the following day, which made our progress to the northward very slow. We were accompanied by a great number of the natives in their canoes, and Terreeoboo gave a fresh proof of his friendship to Captain Cook by a large present of hogs and vegetables that was sent after him.

In the night of the 5th, having a light breeze off the land, we made some way to the northward; and in the morning of the 6th, having passed the westernmost point of the island, we found ourselves abreast of a deep bay called by the natives Toe-yah-yah. We had great hopes that this bay would furnish us with a safe and commodious harbour, as we saw to the north-east several fine streams of water, and the whole had the appearance of being well sheltered. These observations agreeing with the accounts given us by Koah, who accompanied Captain Cook, and had changed his name, out of compliment to us, into "Britannee," the pinnace was hoisted out, and the master, with "Britannee" for his guide, was sent to examine the bay, whilst the ships worked up after them. In the afternoon the weather became gloomy, and the gusts of wind that blew off the land, were so violent as to make it necessary to take in all the sails, and bring to under the mizzen-staysail. All the canoes left us at the beginning of the gale, and Mr Bligh, on his return, had the satisfaction of saving an old woman and two men, whose canoe had been overset by the violence of the wind as they were endeavouring to gain the shore. Besides these distressed people, we had a great many women on board whom the natives had left behind in their hurry to shift for themselves. The master reported to Captain Cook that he had landed at the only village he saw, on the north side of the bay, where he was directed to some wells of water, but found they would by no means answer our purpose; that he afterward proceeded farther into the bay, which runs inland to a great depth, and stretches toward the foot of a very conspicuous high mountain, situated on the north-west end of the island; but that instead of meeting with safe anchorage, as "Britannee" had taught him to expect, he found the shores low and rocky, and a flat bed of coral rocks running along the coast and extending upwards of a mile from the land, on the outside of which the depth of water was twenty fathoms over a sandy bottom; and that, in the meantime "Britannce" had contrived to slip away, being afraid of returning, as we imagined, because his information had not proved true and successful.

In the evening, the weather being more moderate, we again made sail; but about midnight it blew so violently as to split both the fore and main topsails. On the morning of the 7th we bent fresh sails, and had fair weather and a light breeze. At noon the latitude by observation was 20° 1' N., the W. point of the island bearing S. 7° E., and the NW. point N. 38° E. As we were at this time four or five leagues from the shore, and the weather very unsettled, none of the canoes would venture out, so that our guests were obliged to remain with us, much indeed to their dissatisfaction, for they were all sea-sick, and many of them had left young children behind them. In the afternoon, though the weather was still squally, we stood in for the land, and being about three leagues from it we saw a canoe with two men paddling toward us, which we immediately conjectured had been driven off the shore by the late boisterous weather, and therefore stopped the ship's way in order to take them in. These poor wretches were so entirely exhausted with fatigue, that had not one of the natives on board, observing their weakness, jumped into the canoe to their assistance, they would scarcely have been able to fasten it to the rope we had thrown out for that purpose. It was with difficulty we got them up the ship's side, together with a child about four years old, which they had lashed under the thwarts of the canoe, where it had lain with only its head above water. They told us they had left the shore the morning before, and had been from that time without food or water. The usual precautions were taken in giving them victuals, and the child being committed to the care of one of the women, we found them all next morning perfectly recovered.

At midnight a gale of wind came on which obliged us to double reef the top-sails and get down the top-gallant yards. On the 8th at daybreak, we found that the fore-mast had again given way, the fishes which were put on the head in King George's or Nootka Sound, on the coast of America, being sprung, and the parts so very defective as to make it absolutely necessary to replace them, and of course to unstep the mast. In this difficulty, Captain Cook was for some time in doubt whether he should run the chance of meeting with a harbour in the islands to leeward, or return to Karakakooa. That bay was not so remarkably commodious in any respect but that a better might probably be expected, both for the purpose of repairing the masts and for procuring refreshments, of which it was imagined that the neighbourhood of Karakakooa had been already pretty well drained. On the other hand, it was considered as too great a risk to leave a place that was tolerably sheltered, and which, once left could not be regained, for the mere hopes of meeting with a better, the failure of which might perhaps have left us without resource. We therefore continued standing on towards the land, in order to give the natives an opportunity of releasing their friends on board from their confinement; and at noon, being within a mile of the shore, a few canoes came off to us, but so crowded with people that there was not room in them for any of our guests. We therefore hoisted out the pinnace to carry them on shore; and the master who went with them, had directions to examine the south coasts of the bay for water, but returned without finding any.

The winds being variable, and a current setting strong to the northward, we made but little progress in our return; and at 8 o'clock in the evening of the 9th it began to blow very hard from the SE., which obliged us to close reef the top-sails; and at two in the morning of the 10th, in a heavy squall, we found ourselves close in with the breakers that lie to the northward of the west point of Owhyhee. We had just room to haul off and avoid them, and fired several guns to apprise the Discovery of the danger. In the forenoon, the weather was more moderate, and a few canoes came off to us, from which we learned that the late storms had done much mischief, and that several large canoes had been lost. During the remainder of the day we kept beating to windward, and before night we were within a mile of the bay; but not choosing to run on while it was dark, we stood off and on till daylight next morning, when we dropped anchor nearly in the same place as before.

CHAPTER III.

WE were employed the whole of the 11th and part of the 12th in getting out the fore-mast and sending it with the carpenters on shore. Besides the damage which the head of the mast had sustained, we found the heel exceedingly rotten, having a large hole up the middle of it capable of holding four or five cocoa-nuts. It was not however, thought necessary to shorten it, and fortunately the logs of red toa-wood which had been cut at Eimeo for anchor-stocks were found fit to replace the sprung part of the fishes. As these repairs were likely to take up several days, Mr Bayly and myself got the astronomical apparatus on shore, and pitched our tents on the "morai;" having with us a guard of a corporal and six marines. We renewed our friendly correspondence with the priests, who, for the greater security of the workmen and their tools, tabooed the place where the mast lay, sticking their wands round it as before. The sail-makers were also sent on shore to repair the damages which had taken place in their department during the late gales. They were lodged in a house adjoining to the "morai," that was lent us by the priests. Such were our arrangements on shore. I shall now proceed to the account of those other transactions with the natives which led by degrees to the fatal catastrophe of the 14th.

Upon coming to anchor we were surprised to find our reception very different from what it had been on our first arrival; no shouts, no bustle, no confusion, but a solitary bay, with only here and there a canoe stealing close along the shore. The impulse of curiosity, which had before operated to so great a degree, might now indeed be supposed to have ceased; but the hospitable treatment we had invariably met with, and the friendly footing on which we parted, gave us some reason to expect that they would again have flocked about us with great joy on our return. We were forming various conjectures upon the occasion of this extraordinary appearance, when our anxiety was at length relieved by the return of a boat which had been sent on shore, and brought us word that Terreeoboo was absent and had left the bay under the taboo.

Though this account appeared very satisfactory to most of us, yet others were of opinion, or rather perhaps have been led by subsequent events to imagine, that there was something at this time, very suspicious in the behaviour of the natives; and that the interdiction of all intercourse with us, on pretence of the King's absence, was only to give him time to consult with his chiefs in what manner it might be proper to treat us. Whether these suspicions were well founded, or the account given by the natives was the truth, we were never able to ascertain. For though it is not improbable that our sudden return, for which they could see no apparent cause, and the necessity of which we afterward found it very difficult to make them comprehend, might occasion some alarm; yet the unsuspicious conduct of Terreeoboo, who on his supposed arrival the next morning came immediately to visit Captain Cook, and the consequent return of the natives to their former friendly intercourse with us, are strong proofs that they neither meant nor apprehended any change of conduct.

In support of this opinion I may add the account of another accident, precisely of the same kind, which happened to us on our first visit, the day before the arrival of the King. A native had sold a hog on board the Resolution, and taken the price agreed on, when Pareea, passing by, advised the man not to part with the hog without an advanced price. For this he was sharply spoken to and pushed away; and the taboo being soon after laid on the bay, we had at first no doubt but that it was in consequence of the offence given to the chief. Both these accidents serve to show how very difficult it is to draw any certain conclusion from the actions of people with whose customs as well as language we are so imperfectly acquainted; at the same time, some idea may be formed from them of the difficulties, at the first view, perhaps, not very apparent, which those have to encounter who, in all their transactions with these strangers, have to steer their course amidst so much uncertainty, where a trifling error may be attended with even the most fatal consequences. However true or false our conjectures may be, things went on in their usual quiet course till the afternoon of the 13th.

Towards the evening of that day, the officer who commanded the watering party of the Discovery, came to inform me that several chiefs had assembled at the well near the beach, driving away the natives whom he had hired to assist the sailors in rolling down the casks to the shore. He told me, at the same time, that he thought their behaviour extremely suspicious, and that they meant to give him some further disturbance. At his request therefore, I sent a marine along with him, but suffered him to take only his side arms. In a short time the officer returned, and on his acquainting me that the islanders had armed themselves with stones, and were growing very tumultuous, I went myself to the spot, attended by a marine with his musket. Seeing us approach, they threw away their stones, and on my speaking to some of the chiefs, the mob were driven away, and those who chose it were suffered to assist in filling the casks. Having left things quiet here, I went to meet Captain Cook, whom I saw coming on shore in the pinnace. I related to him what had just passed; and he ordered me, in case of their beginning to throw stones or behave insolently, immediately to fire a ball at the offenders. I accordingly gave orders to the corporal to have the pieces of the sentinels loaded with ball instead of small shot. Soon after our return to the tents, we were alarmed by a continued fire of muskets from the Discovery, which we observed to be directed at a canoe that we saw paddling towards the shore in great haste, pursued by one of our small boats. We immediately concluded that the firing was in consequence of some theft, and Captain Cook ordered me to follow him with a marine armed, and to endeavour to seize the people as they came on shore. Accordingly we ran towards the place where we supposed the canoe would land, but were too late, the people having quitted it and made their escape into the country before our arrival. We were at this time ignorant that the goods had been already restored; and as we thought it probable, from the circumstances we had at first observed, that they might be of importance, were unwilling to relinquish our hopes of recovering them. Having therefore inquired of the natives which way the people had fled, we followed them till it was near dark, when, judging ourselves to be about three miles from the tents, and suspecting that the natives who frequently encouraged us in the pursuit were amusing us with false information, we thought it in vain to continue our search any longer, and returned to the beach.

During our absence, a difference of a more serious and unpleasant nature had happened. The officer who had been sent in the small boat, and was returning on board with the goods which had been restored, observing Captain Cook and me engaged in the pursuit of the offenders, thought it his duty to seize the canoe, which was left drawn up on the shore. Unfortunately this canoe belonged to Pareea, who, arriving at the same moment from on board the Discovery, claimed his property with many protestations of his innocence. The officer refusing to give it up, and being joined by the crew of the pinnace, which was waiting for Captain Cook, a scuffle ensued, in which Pareea was knocked down by a violent blow on the head with an oar. The natives who were collected about the spot, and had hitherto been peaceable spectators, immediately attacked our people with such a shower of stones, as forced them to retreat with great precipitation, and swim off to a rock at some distance from the shore. The pinnace was immediately ransacked by the islanders; and but for the timely interposition of Pareea, who seemed to have recovered from the blow, and forgotten it at the same

instant, would soon have been entirely demolished. Having driven away the crowd, he made signs to our people that they might come and take possession of the pinnace, and that he would endeavour to get back the things which had been taken out of it. After their departure, he followed them in his canoe with a midshipman's cap, and some other trifling articles of the plunder, and, with much apparent concern at what had happened, asked if the "Orono" would kill him, and whether he would permit him to come on board the next day? On being assured that he should be well received, he joined noses (as their custom is) with the officers in token of friendship, and paddled over to the village of Kowrowa.

When Captain Cook was informed of what had passed, he expressed much uneasiness at it, and as we were returning on board—"I am afraid," said he, "that these people will oblige me to use some violent measures; for," he added, "they must not be left to imagine that they have gained an advantage over us." However, as it was too late to take any steps this evening, he contented himself with giving orders that every man and woman on board should be immediately turned out of the ship. As soon as this order was executed, I returned on shore; and our former confidence in the natives being now much abated by the events of the day, I posted a double guard on the "morai," with orders to call me if they saw any men lurking about the beach. At about 11 o'clock five islanders were observed creeping round the bottom of the "morai;" they seemed very cautious in approaching us, and at last, finding themselves discovered, retired out of sight. About midnight, one of them venturing up close to the observatory, the sentinel fired over him, on which the man fled and we passed the remainder of the night without further disturbance.

Next morning, at daylight, I went on board the Resolution for the timekeeper, and in my way was hailed by the Discovery, and informed that their cutter had been stolen during the night from the buoy where it was moored. When I arrived on board I found the marines arming, and Captain Cook loading his double-barrelled gun. Whilst I was relating to him what had happened to us in the night, he interrupted me with some eagerness, and acquainted me with the loss of the Discovery's cutter, and with the preparations he was making for its recovery. It had been his usual practice, whenever anything of consequence was lost at any of the islands in this ocean, to get the king or some of the principal "Erees," on board, and to keep them as hostages till it was restored. This method, which had been always attended with success, he meant to pursue on the present occasion; and, at the same time, had given orders to stop all the canoes that should attempt to leave the bay, with an intention of seizing and destroying them if he could not recover the cutter by peaceable means. Accordingly, the boats of both ships, well manned and armed, were stationed across the bay; and before I left the ship some great guns had been fired at two large canoes that were attempting to make their escape.

It was between 7 and 8 o'clock when we quitted the ship together; Captain Cook in the pinnace, having Mr Phillips and nine marines with him, and myself in the small boat. The last orders I received from him were to quiet the minds of the natives on our side of the bay, by assuring them they should not be hurt; to keep my people together; and to be on my guard. We then parted; the Captain went toward Kowrowa, where the King resided, and I proceeded to the beach. My first care on going ashore was to give strict orders to the marines to remain within their tent, to load their pieces with ball, and not to quit their arms. Afterward I took a walk to the huts of old Kaoo and the priests, and explained to them as well as I could the object of the hostile preparations, which had exceedingly alarmed them. I found that they had already heard of the cutter's being stolen, and I assured them, that though Captain Cook was resolved to recover it, and to punish the authors of the theft, yet that they and the people of the village on our side need not be under the smallest apprehension of suffering any evil from us. I desired the priests to explain this to the people, and to tell them not to be alarmed, but to continue peaceable and quiet. Kaoo asked me with great earnestness if Terreeoboo was to be hurt. I assured him he was not; and both he and the rest of his brethren seemed much satisfied with this assurance.

In the meantime, Captain Cook having called off the launch, which was stationed at the north point of the bay, and taken it along with him, proceeded to Kowrowa, and landed with the lieutenant and nine marines. He immediately marched into the village, where he was received with the usual marks of respect, the people prostrating themselves before him, and bringing their accustomed offerings of small hogs. Finding that there was no suspicion of his design, his next step was to inquire for Terreeoboo, and the two boys, his sons, who had been his constant guests on board the Resolution. In a short time the boys returned along with the natives who had been sent in search of them, and immediately led Captain Cook to the house where the King had slept. They found the old man just awoke from sleep; and after a short conversation about the loss of the cutter, from which Captain Cook was convinced that he was in nowise privy to it, he invited him to return in the boat and spend the day on board the Resolution. To this proposal the King readily consented, and immediately got up to accompany him.

Things were in this prosperous train, the two boys being already in the pinnace, and the rest af the party having advanced near the water-side, when an elderly woman called Kaneekabareea, the mother of the boys, and one of the King's favourite wives, came after him, and with many tears and entreaties, besought him not to go on board. At the same time, two chiefs, who came along with her, laid hold of him, and insisting that he should go no farther, forced him to sit down. The natives, who were collecting in prodigious numbers along the shore, and had probably been alarmed by the firing of the great guns, and the appearances of hostility in the bay, began to throng round Capain Cook and their King. In this situation the lieutenant of marines, observing that his men were huddled close together in the crowd, and thus incapable of using their arms if any occasion should require it, proposed to the Captain to draw them up along the rocks close to the water's edge ; and the crowd readily making way for them to pass, they were drawn up in a line at the distance of about thirty yards from the place where the King was sitting. All this time, the old King remained on the ground, with the strongest marks of terror and dejection in his countenance : Captain Cook, not willing to abandon the object for which he had come on shore, continuing to urge him in the most pressing manner to proceed ; whilst, on the other hand, whenever the King appeared inclined to follow him, the chiefs, who stood round him interposed, at first with prayers and entreaties, but afterwards, having recourse to force and violence, insisted on his staying where he was. Captain Cook, therefore, finding that the alarm had spread too generally, and that it was in vain to think any longer of getting him off without bloodshed, at last gave up the point, observing to Mr Phillips that it would be impossible to compel him to go on board without the risk of killing a great number of the inhabitants.

Though the enterprise which had carried Captain Cook on shore had now failed and was abandoned, yet his person did not appear to have been in the least danger till an accident happened which gave a fatal turn to the affair. The boats which had been stationed across the bay having fired at some canoes that were attempting to get out, unfortunately had killed a chief of the first rank. The news of his death arrived at the village where Captain Cook was, just as he had left the King, and was walking slowly toward the shore. The ferment it occasioned was very conspicuous, the women and children were immediately sent off, and the men put on their war-mats and armed themselves with spears and stones. One of the natives, having in his hands a stone and a long iron spike (which they call a "pahooa"), came up to the Captain, flourishing his weapon by way of defiance, and threatening to throw the stone. The Captain desired him to desist ; but the man persisting in his insolence, he was at length provoked to fire a load of small shot. The man having his mat on, which the shot was not able to penetrate, this had no other effect than to irritate and encourage them. Several stones were thrown at the marines ; and one of the "Erees" attempted to stab Mr Phillips with his "pahooa," but failed in the attempt, and received from him a blow with the butt end of his musket. Captain Cook now fired his second barrel, loaded with ball, and killed one of the foremost of the natives. A general attack with stones immediately followed, which was answered by a discharge of musketry from the marines and the people in the boats. The islanders, contrary to the expectations of every one, stood the fire with great firmness ; and before the marines had time to reload they broke in upon them with dreadful shouts and yells. What followed was a scene of the utmost horror and confusion. Four of the marines were cut off amongst the rocks in their retreat, and fell a sacrifice to the fury of the enemy ; three more were dangerously wounded ; and the lieutenant, who had received a stab between the shoulders with a "pahooa," having fortunately reserved his fire, shot the man who had wounded him just as he was going to repeat his blow. Our unfortunate commander, the last time he was seen distinctly, was standing at the water's edge and calling out to the boats to cease firing and to pull in. If it be true, as some of those who were present have imagined, that the marines and boatmen had fired without his orders, and that he was desirous of preventing any further bloodshed, it is not improbable that his humanity on this occasion proved fatal to him. For it was remarked that whilst he faced the natives none of them had offered him any violence, but that having turned about to give his orders to the boats, he was stabbed in the back, and fell with his face into the water. On seeing him fall, the islanders set up a great shout, and his body was immediately dragged on shore and surrounded by the enemy, who, snatching the dagger out of each other's hands, showed a savage eagerness to have a share in his destruction.

Thus fell our great and excellent commander! After a life of so much distinguished and successful enterprise, his death, as far as regards himself, cannot be reckoned premature, since he lived to finish the great work for which he seems to have been designed, and was rather removed from the enjoyment than cut off from the acquisition of glory. How sincerely his loss was felt and lamented by those who had so long found their general security in his skill and conduct, and every consolation under their hardships in his tenderness and humanity, it is neither necessary nor possible for me to describe; much less shall I attempt to paint the horror with which we were struck, and the universal dejection and dismay which followed so dreadful and unexpected a calamity.[1]

CHAPTER IV.

IT has been already related that four

---

[1] Captain King occupies the rest of the Chapter with a sketch of his great chief's career and an eulogium on his abilities, achievements, and character, that is stamped with the eloquence of heartfelt affection and esteem.

of the marines who attended Captain Cook were killed by the islanders on the spot. The rest, with Mr Phillips, their lieutenant, threw themselves into the water, and escaped under cover of a smart fire from the boats. On this occasion a remarkable instance of gallant behaviour and of affection for his men was shown by that officer; for he had scarcely got into the boat, when seeing one of the marines, who was a bad swimmer, struggling in the water, and in danger of being taken by the enemy, he immediately jumped into the sea to his assistance, though much wounded himself; and after receiving a blow on the head from a stone, which had nearly sent him to the bottom, he caught the man by the hair and brought him safe off. Our people continued for some time to keep up a constant fire from the boats (which during the whole transaction were not more than twenty yards from the land), in order to afford their unfortunate companions, if any of them should still remain alive, an opportunity of escaping. These efforts, seconded by a few guns that were fired at the same time from the Resolution, having forced the natives at last to retire, a small boat manned by five of our young midshipmen pulled towards the shore, where they saw the bodies, without any signs of life, lying on the ground; but judging it dangerous to attempt to bring them off with so small a force, and their ammunition being nearly expended, they returned to the ships, leaving them in possession of the islanders, together with ten stands of arms.

As soon as the general consternation which the news of this calamity occasioned throughout both crews had a little subsided, their attention was called to our party at the "morai," where the mast and sails were on shore with a guard of only six marines. It is impossible for me to describe the emotions of my own mind during the time these transactions had been carrying on at the other side of the bay. Being at the distance only of a short mile from the village of Kowrowa, we could see distinctly an immense crowd collected on the spot where Captain Cook had just before landed. We heard the firing of the musketry, and could perceive some extraordinary bustle and agitation in the multitude. We afterward saw the natives flying, the boats retire from the shore, and passing and repassing in great stillness between the ships. I must confess that my heart soon misgave me. Where a life so dear and valuable was concerned, it was impossible not to be alarmed by appearances both new and threatening. But besides this, I knew that a long and uninterrupted course of success in his transactions with the natives of these seas had given the Captain a degree of confidence that I was always fearful might, at some unlucky moment, put him too much off his guard; and I now saw all the dangers to which that confidence might lead, without receiving much consolation from considering the experience that had given rise to it. My first care, on hearing the muskets fired, was to assure the people who were assembled in considerable numbers round the wall of our consecrated field, and seemed equally at a loss with ourselves how to account for what they had seen and heard, that they should not be molested; and that at all events I was desirous of continuing on peaceable terms with them. We remained in this posture till the boats had returned on board, when Captain Clerke observing through his telescope that we were surrounded by the natives, and apprehending they meant to attack us, ordered two four-pounders to be fired at them. Fortunately these guns, though well aimed, did no mischief, and yet gave the natives a convincing proof of their power. One of the balls broke a cocoanut tree in the middle under which a party of them were sitting; and the other shivered a rock that stood in an exact line with them. As I had just before given them the strongest assurances of their safety, I was exceedingly mortified at this act of hostility; and, to prevent a repetition of it, immediately despatched a boat to acquaint Captain Clerke that at present I was

on the most friendly terms with the natives; and that, if occasion should hereafter arise for altering my conduct toward them, I would hoist a jack as a signal for him to afford us all the assistance in his power.

We expected the return of the boat with the utmost impatience; and after remaining a quarter of an hour under the most torturing anxiety and suspense, our fears were at length confirmed by the arrival of Mr Bligh, with orders to strike the tents as quickly as possible and to send the sails that were repairing on board. Just at the same moment our friend Kaireekeea, having also received intelligence of the death of Captain Cook from a native who had arrived from the other side of the bay, came to me with great sorrow and dejection in his countenance, to inquire if it was true. Our situation was at this time extremely critical and important; not only our own lives, but the event of the expedition and the return of at least one of the ships being involved in the same common danger. We had the mast of the Resolution, and the greatest part of our sails, on shore, under the protection of only six marines; their loss would have been irreparable; and though the natives had not as yet shown the smallest disposition to molest us, yet it was impossible to answer for the alteration which the news of the transaction at Kowrowa might produce. I therefore thought it prudent to dissemble my belief of the death of Captain Cook, and to desire Kaireekeea to discourage the report lest either the fear of our resentment, or the successful example of their countrymen, might lead them to seize the favourable opportunity which at this time offered itself of giving us a second blow. At the same time, I advised him to bring old Kaoo and the rest of the priests into a large house that was close to the " morai," partly out of regard to their safety in case it should have been found necessary to proceed to extremities, and partly to have him near us in order to make use of his authority with the people if it could be instrumental in preserving peace.

Having placed the marines on the top of the "morai," which formed a strong and advantageous post, and left the command with Mr Bligh, giving him the most positive directions to act entirely on the defensive, I went on board the Discovery in order to represent to Captain Clerke the dangerous situation of our affairs. As soon as I quitted the spot the natives began to annoy our people with stones, and I had scarcely reached the ship before I heard the firing of the marines. I therefore returned instantly on shore, where I found things growing every moment more alarming. The natives were arming and putting on their mats, and their numbers increased very fast. I could also perceive several large bodies marching towards us along the cliff which separates the village of Kakooa from the north side of the bay, where the village of Kowrowa is situated. They began at first to attack us with stones from behind the walls of their enclosures, and finding no resistance on our part, they soon grew more daring. A few resolute fellows, having crept along the beach under cover of the rocks, suddenly made their appearance at the foot of the "morai," with a design, as it seemed, of storming it on the side next the sea, which was its only accessible part; and were not dislodged till after they had stood a considerable number of shot and seen one of their party fall. The bravery of one of these assailants well deserves to be particularly mentioned. For having returned to carry off his companion amidst the fire of our whole party, a wound which he received made him quit the body and retire; but in a few minutes he again appeared, and being again wounded, he was obliged a second time to retreat. At this moment I arrived at the "morai," and saw him return the third time, bleeding and faint; and being informed of what had happened, I forbade the soldiers to fire, and he was suffered to carry off his friend, which he was just able

to perform, and then fell down himself and expired.

About this time, a strong reinforcement from both ships having landed, the natives retreated behind their walls, which giving me access to our friendly priests, I sent one of them to endeavour to bring their countrymen to some terms, and to propose to them that if they would desist from throwing stones I would not permit our men to fire. This truce was agreed to, and we were suffered to launch the mast and carry off the sails and our astronomical apparatus unmolested. As soon as we had quitted the "morai," they took possession of it, and some of them threw a few stones, but without doing us any mischief. It was half-an-hour past 11 o'clock when I got on board the Discovery, where I found no decisive plan had been adopted for our future proceedings. The restitution of the boat, and the recovery of the body of Captain Cook, were the objects which on all hands we agreed to insist on; and it was my opinion that some vigorous steps should be taken in case the demand of them was not immediately complied with.

Though my feelings on the death of a beloved and honoured friend may be suspected to have had some share in this opinion, yet there were certainly other reasons, and those of the most serious kind, that had considerable weight with me. The confidence which their success in killing our chief and forcing us to quit the shore must naturally have inspired, and the advantage, however trifling, which they had obtained over us the preceding day, would, I had no doubt, encourage them to make some further dangerous attempts; and the more especially as they had little reason, from what they had hitherto seen, to dread the effects of our fire-arms. Indeed, contrary to the expectations of every one, this sort of weapon had produced no signs of terror in them. On our side, such was the condition of the ships, and the state of discipline amongst us, that had a vigorous attack been made on us in the night it would have been impossible to answer for the consequences. In these apprehensions I was supported by the opinion of most of the officers on board, and nothing seemed to me so likely to encourage the natives to make the attempt as the appearance of our being inclined to an accommodation which they could only attribute to weakness or fear.

In favour of more conciliatory measures, it was justly urged that the mischief was done, and irreparable; that the natives had a strong claim to our regard on account of their former friendship and kindness, and the more especially as the late melancholy accident did not appear to have arisen from any premeditated design; that, on the part of Terreeoboo, his ignorance of the theft, his readiness to accompany Captain Cook on board, and his having actually sent his two sons into the boat, must free him from the smallest degree of suspicion; that the conduct of his women and the " Erees " might easily be accounted for, from the apprehensions occasioned by the armed force with which Captain Cook came on shore, and the hostile preparations in the bay, appearances so different from the terms of friendship and confidence in which both parties had hitherto lived, that the arming of the natives was evidently with a design to resist the attempt, which they had some reason to imagine would be made, to carry off their King by force, and was naturally to be expected from a people full of affection and attachment to their chiefs. To these motives of humanity others of a prudential nature were added; that we were in want of water and other refreshments; that our fore-mast would require six or eight days' work before it could be stepped; that the spring was advancing apace, and that the speedy prosecution of our next northern expedition ought now to be our sole object; that therefore to engage in a vindictive contest with the inhabitants might not only lay us under the imputation of unnecessary cruelty, but would occasion an unavoidable delay in the equipment of the ships. In this latter opinion Cap-

tain Clerke concurred, and though I was convinced that an early display of vigorous resentment would more effectually have answered every object both of prudence and humanity, I was not sorry that the measures I had recommended were rejected. For though the contemptuous behaviour of the natives, and their subsequent opposition to our necessary operations on shore, arising I have no doubt from misconstruction of our lenity, compelled us at last to have recourse to violence in our own defence; yet I am not so sure that the circumstances of the case would, in the opinion of the world, have justified the use of force on our part in the first instance. Cautionary rigour is at all times invidious, and has this additional objection to it, that the severity of a preventive course, when it best succeeds, leaves its expediency the least apparent.

During the time we were thus engaged in concerting some plan for our future conduct, a prodigious concourse of natives still kept possession of the shore; and some of them came off in canoes, and had the boldness to approach within pistol-shot of the ships and to insult us by various marks of contempt and defiance. It was with great difficulty we could restrain the sailors from the use of their arms on these occasions; but as pacific measures had been resolved on, the canoes were suffered to return unmolested. In pursuance of this plan, it was determined that I should proceed towards the shore with the boats of both ships, well manned and armed, with a view to bring the natives to a parley, and if possible to obtain a conference with some of the chiefs. If this attempt succeeded, I was to demand the dead bodies, and particularly that of Captain Cook; to threaten them with our vengeance in case of a refusal; but by no means to fire unless attacked, and not to land on any account whatever. These orders were delivered to me before the whole party and in the most positive manner.

I left the ships about 4 o'clock in the afternoon, and as we approached the shore I perceived every indication of a hostile reception. The whole crowd of natives was in motion, the women and children retiring, the men putting on their war-mats and arming themselves with long spears and daggers. We also observed that since the morning they had thrown up stone breastworks along the beach where Captain Cook had landed, probably in expectation of an attack at that place; and as soon as we were within reach they began to throw stones at us with slings, but without doing any mischief. Concluding, therefore, that all attempts to bring them to a parley would be in vain unless I first gave them some ground for mutual confidence, I ordered the armed boats to stop and went on in the small boat alone, with a white flag in my hand, which, by a general cry of joy from the natives, I had the satisfaction to find was instantly understood. The women immediately returned from the side of the hill whither they had retired; the men threw off their mats; and all sat down together by the water-side, extending their arms and inviting me to come on shore.

Though this behaviour was very expressive of a friendly disposition, yet I could not help entertaining some suspicions of its sincerity. But when I saw Koah, with a boldness and assurance altogether unaccountable, swimming off towards the boat with a white flag in his hand, I thought it necessary to return this mark of confidence, and therefore received him into the boat, though armed, a circumstance which did not tend to lessen my suspicions. I must confess I had long harboured an unfavourable opinion of this man. The priests had always told us that he was of a malicious disposition, and no friend of ours; and the repeated detections of his fraud and treachery had convinced us of the truth of their representations. Add to all this, the shocking transaction of the morning, in which he was seen acting a principal part, made me feel the utmost horror at finding myself so near him; and as he came up to me with feigned

tears and embraced me, I was so distrustful of his intentions that I could not help taking hold of the point of the "pahooah" which he held in his hand and turning it from me. I told him that I had come to demand the body of Captain Cook, and to declare war against them unless it was instantly restored. He assured me this should be done as soon as possible, and that he would go himself for that purpose; and, after begging of me a piece of iron with much assurance, as if nothing extraordinary had happened, he leaped into the sea and swam ashore, calling out to his countrymen that we were all friends again.

We waited near an hour with great anxiety for his return, during which time the rest of the boats had approached so near the shore as to enter into conversation with a party of the natives at some distance from us, by whom they were plainly given to understand that the body had been cut to pieces and carried up the country; but of this circumstance I was not informed till our return to the ships. I began now to express some impatience at Koah's delay, upon which the chiefs pressed me exceedingly to come on shore, assuring me that if I would go myself to Terreeoboo the body would certainly be restored to me. When they found they could not prevail on me to land, they attempted, under a pretence of wishing to converse with more ease, to decoy our boat among some rocks where they would have had it in their power to cut us off from the rest. It was no difficult matter to see through these artifices, and I was therefore strongly inclined to break off all further communication with them, when a chief came to us who was the particular friend of Captain Clerke and of the officers of the Discovery, on board which ship he had sailed when we last left the bay, intending to take his passage to Mowee. He told us he came from Terreeoboo to acquaint us, that the body was carried up the country, but that it should be brought to us the next morning.

There appeared a great deal of sincerity in his manner, and being asked if he told a falsehood, he hooked his two fore-fingers together, which is understood amongst these islanders as the sign of truth, in the use of which they are very scrupulous.

As I was now at a loss in what manner to proceed, I sent Mr Vancouver to acquaint Captain Clerke with all that had passed; that my opinion was, they meant not to keep their word with us, and were so far from being sorry at what had happened, that on the contrary they were full of spirits and confidence on account of their late success, and sought only to gain time till they could contrive some scheme for getting us into their power. Mr Vancouver came back with orders for me to return on board; having first given the natives to understand that if the body was not brought the next morning the town should be destroyed. When they saw that we were going off they endeavoured to provoke us by the most insulting and contemptuous gestures. Some of our people said they could distinguish several of the natives parading about in the clothes of our unfortunate comrades; and among them a chief brandishing Captain Cook's hanger, and a woman holding the scabbard. Indeed, there can be no doubt but that our behaviour had given them a mean opinion of our courage; for they could have but little notion of the motives of humanity that directed it.

In consequence of the report I made to Captain Clerke of what I conceived to be the present temper and disposition of the islanders, the most effectual measures were taken to guard against any attack they might make in the night. The boats were moored with top-chains; additional sentinels were posted on both ships; and guard boats were stationed to row round them, in order to prevent the natives from cutting the cables. During the night we observed a prodigious number of lights on the hills, which made some of us imagine they were removing their effects back into the country in consequence of our threats. But I rather believed them to have been the sacrifices that were performing on account of the war in which they imagined themselves about to be engaged; and most probably the bodies of our slain countrymen were at that time burning. We afterward saw fires of the same kind as we passed the Island of Morotoi, and which, we were told by some natives then on board, were made on account of the war they had declared against a neighbouring island. And this agrees with what we learned amongst the Friendly and Society Isles, that previous to any expedition against an enemy, the chiefs always endeavoured to animate and inflame the courage of the people by feasts and rejoicings in the night.

We remained the whole night undisturbed except by the howlings and lamentations which were heard on shore; and early the next morning, Koah came alongside the Resolution with a present of cloth and a small pig, which he desired leave to present to me. I have mentioned before that I was supposed by the natives to be the son of Captain Cook; and as he in his lifetime had always suffered them to believe it, I was probably considered as the chief after his death. As soon as I came on deck I questioned him about the body; and, on his returning me nothing but evasive answers, I refused to accept his presents, and was going to dismiss him with some expressions of anger and resentment, had not Captain Clerke, judging it best at all events to keep up the appearance of friendship, thought it more proper that he should be treated with the usual respect. This treacherous fellow came frequently to us during the course of the forenoon with some trifling present or other; and as I always observed him eyeing every part of the ship with great attention, I took care he should see we were well prepared for our defence. He was exceedingly urgent both with Captain Clerke and myself to go on shore, laying all the blame of the detention of the bodies on the other chiefs, and assuring us that everything might be settled to our satisfaction by a personal interview with Terreeoboo.   However, his conduct was too suspicious to make it prudent to comply with this request; and, indeed, a fact came afterward to our knowledge which proved the entire falsehood of his pretensions.   For we were told that immediately after the action in which Captain Cook was killed, the old King had retired to a cave in the steep part of the mountain that hangs over the bay, which was accessible only by the help of ropes, and where he remained for many days, having his victuals let down to him by cords.

When Koah returned from the ships, we could perceive that his countrymen, who had been collected by break of day in vast crowds on the shore, thronged about him with great eagerness, as if to learn the intelligence he had acquired, and what was to be done in consequence of it.   It is very probable that they expected we should attempt to put our threats in execution; and they seemed fully resolved to stand their ground.   During the whole morning we heard conches blowing in different parts of the coast; large parties were seen marching over the hills; and, in short, appearances were so alarming that we carried out a stream anchor, to enable us to haul the ship abreast of the town in case of an attack, and stationed boats off the north point of the bay to prevent a surprise from that quarter.   The breach of their engagement to restore the bodies of the slain, and the warlike posture in which they at this time appeared, occasioned fresh debates amongst us concerning the measures next to be pursued.   It was at last determined that nothing should be suffered to interfere with the repair of the mast, and the preparations for our departure; but that we should nevertheless continue our negotiations for the recovery of the bodies.   The greatest part of the day was taken up in getting the fore-mast into a proper situation on deck for the carpenters to work upon it, and in making the necessary alterations in the commissions of the officers.   The command of the expedition having devolved upon Captain Clerke, he removed on board the Resolution, appointed Lieutenant Gore to be captain of the Discovery, and promoted Mr Harvey, a midshipman who had been with Captain Cook in his two last voyages, to the vacant lieutenancy.   During the whole day we met with no interruption from the natives; and at night the launch was again moored with a top-chain, and guard boats stationed round both ships as before.

About 8 o'clock, it being very dark, a canoe was heard paddling toward the ship, and as soon as it was seen both the sentinels on deck fired into it.   There were two persons in the canoe, and they immediately roared out "Tinnee" (which was the way in which they pronounced my name), and said they were friends, and had something for me belonging to Captain Cook.   When they came on board, they threw themselves at our feet, and appeared exceedingly frightened.   Luckily neither of them was hurt, notwithstanding the balls of both pieces had gone through the canoe.   One of them was the person whom I have before mentioned under the name of the taboo man, who constantly attended Captain Cook, with the circumstances of ceremony I have already described, and who, though a man of rank in the island, could scarcely be hindered from performing the lowest offices of a menial servant.   After lamenting with abundance of tears the loss of the "Orono," he told us that he had brought us a part of his body.   He then presented to us a small bundle wrapped up in cloth, which he brought under his arm; and it is impossible to describe the horror which seized us on finding in it a piece of human flesh about nine or ten pounds weight.   This, he said, was all that remained of the body; that the rest was cut to pieces and burnt, but that the head and all the bones, except what belonged to the trunk, were in the possession of Terreeoboo and the other "Erees;" that what we saw had been allotted to Kaoo, the chief of the priests, to be made use of in some religious ceremony ; and that he had sent it as a proof of his innocence and attachment to us.

This afforded an opportunity of informing ourselves whether they were cannibals, and we did not neglect it. We first tried by many indirect questions, put to each of them apart, to learn in what manner the rest of the bodies had been disposed of ; and finding them very constant in one story, that after the flesh had been cut off it was all burnt, we at last put the direct question, whether they had not eat some of it. They immediately showed as much horror at the idea as any European would have done ; and asked very naturally if that was the custom amongst us. They afterward asked us with great earnestness and apparent apprehension, "When the 'Orono' would come again ? and what he would do to them on his return ?" The same inquiry was frequently made afterward by others ; and this idea agrees with the general tenor of their conduct toward him, which showed that they considered him as a being of a superior nature. We pressed our two friendly visitors to remain on board till morning, but in vain. They told us that if this transaction should come to the knowledge of the King or chiefs, it might be attended with the most fatal consequences to their whole society, in order to prevent which they had been obliged to come off to us in the dark ; and that the same precaution would be necessary in returning on shore. They informed us further, that the chiefs were eager to revenge the death of their countrymen ; and particularly cautioned us against trusting Koah, who, they said, was our mortal and implacable enemy, and desired nothing more ardently than an opportunity of fighting us, to which the blowing of the conches we had heard in the morning was meant as a challenge. We learned from these men that seventeen of their countrymen were killed in the first action at Kowrowa, of whom five were chiefs ; and that Kaneena and his brother, our very particular friends, were unfortunately of that number. Eight, they said, were killed at the observatory, three of whom were also of the first rank. About 11 o'clock our two friends left us, and took the precaution to desire that our guard boat might attend them till they had passed the Discovery, lest they should again be fired upon, which might alarm their countrymen on shore, and expose them to the danger of being discovered. This request was complied with, and we had the satisfaction to find that they got safe and undiscovered to land.

During the remainder of this night we heard the same loud howling and lamentations as in the preceding one. Early in the morning we received another visit from Koah. I must confess I was a little piqued to find that, notwithstanding the most evident marks of treachery in his conduct, and the positive testimony of our friends the priests, he should still be permitted to carry on the same farce, and to make us at least appear to be the dupes of his hypocrisy. Indeed, our situation was become extremely awkward and unpromising ; none of the purposes for which this pacific course of proceeding had been adopted having hitherto been in the least forwarded by it. No satisfactory answer whatever had been given to our demands ; we did not seem to be at all advanced toward a reconciliation with the islanders ; they still kept in force on the shore, as if determined to resist any attempts we might make to land ; and yet the attempt was become absolutely necessary, as the completing our supply of water would not admit of any longer delay.

However, it must be observed, in justice to the conduct of Captain Clerke, that it was very probable, from the great numbers of the natives and from the resolution with which they seemed to expect us, an attack could not have been made without some danger ; and that the loss of a very few men might have been severely felt by us during the remaining course of our voyage. Whereas the delaying the execution of our threats, though on the one hand it lessened their opinion of our prowess, had the effect of causing them to disperse on the other. For this day, about noon, finding us persist in our inactivity, great bodies of them, after blowing their conches and using every mode of defiance, marched off over the hills, and never appeared afterward. Those, however, who remained were not the less daring and insolent. One man had the audacity to come within musket shot, ahead of the ship; and after slinging several stones at us, he waved Captain Cook's hat over his head, whilst his countrymen on shore were exulting and encouraging his boldness. Our people were all in a flame at this insult, and coming in a body on the quarter-deck, begged they might no longer be obliged to put up with these repeated provocations, and requested me to obtain permission for them from Captain Clerke to avail themselves of the first fair occasion of revenging the death of their commander. On my acquainting him with what was passing, he gave orders for some great guns to be fired at the natives on shore, and promised the crew that if they should meet with any molestation at the watering-place the next day they should then be left at liberty to chastise them.

It is somewhat remarkable that before we could bring our guns to bear the islanders had suspected our intentions, from the stir they saw in the ship, and had retired behind their houses and walls. We were therefore obliged to fire, in some measure, at random; notwithstanding which our shot produced all the effects that could have been desired. For soon after we saw Koah paddling toward us with extreme haste, and on his arrival we learned that some people had been killed, and amongst the rest Maihamaiha, a principal chief and a near relation of the King.[1] Soon after the

arrival of Koah, two boys swam off from the "morai" toward the ships, having each a long spear in his hand; and after they had approached pretty near they began to chant a song in a very solemn manner, the subject of which, from their often mentioning the word "Orono" and pointing to the village where Captain Cook was killed, we concluded to be the late calamitous disaster. Having sung in a plaintive strain for about twelve or fifteen minutes, during the whole of which time they remained in the water, they went on board the Discovery and delivered their spears; and after making a short stay returned on shore. Who sent them, or what was the object of this ceremony, we were never able to learn.

At night, the usual precautions were taken for the security of the ships; and as soon as it was dark our two friends who had visited us the night before came off again. They assured us that though the effects of our great guns this afternoon, had terrified the chiefs exceedingly, they had by no means laid aside their hostile intentions, and advised us to be on our guard. The next morning the boats of both ships were sent ashore for water; and the Discovery was warped close to the beach in order to cover that service. We soon found that the intelligence which the priests had sent us was not without foundation; and that the natives were resolved to take every opportunity of annoying us when it could be done without much risk. Throughout all this group of islands, the villages for the most part are situated near the sea, and the adjacent ground is enclosed with stone walls about three feet high. These we at first imagined were intended for the division of property; but we now discovered that they served, and pro-

---

[1] The word "matee" is commonly used, in the language of these islands, to express either killing or wounding; and we were afterward told that this chief had only received a slight blow on the face from a stone which had been struck by one of the balls.—*Note in Original Edition.*

bably were principally designed, for a defence against invasion. They consist of loose stones, and the inhabitants are very dexterous in shifting them with great quickness to such situations as the direction of the attack may require. In the sides of the mountain which hangs over the bay they have also little holes or caves of considerable depth, the entrance of which is secured by a fence of the same kind. From behind both these defences the natives kept perpetually harassing our waterers with stones; nor could the small force we had on shore, with the advantage of muskets, compel them to retreat.

In this exposed situation our people were so taken up in attending to their own safety, that they employed the whole forenoon in filling only one ton of water. As it was therefore impossible to perform this service till their assailants were driven to a greater distance, the Discovery was ordered to dislodge them with her great guns; which being effected by a few discharges, the men landed without molestation. However, the natives soon after made their appearance again in their usual mode of attack; and it was now found absolutely necessary to burn down some straggling houses near the wall behind which they had taken shelter. In executing these orders I am sorry to add that our people were hurried into acts of unnecessary cruelty and devastation. Something ought certainly to be allowed to their resentment of the repeated insults and contemptuous behaviour of the islanders, and to the natural desire of revenging the loss of their commander. But at the same time their conduct served strongly to convince me that the utmost precaution is necessary in trusting, though but for a moment, the discretionary use of arms in the hands of private seamen or soldiers on such occasions. The rigour of discipline and the habits of obedience by which their force is kept directed to its proper objects lead them naturally enough to conceive that whatever they have the power they have also the right to do. Actual disobedience being

almost the only crime for which they are accustomed to expect punishment, they learn to consider it as the only measure of right and wrong; and hence are apt to conclude that what they can do with impunity they may do with justice and honour. So that the feelings of humanity which are inseparable from us all, and that generosity toward an unresisting enemy which at other times is the distinguishing mark of brave men, become but weak restraints to the exercise of violence when opposed to the desire they naturally have of showing their own independence and power.

I have already mentioned that orders had been given to burn only a few straggling huts which afforded shelter to the natives. We were therefore a good deal surprised to see the whole village on fire; and before a boat that was sent to stop the progress of the mischief could reach the shore, the houses of our old and constant friends the priests were all in flames. I cannot enough lament the illness that confined me on board this day. The priests had always been under my protection; and unluckily the officers who were then on duty, having been seldom on shore at the "morai," were not much acquainted with the circumstances of the place. Had I been present myself, I might probably have been the means of saving their little society from destruction. Several of the natives were shot in making their escape from the flames; and our people cut off the heads of two of them and brought them on board. The fate of one poor islander was much lamented by us all. As he was coming to the well for water he was shot at by one of the marines. The ball struck his calibash, which he immediately threw from him and fled. He was pursued into one of the caves I have before described, and no lion could have defended his den with greater courage and fierceness; till at last, after having kept two of our people at bay for a considerable time, he expired, covered with wounds. It was this accident that first brought us acquainted with the use of these caverns. At this time, an elderly man was taken prisoner, bound, and sent on board in the same boat with the heads of his two countrymen. I never saw horror so strongly pictured as in the face of this man, nor so violent a transition to extravagant joy as when he was untied and told he might go away in safety. He showed us he did not want gratitude, as he frequently afterward returned with presents of provisions, and also did us other services.

Soon after the village was destroyed we saw coming down the hill a man attended by fifteen or twenty boys holding pieces of white cloth, green boughs, plantains, &c., in their hands. I knew not how it happened that this peaceful embassy, as soon as they were within reach, received the fire of a party of our men. This, however, did not stop them. They continued their procession, and the officer on duty came up in time to prevent a second discharge. As they approached nearer, it was found to be our much-esteemed friend Kaireekeea, who had fled on our first setting fire to the village, and had now returned and desired to be sent on board the Resolution. When he arrived, we found him exceedingly grave and thoughtful. We endeavoured to make him understand the necessity we were under of setting fire to the village, by which his house and those of his brethren were unintentionally consumed. He expostulated a little with us on our want of friendship and on our ingratitude. And indeed it was not till now that we learned the whole extent of the injury we had done them. He told us that, relying on the promises I had made them, and on the assurances they had afterward received from the men who had brought us the remains of Captain Cook, they had not removed their effects back into the country with the rest of the inhabitants, but had put everything that was valuable of their own, as well as what they had collected from us, into a house close to the "moral," where they had the mortification to see it all set on fire by ourselves. On coming on board he had seen the heads of his countrymen lying on the deck, at which he was exceedingly shocked, and desired with great earnestness that they might be thrown overboard. This request Captain Clerke instantly ordered to be complied with.

In the evening the watering party returned on board, having met with no further interruption. We passed a gloomy night, the cries and lamentations we heard on shore being far more dreadful than ever. Our only consolation was the hope that we should have no occasion in future for a repetition of such severities. It is very extraordinary that amidst all these disturbances the women of the island who were on board never offered to leave us, nor discovered the smallest apprehensions either for themselves or their friends ashore. So entirely unconcerned did they appear, that some of them who were on deck when the town was in flames seemed to admire the sight, and frequently cried out that it was "maitai," or very fine.

Bancroft Library

The next morning Koah came off as usual to the ships. As there existed no longer any necessity for keeping terms with him, I was allowed to have my own way. When he approached towards the side of the ship, singing his song, and offering me a hog and some plantains, I ordered him to keep off, cautioning him never to appear again without Captain Cook's bones, lest his life should pay the forfeit of his frequent breach of promise. He did not appear much mortified with this reception, but went immediately onshore and joined a party of his countrymen who were pelting the waterers with stones. The body of the young man who had been killed the day before was found this morning lying at the entrance of the cave, and some of our people went and threw a mat over it. Soon after which they saw some men carrying him off on their shoulders, and could hear them singing, as they marched, a mournful song.

The natives being at last convinced

that it was not the want of ability to punish them which had hitherto made us tolerate their provocations, desisted from giving us any further molestation; and in the evening a chief called Eappo, who had seldom visited us, but whom we knew to be a man of the very first consequence, came with presents from Terreeoboo to sue for peace. These presents were received, and he was dismissed with the same answer which had before been given, that until the remains of Captain Cook should be restored no peace would be granted. We learned from this person that the flesh of all the bodies of our people, together with the bones of the trunks, had been burned; that the limb bones of the marines had been divided amongst the inferior chiefs; and that those of Captain Cook had been disposed of in the following manner: the head, to a great chief called Kahoo-opeon; the hair, to Maia-maia; and the legs, thighs, and arms, to Terreeoboo. After it was dark, many of the inhabitants came off with roots and other vegetables, and we also received two large presents of the same articles from Kaireekeea.

The 19th was chiefly taken up in sending and receiving the messages which passed between Captain Clerke and Terreeoboo. Eappo was very pressing that one of our officers should go on shore, and in the meantime offered to remain as a hostage on board. This request, however, it was not thought proper to comply with; and he left us with a promise of bringing the bones the next day. At the beach the waterers did not meet with the least opposition from the natives, who, notwithstanding our cautious behaviour, came amongst us again without the smallest appearance of diffidence or apprehension. Early in the morning of the 20th we had the satisfaction of getting the fore-mast stepped. It was an operation attended with great difficulty and some danger, our ropes being so exceedingly rotten that the purchase gave way several times.

Between 10 and 11 o'clock we saw a great number of people descending the hill which is over the beach in a kind of procession, each man carrying a sugar-cane or two on his shoulders, and bread-fruit, "taro," and plantains in his hand. They were preceded by two drummers, who, when they came to the water-side, sat down by a white flag, and began to beat their drums, while those who had followed them advanced one by one; and, having deposited the presents they had brought, retired in the same order. Soon after, Eappo came in sight in his long feathered cloak, bearing something with great solemnity in his hands; and having placed himself on a rock, he made signs for a boat to be sent him. Captain Clerke conjecturing that he had brought the bones of Captain Cook, which proved to be the fact, went himself in the pinnace to receive him, and ordered me to attend him in the cutter. When we arrived at the beach, Eappo came into the pinnace and delivered to the Captain the bones, wrapped up in a large quantity of fine new cloth, and covered with a spotted cloak of black and white feathers. He afterward attended us to the Resolution, but could not be prevailed upon to go on board; probably not choosing, from a sense of decency, to be present at the opening of the bundle. We found in it both the hands of Captain Cook entire, which were well known from a remarkable scar on one of them that divided the thumb from the forefinger the whole length of the metacarpal bone; the skull, but with the scalp separated from it, and the bones that form the face wanting; the scalp, with the hair upon it cut short, and the ears adhering to it; the bones of both arms, with the skin of the fore-arms hanging to them; the thigh and leg bones joined together, but without the feet. The ligaments of the joints were entire, and the whole bore evident marks of having been in the fire, except the hands, which had the flesh left upon them, and were cut in several places and crammed with salt, apparently with an intention of preserving them. The scalp had a cut in the back part of it, but the skull was free from any fracture. The lower jaw and feet, which were wanting, Eappo told us had been seized by different chiefs, and that Terreeoboo was using every means to recover them.

The next morning Eappo and the King's son came on board, and brought with them the remaining bones of Captain Cook, the barrels of his gun, his shoes, and some other trifles that belonged to him. Eappo took great pains to convince us that Terreeoboo, Maiha-maiha, and himself were most heartily desirous of peace; that they had given us the most convincing proof of it in their power; and that they had been prevented from giving it sooner by the other chiefs, many of whom were still our enemies. He lamented with the greatest sorrow the death of six chiefs we had killed, some of whom, he said, were amongst our best friends. The cutter, he told us, was taken away by Pareea's people, very probably in revenge for the blow that had been given him, and it had been broken up the next day. The arms of the marines, which we had also demanded, he assured us had been carried off by the common people, and were irrecoverable; the bones of the chief alone having been preserved as belonging to Terreeoboo and the "Erees." Nothing now remained but to perform the last offices to our great and unfortunate commander. Eappo was dismissed with orders to taboo all the bay; and in the afternoon, the bones having been put into a coffin and the service read over them, they were committed to the deep with the usual military honours. What our feelings were on this occasion, I leave the world to conceive; those who were present know that it is not in my power to express them.

During the forenoon of the 22d not a canoe was seen paddling in the bay, the taboo which Eappo had laid on it the day before at our request not being yet taken off. At length Eappo came off to us. We assured him that we were now entirely satisfied, and that, as the "Orono" was buried, all remembrance of what had passed was buried with him. We afterward desired him to take off the taboo, and to make it known that the people might bring their provisions as usual. The ships were soon surrounded with canoes, and many of the chiefs came on board expressing great sorrow at what happened and their satisfaction at our reconciliation. Several of our friends who did not visit us sent presents of large hogs and other provisions. Amongst the rest came the old treacherous Koah, but was refused admittance.

As we had now everything ready for sea, Captain Clerke, imagining that if the news of our proceedings should reach the islands to leeward before us it might have a bad effect, gave orders to unmoor. About eight in the evening we dismissed all the natives, and Eappo and the friendly Kaireekeea took an affectionate leave of us. We immediately weighed and stood out of the bay. The natives were collected on the shore in great numbers, and as we passed along, received our last farewells with every mark of affection and goodwill.

CONCLUSION.

[Nothing now remains but to give an outline of the last twenty-one months' voyage of the Resolution and Discovery, until their arrival in England in October 1780; and, as before, the synopsis has been taken from the Cabinet Cyclopædia, "Maritime and Inland Discovery," vol. iii., pp. 86-92.]

"After leaving Owhyhee, the ships touched at the Island of Atooe, which was found desolated by a war originating in the claims of different chiefs to the goats which Captain Cook had put on shore. These animals had increased to six when the war broke out on their account, in the course of which they were all destroyed. The history of the introduction of useful animals into the South Sea Islands affords many parallel instances of human blindness, and of that barbarous degree of envy and rapacity which destroys a treasure rather than leave it in the possession of a rival.

"Captain Clerke proceeded now to execute the intentions of his late commander, by repeating the attempt to find a passage through the Northern Ocean. He touched at the harbour of St Peter and St Paul in Awatska Bay, where he was treated by the Russians with unbounded hospitality; and then passing Behring's Strait a second time, penetrated as far as 70° 33′ N., where the same obstacle which had prevented the progress of the ships the preceding year forbade him to advance any farther. He met here with a firm barrier of ice, seven leagues farther to the south than that which had stopped the progress of Captain Cook. The impossibility of a passage by the north was now thought to be sufficiently proved, and it was resolved to proceed homewards; the chief purpose of the expedition having been thus answered. This resolution of the officers diffused among the crews, who were now heartily tired of the length of the voyage, as lively a joy as if the ships, instead of having nearly the whole earth to compass, were already arrived in the British Channel. When the ships had just reached Kamtschatka, Captain Clerke died of a decline; he had already circumnavigated the globe three times, having sailed first with Commodore Byron, and afterwards with Captain Cook. Captain Gore now succeeded to the command of the expedition, and Lieutenant King took the command of the Discovery. Their voyage to China was not productive of any important geographical results. In navigating these stormy seas they found it necessary to keep at a distance from land, and were thus baffled by constant tempestuous weather in their attempt to survey the coasts of Japan.

"On the 3d of December our navigators arrived at Macao, where they first became acquainted with the events which had taken place in Europe since their departure, and of the war which had broken out be-tween Great Britain and France. A rumour of the generous conduct of the latter Goverment at the same time reached them; an order had been issued in March 1779, by the Minister of the Marine at Paris, to all the commanders of French ships, acquainting them with the expedition and destination of Captain Cook, and instructing them to treat that celebrated navigator wherever they should meet him, as a commander of a neutral and allied power. This measure, so honourable to the nation which adopted it, is said to have originated in the enlightened mind of the celebrated Turgot. Dr Franklin, who at that time resided at Paris as Ambassador from the United States, had a short time before issued a requisition, in which he earnestly recommended the commanders of American armed vessels not to consider Captain Cook as an enemy; but he had no authority to enforce his recommendation, and the Government of the United States had not the magnanimity to adopt it.

"While the ships lay in the River of Canton, the sailors carried on a brisk trade with the Chinese for the sea-otter skins which they had brought with them from the north-west coast of America, and which were every day rising in their value. 'One of our seamen,' says Lieutenant King, 'sold his stock alone for 800 dollars; and a few prime skins, which were clean and had been well preserved, were sold for 120 each. The whole amount of the value, in specie and goods, that was got for the furs in both ships, I am confident, did not fall short of £2000 sterling; and it was generally supposed that at least two-thirds of the quantity we had originally got from the Americans were spoiled and worn out, or had been given away, or otherwise disposed of in Kamtschatka. When, in addition to these facts, it is remembered that the furs were at first collected without our having any idea of their real value; that the greatest part had been worn by the Indians from whom we purchased them; that they were afterwards preserved with little care, and frequently used for bedclothes and other purposes; and that probably we had not got the full value for them in China; the advantages that might be derived from a voyage to that part of the American coast, undertaken with commercial views, appeared to me of a degree of importance sufficient to call for the attention of the public.' These observations of Lieutenant King point to that which eventually proved to be the most important result of this expedition. A great branch of trade in the Pacific Ocean, which had hitherto escaped the notice of the nations most interested in its development, and possessing establishments most conveniently situated for carrying it on, was suddenly discovered, and soon after vigorously prosecuted by a maritime people from the opposite side of the globe. The crews of both ships were astonished, as well as overjoyed, at the price paid them for their furs by the Chinese; and their rage to return to Cook's River, in order to procure a cargo of skins, proceeded at one time almost to mutiny. A few, indeed, contrived to desert, and were among the first adventurers who crossed the Pacific Ocean in the newly discovered fur trade. The seamen thus unexpectedly enriched soon underwent a total metamorphosis; they arrived at Macao in rags, many of them having inconsiderately sold their clothing in the South Sea Islands; but, before they left that harbour, they were decked out in gaudy silks and other Chinese finery. Nothing of importance occurred during the remainder of their voyage home; and on the 4th of October, the ships arrived safe at the Nore, after an absence of four years, two months, and twenty-two days. In the whole course of the voyage the Resolution lost but five men by sickness, of whom three were in a precarious state of health when the expedition left England; the Discovery did not lose a man.

" In order to estimate the merits of Captain Cook, it will be only necessary to survey generally the extent and nature of his discoveries, and to examine what influence they exerted immediately on the commercial enterprise of nations. In the extent of the coasts which he surveyed or discovered, he far surpasses every other navigator. The eastern coast of New Holland, 2000 miles in extent, was totally unknown till he traced it; escaping from the dangers of that intricate navigation solely by his cool intrepidity and the resources of his skill. He also circumnavigated New Zealand, the eastern and southern parts of which were quite unknown, and supposed by many to be united to the Terra Australis Incognita. New Caledonia and Norfolk Island were both discovered by him; and the New Hebrides, from his labours, first assumed a definite shape in our maps. He rendered an essential service to geography also by his circumnavigating the globe in a high southern latitude; for, though the exertions and dangers of that difficult navigation were not repaid by any brilliant discoveries, it set at rest a question which had for ages divided the opinions of speculative geographers. Sandwich Land, or Southern Thule, may be numbered among his discoveries, although it is probably the land which Gerritz had descried a century before.

" His discoveries on the north-west coast of America were still more important and more extensive. In one voyage, he effected more than the Spanish navigators had been able to accomplish in the course of two centuries. In sailing through Behring's Strait, he determined the proximity of Asia and America, which Behring himself had failed to perceive; and he assigned the coast of the Tshuktzki to its true place, which, in many maps of his time, was placed some degrees too far to the westward.

" It is needless to recapitulate here the large additions which he made to our knowledge of the groups of islands scattered through the Pacific Ocean. Some of the Society and Friendly Islands were known before his time; but he carefully surveyed those archipelagoes, and fixed the positions of the chief islands, such as Otaheite and Tongataboo, with an accuracy equal to that of a European observatory. He prided himself especially on having discovered the Sandwich Islands, and there is no good reason to refuse him that honour; for even if it be true that a Spanish navigator, named Gali, discovered those islands in 1576, and that he gave to Owhyhee the name of Mesa or Table Mountain, which is marked in old Spanish charts twenty-two degrees to the west of the Sandwich Islands, but in the same latitude with them; yet no stress can be laid on a discovery from which mankind derived no knowledge. The Spaniards seem soon to have totally forgotten the Sandwich Islands, if they ever knew them, notwithstanding the advantages which they might have derived from those islands in their frequent voyages from New Spain to Manilla. Anson and many other navigators might have been spared infinite distress and suffering in their voyages across the Pacific had anything certain been known of the existence and situation of the Sandwich Islands.

"But Cook's merit is not more conspicuous in the extent of his discoveries, than in the correctness with which he laid down the position of every coast of which he caught a glimpse. His surveys afford the materials of accurate geography. He adopted in practice every improvement suggested by the progress of science; and instead of committing errors amounting to two or three degrees of longitude, like most of his predecessors, his determinations were such as to be considered accurate even at the present day. Nor was this the merit of the astronomers who accompanied him on his expeditions. He was himself a skilful observer, and at the same time so vigilant and indefatigable, that no opportunity ever escaped him of ascertaining his true place. He possessed in an eminent degree the sagacity peculiar to seamen; and in his conjectures respecting the configurations of coasts he very rarely erred. La Perouse, who was a highly accomplished seaman, always mentions the name of

Cook with the warmest admiration, and frequently alludes to the remarkable correctness of his surveys. Crozet, also, who wrote the narrative of Marion's voyage, speaking of Cook's survey of the shores of New Zealand, says—'That its exactness and minuteness of detail astonished him beyond expression;' but Cook's skill as a marine surveyor may be still better estimated from the chart which, at the commencement of his career, he constructed of the coasts of Newfoundland; and of that chart, Captain Frederick Bullock, the able officer who has recently[1] completed the survey of Newfoundland, speaks in those terms of warm commendation which a man of ability naturally bestows on whatever is excellent.

"From the second expedition of Cook may be dated the art of preserving the health of the seamen in long voyages. Before that time, navigators who crossed the Pacific hurried precipitately by the shortest course to the Ladrones or the Philippine Islands; and yet they rarely reached home without the loss of a large proportion of their crew. Cook, on the other hand, felt himself perfectly at home on the ocean; he did not care to limit his voyages either in space of time or of distance; he sailed through every climate, crossing both the arctic and antarctic circles; and proved that a voyage of four years' duration does not necessarily affect the health of seamen. This was a discovery of far greater importance than that of a new continent could have been. By his banishing the terror that arose from the frightful mortality that previously attended on long voyages, he has mainly contributed to the boldness of navigation which distinguishes the present day.

"Among the immediate effects of Captain Cook's voyages, the most important was the establishment of a colony at Botany Bay. That great navigator seems to have contracted a partiality towards the New Zealanders; he admired their generosity,

---

[1] This was published in 1831.

their manly carriage, and their intelligence. Their country appeared to him fertile; abounding in commodities which might become valuable in commerce; and he hints, though with diffidence, at the possibility of a trade being carried on between Europe and New Zealand. His observations on this subject had influence, no doubt, on the minds of the English ministers, and they resolved on establishing a colony at New Holland; and the result has justified Cook's sanguine anticipations.[1] The fur trade also, which soon caused such a concourse of European shipping in the Pacific Ocean, originated with this third voyage; but his familiarity with the South Sea Islanders, the trade which he established with them, and the practice which he commenced of purchasing sea stores from them, have had, perhaps, a still stronger influence on navigation in the Pacific.

"Finally, to complete the eulogium on this great navigator, it will be sufficient to enumerate some of the distinguished seamen who served under him, such as Vancouver, Broughton, Bligh, Burney, Colnett, Portlock, Dixon, &c.; these men learned under Cook the arduous duties of their profession, and they always spoke of him with unqualified admiration and respect."

---

[1] Infinitely more so, in this third quarter of the nineteenth century.

END OF COOK'S VOYAGES.

www.ingramcontent.com/pod-product-compliance
Lightning Source LLC
Chambersburg PA
CBHW031127120726
47905CB00006B/1595